The Annotated

SENSE AND SENSIBILITY

Annotated and Edited by

DAVID M. SHAPARD

David M. Shapard is the author of *The Annotated Pride and Prejudice* and *The Annotated Persuasion*. He graduated with a Ph.D. in European History from the University of California at Berkeley; his specialty was the eighteenth century. Since then he has taught at several colleges. He lives in upstate New York.

ALSO BY DAVID M. SHAPARD

The Annotated Pride and Prejudice

The Annotated Persuasion

The Annotated

SENSE

AND

SENSIBILITY

A young woman reading a book outdoors.

[From *The Repository of arts, literature, fashions, manufactures, &c*, Vol. XIV (1815), p. 240]

The Annotated

SENSE

AND

SENSIBILITY

———

JANE AUSTEN

Annotated and Edited, with an Introduction, by

DAVID M. SHAPARD

ANCHOR BOOKS
A Division of Random House, Inc.
New York

AN ANCHOR BOOKS ORIGINAL, MAY 2011

Library of Congress Cataloging-in-Publication Data
Austen, Jane, 1775–1817.
[Sense and sensibility]
The annotated Sense and sensibility / by Jane Austen ;
annotated and edited, with an introduction, by David M.
Shapard. —1st ed.
p. cm.
Includes bibliographical references.
ISBN 978-0-307-39076-9
1. Young women—England—Fiction.
2. Sisters—England—Fiction.   3. Gentry—England—
Fiction.   4. Inheritance and succession—Fiction.
5. Mate selection—Fiction. 6. Man-woman relationships—
Fiction.   7. England—Social life and customs—
19th century—Fiction.   8. Austen, Jane, 1775–1817.
Sense and sensibility.   9. Domestic fiction.
I. Shapard, David M.   II. Title.
PR4034.S4 2011a
823'.7—dc22
2011002249

Book design by Rebecca Aidlin
Maps by R. Bull

www.anchorbooks.com

Printed in the United States of America

Contents

———

SENSE AND SENSIBILITY

VOLUME I

(Note: The following chapter headings are not found in the novel.
They are added here by the editor to assist the reader.)

VOLUME II

Illustrations

Notes to the Reader

The *Annotated Sense and Sensibility* contains several
features that the reader should be aware of:

Literary interpretations: the comments on the techniques and
themes of the novel, more than other types of entries, represent the
personal views and interpretations of the editor. Such views have
been carefully considered, but inevitably they will still provoke
disagreement among some readers. I can only hope that even in
those cases the opinions expressed provide useful food for thought.

Differences of meaning: many words then, like many words now,
had multiple meanings. The meaning of a word that is given at
any particular place is intended only to apply to the way the word
is used there; it does not represent a complete definition of the
word in the language of the time. Thus some words are defined
differently at different points, while many words are defined only
in certain places, since in other places they are used in ways that
remain familiar today.

Repetitions: this book has been designed so it can be used as a
reference. For this reason many entries refer the reader to other
pages where more complete information about a topic exists.
This, however, is not practical for definitions of words, so definitions of the same word are repeated at various appropriate points.

Acknowledgments

My principal expression of gratitude must go, as before, to my editor, Diana Secker Tesdell. She has proved an invaluable source of advice and assistance during every phase of the book; she has responded patiently to my numerous queries, has identified problems in what I submitted, has suggested better ways of expressing my thoughts, and has added her own plentiful insights into the novel. I am also grateful to Nicole Pedersen, as well as to others at Anchor Books, for the extensive efforts required for the preparation of such a complicated manuscript.

Additional thanks should go to the staff of the Bethlehem Public Library, the New York State Library, and the New York Public Library for helping me procure the materials essential for my research, with particular appreciation for the efforts of Gordon Noble at the first institution.

Finally, I must thank my mother and other members of my family for their continued encouragement and support in my endeavors.

Introduction

Sense and Sensibility was Jane Austen's first published novel. Its appearance, in 1811 when she was thirty-five, marked the formal beginning of her literary career, but that career, and this novel itself, originated in much earlier, unpublished literary efforts.

Jane Austen was born on December 16, 1775, in Hampshire, a county in southern England. Her father, George Austen, was a clergyman and her mother, Cassandra Leigh Austen, whose father was also a clergyman, came from a family consisting principally of landed gentry; thus Jane Austen grew up among the social class she consistently depicts in her novels. The Austens were a large family of six boys and two girls, and they valued books and education. Her father supplemented his income by running a school for boys, and several of her brothers tried their hands at literary composition. The family also encouraged Jane's literary efforts, the first surviving examples of which date to when she was thirteen. Her earliest writings were highly comical, and show the influence of other literary works of the time, many of which she satirized. As she matured, she wrote longer and more serious works, which reveal an increasing interest in the delineation of character.

One of these longer works was an early version of *Sense and Sensibility*. According to the later reminiscences of family members this early version, *Elinor and Marianne*, was written in the form of letters, a popular literary device of the time that she used for some of her other early writings. It was probably done in 1795, when she was nineteen.[1] Late in 1796 she began *First Impressions*, which many years later became *Pride and Prejudice*. Her father sent the manuscript to a publisher, but it was rejected. Toward the end of 1797 she returned to *Elinor and Marianne*, modifying it and changing its name to *Sense and Sensibility*. She followed this with a new novel, *Susan*; it was also submitted to a publisher, who purchased the rights but never published it. Many years later it appeared, without significant modifications, as *Northanger Abbey*.

During this time Jane Austen continued to live with her parents and her sister, Cassandra, in her childhood home in Steventon, Hampshire. Her surviving letters indicate regular attendance at balls and other social events, and an interest in men, but no sustained romance or offer of marriage. The first known major event of her life occurred in 1801, when her father retired and moved the family to the popular spa and resort town of Bath. The family lived there, at various addresses, for the next four years. In 1805 Mr. Austen died, after which Mrs. Austen and her two daughters left Bath, settling eventually in Southampton, a port city in Hampshire. During this whole period Jane Austen did not complete any other novels, though she began at least one, the fragment called *The Watsons*. She also rejected, after briefly

---

[1] For more on the issue of the date, see note 2. One scholar, D. W. Harding, has argued cogently, though necessarily speculatively, that this initial version was not in the form of letters. He reasons that the final version of *Sense and Sensibility* devotes less space to letters than most of Jane Austen's novels, and, since there is no character to function as the recipient of a continual and frank correspondence from the main character, Elinor, it is difficult to see how the story as it now stands could have been told in this manner. Instead he guesses that the sole source for this idea, Caroline Austen—whose brief memoir *My Aunt Jane* was composed more than fifty years after Jane Austen's death and relied on what she heard from others for the subject's early life— confused *Elinor and Marianne* with the initial version of *Pride and Prejudice* (see above). The latter novel is a much better candidate for an original epistolary composition, since the completed version employs letters heavily, far more than in any other Austen novel, and provides the heroine with two characters, her sister and her aunt, who together could have received her correspondence over the course of the novel.

accepting, her one known offer of marriage. Finally, in 1809, she and her mother and sister were able to move into a cottage owned by her brother Edward in the quiet village of Chawton in Hampshire.

This new setting gave her the opportunity to devote herself more fully to writing. In 1810 she finished *Sense and Sensibility*; in October 1811 it appeared, though with a title page that simply said, "By a Lady." It enjoyed modest sales, along with a couple of favorable reviews. January 1813 saw the publication of *Pride and Prejudice*, identified as "By the Author of 'Sense and Sensibility.'" It experienced even greater success, and in 1814 and 1815 *Mansfield Park* and *Emma*, both completely new compositions, appeared. Unfortunately, in 1816 she grew increasingly ill; her ailment has not been identified for certain, though many have suggested it was what is now known as Addison's disease, an endocrine disorder caused by a malfunction of the adrenal glands. She did manage during this period to finish one more novel, *Persuasion*, and to begin another, *Sanditon*. Eventually, however, she grew too weak to write, and on July 18, 1817, she died in the town of Winchester in Hampshire. *Persuasion* and *Northanger Abbey* were published later in the year, along with a brief biographical notice by her brother Henry that finally revealed her identity to the world.

Sense and Sensibility is in some ways the most didactic of all Jane Austen's novels. It is one of three whose titles consist of the names of abstract concepts, the others being *Pride and Prejudice* and *Persuasion*. This signals from the start that a moral message will be central to the story. But while the ideas that pride and prejudice are dangerous and that it is good to be somewhat but not too susceptible to persuasion are not particularly controversial, *Sense and Sensibility* engages in a contentious debate of its day and takes a stance at odds with a prominent cultural trend.

The term "sensibility" first appeared in English in the fifteenth century, used for either mental awareness or the power of sensation or perception. In the eighteenth century the term assumed additional meanings, and became more widely used. It came to denote a person's general emotional consciousness or feelings, as well as, most significantly, a particular acuteness and sensitivity of feeling. This extra sensitivity could mean various things: among the feelings that were identified as especially strong in a person of sensibility were compassion for suffering and the unfortunate, empathy with others' feelings, love of natural beauty, delicate artistic taste, and instinctive aversion toward immorality. Many argued that these qualities had become more pronounced in their own time, and that this signaled the progressive improvement and refinement of society. Sensibility was also believed by many to be more prevalent among the affluent and educated classes and among women. Much of the literature of sensibility emphasized the feminine nature of its qualities, and extolled women for being naturally more tender, delicate, emotional, and morally pure, especially when it came to sexual morality.

Important strains of eighteenth-century thought inspired and informed ideas of sensibility. One of these was the tendency among philosophers to explain human consciousness and knowledge as the product of sensations and experiences, rather than divine inspiration or rational deduction. Another, the theory of the moral sense, was an influential philosophical doctrine that explained morality as the product of an instinctive sense of benevolence in human beings. This sense allowed people to understand moral principles, served as proof of the validity of moral laws, and gave people a reason to act morally, since such actions would naturally produce pleasure while immoral actions would produce pain. Most of the major philosophers of the century advocated one or both of the above doctrines.

Even more influential in spreading the cult of sensibility were the novelists of the time. It was during the eighteenth century that the novel emerged as a major literary genre, one that attracted both a large readership and a host of writers to cater to that audience. The novel, thanks to the opportunity it provided for intensive exploration of inner emotion, proved to be an ideal vehicle for advocates of sensibility. Samuel Richardson, the most popular of all eighteenth-century novelists, one who more than anyone

made the genre influential and respectable and who exercised a
critical influence on Jane Austen, created potent representations
of sensibility in his work. His first two novels, *Pamela* (1740) and
Clarissa (1748), both concern highly virtuous and beautiful young
women who are subject to a series of cruel trials, principally
involving powerful men who wish to rob them of their virginity.
Both heroines are creatures of acute feeling and sensibility, and
the novels, especially *Clarissa*, devote considerable space to the
elaborate exposition of their feelings, often at the expense of plot
movement. Both novels also show the heroines' purity and virtue
exercising a powerful influence on the feelings of others, and
inspiring them to better conduct. Richardson's last novel, *Sir
Charles Grandison* (1754), concerns a man who is a model of sensitivity and tenderness; a central purpose of the book was to show
that such qualities, even if particularly associated with women,
were compatible with manliness.

The two other leading novelists of the mid-eighteenth century,
Henry Fielding and Laurence Sterne, also express approval of
important elements of sensibility in their works. Fielding satirizes
some parts of Richardson and rejects an ideal of extreme tenderness and delicacy, especially for men. Yet both his heroes and
heroines are creatures of strong emotion, whose good actions
spring more from instinctive generosity than from reason. Sterne
goes even farther in this direction, for his most famous novel, *Tris-
tram Shandy* (1760–67), presents a world of disorder and incoher-
ence in which rational forms of understanding, planning, and
communication are ultimately impossible, and the characters'
benevolent, though frequently illogical, feelings provide the only
possible source of happiness, good actions, and true connection
with their fellow creatures. His other novel, *A Sentimental Journey*
(1768), helped popularize the term "sentimental," which was
recently coined and linked to sensibility. That novel is an almost
plotless chronicle of the hero's intense emotional reactions to a
variety of mundane experiences, in which the quality of feeling is
elevated above every other consideration.

The later decades of the eighteenth century witnessed many

more novels of sensibility. A succession of books appeared with heroes and heroines who displayed the most acute feelings toward the sundry events of life, even the most trivial, and who were designed to evoke similar feelings in the reader. Two of the most popular novels of the 1770s were Henry Mackenzie's *The Man of Feeling* and Goethe's *Sorrows of Young Werther* (sensibility was admired throughout Europe, most notably in France, whose sentimental fiction influenced many English writers). The title characters of both these novels are men of such extreme sensitivity that they are unable to cope with the frequently cruel and harsh world around them, and ultimately die from a broken heart. Both men are presented sympathetically, and the extremity of their misfortunes provoked copious tears from their many readers, tears being considered by that point a great mark of virtue. One woman later remembered reading *The Man of Feeling* when she was fourteen and dreading that she would not cry sufficiently "to gain the credit of proper sensibility."[2] Her reaction is not unique: "contemporary letters and memoirs, especially those of women, show a society very ready to weep and tremble, and to take credit for doing so."[3]

By the end of the eighteenth century there was also an increasing reaction against the cult of sensibility. Its extravagant celebrations of the most extreme emotions inevitably provoked dissent, even among those who approved of sensibility in moderation. Both Mackenzie and Goethe, especially the latter, expressed later reservations about what their popular novels had extolled. Others articulated more complete critiques. Samuel Johnson, one of the leading writers of the time and another important influence on Jane Austen, rejected basing morality on feeling on the grounds of human fallibility and the inevitable unreliability of emotion. His objection stemmed partly from traditional Christian doctrines. Although many advocates of sensibility, most notably Samuel

---

[2] Quoted in Janet Todd, *Sensibility: An Introduction* (London, 1986), p. 146.
[3] J. M. S. Tompkins, *The Popular Novel in England, 1770–1800* (London, 1932), p. 107.

"The Triumph of Sentiment": a satire on the vogue for sentimental literature; here a butcher weeps over The Sorrows of Werther, *even as his wife disembowels a carcass in the background.*

[From Joseph Grego, *Rowlandson the Caricaturist* (London, 1880), Vol. I, p. 210]

Richardson, were devout Christians whose writings contained strong religious elements, central aspects of sensibility clashed with fundamental tenets of orthodox Christianity. Traditional Christian doctrine emphasized the inherent sinfulness of humanity, the importance of controlling our often sinful passions, and the need to rely on divine guidance rather than personal sentiments in determining right from wrong.

During the 1780s, and even more so the 1790s, a series of novels appeared explicitly denouncing sensibility. In them one or more characters of ardent emotion, often inspired by ideals of sensibility, are led by these ideals or their own feelings into foolish, self-destructive, or even immoral behavior. Sometimes the character ultimately sees the error of his or her ways and reforms, sometimes not. One of these books, Jane West's *A Gossip's Story*, probably exercised some influence on *Sense and Sensibility*. It concerns two sisters, Louisa and Marianne Dudley, who repre-

sent, respectively, rational sense and excessive sensibility. Marianne Dudley, like Austen's Marianne Dashwood, is led by that
sensibility to bestow her love imprudently, and in her case there is
no final redemption; meanwhile, her sensible sister avoids trouble
and finds happiness.[4]

Other novels take a mixed position, while still showing the
strong influence of the issue. Ann Radcliffe, whose gothic horror
novels were bestsellers of the 1790s (and were satirized in
Northanger Abbey), strives hard to arouse emotions in the reader,
including those of sentimental pity, and devotes considerable
space to fulsome evocations of the beauties of nature similar to
those found in writers who advocate sensibility. But she also deliv-
ers a consistent moral message about the need for rational self-
control in her heroines as they confront various terrors and trials.
The political climate of the 1790s, marked by the fierce reactions
to the French Revolution, also shaped debate on these issues.
Because novels of sensibility gave primacy to individual standards
over social mores, many conservative writers in this period castigated them for allegedly encouraging radicalism. There was no
strict political correlation, however; for the leading conservative
book of the decade, Edmund Burke's *Reflections on the Revolu-*

---

[4] The principal objection to this novel as the original source of *Sense and
Sensibility* is timing. *A Gossip's Story* appeared in 1796; *Elinor and Marianne*, Austen's initial draft, was supposedly composed in the same period as
her sister's engagement, identified as 1795. But this dating, based on family
memories of years later, is flexible enough to allow for the possibility of a
composition in 1796, after the appearance of West's novel. Even if that is not
correct, Austen's revision of the novel in 1797 and 1798 (see above) could definitely have been influenced by West, an author whom Austen's letters indicate she had read. The initial meeting of Marianne and her lover in *A
Gossip's Story* suggests some direct inspiration; he rescues Marianne from an
accident—by stopping her runaway horse—and afterward calls on her.
There they experience a "happy union of minds," from discovering that their
opinions completely coincide, especially in their romantic tastes and love of
music. For more on this point, see J. M. S. Tompkins, "*Elinor and Marianne*:
A Note on Jane Austen," *The Review of English Studies* 16, no. 61 (Jan. 1940),
pp. 33–43.

tion in France, contains strong appeals to sentimental feelings, while many radical writers openly eschewed the idea of sensibility.

This cultural context suggests why Jane Austen would have been stirred in the latter part of the 1790s to begin a novel exploring sensibility. Marianne Dashwood's feelings and ideas exemplify central principles espoused by its advocates, while the miseries she inflicts on herself and others echo those evoked or portrayed by its critics. The years after 1800, when Jane Austen was revising the novel, saw explicit discussion of sensibility fade. But the underlying issues remained, for most of the main elements of the doctrine were replicated in Romanticism, which emerged during these years as the dominant force in much of the art, literature, and thought of the Western world. The final version of the novel reveals an awareness of these new trends by mentioning Sir Walter Scott, whose Romantic narrative poems were the greatest sellers of the age, as one of Marianne's favorite writers, and by satirizing the Romantic taste for the cottage, a new fad among the wealthy in England in the years after 1800. While it is not certain whether Austen would have set out to write a novel criticizing sensibility during this later period, she undoubtedly sensed, with justification, that the issues it raised and the points it made remained highly pertinent.

Jane Austen's interest in exploring the value of sensibility shapes the entire plot of the novel, as well as many of its other features. Most strikingly, it results in the only Austen novel with two heroines. In every other novel one person is the focus; here, though everything is told from Elinor's perspective, Marianne is consistently present and the sisters' respective stories are given equal weight. The novel follows a pattern of regularly switching back and forth, after approximately equal intervals, between each sister. It also provides parallel developments within the two story lines, by having each sister face the loss of the man she loves. Thus the very different reactions of the two demonstrate the relative strengths of sense and sensibility.

In making this comparison the author portrays Elinor's sense more sympathetically than Marianne's sensibility. The extent of the author's partiality is a matter of controversy. Many critics argue that the novel shows both heroines as excessive in their particular quality, and that just as Marianne must learn greater sense, Elinor must develop greater sensibility. Yet Elinor is never shown to be deficient in feeling. The paragraph in the opening chapter makes this clear: "She had an excellent heart;—her disposition was affectionate, and her feelings were strong, but she knew how to govern them." It is this governance of one's feelings, not their absence, that marks the sense represented by Elinor. Her strong feelings appear at various points in the novel, when she learns of Edward's prior engagement, witnesses Marianne's rejection by Willoughby, attends Marianne in her illness, or learns of Edward's unexpected release from Lucy. But, here and elsewhere, her strong self-control keeps her feelings from ever being as manifest as Marianne's. Nor does anything in the novel call her sense into serious question. The errors she makes are few and minor, and do not result from any particular defect of sense. Moreover, while Marianne is forced eventually to acknowledge her grave errors and resolve on a completely different course, Elinor is able, with full justification, to dispense the same basic wisdom at the end as she has been laying down from the beginning. She in fact embodies the basic ideal Jane Austen develops in all her novels, one in which genuine and acute feeling, a quality the author never disparages, is balanced and restrained by the equally important principles of self-control, reason, respect for social rules, and willingness to put others before oneself—all of which Marianne must learn.

In extolling Elinor at the expense of Marianne the novel does not condemn the latter's basic character. It shows her many attractive qualities, treats her sympathetically throughout, and eventually arranges a fate for her that is as happy as her sister's. In her love of those around her, her sense of right and wrong, her generosity, intelligence, education, eloquence, and artistic talents and tastes, Marianne is comparable to Elinor. The most significant difference, from which other differences flow, is in their respective adherence to the principles of sense or sensibility. As in a scientific experiment, Jane Austen has made her two subjects of study as similar as possible, in their attributes, their backgrounds, and their romantic experiences, in order to isolate a single variable, in this case their contrasting principles. Thus, when one acts so rightly and the other so wrongly, the only explanation lies in that variable, and the proof of the superiority of one principle is complete—insofar as such a thing is possible in a work of fiction. Marianne's good qualities also give her failures a particular poignancy, by showing how someone with such deep love for her mother and sister can end up inflicting great misery on them, or how someone of such high intelligence can descend to great folly.

Moreover, both Elinor and Marianne are far more than simple representatives of intellectual positions. The didactic imperative of the novel is balanced by the imperative, always central for Jane Austen, of creating fully believable and complex characters. Elinor and Marianne are, like all Austen characters, especially the main ones, realistic and vivid individuals. It is because of this that the reader cares about them so much and that the novel has continued to attract so many readers, long after the specific controversies surrounding sensibility have faded and other works addressing that controversy, such as West's *A Gossip's Story*, have sunk into obscurity.

These dual imperatives of the author are also manifest in another feature of the novel, its general tone, which is darker and more acerbic than that of any other Austen novels. This reflects the seriousness of its subject. The tone also allows the author to test the heroines' respective principles by plunging them into a variety of difficult ordeals, and to explore darker aspects of human behavior and experiences more fully than she does elsewhere.

This graver tone is established at the beginning of the novel. The plot is set in motion by two deaths, that of the heroines' great-uncle and their beloved father, and two terrible acts of injustice toward the heroines: their great-uncle's refusal to repay their assiduous attentions to him with a decent inheritance and their wealthy brother's refusal to honor his promise to his father to assist them. This is soon followed by the heroines' displacement from their grand home and familiar neighborhood to a much less spacious and less comfortable cottage, located far away. No other Austen heroine lives in such straitened circumstances; even the other two who have little or no fortune, Elizabeth Bennet and Fanny Price, inhabit fine houses with a full complement of servants and luxuries.

The heroines also confront a uniquely unpleasant set of characters over the course of the story. Like all Austen novels, *Sense and Sensibility* offers an array of supporting characters who are in some respects foolish or vulgar or absurd—Sir John and Lady Middleton, Mr. and Mrs. Palmer, Mrs. Jennings, Anne Steele. They provide comic relief to the reader while causing mild annoyance to the heroines. But to this Austen has added another half dozen characters, most of whom play an important role in the plot, who are distinctly nasty and selfish—Willoughby, Mrs. Ferrars, John Dashwood, Fanny Dashwood, Robert Ferrars, and Lucy Steele. The last three exhibit no redeeming characteristics whatsoever. All this means that the heroines spend much of the time being forced to witness despicable specimens of humanity and subjected to various forms of mistreatment. Nor does the reader even have the relief of seeing justice done to those who are selfish and cruel, for by the novel's end all of the characters have prospered. *Sense and Sensibility* is the only novel in which Jane Austen does not take care to mete out general just deserts, which arguably reflects a greater realism, for in the other novels Austen can become a little heavy-handed in allotting justice to all.

The heroines' romantic trials also surpass those found in the other novels. Marianne suffers from encountering a figure who appears in every Austen novel except *Northanger Abbey*—the charming man who woos the heroine before proving untrustworthy in some respect. Willoughby, however, stands out as the most attractive of all these charmers, with his combination of physical beauty, intelligence, musical talents, and great energy. He also woos the heroine more ardently than any other, with the exception of Henry Crawford in *Mansfield Park*. His desirability and

Marianne's own incautious enthusiasm make her, unlike all the other heroines in question, fall deeply in love. At the same time, the disappointment he inflicts is far worse than his analogues. He does not simply drift away or turn out to be engaged elsewhere. He abandons Marianne—abruptly, without explanation, and just after expressing his most fervent devotion—and when she eventually locates him he responds with complete coldness and a letter of egregious callousness. Finally, the revelation of his past wickedness forces Marianne to contemplate that she just missed a terrible fate while also calling into grave question her earlier judgment.

As for Elinor, her trials have a couple of analogues, for Fanny Price and Anne Elliot also must witness the attachment of the man they love to another woman. Elinor, however, is the only one to suffer from the dishonorable usage of being wooed, albeit hesitantly, while the man is engaged to another. In contrast, Fanny's love always treats her kindly; Anne suffers from her love's cold aloofness, but she knows that this is the natural product of her own earlier rejection of him. Furthermore, Fanny's and Anne's female rivals have some good qualities, whereas Elinor's is one of the most odious characters ever created by Jane Austen. This means that in addition to her own loss, Elinor must anticipate great future misery for her beloved. She is also subject to cruel persecutions by her rival, from being trapped into a painful promise of secrecy to being forced to listen repeatedly to the other woman's gloating and snide remarks—all at a time when Elinor is being mistreated by Edward's relatives due to their misperception of the real situation.

The combined effect of these ordeals is to place the heroines' virtues and flaws in sharper relief. Marianne's sensibility leads her into even greater misery and imprudence than would have occurred under less difficult circumstances, while Elinor's ability to maintain her composure and act correctly shines even more brightly. In fact, Elinor is such a model of good thinking and behavior under duress, despite being only nineteen, that she borders on the implausible. In her case the author's didactic purpose overwhelms her realism on occasion. Yet more often the deep feelings that Elinor also possesses, and that she must struggle continually with in order to maintain her good sense, make her believable, while such feelings and struggles earn her the full love and sympathy of the reader.

Marianne is also able to win such sympathy. Her numerous mistakes and follies threaten to turn the reader against her. But the many good qualities she also displays, including a good share of natural, even if misdirected, sense, make her someone whose fate seems of vital importance. Moreover, she is only seventeen, as well as lacking experience and a sensible parent to provide guidance. Thus while her faults stem from bad doctrine, her fervent adherence to that doctrine and refusal to acknowledge its deficiencies is at least partly the product of her youth and circumstances. This encourages the reader's forgiveness, while also making it plausible that, having been forced to perceive her errors while still young, she will amend her ways and be capable of leading an excellent life. Thus her story, even with its dark sides, can still ultimately fit into the author's fundamentally comic vision of life.

All this has allowed *Sense and Sensibility* to continue attracting readers and sympathetic commentary. It contains the same vivid characters, brilliant dialogues, and skillful plot as all Austen novels. Its unique focus on two heroines, even if at the expense of developing the heroes, gives Austen scope for her most thorough exploration of the relationships between sisters, a subject she knew intimately, since throughout her life she was far closer to her sister, Cassandra, than to any other person. Elinor and Marianne present a superb picture of two sisters who are both united by profound affection and divided by profound differences of opinion. Moreover, with Marianne, Jane Austen has created her closest approximation to a true tragic heroine, someone of great abilities and virtues brought very low, to the point of death, by fatal flaws, and one whose story is capable of arousing both fear and pity in the reader. Finally, the novel offers a deeper and more sustained exploration of a controversial intellectual issue than that seen in any other Austen novels. Nor is the issue a historical relic. While the specific concept of sensibility is no longer a matter of discussion and debate, the general dichotomy of emotion versus reason, self-expression versus self-control, and individual imperatives and desires versus moral and social duties are still matters of vital concern and contention. That the novel manages to combine a serious philosophical argument about such matters with a riveting and emotionally engaging human drama is a testament to its strength, and a good reason for its persistent appeal.

The Annotated

SENSE

AND

SENSIBILITY

VOLUME ONE

Chapter One

*T*he family of Dashwood had been long settled in Sussex.[1] Their estate was large,[2] and their residence was at Norland Park, in the centre of their property, where, for many generations, they had lived in so respectable a manner, as to engage[3] the general good opinion of their surrounding acquaintance. The late owner of this estate was a single man, who lived to a very advanced age, and who for many years of his life, had a constant companion and housekeeper[4] in his sister. But her death, which happened ten years before his own, produced a great alteration in his home; for to supply her loss, he invited and received into his house the family of his nephew Mr. Henry Dashwood, the legal inheritor of the Norland estate,[5] and the person to whom he intended to bequeath it. In the society of his nephew and niece, and their children, the old Gentleman's days were comfortably spent. His attachment to them all increased. The constant attention of Mr. and Mrs. Henry Dashwood to his wishes, which proceeded not merely from interest, but from goodness of heart, gave him every degree of solid comfort which his age could receive; and the cheerfulness of the children added a relish to his existence.

By a former marriage, Mr. Henry Dashwood had one son: by his present lady, three daughters. The son, a steady respectable young man, was amply provided for by the fortune of his mother, which had been large, and half of which devolved on him on his coming of age.[6] By his own marriage, likewise, which happened soon afterwards, he added to his wealth.[7] To him therefore the succession to the Norland estate was not so really important as to

1. *Sussex:* A county south of London (see map, p. 738).

2. The gentry that dominates this and other Jane Austen novels were based in rural estates, whose agricultural profits formed the principal source of their income.

3. *engage:* gain.

4. "Housekeeper" was often used to refer to a high-ranking female servant. Here it means that his sister supervised the household, which would include directing and managing the servants, deciding on meals, ordering supplies for the house, and attending to the needs of residents and guests. These tasks were normally performed by women, so a man without a wife would usually have a sister or other unmarried female relative live with him for this purpose. Since unmarried women rarely had homes of their own, she would benefit by gaining a secure home in which she exercised a position of importance and influence.

5. When a landowner lacked sons, a paternal nephew, as Henry Dashwood's name indicates he is, would normally be the sole heir. The idea was to preserve the family estate intact, and in the male line—if a woman inherited and then married, the estate would become her husband's property, thereby transferring it to a different family. Thus even landowners who had daughters would usually leave the property to a nephew or other male relative.

6. The mother's fortune would have come under the control of her husband upon her marriage, but the marriage settlement would have dictated that the son receive it upon turning twenty-one, the legal age of adulthood. Elaborate financial settlements, concerning the husband and wife and any children they might have, were standard for marriages among the gentry.

7. A woman almost always brought a dowry to a marriage: its size would significantly determine her marital desirability, as will be seen at various points in this novel. In return for the dowry, which would fall under the control of the husband, he, or his family in the event of his death, would be obligated to provide for her. Pin money, a certain annual sum for her personal use, would usually be part of the marriage settlement.
    The dowry here, as revealed later (see p. 698), is ten thousand pounds. Thus it is more than what Mr. Henry Dashwood is shown below to have at his disposal. One mark of Jane Austen's novels is precision about monetary sums, along with an appreciation of the important role money plays in life.

his sisters; for their fortune, independent of what might arise to them from their father's inheriting that property, could be but small. Their mother had nothing, and their father only seven thousand pounds in his own disposal; for the remaining moiety of his first wife's fortune was also secured to her child, and he had only a life interest in it.[8]

The old Gentleman died; his will was read, and like almost every other will, gave as much disappointment as pleasure.[9] He was neither so unjust, nor so ungrateful, as to leave his estate from his nephew; — but he left it to him on such terms as destroyed half the value of the bequest. Mr. Dashwood had wished for it more for the sake of his wife and daughters than for himself or his son: — but to his son, and his son's son, a child of four years old, it was secured, in such a way, as to leave to himself no power of providing for those who were most dear to him, and who most needed a provision, by any charge on the estate,[10] or by any sale of its valuable woods.[11] The whole was tied up for the benefit of this child,[12] who, in occasional visits with his father and mother at Norland,[13] had so far gained on the affections of his uncle, by such attractions as are by no means unusual in children of two or three years old; an imperfect articulation, an earnest desire of having his own way, many cunning tricks, and a great deal of noise, as to outweigh all the value of all the attention which, for years, he had received from his niece and her daughters.[14] He meant not to be unkind however, and, as a mark of his affection for the three girls, he left them a thousand pounds a-piece.

Mr. Dashwood's disappointment was, at first, severe; but his temper was cheerful and sanguine, and he might reasonably hope to live many years, and by living economically, lay by a considerable sum from the produce of an estate already large, and capable of almost immediate improvement.[15] But the fortune, which had been so tardy in coming, was his only one twelvemonth. He survived his uncle no longer; and ten thousand pounds, including the late legacies, was all that remained for his widow and daughters.[16]

His son was sent for, as soon as his danger was known,[17] and to

8. This means Henry Dashwood is able to use the income from the remaining moiety, or half, of his wife's fortune but cannot touch the principal, which will go to his son after he dies. The family of the bride would often secure such an arrangement in the marriage settlement. It ensured that her fortune would ultimately go to her children, even if the husband turned out to be financially irresponsible, or if he, after she died, married again and was persuaded by his second wife to leave all his money to his second set of children.

9. Jane Austen herself, along with the rest of her immediate family, experienced disappointments on learning of the wills of some relatives.

10. He could not give them money from the estate, or money he borrowed using the estate as collateral.

11. Timber was often a leading product of estates. Wood was central to the economy of the time, used to make a variety of items that are currently made of metal or plastic.

12. It was standard practice for estates to be bound by such a settlement. By allowing the current holder of the property only to draw income from it, it ensured the estate would pass intact to the succeeding heir. At the same time, most settlements did not restrict the current holders quite this severely, and while they almost all gave the bulk of the estate to the eldest male of the next generation, they usually made more generous provision for other children than this one.

13. That they paid only "occasional visits" to the man's father and grandfather hints at the lack of family feeling that will shortly be on full display.

14. Jane Austen, while described by nieces and nephews as a kind, attentive aunt, often criticizes in her novels excessive or blind fondness for children.

15. For more than a century many landowners had undertaken improvements to their estates, through clearing unproductive land for cultivation or increasing yields by agricultural innovations. The resulting increases in the food supply and population were important factors in the industrial revolution that began in England in the late eighteenth century. Greater income over the years, along with economical living, would allow Mr. Dashwood to accumulate a substantial sum that he then could pass on to his wife and daughters.

16. This would come from their three thousand pounds and the seven thousand pounds already mentioned as under the father's control.

17. Meaning the danger of his dying soon.

him Mr. Dashwood recommended, with all the strength and urgency which illness could command, the interest of his mother-in-law[18] and sisters.

Mr. John Dashwood had not the strong feelings of the rest of the family; but he was affected by a recommendation of such a nature at such a time, and he promised to do every thing in his power to make them comfortable. His father was rendered easy by such an assurance, and Mr. John Dashwood had then leisure to consider how much there might prudently be in his power to do for them.

He was not an ill-disposed young man, unless to be rather cold hearted, and rather selfish, is to be ill-disposed: but he was, in general, well respected; for he conducted himself with propriety in the discharge of his ordinary duties. Had he married a more amiable woman, he might have been made still more respectable[19] than he was:—he might even have been made amiable[20] himself; for he was very young when he married, and very fond of his wife. But Mrs. John Dashwood was a strong caricature of himself;—more narrow-minded[21] and selfish.

When he gave his promise to his father, he meditated within himself to increase the fortunes of his sisters by the present of a thousand pounds a-piece. He then really thought himself equal to it. The prospect of four thousand a-year, in addition to his present income, besides the remaining half of his own mother's fortune,[22] warmed his heart and made him feel capable of generosity.[23]— "Yes, he would give them three thousand pounds: it would be liberal[24] and handsome! It would be enough to make them completely easy.[25] Three thousand pounds! he could spare so considerable a sum with little inconvenience."—He thought of it all day long, and for many days successively, and he did not repent.[26]

No sooner was his father's funeral over, than Mrs. John Dashwood, without sending any notice of her intention to her mother-in-law, arrived with her child and their attendants. No one could dispute her right to come; the house was her husband's from the moment of his father's decease; but the indelicacy of her conduct

18. *mother-in-law*: stepmother.

19. *respectable*: worthy, decent. The term, like the just-used "propriety," was thoroughly complimentary, with none of the negative connotations sometimes found today.

20. *amiable*: kind, friendly, good-natured. The word then suggested general goodness and not just outward agreeableness.

21. *narrow-minded*: mercenary, parsimonious. In a letter Jane Austen expresses doubt of someone's ability to "persuade a perverse and narrow-minded woman to oblige those whom she does not love" (Jan. 25, 1801).

22. The four thousand would be the income from the estate. His wife's dowry of ten thousand (see p. 698) would, at the standard 5% rate of return on investments then, yield five hundred a year. Since his mother's fortune was described as large, his annual income would now be at least five thousand pounds a year, perhaps even six or seven. This is far more than Mrs. Dashwood, who would get only five hundred pounds a year from her ten thousand.

It is hard to translate these amounts into current terms, for relative costs of things were very different then. Goods tended to cost a great deal, while services, including full-time live-in servants, were relatively cheap. But, allowing for that, a pound then is worth approximately 55 pounds today, which at 2010 rates is the equivalent of 80 to 85 U.S. dollars. This would make John Dashwood's income somewhere around half a million dollars a year. For the time, this would probably put him in the top .1 or .2% of the population.

23. That John Dashwood feels capable of generosity only after inheriting such a considerable fortune signals that he is far from naturally generous.

24. *liberal*: generous.

25. *easy*: comfortable financially.

26. That he thinks of it so continually suggests that he may be finding it difficult to reconcile himself to it.

was so much the greater, and to a woman in Mrs. Dashwood's situation, with only common feelings, must have been highly unpleasing,[27]—but in *her* mind there was a sense of honour so keen, a generosity so romantic, that any offence of the kind, by whomsoever given or received, was to her a source of immoveable disgust.[28] Mrs. John Dashwood had never been a favourite with any of her husband's family; but she had had no opportunity, till the present, of shewing them with how little attention to the comfort of other people she could act when occasion required it.

So acutely did Mrs. Dashwood feel this ungracious behaviour, and so earnestly did she despise her daughter-in-law for it, that, on the arrival of the latter, she would have quitted the house for ever,[29] had not the entreaty of her eldest girl induced her first to reflect on the propriety of going, and her own tender love for all her three children determined her afterwards to stay, and for their sakes avoid a breach with their brother.

Elinor, this eldest daughter whose advice was so effectual, possessed a strength of understanding, and coolness of judgment, which qualified her, though only nineteen,[30] to be the counsellor of her mother, and enabled her frequently to counteract, to the advantage of them all, that eagerness of mind in Mrs. Dashwood which must generally have led to imprudence. She had an excellent heart;—her disposition was affectionate, and her feelings were strong; but she knew how to govern them:[31] it was a knowledge which her mother had yet to learn, and which one of her sisters had resolved never to be taught.

Marianne's abilities were, in many respects, quite equal to Elinor's.[32] She was sensible and clever; but eager in every thing; her sorrows, her joys, could have no moderation. She was generous, amiable, interesting:[33] she was every thing but prudent. The resemblance between her and her mother was strikingly great.

Elinor saw, with concern, the excess of her sister's sensibility;[34] but by Mrs. Dashwood it was valued and cherished. They encouraged each other now in the violence of their affliction. The agony of grief which overpowered them at first, was voluntarily renewed, was sought for, was created again and again.[35] They gave them-

27. Once the house became her husband's Mrs. John Dashwood would take over the position of mistress and housekeeper from Mrs. Dashwood (see above, note 4). This is why nobody disputes her right, but a more delicate, or sensitive, person would have refrained from displacing so quickly a woman who had just lost her husband from a position she had long held.

28. *disgust*: distaste. The word did not have as strong a connotation then.

29. Mrs. Dashwood will often display the same impulsiveness shown here, along with the same tender affection for her children. The impropriety of hastily leaving probably refers to the insult it would be to John Dashwood.

30. In calling Elinor "only nineteen" the author raises a possible point of criticism, namely whether someone of Elinor's youth could display the extraordinary wisdom and self-command that she does throughout the novel.

31. This sentence provides an excellent summation of Elinor's character. She represents the "Sense" of the title, but this does not mean she is a creature of pure reason. She shows at various points the strong feelings mentioned here. What distinguishes her is her willingness and ability to control them and act rationally and sensibly, even in the most trying circumstances.

32. The generally equal abilities of Marianne to Elinor, referring particularly to her intellectual abilities, are an important point, as is Marianne's generally equal goodness. Their acute differences stem from their different outlooks on life and opinions on how to act and feel.

33. *interesting*: engaging; inclined to arouse curiosity or emotion.

34. "Sensibility," a word used often then, had a variety of meanings, with the most important revolving around the capacity for sensation or feeling. It was a term often used positively, by Jane Austen as well, for she never regards an incapacity to feel, something displayed by various characters in her works, as laudable. This is why Elinor regrets only the "excess of her sister's sensibility."

"Sensibility" in the eighteenth century had also come to refer to a broad cultural movement that extolled acute feeling and sensitivity (for more on this background, see introduction). Many literary works expounded and celebrated this idea, even as others criticized it. The cult of sensibility exercised an important influence on, and shared much with, Romanticism, which by Jane Austen's time had become a powerful cultural force in Europe. Thus this novel is responding quite explicitly to contemporary matters of great concern and debate.

35. This indulgence in grief and deliberate cultivation of it would be appropriate for a devotee of sensibility. Its advocates believed in fostering and intensifying a variety of emotions, and saw a capacity for grieving and weeping copiously as a mark of tenderness and virtue.

selves up wholly to their sorrow, seeking increase of wretchedness in every reflection that could afford it,[36] and resolved against ever admitting[37] consolation in future. Elinor, too, was deeply afflicted; but still she could struggle, she could exert herself. She could consult with her brother, could receive her sister-in-law on her arrival, and treat her with proper attention; and could strive to rouse her mother to similar exertion, and encourage her to similar forbearance.

Margaret, the other sister, was a good-humoured well-disposed girl; but as she had already imbibed a good deal of Marianne's romance,[38] without having much of her sense, she did not, at thirteen, bid fair to equal her sisters at a more advanced period of life.

36. They turned to every reflection that would make them more wretched.

37. *admitting:* allowing; permitting themselves.

38. *romance:* imaginative or romantic qualities.

Farnley Hall: a grand country house such as Norland might be.

[From John Preston Neale, *Views of the Seats of Noblemen and Gentlemen*, Vol. V (1822)]

Chapter Two

Mrs. John Dashwood now installed herself mistress of Norland; and her mother and sisters-in-law were degraded to the condition of visitors. As such, however, they were treated by her with quiet civility;[1] and by her husband with as much kindness as he could feel towards any body beyond himself, his wife, and their child. He really pressed them, with some earnestness, to consider Norland as their home; and, as no plan appeared so eligible to Mrs. Dashwood as remaining there till she could accommodate herself with a house in the neighbourhood, his invitation was accepted.

A continuance in a place where every thing reminded her of former delight, was exactly what suited her mind. In seasons of cheerfulness, no temper could be more cheerful than hers, or possess, in a greater degree, that sanguine expectation of happiness which is happiness itself. But in sorrow she must be equally carried away by her fancy, and as far beyond consolation as in pleasure she was beyond alloy.

Mrs. John Dashwood did not at all approve of what her husband intended to do for his sisters. To take three thousand pounds from the fortune of their dear little boy, would be impoverishing him to the most dreadful degree. She begged him to think again on the subject. How could he answer it to himself to rob his child, and his only child too, of so large a sum?[2] And what possible claim could the Miss Dashwoods, who were related to him only by half blood, which she considered as no relationship at all, have on his generosity to so large an amount. It was very well known that no affection was ever supposed to exist between the children of any man by different marriages; and why was he to ruin himself, and their poor little Harry, by giving away all his money to his half sisters?

1.   While she is consistently shown to be a nasty person, especially in the remainder of this chapter, Fanny generally displays decent outward manners. One reason is probably her high social origins, for among the elite, especially in London (where her mother lives), a strong code of etiquette was taught and upheld.

2.   If their son remains an only child, with no siblings to share his inheritance, he will be less harmed by any gift to others. She, however, is so determined to dissuade her husband that she will use any argument, good or bad.

"It was my father's last request to me," replied her husband, "that I should assist his widow and daughters."

"He did not know what he was talking of, I dare say; ten to one but he was light-headed at the time. Had he been in his right senses, he could not have thought of such a thing as begging you to give away half your fortune from your own child."[3]

"He did not stipulate for any particular sum, my dear Fanny;[4] he only requested me, in general terms, to assist them, and make their situation more comfortable than it was in his power to do. Perhaps it would have been as well if he had left it wholly to myself. He could hardly suppose I should neglect them. But as he required the promise, I could not do less than give it: at least I thought so at the time. The promise, therefore, was given, and must be performed. Something must be done for them whenever they leave Norland and settle in a new home."

"Well, then, *let* something be done for them; but *that* something need not be three thousand pounds. Consider," she added, "that when the money is once parted with, it never can return. Your sisters will marry, and it will be gone for ever.[5] If, indeed, it could ever be restored to our poor little boy—"[6]

"Why, to be sure," said her husband, very gravely, "that would make a great difference. The time may come when Harry will regret that so large a sum was parted with. If he should have a numerous family, for instance, it would be a very convenient addition."

"To be sure it would."

"Perhaps, then, it would be better for all parties if the sum were diminished one half.—Five hundred pounds would be a prodigious increase to their fortunes!"

"Oh! beyond any thing great! What brother on earth would do half so much for his sisters, even if *really* his sisters![7] And as it is— only half blood!—But you have such a generous spirit!"

"I would not wish to do any thing mean,"[8] he replied. "One had rather, on such occasions, do too much than too little. No one, at least, can think I have not done enough for them: even themselves, they can hardly expect more."

3. Their income is at least five thousand a year (see p. 7, note 22); they also inherited Norland house and its furnishings (the figures for income would be separate from that). In contrast, three thousand pounds would generate only one hundred and fifty pounds of annual income. Thus it represents only 2% to 3% of their fortune.

4. His use of "my dear Fanny" is a standard formulation in Jane Austen's time, found throughout her novels and letters, and does not indicate any special intimacy and affection, or special formality and pretentiousness.

5. If they married their money would become part of the fortune of their husbands' families.

6. Since her husband has just proclaimed his principal reason for assisting his sisters to be the sanctity of a promise, rather than his own inclination, she has cleverly kept insisting on a contrary moral principle, their duty to their son.

7. If half blood is "no relationship at all," they would not really be his sisters. It is notable that he does not contradict her point.

8. *mean*: stingy, base. It is significant that he has switched from the inescapable obligation of a promise to the vaguer principle of not wishing to be mean.

"There is no knowing what *they* may expect," said the lady, "but we are not to think of their expectations: the question is, what you can afford to do."

"Certainly—and I think I may afford to give them five hundred pounds a-piece. As it is, without any addition of mine, they will each have above three thousand pounds on their mother's death—a very comfortable fortune for any young woman."[9]

"To be sure it is: and, indeed, it strikes me that they can want no addition at all. They will have ten thousand pounds divided amongst them. If they marry, they will be sure of doing well, and if they do not, they may all live very comfortably together on the interest of ten thousand pounds."

"That is very true, and, therefore, I do not know whether, upon the whole, it would not be more advisable to do something for their mother while she lives rather than for them—something of the annuity kind I mean.—My sisters would feel the good effects of it as well as herself. A hundred a year would make them all perfectly comfortable."

His wife hesitated a little, however, in giving her consent to this plan.

"To be sure," said she, "it is better than parting with fifteen hundred pounds at once. But then if Mrs. Dashwood should live fifteen years, we shall be completely taken in."

"Fifteen years! my dear Fanny; her life cannot be worth half that purchase."[10]

"Certainly not; but if you observe, people always live for ever when there is any annuity to be paid them; and she is very stout[11] and healthy, and hardly forty. An annuity is a very serious business; it comes over and over every year, and there is no getting rid of it. You are not aware of what you are doing. I have known a great deal of the trouble of annuities; for my mother was clogged[12] with the payment of three to old superannuated servants by my father's will,[13] and it is amazing how disagreeable she found it. Twice every year these annuities were to be paid; and then there was the trouble of getting it to them; and then one of them was said to have died, and afterwards it turned out to be no such thing.

9. "Above three thousand pounds" refers to what they will have once their mother's seven thousand is divided between them and added to their own thousand apiece; the precision that he and his wife display on money matters indicates how much such matters concern them. Women did usually have smaller fortunes in this society, since property generally went to males and husbands were expected to support their wives. But most women of their class had more than this—his wife brought ten thousand pounds to him—and it was usually needed to attract a husband. Moreover, one would normally not count what a woman would inherit after a parent's death, a procedure that allows John Dashwood to triple their supposed fortune, since it was what a woman had when being courted that counted, and in this society a woman usually needed to marry when fairly young if she was to do so at all.

10. *worth half that purchase*: likely to last half that time. Mrs. Dashwood is now forty. Average life expectancy then was low, though much of the reason was high childhood mortality. A reasonable number of people survived to old age, especially if they had already reached Mrs. Dashwood's age, so John Dashwood's estimate of only several years is probably premature. He may be thinking along those lines because it buttresses his argument about the girls having the expectation of inheritance from their mother.

11. *stout*: strong, robust.

12. *clogged*: encumbered.

13. Such charity to servants who had long worked for the family was common, a product of the strong ethos of upper-class paternalism.

My mother was quite sick of it.[14] Her income was not her own, she said, with such perpetual claims on it; and it was the more unkind in my father, because, otherwise, the money would have been entirely at my mother's disposal, without any restriction whatever.[15] It has given me such an abhorrence of annuities, that I am sure I would not pin myself down to the payment of one for all the world."

"It is certainly an unpleasant thing," replied Mr. Dashwood, "to have those kind of yearly drains on one's income. One's fortune, as your mother justly says, is *not* one's own. To be tied down to the regular payment of such a sum, on every rent day,[16] is by no means desirable: it takes away one's independence."[17]

"Undoubtedly; and after all you have no thanks for it. They think themselves secure, you do no more than what is expected, and it raises no gratitude at all. If I were you, whatever I did should be done at my own discretion entirely. I would not bind myself to allow them any thing yearly. It may be very inconvenient some years to spare a hundred, or even fifty pounds from our own expences."

"I believe you are right, my love; it will be better that there should be no annuity in the case; whatever I may give them occasionally will be of far greater assistance than a yearly allowance, because they would only enlarge their style of living if they felt sure of a larger income, and would not be sixpence the richer for it at the end of the year.[18] It will certainly be much the best way. A present of fifty pounds, now and then, will prevent their ever being distressed for money, and will, I think, be amply discharging my promise to my father."

"To be sure it will. Indeed, to say the truth, I am convinced within myself that your father had no idea of your giving them any money at all. The assistance he thought of, I dare say, was only such as might be reasonably expected of you; for instance, such as looking out for a comfortable small house for them, helping them to move their things,[19] and sending them presents of fish and game,[20] and so forth, whenever they are in season. I'll lay my life that he meant nothing farther; indeed, it would be very strange

14. Most servants' annuities were not very large. Since Fanny's mother is later shown to be a very wealthy woman, these payments probably represented only a fraction of her income. Nor would they have been much trouble, since a person in her position would usually employ someone, whether a family attorney or an agent or steward, to handle such details. That she nonetheless felt deeply aggrieved by the matter provides a hint of her greedy and unpleasant character. It also establishes a strong affinity between herself and her daughter.

15. A widow would often receive only a limited portion of her husband's fortune, or only a regular payment from it while she lived, with the rest going to the heir. Fanny's mother is an exception, and the power this gives her will play a critical role in the story.

16. There were four rent days: Christmas, Lady Day (March 25), Midsummer (June 24), and Michaelmas (September 29). They divided the year into quarters and were when many payments were due. Though Fanny's example concerned twice-annual payments, and it would be perfectly possible to give the Miss Dashwoods annuities that were paid only once a year, he has stretched their possible frequency to four times a year to make them sound as unpleasant as possible.

17. By this point John Dashwood has completely abandoned any discussion of moral considerations to focus solely on his own pleasure and convenience.

18. Pence were one of the three basic British monetary units, along with shillings and pounds. Twelve pence made a shilling, and twenty shillings a pound. Thus sixpence—which was half a shilling and the denomination of a silver coin—was a small amount. He probably chose this specific amount because the sixpence coin had long been one of the most common coins in Britain.

19. People who moved would usually have to hire wagons to transport their things, as well as a carriage and horses to convey themselves. A wealthy man like John Dashwood would certainly own a carriage and horses, and a large estate would probably have wagons or carts that could carry goods. Thus this would be of real assistance to them, though worth much less than the monetary sums discussed.

20. Many estates had fishponds, and many landowners hunted game (though John Dashwood is never described as doing so).

and unreasonable if he did. Do but consider, my dear Mr. Dash-wood,[21] how excessively comfortable your mother-in-law and her daughters may live on the interest of seven thousand pounds, besides the thousand pounds belonging to each of the girls, which brings them in fifty pounds a-year a-piece,[22] and, of course, they will pay their mother for their board out of it. Altogether, they will have five hundred a-year amongst them, and what on earth can four women want for more than that?—They will live so cheap! Their housekeeping will be nothing at all. They will have no carriage, no horses, and hardly any servants;[23] they will keep no company, and can have no expences of any kind! Only conceive how comfortable they will be! Five hundred a-year! I am sure I cannot imagine how they will spend half of it; and as to your giving them more, it is quite absurd to think of it. They will be much more able to give *you* something."

"Upon my word," said Mr. Dashwood, "I believe you are perfectly right. My father certainly could mean nothing more by his request to me than what you say. I clearly understand it now, and I will strictly fulfil my engagement by such acts of assistance and kindness to them as you have described. When my mother removes into another house my services shall be readily given to accommodate her as far as I can. Some little present of furniture too may be acceptable then."

"Certainly," returned Mrs. John Dashwood. "But, however, *one* thing must be considered. When your father and mother moved to Norland, though the furniture of Stanhill was sold, all the china, plate, and linen was saved,[24] and is now left to your mother. Her house will therefore be almost completely fitted up as soon as she takes it."

"That is a material consideration undoubtedly. A valuable legacy indeed! And yet some of the plate would have been a very pleasant addition to our own stock here."

"Yes; and the set of breakfast china is twice as handsome as what belongs to this house.[25] A great deal too handsome, in my opinion, for any place *they* can ever afford to live in. But, however, so it is. Your father thought only of *them*. And I must say this:

21. Husbands and wives in Jane Austen often call each other "Mr." and "Mrs."

22. The 5% rate of return she mentions is found throughout Jane Austen. It was the standard rate on government bonds, which were the investment of choice for money that was not tied up in land (there were 3% and 4% bonds as well, but they were sold at a discount, making the effective return the same). The precision about money displayed by both people in the conversation gives a good clue to their character.

23. Fanny is right about their not having a carriage and horses, and few servants, and this does save them considerable expense. But it also comes with a price, one that Fanny does not pay herself. For example, their lack of a carriage will restrict the range of other families they will be able to visit in their new home.

24. Stanhill is the house they lived in before they came to Norland—most prominent houses and estates were given names. The high cost of moving items would have spurred the sale of the first home's furniture. The china, plate (table utensils), and linen, being more portable, were transferred, and because they were not originally part of Norland they do not automatically remain with the house. Thus Henry Dashwood, trying to give as much as he could to his wife and daughters, left them these items.

25. By this time china, which could include porcelain from England or other European countries, had become a standard possession of the wealthy, and even to a degree those of moderate income. This is indicated by the Dashwoods' having a special set of china just for breakfast. Such sets had become popular: in *Northanger Abbey* the heroine admires one owned by a family she is visiting. For a picture of a London glass and china shop at the time, see the following page.

that you owe no particular gratitude to him, nor attention to his wishes, for we very well know that if he could, he would have left almost every thing in the world to *them*."[26]

This argument was irresistible. It gave to his intentions whatever of decision[27] was wanting before; and he finally resolved, that it would be absolutely unnecessary, if not highly indecorous,[28] to do more for the widow and children of his father, than such kind of neighbourly acts as his own wife pointed out.

26. The dialogue comprising this chapter has always, starting from the first reviews of the novel, been celebrated for its brilliant picture of decency giving way to greed. Its tour de force quality is increased by its consisting almost solely of spoken words, with only the occasional mention of who is speaking. It could be objected, however, that the author, in pursuit of a brilliant effect, has sacrificed realism a little. John Dashwood's change of mind is thoroughly plausible; its complete accomplishment in the course of a single brief exchange is less so, especially considering the careful, deliberate character he shows throughout the novel. Later in her career, when Jane Austen worked in a slightly more subtle and realistic manner, she might have shown the transformation happening over more than one conversation, perhaps interspersed with some time for the character to reflect on what was said and gradually resolve upon a different course.

27. *decision:* determination, resolution.

28. *indecorous:* improper.

A London glass and china shop.

[From *The Repository of arts, literature, fashions, manufactures, &c*, Vol. I (1809), p. 330]

Chapter Three

Mrs. Dashwood remained at Norland several months; not from any disinclination to move when the sight of every well known spot ceased to raise the violent emotion[1] which it produced for a while; for when her spirits began to revive, and her mind became capable of some other exertion than that of heightening its affliction by melancholy remembrances, she was impatient to be gone, and indefatigable in her inquiries for a suitable dwelling in the neighbourhood of Norland; for to remove far from that beloved spot was impossible.[2] But she could hear of no situation that at once answered her notions of comfort and ease, and suited the prudence of her eldest daughter, whose steadier judgment rejected several houses as too large for their income, which her mother would have approved.

Mrs. Dashwood had been informed by her husband of the solemn promise on the part of his son in their favour, which gave comfort to his last earthly reflections. She doubted the sincerity of this assurance no more than he had doubted it himself, and she thought of it for her daughters' sake with satisfaction, though as for herself she was persuaded that a much smaller provision than 7000*l.* would support her in affluence. For their brother's sake too, for the sake of his own heart she rejoiced; and she reproached herself for being unjust to his merit before, in believing him incapable of generosity.[3] His attentive behaviour to herself and his sisters convinced her that their welfare was dear to him,[4] and, for a long time, she firmly relied on the liberality[5] of his intentions.

The contempt which she had, very early in their acquaintance, felt for her daughter-in-law, was very much increased by the farther knowledge of her character, which half a year's residence in her family afforded; and perhaps in spite of every consideration of politeness or maternal affection on the side of the former, the two

1.   *emotion:* agitation, mental distress.

2.   Once she and her daughters actually move into a house they can afford she will find many defects in it, in comparison to the grand house she has enjoyed. Mrs. Dashwood's ignorance and impracticality on money matters will appear at other times.

3.   Her benevolence is shown by her wishing this for the sake of his own heart as well as for her own sake. At the same time, her complete trust in the sincerity of his generosity manifests a naive belief about others' goodness — especially if they proclaim it themselves — that will appear later with more serious consequences.

4.   Thus he continues to be externally attentive even as he secretly renounces any financial assistance. This combination will persist in his treatment of his sisters.

5.   *liberality:* generosity.

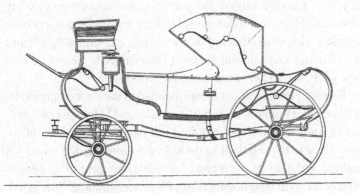

A barouche; the top can fold down, making it an open carriage.
[From T. Fuller, *An Essay on Wheel Carriages* (London, 1828), Plate no. 2]

ladies might have found it impossible to have lived together so long, had not a particular circumstance occurred to give still greater eligibility,[6] according to the opinions of Mrs. Dashwood, to her daughters' continuance at Norland.

This circumstance was a growing attachment between her eldest girl and the brother of Mrs. John Dashwood, a gentleman-like and pleasing young man,[7] who was introduced to their acquaintance soon after his sister's establishment at Norland, and who had since spent the greatest part of his time there.

Some mothers might have encouraged the intimacy from motives of interest, for Edward Ferrars was the eldest son of a man who had died very rich;[8] and some might have repressed it from motives of prudence, for, except a trifling sum, the whole of his fortune depended on the will of his mother.[9] But Mrs. Dashwood was alike uninfluenced by either consideration. It was enough for her that he appeared to be amiable, that he loved her daughter, and that Elinor returned the partiality. It was contrary to every doctrine of her's that difference of fortune should keep any couple asunder who were attracted by resemblance of disposition;[10] and that Elinor's merit should not be acknowledged by every one who knew her, was to her comprehension impossible.

Edward Ferrars was not recommended to their good opinion by any peculiar[11] graces of person[12] or address.[13] He was not hand-some, and his manners[14] required intimacy to make them pleas-ing. He was too diffident to do justice to himself; but when his natural shyness was overcome, his behaviour gave every indica-tion of an open affectionate heart. His understanding[15] was good, and his education had given it solid improvement. But he was neither fitted by abilities nor disposition to answer the wishes of his mother and sister, who longed to see him distinguished—as—they hardly knew what. They wanted him to make a fine figure in the world[16] in some manner or other. His mother wished to inter-est him in political concerns, to get him into parliament,[17] or to see him connected with some of the great men of the day. Mrs. John Dashwood wished it likewise; but in the mean while, till one of these superior blessings could be attained, it would have qui-

6. *eligibility*: desirability, suitableness.

7. The concept of the gentleman was a central one in Jane Austen's society. It referred both to a social status held by all the male characters of this novel (for more, see p. 43, note 29) and to moral qualities, such as honor, courtesy, and generosity, that men of this status were supposed to possess—though not all did. The use of "gentlemanlike" here means that Edward does have those qualities.

8. The attraction would have come from the prevailing practice of leaving most of the family fortune to the eldest son.

9. Thus his mother could choose to leave almost all the fortune to other children (Edward is later revealed to have a younger brother in addition to his sister Fanny). This is why a prudent mother, in Mrs. Dashwood's place, might be reluctant to push for a marriage with Edward.

10. *disposition*: general mental tendencies or bent. The term had a broader connotation then than it does now.

11. *peculiar*: particular.

12. *person*: physical appearance.

13. *address*: outward demeanor, especially in conversation.

14. *manners*: outward bearing or characteristics; general mode of behavior. The word, frequently used in Jane Austen to describe people, also had a broader meaning then.

15. *understanding*: intelligence, intellect.

16. *world*: high or elite society. The term could also have the present sense of the world in general. Both meanings are probably suggested here.

17. Getting elected to Parliament was considered one of the highest honors for any gentleman and was the aspiration of many, whether from genuine interest in politics or from a wish for prestige and influence. For a contemporary picture of the Speaker of the House of Commons, the most powerful of the two houses of Parliament, see p. 33.

eted her ambition to see him driving a barouche.[18] But Edward had no turn for great men or barouches. All his wishes centered in domestic comfort and the quiet of private life.[19] Fortunately he had a younger brother who was more promising.[20]

Edward had been staying several weeks in the house before he engaged much of Mrs. Dashwood's attention; for she was, at that time, in such affliction as rendered her careless of surrounding objects. She saw only that he was quiet and unobtrusive, and she liked him for it. He did not disturb the wretchedness of her mind by ill-timed conversation. She was first called to observe and approve him farther, by a reflection which Elinor chanced one day to make on the difference between him and his sister. It was a contrast which recommended him most forcibly to her mother.

"It is enough," said she; "to say that he is unlike Fanny is enough. It implies every thing amiable. I love him already."

"I think you will like him," said Elinor, "when you know more of him."

"Like him!" replied her mother with a smile. "I can feel no sentiment of approbation inferior to love."

"You may esteem him."

"I have never yet known what it was to separate esteem and love."[21]

Mrs. Dashwood now took pains to get acquainted with him. Her manners were attaching[22] and soon banished his reserve. She speedily comprehended all his merits; the persuasion of his regard for Elinor perhaps assisted her penetration;[23] but she really felt assured of his worth: and even that quietness of manner which militated against all her established ideas of what a young man's address ought to be, was no longer uninteresting when she knew his heart to be warm and his temper[24] affectionate.

No sooner did she perceive any symptom of love in his behaviour to Elinor, than she considered their serious attachment as certain, and looked forward to their marriage as rapidly approaching.[25]

"In a few months, my dear Marianne," said she, "Elinor will in

18. *barouche*: a carriage seating four people whose top could be folded up or down (for a picture, see p. 25). It was an expensive and highly fashionable vehicle, which is why Edward's sister would like to see him driving one. After once riding in a barouche, Jane Austen wrote to her sister, "I liked my solitary elegance, & was ready to laugh all the time, at my being where I was—I could not but feel that I had naturally small right to be parading about London in a Barouche" (May 24, 1813).

19. The two paragraphs describing Edward represent a longer introduction than for any other character in the novel, one that exceeds the introduction for most romantic heroes in Jane Austen. It will soon be supplemented by lengthy speeches or reflections on Edward from Marianne and Elinor. A crucial reason for this is that the plot will consign Edward to a mostly offstage role, preventing the author from presenting his character very fully through his own speech or actions.

20. This last sentence foreshadows later events, in which Robert will end up superseding Edward in more than one way.

21. This exchange highlights a critical difference between Elinor and both her mother and her sister: she makes careful and nuanced distinctions in her reactions to and evaluations of others.

22. *attaching*: engaging; likely to attract or attach someone.

23. *penetration*: quickness or keenness of perception.

24. *temper*: emotional qualities. The term had a broader meaning then.

25. Mrs. Dashwood's haste in anticipating marriage reflects her own impetuous and imaginative nature, but it also reflects a tendency in this society. Marriage was universally considered a good and was entered into by most people, generally at a fairly young age. Moreover, unmarried men and women were subject to various restrictions preventing frequent intimate contact. Thus even mild displays of friendliness and interest between a man and a woman would inspire speculations about a possible marriage.

all probability be settled[26] for life. We shall miss her; but *she* will be happy."

"Oh! mama, how shall we do without her?"

"My love, it will be scarcely a separation. We shall live within a few miles of each other, and shall meet every day of our lives. You will gain a brother, a real, affectionate brother. I have the highest opinion in the world of Edward's heart. But you look grave, Marianne; do you disapprove[27] your sister's choice?"

"Perhaps," said Marianne, "I may consider it with some surprise. Edward is very amiable, and I love him tenderly. But yet— he is not the kind of young man—there is a something wanting—his figure is not striking; it has none of that grace which I should expect in the man who could seriously attach my sister. His eyes want[28] all that spirit,[29] that fire, which at once announce virtue and intelligence.[30] And besides all this, I am afraid, mama, he has no real taste. Music seems scarcely to attract him, and though he admires Elinor's drawings very much, it is not the admiration of a person who can understand their worth.[31] It is evident, in spite of his frequent attention to her while she draws, that in fact he knows nothing of the matter. He admires as a lover, not as a connoisseur. To satisfy me, those characters must be united. I could not be happy with a man whose taste did not in every point coincide with my own. He must enter into all my feelings; the same books, the same music must charm us both.[32] Oh! mama, how spiritless, how tame was Edward's manner in reading to us last night![33] I felt for my sister most severely. Yet she bore it with so much composure, she seemed scarcely to notice it. I could hardly keep my seat. To hear those beautiful lines which have frequently almost driven me wild, pronounced with such impenetrable calmness, such dreadful indifference!"—

"He would certainly have done more justice to simple and elegant prose. I thought so at the time; but you *would* give him Cowper."[34]

"Nay, mama, if he is not to be animated by Cowper!—but we must allow for difference of taste. Elinor has not my feelings, and therefore she may overlook it, and be happy with him. But it

26. *settled*: established in life, especially in marriage.

27. *disapprove*: disapprove of. The verb was often used in this transitive manner then.

28. *want*: lack.

29. *spirit*: ardor, vigor.

30. Marianne shares her mother's preference for boldness and vigor among men (see above), a common preference at the time.

31. He would have been exposed to music by Marianne, as well as to drawing by Elinor. Music and drawing were two of the principal accomplishments taught to young ladies, with most knowing one or the other. The pattern here, in which one sister draws and the other plays an instrument, was often found, including in Jane Austen's own family, where she was the musical one and her sister the visual artist. For a picture of a girl of the time engaged in sketching, see the following page.

32. This ideal of a perfect communion of souls will play a powerful role in Marianne's reactions and behavior during the novel. It is an ideal found in various strands of Romanticism.

33. Reading books aloud was a common practice at the time. Jane Austen refers to it in her letters, including the reading in her family of her own novels. One reason was the high cost of lighting, which meant that in the evening it would often not be possible for everyone in a room to have enough in the way of candles or lamps to see their own book well. Being able to read aloud well was considered a valuable skill, one sometimes included in people's education.

34. William Cowper (pronounced "Cooper") was a poet who lived from 1731 to 1800. He was one of Jane Austen's favorites. His poems celebrate rural life and the beauties of nature in a way that influenced later Romantic poets, though he tended to be less fervent in his enthusiasm. In *Mansfield Park* the somewhat Romantic heroine quotes lines from his poems on two different occasions.

would have broke *my* heart had I loved him, to hear him read with so little sensibility. Mama, the more I know of the world, the more am I convinced that I shall never see a man whom I can really love.[35] I require so much! He must have all Edward's virtues, and his person and manners must ornament his goodness with every possible charm."

"Remember, my love, that you are not seventeen. It is yet too early in life to despair of such an happiness. Why should you be less fortunate than your mother? In one circumstance only, my Marianne, may your destiny be different from her's!"[36]

A girl sketching.
[From Sir Walter Armstrong, *Sir Henry Raeburn* (London, 1901), p. 54]

35. Marianne's expression of despair corresponds to the themes of many Romantic works, which evoke grand ideals and experiences that are doomed never to be fulfilled in the world we actually inhabit.

36. She hopes Marianne will not suffer the loss of her husband so early.

The Speaker of the House of Commons.

[From William Pyne, *Costume of Great Britain* (London, 1804; 1989 reprint), Plate XXXVI]

Chapter Four

"What a pity it is, Elinor," said Marianne, "that Edward should have no taste for drawing."

"No taste for drawing," replied Elinor; "why should you think so? He does not draw himself, indeed, but he has great pleasure in seeing the performances of other people, and I assure you he is by no means deficient in natural taste, though he has not had opportunities of improving it. Had he ever been in the way of learning,[1] I think he would have drawn very well. He distrusts his own judgment in such matters so much, that he is always unwilling to give his opinion on any picture; but he has an innate propriety and simplicity of taste, which in general direct him perfectly right."[2]

Marianne was afraid of offending, and said no more on the subject; but the kind of approbation which Elinor described as excited in him by the drawings of other people, was very far from that rapturous delight, which, in her opinion, could alone be called taste.[3] Yet, though smiling within herself at the mistake, she honoured her sister for that blind partiality to Edward which produced it.[4]

"I hope, Marianne," continued Elinor, "you do not consider him as deficient in general taste. Indeed, I think I may say that you cannot, for your behaviour to him is perfectly cordial, and if *that* were your opinion, I am sure you could never be civil to him."[5]

Marianne hardly knew what to say. She would not wound the feelings of her sister on any account, and yet to say what she did not believe was impossible. At length she replied:

"Do not be offended, Elinor, if my praise of him is not in every thing equal to your sense of his merits. I have not had so many opportunities of estimating the minuter propensities of his mind,[6] his inclinations and tastes as you have; but I have the highest

1.   *in the way of learning:* had the opportunity to learn.

2.   Taste was a concept and attribute much praised and discussed at the time. According to some theories, though not all, simplicity of taste was a positive quality because it connoted an ability to see clearly and to appreciate what was not artificial or overly elaborate and ornate. The diffidence Elinor describes here will continue to characterize Edward generally.

3.   Romantic ideals of taste often emphasized "rapturous delight," for this fit in both with the emphasis on extreme and exalted emotion and with a particular celebration of art as a source of inspiration and salvation.

4.   She can only appreciate and justify Elinor by attributing to her something she considers a virtue—blind partiality—but that Elinor would not regard as virtuous at all.

5.   Elinor's implicit criticism signals one of the persistent differences between her and Marianne, namely the former's strong striving to be civil toward everyone, regardless of her real opinion, and the latter's contrasting refusal, inspired by her own ideal of sincerity.

6.   "Mind" then referred to a person's emotional as well as intellectual attributes.

opinion in the world of his goodness and sense. I think him every thing that is worthy and amiable."

"I am sure," replied Elinor with a smile, "that his dearest friends could not be dissatisfied with such commendation as that. I do not perceive how you could express yourself more warmly."

Marianne was rejoiced to find her sister so easily pleased.[7]

"Of his sense and his goodness," continued Elinor, "no one can, I think, be in doubt, who has seen him often enough to engage him in unreserved conversation. The excellence of his understanding and his principles can be concealed only by that shyness which too often keeps him silent. You know enough of him to do justice to his solid worth. But of his minuter propensities as you call them, you have from peculiar[8] circumstances been kept more ignorant than myself. He and I have been at times thrown a good deal together, while you have been wholly engrossed on the most affectionate principle by my mother.[9] I have seen a great deal of him, have studied his sentiments and heard his opinion on subjects of literature and taste; and, upon the whole, I venture to pronounce that his mind is well-informed, his enjoyment of books exceedingly great, his imagination lively, his observation[10] just[11] and correct, and his taste delicate[12] and pure. His abilities[13] in every respect improve as much upon acquaintance as his manners and person. At first sight, his address is certainly not striking; and his person can hardly be called handsome, till the expression of his eyes, which are uncommonly good, and the general sweetness of his countenance, is perceived. At present, I know him so well, that I think him really handsome; or, at least, almost so. What say you, Marianne?"[14]

"I shall very soon think him handsome, Elinor, if I do not now. When you tell me to love him as a brother, I shall no more see imperfection in his face, than I now do in his heart."

Elinor started at this declaration, and was sorry for the warmth she had been betrayed into, in speaking of him. She felt that Edward stood very high in her opinion. She believed the regard to be mutual; but she required greater certainty of it to make Marianne's conviction of their attachment agreeable to her. She knew

7. Marianne thinks of the praises she has just uttered as being far below her own exalted standard of what constitutes real approval.

8. *peculiar:* special.

9. She could mean their continuing to grieve together over Mr. Dashwood's death (with a possible slight ironic criticism of their indulgence in grief), or Mrs. Dashwood may have deliberately engrossed Marianne in order to give Elinor more time with Edward. Elinor's use of "my mother" to refer to Mrs. Dashwood in front of her own sister, rather than "our mother," is found throughout Jane Austen. She herself, in her letters to her sister, consistently refers to "my mother," "my father," and "my brother."

10. *observation:* faculty of observing or noticing.

11. *just:* exact, accurate.

12. *delicate:* endowed with fine powers of perception and appreciation. The term, often used as one of praise in Jane Austen, had a stronger and broader connotation than it does today.

13. *abilities:* mental powers.

14. Much of this speech, especially in its carefully crafted and balanced sentences, echoes the language found in many philosophical writings or essays of the time. As such, however, it seems excessively formal for an intimate conversation between two young people, even by the more formal standards of the language of the time. Other speeches of Elinor will exhibit the same quality, a product of the author's inclination to make her a representative and mouthpiece of important moral principles.

that what Marianne and her mother conjectured one moment, they believed the next—that with them, to wish was to hope, and to hope was to expect. She tried to explain the real state of the case to her sister.

"I do not attempt to deny," said she, "that I think very highly of him—that I greatly esteem, that I like him."

Marianne here burst forth with indignation—

"Esteem him! Like him! Cold-hearted Elinor! Oh! worse than cold-hearted! Ashamed of being otherwise. Use those words again and I will leave the room this moment."

Elinor could not help laughing. "Excuse me," said she, "and be assured that I meant no offence to you, by speaking, in so quiet a way, of my own feelings. Believe them to be stronger than I have declared; believe them, in short, to be such as his merit, and the suspicion—the hope of his affection for me may warrant, without imprudence or folly. But farther than this you must *not* believe. I am by no means assured of his regard for me. There are moments when the extent of it seems doubtful; and till his sentiments are fully known, you cannot wonder at my wishing to avoid any encouragement of my own partiality, by believing or calling it more than it is. In my heart I feel little—scarcely any doubt of his preference.[15] But there are other points to be considered besides his inclination. He is very far from being independent.[16] What his mother really is we cannot know; but, from Fanny's occasional mention of her conduct and opinions, we have never been disposed to think her amiable; and I am very much mistaken if Edward is not himself aware that there would be many difficulties in his way, if he were to wish to marry a woman who had not either a great fortune or high rank."[17]

Marianne was astonished to find how much the imagination of her mother and herself had outstripped the truth.

"And you really are not engaged to him!" said she. "Yet it certainly soon will happen. But two advantages will proceed from this delay. *I* shall not lose you so soon, and Edward will have greater opportunity of improving that natural taste for your favourite pursuit which must be so indispensably necessary[18] to

15. Elinor, while influenced by her heart, does not judge solely by it. One important reason is that she knows that factors other than personal affection often shape marriage decisions. Her intellectual caution in this case will prove to have justification, though not in the exact way she imagines now.

16. *independent:* independent financially.

17. A mother ambitious for her son, as Mrs. Ferrars was earlier described as being, would wish him to make a financially or socially advantageous marriage. Such a marriage could also help him in his career, since advancement was frequently determined by good connections.

Because most men of Edward's class derived the bulk of their money from inheritance, the threat of disinheritance by his mother is a formidable one. It is exacerbated by his not having entered fully on a career in which he could earn money (for more on this, see pp. 194–196). His mother's opposition would also create a moral barrier, for there was a strong belief in this society, normally shared by a conscientious person like Edward, that while children had the right to choose their mates, their parents retained the right to veto that choice.

18. *indispensably necessary:* absolutely necessary—the phrase, though redundant in a strict sense, is often found in Jane Austen and in the language of the time.

your future felicity. Oh! if he should be so far stimulated by your genius[19] as to learn to draw himself, how delightful it would be!"

Elinor had given her real opinion to her sister. She could not consider her partiality for Edward in so prosperous[20] a state as Marianne had believed it. There was, at times, a want of spirits[21] about him which, if it did not denote indifference, spoke[22] a something almost as unpromising. A doubt of her regard, supposing him to feel it, need not give him more than inquietude. It would not be likely to produce that dejection of mind which frequently attended him. A more reasonable cause might be found in the dependent situation which forbad the indulgence of his affection. She knew that his mother neither behaved to him so as to make his home comfortable[23] at present, nor to give him any assurance that he might form a home for himself, without strictly attending to her views[24] for his aggrandizement. With such a knowledge as this, it was impossible for Elinor to feel easy on the subject. She was far from depending on that result of his preference of her, which her mother and sister still considered as certain. Nay, the longer they were together the more doubtful seemed the nature of his regard; and sometimes, for a few painful minutes, she believed it to be no more than friendship.

But, whatever might really be its limits, it was enough, when perceived by his sister, to make her uneasy; and at the same time, (which was still more common,) to make her uncivil. She took the first opportunity of affronting her mother-in-law on the occasion, talking to her so expressively of her brother's great expectations,[25] of Mrs. Ferrars's resolution that both her sons should marry well, and of the danger attending any young woman who attempted to *draw him in*;[26] that Mrs. Dashwood could neither pretend to be unconscious, nor endeavour to be calm.[27] She gave her an answer which marked her contempt, and instantly left the room, resolving that, whatever might be the inconvenience or expense of so sudden a removal, her beloved Elinor should not be exposed another week to such insinuations.

In this state of her spirits, a letter was delivered to her from the post, which contained a proposal particularly well timed. It was

19. *genius*: ability or talent, especially in a particular area (such as drawing).

20. *prosperous*: flourishing.

21. *want of spirits*: lack of animation or cheerfulness.

22. *spoke*: indicated, revealed.

23. *comfortable*: pleasant, satisfactory.

24. *views*: expectations, intentions.

25. Meaning the prospect and expectation that he will attain a high, or great, social position, and Mrs. Ferrars's intention that he and his brother will marry women of high rank and fortune.

26. The idea of a woman drawing in a man was common in this society. It reflected the high desirability of marriage for women, for in addition to the personal benefits it might provide in any time and place, marriage then gave a woman higher social status, her one possibility of power and influence as mistress of a household, and greater affluence and financial security than she would probably enjoy on her own. For these reasons many women did everything in their power to catch a husband, and almost all women were subject to suspicion of such designs.

27. It is notable that Mrs. Dashwood does not even *endeavor* to remain calm. One reason for her resentment at this insinuation is that, as she explains later (p. 84), she has specifically brought up her daughters not to be the type of women who ensnare men.

the offer of a small house, on very easy terms,[28] belonging to a relation of her own, a gentleman[29] of consequence[30] and property in Devonshire.[31] The letter was from this gentleman himself, and written in the true spirit of friendly accommodation.[32] He understood that she was in need of a dwelling, and though the house he now offered her was merely a cottage,[33] he assured her that every thing should be done to it which she might think necessary, if the situation pleased her. He earnestly pressed her, after giving the particulars of the house and garden, to come with her daughters to Barton Park, the place of his own residence, from whence she might judge, herself, whether Barton Cottage, for the houses were in the same parish,[34] could, by any alteration, be made comfortable to her. He seemed really anxious to accommodate them, and the whole of his letter was written in so friendly a style as could not fail of giving pleasure to his cousin; more especially at a moment when she was suffering under the cold and unfeeling behaviour of her nearer connections.[35] She needed no time for deliberation or inquiry. Her resolution was formed as she read.[36] The situation of Barton, in a county so far distant from Sussex as Devonshire, which, but a few hours before, would have been a sufficient objection to outweigh every possible advantage belonging to the place, was now its first recommendation. To quit the neighbourhood of Norland was no longer an evil; it was an object of desire; it was a blessing, in comparison of the misery of continuing[37] her daughter-in-law's guest: and to remove for ever from that beloved place would be less painful than to inhabit or visit it while such a woman was its mistress. She instantly wrote Sir John Middleton her acknowledgment of his kindness,[38] and her acceptance of his proposal; and then hastened to shew both letters to her daughters, that she might be secure of their approbation before her answer were sent.

Elinor had always thought it would be more prudent for them to settle at some distance from Norland than immediately amongst their present acquaintance. On *that* head, therefore, it was not for her to oppose her mother's intention of removing into Devonshire. The house, too, as described by Sir John, was on so

28. Meaning a low rent, as well as perhaps other generous terms.

29. *gentleman:* a man of genteel status. The basic criterion for such a man was owning enough land that he did not have to work (except for supervising his property), or membership in one of the genteel professions (see p. 194 for a discussion of those professions). A lady, or gentlewoman, was someone whose husband, or father if she were unmarried, was a gentleman.

30. *consequence:* social distinction.

31. *Devonshire:* a county in the southwestern corner of England (see map, p. 738). Jane Austen traveled there twice, but otherwise had no connection with the county. As always in her novels she chooses the locations according to what will work best for the plot, rather than because of any supposed characteristics of the people of the region. She never, even while placing her novels in various counties in the southern half of England, hints at any local characteristics, a tendency that reflects the rise of a common upper-class culture throughout England during the eighteenth century. Devonshire was almost certainly chosen here because its great distance from London will hinder the return home of its main characters later in the novel.

32. *accommodation:* obligingness.

33. A cottage then could mean a house with a number of rooms, as this one has, though it is still much smaller than the grand houses such as Norland that most country gentry inhabited. Landowners would often have smaller houses on their property that they would rent.

34. They both presumably derive their name from the parish. The parish was the basic unit of local government and society in England at this time.

35. *connections:* relatives.

36. Once again she shows her impulsiveness, even on such an important and irreversible decision as this.

37. *continuing:* continuing as. "Continue" by itself was often used in the language of the time, in places where a preposition is currently added.

38. His title means he is either a knight or a baronet. Both titles were granted by the king for meritorious service; the difference was that a knighthood lasted only for the lifetime of the recipient, while a baronetcy was handed down to future descendants. Neither title, unlike the higher-ranking title of lord, conferred any privileges beyond the honor of being called "Sir" and having one's wife called "Lady."

simple a scale, and the rent so uncommonly moderate, as to leave
her no right of objection on either point; and, therefore, though it
was not a plan which brought any charm to her fancy, though it
was a removal from the vicinity of Norland beyond her wishes, she
made no attempt to dissuade her mother from sending her letter
of acquiescence.[39]

*Chawton Cottage: where Jane Austen lived with her mother and sister during the
last period of her life and where she wrote her novels.*

[From Mary Augusta Austen-Leigh, *Personal Aspects of Jane Austen* (New York, 1920), p. 112]

39. Elinor's agreement shows her willingness for self-sacrifice, a willingness she will need frequently over the course of the novel.

A woman in morning dress with a book.

[From *The Repository of arts, literature, fashions, manufactures, &c*, Vol. VI (1811), p. 177]

Chapter Five

No sooner was her answer dispatched, than Mrs. Dashwood indulged herself in the pleasure of announcing to her son-in-law[1] and his wife that she was provided with an house, and should incommode them no longer than till every thing were ready for her inhabiting it.[2] They heard her with surprise. Mrs. John Dashwood said nothing; but her husband civilly hoped that she would not be settled far from Norland. She had great satisfaction in replying that she was going into Devonshire.—Edward turned hastily towards her, on hearing this, and, in a voice of surprise and concern, which required no explanation to her, repeated, "Devonshire! Are you, indeed, going there? So far from hence! And to what part of it?"[3] She explained the situation. It was within four miles northward of Exeter.[4]

"It is but a cottage," she continued, "but I hope to see many of my friends in it. A room or two can easily be added; and if my friends find no difficulty in travelling so far to see me, I am sure I will find none in accommodating them."

She concluded with a very kind invitation to Mr. and Mrs. John Dashwood to visit her at Barton; and to Edward she gave one with still greater affection. Though her late[5] conversation with her daughter-in-law had made her resolve on remaining at Norland no longer than was unavoidable, it had not produced the smallest effect on her in that point to which it principally tended. To separate Edward and Elinor was as far from being her object as ever; and she wished to shew Mrs. John Dashwood by this pointed invitation to her brother, how totally she disregarded her disapprobation of the match.[6]

Mr. John Dashwood told his mother again and again how exceedingly sorry he was that she had taken an house at such a distance from Norland as to prevent his being of any service to her in

1. *son-in-law*: stepson.

2. While giving herself pleasure, her hastiness means that, if these plans were to fall through for some reason, she and her daughters would be left in a difficult position.

3. As his words indicate, part of the reason for Edward's shock is the great distance from Sussex to Devonshire (see map, p. 738), and the consequent separation of himself from Elinor. This is why, for Mrs. Dashwood, his state "required no explanation." But his strong initial exclamation, a contrast to his generally soft-spoken manner, and his concluding question as to which part of Devonshire, something that would make little difference in his separation from Elinor, suggest something more.

4. Exeter is the county seat of Devonshire. For its location, see maps, pp. 738 and 739.

5. *late*: recent.

6. By giving this invitation to Edward in the presence of his sister, Mrs. Dashwood, though relieving her own feelings, is putting him in an awkward position, since he presumably knows his sister disapproves of his interest in Elinor.

removing her furniture. He really felt conscientiously vexed on the occasion; for the very exertion to which he had limited the performance of his promise to his father was by this arrangement rendered impracticable.[7]—The furniture was all sent round by water.[8] It chiefly consisted of household linen, plate, china, and books, with an handsome pianoforte of Marianne's. Mrs. John Dashwood saw the packages depart with a sigh: she could not help feeling it hard that as Mrs. Dashwood's income would be so trifling in comparison with their own, she should have any handsome article of furniture.[9]

Mrs. Dashwood took the house for a twelvemonth; it was ready furnished, and she might have immediate possession. No difficulty arose on either side in the agreement; and she waited only for the disposal of her effects at Norland, and to determine her future household,[10] before she set off for the west; and this, as she was exceedingly rapid in the performance of every thing that interested her, was soon done.—The horses which were left her by her husband, had been sold soon after his death, and an opportunity now offering of disposing of her carriage, she agreed to sell that likewise at the earnest advice of her eldest daughter. For the comfort of her children, had she consulted only her own wishes, she would have kept it; but the discretion of Elinor prevailed.[11] *Her* wisdom too limited the number of their servants to three; two maids and a man, with whom they were speedily provided from amongst those who had formed their establishment[12] at Norland.[13]

The man and one of the maids were sent off immediately into Devonshire, to prepare the house for their mistress's arrival;[14] for as Lady Middleton was entirely unknown to Mrs. Dashwood, she preferred going directly to the cottage to being a visitor at Barton Park; and she relied so undoubtingly on Sir John's description of the house, as to feel no curiosity to examine it herself till she entered it as her own. Her eagerness to be gone from Norland was preserved from diminution by the evident satisfaction of her daughter-in-law in the prospect of her removal; a satisfaction which was but feebly attempted to be concealed under a cold

7. His genuine vexation indicates some decency in him. At the same time, he does not make any attempt to substitute another form of assistance.

8. At this time transportation by water was considerably cheaper than transportation by land, which had to go by slow horse and wagon. For this reason much of the internal trade of Britain was conducted by sea. In this case, since both Sussex and Devonshire are on the southern coast of England, the route by water is almost the same length as the route by land, making the former far more economical.

9. The idea that one's possessions should correspond to one's income and social position was a common one then, used especially to justify the purchase of fancy items by those of high income and position. Few, however, would apply the principle in as petty a fashion as Mrs. John Dashwood; most would also make extra allowances for Mrs. Dashwood because she has come down from a high social position.

10. Meaning to select her servants.

11. This would both gain her money from the sale and save her the expenses of maintaining a carriage. Such expenses would include frequent repairs, due to the damage produced by the rough roads of the time, and the cost of a servant to drive the carriage, for women did not drive themselves. At the same time, owning a carriage was the only means of traveling regularly beyond the immediate radius of one's home, and it was a critical mark of genteel status, so Mrs. Dashwood was naturally reluctant to part with hers. A similar need to economize was presumably the reason for the earlier sale of their horses; she could have continued to use her carriage without owning horses, by renting them when required.

12. *establishment*: organized staff or servants.

13. A book of the time stated "three females and a boy" to be the appropriate staff for someone with Mrs. Dashwood's income, five hundred a year. (Samuel and Sarah Adams, *The Complete Servant*, p. 16). Since adult male servants cost considerably more than either women or boys, her staff roughly follows the recommendation. The much larger size of the Dashwoods' staff at Norland would make it easy to select three among them. Servants often stayed with the same employers, though in this case the servants would have been agreeing to move far away from their homes (and the cost of travel would keep them from returning to see family or friends). Mrs. Dashwood, who would certainly be a generous and kind employer, may have found it easier to persuade servants to accept her offer than most people would have.

14. They would have been sent off via public coaches, an elaborate network of which spanned England. Their preparations would have included unpacking and arranging the household possessions, cleaning the house,

invitation to her to defer her departure. Now was the time when her son-in-law's promise to his father might with particular propriety be fulfilled. Since he had neglected to do it on first coming to the estate, their quitting his house might be looked on as the most suitable period for its accomplishment. But Mrs. Dashwood began shortly to give over[15] every hope of the kind, and to be convinced, from the general drift of his discourse, that his assistance extended no farther than their maintenance for six months at Norland. He so frequently talked of the increasing expenses of housekeeping, and of the perpetual demands upon his purse, which a man of any consequence in the world was beyond calculation exposed to, that he seemed rather to stand in need of more money himself than to have any design of giving money away.[16]

In a very few weeks from the day which brought Sir John Middleton's first letter to Norland, every thing was so far settled in their future abode as to enable Mrs. Dashwood and her daughters to begin their journey.

Many were the tears shed by them in their last adieus to a place so much beloved. "Dear, dear Norland!" said Marianne, as she wandered alone before the house, on the last evening of their being there; "when shall I cease to regret you!—when learn to feel a home elsewhere!—Oh! happy house, could you know what I suffer in now viewing you from this spot, from whence perhaps I may view you no more!—And you, ye well-known trees!—but you will continue the same.—No leaf will decay because we are removed, nor any branch become motionless although we can observe you no longer!—No; you will continue the same; unconscious of the pleasure or the regret you occasion, and insensible of any change in those who walk under your shade!—But who will remain to enjoy you?"[17]

and buying food and other essentials. People of the Dashwoods' class would generally not perform such mundane tasks themselves.

15. *give over*: give up, abandon.

16. A man of consequence, or importance, especially if a prominent landowner, was expected to fulfill certain social duties, including charity to the local poor and hospitality to the neighborhood. But those expenses would not be that onerous for someone with John Dashwood's income. His own greed undoubtedly makes him feel their sting more than most, while the general wish he consistently manifests of being respectable and avoiding any obvious breach of his obligations would keep him from simply disregarding such demands.

17. Marianne's speech expresses the love for and idealization of nature found in much Romantic writing. It also replicates the fulsome encomiums uttered by the heroines of various novels of the time, such as the very popular ones by Ann Radcliffe, whose sentimental and melodramatic excesses are satirized in *Northanger Abbey*.

Chapter Six

*T*he first part of their journey was performed in too melancholy a disposition to be otherwise than tedious and unpleasant. But as they drew towards the end of it, their interest in the appearance of a country which they were to inhabit overcame their dejection, and a view of Barton Valley as they entered it gave them cheerfulness. It was a pleasant fertile spot, well wooded, and rich in pasture. After winding along it for more than a mile, they reached their own house. A small green court[1] was the whole of its demesne[2] in front; and a neat[3] wicket gate[4] admitted them into it.

As a house, Barton Cottage, though small, was comfortable and compact; but as a cottage it was defective, for the building was regular, the roof was tiled, the window shutters were not painted green, nor were the walls covered with honeysuckles.[5] A narrow passage led directly through the house into the garden behind. On each side of the entrance was a sitting room,[6] about sixteen feet square; and beyond them were the offices[7] and the stairs. Four bed-rooms and two garrets formed the rest of the house. It had not been built many years[8] and was in good repair. In comparison of Norland, it was poor and small indeed! — but the tears which recollection called forth as they entered the house were soon dried away. They were cheered by the joy of the servants on their arrival, and each for the sake of the others resolved to appear happy. It was very early in September; the season was fine, and from first seeing the place under the advantage of good weather, they received an impression in its favour which was of material service in recommending it to their lasting approbation.[9]

The situation[10] of the house was good. High hills rose immediately behind, and at no great distance on each side; some of which were open downs,[11] the others cultivated and woody. The village of Barton was chiefly on one of these hills, and formed a

1.   *court*: courtyard, enclosure.

2.   *demesne*: land in front of a house. The term was normally applied to land occupied by the owner, and often when speaking of wealthy and high-ranking people. Hence the term here, for the Dashwoods' humble rented cottage, is probably meant ironically.

3.   *neat*: well-made; attractive but simple.

4.   *wicket gate*: small gate for people on foot to enter a field or enclosure.

5.   This is irony at the expense of the common Romantic celebration of irregular, rustic cottages. For more on such ideas, and their popularity in this period, see p. 469, note 35).

6.   *sitting room*: living room. The term could be applied to any room for general use. Two sitting rooms were considered an absolute minimum for decent social life: one room would be the best room, in which company would be received and entertained, and the other would be the everyday room for the family itself.

7.   *offices*: rooms or parts of the house devoted to necessary household tasks, such as the kitchen, pantry, laundry room, and cellar.

8.   *many years*: many years ago.

9.   Devonshire is one of the rainiest counties in England, thanks to the moist air coming from the nearby ocean. Its rainiest seasons are autumn and winter, which is why its being "very early in September" makes it more likely to be dry. They will soon experience many wet days.

10. *situation*: position, location.

11. *downs*: expanse of elevated land, especially treeless lands used for pasture, a prominent feature of the countryside around Barton. Devonshire, like the rest of western England, was dominated at this time by open pasture, in contrast to eastern and south central England, which consisted primarily of land planted with crops. Jane Austen, who came from a crop-growing county, Hampshire, could have noticed the different nature of the Devonshire terrain when she visited there. In her first trip there, she stayed at the seaside resort of Sidmouth, which, like her fictional Barton, is close to Exeter (though in the opposite direction), and the countryside near it contained rolling hills, topped by open commons (probably used for pasture).

pleasant view from the cottage windows. The prospect[12] in front was more extensive; it commanded the whole of the valley, and reached into the country beyond. The hills which surrounded the cottage terminated the valley in that direction; under another name, and in another course, it branched out again between two of the steepest of them.

With the size and furniture of the house Mrs. Dashwood was upon the whole well satisfied; for though her former style of life rendered many additions to the latter indispensable, yet to add and improve was a delight to her; and she had at this time ready money enough to supply all that was wanted of greater elegance to the apartments.[13] "As for the house itself, to be sure," said she, "it is too small for our family, but we will make ourselves tolerably comfortable for the present, as it is too late in the year for improvements. Perhaps in the spring, if I have plenty of money, as I dare say I shall, we may think about building. These parlours[14] are both too small for such parties[15] of our friends as I hope to see often collected here; and I have some thoughts of throwing the passage into one of them with perhaps a part of the other, and so leave the remainder of that other for an entrance; this, with a new drawing room which may be easily added, and a bedchamber and garret above, will make it a very snug[16] little cottage. I could wish the stairs were handsome.[17] But one must not expect every thing; though I suppose it would be no difficult matter to widen them. I shall see how much I am before-hand[18] with the world in the spring, and we will plan our improvements accordingly."

In the mean time, till all these alterations could be made from the savings of an income of five hundred a-year by a woman who never saved in her life,[19] they were wise enough to be contented with the house as it was; and each of them was busy in arranging their particular concerns, and endeavouring, by placing around them their books and other possessions, to form themselves a home. Marianne's pianoforte[20] was unpacked and properly disposed of; and Elinor's drawings were affixed to the walls of their sitting room.

In such employments as these they were interrupted soon after

12. *prospect*: view.

13. *apartments*: rooms.

14. *parlours*: the sitting rooms already mentioned. "Parlour" was mostly used for a small room of that type; a more spacious and luxurious one would be called a drawing room. Mrs. Dashwood is probably using the term, rather than the more all-inclusive "sitting room," from her consciousness of how much these rooms differ from the equivalent ones at Norland. Thus she proceeds in the same sentence to complain of the rooms' smallness, and to speak of adding a drawing room. For a picture of a drawing room, see p. 143.

15. *parties*: social gatherings, especially at a private home. The term then could refer to even the smallest or quietest gathering.

16. *snug*: comfortable. The word was used more generally as a term of praise then, but it also had the current connotation of coziness in a small space, in which case Mrs. Dashwood's thinking the cottage will be snug after such sizable expansions is a little silly. But from her perspective as the former mistress of a grand country house, even such an expanded cottage might seem snug in this sense, as well as more generally comfortable.

17. *handsome*: decent-sized, reasonably large. The stairs are later described by Elinor as dark and narrow (p. 138).

18. *am before-hand*: have more than sufficient means or extra money.

19. Five hundred a year would be a pitiful amount for making such extensive alterations, especially since much of it would have to go toward daily living expenses. Even very wealthy landowners could run into serious debt from the cost of improvements to their houses, though their construction would be on a much grander scale.

Jane Austen would have an excellent sense of how much Mrs. Dashwood could afford, for in the last part of her life, the time when this and other novels were published, she was in a very similar situation. She and her mother and sister inhabited a house of comparable size, also called a cottage, and enjoyed around the same level of wealth, having a little less than five hundred a year in income but also not having to pay rent on the house (since it was owned by Jane Austen's brother). For a picture of the cottage they inhabited, see p. 44.

20. *pianoforte*: piano. Pianoforte was the original name for a piano. By this time it had become the most popular of all musical instruments, and young ladies who learned to play an instrument were most likely to choose the piano. Jane Austen learned to play, and normally practiced on it every morning. For a picture of a pianoforte, see p. 66.

breakfast the next day by the entrance of their landlord, who called to welcome them to Barton, and to offer them every accommodation from his own house and garden in which their's might at present be deficient. Sir John Middleton was a good looking man about forty. He had formerly visited at Stanhill, but it was too long ago for his young cousins to remember him.[21] His countenance was thoroughly good-humoured; and his manners were as friendly as the style of his letter. Their arrival seemed to afford him real satisfaction, and their comfort to be an object of real solicitude to him. He said much of his earnest desire of their living in the most sociable terms with his family, and pressed them so cordially to dine at Barton Park every day till they were better settled at home, that, though his entreaties were carried to a point of perseverance beyond civility, they could not give offence. His kindness was not confined to words; for within an hour after he left them, a large basket full of garden stuff[22] and fruit arrived from the park, which was followed before the end of the day by a present of game.[23] He insisted moreover on conveying all their letters to and from the post for them,[24] and would not be denied the satisfaction of sending them his newspaper every day.[25]

Lady Middleton had sent a very civil message by him, denoting her intention of waiting on[26] Mrs. Dashwood as soon as she could be assured that her visit would be no inconvenience; and as this message was answered by an invitation equally polite, her lady-ship was introduced to them the next day.[27]

They were of course very anxious to see a person on whom so much of their comfort at Barton must depend; and the elegance of her appearance was favourable to their wishes. Lady Middleton was not more than six or seven and twenty; her face was hand-some, her figure tall and striking, and her address[28] graceful. Her manners had all the elegance which her husband's wanted. But they would have been improved by some share of his frankness and warmth; and her visit was long enough to detract something from their first admiration, by shewing that though perfectly well-bred,[29] she was reserved, cold, and had nothing to say for herself beyond the most common-place inquiry or remark.

21. The Dashwoods had moved from Stanhill to Norland ten years before the death of old Mr. Dashwood (see pp. 2–4). Since the oldest of the Miss Dashwoods, Elinor, is nineteen, they would have all been young at the time of Sir John's visit.

22. *stuff*: produce.

23. Sir John, who is soon revealed to be a zealous hunter, would be likely to have game to spare. At the same time, his bringing them game, as well as produce, on the first day of their arrival contrasts favorably with John Dashwood's vague intention of "sending them presents of fish and game, and so forth, whenever they are in season" (p. 18).

24. Regular mail service had become a standard part of English life by this time. But outside of London there was no home delivery, so people had to send or receive mail at the local post office. Here that would likely be in the local village, which would be a walk up the adjacent hills for the carriageless Dashwood family.

25. Newspapers had also become a common feature of English life, but they were expensive. It was not unusual for neighbors to share their newspapers to save money: during Jane Austen's youth a more affluent neighbor of the Austens shared his with the family.

26. *waiting on*: visiting.

27. Their reciprocal notes represent standard etiquette of introduction. Lady Middleton is consistently shown to be very conscious of proper etiquette.

28. *address*: outward bearing and manner.

29. *well-bred*: polite, courteous.

Conversation however was not wanted,[30] for Sir John was very chatty, and Lady Middleton had taken the wise precaution of bringing with her their eldest child, a fine little boy about six years old, by which means there was one subject always to be recurred to by the ladies in case of extremity, for they had to inquire his name and age, admire his beauty, and ask him questions which his mother answered for him, while he hung about her and held down his head, to the great surprise of her ladyship, who wondered at his being so shy before company as he could make noise enough at home. On every formal visit a child ought to be of the party, by way of provision for discourse.[31] In the present case it took up ten minutes to determine whether the boy were most like his father or mother, and in what particular he resembled either, for of course every body differed, and every body was astonished at the opinion of the others.

An opportunity was soon to be given to the Dashwoods of debating on the rest of the children, as Sir John would not leave the house without securing their promise of dining at the park the next day.[32]

Coleshill House: a country house such as the Middletons could inhabit.

[From John Preston Neale, *Views of the Seats of Noblemen and Gentlemen*, Vol. V (1822)]

30. *wanted*: lacking.

31. Formal visits of introduction followed a strict etiquette, which included a fifteen-minute time limit. The consciousness of this limit, along with the participants' lack of familiarity with one another, tended to make conversation rather banal, so a "provision for discourse," that is, something supplying material for discussion, would be very useful.

32. This indicates the difference between Sir John and his wife. He was earlier mentioned as carrying his friendly entreaties "to a point of perseverance beyond civility." The same spirit now leads him to press them to return the visit, rather than inviting them back in the formal manner employed already by Lady Middleton.

A picnic; the clothing is from a slightly earlier period.

[From Joseph Grego, *Rowlandson the Caricaturist* (London, 1880), vol. II, p. 316]

Chapter Seven

*B*arton Park was about half a mile from the cottage. The ladies had passed near it in their way along the valley, but it was screened from their view at home by the projection of an hill. The house was large and handsome; and the Middletons lived in a style of equal hospitality and elegance. The former was for Sir John's gratification, the latter for that of his lady. They were scarcely ever without some friends staying with them in the house, and they kept more company of every kind than any other family in the neighbourhood. It was necessary to the happiness of both; for however dissimilar in temper and outward behaviour, they strongly resembled each other in that total want of talent and taste which confined their employments, unconnected with such as society produced, within a very narrow compass. Sir John was a sportsman,[1] Lady Middleton a mother. He hunted and shot, and she humoured her children; and these were their only resources.[2] Lady Middleton had the advantage of being able to spoil her children all the year round, while Sir John's independent employments were in existence only half the time.[3] Continual engagements at home and abroad,[4] however, supplied all the deficiencies of nature and education;[5] supported the good spirits of Sir John, and gave exercise to the good-breeding of his wife.

Lady Middleton piqued[6] herself upon the elegance of her table, and of all her domestic arrangements; and from this kind of vanity was her greatest enjoyment in any of their parties. But Sir John's satisfaction in society was much more real; he delighted in collecting about him more young people than his house would hold, and the noisier they were the better was he pleased. He was a blessing to all the juvenile part of the neighbourhood, for in summer he was for ever forming parties to eat cold ham and chicken out of doors,[7] and in winter his private

1.   *sportsman:* man who hunts. The principal forms of sport were hunting land animals, especially foxes and hares, with horses and dogs, and shooting game birds such as partridges and pheasants. Only the former was called "hunting" in current parlance, which is why the next sentence says he "hunted and shot." These activities were extremely popular among English country gentlemen like Sir John, though not all were as fervently devoted to them as he is.

2.   *resources:* means of relaxation or entertainment.

3.   Shooting was legal from September 1 to January 31; hunting was restricted to certain periods, usually late fall and winter, by custom.

4.   *abroad:* outside one's house; out of doors.

5.   In discussing people's character, Jane Austen consistently emphasizes the importance of both nature and education, with the latter often meaning general upbringing as well as formal schooling.

6.   *piqued:* prided.

7.   Eating out of doors had become increasingly popular. The term "picnic" (used in *Emma*) first appeared during the mid-eighteenth century and gradually attained wider circulation along with what it designated. For a picture of a late eighteenth-century picnic, see the preceding page.

Shooting a pheasant.

[From William Henry Scott, *British Field Sports* (London, 1818), p. 232]

balls[8] were numerous enough for any young lady who was not suffering under the insatiable appetite of fifteen.[9]

The arrival of a new family in the country was always a matter of joy to him, and in every point of view he was charmed with the inhabitants he had now procured for his cottage at Barton. The Miss Dashwoods were young, pretty, and unaffected.[10] It was enough to secure his good opinion; for to be unaffected was all that a pretty girl could want to make her mind as captivating as her person. The friendliness of his disposition made him happy in accommodating those, whose situation might be considered, in comparison with the past, as unfortunate. In shewing kindness to his cousins therefore he had the real satisfaction of a good heart; and in settling a family of females only in his cottage, he had all the satisfaction of a sportsman; for a sportsman, though he esteems only those of his sex who are sportsmen likewise, is not often desirous of encouraging their taste by admitting them to a residence within his own manor.[11]

Mrs. Dashwood and her daughters were met at the door of the house by Sir John, who welcomed them to Barton Park with unaffected sincerity; and as he attended them to the drawing room repeated to the young ladies the concern which the same subject had drawn from him the day before, at being unable to get any smart[12] young men to meet them. They would see, he said, only one gentleman there besides himself; a particular friend who was staying at the park, but who was neither very young nor very gay. He hoped they would all excuse the smallness of the party, and could assure them it should never happen so again. He had been to several families that morning in hopes of procuring some addition to their number, but it was moonlight and every body was full of engagements.[13] Luckily Lady Middleton's mother had arrived at Barton within the last hour, and as she was a very cheerful agreeable woman, he hoped the young ladies would not find it so very dull as they might imagine. The young ladies, as well as their mother, were perfectly satisfied with having two entire strangers of the party, and wished for no more.

8. *private balls:* balls occurring in a private residence. Public balls were ones held in assembly rooms, which had become a standard feature of English towns by this time. Public balls simply required the purchase of a ticket or a subscription. This made them less exclusive than private balls, and thus less desirable in some people's eyes.

9. Fifteen was generally the age at which a young lady would be permitted to go to balls. The wording suggests the strong desire of young ladies for dancing, something exhibited at various points in Austen's novels.

10. "Unaffected," usually with a particular connotation of unpretentious, is a common term of praise in Jane Austen.

11. A manor is a unit of land with tenants on it. At this time the term was used particularly in connection with the right to shoot game. By law this right was restricted to men owning an estate worth at least a hundred pounds a year; however, any lord of the manor, i.e., landowner with tenants, could authorize another person to kill game on his land by conferring on him the deputation of gamekeeper. Thus, were Sir John to rent the cottage to a genteel family including men he would face a dilemma. While he would not be legally obligated to grant shooting rights to the men, it would be awkward and seem discourteous to refuse, since shooting was such a basic pastime of gentlemen. But other sportsmen within his domain would compete with Sir John for the available supply of game birds. This had become an important issue during this time, thanks to improved methods of killing game, including better guns. Dedicated sportsmen had responded by establishing preserves where birds could breed more easily, and by taking various steps to prevent animals, poachers, or other gentlemen from killing the birds. Even still, any particular landowner's property would contain a finite supply.

Women rarely participated in outdoor sports then, and never shot, so they would present no difficulty along these lines.

12. *smart:* fashionable, especially in being well dressed and clever or witty in conversation.

13. This means it was at or near the full moon, a time when people were far more likely to have evening engagements. The reason was that the moon was the only good source of light for traveling after dark. There were no streetlights, and in the countryside there would be only occasional light coming from houses or other buildings; carriages had lamps and people could carry torches, but both of these provided only limited illumination. In a letter Jane Austen speaks of walking home from a ball, and not needing a lantern, "as the Moon was up" (Sept. 14, 1804).

Mrs. Jennings, Lady Middleton's mother, was a good-humoured, merry, fat, elderly woman, who talked a great deal, seemed very happy, and rather vulgar. She was full of jokes and laughter, and before dinner was over had said many witty things on the subject of lovers and husbands; hoped they had not left their hearts behind them in Sussex, and pretended to see them blush whether they did or not. Marianne was vexed at it for her sister's sake, and turned her eyes towards Elinor to see how she bore these attacks, with an earnestness which gave Elinor far more pain than could arise from such common-place raillery as Mrs. Jennings's.

Colonel Brandon, the friend of Sir John, seemed no more adapted by resemblance of manner to be his friend, than Lady Middleton was to be his wife, or Mrs. Jennings to be Lady Middleton's mother.[14] He was silent and grave. His appearance however was not unpleasing, in spite of his being in the opinion of Marianne and Margaret an absolute old bachelor, for he was on the wrong side of five and thirty; but though his face was not handsome his countenance was sensible, and his address was particularly gentlemanlike.[15]

There was nothing in any of the party which could recommend them as companions to the Dashwoods; but the cold insipidity of Lady Middleton was so particularly repulsive,[16] that in comparison of it the gravity of Colonel Brandon, and even the boisterous mirth of Sir John and his mother-in-law was interesting. Lady Middleton seemed to be roused to enjoyment only by the entrance of her four noisy children after dinner, who pulled her about, tore her clothes, and put an end to every kind of discourse except what related to themselves.[17]

In the evening, as Marianne was discovered to be musical, she was invited to play. The instrument was unlocked,[18] every body prepared to be charmed, and Marianne, who sang very well, at their request went through the chief of the songs which Lady Middleton had brought into the family on her marriage, and which perhaps had lain ever since in the same position on the

14. One reason for these sharp differences could be the limited social opportunities of genteel people. They would socialize only with others of their class, and since most of them made their money from owning large parcels of land, there would rarely be dense concentrations of them in the rural areas in which they mostly lived. Moreover, social life in each rural area was limited by the slowness and discomfort of carriages, especially over the often poorly maintained local dirt roads. All this restricted people's frequent contacts to a small number of nearby families, the situation consistently depicted by Jane Austen. With few to choose among, they might often befriend, or marry, someone very different in tastes and personality.

The lack of resemblance of Mrs. Jennings and her daughter is more puzzling, and has led to some questioning by critics. They do share the trait of limited intelligence. As for their almost opposite manners, one reason could be something Jane Austen noted in a letter: "Like other young Ladies she is considerably genteeler than her Parents" (Sept. 14, 1804). This happened partly because young ladies were increasingly sent to fashionable schools where elegant manners and tastes were taught and encouraged. This could produce a particularly large gap between parent and child in the case of someone like Lady Middleton, whose father was a merchant (see p. 282), an occupation not considered genteel at all, and whose mother's likely similar origin is indicated by her less polished behavior. The money Mr. Jennings made probably inspired social ambitions for his children and, in a common procedure, led him to send them to expensive schools, where they could learn more genteel ways and form friendships with those of higher rank. Mrs. Jennings's other daughter attends such a school (p. 296), and Lady Middleton probably did as well, where she could have imbibed her very different standards and behavior.

15. In contrast to the other new characters just presented, Colonel Brandon is given only a brief description, and one focused on his appearance. This keeps him mysterious and sets the stage for later, and often surprising, revelations concerning him and his past.

16. *repulsive:* repellent. The term had a less harsh meaning then.

17. The children would have been with a servant, most likely their nursery maid, whose job was to supervise children, especially very young ones. The spoiled character of the Middleton children will appear consistently.

18. The instrument is the pianoforte; the term, often used, signals the piano's popularity. Because pianos of the time were fragile and easily damaged, they would often be kept closed, or even locked. In the case of the Middletons, locking would be desirable, since their children could open an unlocked one and tinker with it. See next page for a picture of a pianoforte.

pianoforté,[19] for her ladyship had celebrated that event by giving up music, although by her mother's account she had played extremely well, and by her own was very fond of it.[20]

Marianne's performance was highly applauded. Sir John was loud in his admiration at the end of every song, and as loud in his conversation with the others while every song lasted. Lady Middleton frequently called him to order, wondered how any one's attention could be diverted from music for a moment, and asked Marianne to sing a particular song which Marianne had just finished.[21] Colonel Brandon alone, of all the party, heard her without being in raptures. He paid her only the compliment of attention; and she felt a respect for him on the occasion, which the others had reasonably forfeited by their shameless want of taste.[22] His pleasure in music, though it amounted not to that extatic delight which alone could sympathize with her own, was estimable when contrasted against the horrible insensibility[23] of the others; and she was reasonable enough to allow that a man of five and thirty might well have outlived all acuteness of feeling and every exquisite[24] power of enjoyment. She was perfectly disposed to make every allowance for the colonel's advanced state of life which humanity required.

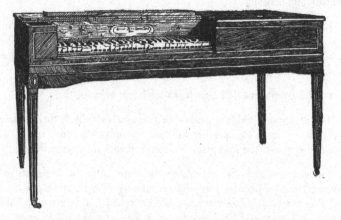

A pianoforte of the time.

[From Esther Singleton, *The Furniture of Our Forefathers*, (New York, 1916), p. 585]

19. The songs would be pieces of printed music. There was a great deal of printed music for sale then, either in single sheets or larger volumes, while many people, because of the cost of this music, copied pieces themselves. Jane Austen had a large collection of songs and other pieces, including many she had copied. That Marianne goes through the chief, i.e. greater part, of Lady Middleton's collection in one evening suggests it is not very large. At the same time, Marianne's ability to play, and to sing at the same time, a series of songs that she presumably has not seen previously, and without any apparent time to study them, suggests a great deal of musical talent.

20. Playing music was a skill often taught to young ladies, especially at the sort of girls' school that Lady Middleton probably attended. It was an accomplishment considered good in itself, but it was also valued as being attractive to men. Hence it was not unusual for ladies to give up music after marriage: *Emma* contains a character who speaks of how she will be forced to do this now that she has been wed, even though she also professes her great love of music. In a youthful story, "Catharine, or the Bower," Jane Austen, in speaking of a fashionable young lady, says that, "twelve Years had been dedicated to the acquirement of Accomplishments [including music] which were now to be displayed and in a few Years entirely neglected." Lady Middleton's abandonment of music would be another reason for their pianoforte to remain locked.

21. The reactions of Sir John and Lady Middleton, especially the latter, are also depicted elsewhere in Jane Austen. Many profess great appreciation of music, for such appreciation was a mark of refined taste in this society. Thus when the instrument was unlocked everybody was "prepared to be charmed." But far from everybody actually enjoyed it sufficiently to listen. At a later musical party in London the narrator will explain there were "a great many people who had real taste for the performance, and a great many more who had none at all" (p. 464).

22. This is the first indication of a possible affinity between Colonel Brandon and Marianne, though at this stage she recognizes it only slightly.

23. *insensibility*: indifference. Marianne's description of this attitude as "horrible" suggests the vehemence of her reaction and her extreme fastidiousness regarding the ordinary run of humanity.

24. *exquisite*: intense, exalted.

Chapter Eight

*M*rs. Jennings was a widow, with an ample jointure.[1] She had only two daughters, both of whom she had lived to see respectably married, and she had now therefore nothing to do but to marry all the rest of the world.[2] In the promotion of this object she was zealously active, as far as her ability reached; and missed no opportunity of projecting weddings among all the young people of her acquaintance. She was remarkably quick in the discovery of attachments, and had enjoyed the advantage of raising the blushes and the vanity of many a young lady by insinuations of her power over such a young man; and this kind of discernment enabled her soon after her arrival at Barton decisively to pronounce that Colonel Brandon was very much in love with Marianne Dashwood. She rather suspected it to be so, on the very first evening of their being together, from his listening so attentively while she sang to them; and when the visit was returned by the Middletons' dining at the cottage,[3] the fact was ascertained[4] by his listening to her again. It must be so. She was perfectly convinced of it. It would be an excellent match, for *he* was rich and *she* was handsome.[5] Mrs. Jennings had been anxious to see Colonel Brandon well married, ever since her connection with Sir John first brought him to her knowledge; and she was always anxious to get a good husband for every pretty girl.

The immediate advantage to herself was by no means inconsiderable, for it supplied her with endless jokes against them both. At the park she laughed at the colonel, and in the cottage at Marianne. To the former her raillery was probably, as far as it regarded only himself, perfectly indifferent; but to the latter it was at first incomprehensible; and when its object was understood, she hardly knew whether most to laugh at its absurdity, or censure its impertinence, for she considered it as an unfeeling reflection on

1. A jointure was an annual payment made to a widow. It was generally stipulated in the marriage settlement to ensure that the wife, if she outlasted the husband, would have some provision, since her fortune became part of his property upon marriage and that property usually went to his heir on his death. Among the landowning class the jointure was frequently fixed at 10% of the dowry, the idea being that the average wife, who was usually younger than the husband, would outlive him by ten years; thus she would receive back her original contribution. It is not clear if this procedure was followed in Mrs. Jennings's case, for her husband, a merchant, came from a lower social class, in which marriage settlements were less common. That he left her plenty of money is later shown by her fine house in London.

2. Getting her daughters married, if she had any, was a vital business of a mother in this society. Marriage was a powerful imperative for young women, and mothers were the ones who had principal care of their daughters. *Pride and Prejudice* centers around a family whose mother's overwhelming preoccupation is finding husbands for her five daughters. Thus Mrs. Jennings's current matchmaking is a natural extension of previous habits.

3. It was standard etiquette to return a visit in this manner, and more generally for families to alternate who dined at whose house.

4. *ascertained:* learned for certain.

5. "Handsome" is often used in Jane Austen to describe women. It had no masculine connotation at this time.

the colonel's advanced years, and on his forlorn condition as an old bachelor.

Mrs. Dashwood, who could not think a man five years younger than herself, so exceedingly ancient as he appeared to the youthful fancy of her daughter, ventured to clear Mrs. Jennings from the probability of wishing to throw ridicule on his age.

"But at least, mama, you cannot deny the absurdity of the accusation, though you may not think it intentionally ill-natured. Colonel Brandon is certainly younger than Mrs. Jennings, but he is old enough to be *my* father; and if he were ever animated enough to be in love, must have long outlived every sensation of the kind. It is too ridiculous! When is a man to be safe from such wit,[6] if age and infirmity will not protect him?"

"Infirmity!" said Elinor, "do you call Colonel Brandon infirm? I can easily suppose that his age may appear much greater to you than to my mother; but you can hardly deceive yourself as to his having the use of his limbs!"

"Did not you hear him complain of the rheumatism?[7] and is not that the commonest infirmity of declining life?"

"My dearest child," said her mother laughing, "at this rate you must be in continual terror of *my* decay; and it must seem to you a miracle that my life has been extended to the advanced age of forty."

"Mama, you are not doing me justice. I know very well that Colonel Brandon is not old enough to make his friends yet apprehensive of losing him in the course of nature. He may live twenty years longer.[8] But thirty-five has nothing to do with matrimony."

"Perhaps," said Elinor, "thirty-five and seventeen had better not have any thing to do with matrimony together. But if there should by any chance happen to be a woman who is single at seven and twenty, I should not think Colonel Brandon's being thirty-five any objection to his marrying *her*."

"A woman of seven and twenty," said Marianne, after pausing a moment, "can never hope to feel or inspire affection again,[9] and if her home be uncomfortable, or her fortune small, I can suppose that she might bring herself to submit to the offices[10] of a nurse,[11]

6. *wit*: teasing; fanciful remarks.

7. *rheumatism*: term used frequently then for all forms of arthritis and related ailments.

8. For a similar attitude toward life expectancy, see p. 16.

9. By her late twenties a woman lost her prime marital eligibility in this society. This is why Elinor says, "if there should by any chance happen to be a woman who is single at seven and twenty." Jane Austen herself had an offer of marriage just before this age, and after turning it down basically resigned herself to remaining single the rest of her life. At the same time, some women did marry at an older age, and few would dismiss the possibility of love for a woman of twenty-seven as sweepingly as Marianne does.

10. *offices*: duties.

11. Most nursing was performed at home at this time, and usually by women. Since almost all medical care was administered at home as well, most women would become practiced at nursing over the course of their lives.

for the sake of the provision and security of a wife. In his marrying such a woman therefore there would be nothing unsuitable. It would be a compact of convenience, and the world would be satisfied. In my eyes it would be no marriage at all, but that would be nothing. To me it would seem only a commercial exchange, in which each wished to be benefited at the expense of the other."[12]

"It would be impossible, I know," replied Elinor, "to convince you that a woman of seven and twenty could feel for a man of thirty-five any thing near enough to love, to make him a desirable companion to her. But I must object to your dooming Colonel Brandon and his wife to the constant confinement of a sick chamber, merely because he chanced to complain yesterday (a very cold damp day) of a slight rheumatic feel in one of his shoulders."

"But he talked of flannel waistcoats,"[13] said Marianne; "and with me a flannel waistcoat is invariably connected with aches, cramps, rheumatisms, and every species of ailment that can afflict the old and the feeble."

"Had he been only in a violent fever, you would not have despised him half so much. Confess, Marianne, is not there something interesting to you in the flushed cheek, hollow eye, and quick pulse of a fever?"[14]

Soon after this, upon Elinor's leaving the room, "Mama," said Marianne, "I have an alarm on the subject of illness, which I cannot conceal from you. I am sure Edward Ferrars is not well. We have now been here almost a fortnight, and yet he does not come. Nothing but real indisposition could occasion this extraordinary delay. What else can detain him at Norland?"

"Had you any idea of his coming so soon?" said Mrs. Dashwood. "I had none. On the contrary, if I have felt any anxiety at all on the subject, it has been in recollecting that he sometimes shewed a want of pleasure and readiness in accepting my invitation, when I talked of his coming to Barton. Does Elinor expect him already?"

"I have never mentioned it to her, but of course she must."

"I rather think you are mistaken, for when I was talking to her

12. Many marriages then contained this element of exchange and were often acknowledged as such; few had any qualms about discussing the monetary or other practical benefits of marriage. But there was also a general belief in the need for genuine affection, if not necessarily the intense romantic passion that Marianne considers essential.

13. *waistcoats:* vests. Waistcoats were a basic part of male attire of the time; see picture below for an example.

14. The cult of sensibility often involved a fascination with acute illness, which provoked feelings of compassion and could seem a sign of special spiritual qualities.

A man in contemporary dress.

[From Max von Boehn, *Modes & Manners of the Nineteenth Century*, Vol. I (London, 1909), p. 132]

yesterday of getting a new grate for the spare bedchamber,[15] she observed that there was no immediate hurry for it, as it was not likely that the room would be wanted for some time."

"How strange this is! what can be the meaning of it! But the whole of their behaviour to each other has been unaccountable! How cold, how composed were their last adieus! How languid their conversation the last evening of their being together! In Edward's farewell there was no distinction between Elinor and me: it was the good wishes of an affectionate brother to both. Twice did I leave them purposely together in the course of the last morning, and each time did he most unaccountably follow me out of the room. And Elinor, in quitting Norland and Edward, cried not as I did. Even now her self-command is invariable. When is she dejected or melancholy? When does she try to avoid society, or appear restless and dissatisfied in it?"[16]

15. She would mean a grate for the fireplace.

16. Marianne will manifest both these tendencies after she experiences a painful separation.

Chapter Nine

The Dashwoods were now settled at Barton with tolerable comfort to themselves. The house and the garden, with all the objects surrounding them, were[1] now become familiar, and the ordinary pursuits which had given to Norland half its charms, were engaged in again with far greater enjoyment than Norland had been able to afford, since the loss of their father. Sir John Middleton, who called on them every day for the first fortnight, and who was not in the habit of seeing much occupation at home, could not conceal his amazement on finding them always employed.

Their visitors, except those from Barton Park, were not many; for, in spite of Sir John's urgent entreaties that they would mix more in the neighbourhood, and repeated assurances of his carriage being always at their service, the independence of Mrs. Dashwood's spirit overcame the wish of society for her children; and she was resolute in declining to visit any family beyond the distance of a walk. There were but few who could be so classed; and it was not all of them that were attainable. About a mile and a half from the cottage, along the narrow winding valley of Allenham, which issued from that of Barton, as formerly described,[2] the girls had, in one of their earliest walks, discovered an ancient respectable looking mansion, which, by reminding them a little of Norland, interested their imagination and made them wish to be better acquainted with it. But they learnt, on inquiry, that its possessor, an elderly lady of very good character,[3] was unfortunately too infirm to mix with the world, and never stirred from home.

The whole country about them abounded in beautiful walks. The high downs which invited them from almost every window of the cottage to seek the exquisite enjoyment of air on their sum-

1. *were*: had. Forming the past tense with "to be" rather than "to have" was a traditional usage still found on occasion in the language of this time.

2. The author refers to the initial description of Barton on pp. 52–54.

3. *character*: reputation.

Howsham Hall: an older country house, such as Allenham is described as being.

[From John Preston Neale, *Views of the Seats of Noblemen and Gentlemen*, Vol. V (1822)]

mits, were an happy alternative when the dirt of the valleys beneath shut up their superior beauties; and towards one of these hills did Marianne and Margaret one memorable morning direct their steps, attracted by the partial sunshine of a showery sky, and unable longer to bear the confinement which the settled rain of the two preceding days had occasioned. The weather was not tempting enough to draw the two others from their pencil and their book,[4] in spite of Marianne's declaration that the day would be lastingly fair, and that every threatening cloud would be drawn off from their hills; and the two girls set off together.

They gaily ascended the downs, rejoicing in their own penetration[5] at every glimpse of blue sky; and when they caught in their faces the animating gales of an high southwesterly wind,[6] they pitied the fears which had prevented their mother and Elinor from sharing such delightful sensations.

"Is there a felicity in the world," said Marianne, "superior to this?—Margaret, we will walk here at least two hours."

Margaret agreed, and they pursued their way against the wind, resisting it with laughing delight for about twenty minutes longer, when suddenly the clouds united over their heads, and a driving rain set full in their face.[7]—Chagrined and surprised, they were obliged, though unwillingly, to turn back, for no shelter was nearer than their own house. One consolation however remained for them, to which the exigence of the moment gave more than usual propriety; it was that of running with all possible speed down the steep side of the hill which led immediately to their garden gate.[8]

They set off. Marianne had at first the advantage, but a false step brought her suddenly to the ground, and Margaret, unable to stop herself to assist her, was involuntarily hurried along, and reached the bottom in safety.

A gentleman carrying a gun, with two pointers playing round him,[9] was passing up the hill and within a few yards of Marianne, when her accident happened. He put down his gun and ran to her assistance. She had raised herself from the ground, but her foot had been twisted in the fall, and she was scarcely able to stand.

4.   The pencil would be Elinor's for drawing.

5.   *penetration*: astuteness, discernment (in guessing the weather would stay fair).

6.   Southwesterly winds, which are frequent in this part of England, would be especially likely to produce rain because they would be coming from the Atlantic Ocean.

7.   This sequence of ecstatic delight followed by sharp disappointment when reality does not fulfill their expectations could be seen as a good allegory of the fate of Marianne's romantic enthusiasm.

8.   It was not considered proper for ladies to run, and running swiftly down a hill could be especially improper because of the likelihood that it would lift their skirts. In one of Jane Austen's youthful works, "Letter the Third," an acerbic older lady condemns a young lady as being one of those who "never mind what weather you trudge in, or how the wind shews [*sic*] your legs."

9.   Pointers were the standard dogs to accompany men out shooting. The task of the pointer, as the name implies, was to locate the birds and then to indicate their location to the shooter by pointing at them. For a picture of pointers, see p. 87.

The gentleman offered his services, and perceiving that her modesty declined what her situation rendered necessary, took her up in his arms without farther delay,[10] and carried her down the hill. Then passing through the garden, the gate of which had been left open by Margaret, he bore her directly into the house, whither Margaret was just arrived,[11] and quitted not his hold till he had seated her in a chair in the parlour.

Elinor and her mother rose up in amazement at their entrance, and while the eyes of both were fixed on him with an evident wonder and a secret admiration which equally sprung from his appearance, he apologized for his intrusion by relating its cause, in a manner so frank and so graceful, that his person, which was uncommonly handsome, received additional charms from his voice and expression. Had he been even old, ugly, and vulgar, the gratitude and kindness of Mrs. Dashwood would have been secured by any act of attention to her child; but the influence of youth, beauty, and elegance, gave an interest to the action which came home to her feelings.

She thanked him again and again; and with a sweetness of address which always attended her, invited him to be seated. But this he declined, as he was dirty and wet. Mrs. Dashwood then begged to know to whom she was obliged. His name, he replied, was Willoughby, and his present home was at Allenham, from whence he hoped she would allow him the honour of calling tomorrow to inquire after Miss Dashwood. The honour was readily granted, and he then departed, to make himself still more interesting, in the midst of an heavy rain.

His manly beauty and more than common gracefulness were instantly the theme of general admiration, and the laugh which his gallantry raised against Marianne, received particular spirit from his exterior attractions. —Marianne herself had seen less of his person than the rest, for the confusion which crimsoned over her face, on his lifting her up,[12] had robbed her of the power of regarding him after their entering the house. But she had seen enough of him to join in all the admiration of the others, and with an energy which always adorned her praise. His person and air[13]

10. Being picked up by a man would be considered completely improper, which is why Marianne's modesty prevents her from asking, or even signaling, him to do that. According to some contemporary conduct guides, a woman should avoid even touching the hand of a man who is not a family member.

11. Margaret is presumably about to ask for assistance.

12. She would be blushing and confused because of the immodesty involved in being lifted up.

13. *air*: outward character, manner.

A man going out shooting.

[From William Henry Scott, *British Field Sports* (London, 1818), p. 53]

were equal to what her fancy had ever drawn for the hero of a favourite story;[14] and in his carrying her into the house with so little previous formality, there was a rapidity of thought which particularly recommended the action to her.[15] Every circumstance belonging to him was interesting.[16] His name was good, his residence was in their favourite village, and she soon found out that of all manly dresses[17] a shooting-jacket was the most becoming.[18] Her imagination was busy, her reflections were pleasant, and the pain of a sprained ancle was disregarded.

Sir John called on them as soon as the next interval of fair weather that morning allowed him to get out of doors; and Marianne's accident being related to him, he was eagerly asked whether he knew any gentleman of the name of Willoughby at Allenham.

"Willoughby!" cried Sir John; "what, is *he* in the country?[19] That is good news however; I will ride over to-morrow, and ask him to dinner on Thursday."

"You know him then," said Mrs. Dashwood.

"Know him! to be sure I do. Why, he is down here every year."

"And what sort of a young man is he?"

"As good a kind of fellow as ever lived, I assure you.[20] A very decent shot, and there is not a bolder rider in England."[21]

"And is *that* all you can say for him?" cried Marianne, indignantly. "But what are his manners[22] on more intimate acquaintance? What his pursuits, his talents and genius?"[23]

Sir John was rather puzzled.

"Upon my soul," said he, "I do not know much about him as to all *that*. But he is a pleasant, good humoured fellow, and has got the nicest little black bitch of a pointer I ever saw.[24] Was she out with him to-day?"

But Marianne could no more satisfy him as to the colour of Mr. Willoughby's pointer, than he could describe to her the shades of his mind.[25]

"But who is he?" said Elinor. "Where does he come from? Has he a house at Allenham?"[26]

14. In addition, the dramatic rescue itself—though not that unlikely an event, since she is often out walking and he, as soon revealed, is often out hunting—fits the manner in which such storybook heroes appear, as does the suddenness and mysteriousness of his appearance and departure. Since much of Marianne's Romanticism has been formed by books, it is appropriate that her first meeting with an eligible young man should correspond to what she has read.

15. His rapidity, and her approval of it, cause them both to form a complete contrast with Edward and Elinor.

16. *interesting*: likely to arouse curiosity or emotion. The term had a stronger connotation at this time than it does today.

17. *dresses*: costumes, garb.

18. A shooting jacket was an informal jacket used for outdoor sport. Standard men's jackets or coats were fairly stiff and formal, making them less practicable for such activity.

19. *country*: county.

20. This praise is of limited value, for Sir John expresses similar enthusiasm about almost everyone.

21. Several outdoor sports, including foxhunting, involved following on horseback a fleet of swift running dogs and their prey. A bold rider was someone willing to move quickly despite all obstacles and dangers, the most significant of which were fences and streams that had to be jumped. Serious accidents did occur as part of these hunts, so it would require boldness, if not recklessness at times, to advance swiftly. Willoughby will show some similar characteristics in other aspects of his behavior. For a contemporary picture of foxhunting, see p. 86.

22. *manners*: general outward conduct and demeanor.

23. *genius*: natural abilities; quality of mind.

24. Dogs of both sexes were used by sportsmen. For a picture of a black pointer, though a male, see p. 87.

25. *mind*: inner character.

26. Elinor has the practical sense to ask Sir John some basic questions nobody else has posed, and they are also ones, unlike Marianne's, that he can answer.

On this point Sir John could give more certain intelligence; and he told them that Mr. Willoughby had no property of his own in the country; that he resided there only while he was visiting the old lady at Allenham Court,[27] to whom he was related, and whose possessions he was to inherit;[28] adding, "Yes, yes, he is very well worth catching, I can tell you, Miss Dashwood;[29] he has a pretty little estate of his own in Somersetshire[30] besides; and if I were you, I would not give him up to my younger sister in spite of all this tumbling down hills. Miss Marianne[31] must not expect to have all the men to herself. Brandon will be jealous, if she does not take care."

"I do not believe," said Mrs. Dashwood, with a good humoured smile, "that Mr. Willoughby will be incommoded by the attempts of either of *my* daughters towards what you call *catching him*. It is not an employment to which they have been brought up.[32] Men are very safe with us, let them be ever so rich. I am glad to find, however, from what you say, that he is a respectable young man, and one whose acquaintance will not be ineligible."

"He is as good a sort of fellow, I believe, as ever lived," repeated Sir John. "I remember last Christmas, at a little hop at the park, he danced from eight o'clock till four, without once sitting down."[33]

"Did he indeed?" cried Marianne, with sparkling eyes, "and with elegance, with spirit?"

"Yes; and he was up again at eight to ride to covert."[34]

"That is what I like; that is what a young man ought to be. Whatever be his pursuits, his eagerness in them should know no moderation, and leave him no sense of fatigue."

"Aye, aye, I see how it will be," said Sir John, "I see how it will be. You will be setting your cap at him now, and never think of poor Brandon."

"That is an expression, Sir John," said Marianne, warmly, "which I particularly dislike. I abhor every common-place phrase by which wit is intended;[35] and 'setting one's cap at a man,' or 'making a conquest,' are the most odious of all. Their tendency is

27. Allenham was identified above as the valley "which issued from that of Barton" (p. 76), and which contained an ancient mansion inhabited by an elderly lady. Large country houses often had names ending in "Court" or "Park."

28. It is later revealed that while he has reasonable expectations of inheriting her property, it is not assured to him.

29. *Miss Dashwood*: Elinor. Sir John would never call her "Elinor" because only family members would use first names. "Miss + Last Name" is always used for the eldest unmarried daughter of a family.

30. *Somersetshire*: a county immediately northeast of Devonshire. See map, p. 739.

31. *Miss Marianne*: younger unmarried daughters were normally called or referred to as "Miss + First Name." The only exception would be if no elder sister were present, when her last name only could be used. After Willoughby carried Marianne home he referred to her, before Elinor, as "Miss Dashwood," but he could not know that Marianne was a younger sister.

32. Mrs. Dashwood earlier expressed her indignation at Mrs. John Dashwood's accusation that Elinor was trying to ensnare Edward (see p. 40). Her use of "employment" here is appropriate, for finding a husband was a serious business for young ladies in this society, and one that some pursued with great determination and a strong hope for gain.

33. Dances often lasted very late. In a letter Jane Austen describes a ball from which they returned home "before 5" (Nov. 20, 1800), and in *Mansfield Park* a young man of an enthusiastic and energetic character says at a ball, when it is already three o'clock, "Why, the sport is but just begun. I hope we shall keep it up these [next] two hours."
Sir John, in saying "hop" for dance, is using slang of the time.

34. He means foxhunting. Coverts were hiding places, usually thickets, for wild animals, and were frequently associated with foxes. Foxhunts traditionally began at the beginning of the day, which would be around eight o'clock in England during the late fall and winter, the normal season for hunting (as well as the most common time of year for dances). Foxes, having fed during the night, would be slowed by their full bellies in the morning and thus be easier to catch.

35. Marianne will proclaim elsewhere her aversion to commonplace phrases (p. 184), while she often speaks critically of wit, or words meant to be cleverly jesting or teasing. "Setting one's cap at a man" was a familiar expression referring to a woman's pursuit of a man; its origin is not certain.

gross[36] and illiberal;[37] and if their construction could ever be deemed clever, time has long ago destroyed all its ingenuity."

Sir John did not much understand this reproof; but he laughed as heartily as if he did, and then replied,

"Aye, you will make conquests enough, I dare say, one way or other. Poor Brandon! he is quite smitten already, and he is very well worth setting your cap at,[38] I can tell you, in spite of all this tumbling about and spraining of ancles."[39]

Foxhunting: the picture shows the risky or bold riding the sport could involve.
[From William Henry Scott, *British Field Sports* (London, 1818), p. 419]

36. *gross:* unrefined, uncultured.

37. *illiberal:* sordid.

38. Sir John's total obliviousness to what Marianne has just said suggests the large gap between her own exalted standards and the majority of humanity. His words, from someone who does not seem particularly mercenary, show the strong presumption in this society that most women were out to "make conquests" of men.

39. His reference to "tumbling about," echoing one he just made to Elinor, indicates his sense of how much such an action could promote sexual attraction because of the romantic rescue it would inspire, and perhaps also because of the intimate physical contact it would lead to, in a society in which such contact was rare.

Two pointers: in this case, unlike in Willoughby's, the black pointer is a male, while the white one is female.

[From W. B. Daniel, *Rural Sports*, Vol. 3 (London, 1807), p. 336]

Chapter Ten

Marianne's preserver, as Margaret, with more elegance than precision, stiled Willoughby, called at the cottage early the next morning to make his personal inquiries.[1] He was received by Mrs. Dashwood with more than politeness; with a kindness which Sir John's account of him and her own gratitude prompted; and every thing that passed during the visit, tended to assure him of the sense, elegance, mutual affection, and domestic comfort of the family to whom accident had now introduced him. Of their personal charms he had not required a second interview to be convinced.

Miss Dashwood had a delicate complexion, regular features, and a remarkably pretty figure. Marianne was still handsomer. Her form, though not so correct as her sister's, in having the advantage of height was more striking; and her face was so lovely, that when in the common cant of praise she was called a beautiful girl, truth was less violently outraged than usually happens. Her skin was very brown,[2] but from its transparency, her complexion was uncommonly brilliant;[3] her features were all good; her smile was sweet and attractive, and in her eyes, which were very dark, there was a life, a spirit, an eagerness which could hardly be seen without delight. From Willoughby their expression was at first held back, by the embarrassment which the remembrance of his assistance created. But when this passed away, when her spirits became collected, when she saw that to the perfect good-breeding of the gentleman, he united frankness and vivacity, and above all, when she heard him declare that of music and dancing he was passionately fond,[4] she gave him such a look of approbation as secured the largest share of his discourse to herself for the rest of his stay.

It was only necessary to mention any favourite amusement to

1. He is later described as not usually rising early (p. 124), so this indicates some interest in Marianne on his part.

2. *Her skin was very brown:* she was dark-complexioned.

3. An 1811 book on beauty, *The Mirror of the Graces*, speaks of "the transparent surface of a clear skin" as one of the finest assets a woman can have.

4. Willoughby's fondness for music is demonstrated later by his singing, and even more by his writing out music (p. 158), which requires training and practice. It also establishes a strong link between him and Marianne, for in this society men rarely learned music or developed musical skills. Men also generally show less interest in dancing in Austen novels.

A young woman reading music.

[From *The Repository of arts, literature, fashions, manufactures, &c*, Vol. X (1813), p. 242]

engage her to talk. She could not be silent when such points were introduced, and she had neither shyness nor reserve in their discussion. They speedily discovered that their enjoyment of dancing and music was mutual, and that it arose from a general conformity of judgment in all that related to either. Encouraged by this to a further examination of his opinions, she proceeded to question him on the subject of books; her favourite authors were brought forward and dwelt upon with so rapturous a delight, that any young man of five and twenty must have been insensible indeed, not to become an immediate convert to the excellence of such works, however disregarded before. Their taste was strikingly alike. The same books, the same passages were idolized by each — or if any difference appeared, any objection arose, it lasted no longer than till the force of her arguments and the brightness of her eyes could be displayed. He acquiesced in all her decisions, caught all her enthusiasm; and long before his visit concluded, they conversed with the familiarity of a long-established acquaintance.[5]

"Well, Marianne," said Elinor, as soon as he had left them, "for *one* morning I think you have done pretty well. You have already ascertained Mr. Willoughby's opinion in almost every matter of importance. You know what he thinks of Cowper and Scott;[6] you are certain of his estimating their beauties as he ought, and you have received every assurance of his admiring Pope no more than is proper.[7] But how is your acquaintance to be long supported, under such extraordinary dispatch of every subject for discourse? You will soon have exhausted each favourite topic. Another meeting will suffice to explain his sentiments on picturesque beauty, and second marriages,[8] and then you can have nothing farther to ask." —

"Elinor," cried Marianne, "is this fair? is this just? are my ideas so scanty? But I see what you mean. I have been too much at my ease, too happy, too frank. I have erred against every commonplace notion of decorum;[9] I have been open and sincere where I ought to have been reserved, spiritless, dull, and deceitful: — had I

5.   The paragraph suggests that, except for the initial subjects of dancing and music, the perfect concord they reach is the product of his agreeing to her assertions. Marianne had earlier stated, "I could not be happy with a man whose taste did not in every point coincide with my own" (p. 30). In this conversation she probably conveys this attitude to Willoughby, along with opinions on specific books, and he, inspired by her beauty and enthusiasm, is happy to present himself as the man she wishes him to be. His real nature is still unclear: it is notable that the narrator has so far only sketched his appearance and said nothing about his character.

6.   Cowper was mentioned earlier as one of Marianne's favorite poets (p. 30). Sir Walter Scott (1771–1832) had published more recently, and his long narrative poems were the greatest literary sellers of the age. The ones that had appeared by the time of this novel were *The Lay of the Last Minstrel* (1805), *Marmion* (1808), and *The Lady of the Lake* (1810). The latter two are the subject of a conversation in *Persuasion* between the heroine and a young man of Romantic tastes similar to Marianne's, while lines from the first are quoted by the heroine of *Mansfield Park*, who also shares some of Marianne's tastes. All three poems are set in sixteenth-century Scotland—the type of remote setting popular in much Romantic literature—and are highly dramatic tales of love and war that also contain a variety of tender songs.

7.   Alexander Pope (1688–1744) was the leading poet of his age in England, and one still widely read and respected at the time of this novel. In a letter Jane Austen, with an evident expectation that the recipient will catch the reference, paraphrases a famous line of his and then adds, "There has been one infallible Pope in the World" (Oct. 26, 1813). His poems, both in their form and content, express a restrained and rationalistic spirit that is utterly different from Marianne's. Thus, while his prestige and genuine skill were strong enough to make her read him and admire him to a degree, she does not rate him too highly or wish others to do so.

8.   These are both subjects on which Marianne has strong opinions that will be discussed later.

9.   The commonplace notion of decorum she probably means is that limiting introductory visits to fifteen minutes, in which banalities are mostly exchanged (see p. 59, note 31). But her behavior has also violated more serious principles of contemporary decorum. One is the courtesy to include all in the conversation: the description of her lengthy exchange with Willoughby suggests it was exclusively between them. Another is female modesty and caution. Conduct books of the time frequently warn women against being too forward and encouraging in their behavior toward men, because many men were happy to gain female affections without having honorable intentions toward them.

talked only of the weather and the roads,[10] and had I spoken only once in ten minutes, this reproach would have been spared."

"My love," said her mother, "you must not be offended with Elinor—she was only in jest.[11] I should scold her myself, if she were capable of wishing to check the delight of your conversation with our new friend."—Marianne was softened in a moment.[12]

Willoughby, on his side, gave every proof of his pleasure in their acquaintance, which an evident wish of improving it could offer. He came to them every day. To inquire after Marianne was at first his excuse; but the encouragement of his reception, to which every day gave greater kindness, made such an excuse unnecessary before it had ceased to be possible, by Marianne's perfect recovery. She was confined for some days to the house; but never had any confinement been less irksome. Willoughby was a young man of good abilities, quick imagination, lively[13] spirits, and open, affectionate manners. He was exactly formed to engage Marianne's heart, for with all this, he joined not only a captivating person, but a natural ardour of mind which was now roused and increased by the example of her own, and which recommended him to her affection beyond every thing else.[14]

His society became gradually her most exquisite enjoyment. They read, they talked, they sang together; his musical talents were considerable;[15] and he read with all the sensibility and spirit which Edward had unfortunately wanted.[16]

In Mrs. Dashwood's estimation, he was as faultless as in Marianne's; and Elinor saw nothing to censure in him but a propensity, in which he strongly resembled and peculiarly delighted her sister, of saying too much what he thought on every occasion, without attention to persons or circumstances. In hastily forming and giving his opinion of other people, in sacrificing general politeness to the enjoyment of undivided attention where his heart was engaged,[17] and in slighting too easily the forms of worldly propriety, he displayed a want of caution which Elinor could not approve, in spite of all that he and Marianne could say in its support.[18]

Marianne began now to perceive that the desperation which

10. The state of the roads was, along with the weather, a central subject of the ordinary banal conversation that Marianne scorns. Roads in the country, made of dirt and inconsistently maintained by local authorities, were frequently in bad shape, thereby affecting people's daily travel.

11. Mrs. Dashwood is right about Elinor's jesting tone—and Marianne's inability to perceive this is part of her general humorlessness. But Elinor's words also hint at important points, ones Mrs. Dashwood fails to perceive, probably because she shares some of the same propensities. Elinor, in speaking ironically of the perfect concord Marianne and Willoughby have achieved in their first talk, is clearly suggesting the difficulty of really achieving such concord and complete knowledge of another person in such a brief span. Elinor herself is consistently shown taking time and care in her evaluations of others, and her judgments usually prove to be more accurate than her sister's.

12. Marianne's immediate softening indicates a positive side of her seen at other points: though quick to take offense, she can also easily relent.

13. *lively*: vivacious, lighthearted, merry. For more on the partially different meaning of the term then, which has an important bearing on Willoughby's character and behavior, see p. 176.

14. Once more Willoughby is being shaped by Marianne's influence. The brief description of Willoughby in this passage represents the last verdict on him presented by the narrator—and it mostly concerns his external features and his effect on Marianne. It will only be much later in the novel that a combination of his actions, the revelations of another person, and, most important, his own confession give a full picture of his character. Until then he remains a man of mystery, seen primarily through the prisms of Marianne's enthused imagination (in which she will soon be joined by Mrs. Dashwood) and Elinor's fluctuating and uncertain attempts at evaluation.

15. As mentioned in note 4 above, men in this society did not frequently cultivate music, so his talents and his singing mark him as distinctive.

16. He would be reading aloud, a common activity then (see p. 31, note 33).

17. His haste in judging others and neglecting them to focus solely on Marianne replicates her procedure toward him in their initial conversation.

18. Marianne would support their behavior from her genuine conviction, basic to her outlook, on the primacy of individual feelings over social rules. Willoughby, whatever his real opinions, would have a natural incentive to argue the same, both from agreement with her and from a wish to justify his own behavior.

had seized her at sixteen and a half, of ever seeing a man who could satisfy her ideas of perfection, had been rash and unjustifiable.[19] Willoughby was all that her fancy had delineated in that unhappy hour and in every brighter period, as capable of attaching her; and his behaviour declared his wishes to be in that respect as earnest, as his abilities were strong.

Her mother too, in whose mind not one speculative thought of their marriage had been raised, by his prospect of riches, was led before the end of a week to hope and expect it; and secretly to congratulate herself on having gained two such sons-in-law as Edward and Willoughby.

Colonel Brandon's partiality for Marianne, which had so early been discovered by his friends, now first became perceptible to Elinor, when it ceased to be noticed by them. Their attention and wit were drawn off[20] to his more fortunate rival; and the raillery which the other had incurred before any partiality arose, was removed when his feelings began really to call for the ridicule so justly annexed to sensibility.[21] Elinor was obliged, though unwillingly, to believe that the sentiments which Mrs. Jennings had assigned him for her own satisfaction, were now actually excited by her sister; and that however a general resemblance of disposition between the parties might forward the affection of Mr. Willoughby, an equally striking opposition of character was no hindrance to the regard of Colonel Brandon. She saw it with concern; for what could a silent man of five and thirty hope, when opposed by a very lively one of five and twenty? and as she could not even wish him successful, she heartily wished him indifferent. She liked him—in spite of his gravity and reserve, she beheld in him an object of interest. His manners, though serious, were mild; and his reserve appeared rather the result of some oppression of spirits, than of any natural gloominess of temper. Sir John had dropt hints of past injuries and disappointments, which justified her belief of his being an unfortunate man, and she regarded him with respect and compassion.

Perhaps she pitied and esteemed him the more because he was slighted by Willoughby and Marianne, who, prejudiced against

19. Despair about the possibility of finding ideal perfection in the world was a strand in much Romantic thinking. Here, as the fervent conclusion of someone only sixteen and a half, it appears to particular disadvantage.

20. *drawn off*: diverted, turned.

21. This last clause is probably ironic on the author's part. While Austen does over the course of the novel criticize many aspects of sensibility, seen as a cultural trend or set of ideas, here the word simply means strong feelings, in particular feelings of love, and the "just ridicule" is what people like Mrs. Jennings and Sir John delight in inflicting on all those appearing to be in love.

Selling a horse.

[From William Combe, *The Tour of Doctor Syntax in Search of the Picturesque* (London, 1817; 1903 reprint), p. 134]

him for being neither lively nor young, seemed resolved to under-value his merits.

"Brandon is just the kind of man," said Willoughby one day, when they were talking of him together, "whom every body speaks well of, and nobody cares about; whom all are delighted to see, and nobody remembers to talk to."

"That is exactly what I think of him," cried Marianne.

"Do not boast of it, however," said Elinor, "for it is injustice in both of you. He is highly esteemed by all the family at the park, and I never see him myself without taking pains to converse with him."

"That he is patronized by *you*," replied Willoughby, "is certainly in his favour; but as for the esteem of the others, it is a reproach in itself. Who would submit to the indignity of being approved by such women as Lady Middleton and Mrs. Jennings, that could command the indifference of any body else?"[22]

"But perhaps the abuse of such people as yourself and Marianne, will make amends for the regard of Lady Middleton and her mother. If their praise is censure, your censure may be praise, for they are not more undiscerning, than you are prejudiced and unjust."

"In defence of your protegé you can even be saucy."

"My protegé, as you call him, is a sensible man; and sense will always have attractions for me. Yes, Marianne, even in a man between thirty and forty. He has seen a great deal of the world; has been abroad;[23] has read, and has a thinking mind. I have found him capable of giving me much information on various subjects, and he has always answered my inquiries with the readiness of good-breeding and good nature."[24]

"That is to say," cried Marianne contemptuously, "he has told you that in the East Indies[25] the climate is hot, and the mosquitoes are troublesome."

"He *would* have told me so, I doubt not, had I made any such inquiries, but they happened to be points on which I had been previously informed."

"Perhaps," said Willoughby, "his observations may have extended to the existence of nabobs, gold mohrs, and palanquins."[26]

22. Willoughby does not simply have a low opinion of Lady Middleton and Mrs. Jennings, as Elinor also does to a great degree, but he openly expresses complete contempt, even as he continues to partake happily of the Middletons' frequent hospitality. As for his dislike of Colonel Brandon, it takes on ironic significance in light of later events that will place the two men in an unexpected position regarding each other.

23. It was unusual for people in England then to have spent time out of the country. Travel was very expensive and difficult, and during this period in particular venturing to Europe, the closest overseas destination, was rarely possible because of the continual wars between Britain and Napoleonic France, which controlled much of the continent. Jane Austen never went abroad, and though many of her characters are very wealthy, few are ever described as having left the country, except for naval officers, whose travels are often restricted to overseas bases and ports.

24. A later passage (p. 400) contrasts good breeding, or politeness, with good nature, indicating that while the latter is more worthwhile, the former still has value. Here there is fortunately no opposition.

25. The East Indies refers to India and the islands of Southeast Asia. It is later revealed that Colonel Brandon spent several years serving the army in India, which was a British colony then.

26. These are all features of India. The word "nabobs," which originally referred to high Indian officials, by this time mostly meant people from Britain who acquired great wealth in India. Gold mohrs, or mohurs, were the principal coins used in British India. Palanquins were covered litters on which people were carried by means of poles extending from them; British people living in India sometimes used them. Willoughby, who is unlikely to have been to India himself, could have learned of these things from other men who had been to India, from travel books, of which there were many then, or from a number of popular novels that were set in India. Jane Austen herself also could have acquired familiarity with these matters from her sister-in-law, Eliza de Feuillide, who was born in India and whose mother lived there for a number of years.

"I may venture to say that *his* observations have stretched much farther than *your* candour.[27] But why should you dislike him?"

"I do not dislike him. I consider him, on the contrary, as a very respectable man, who has every body's good word and nobody's notice; who has more money than he can spend,[28] more time than he knows how to employ,[29] and two new coats every year."[30]

"Add to which," cried Marianne, "that he has neither genius,[31] taste, nor spirit.[32] That his understanding[33] has no brilliancy,[34] his feelings no ardour, and his voice no expression."[35]

"You decide on his imperfections so much in the mass," replied Elinor, "and so much on the strength of your own imagination, that the commendation I am able to give of him is comparatively cold and insipid. I can only pronounce him to be a sensible man, well-bred, well-informed, of gentle address, and I believe possessing an amiable heart."

. "Miss Dashwood," cried Willoughby, "you are now using me unkindly. You are endeavouring to disarm me by reason, and to convince me against my will. But it will not do. You shall find me as stubborn as you can be artful.[36] I have three unanswerable reasons for disliking Colonel Brandon: he has threatened me with rain when I wanted it to be fine; he has found fault with the hanging of my curricle,[37] and I cannot persuade him to buy my brown mare.[38] If it will be any satisfaction to you, however, to be told, that I believe his character to be in other respects irreproachable, I am ready to confess it. And in return for an acknowledgment, which must give me some pain, you cannot deny me the privilege of disliking him as much as ever."[39]

27. *candour*: fairness, generosity in judging others.

28. Willoughby is later revealed to spend more than he has, so he may envy someone in the opposite position.

29. Landed gentlemen usually had a lot of leisure time, so Brandon is hardly worthy of particular censure in this respect.

30. This would be another mark of Brandon's affluence, for clothing was expensive then, and the most common form of men's coat, a greatcoat, would be costlier than most articles because its length required large amounts of fabric. But it is doubtful if Willoughby has any basis for knowing that Colonel Brandon really buys two new coats a year.

31. *genius*: talent, natural ability.

32. *spirit*: ardor, vigor, vivacity.

33. *understanding*: intellect.

34. *brilliancy*: sparkle.

35. *expression*: ability to express feeling. Marianne and Willoughby are united in their criticism of Colonel Brandon, but they show their different characters by the ways they express it, she directly and seriously and he with exaggeration and playful irony.

36. *artful*: clever, skillful.

37. *curricle*: an open carriage (see p. 129, note 28, and picture on the next page). Hanging refers to how high the body of the carriage is suspended. In Jane Austen's youthful story, "Three Sisters," a prospective bride and groom argue over whether the carriage they purchase upon marriage will be hung high or low.

38. Buying and selling horses was a common concern of gentlemen, for they used horses frequently to pull their carriages, hunt, or simply ride, either as recreation or as a means of transport. For a picture of selling a horse, see p. 95.

39. Willoughby's clever, self-deprecating humor implicitly acknowledges his injustice toward Colonel Brandon, but it also serves to disarm serious criticism of that injustice. A character in *Mansfield Park*, Mary Crawford, uses a similar procedure to sugar over less than admirable actions.

Chapter Eleven

*L*ittle had Mrs. Dashwood or her daughters imagined, when they first came into Devonshire, that so many engagements would arise to occupy their time as shortly presented themselves, or that they should have such frequent invitations and such constant visitors as to leave them little leisure for serious employment. Yet such was the case. When Marianne was recovered, the schemes of amusement[1] at home and abroad, which Sir John had been previously forming, were put in execution. The private balls at the park then began,[2] and parties on the water were made and accomplished as often as a showery October would allow.[3] In every meeting of the kind Willoughby was included; and the ease[4] and familiarity[5] which naturally attended these parties were exactly calculated[6] to give increasing intimacy to his acquaintance with the Dashwoods, to afford him opportunity of witnessing the excellencies of Marianne, of marking his animated admiration of her, and of receiving, in her behaviour to himself, the most pointed assurance of her affection.

Elinor could not be surprised at their attachment. She only wished that it were less openly shewn; and once or twice did venture to suggest the propriety of some self-command to Marianne. But Marianne abhorred all concealment where no real disgrace could attend unreserve; and to aim at the restraint of sentiments which were not in themselves illaudable, appeared to her not merely an unnecessary effort, but a disgraceful subjection of reason to common-place and mistaken notions. Willoughby thought the same; and their behaviour, at all times, was an illustration of their opinions.

When he was present she had no eyes for any one else. Every thing he did, was right. Every thing he said, was clever. If their evenings at the park were concluded with cards, he cheated him-

1.   *schemes of amusement:* plans or projects of enjoyment.

2.   For private balls, see p. 63, note 8. The facing passage there spoke of Sir John's organizing balls in the winter and outdoor excursions in the summer, but obviously he is happy to organize as much as is feasible, whatever the time of year.

3.   The plan for a later outing includes sailing on a large body of water. For the rainy weather prevailing in Devonshire, especially at this time of year, see p. 53, note 9.

4.   *ease:* lack of restraint; informality.

5.   *familiarity:* intimate or friendly intercourse.

6.   *calculated:* suited.

A curricle (Ashtead Park, a country house, is in the background).

[From John Preston Neale, *Views of the Seats of Noblemen and Gentlemen,* Vol. V (1822)]

self and all the rest of the party to get her a good hand. If dancing formed the amusement of the night, they were partners for half the time; and when obliged to separate for a couple of dances, were careful to stand together and scarcely spoke a word to any body else.[7] Such conduct made them of course most exceedingly laughed at; but ridicule could not shame, and seemed hardly to provoke them.[8]

Mrs. Dashwood entered into all their feelings with a warmth which left her no inclination for checking this excessive display of them. To her it was but the natural consequence of a strong affection in a young and ardent mind.

This was the season of happiness to Marianne. Her heart was devoted to Willoughby, and the fond attachment to Norland, which she brought with her from Sussex, was more likely to be softened than she had thought it possible before, by the charms which his society bestowed on her present home.

Elinor's happiness was not so great. Her heart was not so much at ease, nor her satisfaction in their amusements so pure. They afforded her no companion that could make amends for what she had left behind, nor that could teach her to think of Norland with less regret than ever. Neither Lady Middleton nor Mrs. Jennings could supply to her the conversation she missed; although the latter was an everlasting talker, and from the first had regarded her with a kindness which ensured her a large share of her discourse. She had already repeated her own history to Elinor three or four times; and had Elinor's memory been equal to her means of improvement,[9] she might have known very early in their acquaintance, all the particulars of Mr. Jennings's last illness, and what he said to his wife a few minutes before he died. Lady Middleton was more agreeable than her mother, only in being more silent. Elinor needed little observation to perceive that her reserve was a mere calmness of manner with which sense had nothing to do. Towards her husband and mother she was the same as to them; and intimacy was therefore neither to be looked for nor desired. She had nothing to say one day that she had not said the day before. Her insipidity was invariable, for even her spirits were

7. Dancing etiquette dictated changing partners over the course of the evening. Dancing more than once with the same partner was generally permissible, but only after first dancing with other people. The suggestion here is that Marianne and Willoughby dance only with each other, alternating pairs of dances in which they are able to dance together with ones in which they both stand aside. Dances were performed in pairs, which is why it speaks of their separating for "a couple of dances"; the two dances usually lasted around half an hour, after which one would sit down or partner with someone else for the next pair.

8. Their behavior is similar to that of the foolish heroine and her friends in *Love and Friendship*, Jane Austen's youthful satire of the excesses of sensibility. The heroine explains, "In the society of my Edward & this Amiable Pair, I passed the happiest moments of my Life: Our time was most delightfully spent, in mutual Protestations of Freindship [sic], and in vows of unalterable Love, in which we were secure from being interrupted, by intruding & disagreeable Visitors, as Augustus & Sophia had on their first Entrance in the Neighbourhood, taken due care to inform the surrounding Families, that as their Happiness centered wholly in themselves, they wished for no other society." In contrast, in her novels Austen upholds an ideal in which love between two people goes along with continuing affection and attention toward a larger circle of friends and family.

9. *means of improvement:* opportunities for education or cultivation. The phrase is meant ironically, since learning the details of Mrs. Jennings's history hardly constitutes real improvement of the mind.

always the same; and though she did not oppose the parties arranged by her husband, provided every thing were conducted in style and her two eldest children attended her, she never appeared to receive more enjoyment from them, than she might have experienced in sitting at home;—and so little did her presence add to the pleasure of the others, by any share in their conversation, that they were sometimes only reminded of her being amongst them by her solicitude about her troublesome boys.

In Colonel Brandon alone, of all her new acquaintance, did Elinor find a person who could in any degree claim the respect of abilities, excite the interest of friendship, or give pleasure as a companion. Willoughby was out of the question. Her admiration and regard, even her sisterly regard, was all his own; but he was a lover; his attentions were wholly Marianne's, and a far less agreeable man might have been more generally pleasing.[10] Colonel Brandon, unfortunately for himself, had no such encouragement to think only of Marianne, and in conversing with Elinor he found the greatest consolation for the total indifference of her sister.

Elinor's compassion for him increased, as she had reason to suspect that the misery of disappointed love had already been known by him. This suspicion was given by some words which accidentally dropt from him one evening at the park, when they were sitting down together by mutual consent, while the others were dancing. His eyes were fixed on Marianne, and, after a silence of some minutes, he said with a faint smile, "Your sister, I understand, does not approve of second attachments."[11]

"No," replied Elinor, "her opinions are all romantic."

"Or rather, as I believe, she considers them impossible to exist."

"I believe she does. But how she contrives it without reflecting on the character of her own father, who had himself two wives, I know not. A few years however will settle her opinions on the reasonable basis of common sense and observation; and then they may be more easy to define and to justify than they now are, by any body but herself."

10. *generally pleasing*: pleasing or agreeable to people in general.

11. Marianne's ideal of a perfect and absolute union of two souls, a common Romantic idea, would naturally lead her to doubt the possibility of anyone achieving a second such union. Elinor will later express her disagreement with the notion, a disagreement shared by Jane Austen herself (see pp. 486–488 and p. 489, note 41).

Mrs. Henry Baring and Children.

[From *The Masterpieces of Lawrence* (London, 1913), p. 39]

"This will probably be the case," he replied; "and yet there is something so amiable[12] in the prejudices of a young mind, that one is sorry to see them give way to the reception of more general opinions."

"I cannot agree with you there," said Elinor. "There are inconveniences attending such feelings as Marianne's, which all the charms of enthusiasm and ignorance of the world cannot atone for. Her systems[13] have all the unfortunate tendency of setting propriety[14] at nought; and a better acquaintance with the world is what I look forward to as her greatest possible advantage."

After a short pause he resumed the conversation by saying—

"Does your sister make no distinction in her objections against a second attachment? or is it equally criminal in every body? Are those who have been disappointed in their first choice, whether from the inconstancy of its object, or the perverseness of circumstances, to be equally indifferent during the rest of their lives?"

"Upon my word, I am not acquainted with the minutia of her principles. I only know that I never yet heard her admit any instance of a second attachment's being pardonable."

"This," said he, "cannot hold; but a change, a total change of sentiments—No, no, do not desire it,—for when the romantic refinements of a young mind are obliged to give way, how frequently are they succeeded by such opinions as are but too common, and too dangerous! I speak from experience. I once knew a lady who in temper and mind greatly resembled your sister, who thought and judged like her, but who from an inforced change—from a series of unfortunate circumstances"—Here he stopt suddenly; appeared to think that he had said too much, and by his countenance gave rise to conjectures, which might not otherwise have entered Elinor's head. The lady would probably have passed without suspicion, had he not convinced Miss Dashwood that what concerned her ought not to escape his lips.[15] As it was, it required but a slight effort of fancy to connect his emotion with the tender recollection of past regard. Elinor attempted no more. But Marianne, in her place, would not have done so little. The

12. *amiable*: attractive, pleasing.

13. *systems*: doctrines, set of principles. The phrase, along with Elinor's reference below to "the minutia of her principles," suggests how much Marianne's beliefs stem not simply from feelings or natural impulses, but from a comprehensive and carefully thought-out body of ideas. They result as much from theory and reading as from instinct.

14. *propriety*: that which is right and proper. The term had a wider scope than it does now, referring to moral principles as well as rules of etiquette.

15. The identity and history of this lady, and their relevance to Marianne, will eventually be disclosed (see pp. 384–388). His warning about the possible dangers of abandoning romantic principles, while clearly reflecting his own attitudes and experience, does not necessarily contradict the general message of the novel, which, even as it ridicules many aspects of Marianne's sensibility, also presents examples of lack of feeling that are more harmful or repulsive, often much more so, than any of Marianne's faults. Mr. and Mrs. John Dashwood's callous selfishness, and to a lesser degree Lady Middleton's cold vacuousness, are two of these, and others will appear.

whole story would have been speedily formed under her active imagination; and every thing established in the most melancholy order of disastrous love.[16]

A military man of the time (General Sir John Moore).

[From Lord Ronald Sutherland Gower, *Sir Thomas Lawrence* (London, 1900), p. 110]

16. Tragic love formed a central subject of much Romantic literature. In this case, Marianne's potential conjectures would actually have some justification.

The interior of a stable.
[From George Williamson, *George Morland: His Life and Works* (London, 1907), p. 62]

Chapter Twelve

As Elinor and Marianne were walking together the next morning the latter communicated a piece of news to her sister, which in spite of all that she knew before of Marianne's imprudence and want of thought, surprised her by its extravagant testimony of both. Marianne told her, with the greatest delight, that Willoughby had given her a horse, one that he had bred himself on his estate in Somersetshire,[1] and which was exactly calculated to carry a woman.[2] Without considering that it was not in her mother's plan to keep any horse, that if she were to alter her resolution in favour of this gift, she must buy another for the servant, and keep a servant to ride it,[3] and after all, build a stable to receive them, she had accepted the present without hesitation, and told her sister of it in raptures.

"He intends to send his groom[4] into Somersetshire immediately for it," she added, "and when it arrives, we will ride every day. You shall share its use with me. Imagine to yourself, my dear Elinor, the delight of a gallop on some of these downs."

Most unwilling was she to awaken from such a dream of felicity, to comprehend all the unhappy truths which attended the affair; and for some time she refused to submit to them. As to an additional servant, the expence would be a trifle;[5] mama she was sure would never object to it; and any horse would do for *him*;[6] he might always get one at the park; as to a stable, the merest shed would be sufficient.[7] Elinor then ventured to doubt the propriety of her receiving such a present from a man so little, or at least so lately known to her. This was too much.

"You are mistaken, Elinor," said she warmly, "in supposing I know very little of Willoughby.[8] I have not known him long indeed, but I am much better acquainted with him, than I am with any other creature in the world, except yourself and mama. It

1.   Breeding horses, sometimes through the mixture of different stocks, was a practice of many country gentlemen.

2.   While horseback riding was not a common pursuit for ladies, some did ride, including all the principal young ladies in *Mansfield Park*. They would need horses considered suitable for a woman: the heroine rides a pony when young, and later her cousin procures a mare that, unlike other horses in his possession, would be fit for her to ride.

3.   She would need to have a servant accompany her, since it would not be proper for a woman to ride on her own.

4.   *groom:* servant whose job was to take care of horses.

5.   The Dashwoods had already limited their staff to three. Since the additional servant would need to be a man (only men could serve as grooms) the expense would be even greater. Male servants commanded significantly higher salaries; also, unlike female servants, they were generally provided with a uniform by their employer and were subject to a special tax.

6.   This is a rather callous attitude toward the servant, especially since his function would require him to keep up with Marianne as she rode.

7.   Given the rainy nature of the climate here, they would have particular need of a good stable, rather than a mere shed. The cost of that, along with the servant, the extra horse, and food and equipment for both horses, would make it prohibitively expensive for the Dashwoods. Willoughby shows both social and financial imprudence in thinking the gift would be appropriate. For a contemporary picture of a stable, see the preceding page.

8.   This is Marianne's first use of "Willoughby" without "Mr." before it. This less formal designation was usually employed only by men speaking of other men. Other Jane Austen heroines always use "Mr." for the man they are interested in, even after they have known him far longer than Marianne has known Willoughby, just as the men always call a woman "Miss" (the principal exception is when a family connection allows both to use first names, as with Elinor and Edward—though even Edward sometimes calls Elinor "Miss Dashwood"). Elinor and Margaret continue to use "Mr. Willoughby," at least for now.

is not time or opportunity that is to determine[9] intimacy;—it is disposition[10] alone. Seven years would be insufficient to make some people acquainted with each other, and seven days are more than enough for others.[11] I should hold myself guilty of greater impropriety in accepting a horse from my brother, than from Willoughby. Of John I know very little, though we have lived together for years; but of Willoughby my judgment has long been formed."

. Elinor thought it wisest to touch that point no more. She knew her sister's temper.[12] Opposition on so tender a subject would only attach her the more to her own opinion. But by an appeal to her affection for her mother, by representing the inconveniences which that indulgent mother must draw on herself, if (as would probably be the case) she consented to this increase of establishment,[13] Marianne was shortly subdued; and she promised not to tempt her mother to such imprudent kindness by mentioning the offer,[14] and to tell Willoughby when she saw him next, that it must be declined.

She was faithful to her word; and when Willoughby called at the cottage, the same day, Elinor heard her express her disappointment to him in a low voice, on being obliged to forego the acceptance of his present. The reasons for this alteration were at the same time related, and they were such as to make further entreaty on his side impossible. His concern however was very apparent; and after expressing it with earnestness, he added in the same low voice—"But, Marianne,[15] the horse is still yours, though you cannot use it now. I shall keep it only till you can claim it. When you leave Barton to form your own establishment in a more lasting home, Queen Mab shall receive you."[16]

This was all overheard by Miss Dashwood; and in the whole of the sentence, in his manner of pronouncing it, and in his addressing her sister by her christian name alone, she instantly saw an intimacy so decided, a meaning so direct, as marked a perfect agreement between them. From that moment she doubted not of their being engaged to each other; and the belief of it created no

9. *is to determine:* is likely to determine, usually determines.

10. *disposition:* general mental character or bent.

11. This represents a good summation of Marianne's prioritizing personal feeling over every other consideration and her belief in a union of souls that makes carefully getting to know someone unnecessary.

12. *temper:* emotional disposition.

13. *establishment:* household staff and facilities.

14. Here, as at other times, Marianne's affection for others and genuine goodness of heart check her excesses.

15. Willoughby's use of Marianne's first name represents an even greater presumption of intimacy than her use of his last name alone. Usually it was only after a marriage proposal was accepted that a man would progress to that. For that same reason Marianne's apparent acquiescence in his usage is a sign of imprudence, for it suggests acknowledgment on her part of an engaged state even though no such state exists. In *Mansfield Park* the heroine, Fanny Price, indicates her displeasure, as rules of propriety would dictate, when a man wooing her calls her "Fanny" rather than "Miss Price."

16. Queen Mab is from *Romeo and Juliet,* the subject of a long speech in which she is described as the "fairies' midwife," a minuscule creature who rides around every night in a tiny vehicle pulled by a gnat to spark dreams within each person she visits. It is later revealed that toward the end of Willoughby's time in Devonshire he and the Dashwood family read *Hamlet* together (p. 162). It is possible they were earlier reading *Romeo and Juliet,* whose tale of passionate young love would have a natural appeal to them, especially to Marianne, and that this inspired Willoughby, in order to honor or please her, to name his horse after Queen Mab, whose fantastical nature could have aroused Marianne's expressed fancy or at least made Willoughby think she would like the name. This choice also indicates the horse is a mare, which would be considered the most suitable for a woman.

other surprise, than that she, or any of their friends, should be left by tempers so frank, to discover it by accident.

Margaret related something to her the next day, which placed this matter in a still clearer light. Willoughby had spent the preceding evening with them, and Margaret, by being left some time in the parlour with only him and Marianne, had had opportunity for observations, which, with a most important face, she communicated to her eldest sister, when they were next by themselves.

"Oh! Elinor," she cried, "I have such a secret to tell you about Marianne. I am sure she will be married to Mr. Willoughby very soon."

"You have said so," replied Elinor, "almost every day since they first met on High-church Down;[17] and they had not known each other a week, I believe, before you were certain that Marianne wore his picture round her neck; but it turned out to be only the miniature[18] of our great uncle."[19]

"But indeed this is quite another thing. I am sure they will be married very soon, for he has got a lock of her hair."

"Take care, Margaret. It may be only the hair of some great uncle of *his*."

"But indeed, Elinor, it is Marianne's. I am almost sure it is, for I saw him cut it off. Last night after tea,[20] when you and mama went out of the room, they were whispering and talking together as fast as could be, and he seemed to be begging something of her, and presently he took up her scissars and cut off a long lock of her hair,[21] for it was all tumbled down her back;[22] and he kissed it, and folded it up in a piece of white paper, and put it into his pocket-book."[23]

From such particulars, stated on such authority, Elinor could not withhold her credit: nor was she disposed to it, for the circumstance was in perfect unison with what she had heard and seen herself.

Margaret's sagacity was not always displayed in a way so satisfactory to her sister. When Mrs. Jennings attacked her one evening at the park, to give the name of the young man who was Elinor's particular favourite, which had been long a matter of

17. This is the name of the nearby open hill where Marianne had her accident and Willoughby rescued her.

18. *miniature*: miniature painting. Miniatures had long been popular, especially for portraits, because their small size allowed them to be worn around the neck, as this one is, to keep the image of the other person always at hand. Their popularity had greatly increased during the late eighteenth century. For a picture of two women looking at one, see p. 249.

19. Her wearing a picture of their great-uncle, despite his having given most of the family inheritance to their half brother, shows her lack of petty resentment. Elinor and Mrs. Dashwood also never manifest the slightest bitterness along those lines.

20. Tea was a meal, not necessarily a large one, taken regularly in the evening. It involved tea or other hot beverages, along with food. Later on, tea is described as occurring at seven o'clock (p. 588). Dinner, the main meal of the day, was served during the late afternoon, while supper, a light meal, was served later in the evening (people of this class did not normally go to bed very early).

21. A lock of hair was frequently used as a memento of love. This is why Margaret is sure it indicates their intention to marry.

22. Women generally had long hair, but most of it was kept pinned up, with nothing falling below the face. Usually a woman would let down her hair only when she had retired for the night. Marianne's wearing hers down in front of a young man would be considered immodest—the principal reason for pinning up hair was to avoid excessive arousal of male lust, the same reason for full-length skirts.

23. *pocket-book*: a small book that could fit into the pocket; it was used by both sexes. The book usually would be for notes or memorandums, and it was a potential storage place for small items. The gradual expansion of this latter function after Jane Austen's time is what led the term eventually to become a synonym for a woman's purse.

great curiosity to her, Margaret answered by looking at her sister, and saying, "I must not tell, may I, Elinor?"

This of course made every body laugh; and Elinor tried to laugh too. But the effort was painful. She was convinced that Margaret had fixed on a person, whose name she could not bear with composure to become a standing joke with Mrs. Jennings.

Marianne felt for her most sincerely; but she did more harm than good to the cause, by turning very red, and saying in an angry manner to Margaret,[24]

"Remember that whatever your conjectures may be, you have no right to repeat them."

"I never had any conjectures about it," replied Margaret; "it was you who told me of it yourself."

This increased the mirth of the company, and Margaret was eagerly pressed to say something more.

"Oh! pray, Miss Margaret, let us know all about it," said Mrs. Jennings. "What is the gentleman's name?"

"I must not tell, ma'am. But I know very well what it is; and I know where he is too."

"Yes, yes, we can guess where he is; at his own house at Norland to be sure. He is the curate of the parish I dare say."[25]

"No, *that* he is not. He is of no profession at all."

"Margaret," said Marianne with great warmth, "you know that all this is an invention of your own, and that there is no such person in existence."

"Well then he is lately dead, Marianne, for I am sure there was such a man once, and his name begins with an F."[26]

Most grateful did Elinor feel to Lady Middleton for observing at this moment, "that it rained very hard," though she believed the interruption to proceed less from any attention to her, than from her ladyship's great dislike of all such inelegant subjects of raillery as delighted her husband and mother.[27] The idea however started by her, was immediately pursued by Colonel Brandon, who was on every occasion mindful of the feelings of others; and much was said on the subject of rain by both of them. Willoughby opened the piano-forte, and asked Marianne to sit down to it;[28] and thus

24. Marianne must try to silence Margaret, for any attempt by Elinor would only draw suspicion on her head. Marianne's vehement attempts testify to her concern for her sister, though, as is often the case, her fervor undermines her good intentions.

25. A curate was someone hired by the clergyman of the parish to live there and perform the duties there. The clergyman would usually do this because he had other parishes he needed to attend to or because he was old and needed to retire someplace else. The latter reason caused Jane Austen's father to hire a curate. Curates were often poorly paid, though as clergymen they were considered gentlemen.

26. Margaret's thoughtless revelation, even though only partial at this point, will end up playing a crucial role in the plot.

27. Raillery, or teasing, about others' love affairs would be considered inelegant, especially because such affairs involved sexual attraction. Of course, it is this, and the opportunity for crude jokes and allusions, that draws Sir John and Mrs. Jennings to the subject.

28. Willoughby's intervention probably results from concern for Elinor, along with perhaps his wish to end the general conversation so he and Marianne can focus completely on each other. He seems to like Elinor, and could certainly be influenced by Marianne's affection for her sister, just on full display.

amidst the various endeavours of different people to quit the topic, it fell to the ground. But not so easily did Elinor recover from the alarm into which it had thrown her.

A party[29] was formed this evening for going on the following day to see a very fine place about twelve miles from Barton, belonging to a brother-in-law of Colonel Brandon,[30] without whose interest[31] it could not be seen, as the proprietor, who was then abroad, had left strict orders on that head. The grounds were declared to be highly beautiful,[32] and Sir John, who was particularly warm in their praise, might be allowed to be a tolerable judge, for he had formed parties to visit them, at least, twice every summer for the last ten years. They contained a noble[33] piece of water;[34] a sail on which was to form a great part of the morning's amusement; cold provisions were to be taken,[35] open carriages only to be employed, and every thing conducted in the usual style of a complete party of pleasure.

To some few of the company, it appeared rather a bold undertaking, considering the time of year, and that it had rained every day for the last fortnight;—and Mrs. Dashwood, who had already a cold, was persuaded by Elinor to stay at home.[36]

29. *party:* group or company of persons, especially one formed for a specific purpose.

30. Colonel Brandon's sister will shortly be mentioned as living overseas, so this man is likely her husband.

31. *interest:* influence, especially as arising from a personal connection.

32. Elaborate landscaping was a major preoccupation of wealthy English landowners.

33. *noble:* splendid, large.

34. It is possible it was created, at least in part. Forming bodies of water, or expanding existing ones, was often central to landscaping grounds.

35. The elaborate gardens and landscaped parks attached to many country houses increased the popularity of eating outdoors.

36. She probably also stayed at home this evening. She is never mentioned during the conversation, and Margaret might not have dared divulge inappropriate secrets about Elinor in their mother's presence.

Wilton House: a country house with water in front, as was popular in the landscaping of the time.

[From John Preston Neale, *Views of the Seats of Noblemen and Gentlemen*, Vol. V (1822)]

Chapter Thirteen

*T*heir intended excursion to Whitwell turned out very differently from what Elinor had expected. She was prepared to be wet through, fatigued, and frightened; but the event was still more unfortunate, for they did not go at all.

By ten o'clock the whole party were assembled at the park, where they were to breakfast.[1] The morning was rather favourable, though it had rained all night, as the clouds were then dispersing across the sky, and the sun frequently appeared. They were all in high spirits and good humour, eager to be happy, and determined to submit to the greatest inconveniences and hardships rather than be otherwise.

While they were at breakfast the letters were brought in.[2] Among the rest there was one for Colonel Brandon;—he took it, looked at the direction,[3] changed colour, and immediately left the room.

"What is the matter with Brandon?" said Sir John.

Nobody could tell.

"I hope he has had no bad news," said Lady Middleton. "It must be something extraordinary that could make Colonel Brandon leave my breakfast table so suddenly."[4]

In about five minutes he returned.

"No bad news, Colonel, I hope"; said Mrs. Jennings, as soon as he entered the room.

"None at all, ma'am, I thank you."

"Was it from Avignon? I hope it is not to say that your sister is worse."[5]

"No, ma'am. It came from town,[6] and is merely a letter of business."

"But how came the hand[7] to discompose you so much, if it was

1.   This was a common breakfast time. It resulted from the generally late hours of wealthy people then (poor people rose and ate much earlier) and their habit of late evening suppers, which would make them less hungry when they awoke.

2.   The letters would have come from the village post office and would now be brought in by the servant. Sir John earlier offered to take the Dashwoods' letters to and from the post (p. 56), so he or a servant of his would presumably go there each day for the Middletons' own mail as well.

3.   *direction:* address (as written on the outside of the letter).

4.   A rare interjection, and a reasonably lengthy one, by Lady Middleton. It naturally results from a perceived fault in decorum by someone at her house, the only subject, along with her children, that rouses any interest in her.

5.   Avignon is a city in southern France. A number of people from Britain had settled there in the eighteenth century. Many wealthy Britons went to live or take extended vacations in Italy or southern France, in part because of the health benefits of a warmer climate. That Mrs. Jennings asks about the condition of Colonel Brandon's sister suggests that is her reason for living there. At the same time, it would be an odd place for someone from Britain to live at this particular juncture, when a long-standing war between Britain and France had cut off most travel between the countries. It is possible she had been trapped in France, as many British citizens were after the outbreak of war. It is also possible the allusion to it is a legacy of Jane Austen's initial draft of the novel, titled *Elinor and Marianne*, in 1795, when the war had only recently begun and might still be considered a fleeting event.

6.   *town:* London.

7.   *hand:* handwriting (of a specific person).

only a letter of business? Come, come, this wo'nt do, Colonel; so let us hear the truth of it."

"My dear Madam,"[8] said Lady Middleton, "recollect what you are saying."

"Perhaps it is to tell you that your cousin Fanny is married?" said Mrs. Jennings, without attending to her daughter's reproof.

"No, indeed, it is not."

"Well, then, I know who it is from, Colonel. And I hope she is well."

"Whom do you mean, ma'am?" said he, colouring[9] a little.

"Oh! you know who I mean."

"I am particularly sorry, ma'am," said he, addressing Lady Middleton, "that I should receive this letter today, for it is on business which requires my immediate attendance in town."[10]

"In town!" cried Mrs. Jennings. "What can you have to do in town at this time of year?"

"My own loss is great," he continued, "in being obliged to leave so agreeable a party; but I am the more concerned, as I fear my presence is necessary to gain your admittance at Whitwell."

What a blow upon them all was this!

"But if you write a note to the housekeeper, Mr. Brandon," said Marianne eagerly, "will it not be sufficient?"[11]

He shook his head.

"We must go," said Sir John. — "It shall not be put off when we are so near it. You cannot go to town till to-morrow, Brandon, that is all."

"I wish it could be so easily settled. But it is not in my power to delay my journey for one day!"

"If you would but let us know what your business is," said Mrs. Jennings, "we might see whether it could be put off or not."

"You would not be six hours later," said Willoughby, "if you were to defer your journey till our return."

"I cannot afford to lose *one* hour." —

Elinor then heard Willoughby say in a low voice to Marianne, "There are some people who cannot bear a party of pleasure. Brandon is one of them. He was afraid of catching cold I dare say,

8. *Madam:* a very formal designation for a casual conversation—Colonel Brandon will shortly use the more informal "ma'am." This may reflect Lady Middleton's usual formality, or her wish, by speaking in this manner, to force her mother to realize the breach of etiquette she is committing through her persistent inquisitiveness.

9. *colouring:* blushing.

10. As the mistress of the house, and thus his hostess while he has been staying there, Lady Middleton is the correct person to whom to address his apology for needing to leave so suddenly and unexpectedly.

11. The housekeeper was the highest-ranking female servant, and frequently the servant in charge of running the household. This would be especially likely when the owner was away. She was also the one who usually showed visitors around the house.

A country house with elaborate grounds around it, such as Whitwell is described as having.

[From Geoffrey Holme, ed., *Early English Water-colour Drawings* (London, 1919), Plate V]

and invented this trick for getting out of it. I would lay fifty guineas[12] the letter was of his own writing."[13]

"I have no doubt of it," replied Marianne.

"There is no persuading you to change your mind, Brandon, I know of old," said Sir John, "when once you are determined on any thing. But, however, I hope you will think better of it. Consider, here are the two Miss Careys come over from Newton, the three Miss Dashwoods walked up from the cottage, and Mr. Willoughby got up two hours before his usual time,[14] on purpose to go to Whitwell."

Colonel Brandon again repeated his sorrow at being the cause of disappointing the party; but at the same time declared it to be unavoidable.

"Well then, when will you come back again?"

"I hope we shall see you at Barton," added her ladyship, "as soon as you can conveniently leave town; and we must put off the party to Whitwell till you return."

"You are very obliging. But it is so uncertain, when I may have it in my power to return, that I dare not engage for it at all."

"Oh! he must and shall come back," cried Sir John. "If he is not here by the end of the week, I shall go after him."

"Aye, so do, Sir John," cried Mrs. Jennings, "and then perhaps you may find out what his business is."

"I do not want to pry into other men's concerns. I suppose it is something he is ashamed of."

Colonel Brandon's horses were announced.[15]

"You do not go to town on horseback, do you?" added Sir John.[16]

"No. Only to Honiton.[17] I shall then go post."[18]

"Well, as you are resolved to go, I wish you a good journey. But you had better change your mind."

"I assure you it is not in my power."

He then took leave of the whole party.

"Is there no chance of my seeing you and your sisters in town this winter, Miss Dashwood?"[19]

"I am afraid, none at all."

12. *guineas:* coins worth a pound and a shilling. Fifty guineas would be a considerable sum to wager. Willoughby's use of such an expression and his selection of such a sizable figure suggest he may be someone who gambles regularly, perhaps for high stakes. Gambling was a common pursuit of those in fashionable London society, especially young men, and what is later revealed about Willoughby makes him a likely candidate for this.

13. Willoughby has already indicated his dislike of Colonel Brandon. His censorious speculation, which conflicts with everything so far seen about Colonel Brandon's character, will become particularly ironic when Colonel Brandon discloses the real reason for his departure.

14. Thus Willoughby normally rises very late. He later says he associated with those wealthier than himself, and the wealthy generally kept late hours.

15. Colonel Brandon has brought horses with him on his visit to Sir John, whether for transportation or for recreation; it was not unusual for gentlemen to own more than one. One of the horses being announced may be for a servant who will accompany him, or it may be that he will simply take one or more horses with him without a rider. If more than one is saddled he could improve his speed by switching horses during the journey.

16. Sir John is surprised at the idea of his going on horseback because it is much slower for long distances—and the journey from Devonshire to London is a very long one—due to a horse's need for frequent rest and refreshment.

17. *Honiton:* a town in eastern Devonshire, approximately fifteen miles east by northeast from Exeter. This means it is on the route to London. Barton is "within four miles northward of Exeter" (p. 46): his going directly to Honiton, rather than first to Exeter, suggests Barton may be northeast of Exeter.

18. Traveling post is the means that all characters in Jane Austen use to travel long distances. By this time an elaborate network had been established in England along all the main roads, with places approximately every ten miles at which a traveler could stop and change horses. This meant that over each stage of a journey the horses could go at maximum speed, after which they could rest and get food and water while a fresh set traveled the next stage. Travelers could use their own carriages or hire a carriage at one of the stopping points—the latter is what Colonel Brandon will do at Honiton, while his own horses will be conveyed home by his servant or someone he hires for the purpose. These stopping points were usually inns in towns, so travelers could also procure food and drink, or spend the night.

19. Many who could afford it went to London during the winter to escape the lack of activities in the country and to enjoy the very active social and cultural life of the capital at that time.

"Then I must bid you farewell for a longer time than I should wish to do."

To Marianne, he merely bowed and said nothing.

"Come, Colonel," said Mrs. Jennings, "before you go, do let us know what you are going about."

He wished her a good morning, and attended by Sir John, left the room.

The complaints and lamentations which politeness had hitherto restrained, now burst forth universally; and they all agreed again and again how provoking it was to be so disappointed.

"I can guess what his business is, however," said Mrs. Jennings exultingly.

"Can you, ma'am?" said almost every body.

"Yes; it is about Miss Williams, I am sure."

"And who is Miss Williams?" asked Marianne.

"What! do not you know who Miss Williams is? I am sure you must have heard of her before. She is a relation of the Colonel's, my dear; a very near relation. We will not say how near, for fear of shocking the young ladies." Then lowering her voice a little, she said to Elinor, "She is his natural daughter."[20]

"Indeed!"

"Oh! yes; and as like him as she can stare. I dare say the Colonel will leave her all his fortune."[21]

When Sir John returned, he joined most heartily in the general regret on so unfortunate an event; concluding however by observing, that as they were all got together, they must do something by way of being happy; and after some consultation it was agreed, that although happiness could only be enjoyed at Whitwell, they might procure a tolerable composure of mind by driving about the country. The carriages were then ordered; Willoughby's was first, and Marianne never looked happier than when she got into it. He drove through the park[22] very fast,[23] and they were soon out of sight; and nothing more of them was seen till their return, which did not happen till after the return of all the rest. They both seemed delighted with their drive, but said only in general terms

20. A natural child is one fathered out of wedlock and hence one that is a man's child by nature, but not legally. The reason Mrs. Jennings lowers her voice and speaks of not shocking the young ladies is that such a subject would be considered completely inappropriate for polite conversation (see also next note), while it was especially inappropriate to discuss anything relating to sex before young ladies. This stemmed partly from a belief in ladies' natural delicacy and partly from a fear that imparting knowledge or raising curiosity about sex among unmarried young women might encourage an interest in the subject that could jeopardize their chastity. For this reason they were sometimes barred from reading racier books until they were married.

It is odd for Mrs. Jennings to tell the secret to Elinor after having worried about the ears of young ladies, for Elinor is only nineteen. It may be that Mrs. Jennings cannot keep herself from telling someone and selects Elinor because she is nearby and is her frequent confidante (see p. 102). It also may be that Elinor's great maturity has made Mrs. Jennings forget her exact age.

21. In the first published edition of the novel the following paragraph followed: "Lady Middleton's delicacy was shocked; and in order to banish so improper a subject as the mention of a natural daughter, she actually took the trouble of saying something herself about the weather." Jane Austen presumably decided the passage was unnecessary.

22. *park*: the large grounds surrounding a prominent country house.

23. Young men were known for driving their carriages fast, and it would be natural for someone as ardent and energetic as Willoughby to drive that way, especially with the possible further motive of thrilling and impressing Marianne.

that they had kept in the lanes, while the others went on the downs.[24]

It was settled that there should be a dance in the evening, and that every body should be extremely merry all day long. Some more of the Careys came to dinner, and they had the pleasure of sitting down nearly twenty to table, which Sir John observed with great contentment. Willoughby took his usual place between the two elder Miss Dashwoods. Mrs. Jennings sat on Elinor's right hand;[25] and they had not been long seated, before she leant behind her and Willoughby, and said to Marianne,[26] loud enough for them both to hear, "I have found you out in spite of all your tricks. I know where you spent the morning."[27]

Marianne coloured, and replied very hastily, "Where, pray?" —

"Did not you know," said Willoughby, "that we had been out in my curricle?"[28]

"Yes, yes, Mr. Impudence,[29] I know that very well, and I was determined to find out *where* you had been to. — I hope you like your house, Miss Marianne. It is a very large one I know, and when I come to see you, I hope you will have new-furnished it,[30] for it wanted it very much, when I was there six years ago."[31]

Marianne turned away in great confusion. Mrs. Jennings laughed heartily; and Elinor found that in her resolution to know where they had been, she had actually made her own woman enquire of Mr. Willoughby's groom,[32] and that she had by that method been informed that they had gone to Allenham, and spent a considerable time there in walking about the garden and going all over the house.

Elinor could hardly believe this to be true, as it seemed very unlikely that Willoughby should propose, or Marianne consent, to enter the house while Mrs. Smith was in it, with whom Marianne had not the smallest acquaintance.

As soon as they left the dining-room,[33] Elinor enquired of her about it; and great was her surprise when she found that every circumstance related by Mrs. Jennings was perfectly true. Marianne was quite angry with her for doubting it.

"Why should you imagine, Elinor, that we did not go there, or

24. The downs would be open hilly areas; the lanes were in lower places between or next to the downs.

25. This would fit with Mrs. Jennings's apparent enjoyment in talking to Elinor. She would be able to seat herself thus because at this time etiquette did not demand alternating men and women at dinners, even formal dinner parties.

26. It would not be good manners to lean behind two other people and talk to someone else.

27. Morning then meant the entire period until dinner, which usually occurred around four or five.

28. A curricle was an open carriage for two people pulled by two horses. It differed from the other main open carriage, a gig, which was pulled by one horse. The extra horse made curricles both faster and more expensive to maintain, and this made them more fashionable and prestigious. (For a picture, see p. 101.) It is natural that Willoughby, who is soon described as living beyond his means, should care more about speed and fashion than expense.

29. *Impudence:* shamelessness.

30. Mrs. Jennings means that once Willoughby and Marianne marry, they will be living at this house—Allenham, where Willoughby is now staying and which he is due to inherit—and will be able to furnish it anew and have visitors like Mrs. Jennings. Their having gone to the house together strongly encourages her to expect an imminent marriage (see note 46 below).

31. The owner of Allenham was earlier described as "an elderly lady . . . too infirm to mix with the world"; that is probably why Mrs. Jennings's last visit was six years ago, when the owner was presumably in better health.

32. The groom would be taking care of Willoughby's horses; Mrs. Jennings's "own woman" would be her servant. Servant gossip was a common means for information to spread, since servants from different houses would frequently talk to one another, as well as to other working people. Usually the servants would spread news on their own initiative, and employers would then hear of it later. Mrs. Jennings is unique in Austen's novels in deploying a servant to make inquiries.

33. The women have left the dining room together and gone to the drawing room. This was standard procedure. The men would normally drink more and talk about topics considered of mostly masculine interest, such as politics, or ones forbidden to discuss before ladies. At some point, the men would rejoin the women.

that we did not see the house? Is not it what you have often wished to do yourself?"

"Yes, Marianne, but I would not go while Mrs. Smith was there, and with no other companion than Mr. Willoughby."

"Mr. Willoughby however is the only person who can have a right to shew that house; and as we went in an open carriage, it was impossible to have any other companion.[34] I never spent a pleasanter morning in my life."

"I am afraid," replied Elinor, "that the pleasantness of an employment does not always evince its propriety."[35]

"On the contrary, nothing can be a stronger proof of it, Elinor; for if there had been any real impropriety in what I did, I should have been sensible[36] of it at the time, for we always know when we are acting wrong, and with such a conviction I could have had no pleasure."[37]

"But, my dear Marianne, as it has already exposed you to some very impertinent[38] remarks, do you not now begin to doubt the discretion of your own conduct?"

"If the impertinent remarks of Mrs. Jennings are to be the proof of impropriety in conduct, we are all offending every moment of all our lives. I value not her censure any more than I should do her commendation. I am not sensible of having done any thing wrong in walking over Mrs. Smith's grounds, or in seeing her house. They will one day be Mr. Willoughby's, and . . ."

"If they were one day to be your own, Marianne, you would not be justified in what you have done."

She blushed at this hint; but it was even visibly gratifying to her; and after a ten minutes' interval of earnest thought, she came to her sister again, and said with great good humour, "Perhaps, Elinor, it *was* rather ill-judged in me to go to Allenham; but Mr. Willoughby wanted particularly to shew me the place; and it is a charming house I assure you. —There is one remarkably pretty sitting room up stairs; of a nice comfortable size for constant use, and with modern furniture it would be delightful.[39] It is a corner room, and has windows on two sides.[40] On one side you look across the bowling-green,[41] behind the house, to a beautiful hang-

34. Willoughby's curricle seats only two comfortably.

35. It would be wrong to go while Mrs. Smith was there because, given her infirmity, it might disturb or inconvenience her. It would be improper to go with only Willoughby because unmarried men and women should not have extensive intimate contact. Even riding alone together in a carriage would be frowned upon: after the heroine of *Northanger Abbey* has ridden in an open carriage with a man, accompanied by her brother and another lady in another carriage, her guardian counsels her to avoid such excursions in the future. Going all over a house together would be worse, both for the extensive contact away from others' eyes and for their probably going into bedrooms together.

36. *sensible:* conscious, aware.

37. Marianne proclaims a succinct version of the Moral Sense, the idea that human beings possess a natural or instinctive sense of goodness that can serve as the foundation of morality. This idea played an important role in eighteenth-century philosophy, espoused in varying forms by many leading thinkers, and was adopted by Romantic writers and proponents of sensibility. Many writers also criticized it, arguing that people's instincts are often not benevolent and that personal feelings are an unreliable guide for morality. Jane Austen is among such critics, as she presents numerous cases in which personal feelings, even among good characters, can lead people astray, and consistently affirms the validity and necessity of objective moral principles, irrespective of feeling. Marianne's own story probably constitutes the author's strongest demonstration of this conviction.

38. *impertinent:* presumptuous, overly familiar.

39. Most country houses had at least some rooms with furniture from much earlier periods, for furniture was expensive and older pieces would be handed down through many generations. At the same time, furniture styles continually changed: during the eighteenth century they had steadily become more lightweight and delicate, qualities identified more than once in Jane Austen as superior in elegance.

40. This would give it more light, an important consideration with the limited means of artificial illumination then available.

41. *bowling-green:* a smooth lawn for playing bowls. Jane Austen twice visited a cousin who had a bowling green that was said to be one of the best in England.

ing wood,[42] and on the other you have a view of the church and village,[43] and, beyond them, of those fine bold hills that we have so often admired.[44] I did not see it to advantage, for nothing could be more forlorn than the furniture,—but if it were newly fitted up—a couple of hundred pounds, Willoughby says, would make it one of the pleasantest summer-rooms in England."[45]

Could Elinor have listened to her without interruption from the others, she would have described every room in the house with equal delight.[46]

42. *hanging wood*: wood on a steep slope. The name derived from the tendency of the trees in them to hang down. They were a popular feature of landscaping then.

43. A church was standard in an English village, and its steeple usually made it by far the most prominent feature, especially when seen from a distance.

44. Bold hills were highly praised by advocates of picturesque ideas (for more on these ideas, see pp. 182–186).

45. Two hundred pounds was a substantial sum, and Willoughby's discussion of that with Marianne, and her repeating it now, show a rather cavalier attitude toward money. But if he did inherit Allenham and move in, he would certainly be able to afford this, based on everything indicated about the wealth of the estate.

46. This means she must have seen every room in the house, a sign of the duration of the visit. Such a tour, and Marianne's enthusiastic discussion of all the new arrangements that could be made in the house, would normally be clear indicators of an impending marriage. This is why Mrs. Jennings expressed her expectation of visiting the couple. Household arrangements were central tasks of a wife, and decorating and furnishing would be a natural focus of any new bride (who would also wish to complete such tasks before any children arrived). In showing Marianne the house in this manner, and talking of new furniture, Willoughby is giving her a clear indication of his intentions, while Marianne's words to Elinor convey a confident expectation along the same lines.

Chapter Fourteen

*T*he sudden termination of Colonel Brandon's visit at the park, with his steadiness in concealing its cause, filled the mind and raised the wonder of Mrs. Jennings for two or three days; she was a great wonderer, as every one must be who takes a very lively interest in all the comings and goings of all their acquaintance. She wondered with little intermission what could be the reason of it; was sure there must be some bad news, and thought over every kind of distress that could have befallen him, with a fixed determination that he should not escape them all.

"Something very melancholy must be the matter, I am sure," said she. "I could see it in his face. Poor man! I am afraid his circumstances may be bad. The estate at Delaford was never reckoned more than two thousand a year,[1] and his brother left every thing sadly involved.[2] I do think he must have been sent for about money matters, for what else can it be? I wonder whether it is so. I would give any thing to know the truth of it. Perhaps it is about Miss Williams—and, by the bye, I dare say it is, because he looked so conscious when I mentioned her.[3] May be she is ill in town; nothing in the world more likely, for I have a notion she is always rather sickly. I would lay any wager it is about Miss Williams. It is not so very likely he should be distressed in his circumstances *now*, for he is a very prudent man, and to be sure must have cleared the estate by this time.[4] I wonder what it can be! May be his sister is worse at Avignon, and has sent for him over. His setting off in such a hurry seems very like it. Well, I wish him out of all his trouble with all my heart, and a good wife into the bargain."

So wondered, so talked Mrs. Jennings. Her opinion varying with every fresh conjecture, and all seeming equally probable as they arose. Elinor, though she felt really interested in the welfare

1. This represents a very good income, but not an enormous one as landed estates went. In the society depicted by Jane Austen everyone has a clear idea of others' income, and most have no hesitation about discussing these sums openly.

2. *involved*: entangled. Many landowners fell into serious debt: *Persuasion* centers around a family that is forced to rent its house and move elsewhere because of crippling debts. Later Colonel Brandon will explain that in his father's time his family's estate was greatly burdened with debt, and his elder brother, who inherited it, was an irresponsible person. Delaford, the village where the estate and Colonel Brandon's home are located, is later described as being in Dorsetshire, the county directly east of Devonshire (see map, p. 739).

3. Miss Williams is the natural daughter Mrs. Jennings mentioned earlier. Her explicit mention of Miss Williams occurred after Colonel Brandon left, but earlier, when Mrs. Jennings said, "I hope she is well," Colonel Brandon blushed, and she replied, "Oh! you know who I mean" (p. 122).

4. Meaning cleared any debts or mortgages on the estate.

of Colonel Brandon, could not bestow all the wonder on his going so suddenly away, which Mrs. Jennings was desirous of her feeling; for besides that the circumstance did not in her opinion justify such lasting amazement or variety of speculation, her wonder was otherwise disposed of. It was engrossed by the extraordinary silence of her sister and Willoughby on the subject, which they must know to be peculiarly[5] interesting to them all. As this silence continued, every day made it appear more strange and more incompatible with the disposition of both. Why they should not openly acknowledge to her mother and herself, what their constant behaviour to each other declared to have taken place, Elinor could not imagine.

She could easily conceive that marriage might not be immediately in their power; for though Willoughby was independent,[6] there was no reason to believe him rich. His estate had been rated by Sir John at about six or seven hundred a year; but he lived at an expense to which that income could hardly be equal,[7] and he had himself often complained of his poverty.[8] But for this strange kind of secrecy maintained by them relative to their engagement, which in fact concealed nothing at all, she could not account; and it was so wholly contradictory to their general opinions and practice,[9] that a doubt sometimes entered her mind of their being really engaged, and this doubt was enough to prevent her making any inquiry of Marianne.[10]

Nothing could be more expressive of attachment to them all, than Willoughby's behaviour. To Marianne it had all the distinguishing tenderness which a lover's heart could give, and to the rest of the family it was the affectionate attention of a son and a brother. The cottage seemed to be considered and loved by him as his home; many more of his hours were spent there than at Allenham; and if no general engagement collected them at the park,[11] the exercise which called him out in the morning was almost certain of ending there, where the rest of the day was spent by himself at the side of Marianne, and by his favourite pointer at her feet.

One evening in particular, about a week after Colonel Brandon

5. *peculiarly*: particularly.

6. *independent*: independent financially.

7. His carriage and his horses—and a later conversation suggests he also has horses for hunting—would by themselves represent a considerable expense. He is also spoken of as traveling to various places. All this is why, though a single man, he cannot live within an income that is greater than that of Mrs. Dashwood and her children.

8. People in Jane Austen's novels sometimes speak of poverty, but what they always mean is an income insufficient for the genteel ranks of society, not a lack of basic necessities.

9. Their conduct represents a reversal of their usual position. They, especially Marianne, have lauded the virtue of sincerity, against the social rules that counsel disguising one's true feelings when politeness requires it. But when it comes to engagements, society's rules dictate openness—public proclamation validates an engagement and gives it practical force—and Marianne and Willoughby seem to be practicing secrecy.

10. She does not inquire to avoid embarrassing or discomforting her sister if no engagement actually exists. Were Elinor sure of the engagement, she would naturally inquire: in *Pride and Prejudice* a similarly close pair of sisters tell each other immediately of their engagements, in part for the great mutual pleasure of talking at length about them.

11. The park is Barton Park, the Middletons' home. The necessity for even an apparently engaged couple to participate fully in general activities demonstrates the extent of prevailing social obligations.

had left the country, his heart seemed more than usually open to every feeling of attachment to the objects around him; and on Mrs. Dashwood's happening to mention her design of improving the cottage in the spring, he warmly opposed every alteration of a place which affection had established as perfect with him.

"What!" he exclaimed—"Improve this dear cottage! No. *That* I will never consent to. Not a stone must be added to its walls, not an inch to its size, if my feelings are regarded."[12]

"Do not be alarmed," said Miss Dashwood, "nothing of the kind will be done; for my mother will never have money enough to attempt it."

"I am heartily glad of it," he cried. "May she always be poor, if she can employ her riches no better."

"Thank you, Willoughby.[13] But you may be assured that I would not sacrifice one sentiment of local attachment of yours, or of any one whom I loved, for all the improvements in the world.[14] Depend upon it that whatever unemployed sum may remain, when I make up[15] my accounts in the spring, I would even rather lay it uselessly by than dispose of it in a manner so painful to you. But are you really so attached to this place as to see no defect in it?"

"I am," said he. "To me it is faultless. Nay, more, I consider it as the only form of building in which happiness is attainable, and were I rich enough, I would instantly pull Combe down, and build it up again in the exact plan of this cottage."

"With dark narrow stairs,[16] and a kitchen that smokes,[17] I suppose," said Elinor.

"Yes," cried he in the same eager tone, "with all and every thing belonging to it;—in no one convenience or *in*convenience about it, should the least variation be perceptible. Then, and then only, under such a roof, I might perhaps be as happy at Combe as I have been at Barton."

"I flatter myself," replied Elinor, "that even under the disadvantage of better rooms and a broader staircase, you will hereafter find your own house as faultless as you now do this."

"There certainly are circumstances," said Willoughby, "which

12. Willoughby is probably engaging in a measure of deliberate, and generally understood, exaggeration. But his words over the course of the conversation suggest he is mostly serious, and if so he is showing, amidst his expressions of affection toward the family, a preference for his own feelings—which, notably, he commenced the conversation by referring to—above the good of the Dashwoods.

13. Calling him simply "Willoughby," with no "Mr.," signals a significant step toward intimacy on her part. She may already be considering him a member of the family. Elinor, perhaps following her mother's lead, will use the same designation after this.

14. Mrs. Dashwood, while never willing to give up planned improvements because of the substantial practical barrier of insufficient funds, immediately makes a complete renunciation when someone adduces sentimental reasons for doing so.

15. *make up*: balance, put in order.

16. The darkness of stairs, often related to their narrowness, was a common issue in houses then. Limited artificial lighting meant staircases were frequently dark, and this would make them difficult to use, especially for women in long dresses.

17. This means that the kitchen fireplace, which would be large and frequently burning very hot for cooking, emitted smoke into the room. This was another common problem. Better designs of fireplaces and chimneys had appeared to curb smokiness—one of the most significant, a Rumford, is mentioned in *Northanger Abbey*—but simpler dwellings frequently lacked them.

might greatly endear it to me;[18] but this place will always have one claim on my affection, which no other can possibly share."

Mrs. Dashwood looked with pleasure at Marianne, whose fine eyes were fixed so expressively on Willoughby, as plainly denoted how well she understood him.

"How often did I wish," added he, "when I was at Allenham this time twelvemonth, that Barton cottage were inhabited! I never passed within view of it without admiring its situation, and grieving that no one should live in it. How little did I then think that the very first news I should hear from Mrs. Smith, when I next came into the country, would be that Barton cottage was taken: and I felt an immediate satisfaction and interest in the event, which nothing but a kind of prescience of what happiness I should experience from it, can account for. Must it not have been so, Marianne?" speaking to her in a lowered voice. Then continuing his former tone, he said, "And yet this house you would spoil, Mrs. Dashwood? You would rob it of its simplicity by imaginary improvement! and this dear parlour, in which our acquaintance first began, and in which so many happy hours have been since spent by us together, you would degrade to the condition of a common entrance,[19] and every body would be eager to pass through the room which has hitherto contained within itself, more real accommodation and comfort than any other apartment of the handsomest dimensions in the world could possibly afford."

Mrs. Dashwood again assured him that no alteration of the kind should be attempted.

"You are a good woman," he warmly replied. "Your promise makes me easy. Extend it a little farther, and it will make me happy. Tell me that not only your house will remain the same, but that I shall ever find you and yours as unchanged as your dwelling; and that you will always consider me with the kindness which has made every thing belonging to you so dear to me."

The promise was readily given, and Willoughby's behaviour during the whole of the evening declared at once his affection and happiness.

18. He means the circumstance of Marianne's joining him in his new house as his wife. The implication would be clearly understood by all, though since it is not an explicit declaration, it is not, strictly speaking, an actual avowal of engagement.

19. Parlours were small sitting rooms, and Mrs. Dashwood's plans included building a larger drawing room and turning the existing parlour into an anteroom of the new drawing room (see p. 54). For a picture of a contemporary drawing room, see the following page.

"Shall we see you to-morrow to dinner?" said Mrs. Dashwood when he was leaving them. "I do not ask you to come in the morning, for we must walk to the park, to call on Lady Middleton."[20]

He engaged to be with them by four o'clock.[21]

20. They may visit Lady Middleton regularly as part of neighborly kindness, or this may be in return for a specific visit of hers.

21. Morning meant most of the day then, so four o'clock would be the earliest he could come.

A drawing room of the time.

[From K. Warren Clouston, *The Chippendale Period in English Furniture* (New York, 1897), p. 149]

Chapter Fifteen

Mrs. Dashwood's visit to Lady Middleton took place the next day, and two of her daughters went with her; but Marianne excused herself from being of the party under some trifling pretext of employment;[1] and her mother, who concluded that a promise had been made by Willoughby the night before of calling on her while they were absent, was perfectly satisfied with her remaining at home.

On their return from the park they found Willoughby's curricle and servant in waiting at the cottage,[2] and Mrs. Dashwood was convinced that her conjecture had been just. So far it was all as she had foreseen; but on entering the house she beheld what no foresight had taught her to expect. They were no sooner in the passage than Marianne came hastily out of the parlour apparently in violent affliction, with her handkerchief at her eyes;[3] and without noticing them ran up stairs. Surprised and alarmed they proceeded directly into the room she had just quitted, where they found only Willoughby, who was leaning against the mantle-piece with his back towards them. He turned round on their coming in, and his countenance shewed that he strongly partook of the emotion which overpowered Marianne.

"Is any thing the matter with her?" cried Mrs. Dashwood as she entered—"is she ill?"

"I hope not," he replied, trying to look cheerful; and with a forced smile presently added, "It is I who may rather expect to be ill—for I am now suffering under a very heavy disappointment!"[4]

"Disappointment!"

"Yes, for I am unable to keep my engagement with you. Mrs. Smith has this morning exercised the privilege of riches upon a poor dependant cousin, by sending me on business to London.[5] I have just received my dispatches, and taken my farewel of Allen-

1. The employment could refer to minor household duties: with only three servants they would have to perform some household tasks. Jane Austen, in a similar situation with her sister and her mother, had a few responsibilities, including supervision of kitchen stores. The serious work of cooking and cleaning was still left to the servants.

2. Gentlemen were often accompanied by servants. In this case, the servant may be his groom, who would take care of the curricle's horses.

3. Women generally carried handkerchiefs then. Jane Austen's House Museum in Chawton, England, possesses a handkerchief of Jane Austen's sister, embroidered by Jane herself.

4. Willoughby immediately reverts to his own feelings of distress, just as his parting words below refer to not tormenting himself longer by remaining. He never speaks of Marianne's obvious sufferings, which he has just witnessed.

5. This could mean some financial or legal business of Mrs. Smith's; such business, even for people who lived in the country, was often conducted in London. The phrase is sufficiently vague to provide a good all-purpose rationale for leaving.

ham; and by way of exhilaration I am now come to take my farewel of you."

"To London![6]—and are you going this morning?"

"Almost this moment."

"This is very unfortunate. But Mrs. Smith must be obliged;— and her business will not detain you from us long I hope."

He coloured as he replied, "You are very kind, but I have no idea[7] of returning into Devonshire immediately. My visits to Mrs. Smith are never repeated within the twelvemonth."

"And is Mrs. Smith your only friend?[8] Is Allenham the only house in the neighbourhood to which you will be welcome? For shame, Willoughby. Can you wait for an invitation here?"

His colour increased; and with his eyes fixed on the ground he only replied, "You are too good."

Mrs. Dashwood looked at Elinor with surprise. Elinor felt equal amazement. For a few moments every one was silent. Mrs. Dashwood first spoke.

"I have only to add, my dear Willoughby, that at Barton cottage you will always be welcome; for I will not press you to return here immediately, because you only can judge how far *that* might be pleasing to Mrs. Smith;[9] and on this head I shall be no more disposed to question your judgment than to doubt your inclination."

"My engagements at present," replied Willoughby confusedly, "are of such a nature—that—I dare not flatter myself"—[10]

He stopt. Mrs. Dashwood was too much astonished to speak, and another pause succeeded. This was broken by Willoughby, who said with a faint smile, "It is folly to linger in this manner. I will not torment myself any longer by remaining among friends whose society it is impossible for me now to enjoy."

He then hastily took leave of them all and left the room. They saw him step into his carriage, and in a minute it was out of sight.

Mrs. Dashwood felt too much for speech, and instantly quitted the parlour to give way in solitude to the concern and alarm which this sudden departure occasioned.

Elinor's uneasiness was at least equal to her mother's. She thought of what had just passed with anxiety and distrust.

6. London would be a considerable distance to travel from Devonshire: a later journey by other characters takes more than two days (p. 294).

7. *idea*: thought.

8. "Friend" then often included relatives.

9. Presumably Mrs. Smith might be offended by his staying with the Dashwoods rather than with her.

10. The reason for Willoughby's confusion will be revealed later (pp. 602–606).

Willoughby's behaviour in taking leave of them, his embarrass-ment, and affectation of cheerfulness, and, above all, his unwill-ingness to accept her mother's invitation, a backwardness[11] so unlike a lover, so unlike himself, greatly disturbed her. One moment she feared that no serious design had ever been formed on his side; and the next that some unfortunate quarrel had taken place between him and her sister;—the distress in which Mari-anne had quitted the room was such as a serious quarrel could most reasonably account for, though when she considered what Marianne's love for him was, a quarrel seemed almost impossible.

But whatever might be the particulars of their separation, her sister's affliction was indubitable; and she thought with the ten-derest compassion of that violent sorrow which Marianne was in all probability not merely giving way to as a relief, but feeding and encouraging as a duty.[12]

In about half an hour her mother returned, and though her eyes were red, her countenance was not uncheerful.

"Our dear Willoughby is now some miles from Barton, Elinor," said she, as she sat down to work,[13] "and with how heavy a heart does he travel?"

"It is all very strange. So suddenly to be gone! It seems but the work of a moment. And last night he was with us so happy, so cheerful, so affectionate? And now after only ten minutes notice—Gone too without intending to return!—Something more than what he owned[14] to us must have happened. He did not speak, he did not behave like himself. *You* must have seen the difference as well as I. What can it be? Can they have quarrelled? Why else should he have shewn such unwillingness to accept your invitation here?"—[15]

"It was not inclination that he wanted, Elinor; I could plainly see *that*. He had not the power of accepting it. I have thought it all over I assure you, and I can perfectly account for every thing that at first seemed strange to me as well as to you."

"Can you indeed?"

"Yes. I have explained it to myself in the most satisfactory way;—but you, Elinor, who love to doubt where you can—It will

11. *backwardness*: reluctance, hesitation.

12. This replicates the behavior of Marianne and Mrs. Dashwood after the death of Mr. Dashwood (pp. 8–10).

13. This probably means needlework, which was often called simply "work" because it was such a central task of women.

14. *owned*: acknowledged.

15. Elinor's suspicion of Willoughby's inexplicable behavior will eventually be confirmed.

not satisfy *you*, I know; but you shall not talk *me* out of my trust in it. I am persuaded that Mrs. Smith suspects his regard for Marianne, disapproves of it, (perhaps because she has other views for him,) and on that account is eager to get him away;[16]—and that the business which she sends him off to transact, is invented as an excuse to dismiss him. This is what I believe to have happened. He is moreover aware that she *does* disapprove the connection,[17] he dares not therefore at present confess to her his engagement with Marianne, and he feels himself obliged, from his dependent situation, to give into her schemes, and absent himself from Devonshire for a while.[18] You will tell me, I know, that this may, or may *not* have happened; but I will listen to no cavil, unless you can point out any other method of understanding the affair as satisfactory as this. And now, Elinor, what have you to say?"

"Nothing, for you have anticipated my answer."

"Then you would have told me, that it might or might not have happened. Oh! Elinor, how incomprehensible are your feelings! You had rather take evil upon credit than good. You had rather look out for misery for Marianne and guilt for poor Willoughby, than an apology[19] for the latter. You are resolved to think him blameable, because he took leave of us with less affection than his usual behaviour has shewn. And is no allowance to be made for inadvertence,[20] or for spirits depressed by recent disappointment? Are no probabilities to be accepted, merely because they are not certainties? Is nothing due to the man whom we have all so much reason to love, and no reason in the world to think ill of? To the possibility of motives unanswerable in themselves, though unavoidably secret for a while? And, after all, what is it you suspect him of?"

"I can hardly tell you myself.—But suspicion of something unpleasant is the inevitable consequence of such an alteration as we have just witnessed in him. There is great truth, however, in what you have now urged of the allowances which ought to be made for him, and it is my wish to be candid[21] in my judgment of every body. Willoughby may undoubtedly have very sufficient reasons for his conduct, and I will hope that he has. But it would have been more like Willoughby to acknowledge them at once.

16. People often had ambitious views, or expectations, for their children or heirs. This was seen earlier with the expectations of Edward by his mother and sister. In Mrs. Smith's case, she could be hoping that Willoughby will marry a wealthy or socially prominent woman, which Marianne is not.

17. *connection:* engagement. The term was often used then in this way, a sign of how much marriage was seen as a linking of families.

18. Willoughby's inability to meet his current expenses, not to mention the greater expense of supporting a wife, would require him to maintain Mrs. Smith's favor so that she does not disinherit him.

19. *apology:* justification, explanation.

20. *inadvertence:* inattention, carelessness.

21. *candid:* fair, generous.

Secrecy may be advisable; but still I cannot help wondering at its being practised by him."

"Do not blame him, however, for departing from his character, where the deviation is necessary. But you really do admit the justice of what I have said in his defence?—I am happy—and he is acquitted."

"Not entirely. It may be proper to conceal their engagement (if they *are* engaged) from Mrs. Smith—and if that is the case, it must be highly expedient for Willoughby to be but little in Devonshire at present. But this is no excuse for their concealing it from us."

"Concealing it from us! my dear child, do you accuse Willoughby and Marianne of concealment? This is strange indeed, when your eyes have been reproaching them every day for incautiousness."

"I want no proof of their affection," said Elinor; "but of their engagement I do."[22]

"I am perfectly satisfied of both."

"Yet not a syllable has been said to you on the subject, by either of them."

"I have not wanted syllables where actions have spoken so plainly. Has not his behaviour to Marianne and to all of us, for at least the last fortnight,[23] declared that he loved and considered her as his future wife,[24] and that he felt for us the attachment of the nearest relation? Have we not perfectly understood each other? Has not my consent been daily asked by his looks, his manner, his attentive and affectionate respect?[25] My Elinor, is it possible to doubt their engagement? How could such a thought occur to you? How is it to be supposed that Willoughby, persuaded as he must be of your sister's love, should[26] leave her, and leave her perhaps for months, without telling her of his affection;—that they should part without a mutual exchange of confidence?"

"I confess," replied Elinor, "that every circumstance except *one* is in favour of their engagement; but that *one* is the total silence of both on the subject, and with me it almost outweighs every other."

"How strange this is! You must think wretchedly indeed of Willoughby, if after all that has openly passed between them, you

22. The prevailing rules of society, which Elinor endorses, stated that an unmarried man and woman should avoid open or effusive displays of affection in order to keep them, especially her, from dangerously committing their hearts before being certain of the other's commitment. Once they are engaged, however, they should proclaim the fact clearly to others, ensuring that neither would be able to renounce the agreement without suffering censure or other serious social consequences.

23. Willoughby and Marianne have known each other approximately a month (see chronology, pp. 712–713); hence, according to Mrs. Dashwood's calculation, it was around the halfway point of their acquaintance that the signs of his love became unmistakable.

24. For a man to indicate, whether by word or deed, that he loved a woman was in effect to announce his engagement. Normally a man would never tell a woman explicitly of his love until the actual proposal.

25. The prevailing belief was that young people had the right to court, within certain limits, and to make their own marital choice, but parental consent was still needed before an engagement was final. This is why Elinor emphasizes that neither of them has spoken to Mrs. Dashwood. Usually the man made a formal request to the woman's father, or mother if no father existed. Mrs. Dashwood understands the general rule, but, happy to dispense with formalities, she is willing to consider Willoughby's prior behavior as a sufficient request.

26. *should*: would.

can doubt the nature of the terms on which they are together.[27] Has he been acting a part in his behaviour to your sister all this time? Do you suppose him really indifferent to her?"

"No, I cannot think that. He must and does love her I am sure."

"But with a strange kind of tenderness, if he can leave her with such indifference, such carelessness of the future, as you attribute to him."

"You must remember, my dear mother, that I have never considered this matter as certain. I have had my doubts, I confess; but they are fainter than they were, and they may soon be entirely done away. If we find they correspond, every fear of mine will be removed."[28]

"A mighty concession indeed! If you were to see them at the altar, you would suppose they were going to be married.[29] Ungracious girl! But I require no such proof. Nothing in my opinion has ever passed to justify doubt; no secrecy has been attempted; all has been uniformly open and unreserved. You cannot doubt your sister's wishes. It must be Willoughby therefore whom you suspect. But why? Is he not a man of honour and feeling?[30] Has there been any inconsistency on his side to create alarm? can he be deceitful?"

"I hope not, I believe not," cried Elinor. "I love Willoughby, sincerely love him; and suspicion of his integrity cannot be more painful to yourself than to me. It has been involuntary, and I will not encourage it. I was startled, I confess, by the alteration in his manners this morning;—he did not speak like himself, and did not return your kindness with any cordiality. But all this may be explained by such a situation of his affairs as you have supposed. He had just parted from my sister, had seen her leave him in the greatest affliction; and if he felt obliged, from a fear of offending Mrs. Smith, to resist the temptation of returning here soon, and yet aware that by declining your invitation, by saying that he was going away for some time, he should seem to act an ungenerous,[31] a suspicious part by our family, he might well be embarrassed and disturbed. In such a case, a plain and open avowal of his difficulties would have been more to his honour I think, as well as more consistent with his general character;—but I will not raise objections against any one's conduct on so illiberal[32] a foundation, as a

27. If they were not engaged, Willoughby's behavior would be wretched, since he has given clear signs of intending to marry Marianne. Thus he would have been toying with both her heart and her reputation, since he has also signaled his intentions to their circle of friends.

28. A strict and universally understood rule in this society was that unmarried men and women, unless linked by family ties, could never correspond without being engaged. A critical reason was to prevent illicit love affairs, the same type of consideration that forbade prolonged personal contact away from the presence and supervision of others.

29. She speaks of an altar because by law all marriages had to be performed in an Anglican church (except for those of Quakers and Jews, which would not be pertinent here).

30. *feeling*: tenderness, compassion.

31. *ungenerous*: ignoble.

32. *illiberal*: narrow-minded.

difference in judgment from myself, or a deviation from what I may think right and consistent."[33]

"You speak very properly. Willoughby certainly does not deserve to be suspected. Though *we* have not known him long, he is no stranger in this part of the world; and who has ever spoken to his disadvantage?[34] Had he been in a situation to act independently and marry immediately, it might have been odd that he should leave us without acknowledging every thing to me at once: but this is not the case. It is an engagement in some respects not prosperously[35] begun, for their marriage must be at a very uncertain distance;[36] and even secrecy, as far as it can be observed, may now be very advisable."

They were interrupted by the entrance of Margaret; and Elinor was then at liberty to think over the representations[37] of her mother, to acknowledge the probability of many, and hope for the justice of all.[38]

They saw nothing of Marianne till dinner time, when she entered the room and took her place at the table without saying a word. Her eyes were red and swollen; and it seemed as if her tears were even then restrained with difficulty. She avoided the looks of them all, could neither eat nor speak, and after some time, on her mother's silently pressing her hand with tender compassion, her small degree of fortitude was quite overcome, she burst into tears and left the room.

This violent oppression of spirits continued the whole evening. She was without any power, because she was without any desire of command over herself. The slightest mention of any thing relative to Willoughby overpowered her in an instant; and though her family were most anxiously attentive to her comfort, it was impossible for them, if they spoke at all, to keep clear of every subject which her feelings connected with him.

33. Elinor's hesitation to pronounce judgment contrasts with Marianne, who is quick to judge others and to condemn those with a different outlook.

34. This was an important principle in this society: people's reputation was considered a vital clue to their character. But that principle is vitiated in this case by the lack of discernment and discriminating standards of those who are most likely to have known Willoughby long—Sir John, Lady Middleton, and Mrs. Jennings. Colonel Brandon would be a more reliable judge, but there is no indication that he had any contact with Willoughby prior to this visit to the Middletons. Moreover, Willoughby himself said he stayed at Allenham only a limited time each year, so even those resident here have not had continual opportunities to observe and evaluate him.

35. *prosperously*: favorably, auspiciously.

36. *distance*: distance in time.

37. *representations*: explanations, arguments.

38. The careful parallel construction of this sentence, in which each of the three clauses has a succession of the same basic parts of speech, strongly echoes the language of one of Jane Austen's favorite writers, Samuel Johnson. There are a number of such examples in this novel, more than in almost any other; one reason may be that this is probably her most didactic novel, and much of Johnson's corpus consists of moral essays in which he enunciates general principles of conduct, including many with a strong affinity to Elinor's.

Chapter Sixteen

Marianne would have thought herself very inexcusable had she been able to sleep at all the first night after parting from Willoughby. She would have been ashamed to look her family in the face the next morning, had she not risen from her bed in more need of repose than when she lay down in it.[1] But the feelings which made such composure a disgrace, left her in no danger of incurring it. She was awake the whole night, and she wept the greatest part of it. She got up with an headache, was unable to talk, and unwilling to take any nourishment; giving pain every moment to her mother and sisters, and forbidding all attempt at consolation from either.[2] Her sensibility was potent enough!

When breakfast was over she walked out by herself, and wandered about the village of Allenham, indulging the recollection of past enjoyment and crying over the present reverse for the chief[3] of the morning.

The evening passed off in the equal indulgence of feeling. She played over every favourite song that she had been used to play to Willoughby, every air[4] in which their voices had been oftenest joined, and sat at the instrument gazing on every line of music that he had written out for her,[5] till her heart was so heavy that no farther sadness could be gained; and this nourishment of grief was every day applied. She spent whole hours at the pianoforte alternately singing and crying; her voice often totally suspended by her tears. In books too, as well as in music, she courted the misery which a contrast between the past and present was certain of giving. She read nothing but what they had been used to read together.

Such violence of affliction indeed could not be supported for ever; it sunk within a few days into a calmer melancholy; but these employments, to which she daily recurred, her solitary

1. Romantic doctrines emphasized the importance of experiencing all passions to the full, and the affliction following misfortune in love would be one of the most natural and powerful of all. Moreover, lack of sorrow would indicate lack of real love, leading in turn to an indictment of insincerity and a failure to experience the most exalted and vital of all human passions.

2. Thus she is hurting others as well as herself.

3. *chief*: greater part.

4. *air*: musical air or melody.

5. Writing out music was a common practice then among those skilled

A woman walking outdoors; upper-class ladies would often wear such fancy attire when taking a walk.

[From Sir Walter Armstrong, *Lawrence* (London, 1913), p. 46]

walks and silent meditations, still produced occasional effusions of sorrow as lively as ever.

No letter from Willoughby came; and none seemed expected by Marianne. Her mother was surprised, and Elinor again became uneasy. But Mrs. Dashwood could find explanations whenever she wanted them, which at least satisfied herself.

"Remember, Elinor," said she, "how very often Sir John fetches our letters himself from the post, and carries them to it. We have already agreed that secrecy may be necessary, and we must acknowledge that it could not be maintained if their correspondence were to pass through Sir John's hands."[6]

Elinor could not deny the truth of this, and she tried to find in it a motive sufficient for their silence. But there was one method so direct, so simple, and in her opinion so eligible[7] of knowing the real state of the affair, and of instantly removing all mystery, that she could not help suggesting it to her mother.

"Why do you not ask Marianne at once," said she, "whether she is or is not engaged to Willoughby? From you, her mother, and so kind, so indulgent a mother, the question could not give offence. It would be the natural result of your affection for her. She used to be all unreserve, and to you more especially."

"I would not ask such a question for the world. Supposing it possible that they are not engaged, what distress would not such an inquiry inflict! At any rate it would be most ungenerous. I should never deserve her confidence again, after forcing from her a confession of what is meant at present to be unacknowledged to any one.[8] I know Marianne's heart: I know that she dearly loves me, and that I shall not be the last to whom the affair is made known, when circumstances make the revealment[9] of it eligible. I would not attempt to force the confidence of any one; of a child much less; because a sense of duty would prevent the denial which her wishes might direct."

Elinor thought this generosity overstrained, considering her sister's youth, and urged the matter farther, but in vain;[10] common sense, common care, common prudence, were all sunk in Mrs. Dashwood's romantic delicacy.

enough to do it; Jane Austen wrote out many pieces of music. An important reason was the expense of printed music. As a substitute people would copy music owned by others: Willoughby, who has more disposable income than Marianne and has frequently been in London, where it would be easy to procure printed music, has presumably copied for Marianne some of his pieces. This indicates some dedication to her, for copying music, in the admission even of dedicated musicians, was time-consuming and tedious, though it is not clear how much music he has copied; the statement that she gazed on every line written out might suggest that the lines were not many.

6. Sir John would notice Willoughby's name on the outside of any letter sent by Marianne and might recognize Willoughby's handwriting on any letter to her (he would not learn anything from a return address, for those were not placed on letters then). He would certainly not hesitate to tell everyone what he saw.

7. *eligible*: suitable, proper.

8. If Marianne is engaged, she would be caught painfully between two obligations, that of keeping the engagement secret and that of obeying her mother. Mrs. Dashwood's words suggest an expectation that Marianne would comply with her mother's command, but that, by behaving more as an authority figure than a friend, Mrs. Dashwood would be forfeiting her right to have Marianne confide in her.

9. *revealment*: disclosure.

10. Elinor refers to a basic principle of treating people differently according to age, something seen in every aspect of this society. Greater youth means less ability to judge rationally, and thus greater justification for interference in that person's affairs.

It was several days before Willoughby's name was mentioned before Marianne by any of her family; Sir John and Mrs. Jennings, indeed, were not so nice;[11] their witticisms added pain to many a painful hour;—but one evening, Mrs. Dashwood, accidentally taking up a volume of Shakespeare, exclaimed,

"We have never finished Hamlet, Marianne; our dear Willoughby went away before we could get through it.[12] We will put it by, that when he comes again . . . But it may be months, perhaps, before *that* happens."

"Months!" cried Marianne, with strong surprise. "No—nor many weeks."

Mrs. Dashwood was sorry for what she had said; but it gave Elinor pleasure, as it produced a reply from Marianne so expressive of confidence in Willoughby and knowledge of his intentions.

One morning, about a week after his leaving the country, Marianne was prevailed on to join her sisters in their usual walk, instead of wandering away by herself. Hitherto she had carefully avoided every companion in her rambles.[13] If her sisters intended to walk on the downs, she directly[14] stole away towards the lanes;[15] if they talked of the valley, she was as speedy in climbing the hills, and could never be found when the others set off. But at length she was secured by the exertions of Elinor, who greatly disapproved such continual seclusion. They walked along the road through the valley, and chiefly in silence, for Marianne's *mind* could not be controuled, and Elinor, satisfied with gaining one point, would not then attempt more. Beyond the entrance of the valley, where the country, though still rich, was less wild and more open,[16] a long stretch of the road which they had travelled on first coming to Barton, lay before them; and on reaching that point, they stopped to look around them, and examine a prospect[17] which formed the distance of their view from the cottage, from a spot which they had never happened to reach in any of their walks before.[18]

Amongst the objects in the scene, they soon discovered an animated one; it was a man on horseback riding towards them.[19] In a

11. *nice*: scrupulous, sensitive.

12. They would have been reading it aloud together, perhaps with different people speaking various parts. Another play of Shakespeare is read aloud in *Mansfield Park*. *Hamlet* would be a logical choice for them, especially for Marianne, since she is the most passionate about literature and her enthusiasms were already shown to guide Willoughby. In addition to long being one of Shakespeare's most popular plays, *Hamlet* exercised a particular appeal to advocates of Romanticism, who identified strongly with the central character's melancholy, tendency toward brooding reflectiveness, isolation from others, and disgust with the corrupt world around him. It is also probable that Marianne, who almost never jokes or laughs, would prefer tragedy to comedy; an earlier incident suggested the family, or at least she and Willoughby, were possibly reading *Romeo and Juliet* (p. 113, note 16).

13. The pursuit of solitude, often to the point of completely abandoning society, is a theme found in many Romantic writings.

14. *directly*: immediately.

15. As mentioned before, the lanes were below the downs. This clause forms the complement to the next one, suggesting that whether they went high or low, she went the other way.

16. The valley was described initially as well wooded, so a less wild and more open area probably means farmed fields. Its openness would give them the extensive view mentioned next.

17. *prospect*: scene.

18. Elinor also enjoys the beauties of nature, even if she speaks of them less enthusiastically than Marianne. Jane Austen shows a definite appreciation of natural beauty in her own letters.

19. Since carriages were usually employed for long-distance travel, this suggests that he has not traveled from a great distance.

few minutes they could distinguish him to be a gentleman;[20] and in a moment afterwards Marianne rapturously exclaimed,

"It is he; it is indeed;—I know it is!"—And was hastening to meet him, when Elinor cried out,

"Indeed, Marianne, I think you are mistaken. It is not Willoughby. The person is not tall enough for him, and has not his air."[21]

"He has, he has," cried Marianne, "I am sure he has. His air, his coat, his horse. I knew how soon he would come."

She walked eagerly on as she spoke; and Elinor, to screen Marianne from particularity,[22] as she felt almost certain of its not being Willoughby, quickened her pace and kept up with her. They were soon within thirty yards of the gentleman. Marianne looked again; her heart sunk within her; and abruptly turning round, she was hurrying back, when the voices of both her sisters were raised to detain her, a third, almost as well known as Willoughby's, joined them in begging her to stop, and she turned round with surprise to see and welcome Edward Ferrars.

He was the only person in the world who could at that moment be forgiven for not being Willoughby; the only one who could have gained a smile from her; but she dispersed her tears to smile on *him*, and in her sister's happiness forgot for a time her own disappointment.

He dismounted, and giving his horse to his servant,[23] walked back with them to Barton, whither he was purposely coming to visit them.

He was welcomed by them all with great cordiality, but especially by Marianne, who shewed more warmth of regard in her reception of him than even Elinor herself. To Marianne, indeed, the meeting between Edward and her sister was but a continuation of that unaccountable coldness which she had often observed at Norland in their mutual behaviour. On Edward's side, more particularly, there was a deficiency of all that a lover ought to look and say on such an occasion. He was confused, seemed scarcely sensible of pleasure in seeing them, looked neither rapturous nor gay, said little but what was forced from him by ques-

20. He might be distinguished as a gentleman by his clothing, which differed greatly between classes. The most distinctive marks of a gentleman to be seen from a distance would be his stiff top hat and his tailored coat (or, if cold enough, his very long outer greatcoat), none of which would be worn by a laboring man. It also turns out he is accompanied by a servant, something common for gentlemen traveling.

21. *air*: outward character or demeanor.

22. *particularity*: peculiarity.

23. The servant could both take care of his horses and serve as his valet, one who took care of his master's possessions, especially his clothes, and helped him dress. The functions were often combined.

tions, and distinguished Elinor by no mark of affection.[24] Marianne saw and listened with increasing surprise. She began almost to feel a dislike of Edward; and it ended, as every feeling must end with her, by carrying back her thoughts to Willoughby, whose manners formed a contrast sufficiently striking to those of his brother elect.[25]

After a short silence which succeeded the first surprise and inquiries of meeting, Marianne asked Edward if he came directly from London. No, he had been in Devonshire a fortnight.

"A fortnight!" she repeated, surprised at his being so long in the same county with Elinor without seeing her before.

He looked rather distressed as he added, that he had been staying with some friends near Plymouth.[26]

"Have you been lately in Sussex?" said Elinor.

"I was at Norland about a month ago."

"And how does dear, dear Norland look?" cried Marianne.

"Dear, dear Norland," said Elinor, "probably looks much as it always does at this time of year. The woods and walks thickly covered with dead leaves."

"Oh!" cried Marianne, "with what transporting[27] sensations have I formerly seen them fall! How have I delighted, as I walked, to see them driven in showers about me by the wind! What feelings have they, the season, the air altogether inspired! Now there is no one to regard them. They are seen only as a nuisance, swept hastily off, and driven as much as possible from the sight."[28]

"It is not every one," said Elinor, "who has your passion for dead leaves."

"No; my feelings are not often shared, not often understood. But *sometimes* they are."[29]—As she said this, she sunk into a reverie for a few moments;—but rousing herself again, "Now, Edward," said she, calling his attention to the prospect, "here is Barton valley. Look up it, and be tranquil if you can.[30] Look at those hills! Did you ever see their equals? To the left is Barton park, amongst those woods and plantations.[31] You may see one end of the house. And there, beneath that farthest hill, which rises with such grandeur, is our cottage."

24. The reason for Edward's dejection will be revealed later (p. 250).

25. *brother elect*: chosen or selected brother, or, in this case, brother-in-law.

26. Plymouth is at the western edge of Devonshire. This is why he has been able to come on horseback, though such a journey would still take many hours. His dejected mood, which turns out to be a product of his experience in Plymouth, may have made him happy for the opportunity for a long ride.

27. *transporting*: overwhelming, ecstatic.

28. Marianne's speech, with its succession of short, emphatic sentences and frequent exclamation marks, gives a sense of her excitable character. It contrasts with Elinor's more sober choice of words and tendency toward longer, more intricate sentences.

29. The "*sometimes*" refers to Willoughby, who often proclaimed his full agreement with Marianne's ideas. The idea of not being understood or having one's feelings shared by the rest of the world was commonly expressed by Romantic writers.

30. This represents a particular vision of natural beauty and its effects. An opposing view celebrated the beauties of nature in part for the tranquillity they might induce, whether as a relief from the cares of existence or as a soothing proof of the harmony of creation.

31. *plantations*: woods of planted trees, generally established to produce timber, and thus often consisting of uniform types of trees. Marianne is distinguishing them from regular woods that have developed without such guidance.

"It is a beautiful country," he replied; "but these bottoms[32] must be dirty in winter."[33]

"How can you think of dirt, with such objects before you?"

"Because," replied he, smiling, "among the rest of the objects before me, I see a very dirty lane."

"How strange!" said Marianne to herself as she walked on.

"Have you an agreeable neighbourhood here? Are the Middletons pleasant people?"

"No, not at all," answered Marianne, "we could not be more unfortunately situated."

"Marianne," cried her sister, "how can you say so? How can you be so unjust? They are a very respectable family, Mr. Ferrars; and towards us have behaved in the friendliest manner. Have you forgot, Marianne, how many pleasant days we have owed to them?"

"No," said Marianne in a low voice, "nor how many painful moments."

Elinor took no notice of this, and directing her attention to their visitor, endeavoured to support something like discourse with him by talking of their present residence, its conveniences, &c. extorting from him occasional questions and remarks. His coldness and reserve mortified her severely; she was vexed and half angry;[34] but resolving to regulate her behaviour to him by the past rather than the present, she avoided every appearance of resentment or displeasure, and treated him as she thought he ought to be treated from the family connection.[35]

32. *bottoms:* low-lying land, valleys.

33. Edward's prosaic reply, in addition to representing his genuinely different perspective on nature (shortly explained on p. 184), may reflect his current gloominess, which makes him inclined to see the less pleasant aspects even of beautiful scenery. It also may be a reaction against Marianne's fervent advocacy of her particular way of regarding the scene. The smile that accompanies his next remark suggests some irony regarding her insistent enthusiasm.

34. Her reaction reveals that Elinor can also experience strong feelings from romantic disappointment, even as her behavior shows her different way of treating those feelings.

35. As their brother's brother-in-law he deserves courtesy regardless of any possible romantic tie with Elinor.

Chapter Seventeen

M rs. Dashwood was surprised only for a moment at seeing him; for his coming to Barton was, in her opinion, of all things the most natural. Her joy and expressions of regard long outlived her wonder. He received the kindest welcome from her; and shyness, coldness, reserve could not stand against such a reception. They had begun to fail him before he entered the house, and they were quite overcome by the captivating manners of Mrs. Dashwood. Indeed a man could not very well be in love with either of her daughters, without extending the passion to her; and Elinor had the satisfaction of seeing him soon become more like himself. His affections seemed to reanimate towards them all, and his interest in their welfare again became perceptible. He was not in spirits[1] however; he praised their house, admired its prospect, was attentive, and kind; but still he was not in spirits. The whole family perceived it, and Mrs. Dashwood, attributing it to some want of liberality[2] in his mother, sat down to table indignant against all selfish parents.[3]

"What are Mrs. Ferrars's views for you at present, Edward?" said she, when dinner was over and they had drawn round the fire; "are you still to be a great orator in spite of yourself?"[4]

"No. I hope my mother is now convinced that I have no more talents than inclination for a public life!"[5]

"But how is your fame to be established? for famous you must be to satisfy all your family; and with no inclination for expense,[6] no affection for strangers, no profession, and no assurance,[7] you may find it a difficult matter."

"I shall not attempt it. I have no wish to be distinguished; and I have every reason to hope I never shall. Thank Heaven! I cannot be forced into genius and eloquence."

1. *in spirits:* cheerful, happy.

2. *want of liberality:* lack of generosity, especially financial; or lack of broad-mindedness, possibly referring in this case to Mrs. Ferrars's ideas on what course Edward should pursue.

3. In contrast to Willoughby and Marianne's frequent practice, Edward will converse with the entire Dashwood family throughout his visit.

4. Mrs. Dashwood, as the head of the family, would normally initiate inquiries to a guest who has just arrived.

5. Being a good orator was an important skill for those seeking success in public life, for such a life usually involved being a member of Parliament, where eloquence in debate was invaluable for advancing a member's reputation and influence. For a picture of a debate in Parliament, see p. 219.

6. Extravagance could produce a sort of distinction among sections of upper-class society; aristocratic norms celebrated qualities often associated with such expenditure, such as fine taste in possessions or generosity to friends, while regarding insolvency or serious debts as minor flaws.

7. *assurance:* audacity, cockiness, self-confidence. The word could be used in both a positive and a negative sense.

A London bookshop.

[From *The Repository of arts, literature, fashions, manufactures, &c,* Vol. I (1809), p. 251]

"You have no ambition, I well know. Your wishes are all moderate."

"As moderate as those of the rest of the world, I believe. I wish as well as every body else to be perfectly happy; but like every body else it must be in my own way. Greatness[8] will not make me so."

"Strange if it would!" cried Marianne. "What have wealth or grandeur to do with happiness?"

"Grandeur has but little," said Elinor, "but wealth has much to do with it."[9]

"Elinor, for shame!" said Marianne; "money can only give happiness where there is nothing else to give it. Beyond a competence,[10] it can afford no real satisfaction, as far as mere self is concerned."

"Perhaps," said Elinor, smiling, "we may come to the same point. *Your* competence and *my* wealth are very much alike, I dare say; and without them, as the world goes now, we shall both agree that every kind of external comfort must be wanting. Your ideas are only more noble than mine.[11] Come, what is your competence?"

"About eighteen hundred or two thousand a-year; not more than *that*."[12]

Elinor laughed. "*Two* thousand a-year! *One* is my wealth! I guessed how it would end."[13]

"And yet two thousand a-year is a very moderate income," said Marianne. "A family[14] cannot well be maintained on a smaller. I am sure I am not extravagant in my demands. A proper establishment of servants,[15] a carriage, perhaps two,[16] and hunters,[17] cannot be supported on less."[18]

Elinor smiled again, to hear her sister describing so accurately their future expenses at Combe Magna.

"Hunters!" repeated Edward—"But why must you have hunters? Every body does not hunt."

Marianne coloured as she replied, "But most people do."[19]

"I wish," said Margaret, striking out a novel thought, "that somebody would give us all a large fortune apiece!"

8. *Greatness*: high rank or social position.

9. While Jane Austen never argues that money is the main source of happiness, and criticizes those, like John and Fanny Dashwood, who are obsessed with wealth, she also consistently presents an appreciation of money as natural and a sign of good practical sense.

10. *competence*: sufficiency of means.

11. Marianne proclaims more exalted principles, but when applied to concrete cases, they amount to the same.

12. Less than one percent of the population at the time enjoyed this level of income.

13. Even Elinor's one thousand a year is far above the incomes of most people, though she is calling it wealth rather than a mere competence. Both are judging by the standards of the genteel ranks of society.

14. *family*: household. This could include the staff of servants.

15. A family of the income she suggests would usually have around a dozen servants.

16. Most genteel families owned a carriage, but only very wealthy ones owned two. The costs of the carriages themselves, the taxes on them (which were higher per carriage the more one owned), the horses to pull them, and the servants needed to drive them would add up to a considerable expense.

17. *hunters*: horses used for hunting. This means especially horses suitable for the rapid rides and frequent jumps involved in foxhunting. The skill and strength required for this made hunters especially expensive. Willoughby has undoubtedly told Marianne of his interest in hunters.

18. Marianne, after proclaiming her disdain for wealth, an attitude found in various Romantic writers, ends up expressing very expensive desires. Possible reasons for this are her poor sense of practical matters, in which she follows her mother, her inclination to focus on her wishes and feelings without regard to external obstacles, and the influence of Willoughby, who could have inspired Marianne with his own expensive tastes.

19. She means most men of gentility. The popularity of hunting among gentlemen means that, in those terms, her statement may be true, or close to true.

"Oh that they would!" cried Marianne, her eyes sparkling with animation, and her cheeks glowing with the delight of such imaginary happiness.[20]

"We are all unanimous in that wish, I suppose," said Elinor, "in spite of the insufficiency of wealth."

"Oh dear!" cried Margaret, "how happy I should be! I wonder what I should do with it!"

Marianne looked as if she had no doubt on that point.

"I should be puzzled to spend a large fortune myself," said Mrs. Dashwood, "if my children were all to be rich without my help."

"You must begin your improvements on this house," observed Elinor, "and your difficulties will soon vanish."

"What magnificent orders would travel from this family to London," said Edward, "in such an event![21] What a happy day for booksellers, music-sellers,[22] and print-shops![23] You, Miss Dashwood, would give a general commission for every new print of merit to be sent you—and as for Marianne, I know her greatness of soul, there would not be music enough in London to content her. And books!—Thomson, Cowper, Scott[24]—she would buy them all over and over again; she would buy up every copy, I believe, to prevent their falling into unworthy hands;[25] and she would have every book that tells her how to admire an old twisted tree.[26] Should not you, Marianne? Forgive me, if I am very saucy. But I was willing to shew you that I had not forgot our old disputes."[27]

"I love to be reminded of the past, Edward—whether it be melancholy or gay, I love to recall it—and you will never offend me by talking of former times.[28] You are very right in supposing how my money would be spent—some of it, at least—my loose cash would certainly be employed in improving my collection of music and books."

"And the bulk of your fortune would be laid out[29] in annuities on the authors or their heirs."[30]

"No, Edward, I should have something else to do with it."[31]

"Perhaps then you would bestow it as a reward on that person who wrote the ablest defence of your favourite maxim, that no

20. A further contradiction of her just-proclaimed indifference to wealth.

21. London's shops were far superior to those in the rest of England. People from the provinces, especially rural areas, would do much of their shopping in London if they had opportunities to travel there.

22. *music-sellers:* stores selling printed sheets of music.

23. *print-shops:* shops selling prints, i.e., pictures made from engravings. Prints, often derived from the works of prominent painters, were very popular then. Amateur artists like Elinor would seek them not simply, or principally, from appreciation, but because copying prints was a common activity among those who drew. For a picture of one, see p. 179.

24. Marianne's love for Cowper and Scott has already appeared (pp. 30 and 90). James Thomson (1700–1748) was most noted for his long poem *The Seasons*, which expresses a strong love for nature. Lines from it, along with lines from Pope, Thomas Gray, and Shakespeare, are mentioned as ones that the heroine of *Northanger Abbey* learned as part of her literary education.

25. The cult of sensibility celebrated souls sensitive and tender enough to have the correct, fully developed feelings and disdained those, perhaps the great majority, who lacked such sensitivity.

26. For Marianne's reasons for admiring twisted trees, see p. 187, note 16.

27. Edward's ready citing of several principles of Marianne, and his reference to their old disputes, suggest how inclined she is to proclaim and debate her doctrines.

28. Many Romantic writings, especially poems, focused on reliving or extolling the experiences and feelings of the past.

29. *laid out:* spent, expended.

30. Providing annuities to authors was a long-standing tradition among the wealthy, though by this time the practice was lessening and more authors were relying on the marketplace for sustenance.

31. She may mean help provide means for Willoughby to marry her, if she knows or believes that this is the reason he left and has not returned.

one can ever be in love more than once in their life[32]—for your opinion on that point is unchanged, I presume?".

"Undoubtedly. At my time of life opinions are tolerably fixed. It is not likely that I should now see or hear anything to change them."

"Marianne is as stedfast as ever, you see," said Elinor,. "she is not at all altered."[33]

"She is only grown a little more grave than she was."

"Nay, Edward," said Marianne, "*you* need not reproach me. You are not very gay yourself."

"Why should you think so!" replied he, with a sigh. "But gaiety never was a part of *my* character."

"Nor do I think it a part of Marianne's," said Elinor; "I should hardly call her a lively girl—she is very earnest, very eager in all she does—sometimes talks a great deal and always with animation—but she is not often really merry."[34]

"I believe you are right," he replied, "and yet I have always set her down as[35] as a lively girl."

"I have frequently detected myself in such kind of mistakes," said Elinor, "in a total misapprehension of character in some point or other: fancying people so much more gay or grave, or ingenious[36] or stupid[37] than they really are, and I can hardly tell why, or in what the deception originated. Sometimes one is guided by what they say of themselves, and very frequently by what other people say of them, without giving oneself time to deliberate and judge."[38]

"But I thought it was right, Elinor," said Marianne, "to be guided wholly by the opinion of other people. I thought our judgments were given us merely to be subservient to those of our neighbours. This has always been your doctrine, I am sure."

"No, Marianne, never. My doctrine has never aimed at the subjection of the understanding. All I have ever attempted to influence has been the behaviour. You must not confound my meaning. I am guilty, I confess, of having often wished you to treat our acquaintance in general with greater attention; but when

32. For Marianne's views on second attachments, see p. 104.

33. Elinor's use of "stedfast" [sic] implies the determined effort Marianne makes to avoid any bending or retreat in her ideas. It also may signal Elinor's frustration with this quality, which would only be exacerbated by hearing her sister declare that at only seventeen her opinions are fixed.

34. Elinor's explanation indicates the different meaning of "lively" then, for while it connoted vivacity and animation, it also involved merriness and gaiety. Thus the energetic but serious Marianne is not lively; in contrast, the word is frequently applied to the lighthearted and witty heroine of *Pride and Prejudice*, Elizabeth Bennet.

35. *set her down as:* considered her to be.

36. *ingenious:* clever, talented, discerning.

37. *stupid:* slow-witted, dull. The word did not have as harsh a connotation then.

38. Elinor's admission of her frequent errors in judging others is ironic in a sense, for over the course of the novel her judgments, while far from perfect, prove superior to those of anyone else. Of course, her very acknowledgment of her fallibility, and awareness of the various ways one can be led to misjudge, are critical reasons for her overall accuracy. At numerous points she is shown taking time to arrive at a verdict, after careful observation of others and contemplation of the factors that might shed light on their character and behavior. This contrasts with Marianne's belief that she can understand Willoughby completely after a brief acquaintance.

have I advised you to adopt their sentiments or conform to their judgment in serious matters?"[39]

"You have not been able then to bring your sister over to your plan of general civility," said Edward to Elinor. "Do you gain no ground?"

"Quite the contrary," replied Elinor, looking expressively at Marianne.[40]

"My judgment," he returned, "is all on your side of the question; but I am afraid my practice is much more on your sister's. I never wish to offend, but I am so foolishly shy, that I often seem negligent, when I am only kept back by my natural aukwardness. I have frequently thought that I must have been intended by nature to be fond of low[41] company, I am so little at my ease among strangers of gentility!"[42]

"Marianne has not shyness to excuse any inattention of hers," said Elinor.

"She knows her own worth too well for false shame," replied Edward. "Shyness is only the effect of a sense of inferiority in some way or other. If I could persuade myself that my manners were perfectly easy[43] and graceful, I should not be shy."

"But you would still be reserved," said Marianne, "and that is worse."

Edward stared—"Reserved! Am I reserved, Marianne?"

"Yes, very."

"I do not understand you," replied he, colouring. "Reserved!— how, in what manner? What am I to tell you? What can you suppose?"[44]

Elinor looked surprised at his emotion, but trying to laugh off the subject, she said to him, "Do not you know my sister well enough to understand what she means? Do not you know she calls every one reserved who does not talk as fast, and admire what she admires as rapturously as herself?"

Edward made no answer. His gravity and thoughtfulness returned on him in their fullest extent—and he sat for some time silent and dull.

39. Elinor's distinction is one often made by Jane Austen, who shares this attitude. The admirable characters in her novels think and judge for themselves, rather than simply accepting others' opinions—though these thoughts and judgments are based on generally established moral, religious, or social principles. At the same time, they always display outward courtesy, even when dealing with people they regard with contempt.

40. Elinor's expressive look is probably sparked by Marianne's recent behavior with Willoughby, in which she showed particular neglect of others and of her social obligations.

41. *low:* socially inferior.

42. Edward's greater comfort among those who are not genteel echoes one of the most popular plays of this time, Oliver Goldsmith's *She Stoops to Conquer* (1773). It centers around a young gentleman who can only approach or talk easily to women of a lower station, which leads a young lady to pretend to be a servant to win his love.

43. *easy:* unembarrassed; free from awkwardness or stiffness.

44. Edward's reaction signals that Marianne has touched a nerve in calling him "reserved." The term then had its current connotation of cold or aloof, but it also meant uncommunicative or not open and frank. It is this that probably arouses him, for, as soon revealed, Edward has powerful reasons not to be communicative or frank about his personal affairs.

A London print shop.

[From *The Repository of arts, literature, fashions, manufactures, &c*, Vol. I (1809), p. 53]

Two landscapes showing the irregular features and the distant haziness valued by advocates of the picturesque (for more, see next chapter).

[From William Gilpin, *Observations on the River Wye* (London, 1800; 2005 reprint), pp. 32 and 75]

Landscapes with a blasted tree and a building in ruins, two other elements valued by advocates of the picturesque.

[From William Gilpin, *Observations on the River Wye* (London, 1800; 2005 reprint), pp. 71 and 47]

Chapter Eighteen

*E*linor saw, with great uneasiness, the low spirits of her friend. His visit afforded her but a very partial satisfaction, while his own enjoyment in it appeared so imperfect. It was evident that he was unhappy; she wished it were equally evident that he still distinguished her by the same affection which once she had felt no doubt of inspiring; but hitherto the continuance of his preference seemed very uncertain; and the reservedness of his manner towards her contradicted one moment what a more animated look had intimated the preceding one.[1]

He joined her and Marianne in the breakfast-room the next morning before the others were down;[2] and Marianne, who was always eager to promote their happiness as far as she could, soon left them to themselves. But before she was half way up stairs she heard the parlour door open, and, turning round, was astonished to see Edward himself come out.

"I am going into the village to see my horses," said he, "as you are not yet ready for breakfast; I shall be back again presently."[3]

Edward returned to them with fresh admiration of the surrounding country; in his walk to the village, he had seen many parts of the valley to advantage; and the village itself, in a much higher situation[4] than the cottage, afforded a general view of the whole, which had exceedingly pleased him. This was a subject which ensured Marianne's attention, and she was beginning to describe her own admiration of these scenes, and to question him more minutely on the objects that had particularly struck him, when Edward interrupted her by saying, "You must not inquire too far, Marianne—remember I have no knowledge in the picturesque,[5] and I shall offend you by my ignorance and want of

1. Elinor notices a lesser interest in her as well as a general state of dejection in Edward. The fluctuating character of his affection for her is something she perceived during their earlier time together at Norland, and it now seems to have become more pronounced.

2. Many houses then had a special room for breakfast. The heavy reliance on the sun for heat and light made a room facing south or east more convenient early in the day. In grander ones it could be a dining room used almost solely for that purpose; here, however, one of the parlors apparently serves as the breakfast room, since in the next sentence Edward opens the parlor door to leave.

3. As already mentioned, breakfast time tended to be around ten, so he might still expect to be back in time. It is possible that Elinor, who has remained in the breakfast room, was taking care of the preparations for breakfast: Jane Austen had that task in her household. The servant would have taken the horses to the village—the Dashwoods having no stable, as a wealthier family would have—and Edward will presumably see what place the servant has hired and ensure that the horses are being cared for properly.

4. *situation:* position, location.

5. The picturesque was a concept that had become very popular at this time. The term first appeared in the early eighteenth century and meant scenery that had the elements of a picture or was fit to be the subject of a picture. A critical inspiration for the concept was the landscapes of the Italian countryside by the seventeenth-century painters Claude Lorrain and Salvator Rosa, whose works were celebrated for presenting an ideally beautiful and poetic vision of nature. The closer actual scenes from nature resembled these paintings, the more likely they were to be called picturesque. In the late eighteenth century the concept grew in popularity and took on further connotations in the hands of certain writers. They identified the picturesque as one of the three main categories of natural beauty, along with the beautiful, used to refer to what was gentle and delicate and harmonious, and the sublime, used to refer to what was vast and overwhelming. The picturesque was used for scenery characterized by irregularity, roughness, and variation, features not fitting into either of the other categories. These ideas had many links with the cult of sensibility and the growing Romanticism of the same period; picturesque scenery was often celebrated for the Romantic emotions it provoked.

taste if we come to particulars. I shall call hills steep, which ought to be bold;[6] surfaces strange and uncouth, which ought to be irregular and rugged; and distant objects out of sight, which ought only to be indistinct through the soft medium of a hazy atmosphere.[7] You must be satisfied with such admiration as I can honestly give. I call it a very fine country—the hills are steep, the woods seem full of fine timber, and the valley looks comfortable[8] and snug—with rich meadows and several neat[9] farm houses scattered here and there. It exactly answers[10] my idea of a fine country because it unites beauty with utility—and I dare say it is a picturesque one too, because you admire it; I can easily believe it to be full of rocks and promontories, grey moss and brush wood,[11] but these are all lost on me. I know nothing of the picturesque."

"I am afraid it is but too true," said Marianne; "but why should you boast of it?"

"I suspect," said Elinor, "that to avoid one kind of affectation, Edward here falls into another. Because he believes many people pretend to more admiration of the beauties of nature than they really feel,[12] and is disgusted with such pretensions, he affects greater indifference and less discrimination in viewing them him-

A traveler sketching a picturesque scene.

[From William Combe, *The Tour of Dr. Syntax in Search of the Picturesque* (London, 1817; 1903 reprint), p. 105]

6.   Marianne had used the very term "bold hills" when describing the view from the room at Allenham (p. 132).

7.   Though Edward begins by admitting his ignorance, along with his want, or lack, of taste, concerning the picturesque, and concludes this speech with the same declaration, his comments reveal a great familiarity with the idea. He recognizes the high value placed on irregularity and ruggedness, and his final words echo the language found in writings of picturesque. The most influential of these writings, William Gilpin's series of guides to the picturesque beauties of various parts of the British Isles, praises haziness for possibly improving scenes, especially by evoking objects in the background in the manner of paintings by Claude Lorrain (for pictures from one of Gilpin's works that show his taste for hazy effects and for irregular or rugged features, see p. 180).

8.   *comfortable:* cheerful, tranquil.

9.   *neat:* well made; attractive but simple.

10.   *answers:* fulfills, satisfies.

11.   These natural features were all believed to add to the picturesque quality of a scene.

12.   Appreciation of picturesque beauty had become a very popular phenomenon by this time. People not only read many writings extolling and expounding the picturesque, but also traveled to various parts of Britain in quest of picturesque beauty. Many would take something called a Claude glass, a rectangular lens through which they could look out to identify which scenes most closely resembled those found in Claude Lorrain paintings, and then appreciate them for their Claudian qualities. The popularity of these tours sparked, in the year after this novel was published, a satire, *The Tour of Dr. Syntax in Search of the Picturesque,* about the misadventures of the title character during his tour; the book went through numerous editions, and Jane Austen refers to it in a letter (March 5, 1814). For pictures from the book, see facing page and p. 189.

self than he possesses. He is fastidious and will have an affectation of his own."[13]

"It is very true," said Marianne, "that admiration of landscape scenery is become a mere jargon. Every body pretends to feel and tries to describe with the taste and elegance of him who first defined what picturesque beauty was. I detest jargon of every kind, and sometimes I have kept my feelings to myself, because I could find no language to describe them in but what was worn and hackneyed out of all sense and meaning."[14]

"I am convinced," said Edward, "that you really feel all the delight in a fine prospect[15] which you profess to feel. But, in return, your sister must allow me to feel no more than I profess. I like a fine prospect, but not on picturesque principles. I do not like crooked, twisted, blasted trees.[16] I admire them much more if they are tall, straight and flourishing. I do not like ruined, tattered cottages. I am not fond of nettles, or thistles, or heath blossoms.[17] I have more pleasure in a snug farm-house than a watchtower— and a troop of tidy, happy villagers please me better than the finest banditti in the world."[18]

Marianne looked with amazement at Edward, with compassion at her sister. Elinor only laughed.[19]

The subject was continued no farther; and Marianne remained thoughtfully silent, till a new object suddenly engaged her attention. She was sitting by Edward, and in taking his tea from Mrs. Dashwood, his hand passed so directly before her, as to make a ring, with a plait of hair in the centre, very conspicuous on one of his fingers.

"I never saw you wear a ring before, Edward," she cried. "Is that Fanny's hair? I remember her promising to give you some. But I should have thought her hair had been darker."[20]

Marianne spoke inconsiderately what she really felt—but when she saw how much she had pained Edward, her own vexation at her want of thought could not be surpassed by his. He coloured very deeply, and giving a momentary glance at Elinor, replied, "Yes; it is my sister's hair. The setting always casts a different shade on it you know."

13. Elinor is misunderstanding Edward a little here, for he has just praised the surrounding countryside and called himself indifferent only to what advocates of the picturesque praised as beautiful. Elinor may be less familiar with the specifics of picturesque theory than the other two, and therefore less careful in distinguishing it from a more general love of nature.

14. Marianne's aversion to repeating what has already been said—something hard to avoid in this case, given the popularity of the picturesque—corresponds to an emphasis in Romanticism on the great importance of originality.

15. *prospect*: view, scene.

16. The picturesque writer William Gilpin, who wrote an entire book on forest scenery, claimed that only trees that are decayed or blasted in some respect can have true picturesque beauty. For a picture of such a tree from one of his books, see p. 181.

17. These last natural features all have the appropriate roughness to qualify as picturesque, as do ruined cottages. Writers on the subject in fact wrote much of ruins, celebrating the powerful aesthetic effects they created and seeking out scenes containing them. For an example of this from Gilpin's work, see picture on p. 181.

18. Banditti, or bands of robbers, as well as gypsies, beggars, or other outcast groups, were believed to make a scene particularly picturesque. Interest in such groups and in watchtowers, towers stationed to allow people to look out for danger, also fit with the interest in violence and crime in much Romantic literature. In expressing his contrary preferences Edward is criticizing picturesque theory on a point that even its proponents admitted to be problematic: some of what it considered aesthetically pleasing, such as decay or destruction or misery, was not pleasing from a moral perspective.

19. Marianne's amazement shows her attachment to the principles he criticized. At the same time, his command of the subject makes it difficult for her to respond. This dialogue is one of the few places in which Edward has a chance to reveal his cleverness and independence of mind, since the plot forces him into an absent or tongue-tied role for much of the novel. It thus plays a useful role in showing the reasons for Elinor's affection for him, including his ability to make her laugh.

20. As seen earlier in the case of Marianne and Willoughby, a woman's hair could serve as a keepsake for someone close to her.

Elinor had met his eye, and looked conscious likewise. That the hair was her own, she instantaneously felt as well satisfied as Marianne; the only difference in their conclusions was, that what Marianne considered as a free gift from her sister, Elinor was conscious must have been procured by some theft or contrivance unknown to herself. She was not in a humour, however, to regard it as an affront, and affecting to take no notice of what passed, by instantly talking of something else, she internally resolved henceforward to catch every opportunity of eyeing the hair and of satisfying herself, beyond all doubt, that it was exactly the shade of her own.

Edward's embarrassment lasted some time, and it ended in an absence of mind still more settled. He was particularly grave the whole morning. Marianne severely censured herself for what she had said; but her own forgiveness might have been more speedy, had she known how little offence it had given her sister.

Before the middle of the day, they were visited by Sir John and Mrs. Jennings, who, having heard of the arrival of a gentleman at the cottage, came to take a survey of the guest. With the assistance of his mother-in-law, Sir John was not long in discovering that the name of Ferrars began with an F. and this prepared a future mine of raillery against the devoted Elinor, which nothing but the newness of their acquaintance with Edward could have prevented from being immediately sprung.[21] But, as it was, she only learned from some very significant looks, how far their penetration,[22] founded on Margaret's instructions, extended.

Sir John never came to the Dashwoods without either inviting them to dine at the park the next day, or to drink tea with them that evening. On the present occasion, for the better entertainment of their visitor, towards whose amusement he felt himself bound to contribute, he wished to engage them for both.

"You *must* drink tea with us to night," said he, "for we shall be quite alone—and to-morrow you must absolutely dine with us, for we shall be a large party."[23]

Mrs. Jennings enforced[24] the necessity. "And who knows but you may raise a dance," said she. "And that will tempt *you*, Miss Marianne."

21. *sprung:* exploded (to release or loosen the contents). The word continues the metaphor of the mine of raillery or teasing.

22. *penetration:* perception, discernment (of Elinor's attachment).

23. Sir John finds a reason for others to join them, no matter what the circumstances. Drinking tea with them would mean coming after dinner.

24. *enforced:* reaffirmed, urged further.

A traveler falling into the water due to excessive concentration on the picturesque scenery.

[From William Combe, *The Tour of Dr. Syntax in Search of the Picturesque* (London, 1817; 1903 reprint), p. 68]

"A dance!" cried Marianne. "Impossible! Who is to dance?"

"Who! why yourselves, and the Careys, and Whitakers to be sure.—What! you thought nobody could dance because a certain person that shall be nameless is gone!"

"I wish with all my soul," cried Sir John, "that Willoughby were among us again."

This, and Marianne's blushing, gave new suspicions to Edward. "And who is Willoughby?" said he, in a low voice, to Miss Dashwood, by whom he was sitting.

She gave him a brief reply. Marianne's countenance was more communicative. Edward saw enough to comprehend, not only the meaning of others, but such of Marianne's expressions as had puzzled him before; and when their visitors left them, he went immediately round to her and said, in a whisper, "I have been guessing. Shall I tell you my guess?"

"What do you mean?"

"Shall I tell you?"

"Certainly."

"Well then; I guess that Mr. Willoughby hunts."

Marianne was surprised and confused, yet she could not help smiling at the quiet archness of his manner, and, after a moment's silence, said,

"Oh! Edward! How can you?—But the time will come I hope.... I am sure you will like him."

"I do not doubt it," replied he, rather astonished at her earnestness and warmth; for had he not imagined it to be a joke for the good of her acquaintance in general, founded only on a something or a nothing between Mr. Willoughby and herself, he would not have ventured to mention it.[25]

25. Thus Edward shows great delicacy in not wanting to hurt someone else's feelings, even though in this case Marianne does not seem really hurt. The episode, like Marianne's mention of the ring, shows the potential danger, even if only a mild one, of speaking without care or discretion.

A gig.

[From G. A. Thrupp, *History of Coaches* (London, 1877), p. 75]

Chapter Nineteen

*E*dward remained a week at the cottage; he was earnestly pressed by Mrs. Dashwood to stay longer; but as if he were bent only on self-mortification, he seemed resolved to be gone when his enjoyment among his friends was at the height. His spirits, during the last two or three days, though still very unequal,[1] were greatly improved—he grew more and more partial to the house and environs—never spoke of going away without a sigh—declared his time to be wholly disengaged—even doubted to what place he should go when he left them—but still, go he must. Never had any week passed so quickly—he could hardly believe it to be gone. He said so repeatedly; other things he said too, which marked the turn of his feelings and gave the lie to his actions. He had no pleasure at Norland; he detested being in town; but either to Norland or London, he must go. He valued their kindness beyond any thing, and his greatest happiness was in being with them. Yet he must leave them at the end of a week, in spite of their wishes and his own, and without any restraint on his time.

Elinor placed all that was astonishing in this way of acting to his mother's account; and it was happy for her that he had a mother whose character was so imperfectly known to her, as to be the general excuse for every thing strange on the part of her son.[2] Disappointed, however, and vexed as she was, and sometimes displeased with his uncertain behaviour to herself, she was very well disposed on the whole to regard his actions with all the candid[3] allowances and generous qualifications, which had been rather more painfully extorted from her, for Willoughby's service,[4] by her mother.[5] His want of spirits, of openness, and of consistency, were most usually attributed to his want of independence,[6] and his better knowledge of Mrs. Ferrars's dispo-

1. *unequal:* uneven, fluctuating.

2. The phrasing of the sentence suggests Elinor's explanation has deficiencies, but it is the best available to her, given her current knowledge. His
mother's opposition to his marriage with Elinor would not necessarily preclude his spending more time with her. His words and actions do not suggest
that he always consults her wishes; moreover, her willingness for him to
remain idle would presumably keep her from inquiring too closely into his
movements. Nor does anything relating to her account for the sense of obligation to leave that he seems to cite repeatedly.

3. *candid:* favorable, benevolent.

4. *service:* benefit.

5. This is a sign that Elinor, though generally the voice of wisdom in the
novel, is not completely wise or objective. At this stage Edward could be
faulted at least as much as Willoughby for his mysterious departure; in fact,
Willoughby, by referring specifically to his cousin's sending him on business
to London, was clearer about the obligation forcing him to go than Edward.
The main way in which Edward is less blameworthy is that, while paying
some attention to Elinor, he has never behaved in a manner clearly indicating his intent to marry her as Willoughby did toward Marianne. Hence his
obligation toward Elinor, and her family, is less.

6. *independence:* financial independence. Edward's financial dependence
does place him in a truly precarious state. The small sum of money that is
later identified as all that is legally secured to him, two thousand pounds,
would not allow him to live in the genteel manner he is accustomed to (at
this point he undoubtedly receives some kind of allowance from his mother
for his spending money). It would be even less capable of supporting a
family—and Elinor, with only a thousand pounds, is in no position to supply
the deficiency. His only other option would be to work, but in any profession
it would be a while before he would be likely to earn enough to make a wife
and children comfortable.

sition[7] and designs. The shortness of his visit, the steadiness of his purpose in leaving them, originated in the same fettered inclination, the same inevitable necessity of temporising with his mother. The old, well established grievance of duty against will,[8] parent against child, was the cause of all. She would have been glad to know when these difficulties were to cease, this opposition was to yield,—when Mrs. Ferrars would be reformed, and her son be at liberty to be happy. But from such vain wishes, she was forced to turn for comfort to the renewal of her confidence in Edward's affection, to the remembrance of every mark of regard in look or word which fell from him while at Barton, and above all to that flattering proof of it which he constantly wore round his finger.

"I think, Edward," said Mrs. Dashwood, as they were at breakfast the last morning, "you would be a happier man if you had any profession to engage your time and give an interest to your plans and actions. Some inconvenience to your friends, indeed, might result from it—you would not be able to give them so much of your time. But (with a smile) you would be materially benefited in one particular at least—you would know where to go when you left them."

"I do assure you," he replied, "that I have long thought on this point, as you think now. It has been, and is, and probably will always be a heavy misfortune to me, that I have had no necessary business to engage me, no profession to give me employment, or afford me any thing like independence. But unfortunately my own nicety,[9] and the nicety of my friends, have made me what I am, an idle, helpless being. We never could agree in our choice of a profession.[10] I always preferred the church, as I still do. But that was not smart enough for my family.[11] They recommended the army. That was a great deal too smart for me.[12] The law was allowed to be genteel enough;[13] many young men, who had chambers in the Temple,[14] made a very good appearance in the first circles, and drove about town in very knowing[15] gigs.[16] But I had no inclination for the law, even in this less abstruse study of it,

7. *dispositions:* plans, arrangements. This was spelled "disposition" in the first edition of the work. The two spellings give different meanings, but either is possible here: in the plural the word would be echoing and reinforcing "designs"; in the singular it would be referring to the general mental character or bent of Mrs. Ferrars.

8. Meaning the duty of obeying one's parent versus one's own inclinations.

9. *nicety:* fastidiousness, scrupulous caution.

10. Edward's list contains the four professions considered genteel, and therefore what a gentleman could pursue without losing his status.

11. Being a clergyman was not considered smart, or fashionable and prestigious, by many. In *Mansfield Park* a woman from elite London society declares that the clergy are nothing. She cites the inability to distinguish oneself in the profession; she could add that it did not offer the same possibility of riches as the others.

12. Army officer was the most prestigious of the professions. One reason was that traditionally it was the particular interest of the nobility, who in medieval times had been defined heavily by their military role. Moreover, it was less meritocratic, and thus more socially exclusive, than the navy. Edward's rejection of it as "too smart" probably plays on the word's meaning of sharp or severe (in reference to wounds) as well as fashionable.

13. By "the law" he means a barrister, the kind of lawyer who could try cases in court. Attorneys, who took care of property matters and constituted the majority of lawyers, were definitely not genteel.

14. The Inner Temple and Middle Temple were two of the four Inns of Court. Anyone wishing to be a barrister had to attend and pass the requirements of one, and many practicing barristers had chambers, or offices, near or in one of them, for they were congregated around the main courts in London.

15. *knowing:* stylish, chic.

16. *gigs:* open carriages pulled by one horse. They were less expensive and prestigious than curricles, but better ones could still allow someone of limited means, as a young lawyer usually would be, to dash around town in relative style—the single horse made them narrow and thus able to advance quickly through the tight spaces and heavy traffic of London. For a picture of a gig, see p. 191.

which my family approved.[17] As for the navy, it had fashion[18] on its side, but I was too old when the subject was first started to enter it[19]—and, at length, as there was no necessity for my having any profession at all, as I might be as dashing and expensive[20] without a red coat[21] on my back as with one, idleness was pronounced on the whole to be the most advantageous and honourable,[22] and a young man of eighteen is not in general so earnestly bent on being busy as to resist the solicitations of his friends to do nothing. I was therefore entered at Oxford and have been properly idle ever since."[23]

"The consequence of which, I suppose, will be," said Mrs. Dashwood, "since leisure has not promoted your own happiness, that your sons will be brought up to as many pursuits, employments, professions, and trades as Columella's."[24]

"They will be brought up," said he, in a serious accent,[25] "to be as unlike myself as is possible. In feeling, in action, in condition, in every thing."

"Come, come; this is all an effusion of immediate want of spirits, Edward. You are in a melancholy humour, and fancy that any one unlike yourself must be happy. But remember that the pain of parting from friends will be felt by every body at times, whatever be their education or state.[26] Know your own happiness. You want nothing but patience—or give it a more fascinating name, call it hope. Your mother will secure to you, in time, that independence you are so anxious for; it is her duty, and it will, it must ere long become her happiness to prevent your whole youth from being wasted in discontent. How much may not a few months do?"

"I think," replied Edward, "that I may defy many months to produce any good to me."

This desponding turn of mind, though it could not be communicated to Mrs. Dashwood,[27] gave additional pain to them all in the parting, which shortly took place, and left an uncomfortable impression on Elinor's feelings especially, which required some trouble and time to subdue. But as it was her determination to subdue it, and to prevent herself from appearing to suffer more than what all her family suffered on his going away, she did not

17. Really studying the law would involve immersion in some very abstruse matters. He probably means that his family approved of his becoming qualified as a barrister but being one only nominally. Qualifying was easy, for the Inns of Court imposed almost no formal study requirements, but attaining real success was difficult and usually took years of effort. Since Edward, as the eldest son, would eventually inherit the family estate, the idea could be for him simply to acquire the prestige of being a barrister, as well as perhaps a general familiarity with legal matters, which would be useful for someone in charge of an estate.

18. *fashion:* social prestige. "Fashion" and "fashionable" were used frequently then to denote the elite sections of society.

19. Aspiring naval officers generally went to sea between eleven and thirteen, or went to the naval academy around the same age.

20. *expensive:* given to lavish expenditure.

21. *red coat:* army uniform. Most army uniforms were red, and, being made partly for impressive and fashionable display, added to the prestige of the army.

22. Idleness was often looked on as honorable, or at least not especially dishonorable, in upper-class society. One reason was that the highest-ranking gentlemen were those whose wealthy estates freed them from any regular employment. Many such men would in fact put great effort into managing their estates, or into political activity, but it was not a necessity for them.

23. Oxford and Cambridge, the only two English universities then, had fairly loose academic requirements, and students there, especially the many upper-class ones, would often study very little. For more, see p. 675, note 9.

24. Columella is the title character of a 1779 novel by Richard Graves. Frustrated with his own idle life, he brings up his sons to a variety of professions.

25. *accent:* tone.

26. Mrs. Dashwood could be using "state" in the then-current sense of social status or position, which would pair it in some respects with education, or she could be using it in the modern sense of general condition or situation.

27. He could not transfer his despondence to her.

adopt the method so judiciously employed by Marianne, on a similar occasion, to augment and fix her sorrow, by seeking silence, solitude, and idleness. Their means were as different as their objects, and equally suited to the advancement of each.

Elinor sat down to her drawing-table[28] as soon as he was out of the house, busily employed herself the whole day, neither sought nor avoided the mention of his name, appeared to interest herself almost as much as ever in the general concerns of the family, and if, by this conduct, she did not lessen her own grief, it was at least prevented from unnecessary increase, and her mother and sisters were spared much solicitude on her account.

Such behaviour as this, so exactly the reverse of her own, appeared no more meritorious to Marianne, than her own had seemed faulty to her. The business of self-command she settled very easily;—with strong affections it was impossible, with calm ones it could have no merit. That her sister's affections *were* calm, she dared not deny, though she blushed to acknowledge it; and of the strength of her own, she gave a very striking proof, by still loving and respecting that sister, in spite of this mortifying conviction.[29]

Without shutting herself up from her family, or leaving the house in determined solitude to avoid them, or laying awake the whole night to indulge meditation, Elinor found every day afforded her leisure enough to think of Edward, and of Edward's behaviour, in every possible variety which the different state of her spirits at different times could produce;[30]—with tenderness, pity, approbation, censure, and doubt. There were moments in abundance, when, if not by the absence of her mother and sisters, at least by the nature of their employments, conversation was forbidden among them,[31] and every effect of solitude was produced. Her mind was inevitably at liberty; her thoughts could not be chained elsewhere; and the past and the future, on a subject so interesting, must be before her, must force her attention, and engross her memory, her reflection, and her fancy.

From a reverie of this kind, as she sat at her drawing-table, she was roused one morning, soon after Edward's leaving them, by

28. *drawing-table:* table whose top leaf could be tilted up to allow one to draw easily on it. It was often called a writing table, for the same feature would also allow people to write more easily on it. For an example, see picture below.

29. This, like so many incidents, shows both the good and bad of Marianne, her rigid and often unrealistic principles along with her genuine affection and benevolence. At the same time, her self-congratulation on her magnanimity is ironic, since Elinor is the one who will show magnanimity in doing everything she can to help her sister despite the latter's grave errors.

30. This shows there is no necessity to engage in contemplation for Marianne's more extreme actions.

31. Employments that could preclude conversation would be Marianne's music, Elinor's drawing, the reading all seem to enjoy, and the studying Margaret would still be young enough to pursue.

A drawing or writing table, with a tilted top to make those tasks easier; this one has a game board that can slide out.

[From *The Repository of arts, literature, fashions, manufactures, &c,* Vol. XI (1814), p. 115]

the arrival of company. She happened to be quite alone. The clos-
ing of the little gate, at the entrance of the green court in front of
the house, drew her eyes to the window, and she saw a large party
walking up to the door. Amongst them were Sir John and Lady
Middleton and Mrs. Jennings, but there were two others, a gentleman and lady, who were quite unknown to her. She was sitting
near the window, and as soon as Sir John perceived her, he left the
rest of the party to the ceremony of knocking at the door, and stepping across the turf,[32] obliged her to open the casement[33] to speak
to him, though the space was so short between the door and the
window, as to make it hardly possible to speak at one without
being heard at the other.

"Well," said he, "we have brought you some strangers. How do
you like them?"

"Hush! they will hear you."

"Never mind if they do. It is only the Palmers. Charlotte is very
pretty, I can tell you. You may see her if you look this way."

As Elinor was certain of seeing her in a couple of minutes, without taking that liberty, she begged to be excused.

"Where is Marianne? Has she run away because we are
come?[34] I see her instrument is open."[35]

"She is walking, I believe."

They were now joined by Mrs. Jennings, who had not patience
enough to wait till the door was opened before she told *her* story.
She came hallooing[36] to the window, "How do you do, my dear?
How does Mrs. Dashwood do? And where are your sisters? What!
all alone! you will be glad of a little company to sit with you. I
have brought my other son and daughter to see you. Only think of
their coming so suddenly! I thought I heard a carriage last night,
while we were drinking our tea, but it never entered my head that
it could be them. I thought of nothing but whether it might not be
Colonel Brandon come back again; so I said to Sir John, I do
think I heard a carriage; perhaps it is Colonel Brandon come back
again" —

Elinor was obliged to turn from her, in the middle of her story,
to receive the rest of the party;[37] Lady Middleton introduced the

32. The turf, or grass, of the green court in front of their house.

33. *casement*: casement window. Such windows, which open in or out using hinges, were the traditional type of window in England. During the eighteenth century they had been largely superseded by sash windows, which open up and down. This cottage was earlier described as fairly new, but because cottages were very traditional structures, there was a natural tendency to include older types of windows.

34. *are come*: have come.

35. The instrument is her piano. As mentioned earlier, the Middletons keep theirs not only closed but locked, thanks to the dangers posed by their children and the fact that Lady Middleton no longer plays (see p. 66, and 67, note 20). Thus he concludes that one that is open must have been just abandoned. In fact, Marianne, like the others, had earlier left Elinor alone.

36. *hallooing*: shouting in order to attract attention.

37. As the only resident of the house now present, she must play the hostess and greet those who are actually entering, in preference to someone speaking to her from outside the window.

two strangers;[38] Mrs. Dashwood and Margaret came down stairs at the same time, and they all sat down to look at one another, while Mrs. Jennings continued her story as she walked through the passage into the parlour, attended by Sir John.

Mrs. Palmer was several years younger than Lady Middleton, and totally unlike her in every respect. She was short and plump, had a very pretty face, and the finest expression of good humour in it that could possibly be.[39] Her manners were by no means so elegant as her sister's, but they were much more prepossessing. She came in with a smile, smiled all the time of her visit, except when she laughed, and smiled when she went away. Her husband was a grave looking young man of five or six and twenty, with an air of more fashion[40] and sense than his wife, but of less willingness to please or be pleased. He entered the room with a look of self-consequence,[41] slightly bowed to the ladies, without speaking a word, and, after briefly surveying them and their apartments,[42] took up a newspaper from the table and continued to read it as long as he staid.[43]

Mrs. Palmer, on the contrary, who was strongly endowed by nature with a turn for being uniformly civil and happy, was hardly seated before her admiration of the parlour and every thing in it burst forth.

"Well! what a delightful room this is! I never saw anything so charming! Only think, mama, how it is improved since I was here last! I always thought it such a sweet place, ma'am! (turning to Mrs. Dashwood,) but you have made it so charming! Only look, sister, how delightful every thing is! How I should like such a house for myself! Should not you, Mr. Palmer?"

Mr. Palmer made her no answer, and did not even raise his eyes from the newspaper.

"Mr. Palmer does not hear me," said she, laughing, "he never does sometimes. It is so ridiculous!"[44]

This was quite a new idea to Mrs. Dashwood, she had never been used to find wit[45] in the inattention of any one, and could not help looking with surprise at them both.

Mrs. Jennings, in the mean time, talked on as loud as she

38. Lady Middleton, unlike her husband and mother, has waited to come into the house before speaking, which would be proper etiquette.

39. In all these respects she is much more like her mother than Lady Middleton is.

40. *fashion:* elegance.

41. *self-consequence:* self-importance.

42. *apartments:* rooms.

43. Men are consistently shown in Jane Austen to be the more avid newspaper readers, probably because only men could vote or participate in politics. Mr. Palmer is soon described as running for Parliament, so he would have particular reason to read newspapers, though he may be turning to one now to avoid talking. Since he is visiting people he has never met before, his reading the newspaper the whole time, and never speaking to them, is a clear breach of good manners.

44. Of all the characters in the novel given much speaking time, the Palmers play the least significant role in the plot. They exist almost purely for comic relief, and in that respect also stand out somewhat in this novel, which is, with the possible exception of *Persuasion,* the least comical of Jane Austen's novels.

45. *wit:* the quality of being cleverly amusing.

could, and continued her account of their surprise, the evening before, on seeing their friends, without ceasing till every thing was told. Mrs. Palmer laughed heartily at the recollection of their astonishment, and every body agreed, two or three times over, that it had been quite an agreeable surprise.

"You may believe how glad we all were to see them," added Mrs. Jennings, leaning forwards towards Elinor, and speaking in a low voice as if she meant to be heard by no one else, though they were seated on different sides of the room; "but, however, I can't help wishing they had not travelled quite so fast, nor made such a long journey of it, for they came all round by London upon account of some business,[46] for you know (nodding significantly and pointing to her daughter) it was wrong in her situation. I wanted her to stay at home and rest this morning,[47] but she would come with us; she longed so much to see you all!"

Mrs. Palmer laughed, and said it would not do her any harm.

"She expects to be confined in February," continued Mrs. Jennings.[48]

Lady Middleton could no longer endure such a conversation, and therefore exerted herself to ask Mr. Palmer if there was any news in the paper.[49]

"No, none at all," he replied, and read on.

"Here comes Marianne," cried Sir John. "Now, Palmer, you shall see a monstrous[50] pretty girl."

He immediately went into the passage, opened the front door, and ushered her in himself. Mrs. Jennings asked her, as soon as she appeared, if she had not been to Allenham; and Mrs. Palmer laughed so heartily at the question, as to shew she understood it. Mr. Palmer looked up on her entering the room, stared at her some minutes, and then returned to his newspaper. Mrs. Palmer's eye was now caught by the drawings which hung round the room. She got up to examine them.

"Oh! dear, how beautiful these are! Well! how delightful! Do but look, mama, how sweet! I declare they are quite charming; I could look at them for ever." And then sitting down again, she very soon forgot that there were any such things in the room.[51]

46. Stopping in London would add substantially to their trip. The direct trip from the Palmers' residence in Somersetshire to Barton is later described as a "long day's journey" (p. 518), while the trip from Barton to London is more than two days (p. 296), and from London to the Palmers' residence more than one (see p. 595, note 12); for a further sense of the extremity of the detour, see maps on pp. 738 and 739. Thus such a trip would be rather reckless of Mr. Palmer, considering both the pains of travel and Mrs. Palmer's pregnancy (see next two notes), and would suggest more than simple rudeness in his treatment of his wife. It is possible, however, that they were in London, where they have a house, for a much longer period before traveling to Barton. Mrs. Palmer shortly explains that their trip here was "quite a sudden thing" that she did not know about until just before they left, which does not seem compatible with London's being a mere stopover on a trip from their Somersetshire home to Barton. Mrs. Jennings may have exaggerated the continuous nature of their journey, and thus its hardships, in order to have a good excuse to introduce the topic of pregnancy into the conversation.

47. Travel could be very hard on people, for the condition of carriages and roads produced bumpy rides. A journey of more than two days by Jane Austen and her mother left the latter "a good deal indisposed" and in need of rest and medicine (Oct. 27, 1798).

48. This means she is expecting a baby in February (it is now early November: see chronology, p. 713). When a woman gave birth, she began her confinement, or lying-in. During this period, which usually lasted a month or a little more, she was kept indoors and inactive, with a nurse to attend her if possible, to minimize the risks to her and the baby. Initially the mother would remain in bed, often shielded from strong light, and then, in gradual stages, she would be allowed to receive more visitors and move about.

49. Lady Middleton intervenes, which for her is an exertion, because pregnancy was in no way an acceptable topic of polite conversation. This is also why Mrs. Jennings makes a pretense of speaking lower to Elinor and first nodding toward her daughter to indicate her meaning.

50. *monstrous:* extremely. This was a popular slang term of the time. It is used only by unpolished characters like Sir John, Mrs. Jennings, and Mrs. Palmer.

51. Her reaction is similar to the affected taste for music Lady Middleton displayed earlier, though Mrs. Palmer's behavior seems less the result of a wish to display her socially approved good taste than the result of her general inclination to praise everything and everyone, regardless of whether she knows anything about the objects of her praise.

When Lady Middleton rose to go away, Mr. Palmer rose also, laid down the newspaper, stretched himself, and looked at them all round.

"My love, have you been asleep?" said his wife, laughing.

He made her no answer; and only observed, after again examining the room, that it was very low pitched, and that the ceiling was crooked. He then made his bow and departed with the rest.[52]

Sir John had been very urgent with them all to spend the next day at the park. Mrs. Dashwood, who did not chuse to dine with them oftener than they dined at the cottage, absolutely refused on her own account; her daughters might do as they pleased.[53] But they had no curiosity to see how Mr. and Mrs. Palmer ate their dinner,[54] and no expectation of pleasure from them in any other way. They attempted, therefore, likewise to excuse themselves; the weather was uncertain and not likely to be good.[55] But Sir John would not be satisfied—the carriage should be sent for them and they must come. Lady Middleton too, though she did not press their mother, pressed them. Mrs. Jennings and Mrs. Palmer joined their entreaties, all seemed equally anxious to avoid a family party;[56] and the young ladies were obliged to yield.

"Why should they ask us?" said Marianne, as soon as they were gone. "The rent of this cottage is said to be low; but we have it on very hard terms, if we are to dine at the park whenever any one is staying either with them, or with us."

"They mean no less to be civil and kind to us now," said Elinor,[57] "by these frequent invitations than by those which we received from them a few weeks ago. The alteration is not in them, if their parties are grown tedious and dull. We must look for the change elsewhere."[58]

52. His bow is a more formal gesture than most people would make on such an occasion.

53. Standard etiquette called for alternating dinner invitations. The Dashwoods' small dwelling and limited resources, as well as their lack of the Middleton family's avidity for social intercourse, probably keep them from inviting the Middletons too frequently, and Mrs. Dashwood, whose desire for independence has already been mentioned (p. 76), does not wish to accept more hospitality than she is extending. Since her daughters are not the ones offering hospitality as mistress of the house, such considerations matter less for them.

54. An invitation for the day would include dinner; since people were often occupied at home during the early part of the day, they would probably arrive midday or later, and dinner usually occurred around four or five o'clock.

55. Lacking a carriage they would have to walk, and on dirt roads and in long skirts. Hence rain would prevent them from going.

56. *family party*: gathering of only the family.

57. Elinor, while not necessarily liking the Middletons' officious invitations any more than Marianne, is able, unlike her sister, to appreciate the kind intentions behind them.

58. The change she means presumably comes from their recent romantic disappointments: Willoughby's mysterious departure and the uncertain affections Edward displayed during his visit. She may hope to provoke Marianne to reveal more of her situation with Willoughby.

Chapter Twenty

As the Miss Dashwoods entered the drawing-room of the park the next day, at one door, Mrs. Palmer came running in at the other, looking as good humoured and merry as before. She took them all most affectionately by the hand, and expressed great delight in seeing them again.

"I am so glad to see you!" said she, seating herself between Elinor and Marianne, "for it is so bad a day I was afraid you might not come, which would be a shocking thing, as we go away again to-morrow. We must go, for the Westons come to us next week you know. It was quite a sudden thing our coming at all, and I knew nothing of it till the carriage was coming to the door, and then Mr. Palmer asked me if I would go with him to Barton. He is so droll! He never tells me any thing! I am so sorry we cannot stay longer; however we shall meet again in town[1] very soon, I hope."

They were obliged to put an end to such an expectation.

"Not go to town!" cried Mrs. Palmer, with a laugh, "I shall be quite disappointed if you do not. I could get the nicest house in the world for you, next door to our's, in Hanover-square.[2] You must come, indeed. I am sure I shall be very happy to chaperon you at any time till I am confined, if Mrs. Dashwood should not like to go into public."[3]

They thanked her; but were obliged to resist all her entreaties.

"Oh! my love," cried Mrs. Palmer to her husband, who just then entered the room—"You must help me to persuade the Miss Dashwoods to go to town this winter."[4]

Her love made no answer; and after slightly bowing to the ladies, began complaining of the weather.

"How horrid all this is!" said he. "Such weather makes every thing and every body disgusting.[5] Dulness is as much produced within doors as without, by rain. It makes one detest all one's

1. *town:* London.

2. *Hanover-square:* a square, built in the early eighteenth century, in May-fair, the wealthiest and most fashionable section of London at the time. (For more, see p. 315, note 23, and map, p. 742.) A London house in such an area, along with his country house, would indicate a fair amount of wealth on Mr. Palmer's part, for London houses cost a lot to buy and maintain.

3. Single women in London would need to be chaperoned, especially to any social events. Mrs. Palmer, though probably not much older than Elinor, could perform that function because she is married.

4. Winter was the season when wealthy people from the country flocked to London.

5. *disgusting:* distasteful.

Hanover Square in London, the residence of the Palmers.
[From E. Beresford Chancellor, *The XVIIIth Century in London* (New York, 1921), p. 251]

acquaintance. What the devil does Sir John mean by not having a billiard room in his house?[6] How few people know what comfort is! Sir John is as stupid[7] as the weather."

The rest of the company soon dropt in.

"I am afraid, Miss Marianne," said Sir John, "you have not been able to take your usual walk to Allenham to-day."

Marianne looked very grave and said nothing.

"Oh! don't be so sly[8] before us," said Mrs. Palmer; "for we know all about it, I assure you; and I admire your taste very much, for I think he is extremely handsome. We do not live a great way from him in the country, you know. Not above ten miles, I dare say."

"Much nearer thirty," said her husband.

"Ah! well! there is not much difference.[9] I never was at his house; but they say it is a sweet pretty place."

"As vile a spot as I ever saw in my life," said Mr. Palmer.

Marianne remained perfectly silent, though her countenance betrayed her interest in what was said.

"Is it very ugly?" continued Mrs. Palmer—"then it must be some other place that is so pretty I suppose."

When they were seated in the dining room, Sir John observed with regret that they were only eight all together.

"My dear," said he to his lady, "it is very provoking that we should be so few. Why did not you ask the Gilberts to come to us to-day?"[10]

"Did not I tell you, Sir John,[11] when you spoke to me about it before, that it could not be done? They dined with us last."[12]

"You and I, Sir John," said Mrs. Jennings, "should not stand upon such ceremony."

"Then you would be very ill-bred,"[13] cried Mr. Palmer.

"My love, you contradict every body,"—said his wife with her usual laugh. "Do you know that you are quite rude?"[14]

"I did not know I contradicted any body in calling your mother ill-bred."

"Aye, you may abuse me as you please," said the good-natured old lady, "you have taken Charlotte off my hands, and cannot give her back again. So there I have the whip hand of[15] you."

6. Billiard tables had become increasingly fashionable in this period, and many country houses had billiard rooms. The title house in *Mansfield Park* does, as did that of Jane Austen's wealthy brother Edward. In a letter from a visit there she declares, "It draws all the gentlemen to it whenever they are within, especially after dinner, so that my B^r Fanny & I have the Library to ourselves in delightful quiet" (Oct. 14, 1813). Sir John's lack of a billiard room may result from his own love of outdoor sports, combined with his interest in being with as much company as possible when indoors. Mr. Palmer's surprise may also reflect his own possibly wealthier background (see note 2 above), for the grander the house the more likely such specialized rooms were. Later, when at his own home, he devotes much of his time to billiards (p. 568).

7. *stupid:* tiresome.

8. *sly:* secretive.

9. This would be a tremendous difference. If the local roads were of reasonable quality, one might cover ten miles in two hours, making occasional visits for the day feasible. Thirty miles would rule that out.

10. As the mistress of the house, Lady Middleton would be the one to issue invitations.

11. Married couples often used such formal designations when speaking to each other.

12. As already mentioned, standard etiquette dictated alternating invitations.

13. *ill-bred:* lacking in manners.

14. His wife's justifiable criticism of his rudeness stands in ironic contrast to his own criticism of Mrs. Jennings's lack of manners. In his behavior Mr. Palmer shows a curious combination of formal correctness, as seen in his bowing both when leaving the Dashwoods and when they arrived here, and indifference to any idea of acting affably toward others.

15. *the whip hand of:* the advantage over.

Charlotte laughed heartily to think that her husband could not get rid of her; and exultingly said, she did not care how cross he was to her, as they must live together.[16] It was impossible for any one to be more thoroughly good-natured, or more determined to be happy than Mrs. Palmer. The studied indifference, insolence, and discontent of her husband gave her no pain: and when he scolded or abused her, she was highly diverted.

"Mr. Palmer is so droll!" said she, in a whisper, to Elinor. "He is always out of humour."

Elinor was not inclined, after a little observation, to give him credit for being so genuinely and unaffectedly ill-natured or ill-bred as he wished to appear. His temper might perhaps be a little soured by finding, like many others of his sex, that through some unaccountable bias in favour of beauty, he was the husband of a very silly woman,—but she knew that this kind of blunder was too common for any sensible man to be lastingly hurt by it.[17]—It was rather a wish of distinction she believed, which produced his contemptuous treatment of every body, and his general abuse of every thing before him. It was the desire of appearing superior to other people. The motive was too common to be wondered at; but the means, however they might succeed by establishing his superiority in ill-breeding, were not likely to attach any one to him except his wife.

"Oh! my dear Miss Dashwood," said Mrs. Palmer soon afterwards, "I have got such a favour to ask of you and your sister. Will you come and spend some time at Cleveland this Christmas? Now, pray do,—and come while the Westons are with us. You cannot think how happy I shall be! It will be quite delightful!—My love," applying to her husband, "don't you long to have the Miss Dashwoods come to Cleveland?"

"Certainly,"—he replied with a sneer—"I came into Devonshire with no other view."

"There now"—said his lady, "you see Mr. Palmer expects you; so you cannot refuse to come."

They both eagerly and resolutely declined her invitation.

"But indeed you must and shall come. I am sure you will like it

16. Divorce was impossible to attain at this time, except under very unusual circumstances, so they are stuck with each other until one dies.

17. Mr. Bennet of *Pride and Prejudice* represents another intelligent man who has married a pretty but silly woman, and who after marriage disdains his wife and takes refuge in silence and sarcasm (Mr. Bennet has the advantage of being more amusing and less openly rude and contemptuous toward others). The wording of this passage suggests it to be a phenomenon the author witnessed frequently. At the same time, in *Northanger Abbey* she underlines the point made here, that a truly sensible man would not be significantly altered by a bad marital choice, for in it Mr. Allen shows consistent good humor and politeness even though he has a wife at least as vacuous as Mrs. Palmer.

of all things. The Westons will be with us, and it will be quite delightful. You cannot think what a sweet place Cleveland is; and we are so gay now, for Mr. Palmer is always going about the country canvassing against[18] the election; and so many people come to dine with us that I never saw before, it is quite charming![19] But, poor fellow! it is very fatiguing to him! for he is forced to make every body like him."

Elinor could hardly keep her countenance[20] as she assented to the hardship of such an obligation.

"How charming it will be," said Charlotte, "when he is in Parliament!—won't it? How I shall laugh! It will be so ridiculous to see all his letters directed to him with an M.P.[21]—But do you know, he says, he will never frank for me?[22] He declares he won't. Don't you, Mr. Palmer?"

Mr. Palmer took no notice of her.

"He cannot bear writing, you know," she continued—"he says it is quite shocking."

"No"; said he, "I never said any thing so irrational. Don't palm all your abuses of language upon me."

"There now; you see how droll he is. This is always the way with him! Sometimes he won't speak to me for half a day together, and then he comes out with something so droll—all about any thing in the world."

She surprised Elinor very much as they returned into the drawing-room by asking her whether she did not like Mr. Palmer excessively.[23]

"Certainly"; said Elinor, "he seems very agreeable."

"Well—I am so glad you do. I thought you would, he is so pleasant; and Mr. Palmer is excessively pleased with you and your sisters I can tell you, and you can't think how disappointed he will be if you don't come to Cleveland.—I can't imagine why you should object to it."

Elinor was again obliged to decline her invitation; and by changing the subject, put a stop to her entreaties. She thought it probable that as they lived in the same county, Mrs. Palmer might be able to give some more particular account of Willoughby's

18. *canvassing against:* campaigning for.

19. Mr. Palmer is running for election to the House of Commons, the larger and more important of the two houses of Parliament (the other was the House of Lords, which at this time still had genuine power). In England, which comprised the majority of the United Kingdom and which dominated Parliament, members were elected either as representatives of entire counties or, more frequently, as representatives of specific boroughs, which differed greatly in size and in qualifications for voting. Mr. Palmer is almost certainly campaigning for a borough seat, because campaigns for county seats were so expensive that they were mostly the province of the high aristocracy. Campaigns for boroughs could also cost a lot, a cost that usually included offering various types of hospitality to voters. This is why so many people now come to dine with the Palmers. For a contemporary picture of a debate in the House of Commons, see p. 219.

20. *keep her countenance:* maintain a straight face.

21. *M.P.:* Member of Parliament. A member would have this placed after his name in formal designations.

22. One privilege of members of Parliament and other important government officials was to frank letters, which meant signing them and getting them sent free of charge. Since postage was expensive—one reason being that the government used the postal service as a source of revenue—the privilege was frequently abused, with friends of the member often using his frank. In a letter Jane Austen, while visiting her brother, mentions a visitor who is a member of Parliament and writes, "If I can, I will get a frank from him & write to you all the sooner" (Oct. 11, 1813). Mr. Palmer's stated refusal to frank for his wife would be very unusual. He may have simply said that to annoy her, or he may happen to be extremely punctilious about obeying the rules, which forbade anyone except the member or official himself from using the frank.

23. The ladies have withdrawn after dinner, leaving the men in the dining room (the term "drawing room" derives from "withdrawing").

general character,[24] than could be gathered from the Middletons' partial acquaintance with him; and she was eager to gain from any one, such a confirmation of his merits as might remove the possibility of fear for Marianne. She began by inquiring if they saw much of Mr. Willoughby at Cleveland, and whether they were intimately acquainted with him.

"Oh! dear, yes; I know him extremely well," replied Mrs. Palmer—"Not that I ever spoke to him indeed; but I have seen him for ever in town. Somehow or other I never happened to be staying at Barton while he was at Allenham. Mama saw him here once before;—but I was with my uncle at Weymouth.[25] However, I dare say we should have seen a great deal of him in Somersetshire, if it had not happened very unluckily that we should never have been in the country[26] together. He is very little at Combe, I believe; but if he were ever so much there, I do not think Mr. Palmer would visit him, for he is in the opposition you know,[27] and besides it is such a way off. I know why you inquire about him, very well; your sister is to marry him. I am monstrous glad of it, for then I shall have her for a neighbour you know."

"Upon my word," replied Elinor, "you know much more of the matter than I do, if you have any reason to expect such a match."

"Don't pretend to deny it, because you know it is what every body talks of. I assure you I heard of it in my way through town."

"My dear Mrs. Palmer!"

"Upon my honour I did.—I met Colonel Brandon Monday morning in Bond-street,[28] just before we left town, and he told me of it directly."

"You surprise me very much. Colonel Brandon tell you of it! Surely you must be mistaken. To give such intelligence to a person who could not be interested in it, even if it were true, is not what I should expect Colonel Brandon to do."

"But I do assure you it was so, for all that, and I will tell you how it happened. When we met him, he turned back and walked with us; and so we began talking of my brother and sister, and one thing and another, and I said to him, 'So, Colonel, there is a new family come to Barton cottage, I hear, and mama sends me word

24. *character:* reputation.

25. Weymouth is a seaside town in Dorsetshire, a county east of Devonshire and southeast of Somersetshire, that had developed into a popular resort in the eighteenth century (see map, p. 739). Two characters in *Emma* meet and become engaged when both are on vacation there. Bathing, or swimming, in the sea had become very popular, both for health and recreation, and many towns along the English coast, especially the southern coast, grew and prospered from the influx of visitors. Jane Austen's last, uncompleted novel, *Sanditon*, satirizes aspects of this popularity, though she herself took several trips to resorts along the sea and enjoyed them.

26. *country:* county. For the location of Somersetshire, see map, p. 739.

27. At this time Britain was dominated by the Tories, who had been, along with the Whigs, one of the two major political camps since the seventeenth century. The principal issues dividing the country during this period were the war with Napoleonic France, which had lasted almost twenty years by this point, and increased political and legal rights for Catholics: the Tories, in contrast to the Whigs, favored vigorous prosecution of the former and opposed the latter, and these positions were supported by both the monarch and the majority of the public. Neither group, however, had a well-developed party organization (that would not happen until a little later in the century) and both were split into various factions. Thus other labels besides Tory and Whig were often used. Moreover, disgust with both groups, which were particularly fragmented and disputatious during these years, caused many people to speak simply of the party in power and the opposition, without dignifying either with a party label. The Tories derived much of their support from the country gentry, the class including most of the characters in this novel, while the Whigs were heavily based in the smaller but higher-ranking aristocracy. It would make more sense for Willoughby to belong to the Whigs than Mr. Palmer, since the former has strong connections in London, where the aristocracy was centered. One cannot be certain, however, that Mrs. Palmer's information about Willoughby is correct, since so much of what she says is inaccurate, including her statements about both the location and the character of Willoughby's home.

28. *Bond-street:* a main street in the Mayfair section of London where Mrs. Palmer has a house. It was one of the principal shopping venues in London at the time, so it would be a logical place for her to meet Colonel Brandon. Later in the novel, when various characters are in London, several chance encounters occur in Bond Street.

they are very pretty, and that one of them is going to be married to Mr. Willoughby of Combe Magna. Is it true, pray? for of course you must know, as you have been in Devonshire so lately.' "

"And what did the Colonel say?"

"Oh!—he did not say much; but he looked as if he knew it to be true, so from that moment I set it down as certain. It will be quite delightful, I declare! When is it to take place?"

"Mr. Brandon was very well I hope."

"Oh! yes, quite well; and so full of your praises, he did nothing but say fine things of you."

"I am flattered by his commendation. He seems an excellent man; and I think him uncommonly pleasing."

"So do I.—He is such a charming man, that it is quite a pity he should be so grave and so dull.[29] Mama says *he* was in love with your sister too.—I assure you it was a great compliment if he was, for he hardly ever falls in love with any body."

"Is Mr. Willoughby much known in your part of Somerset-shire?" said Elinor.

"Oh! yes, extremely well; that is, I do not believe many people are acquainted with him, because Combe Magna is so far off; but they all think him extremely agreeable I assure you. Nobody is more liked than Mr. Willoughby wherever he goes, and so you may tell your sister. She is a monstrous lucky girl to get him, upon my honour; not but that he is much more lucky in getting her, because she is so very handsome and agreeable, that nothing can be good enough for her. However I don't think her hardly at all handsomer than you, I assure you; for I think you both excessively pretty, and so does Mr. Palmer too I am sure, though we could not get him to own[30] it last night."

Mrs. Palmer's information respecting Willoughby was not very material; but any testimony in his favour, however small, was pleasing to her.

"I am so glad we are got acquainted at last," continued Charlotte.—"And now I hope we shall always be great friends. You can't think how much I longed to see you! It is so delightful that you should live at the cottage! Nothing can be like it to be sure!

29. *dull*: sad.

30. *own*: acknowledge, confess.

The House of Commons.

[From Fiona St. Aubyn, *Ackermann's Illustrated London*; illustrations by Augustus Pugin and Thomas Rowlandson (Ware, 1985), p. 37]

And I am so glad your sister is going to be well married! I hope you will be a great deal at Combe Magna. It is a sweet place by all accounts."[31]

"You have been long acquainted with Colonel Brandon, have not you?"

"Yes, a great while; ever since my sister married. — He was a particular friend of Sir John's. I believe," she added in a low voice, "he would have been very glad to have had me, if he could. Sir John and Lady Middleton wished it very much. But mama did not think the match good enough for me,[32] otherwise Sir John would have mentioned it to the Colonel, and we should have been married immediately."

"Did not Colonel Brandon know of Sir John's proposal to your mother before it was made? Had he never owned his affection to yourself?"

"Oh! no; but if mama had not objected to it, I dare say he would have liked it of all things. He had not seen me then above twice, for it was before I left school.[33] However I am much happier as I am. Mr. Palmer is just the kind of man I like."

31. Her husband, who has seen it, just called it a vile spot.

32. This is extremely unlikely. Mrs. Jennings is not snobbish at all and consistently shows a great fondness for Colonel Brandon, so it is hard to imagine her rejecting him as a husband for her daughter. Moreover, even if Colonel Brandon is less wealthy than Mr. Palmer, he still has a fine fortune and his rank as a colonel gives him added social prestige.

33. Most girls from wealthy families went to school for a while, though this varied greatly from family to family. There were no educational requirements by law at the time and no generally agreed upon curriculum, especially in the case of girls, whose schooling was considered less important than boys'. Jane Austen had little formal schooling, though her family placed a great value on education and reading and encouraged her literary interests.

Chapter Twenty-one

*T*he Palmers returned to Cleveland the next day, and the two families at Barton were again left to entertain each other. But this did not last long; Elinor had hardly got their last visitors out of her head, had hardly done wondering at Charlotte's being so happy without a cause, at Mr. Palmer's acting so simply,[1] with good abilities,[2] and at the strange unsuitableness which often existed between husband and wife, before Sir John's and Mrs. Jennings's active zeal in the cause of society, procured her some other new acquaintance to see and observe.

In a morning's excursion to Exeter,[3] they had met with two young ladies, whom Mrs. Jennings had the satisfaction of discovering to be her relations, and this was enough for Sir John to invite them directly to the park, as soon as their present engagements at Exeter were over. Their engagements at Exeter instantly gave way before such an invitation,[5] and Lady Middleton was thrown into no little alarm on the return of Sir John, by hearing that she was very soon to receive a visit from two girls whom she had never seen in her life, and of whose elegance,—whose tolerable gentility even,[6] she could have no proof; for the assurances of her husband and mother on that subject went for nothing at all. Their being her relations too made it so much the worse; and Mrs. Jennings's attempts at consolation were therefore unfortunately founded, when she advised her daughter not to care about their being so fashionable;[7] because they were all cousins and must put up with one another. As it was impossible however now to prevent their coming, Lady Middleton resigned herself to the idea of it, with all the philosophy[8] of a well bred woman, contenting herself with merely giving her husband a gentle reprimand on the subject five or six times every day.

The young ladies arrived, their appearance was by no means

1.   *simply:* foolishly.

2.   *abilities:* mental abilities or endowments.

3.   Since Barton is only four miles from Exeter it would be easy for them to go there for the day, or even part of the day.

4.   *discovering:* revealing, disclosing.

5.   It is likely that those they are staying with at Exeter are of lower social rank. Provincial towns contained local commercial elites and professionals, but usually not many who were truly genteel, for the latter generally resided in the country, or in London or a few other popular resort towns such as Bath.

6.   The distinction between gentility and elegance is often found in Jane Austen. The first means membership in the genteel class and the possession of its basic manners, bearing, dress, and speech (it could also refer to higher moral standards associated with that class, but it is doubtful if that is uppermost in Lady Middleton's mind). The second is something above simple gentility, for it means having a special grace and refinement that only some, even of the highest social ranks, possess.

7.   That is, not to care whether they are of high rank or background.

8.   *philosophy:* philosophical acceptance.

ungenteel or unfashionable. Their dress was very smart, their manners very civil, they were delighted with the house, and in raptures with the furniture,[9] and they happened to be so doatingly fond of children that Lady Middleton's good opinion was engaged in their favour before they had been an hour at the Park. She declared them to be very agreeable girls indeed, which for her ladyship was enthusiastic admiration. Sir John's confidence in his own judgment rose with this animated praise, and he set off directly for the cottage to tell the Miss Dashwoods of the Miss Steeles' arrival, and to assure them of their being the sweetest girls in the world. From such commendation as this, however, there was not much to be learned; Elinor well knew that the sweetest girls in the world were to be met with in every part of England,[10] under every possible variation of form,[11] face, temper, and understanding.[12] Sir John wanted the whole family to walk to the Park directly and look at his guests. Benevolent, philanthropic man! It was painful to him even to keep a third cousin to himself.

"Do come now," said he—"pray come—you must come—I declare you shall come—You can't think how you will like them. Lucy is monstrous pretty, and so good humoured and agreeable! The children are all hanging about her already, as if she was an old acquaintance. And they both long to see you of all things, for they have heard at Exeter that you are the most beautiful creatures in the world; and I have told them it is all very true, and a great deal more. You will be delighted with them I am sure. They have brought the whole coach full of playthings for the children. How can you be so cross as not to come? Why they are your cousins, you know, after a fashion. You are my cousins, and they are my wife's, so you must be related."

But Sir John could not prevail. He could only obtain a promise of their calling at the Park within a day or two, and then left them in amazement at their indifference, to walk home and boast anew of their attractions to the Miss Steeles, as he had been already boasting of the Miss Steeles to them.[13]

When their promised visit to the Park and consequent introduction to these young ladies took place, they found in the appearance

9. *furniture:* furnishings. The term often had a wider meaning then, and in this case it means the Miss Steeles are praising all aspects of the house's interior.

10. Fulsome praise of young ladies is a common practice in Jane Austen's novels. In *Northanger Abbey* a foolish young woman is particularly fond of labeling others the "sweetest creatures," including two girls she met only earlier that day and another about whom she admits, after singing her praises, "there is something amazingly insipid about her."

11. *form:* bodily figure.

12. *temper, and understanding:* emotional and intellectual qualities. Hence the list refers to all important characteristics of a person.

13. Even as Sir John frequently pesters others, often annoyingly, to join in his gatherings, he does not hold it against them when they refuse.

of the eldest, who was nearly thirty, with a very plain and not a sensible face, nothing to admire; but in the other, who was not more than two or three and twenty, they acknowledged considerable beauty; her features were pretty, and she had a sharp quick eye, and a smartness of air,[14] which though it did not give actual elegance or grace, gave distinction to her person.—Their manners were particularly civil, and Elinor soon allowed them credit for some kind of sense, when she saw with what constant and judicious attentions they were making themselves agreeable to Lady Middleton. With her children they were in continual raptures, extolling their beauty, courting their notice, and humouring all their whims; and such of their time as could be spared from the importunate demands which this politeness made on it, was spent in admiration of whatever her ladyship was doing, if she happened to be doing any thing,[15] or in taking patterns of some elegant new dress,[16] in which her appearance the day before had thrown them into unceasing delight. Fortunately for those who pay their court through such foibles, a fond mother, though, in pursuit of praise for her children, the most rapacious of human beings, is likewise the most credulous; her demands are exorbitant; but she will swallow any thing; and the excessive affection and endurance of the Miss Steeles towards her offspring, were viewed therefore by Lady Middleton without the smallest surprise or distrust. She saw with maternal complacency all the impertinent incroachments and mischievous tricks to which her cousins submitted. She saw their sashes untied,[17] their hair pulled about their ears,[18] their workbags[19] searched, and their knives and scissars stolen away,[20] and felt no doubt of its being a reciprocal enjoyment. It suggested no other surprise than that Elinor and Marianne should sit so composedly by, without claiming a share in what was passing.

"John[21] is in such spirits to-day!" said she, on his taking Miss Steele's pocket handkerchief, and throwing it out of window— "He is full of monkey tricks."

And soon afterwards, on the second boy's violently pinching one of the same lady's fingers, she fondly observed, "How playful William is!"

14. *smartness of air:* stylish appearance and manner.

15. These attempts to praise Lady Middleton's only occasional activities signal the desperate nature of their flattery.

16. At this time people generally did not have access to printed patterns for clothing, so they often would take the patterns of other people's dress (a term that could mean various articles of clothing then). Jane Austen refers in her letters to taking patterns of items owned by others.

17. Women frequently wore sashes around their waists then. For an example of a contemporary dress with a prominent sash, see p. 237.

18. Since women's hair was always pinned up, this would loosen their hair and force them to rearrange it later.

19. *work-bags:* bags for embroidery materials and tools. They were made of cloth and could be pulled together at the top to close. Ladies would often carry these with them when visiting to allow them to embroider in company with others.

20. The knives and scissors would be used for embroidery.

21. The eldest boy has been named after his father, a standard practice then.

"And here is my sweet little Annamaria,"[22] she added, tenderly caressing a little girl of three years old, who had not made a noise for the last two minutes; "And she is always so gentle and quiet— Never was there such a quiet little thing!"

But unfortunately in bestowing these embraces, a pin in her ladyship's head dress slightly scratching the child's neck,[23] produced from this pattern of gentleness, such violent screams, as could hardly be outdone by any creature professedly noisy. The mother's consternation was excessive; but it could not surpass the alarm of the Miss Steeles, and every thing was done by all three, in so critical an emergency, which affection could suggest as likely to assuage the agonies of the little sufferer. She was seated in her mother's lap, covered with kisses, her wound bathed with lavender-water,[24] by one of the Miss Steeles, who was on her knees to attend her, and her mouth stuffed with sugar plums[25] by the other. With such a reward for her tears, the child was too wise to cease crying. She still screamed and sobbed lustily, kicked her two brothers for offering to touch her, and all their united soothings were ineffectual till Lady Middleton luckily remembering that in a scene of similar distress last week, some apricot marmalade[26] had been successfully applied for a bruised temple, the same remedy was eagerly proposed for this unfortunate scratch, and a slight intermission of screams in the young lady on hearing it, gave them reason to hope that it would not be rejected.[27]—She was carried out of the room therefore in her mother's arms, in quest of this medicine, and as the two boys chose to follow, though earnestly entreated by their mother to stay behind, the four young ladies were left in a quietness which the room had not known for many hours.

"Poor little creature!" said Miss Steele, as soon as they were gone. "It might have been a very sad accident."

"Yet I hardly know how," cried Marianne, "unless it had been under totally different circumstances. But this is the usual way of heightening alarm, where there is nothing to be alarmed at in reality."

"What a sweet woman Lady Middleton is!" said Lucy Steele.[28]

22. She is presumably the third child and the oldest girl—four children are mentioned for the Middletons, but since the oldest is only six (p. 58), the fourth child, who is never described, is probably a baby. The eldest girl was frequently named after her mother, a procedure not followed here, since Lady Middleton's name is Mary (p. 308). It is possible another close female relative, such as Sir John's mother, is named Anne or Anna and they decided on Annamaria as a way of combining the two names. Over the last century female names ending in "a," which marked them as not being traditional English names and as likely deriving from Latin or Italian, had grown significantly in popularity. Their use in Jane Austen is sometimes a mark of pretension on the part of the family, and the double name of Annamaria, virtually the only such in Austen, is probably meant to signal Lady Middleton's affectation.

23. Women always wore something on their heads, and many, especially wealthy and fashionable women, had elaborate headdresses (for examples, see pictures on pp. 235 and 499). They would often be held together with pins, and since safety pins had not yet been invented, these pins could easily scratch someone too close to the headdress.

24. *lavender-water:* a liquid distilled from lavender flowers that could be used as a perfume or as a medicine for various ailments, either applied externally as here or swallowed.

25. *sugar plums:* small sweets made from boiled sugar and some added flavoring.

26. Apricots were a popular source for marmalade, which was usually eaten as a dessert after dinner.

27. The extreme solicitude shown toward the children here was not that unusual then. Many wealthy parents at this time were fairly indulgent toward their children, though most did not go as far as Lady Middleton.

28. Lucy is distinguished from Miss Steele, indicating that she is younger. Lucy is probably switching to praise of Lady Middleton because her sister's attempt to show her concern for the child met with such a blunt rejoinder from Marianne.

Marianne was silent; it was impossible for her to say what she did not feel, however trivial the occasion; and upon Elinor therefore the whole task of telling lies when politeness required it, always fell. She did her best when thus called on, by speaking of Lady Middleton with more warmth than she felt, though with far less than Miss Lucy.[29]

"And Sir John too," cried the elder sister, "what a charming man he is!"

Here too, Miss Dashwood's commendation, being only simple and just, came in without any eclat.[30] She merely observed that he was perfectly good humoured and friendly.[31]

"And what a charming little family they have! I never saw such fine children in my life.—I declare I quite doat upon them already, and indeed I am always distractedly fond of children."

"I should guess so," said Elinor with a smile, "from what I have witnessed this morning."

"I have a notion," said Lucy, "you think the little Middletons rather too much indulged; perhaps they may be the outside of enough; but it is so natural in Lady Middleton; and for my part, I love to see children full of life and spirits; I cannot bear them if they are tame and quiet."

"I confess," replied Elinor, "that while I am at Barton Park, I never think of tame and quiet children with any abhorrence."

A short pause succeeded this speech, which was first broken by Miss Steele, who seemed very much disposed for conversation, and who now said rather abruptly, "And how do you like Devonshire, Miss Dashwood? I suppose you were very sorry to leave Sussex."

In some surprise at the familiarity of this question, or at least of the manner in which it was spoken,[32] Elinor replied that she was.

"Norland is a prodigious beautiful place, is not it?" added Miss Steele.

"We have heard Sir John admire it excessively," said Lucy,[33] who seemed to think some apology necessary for the freedom[34] of her sister.

"I think every one *must* admire it," replied Elinor, "who ever

29. The issue of how to balance truthfulness and the demands of courtesy often arises in Jane Austen, and her leading characters, committed to both principles, often struggle with it. In general she favors a moderate course. Elinor clearly represents a reasonably happy mean between Marianne's refusal ever to dissemble, even if it means insulting others, and the Miss Steeles' insincere flattery. A further distinction between Elinor and the Miss Steeles is that Elinor's falsehoods or evasions are done to avoid hurting others' feelings, while their mendacity is designed to win the favor of those who might benefit them. They, especially Lucy, will show themselves willing to say unpleasant things to those who are not in a position to confer any benefits.

30. *eclat:* show, acclamation.

31. Elinor is able to satisfy the conflicting demands of truth and politeness fairly well by concentrating on praiseworthy aspects of Sir John's character and omitting any reference to others.

32. It would be considered impolite to ask people you had just met such direct personal questions.

33. In the next chapter Lucy will reveal her reason for not wishing others to learn of her and her sister's familiarity with Norland. Thus she tries to explain it away with a reference to Sir John, though in fact he is unlikely to have ever seen Norland, for his only visit to the Dashwoods came before they had moved there (p. 56).

34. *freedom:* excessive familiarity, overstepping of the normal bounds of conversation.

saw the place; though it is not to be supposed that any one can estimate its beauties as we do."

"And had you a great many smart beaux[35] there? I suppose you have not so many in this part of the world; for my part, I think they are a vast addition always."

"But why should you think," said Lucy, looking ashamed of her sister, "that there are not as many genteel young men in Devonshire as Sussex?"

"Nay, my dear, I'm sure I don't pretend to say that there an't. I'm sure there's a vast many smart beaux in Exeter; but you know, how could I tell what smart beaux there might be about Norland; and I was only afraid the Miss Dashwoods might find it dull at Barton, if they had not so many as they used to have. But perhaps you young ladies may not care about the beaux, and had as lief[36] be without them as with them. For my part, I think they are vastly agreeable, provided they dress smart and behave civil. But I can't bear to see them dirty and nasty. Now there's Mr. Rose at Exeter, a prodigious smart young man, quite a beau, clerk to Mr. Simpson you know,[37] and yet if you do but meet him of a morning, he is not fit to be seen. — I suppose your brother was quite a beau, Miss Dashwood, before he married, as he was so rich?"[38]

"Upon my word," replied Elinor, "I cannot tell you, for I do not perfectly comprehend the meaning of the word. But this I can say, that if he ever was a beau before he married, he is one still, for there is not the smallest alteration in him."

"Oh! dear! one never thinks of married men's being beaux — they have something else to do."

"Lord! Anne," cried her sister, "you can talk of nothing but beaux; — you will make Miss Dashwood believe you think of nothing else." And then to turn the discourse,[39] she began admiring the house and the furniture.

This specimen of the Miss Steeles was enough. The vulgar freedom and folly of the eldest left her no recommendation, and as Elinor was not blinded by the beauty, or the shrewd look of the youngest, to her want of real elegance and artlessness,[40] she left the house without any wish of knowing them better.

35. *beaux:* sweethearts, lovers. It could also mean fashionable men, though Miss Steele is probably using it in the first sense. The only characters who use the term in Jane Austen are vulgar or affected.

36. *lief:* gladly.

37. Mr. Simpson is probably an attorney; "clerk" would refer to his assistant. It could also refer to someone else working in a subordinate position in a business or office. In whatever case, he has relatively low status, for attorneys and businessmen were not considered genteel, and their clerks would be of even lesser standing. Miss Steele's obviously regarding him as a potential mate indicates the Steeles' lower social origins, for people in this society would generally know only people of their own rank.

38. Miss Steele's language reveals her vulgarity, not just by her subject matter but also by her poor grammar (as in the use of "an't" and of "vast" and "civil" as adverbs), her harping on the same points, and her constant use of the same pet terms, here and elsewhere, "beaux," "smart," "vastly," and "prodigious."

39. *turn the discourse:* redirect the conversation.

40. *artlessness:* naturalness, freedom from artificiality.

Not so, the Miss Steeles.—They came from Exeter, well provided with admiration for the use[41] of Sir John Middleton, his
family, and all his relations, and no niggardly proportion was now
dealt out to his fair cousins, whom they declared to be the most
beautiful, elegant, accomplished and agreeable girls they had
ever beheld, and with whom they were particularly anxious to be
better acquainted.—And to be better acquainted therefore, Elinor
soon found was their inevitable lot, for as Sir John was entirely on
the side of the Miss Steeles, their party would be too strong for
opposition, and that kind of intimacy must be submitted to, which
consists of sitting an hour or two together in the same room
almost every day. Sir John could do no more; but he did not know
that any more was required; to be together was, in his opinion, to
be intimate, and while his continual schemes for their meeting
were effectual, he had not a doubt of their being established
friends.

To do him justice, he did every thing in his power to promote
their unreserve, by making the Miss Steeles acquainted with
whatever he knew or supposed of his cousins' situations in the
most delicate particulars,—and Elinor had not seen them more
than twice, before the eldest of them wished her joy on her sister's
having been so lucky as to make a conquest of a very smart beau
since she came to Barton.

"'Twill be a fine thing to have her married so young to be sure,"
said she, "and I hear he is quite a beau, and prodigious handsome.
And I hope you may have as good luck yourself soon,—but perhaps you may have a friend in the corner[42] already."

Elinor could not suppose that Sir John would be more nice[43] in
proclaiming his suspicions of her regard for Edward, than he had
been with respect to Marianne; indeed it was rather his favourite
joke of the two, as being somewhat newer and more conjectural;
and since Edward's visit, they had never dined together, without
his drinking to her best affections with so much significancy and
so many nods and winks, as to excite general attention. The letter
F— had been likewise invariably brought forward, and found pro-

41. *use:* benefit.

42. *friend in the corner:* person who will be a refuge in case of need. This was an old proverbial expression, and a more colloquial one than the polished and educated characters in Jane Austen use.

43. *nice:* delicate, scrupulous.

Two fashionable women.

[From *The Repository of arts, literature, fashions, manufactures, &c*, Vol. IV (1810), p. 301]

ductive of such countless jokes, that its character as the wittiest letter in the alphabet had been long established with Elinor.

The Miss Steeles, as she expected, had now all the benefit of these jokes, and in the eldest of them they raised a curiosity to know the name of the gentleman alluded to, which, though often impertinently expressed, was perfectly of a piece with her general inquisitiveness into the concerns of their family. But Sir John did not sport long with the curiosity which he delighted to raise, for he had at least as much pleasure in telling the name, as Miss Steele had in hearing it.

"His name is Ferrars," said he, in a very audible whisper; "but pray do not tell it, for it's a great secret."

"Ferrars!" repeated Miss Steele; "Mr. Ferrars is the happy man, is he? What! your sister-in-law's brother, Miss Dashwood? a very agreeable young man to be sure; I know him very well."

"How can you say so, Anne?" cried Lucy, who generally made an amendment to all her sister's assertions. "Though we have seen him once or twice at my uncle's, it is rather too much to pretend to know him very well."

Elinor heard all this with attention and surprise. "And who was this uncle? Where did he live? How came they acquainted?" She wished very much to have the subject continued, though she did not chuse to join in it herself; but nothing more of it was said, and for the first time in her life, she thought Mrs. Jennings deficient either in curiosity after petty information,[44] or in a disposition to communicate it. The manner in which Miss Steele had spoken of Edward, increased her curiosity; for it struck her as being rather ill-natured, and suggested the suspicion of that lady's knowing, or fancying herself to know something to his disadvantage. — But her curiosity was unavailing, for no farther notice was taken of Mr. Ferrars's name by Miss Steele when alluded to, or even openly mentioned by Sir John.

44. This unique example of noninquisitiveness on Mrs. Jennings's part will have important ramifications for the plot.

A woman with a sash.

[From *The Repository of arts, literature, fashions, manufactures, &c*, Vol. VIII (1812), p. 174]

Chapter Twenty-two

Marianne, who had never much toleration for any thing like impertinence, vulgarity, inferiority of parts,[1] or even difference of taste from herself, was at this time particularly ill-disposed, from the state of her spirits, to be pleased with the Miss Steeles, or to encourage their advances; and to the invariable coldness of her behaviour towards them, which checked every endeavour at intimacy on their side, Elinor principally attributed that preference of herself which soon became evident in the manners[2] of both, but especially of Lucy, who missed no opportunity of engaging her in conversation, or of striving to improve their acquaintance by an easy[3] and frank communication of her sentiments.

Lucy was naturally clever; her remarks were often just[4] and amusing;[5] and as a companion for half an hour Elinor frequently found her agreeable; but her powers[6] had received no aid from education, she was ignorant and illiterate,[7] and her deficiency of all mental improvement, her want of information in the most common particulars,[8] could not be concealed from Miss Dashwood, in spite of her constant endeavour to appear to advantage. Elinor saw, and pitied her for, the neglect of abilities which education might have rendered so respectable;[9] but she saw, with less tenderness of feeling, the thorough want of delicacy,[10] of rectitude, and integrity of mind, which her attentions, her assiduities, her flatteries at the Park betrayed; and she could have no lasting satisfaction in the company of a person who joined insincerity with ignorance; whose want of instruction prevented their meeting in conversation on terms of equality, and whose conduct towards others, made every shew of attention and deference towards herself perfectly valueless.[11]

"You will think my question an odd one, I dare say," said Lucy

1. *parts*: abilities, talents.

2. *manners*: behavior and demeanor.

3. *easy*: unrestrained, unembarrassed; the term is sometimes used in a pejorative manner, as it is here.

4. *just*: exact, accurate.

5. *amusing*: interesting, entertaining.

6. *powers*: natural abilities.

7. *illiterate*: uneducated.

8. *want of information in the most common particulars*: lack of knowledge about the most ordinary details or facts.

9. *respectable*: worthy of respect.

10. *delicacy*: sensitivity to others' feelings, or to what is proper and appropriate.

11. They are valueless because she showers deference and attention on everyone. Flattery ends up being counterproductive when used on an intelligent person in a position to observe other applications of it.

to her one day as they were walking together from the park to the cottage[12] — "but, pray, are you personally acquainted with your sister-in-law's mother, Mrs. Ferrars?"

Elinor *did* think the question a very odd one, and her countenance expressed it, as she answered that she had never seen Mrs. Ferrars.

"Indeed!" replied Lucy; "I wonder at that, for I thought you must have seen her at Norland sometimes. Then perhaps you cannot tell me what sort of a woman she is?"

"No"; returned Elinor, cautious of giving her real opinion of Edward's mother, and not very desirous of satisfying, what seemed impertinent[13] curiosity — "I know nothing of her."

"I am sure you think me very strange, for inquiring about her in such a way"; said Lucy, eyeing Elinor attentively as she spoke; "but perhaps there may be reasons — I wish I might venture; but however I hope you will do me the justice of believing that I do not mean to be impertinent."

Elinor made her a civil reply, and they walked on for a few minutes in silence. It was broken by Lucy, who renewed the subject again by saying with some hesitation,

"I cannot bear to have you think me impertinently curious. I am sure I would rather do any thing in the world than be thought so by a person whose good opinion is so well worth having as yours.[14] And I am sure I should not have the smallest fear of trusting *you*; indeed I should be very glad of your advice how to manage in such an uncomfortable situation as I am; but however there is no occasion to trouble *you*. I am sorry you do not happen to know Mrs. Ferrars."

"I am sorry I do *not*," said Elinor, in great astonishment, "if it could be of any use to *you* to know my opinion of her. But really, I never understood that you were at all connected with that family, and therefore I am a little surprised, I confess, at so serious an inquiry into her character."

"I dare say you are, and I am sure I do not at all wonder at it. But if I dared tell you all, you would not be so much surprised. Mrs. Ferrars is certainly nothing to me at present, — but the time

12. A walk like this, from the Middletons' residence to the Dashwoods', constitutes their best opportunity of private conversation, which is why Lucy has chosen to introduce an important and intimate topic now.

13. *impertinent*: presumptuous, intrusive.

14. Lucy, frustrated that Elinor's limited response and subsequent silence have thwarted her plans to extend their discussion, is desperate for some other means to continue her chosen topic, and so comes up with this rationale. It is a lame one, for while Elinor displayed some puzzlement at Lucy's question, she indicated no real disapproval or inclination to ask about Lucy's reason; nor does Lucy show herself in general to be a person lacking in confidence or plagued by remorse. But, however feeble the rationale, it is all she has, and she utilizes it.

may come—how soon it will come must depend upon herself—when we may be very intimately connected."[15]

She looked down as she said this, amiably bashful, with only one side glance at her companion to observe its effect on her.

"Good heavens!" cried Elinor, "what do you mean? Are you acquainted with Mr. Robert Ferrars?[16] Can you be—?" And she did not feel much delighted with the idea of such a sister-in-law.

"No"; replied Lucy, "not to Mr. *Robert* Ferrars—I never saw him in my life; but," fixing her eyes upon Elinor, "to his elder brother."

What felt Elinor at that moment? Astonishment, that would have been as painful as it was strong, had not an immediate disbelief of the assertion attended it. She turned towards Lucy in silent amazement, unable to divine the reason or object of such a declaration,[17] and though her complexion varied,[18] she stood firm in incredulity and felt in no danger of an hysterical fit, or a swoon.[19]

"You may well be surprised," continued Lucy; "for to be sure you could have had no idea of it before; for I dare say he never dropped the smallest hint of it to you or any of your family; because it was always meant to be a great secret, and I am sure has been faithfully kept so by me to this hour.[20] Not a soul of all my relations know of it but Anne, and I never should have mentioned it to you, if I had not felt the greatest dependance in the world upon your secrecy; and I really thought my behaviour in asking so many questions about Mrs. Ferrars, must seem so odd, that it ought to be explained.[21] And I do not think Mr. Ferrars can be displeased, when he knows I have trusted you, because I know he has the highest opinion in the world of all your family, and looks upon yourself and the other Miss Dashwoods, quite as his own sisters."[22]—She paused.

Elinor for a few moments remained silent. Her astonishment at what she heard was at first too great for words; but at length forcing herself to speak, and to speak cautiously, she said with a calmness of manner, which tolerably well concealed her surprise and solicitude[23]—"May I ask if your engagement is of long standing?"

"We have been engaged these four years."

15. To be intimately connected would mean to be related by marriage. How soon depends on Mrs. Ferrars because of her son's financial dependence on her.

16. Edward's younger brother was mentioned earlier (p. 28). Because he is younger he is called "Mr. Robert Ferrars," in contrast to Edward's simple "Mr. Ferrars." The distinction is the same as that between the oldest unmarried sister and the younger ones.

17. She cannot understand why Lucy would make such a declaration, having told nobody else of the supposed engagement, and this helps persuade Elinor that it must be false.

18. *complexion varied:* face changed color.

19. Hysterical fits or swoons by heroines were a popular convention of novels of the time, especially sentimental novels (where susceptibility to such swoons could be a positive sign of the heroine's highly developed sensibility). In Jane Austen's youthful satire on sensibility and sentimental novels, *Love and Friendship*, the heroine and her best friend are constantly fainting. In contrast, in her novels the heroines, though often subject to very powerful emotions and strains, never faint.

20. This explains why Lucy has not mentioned it previously.

21. This reason would be grossly insufficient to justify revealing an important secret to someone Lucy has recently met and has no other connection with. Of course, the real reason, which will become apparent, is one that cannot be articulated, namely the wish to warn off Elinor from Edward.

22. A clear hint to Elinor of the only status she should aspire to with regard to Edward.

23. Elinor is now facing, just like her sister, unexpected romantic disappointment. Her struggles with her feelings here indicate that she is experiencing some of the same sufferings, but her response is very different, for Marianne made no attempt at composure. Of course, Marianne was not faced with a hostile stranger before whom she did not wish to embarrass herself. This gives Elinor an extra incentive to remain outwardly calm, though it also makes the revelation more of an ordeal for her, and thus a crucial test of her character.

"Four years!"

"Yes."

Elinor, though greatly shocked, still felt unable to believe it.

"I did not know," said she, "that you were even acquainted till the other day."

"Our acquaintance, however, is of many years date. He was under my uncle's care, you know, a considerable while."

"Your uncle!"

"Yes; Mr. Pratt. Did you never hear him talk of Mr. Pratt?"

"I think I have," replied Elinor, with an exertion of spirits, which increased with her increase of emotion.[24]

"He was four years with my uncle, who lives at Longstaple, near Plymouth.[25] It was there our acquaintance begun, for my sister and me was often staying with my uncle,[26] and it was there our engagement was formed, though not till a year after he had quitted as a pupil;[27] but he was almost always with us afterwards. I was very unwilling to enter into it, as you may imagine, without the knowledge and approbation of his mother; but I was too young and loved him too well to be so prudent as I ought to have been. — Though you do not know him so well as me, Miss Dashwood, you must have seen enough of him to be sensible he is very capable of making a woman sincerely attached to him."

"Certainly," answered Elinor, without knowing what she said; but after a moment's reflection, she added with revived security of Edward's honour and love, and her companion's falsehood — "Engaged to Mr. Edward Ferrars! — I confess myself so totally surprised at what you tell me, that really — I beg your pardon; but surely there must be some mistake of person or name. We cannot mean the same Mr. Ferrars."

"We can mean no other," cried Lucy smiling. "Mr. Edward Ferrars, the eldest son of Mrs. Ferrars of Park-street,[28] and brother of your sister-in-law, Mrs. John Dashwood, is the person I mean; you must allow that I am not likely to be deceived, as to the name of the man on who all my happiness depends."[29]

"It is strange," replied Elinor in a most painful perplexity, "that I should never have heard him even mention your name."

24. *emotion:* agitation, distress.

25. When Edward recently visited the Dashwoods, he had come from Plymouth.

26. Her use of "begun" for "began," "me" for "I," and "was" for "were" demonstrates her poor grammar, which will continue to appear.

27. Edward was being schooled by Mr. Pratt. This was not unusual: many educated men took in boarders and taught them in order to supplement their incomes. When Jane Austen was a girl her father, a well-read clergyman, taught a number of boys at the Austen home. This does lead to the question of how the Miss Steeles are so poorly educated, for their uncle, with whom they have stayed a fair amount, would have needed to be a very learned man to attract as a pupil the eldest son of a very wealthy family, and one whose intelligence would have allowed him to notice any serious deficiencies in his teacher.

28. *Park-street:* a street in the fashionable and expensive Mayfair section of London. That it is the residence mentioned for Mrs. Ferrars indicates that it is her only one, for if she had a country house she would be associated with it, even if she spent much of her time in London. Many wealthy widows resided in London; it offered them ample social and cultural opportunities, and greater independence than rural society, in which rules of propriety and difficulties of transportation often restricted single women's ability to venture outside. Mrs. Jennings also has a house in London, though in her case she has a connection to the city from her earlier life.

29. This final clause, including Lucy's emphatic *I*, represents a clear dig at Elinor, who has apparently been deceived about Edward. The phrase "all my happiness depends" was a common one in connection with marriage. It was especially apt for women, whose social and financial fate was so dependent on a husband, and most especially for a woman like Lucy without money or good social position of her own.

"No; considering our situation, it was not strange. Our first care has been to keep the matter secret. — You knew nothing of me, or my family, and therefore there could be no *occasion* for ever mentioning my name to you, and as he was always particularly afraid of his sister's suspecting any thing, *that* was reason enough for his not mentioning it."[30]

She was silent. — Elinor's security[31] sunk; but her self-command did not sink with it.

"Four years you have been engaged," said she with a firm voice.

"Yes; and heaven knows how much longer we may have to wait. Poor Edward! It puts him quite out of heart."[32] Then taking a small miniature[33] from her pocket,[34] she added, "To prevent the possibility of mistake, be so good as to look at this face. It does not do him justice to be sure, but yet I think you cannot be deceived as to the person it was drew for. — I have had it above these three years."[35]

She put it into her hands as she spoke, and when Elinor saw the painting, whatever other doubts her fear of a too hasty decision, or her wish of detecting falsehood might suffer to linger in her mind, she could have none of its being Edward's face. She returned it almost instantly, acknowledging the likeness.[36]

"I have never been able," continued Lucy, "to give him my picture in return, which I am very much vexed at, for he has been always so anxious to get it![37] But I am determined to sit[38] for it the very first opportunity."

"You are quite in the right"; replied Elinor calmly. They then proceeded a few paces in silence. Lucy spoke first.

"I am sure," said she, "I have no doubt in the world of your faithfully keeping this secret, because you must know of what importance it is to us, not to have it reach his mother; for she would never approve of it, I dare say. I shall have no fortune, and I fancy she is an exceeding proud woman."

"I certainly did not seek your confidence," said Elinor; "but you do me no more than justice in imagining that I may be depended on. Your secret is safe with me; but pardon me if I express some surprise at so unnecessary a communication. You must at least

30. Because of Elinor's connection with Edward's sister, word about his engagement could have reached Fanny through Elinor or other members of her immediate family. Explaining Edward's secrecy is important for Lucy, since his complete silence on the subject constitutes a salient point of doubt about her story.

31. *security*: confidence, assurance.

32. *out of heart*: in a state of dejection, discouragement.

33. *miniature*: miniature painting (see p. 115, note 18 for more). It was popular to carry or wear miniatures of one's beloved; a crucial development in *Persuasion* is sparked by a man's commission to have a miniature of himself framed for his fiancée. Lucy, unlike most with such pictures, cannot wear hers. For a picture of two women looking at a miniature, see next page.

34. Ladies' gowns often had pockets. A woman also would sometimes wear a belt under her gown with pockets suspended from it, to which access was provided by a slit in the gown.

35. *above these three years*: for more than three years.

36. Elinor does not wish to linger on the picture.

37. It is possible that, despite Lucy's words, Edward has not really pressed her to give him a miniature of herself. There will be indications, in this conversation and subsequently, that he is not as committed to the engagement as Lucy claims he is.

38. This was "set" in the first edition, and was changed for the second. It is not clear if this was done by Jane Austen or by the printer. She may have meant it to be "set" to mark Lucy's poor grammar, though she is far from always ungrammatical.

have felt that my being acquainted with it could not add to its safety."

As she said this, she looked earnestly at Lucy, hoping to discover something in her countenance; perhaps the falsehood of the greatest part of what she had been saying; but Lucy's countenance suffered no change.

"I was afraid you would think I was taking a great liberty with you," said she, "in telling you all this. I have not known you long to be sure, personally at least, but I have known you and all your family by description a great while; and as soon as I saw you, I felt almost as if you was an old acquaintance. Besides in the present case, I really thought some explanation was due to you after my making such particular inquiries about Edward's mother; and I am so unfortunate, that I have not a creature whose advice I can ask. Anne is the only person that knows of it, and she has no judgment at all; indeed she does me a great deal more harm than good, for I am in constant fear of her betraying me. She does not know how to hold her tongue, as you must perceive, and I am sure I was in the greatest fright in the world t'other day, when Edward's name was mentioned by Sir John, lest she should out with it all. You can't think how much I go through in my mind from it altogether. I only wonder that I am alive after what I have suffered for Edward's sake these last four years.[39] Every thing in such suspense and uncertainty; and seeing him so seldom—we can hardly meet above twice a-year.[40] I am sure I wonder my heart is not quite broke."

Here she took out her handkerchief; but Elinor did not feel very compassionate.

"Sometimes," continued Lucy, after wiping her eyes, "I think whether it would not be better for us both, to break off the matter entirely." As she said this, she looked directly at her companion.[41] "But then at other times I have not resolution enough for it.[42]—I cannot bear the thoughts of making him so miserable, as I know the very mention of such a thing would do. And on my own account too—so dear as he is to me—I don't think I could be

39. Such hyperbolic expressions are a consistent sign of an untrustworthy character in Jane Austen, since they tend to denote either insincerity or excessive emotion.

40. A sign of Edward's possible ambivalence. Having plenty of leisure, he could visit her more often if he really wished to do so.

41. In looking at Elinor she may be hoping the latter will betray herself by urging Lucy to break the engagement. In their next conversation Lucy will make an even more explicit appeal to Elinor along these lines.

42. Social conventions gave the woman, but not the man, the power to break off an engagement. Hence it is up to Lucy.

Two women looking at a miniature.

[From *The Repository of arts, literature, fashions, manufactures, &c*, Vol. III (1810), p. 389]

equal to it. What would you advise me to do in such a case, Miss Dashwood? What would you do yourself?"[43]

"Pardon me," replied Elinor, startled by the question; "but I can give you no advice under such circumstances. Your own judgment must direct you."

"To be sure," continued Lucy, after a few minutes silence on both sides, "his mother must provide for him sometime or other; but poor Edward is so cast down about it! Did not you think him dreadful low-spirited when he was at Barton? He was so miserable when he left us at Longstaple, to go to you, that I was afraid you would think him quite ill."

"Did he come from your uncle's then, when he visited us?"

"Oh! yes; he had been staying a fortnight with us. Did you think he came directly from town?"

"No," replied Elinor, most feelingly sensible[44] of every fresh circumstance in favour of Lucy's veracity; "I remember he told us, that he had been staying a fortnight with some friends near Plymouth." She remembered too, her own surprise at the time, at his mentioning nothing farther of those friends, at his total silence with respect even to their names.

"Did not you think him sadly out of spirits?" repeated Lucy.

"We did indeed, particularly so when he first arrived."[45]

"I begged him to exert himself for fear you should suspect what was the matter; but it made him so melancholy, not being able to stay more than a fortnight with us, and seeing me so much affected. — Poor fellow! — I am afraid it is just the same with him now; for he writes in wretched spirits. I heard from him just before I left Exeter"; taking a letter from her pocket and carelessly shewing the direction[46] to Elinor.[47] "You know his hand, I dare say, a charming one it is;[48] but that is not written so well as usual. — He was tired, I dare say, for he had just filled the sheet to me as full as possible."[49]

Elinor saw that it *was* his hand, and she could doubt no longer. The picture, she had allowed herself to believe, might have been accidentally obtained; it might not have been Edward's gift; but a correspondence between them by letter, could subsist only under

43. Of course, Elinor's own situation bears significant similarities. Lucy, who probably hopes that her disclosure will prompt Elinor to contact Edward and sever whatever understanding or friendly relationship they have established, may be hoping to gauge the possibility of that through her last question.

44. *feelingly sensible*: sensitively or acutely aware.

45. Elinor means to suggest that it was his time with Lucy that most depressed him. In fact, he did improve during the course of his stay with the Dashwoods, with his enjoyment being "at the height" at the end of his stay. This is a strong indication that it was his engagement to Lucy, rather than his inability to marry, that caused his despondency. More generally, it is difficult to understand why he would have paid such attention to Elinor, or even visited the Dashwoods at all, if he truly loved Lucy and were only waiting to persuade his mother to consent to the match.

46. *direction*: address.

47. Lucy's ready deployment of this and other proofs indicate that she has come fully prepared for this battle.

48. An attractive and well-formed hand, or handwriting, was highly regarded then. People could be taught good penmanship in school, and books provided models of handwriting to emulate.

49. Because postage was expensive, and was assessed by weight, people would generally try to fill their sheets of paper in order to avoid having to add another one. Jane Austen in her own letters used a variety of expedients to fit as much information as possible on each sheet.

Edward may have written the address poorly from lack of enthusiasm for Lucy, which made him take less effort, rather than tiredness.

a positive engagement, could be authorised by nothing else;[50] for a few moments, she was almost overcome—her heart sunk within her, and she could hardly stand; but exertion was indispensably necessary, and she struggled so resolutely against the oppression[51] of her feelings, that her success was speedy, and for the time complete.[52]

"Writing to each other," said Lucy, returning the letter into her pocket, "is the only comfort we have in such long separations. Yes, I have one other comfort in his picture; but poor Edward has not even *that*. If he had but my picture, he says he should be easy. I gave him a lock of my hair set in a ring when he was at Longstaple last, and that was some comfort to him, he said, but not equal to a picture.[53] Perhaps you might notice the ring when you saw him?"

"I did"; said Elinor, with a composure of voice, under which was concealed an emotion and distress beyond any thing she had ever felt before. She was mortified, shocked, confounded.[54]

Fortunately for her, they had now reached the cottage, and the conversation could be continued no farther. After sitting with them a few minutes, the Miss Steeles returned to the Park, and Elinor was then at liberty to think and be wretched.

END OF VOL. I

50. The letter constitutes an important proof of the engagement, because unmarried and unrelated men and women could correspond only if they were engaged. Elinor knows that Edward is too conscientious to violate such a rule.

51. *oppression*: overpowering depression.

52. Elinor's success in quickly steadying her feelings, even under these circumstances, attests to her personal strength. At the same time, it inevitably makes those feelings less palpable to the reader. This is the problem with having a heroine who functions in part to exemplify a moral and intellectual ideal. The heroines of *Mansfield Park* and *Persuasion* are also virtuous and wise, but their sufferings under painful feelings are presented much more fully and acutely.

53. Lucy may have chosen to give him a lock of hair rather than a miniature because the former is less expensive—or it could have been simply from lacking the time to procure the latter. It would seem this was the first time she gave him such a memento, possibly because his possession of one would increase the risk of detection. She may have changed her policy after observing him during his recent visit: if he was in lower spirits than previously, perhaps because Elinor had given him a taste of a better alternative, she could have noticed and decided to insist on his accepting a keepsake; she would be especially likely if his unhappiness had made him raise the topic of ending the engagement. This also may be why, having seen the threat from Elinor, she speaks of sitting for a miniature portrait. All these attempts to bind him, as well as her multiple demonstrations to Elinor of the engagement, would be further motivated by her knowledge that its secret nature makes it more precarious. A crucial reason for making an engagement public was to prevent, through social pressure, either person from renouncing it. No such mechanism exists in this case; Lucy can rely only on Edward's honor, and she, not being honorable herself, is probably inclined to doubt the strength of such a force.

54. Here Elinor does give way more completely to unpleasant feelings, though they are simply mentioned rather than fully presented.

VOLUME TWO

Chapter One

*H*owever small Elinor's general dependance on Lucy's veracity might be, it was impossible for her on serious reflection to suspect it in the present case, where no temptation could be answerable[1] to the folly of inventing a falsehood of such a description. What Lucy had asserted to be true, therefore, Elinor could not, dared not longer doubt; supported as it was too on every side by such probabilities and proofs, and contradicted by nothing but her own wishes.[2] Their opportunity of acquaintance in the house of Mr. Pratt was a foundation for the rest, at once indisputable and alarming; and Edward's visit near Plymouth, his melancholy state of mind, his dissatisfaction at his own prospects, his uncertain behaviour towards herself,[3] the intimate knowledge of the Miss Steeles as to Norland and their family connections, which had often surprised her, the picture, the letter, the ring, formed altogether such a body of evidence, as overcame every fear of condemning him unfairly, and established as a fact, which no partiality could set aside, his ill-treatment of herself.[4]—Her resentment of such behaviour, her indignation at having been its dupe, for a short time made her feel only for herself; but other ideas, other considerations soon arose. Had Edward been intentionally deceiving her? Had he feigned a regard for her which he did not feel? Was his engagement to Lucy, an engagement of the heart? No; whatever it might once have been, she could not believe it such at present.[5] His affection was all her own.[6] She could not be deceived in that. Her mother, sisters, Fanny, all had been conscious of his regard for her at Norland;[7] it was not an illusion of her own vanity. He certainly loved her. What a softener of

1. *answerable to:* sufficient for.

2. Even in this, the greatest emotional trial she has faced, Elinor still rationally accepts the facts.

3. She had noticed his uncertain and fluctuating behavior both at Norland and at Barton.

4. He treated her badly by indicating his affection toward her even though he was engaged elsewhere. This would be especially serious because of the tremendous social and economic importance of marriage for a woman and because a young lady's marital eligibility lasted a limited time. If she wasted much of the time by pining for a man she could never have, she might lose her chance permanently.

5. Their having been engaged four years increases the possibility that their mutual affection, or at least his affection for her, could have declined. Its endurance also suggests that at least one of them has not been especially eager to overcome the barriers in their way.

6. Edward's behavior supports this conclusion. His vacillation toward her would have been a natural product of the conflict between his attraction to her and his knowledge that he needed to draw back and avoid intimacy. Thus when he visited the Dashwoods he felt bound to leave despite the admitted enjoyment he experienced there; he had spoken of his duty, without explaining what it was, and Elinor had struggled to find a good explanation for his departure. Even his hesitation to choose a profession might result in part from his reluctance to take a step that, by providing him with a more regular income, would advance the day of his marriage to Lucy.

7. Elinor is not simply relying on her own feelings, but supplementing them with other people's perceptions and opinions.

the heart was this persuasion! How much could it not tempt her to forgive![8] He had been blameable, highly blameable, in remaining at Norland after he first felt her influence over him to be more than it ought to be. In that, he could not be defended; but if he had injured her, how much more had he injured himself; if her case were pitiable, his was hopeless. His imprudence had made her miserable for a while; but it seemed to have deprived himself of all chance of ever being otherwise. She might in time regain tranquillity; but *he*, what had he to look forward to? Could he ever be tolerably happy with Lucy Steele;[9] could he, were his affection for herself out of the question, with his integrity, his delicacy, and well-informed[10] mind, be satisfied with a wife like her — illiterate,[11] artful,[12] and selfish?

The youthful infatuation of nineteen would naturally blind him to every thing but her beauty and good nature;[13] but the four succeeding years — years, which if rationally spent, give such improvement to the understanding, must have opened his eyes to her defects of education, while the same period of time, spent on her side in inferior society and more frivolous pursuits,[14] had perhaps robbed her of that simplicity, which might once have given an interesting[15] character to her beauty.

If in the supposition of his seeking to marry herself, his difficulties from his mother had seemed great, how much greater were they now likely to be, when the object of his engagement was undoubtedly inferior in connections,[16] and probably inferior in fortune to herself.[17] These difficulties, indeed, with an heart so alienated from Lucy, might not press very hard upon his patience,[18] but melancholy was the state of the person, by whom the expectation of family opposition and unkindness, could be felt as a relief!

As these considerations occurred to her in painful succession, she wept for him, more than for herself. Supported by the conviction of having done nothing to merit her present unhappiness, and consoled by the belief that Edward had done nothing to forfeit her esteem, she thought she could even now, under the first smart of the heavy blow, command herself enough to guard every

8. To the degree that Elinor's softening results from being flattered by his love, this would indicate her susceptibility to normal weaknesses, something not often seen over the course of the novel.

9. It is a sign of her love for him and her genuine goodness that even after learning of the wrong he has committed toward her, and of the probability she will never marry him, a good deal of her thoughts center around his welfare rather than her own.

10. *well-informed*: educated, enlightened.

11. *illiterate*: uneducated.

12. *artful*: cunning, deceitful.

13. Meaning her outward pleasantness and affability.

14. The Steeles' behavior and speech consistently indicate their lower social origins and the lack of polish and education among those they have been living with.

15. *interesting*: fascinating, engaging.

16. *connections*: family connections or relations. This was very important in this society.

17. No wealth is ever ascribed to the Steeles, and Jane Austen is usually very specific about her characters' fortunes. Moreover, the eagerness with which they accepted the Middletons' invitation and their unceasing flattery of their hostess suggest people in difficult circumstances, willing to do anything to live among more affluent people and strengthen their ties with them.

18. If he does not wish to marry her, he might be happy that her poor background and circumstances rule out marriage at present.

suspicion of the truth from her mother and sisters. And so well was she able to answer her own expectations, that when she joined them at dinner only two hours after she had first suffered the extinction of all her dearest hopes, no one would have supposed from the appearance of the sisters, that Elinor was mourning in secret over obstacles which must divide her for ever from the object of her love,[19] and that Marianne was internally dwelling on the perfections of a man, of whose whole heart she felt thoroughly possessed,[20] and whom she expected to see in every carriage which drove near their house.[21]

The necessity of concealing from her mother and Marianne, what had been entrusted in confidence to herself, though it obliged her to unceasing exertion, was no aggravation of Elinor's distress. On the contrary it was a relief to her, to be spared the communication of what would give such affliction to them, and to be saved likewise from hearing that condemnation of Edward, which would probably flow from the excess of their partial affection for herself, and which was more than she felt equal to support.

From their counsel, or their conversation she knew she could receive no assistance, their tenderness and sorrow must add to her distress, while her self-command would neither receive encouragement from their example nor from their praise.[22] She was stronger alone, and her own good sense so well supported her, that her firmness was as unshaken, her appearance of cheerfulness as invariable, as with regrets so poignant and so fresh, it was possible for them to be.

Much as she had suffered from her first conversation with Lucy on the subject, she soon felt an earnest wish of renewing it; and this for more reasons than one. She wanted to hear many particulars of their engagement repeated again, she wanted more clearly to understand what Lucy really felt for Edward, whether there were any sincerity in her declaration of tender regard for him,[23] and she particularly wanted to convince Lucy, by her readiness to enter on the matter again, and her calmness in conversing on it, that she was no otherwise interested in it than as a friend, which

19. Her poise contrasts sharply with Marianne's behavior after Willoughby's departure.

20. The wording suggests that Marianne still manifests outward signs of distress, even as she retains hope and faith within.

21. Carriages made a fair amount of noise, and the wording implies that Marianne may look out the window whenever she hears one to see if it contains Willoughby.

22. This again contrasts with Marianne, who receives tremendous support and succor from Elinor over the course of the novel. That Elinor believes that communicating her secret to Mrs. Dashwood and Marianne would only add to her distress reveals their flaws as a mother and a sister.

23. Elinor's self-command, by allowing her to speak calmly to Lucy, will help her gain valuable information.

she very much feared her involuntary agitation, in their morning discourse, must have left at least doubtful.[24] That Lucy was disposed to be jealous of her, appeared very probable; it was plain that Edward had always spoken highly in her praise, not merely from Lucy's assertion, but from her venturing to trust her on so short a personal acquaintance, with a secret, so confessedly and evidently important.[25] And even Sir John's joking intelligence[26] must have had some weight. But indeed, while Elinor remained so well assured within herself of being really beloved by Edward, it required no other consideration of probabilities to make it natural that Lucy should be jealous; and that she was so, her very confidence[27] was a proof. What other reason for the disclosure of the affair could there be, but that Elinor might be informed by it of Lucy's superior claims on Edward, and be taught to avoid him in future? She had little difficulty in understanding thus much of her rival's intentions, and while she was firmly resolved to act by her as every principle of honour and honesty directed, to combat her own affection for Edward and to see him as little as possible; she could not deny herself the comfort of endeavouring to convince Lucy that her heart was unwounded. And as she could now have nothing more painful to hear on the subject than had already been told, she did not mistrust her own ability of going through a repetition of particulars with composure.

But it was not immediately that an opportunity of doing so could be commanded, though Lucy was as well disposed as herself to take advantage of any that occurred; for the weather was not often fine enough to allow of their joining in a walk, where they might most easily separate themselves from the others; and though they met at least every other evening either at the park or cottage, and chiefly at the former, they could not be supposed to meet for the sake of conversation.[28] Such a thought would never enter either Sir John or Lady Middleton's head, and therefore very little leisure was ever given for general chat, and none at all for particular discourse.[29] They met for the sake of eating, drinking, and laughing together, playing at cards, or consequences,[30] or any other game that was sufficiently noisy.

24. This suggests a less than ideal pride in Elinor. She presumably felt that Lucy had gotten the better of her in their earlier conversation because of Elinor's shock at the news, and she would like to reverse that, from a wish to look better in Lucy's eyes and perhaps in her own eyes as well.

25. Since Elinor could divulge the secret, the only justification for the risk would be to prevent the even greater danger of a firmer attachment between Edward and Elinor.

26. *intelligence:* information (about Edward's affection).

27. *confidence:* confiding in Elinor.

28. Private conversation is often difficult in Jane Austen's novels, for there is a great emphasis on general sociability.

29. *particular discourse:* separate or private conversation.

30. *consequences:* a game in which a group of people tell collectively the story of a romance between a hypothetical gentleman and lady, from its beginning to its ultimate consequences, by having each person contribute a piece of information to the story without knowing what the others have contributed. Such a game, in which a great deal of confusion and laughable or absurd stories could easily result, would naturally appeal to the taste of Sir John.

A hot water jug and a creamer from the time.

[From MacIver Percival, *Old English Furniture and Its Surroundings* (New York, 1920), pp. 176 and 177]

One or two meetings of this kind had taken place, without affording Elinor any chance of engaging Lucy in private, when Sir John called at the cottage one morning, to beg in the name of charity, that they would all dine with Lady Middleton that day, as he was obliged to attend the club at Exeter,[31] and she would otherwise be quite alone, except her mother and the two Miss Steeles. Elinor, who foresaw a fairer[32] opening for the point she had in view, in such a party[33] as this was likely to be, more at liberty among themselves under the tranquil and well-bred direction of Lady Middleton than when her husband united them together in one noisy purpose, immediately accepted the invitation; Margaret, with her mother's permission, was equally compliant, and Marianne, though always unwilling to join any of their parties, was persuaded by her mother, who could not bear to have her seclude herself from any chance of amusement, to go likewise.

The young ladies went, and Lady Middleton was happily preserved from the frightful solitude which had threatened her. The insipidity of the meeting was exactly such as Elinor had expected; it produced not one novelty of thought or expression,[34] and nothing could be less interesting than the whole of their discourse both in the dining parlour and drawing room: to the latter, the children accompanied them, and while they remained there, she was too well convinced of the impossibility of engaging Lucy's attention to attempt it.[35] They quitted it only with the removal of the tea-things.[36] The card-table was then placed,[37] and Elinor

A teapot.

[From MacIver Percival, *Old English Furniture and Its Surroundings* (New York, 1920), p. 177]

31. Clubs and associations were a basic part of English life at this time. They had been steadily growing in number for more than a century and by this point there were more than a thousand in England. Originally they had existed mostly for drinking and socializing, but as time went on many clubs dedicated to various political, religious, charitable, educational, scientific, or cultural purposes had sprouted, with some developing a national organization as well. At the same time many remained primarily local drinking clubs, and Sir John seems most likely to be a member of one like this. The only more specialized type he might gravitate toward would be a sporting club; such clubs played an increasing role in organizing and managing sporting events like foxhunts. The great majority of clubs was exclusively male, and often valued for the chance they provided for socializing solely with one's own sex. They also were overwhelmingly centered in towns and cities, though ones in relatively small towns like Exeter would draw heavily on people from nearby rural areas. Sir John's club was probably dominated by landed gentlemen like himself, with a possible mixture of wealthier professionals and merchants—while clubs tended to replicate the existing social structure, they usually did not enforce rigid class divisions, and Sir John seems like someone happy to mix with a variety of people.

32. *fairer*: better, less obstructed.

33. *party*: gathering.

34. No new idea was uttered, nor anything novel in the choice of words or phrasing.

35. Lucy would be too devoted to entertaining and indulging the children to concentrate on anything else.

36. Tea would take place an hour or two after dinner. The tea things would include an urn or pot with boiling water, the tea itself, sugar, milk or cream and a creamer to serve it, utensils, cups, saucers, and plates. There would also be snack items for eating, such as breads and cakes; that would be one reason the children would have stayed for it. For a picture of tea things from the time, see the facing page, the previous page, and the following page.

37. Card tables had been popular for at least a century prior to this novel. The top folded in half, allowing the table to be stored compactly. The top was usually covered with a material such as leather to make it less slick. For a picture of such a card table, see p. 268.

began to wonder at herself for having ever entertained a hope of finding time for conversation at the park. They all rose up in preparation for a round game.[38]

"I am glad," said Lady Middleton to Lucy, "you are not going to finish poor little Annamaria's basket this evening; for I am sure it must hurt your eyes to work fillagree[39] by candlelight.[40] And we will make the dear little love some amends for her disappointment to-morrow, and then I hope she will not much mind it."[41]

This hint was enough, Lucy recollected herself instantly and replied, "Indeed you are very much mistaken, Lady Middleton; I am only waiting to know whether you can make your party without me,[42] or I should have been at my fillagree already. I would not disappoint the little angel for all the world, and if you want me at the card-table now, I am resolved to finish the basket after supper."[43]

"You are very good, I hope it won't hurt your eyes—will you ring the bell[44] for some working candles?[45] My poor little girl would be sadly disappointed, I know, if the basket was not finished to-morrow, for though I told her it certainly would not, I am sure she depends upon having it done."

Lucy directly drew her work table near her and reseated herself

A cup and saucer.

[From MacIver Percival, *Old English Furniture and Its Surroundings* (New York, 1920), Plate XIV, no. 4]

38. *round game:* game of cards for any number of players. In contrast, whist, the most popular card game at the time, was for four people only. Round games would naturally appeal to the Middletons because they allowed large numbers to play, with no worries about how many people had been invited. Moreover, most round games were less challenging than whist, thereby requiring less mental effort and allowing for greater conversation.

39. *fillagree:* sometimes spelled "filigree," this referred originally to delicate jewel work, usually done in gold. Here it means work done in paper in imitation of metal filigree. This had become a popular pastime for ladies. It involved taking very thin strips of stiff paper or parchment, which had been gilded or tilted, and then rolling or folding them into elaborate shapes. They would then be glued to the surface of an object such as a box or a basket. Such decorative activities were often taught to young ladies in school.

40. Candles, the principal form of artificial illumination at the time, were expensive. Even in wealthy homes, where more and better-quality candles were used, rooms would not be brightly lit in the evening. This could create eyestrain when performing as intricate a task as filigree.

41. Lady Middleton's heavy-handed irony is an attempt to reconcile her only real interests, pleasing her spoiled children and following correct etiquette — the latter would forbid openly demanding that somebody make an effort or a sacrifice for the sake of one's child.

42. Meaning whether Lady Middleton will have enough for her card game. Since they are playing a game in which numbers are flexible, and there are seven people here (see note 52 below), such a worry has little basis. But Lucy needs to make some excuse for her neglect of a task she now professes a great devotion to completing.

43. Supper, a light meal, will come later in the evening, after they have played cards, which is why Lucy says she would wait until after supper if she were needed at cards.

44. *ring the bell:* pull a cord that makes a bell ring. Large country houses had elaborate systems of bells and pulleys that caused a bell to ring in the servants' quarters, showing in which room somebody had requested service.

45. Candles made of wax or spermaceti (sperm whale oil) provided stronger illumination than the tallow candles most commonly used. Such better candles, especially if collected in sufficient numbers to provide strong light, cost more, but Lady Middleton is clearly happy to incur the expense for the sake of her child. Pieces of furniture where work was done that required substantial light often had fittings built into them to hold candles, ensuring the candles would be reasonably low and remain secure.

with an alacrity and cheerfulness which seemed to infer[46] that she could taste no greater delight than in making a fillagree basket for a spoilt child.[47]

Lady Middleton proposed a rubber of Casino[48] to the others. No one made any objection but Marianne, who, with her usual inattention to the forms of general civility, exclaimed, "Your lady-ship will have the goodness to excuse *me*—you know I detest cards.[49] I shall go to the piano-forté; I have not touched it since it was tuned.[50] And without farther ceremony, she turned away and walked to the instrument.

Lady Middleton looked as if she thanked heaven that *she* had never made so rude a speech.

"Marianne can never keep long from that instrument you know, ma'am," said Elinor, endeavouring to smooth away the offence; "and I do not much wonder at it; for it is the very best toned piano-forté I ever heard."[51]

The remaining five were now to draw their cards.[52]

"Perhaps," continued Elinor, "if I should happen to cut out, I may be of some use to Miss Lucy Steele, in rolling her papers for her;[53] and there is so much still to be done to the basket, that it must be impossible I think for her labour singly, to finish it this evening. I should like the work exceedingly, if she would allow me a share in it."

"Indeed I shall be very much obliged to you for your help," cried Lucy, "for I find there is more to be done to it than I thought there was; and it would be a shocking thing to disappoint dear Annamaria after all."

"Oh! that would be terrible indeed," said Miss Steele—"Dear little soul, how I do love her!"

"You are very kind," said Lady Middleton to Elinor: "and as you really like the work, perhaps you will be as well pleased not to cut in[54] till another rubber,[55] or will you take your chance[56] now?"

Elinor joyfully profited by the first of these proposals, and thus by a little of that address,[57] which Marianne could never conde-scend to practise, gained her own end, and pleased Lady Middle-ton at the same time. Lucy made room for her with ready

46. *infer:* imply.

47. This reminder of Lucy's frequent insincerity forms a useful prelude to the exchange between her and Elinor that follows.

48. In casino the players take turns laying cards down on the table, trying to match cards already played in order to win them. Varying numbers of people can play, either on their own or in partnerships.

49. Marianne is being uncivil both in the manner of her refusal, bluntly expressing disgust for a pursuit that her hostess has proposed, and in its substance. Cards were a very popular pastime then and a basic part of social life, so most people would play some even if they did not really enjoy it.

50. It had probably not been tuned during the years when it lay neglected by Lady Middleton, but Marianne's devotion to music would have prompted greater attention to its proper workings, most likely out of consideration for her—since none of the family displays any real appreciation of music, they would not worry much about its being in tune for their own sake. Hence Marianne's reference to what the Middletons have done for her stands in ironic contrast to her refusal here to oblige Lady Middleton.

51. Elinor displays her own insincerity here—and she will display more in her exchange with Lucy—but hers comes from consideration of Lady Middleton's feelings, and her sister's standing among the others, rather than from concern for flattering someone whose favor she seeks.

52. The remaining five, without Lucy and Marianne, are Lady Middleton, Mrs. Jennings, Miss Steele, Elinor, and Margaret.

53. Rolling papers is a central part of the filigree work Lucy has undertaken (see note 39 above).

54. *cut in:* join in (a card game). In whist, where the term was often used, cutting in would mean replacing someone else, who would then "cut out." But in casino, where numbers were not fixed, this would not necessarily be the case.

55. *rubber:* a set of card games, usually three and sometimes five. The goal would be to win the most over the course of the rubber, so one would not wish for someone to join the game in the middle of a rubber.

56. *take your chance:* seize your opportunity (to join the card game now).

57. *address:* dexterity, adroitness.

attention, and the two fair rivals were thus seated side by side at the same table, and with the utmost harmony engaged in forwarding the same work.[58] The piano-forté, at which Marianne, wrapt up in her own music and her own thoughts, had by this time forgotten that any body was in the room besides herself, was luckily so near them that Miss Dashwood now judged, she might safely, under the shelter of its noise, introduce the interesting subject, without any risk of being heard at the card-table.

A contemporary card table.

[From K. Warren Clouston, *The Chippendale Period in English Furniture* (New York, 1897), p. 152]

58. The sentence suggests what will continue to be the relationship of Elinor and Lucy, an outward show of great friendship and concord combined with animosity and conflict beneath the surface, especially on Lucy's part.

A young woman receiving a letter.

[From *The Repository of arts, literature, fashions, manufactures, &c*, Vol. X (1813), p. 300]

Chapter Two

*I*n a firm, though cautious tone, Elinor thus began.

"I should be undeserving of the confidence you have honoured me with, if I felt no desire for its continuance, or no farther curiosity on its subject. I will not apologize therefore for bringing it forward again."[1]

"Thank you," cried Lucy warmly, "for breaking the ice; you have set my heart at ease by it; for I was somehow or other afraid I had offended you by what I told you that Monday."

"Offended me! How could you suppose so? Believe me," and Elinor spoke it with the truest sincerity, "nothing could be farther from my intention, than to give you such an idea.[2] Could you have a motive for the trust, that was not honourable and flattering to me?"[3]

"And yet I do assure you," replied Lucy, her little sharp eyes full of meaning, "there seemed to me to be a coldness and displeasure in your manner, that made me quite uncomfortable. I felt sure that you was angry with me; and have been quarrelling with myself ever since, for having took such a liberty as to trouble you with my affairs. But I am very glad to find it was only my own fancy, and that you do not really blame me. If you knew what a consolation it was to me to relieve my heart by speaking to you of what I am always thinking of every moment of my life, your compassion would make you overlook every thing else I am sure."

"Indeed I can easily believe that it was a very great relief to you, to acknowledge your situation to me, and be assured that you shall never have reason to repent it. Your case is a very unfortunate one; you seem to me to be surrounded with difficulties, and you will have need of all your mutual affection to support you under them. Mr. Ferrars,[4] I believe, is entirely dependent on his mother."

"He has only two thousand pounds of his own; it would be

1. Elinor's language here is rather formal, even for her. Such language may be intended to help control her emotions during the conversation, a difficult but vitally important task. It also serves to point up the contrast between her and Lucy, who will continue to speak less formally and elaborately, to use bad grammar at times, and to employ colloquial expressions—such as "breaking the ice" in her next line—that Elinor would not use.

2. Elinor's words are strictly speaking true, for she is determined to avoid appearing to Lucy as if she were offended, or affected in any way, by her revelation about Edward. This is why she spoke "with the truest sincerity." But they are also misleading, for they suggest affection and concern for Lucy as her motive. Throughout this conversation Elinor will resort to subtle forms of insincerity, as she tries to combat and vanquish someone who frequently employs the most flagrant forms of it.

3. Her trust would be honorable and flattering because it would signify Lucy's strong confidence in Elinor's discretion and scrupulousness—yet both women know that Lucy did indeed have another motive.

4. Elinor, here and later, calls Edward "Mr. Ferrars," though she uses his first name when speaking to her sister (who uses his first name in speaking to anyone about him). She will also use this more formal designation when speaking of him to Mrs. Jennings. She may think that, since her family relationship to him is not that close, it would be presumptuous to use his first name to a person outside the family.

madness to marry upon that, though for my own part, I could give up every prospect of more without a sigh.[5] I have been always used to a very small income, and could struggle with any poverty for him; but I love him too well to be the selfish means of robbing him, perhaps, of all that his mother might give him if he married to please her.[6] We must wait, it may be for many years. With almost every other man in the world, it would be an alarming prospect;[7] but Edward's affection and constancy nothing can deprive me of I know."

"That conviction must be every thing to you; and he is undoubtedly supported by the same trust in your's. If the strength of your reciprocal attachment had failed, as between many people and under many circumstances it naturally would during a four years' engagement, your situation would have been pitiable indeed."[8]

Lucy here looked up; but Elinor was careful in guarding her countenance from every expression that could give her words a suspicious tendency.

"Edward's love for me," said Lucy, "has been pretty well put to the test, by our long, very long absence since we were first engaged, and it has stood the trial so well, that I should be unpardonable to doubt it now. I can safely say that he has never gave me one moment's alarm on that account from the first."[9]

Elinor hardly knew whether to smile or sigh at this assertion.[10]

Lucy went on. "I am rather of a jealous temper too by nature, and from our different situations in life, from his being so much more in the world[11] than me, and our continual separation, I was enough inclined for suspicion, to have found out the truth in an instant, if there had been the slightest alteration in his behaviour to me when we met, or any lowness of spirits that I could not account for, or if he had talked more of one lady than another, or seemed in any respect less happy at Longstaple than he used to be.[12] I do not mean to say that I am particularly observant or quick-sighted in general, but in such a case I am sure I could not be deceived."

5. This statement, which will eventually prove to be the exact opposite of the truth, constitutes an automatic sign of Lucy's falsity, for even good, non-mercenary characters in Jane Austen make no pretense of complete indifference to money.

6. Mrs. Ferrars is later revealed to have an estate worth a thousand a year, as well as other substantial sums of money. If Edward were deprived of that, he, and any bride of his, would be suffering a great loss.

7. While convention dictated that a man should not break an engagement, he still could. The worst he could suffer, in addition to social disapproval, would be a legal suit for breach of promise, which would cause him embarrassment and, if he lost, force him to pay a fine. Since this could be less painful than a long engagement or disinheritance, a woman would have grounds for worrying about a man's continued fidelity, if she did not trust his honor.

8. A pointed remark for Lucy, for while Elinor speaks as if there is no reason to doubt the persistence of their reciprocal attachment, she and Lucy both know that Edward's attachment for Lucy has wavered because of his interest in Elinor. If that were not the case, Lucy would never have made her communication in the first place.

9. This statement, like her looking up at Elinor after the latter's words, signifies that Lucy fully understands Elinor's meaning. To refute it she begins with her strongest argument, Edward's willingness to persist for years in the engagement. But, presumably feeling this is insufficient, she is forced to conclude with a patent lie about having never felt alarm.

10. Her smile would be at the absurdity of the statement, and her sigh presumably at what it shows about Lucy's character, and thus Edward's potential fate.

11. *being so much more in the world*: circulating so much more among people, and among elite society in particular.

12. This assertion is contradicted not only by Lucy's decision to warn off Elinor, but also by her own words in their previous exchange, for she had made a point of mentioning Edward's acute despondency during his last visit at Longstaple. Her resort to such a clear falsehood shows how much Elinor's last remark has stung her, as does the lengthy and repetitive nature of these two consecutive statements—taken together, since Elinor has said nothing in between, they constitute Lucy's longest speech of this conversation. Moreover, she is unable to adduce any specific act of Edward's that constitutes proof of his continued affection for her.

"All this," thought Elinor, "is very pretty; but it can impose upon[13] neither of us."

"But what," said she after a short silence,[14] "are your views?[15] or have you none but that of waiting for Mrs. Ferrars' death, which is a melancholy and shocking extremity?—Is her son determined to submit to this, and to all the tediousness of the many years of suspense[16] in which it may involve you, rather than run the risk of her displeasure for a while by owning[17] the truth?"

"If we could be certain that it would be only for a while! But Mrs. Ferrars is a very headstrong proud woman, and in her first fit of anger upon hearing it, would very likely secure every thing to Robert,[18] and the idea of that, for Edward's sake, frightens away all my inclination for hasty measures."

"And for your own sake too, or you are carrying your disinterestedness beyond reason."

Lucy looked at Elinor again, and was silent.[19]

"Do you know Mr. Robert Ferrars?" asked Elinor.

"Not at all—I never saw him; but I fancy he is very unlike his brother—silly and a great coxcomb."[20]

"A great coxcomb!" repeated Miss Steele, whose ear had caught those words by a sudden pause in Marianne's music.— "Oh! they are talking of their favourite beaux, I dare say."

"No, sister," cried Lucy, "you are mistaken there, our favourite beaux are *not* great coxcombs."

"I can answer for it that Miss Dashwood's is not," said Mrs. Jennings, laughing heartily; "for he is one of the modestest, prettiest[21] behaved young men I ever saw; but as for Lucy, she is such a sly[22] little creature, there is no finding out who *she* likes."

"Oh!" cried Miss Steele, looking significantly round at them, "I dare say Lucy's beau is quite as modest and pretty behaved as Miss Dashwood's."

Elinor blushed in spite of herself. Lucy bit her lip, and looked angrily at her sister. A mutual silence took place for some time. Lucy first put an end to it by saying in a lower tone, though Marianne was then giving them the powerful protection of a very magnificent concerto[23] —

13. *impose upon*: deceive.

14. The silence indicates a shift in the conversation toward Elinor's advantage. Lucy was presumably hoping for Elinor to reply, but the latter felt no reason to respond to words whose falseness she had clearly perceived. Since Lucy does not have any further arguments to make to impress her listener, Elinor is able to turn to posing questions, including ones that might even give her valuable information about Edward.

15. *views*: expectations; plans.

16. *suspense*: uncertainty, delay.

17. *owning*: confessing.

18. Mrs. Ferrars could bequeath all her fortune and property to Robert. That this is the sole reason Lucy gives for the lengthy delay in their engagement shows that this is uppermost in her mind, and that such financial considerations overshadow the hardships of long waiting that Elinor has just evoked.

19. Lucy's silence is a further indication that Elinor is getting the better of her, in this case by pointing out the contradiction between Lucy's pose of thinking solely of Edward and her evident concern for her own financial interest.

20. *coxcomb*: conceited, foolish man, excessively concerned with his appearance and inclined to show off; fop.

21. *prettiest*: best.

22. *sly*: secretive.

23. *concerto*: musical piece. The term then could apply to a variety of musical compositions, rather than just ones involving a solo instrument and an orchestra, as it usually does today.

"I will honestly tell you of one scheme which has lately come into my head, for bringing matters to bear; indeed I am bound to let you into the secret, for you are a party concerned.[24] I dare say you have seen enough of Edward to know that he would prefer the church to every other profession; now my plan is that he should take orders[25] as soon as he can, and then through your interest,[26] which I am sure you would be kind enough to use out of friendship for him, and I hope out of some regard to me, your brother might be persuaded to give him Norland living;[27] which I understand is a very good one,[28] and the present incumbent not likely to live a great while.[29] That would be enough for us to marry upon, and we might trust to time and chance for the rest."

"I should be always happy," replied Elinor, "to shew any mark of my esteem and friendship for Mr. Ferrars;[30] but do not you perceive that my interest on such an occasion would be perfectly unnecessary? He is brother to Mrs. John Dashwood—*that* must be recommendation enough to her husband."

"But Mrs. John Dashwood would not much approve of Edward's going into orders."

"Then I rather suspect that my interest would do very little."

They were again silent for many minutes. At length Lucy exclaimed with a deep sigh,

"I believe it would be the wisest way to put an end to the business at once by dissolving the engagement.[31] We seem so beset with difficulties on every side, that though it would make us miserable for a time, we should be happier perhaps in the end. But you will not give me your advice, Miss Dashwood?"

"No"; answered Elinor, with a smile, which concealed very agitated feelings,[32] "on such a subject I certainly will not. You know very well that my opinion would have no weight with you, unless it were on the side of your wishes."

"Indeed you wrong me," replied Lucy with great solemnity; "I know nobody of whose judgment I think so highly as I do of yours; and I do really believe, that if you was to say to me, 'I advise you by all means to put an end to your engagement with Edward Ferrars,

24. She presumably means Elinor is a party concerned because of her friendship with Edward, or her family connection with him.

25. *take orders:* become ordained as a clergyman.

26. *interest:* influence, especially through personal connections.

27. The living is the position of clergyman for a parish. The right to appoint people, who had to be qualified clergy, to these positions was not controlled by the church, but by a variety of individuals or other entities. This right was effectively a piece of property, which could be passed on to one's heirs or bought and sold. Wealthy landowning families controlled a large number of livings, and were especially likely to control one for the parish in which they resided, as is the case here with John Dashwood and is later revealed to be the case with Colonel Brandon. The personal influence Lucy refers to was critical for appointments, for those making them were most likely to choose a person who was a family member or friend, or was recommended by someone connected to them. This system, though subject to some criticism, was generally accepted, in part because most institutions in this society were governed primarily by patronage and personal connections.

28. The holder of the living enjoys a very good income. This would come from tithes the parishioners were obligated to pay and profits of glebe land, which the holder of the living could farm. Incomes varied significantly from one living to another, due to the great differences in the population and wealth of parishes, which would determine the amount of the tithes collected, as well as to the differences in the size of glebe land.

29. Since appointments to clerical positions were for life, they would normally become vacant only when the current holder, or incumbent, died. Even those who had become too old to perform the duties effectively would usually hire a curate (see p. 117, note 25), rather than resign.

30. She speaks of friendship only for Edward, though Lucy had mentioned Elinor's possible regard for herself.

31. Lucy, as the woman, would be the one to decide to do this, though she certainly could do it in consultation with Edward if she wished.

32. Elinor conceals her emotions, probably from a sense that Lucy's words are meant to solicit a reaction that reveals Elinor's true feelings for Edward and puts her in an embarrassed position.

it will be more for the happiness of both of you,' I should resolve upon doing it immediately."

Elinor blushed for the insincerity of Edward's future wife, and replied, "This compliment would effectually frighten me from giving any opinion on the subject had I formed one. It raises my influence much too high; the power of dividing two people so tenderly attached is too much for an indifferent person."[33]

"'Tis because you are an indifferent person," said Lucy, with some pique, and laying a particular stress on those words, "that your judgment might justly have such weight with me. If you could be supposed to be biassed in any respect by your own feelings, your opinion would not be worth having."[34]

Elinor thought it wisest to make no answer to this, lest they might provoke each other to an unsuitable increase of ease[35] and unreserve;[36] and was even partly determined never to mention the subject again. Another pause therefore of many minutes' duration, succeeded this speech, and Lucy was still the first to end it.

"Shall you be in town this winter, Miss Dashwood?" said she with all her accustomary[37] complacency.

"Certainly not."

"I am sorry for that," returned the other, while her eyes brightened at the information, "it would have gave me such pleasure to meet you there! But I dare say you will go for all that. To be sure, your brother and sister will ask you to come to them."

"It will not be in my power to accept their invitation if they do."

"How unlucky that is! I had quite depended upon meeting you there. Anne and me are to go the latter end of January to some relations who have been wanting us to visit them these several years! But I only go for the sake of seeing Edward.[38] He will be there in February, otherwise London would have no charms for me; I have not spirits for it."

Elinor was soon called to the card-table by the conclusion of the first rubber,[39] and the confidential discourse of the two ladies was therefore at an end, to which both of them submitted without any reluctance, for nothing had been said on either side, to make them dislike each other less than they had done before; and Eli-

33. In calling them "so tenderly attached" Elinor is employing stronger and more obvious sarcasm than she has used until now. It may be the result of the agitation caused by Lucy's last question, or simply from cumulative annoyance as she talks further to Lucy.

34. Lucy's words also reveal increased annoyance with Elinor, though, in a sign of the latter's relative triumph in this conversation, Lucy alone shows her annoyance through the tone of her voice.

35. *ease:* lack of restraint; informality.

36. Their increasingly sharp words might escalate into more open avowals of their real feelings toward each other.

37. *accustomary:* usual.

38. Lucy explicitly declares her indifference toward these relations, even though she is obviously intending to make use of their hospitality. When not attempting to flatter or deceive someone, her own words frequently display her underlying lack of regard for others.

39. The rubber of casino (see p. 266 and p. 267, note 55).

nor sat down to the card-table with the melancholy persuasion
that Edward was not only without affection for the person who
was to be his wife; but that he had not even the chance of being
tolerably happy in marriage, which sincere affection on *her* side
would have given, for self-interest alone could induce a woman to
keep a man to an engagement, of which she seemed so thoroughly aware that he was weary.[40]

From this time the subject was never revived by Elinor, and
when entered on by Lucy, who seldom missed an opportunity of
introducing it, and was particularly careful to inform her confidante, of her happiness whenever she received a letter from
Edward,[41] it was treated by the former with calmness and caution,
and dismissed as soon as civility would allow; for she felt such conversations to be an indulgence which Lucy did not deserve, and
which were dangerous to herself.[42]

The visit of the Miss Steeles at Barton Park was lengthened far
beyond what the first invitation implied. Their favour increased,
they could not be spared; Sir John would not hear of their going;
and in spite of their numerous and long arranged engagements in
Exeter, in spite of the absolute necessity of their returning to fulfil
them immediately, which was in full force at the end of every
week, they were prevailed on to stay nearly two months at the
park,[43] and to assist in the due celebration of that festival which
requires a more than ordinary share of private balls and large dinners to proclaim its importance.[44]

40. Lucy's having felt the need to warn Elinor away by revealing the engagement constitutes the strongest proof that she knows Edward is weary of it. Further proof appeared in this conversation through Lucy's evident animosity toward Elinor and her inability to mention anything indicating Edward's continued regard, even after implicitly challenged on the point by Elinor.

41. Lucy could receive these letters without sacrificing the secrecy of her engagement because none of the people with whom she is now staying would know Edward's handwriting. People did not write a return address on letters then, only the name of the recipient. Letters did show a postmark, but Edward seems to spend much of his time in London, and a postmark from there, even if it excited the curiosity of Mrs. Jennings or Sir John, could easily be explained as coming from the relations in London that Lucy has just mentioned.

42. They could be dangerous by inciting her to speak to Lucy in a way that would violate good manners, or, perhaps even more likely, by reminding her of her disappointment with Edward and kindling resentment toward him or regrets about her own situation. She was earlier shown trying to suppress her feelings of disappointment after Edward's visit.

43. Presumably they prefer the Middletons because of their superior wealth and status—for the probable social inferiority of their relatives at Exeter, see p. 223, note 5. Over the course of the novel they repeatedly drop one group of people for another whenever it seems advantageous.

44. This would be Christmas (see chronology, p. 713). At this time Christmas was celebrated principally through parties and feasting. Gift giving, trees, cards, and special decorations did not arise until later in the nineteenth century.

Chapter Three

*T*hough Mrs. Jennings was in the habit of spending a large portion of the year at the houses of her children and friends, she was not without a settled habitation of her own. Since the death of her husband, who had traded with success in a less elegant part of the town, she had resided every winter in a house in one of the streets near Portman-square.[1] Towards this home, she began on the approach of January to turn her thoughts, and thither she one day abruptly, and very unexpectedly by them, asked the elder Miss Dashwoods to accompany her. Elinor, without observing the varying complexion of her sister, and the animated look which spoke[2] no indifference to the plan, immediately gave a grateful but absolute denial for both, in which she believed herself to be speaking their united inclinations. The reason alledged was their determined resolution of not leaving their mother at that time of the year. Mrs. Jennings received the refusal with some surprize, and repeated her invitation immediately.

"Oh! Lord, I am sure your mother can spare you very well, and I *do* beg you will favour me with your company, for I've quite set my heart upon it. Don't fancy that you will be any inconvenience to me, for I shan't put myself at all out of my way for you. It will only be sending Betty by the coach, and I hope I can afford *that*.[3] We three shall be able to go very well in my chaise;[4] and when we are in town, if you do not like to go wherever I do, well and good, you may always go with one of my daughters.[5] I am sure your mother will not object to it; for I have had such good luck in getting my own children off my hands, that she will think me a very fit person to have the charge of you; and if I don't get one of you at least well married before I have done with you, it shall not be my fault.[6] I shall speak a good word for you to all the young men, you may depend upon it."[7]

1.   Portman Square is in an elegant part of London; for more on this, see p. 315, note 23. For the location of the square, see map, p. 742; for a picture, see p. 291.

2.   *spoke:* indicated, revealed.

3.   Betty is her servant. Many wealthy women would be accompanied wherever they went by lady's maids, who took care of their mistresses' clothes and helped them with dressing and grooming. Betty, however, is not such a maid, though she may perform some of the same functions, for a lady's maid was an upper servant, which would give her the right to be called by her last name rather than her first. Betty was a common name for servants, who often had diminutives as names: according to one scholar (Maggie Lane), most poorer women of the time with the name had been christened simply "Betty," rather than "Elizabeth." The former name was correspondingly shunned by the wealthy, even as the latter remained popular: Elizabeth Bennet, the heroine of *Pride and Prejudice,* is only called "Elizabeth," "Eliza," or "Lizzy."
  Betty would be sent by the public coach because the chaise (see next note) seats only three people, so there would be no room for her if Elinor and Marianne came. The fare for a coach ride would be a modest sum for someone like Mrs. Jennings, who is wealthy enough to own an elegant house in London. For a picture of a public coach, see p. 403.

4.   A chaise was a small enclosed carriage (for a picture, see p. 287). Whereas a coach had two seats, each with room for three that faced one another, a chaise had one such seat facing forward. It was the vehicle most commonly used by people traveling post (see p. 125, note 18). Its being enclosed meant protection from cold and rain, while its small size meant it could go faster than a coach. Mrs. Jennings would be renting a chaise, the most common procedure for those traveling post.

5.   One of them could serve as chaperone (see p. 209, note 3).

6.   Mrs. Jennings assumes, like most people in this society, that a mother's principal concern for her daughters is that they find husbands.

7.   She probably figures that all those who have shown an interest in Marianne and Elinor—Willoughby, Colonel Brandon, and Edward—will be in London for the winter. At the same time, the vagueness of her words suggests she would be happy to look out for any potential mates; further incidents will show Mrs. Jennings assuming that other people are not too choosy about whom they will marry.

"I have a notion," said Sir John, "that Miss Marianne would not object to such a scheme, if her elder sister would come into[8] it. It is very hard indeed that she should not have a little pleasure, because Miss Dashwood does not wish it. So I would advise you two, to set off for town, when you are tired of Barton, without saying a word to Miss Dashwood about it."

"Nay," cried Mrs. Jennings, "I am sure I shall be monstrous glad of Miss Marianne's company, whether Miss Dashwood will go or not, only the more the merrier say I, and I thought it would be more comfortable[9] for them to be together; because if they got tired of me, they might talk to one another, and laugh at my odd ways behind my back.[10] But one or the other, if not both of them, I must have. Lord bless me! how do you think I can live poking[11] by myself, I who have been always used till this winter to have Charlotte with me.[12] Come, Miss Marianne, let us strike hands upon the bargain, and if Miss Dashwood will change her mind by and bye, why so much the better."[13]

"I thank you, ma'am, sincerely thank you," said Marianne, with warmth; "your invitation has insured my gratitude for ever, and it would give me such happiness, yes almost the greatest happiness I am capable of, to be able to accept it. But my mother, my dearest, kindest mother,—I feel the justice of what Elinor has urged, and if she were to be made less happy, less comfortable by our absence—Oh! no, nothing should tempt me to leave her. It should not, must not be a struggle."

Mrs. Jennings repeated her assurance that Mrs. Dashwood could spare them perfectly well; and Elinor, who now understood her sister, and saw to what indifference to almost every thing else, she was carried by her eagerness to be with Willoughby again,[14] made no farther direct opposition to the plan, and merely referred it to her mother's decision, from whom however she scarcely expected to receive any support in her endeavour to prevent a visit, which she could not approve of for Marianne, and which on her own account she had particular reasons to avoid.[15] Whatever Marianne was desirous of, her mother would be eager to promote—she could not expect to influence the latter to cautious-

8. *come into*: agree with, accede to.

9. *comfortable*: pleasant, enjoyable.

10. From this point forward Mrs. Jennings plays a more important role. While her basic character remains the same, the more positive aspects of her nature, particularly her generosity and good humor, come more to the fore. Her offer to take Elinor and Marianne, and her talking merrily of how they could laugh at her behind her back, highlight those qualities.

11. *poking*: puttering around.

12. Charlotte (Mrs. Palmer) would have lived with her mother during previous winters because she was still unmarried. Her being pregnant now with her first child indicates that her marriage was recent, for since children were seen as a central purpose of marriage, and birth control was rarely practiced, couples generally began having babies soon after the wedding.

13. As always in Jane Austen, the language employed by Mrs. Jennings gives a good sense of her character. Her use of a slang term like "monstrous," frequent recourse to colloquial expressions like "the more the merrier" and "let us strike hands," and her saying "Lord"—an invocation often in her mouth that was generally regarded as improper—mark her speech as far from polished and elegant. The speech of most characters, especially intelligent ones like Elinor, do not include any of these features.

14. Marianne may expect Willoughby to be in London because he identified that as his destination when he left (though he did not say how long he would be there), or because he had told her he intended to be there in the winter, or simply because she knows that many people go to London then. The mention of Willoughby and Marianne's feelings toward him indicates that the story, after having focused on Elinor's situation for a number of chapters, is now shifting back to the younger sister. There will be several more shifts until the end.

15. On her own account she wishes to avoid seeing Edward, especially in the presence of Lucy. As for Marianne, Elinor's thoughts about her and Willoughby have not been described since his abrupt departure and her debates with her mother on the subject. But Willoughby's continued absence and silence would certainly increase her doubts about his intentions, and she probably fears that pursuing him to London is likely to lead Marianne to disappointment, while encouraging her to keep focusing on a matter that causes her distress.

ness of conduct in an affair, respecting which she had never been able to inspire her with distrust; and she dared not explain the motive of her own disinclination for going to London. That Marianne, fastidious as she was, thoroughly acquainted with Mrs. Jennings's manners, and invariably disgusted by them, should overlook every inconvenience of that kind, should disregard whatever must be most wounding to her irritable feelings, in her pursuit of one object, was such a proof, so strong, so full of the importance of that object to her, as Elinor, in spite of all that had passed, was not prepared to witness.[16]

On being informed of the invitation, Mrs. Dashwood, persuaded that such an excursion would be productive of much amusement[17] to both her daughters, and perceiving through all her affectionate attention to herself, how much the heart of Marianne was in it, would not hear of their declining the offer upon *her* account; insisted on their both accepting it directly,[18] and then began to foresee with her usual cheerfulness, a variety of advantages that would accrue to them all, from this separation.

"I am delighted with the plan," she cried, "it is exactly what I could wish. Margaret and I shall be as much benefited by it as yourselves. When you and the Middletons are gone, we shall go on so quietly and happily together with our books and our music! You will find Margaret so improved when you come back again![19] And I have a little plan of alteration for your bedrooms too, which may now be performed without inconvenience to any one. It is very right that you *should* go to town; I would have every young woman of your condition in life, acquainted with the manners and amusements of London.[20] You will be under the care of a motherly good sort of woman, of whose kindness to you I can have no doubt. And in all probability you will see your brother, and whatever may be his faults, or the faults of his wife, when I consider whose son he is, I cannot bear to have you so wholly estranged from each other."

"Though with your usual anxiety for our happiness," said Elinor, "you have been obviating every impediment to the present

16. Elinor fears what these strong feelings portend, in the event that Marianne's hopes are not fulfilled.

17. *amusement*: enjoyment.

18. *directly*: immediately.

19. Mrs. Dashwood is educating Margaret at home (being thirteen she is not finished yet). This was common for girls and would be particularly likely in a case like this in which the mother is highly capable of teaching—Mrs. Dashwood's polished and articulate speech, her high social background, and the excellent learning displayed by her two oldest daughters all suggest that she is well educated—but in no position to afford a fine school. One reason for Mrs. Dashwood to expect great improvement in Margaret while the others are gone, in addition to her inveterate optimism about everything, is that Margaret has undoubtedly spent a large amount of time away from home, and her studies, due to the frequent social events sponsored by the Middletons.

20. London offered a vast array of plays, concerts, and public spectacles, and these could provide young women of their condition, i.e., social rank, with enjoyment and cultural polish. As for manners, those of elite London society were considered the height of elegance and refinement, and their beneficial influence was extolled by many writers.

A *chaise*.

[From G. A. Thrupp, *History of Coaches* (London, 1877), p. 77]

scheme which occurred to you,[21] there is still one objection which, in my opinion, cannot be so easily removed."

Marianne's countenance sunk.

"And what," said Mrs. Dashwood, "is my dear prudent Elinor going to suggest? What formidable obstacle is she now to bring forward? Do not let me hear a word about the expense of it."[22]

"My objection is this; though I think very well of Mrs. Jennings's heart, she is not a woman whose society can afford us pleasure, or whose protection[23] will give us consequence."[24]

"That is very true," replied her mother; "but of her society, separately from that of other people, you will scarcely have any thing at all, and you will almost always appear in public with Lady Middleton."[25]

"If Elinor is frightened away by her dislike of Mrs. Jennings," said Marianne, "at least it need not prevent *my* accepting her invitation. I have no such scruples,[26] and I am sure, I could put up with every unpleasantness of that kind with very little effort."

Elinor could not help smiling at this display of indifference towards the manners of a person, to whom she had often had difficulty in persuading Marianne to behave with tolerable politeness: and resolved within herself, that if her sister persisted in going, she would go likewise, as she did not think it proper that Marianne should be left to the sole guidance of her own judgment, or that Mrs. Jennings should be abandoned to the mercy of Marianne for all the comfort of her domestic hours.[27] To this determination she was the more easily reconciled, by recollecting, that Edward Ferrars, by Lucy's account, was not to be in town before February; and that their visit, without any unreasonable abridgment, might be previously finished.

"I will have you *both* go," said Mrs. Dashwood; "these objections are nonsensical. You will have much pleasure in being in London, and especially in being together; and if Elinor would ever condescend[28] to anticipate enjoyment, she would foresee it there from a variety of sources; she would perhaps expect some from improving her acquaintance with her sister-in-law's family."[29]

21. This is a diplomatic way for Elinor to hint critically at her mother's tendency to overlook every possible impediment or drawback to a pleasant scheme. One example of this tendency appears above in her mother's talk of being able to alter the bedrooms, which, given everything that has appeared about their finances, is almost certainly not feasible.

22. Mrs. Dashwood's quick dismissal of the entire matter of cost indicates her impracticality. It may not cost much, since they will be staying with Mrs. Jennings, but one cannot be automatically sure of that, especially given the expensiveness of London.

23. *protection*: patronage, tutelage.

24. *consequence*: social importance or position. Since they will be Mrs. Jennings's effective dependents while there, her vulgarity will reflect on them socially. That Elinor should consider this an objection worth raising, and that Mrs. Dashwood should feel compelled to answer it, indicates how much even the most high-minded people in this society value social status.

25. Going in public with Lady Middleton would be preferable because of her far superior manners and social polish.

26. *scruples*: hesitations.

27. This decision underlines Elinor's self-sacrificing character. It is also essential to the development of the entire plot.

28. *condescend*: consent.

29. This could mean Edward, though Elinor already knows him well, or Edward's brother, about whom they know little, or Mrs. Ferrars, though after all that has been heard to her detriment, it is doubtful that one could rationally anticipate enjoyment from becoming acquainted with her.

Elinor had often wished for an opportunity of attempting to weaken her mother's dependence on the attachment of Edward and herself, that the shock might be the less when the whole truth were revealed, and now on this attack, though almost hopeless of success, she forced herself to begin her design by saying, as calmly as she could, "I like Edward Ferrars very much, and shall always be glad to see him; but as to the rest of the family, it is a matter of perfect indifference to me, whether I am ever known to them or not."

Mrs. Dashwood smiled and said nothing. Marianne lifted up her eyes in astonishment, and Elinor conjectured that she might as well have held her tongue.

After very little farther discourse, it was finally settled that the invitation should be fully accepted. Mrs. Jennings received the information with a great deal of joy, and many assurances of kindness and care; nor was it a matter of pleasure merely to her. Sir John was delighted; for to a man, whose prevailing anxiety was the dread of being alone, the acquisition of two, to the number of inhabitants in London, was something. Even Lady Middleton took the trouble of being delighted, which was putting herself rather out of her way; and as for the Miss Steeles, especially Lucy, they had never been so happy in their lives as this intelligence made them.[30]

Elinor submitted to the arrangement which counteracted her wishes, with less reluctance than she had expected to feel. With regard to herself, it was now a matter of unconcern whether she went to town or not, and when she saw her mother so thoroughly pleased with the plan, and her sister exhilarated by it in look, voice, and manner, restored to all her usual animation, and elevated to more than her usual gaiety, she could not be dissatisfied with the cause, and would hardly allow herself to distrust the consequence.[31]

Marianne's joy was almost a degree beyond happiness, so great was the perturbation of her spirits and her impatience to be gone. Her unwillingness to quit her mother was her only restorative to calmness; and at the moment of parting, her grief on that score

30. The hyperbole of their enthusiasm contrasts sharply with Lucy's look of delight when Elinor told her earlier she would not go to London (p. 278).

31. Meaning to mistrust or fear what might result from Marianne's attempt to see Willoughby again.

Portman Square in London; Mrs. Jennings's residence is near here.

[From *The Repository of arts, literature, fashions, manufactures, &c*, Vol. X (1813), p. 105]

was excessive. Her mother's affliction was hardly less, and Elinor was the only one of the three, who seemed to consider the separation as any thing short of eternal.

Their departure took place in the first week in January. The Middletons were to follow in about a week. The Miss Steeles kept their station at the park, and were to quit it only with the rest of the family.[32]

A contemporary view of London.

[From *The Repository of arts, literature, fashions, manufactures, &c*, Vol. VII (1812), p. 223]

32. Soon almost all the characters will appear in London, and remain there for much of the rest of the novel. As already mentioned, London was very busy in the winter and attracted many people. For some, such as John Dashwood and his wife, it would be a natural venue because they live in the nearby county of Sussex. For the Middletons it would be more unusual, given the long travel time between Devonshire and London. Wealthy families in the western part of England would be more likely to go to Bath for the winter, as important characters in both *Northanger Abbey* and *Persuasion* do, because of its greater proximity (see map, p. 738). Bath was the leading resort town in England, and while not as busy as London, it offered plenty of entertainment and social life, at a lower cost. The probable reason for the exception here is that Mrs. Jennings and the Palmers both have a house in London, the former because of her earlier residence there and the latter most likely because of his ambition to serve in Parliament. This could easily induce the Middletons to go there as well to be close to their relations.

Carriages stopping at an inn.

[From Joseph Grego, *Rowlandson the Caricaturist*, Vol. I (London, 1880), p. 213]

Chapter Four

*E*linor could not find herself in the carriage with Mrs. Jennings, and beginning a journey to London under her protection, and as her guest, without wondering at her own situation, so short had their acquaintance with that lady been, so wholly unsuited were they in age and disposition, and so many had been her objections against such a measure only a few days before! But these objections had all, with that happy ardour of youth which Marianne and her mother equally shared, been overcome or overlooked; and Elinor, in spite of every occasional doubt of Willoughby's constancy, could not witness the rapture of delightful expectation which filled the whole soul and beamed in the eyes of Marianne, without feeling how blank was her own prospect, how cheerless her own state of mind in the comparison, and how gladly she would engage in the solicitude of Marianne's situation to have the same animating object in view, the same possibility of hope. A short, a very short time however must now decide what Willoughby's intentions were; in all probability he was already in town. Marianne's eagerness to be gone declared her dependance on finding him there; and Elinor was resolved not only upon gaining every new light as to his character which her own observation or the intelligence of others could give her, but likewise upon watching his behaviour to her sister with such zealous attention, as to ascertain what he was and what he meant, before many meetings had taken place. Should the result of her observations be unfavourable, she was determined at all events to open the eyes of her sister; should it be otherwise, her exertions would be of a different nature—she must then learn to avoid every selfish comparison, and banish every regret which might lessen her satisfaction in the happiness of Marianne.[1]

They were three days on their journey,[2] and Marianne's behav-

1. That this would require exertion indicates that Elinor's goodness is not simply a natural and automatic attribute, but something she must continually attain by struggling to suppress other impulses. This is consistently the case for Jane Austen's heroines.

2. The distance from Barton, four miles north of Exeter, to London would be around 175 miles by the main roads of the time. The standard speed on main roads was seven to eight miles per hour if using two horses, as most people did. This would mean a journey of between twenty-two and twenty-five hours: they probably spent around nine hours each day on the road the first two days, and the remainder on the third day (they are described below as arriving at three o'clock). These times, while very slow from our perspective, were a considerable improvement over earlier ages, a product of better carriages and, especially, advances in road design and construction. Jane Austen is always very accurate about the amount of time required to travel someplace; in a letter to a niece, in which she comments on the niece's draft of a novel, she criticizes her for having people travel in one day between two towns that are actually two days apart (Aug. 18, 1814).

iour as they travelled was a happy[3] specimen of what her future complaisance[4] and companionableness to Mrs. Jennings might be expected to be. She sat in silence almost all the way, wrapt in her own meditations, and scarcely ever voluntarily speaking, except when any object of picturesque beauty within their view drew from her an exclamation of delight exclusively addressed to her sister. To atone for this conduct therefore, Elinor took immediate possession of the post of civility which she had assigned herself, behaved with the greatest attention to Mrs. Jennings, talked with her, laughed with her, and listened to her whenever she could;[5] and Mrs. Jennings on her side treated them both with all possible kindness, was solicitous on every occasion for their ease and enjoyment, and only disturbed that she could not make them choose their own dinners at the inn,[6] nor extort a confession of their preferring salmon to cod, or boiled fowls to veal cutlets.[7] They reached town by three o'clock the third day, glad to be released, after such a journey, from the confinement of a carriage, and ready to enjoy all the luxury of a good fire.[8]

The house was handsome[9] and handsomely fitted up, and the young ladies were immediately put in possession of a very comfortable apartment.[10] It had formerly been Charlotte's, and over the mantlepiece still hung a landscape in coloured silks[11] of her performance, in proof of her having spent seven years at a great[12] school in town to some effect.[13]

As dinner was not to be ready in less than two hours from their arrival, Elinor determined to employ the interval in writing to her mother, and sat down for that purpose. In a few moments Marianne did the same. "I am writing home, Marianne," said Elinor; "had not you better defer your letter for a day or two?"

"I am *not* going to write to my mother," replied Marianne hastily, and as if wishing to avoid any farther inquiry. Elinor said no more; it immediately struck her that she must then be writing to Willoughby, and the conclusion which as instantly followed was, that however mysteriously they might wish to conduct the affair, they must be engaged.[14] This conviction, though not entirely satisfactory,[15] gave her pleasure, and she continued her

3. *happy*: fitting, appropriate.

4. *complaisance*: civility, willingness to please others.

5. Elinor frequently makes up for Marianne's deficiencies in civility. It is one reason Marianne is able to be rude or inconsiderate without suffering many negative consequences.

6. They probably just took whatever standard fare was being offered or deferred to Mrs. Jennings's choice.

7. As this list indicates, the diet of wealthy people in England then was heavily centered on meat and fish.

8. It is now January, and carriages then had no heat (though people did use very warm coverings).

9. *handsome*: moderately large.

10. "Apartment" most frequently meant room then, but it could mean a suite of rooms. Country houses often had apartments consisting of a bedroom and a dressing room, and perhaps a large closet. But in town houses, where space was far more limited, people were more likely just to have a bedroom, and this is probably the case with Elinor and Marianne.

11. *landscape in coloured silks*: silk embroidery of a landscape scene.

12. *great*: prestigious (especially in a social sense).

13. Girls from wealthy families would often go to schools. Those in London were especially prestigious, though the main reason Charlotte attended one may have been because her parents lived there. The focus of these schools was teaching accomplishments, which could include foreign languages (usually French or Italian), drawing, music, dance, or decorative activities like embroidery. That the best proof of Charlotte's seven years is a piece of embroidery suggests that the education she received was of limited value.

14. As already mentioned, correspondence between unmarried men and women was permitted only if they were engaged. Presumably Elinor did not witness any letters from Marianne to Willoughby while they were at home.

15. The reason it is not entirely satisfactory is probably that Willoughby's prolonged absence and silence have made her doubt his affection for Marianne. Thus if they are engaged Marianne could be binding herself to a man who would not prove to be an ideal husband.

letter with greater alacrity. Marianne's was finished in a very few minutes; in length it could be no more than a note: it was then folded up, sealed and directed with eager rapidity.[16] Elinor thought she could distinguish a large W. in the direction, and no sooner was it complete than Marianne, ringing the bell,[17] requested the footman[18] who answered it, to get that letter conveyed for her to the two-penny post.[19] This decided the matter at once.

Her spirits still continued very high, but there was a flutter in them which prevented their giving much pleasure to her sister, and this agitation increased as the evening drew on. She could scarcely eat any dinner, and when they afterwards returned to the drawing room, seemed anxiously listening to the sound of every carriage.

It was a great satisfaction to Elinor that Mrs. Jennings, by being much engaged in her own room, could see little of what was passing. The tea things were brought in, and already had Marianne been disappointed more than once by a rap at a neighbouring door,[20] when a loud one was suddenly heard which could not be mistaken for one at any other house.[21] Elinor felt secure of its announcing Willoughby's approach, and Marianne starting up moved towards the door.[22] Every thing was silent; this could not be borne many seconds, she opened the door, advanced a few steps towards the stairs,[23] and after listening half a minute, returned into the room in all the agitation which a conviction of having heard him would naturally produce; in the extasy of her feelings at that instant she could not help exclaiming, "Oh! Elinor, it is Willoughby, indeed it is!" and seemed almost ready to throw herself into his arms, when Colonel Brandon appeared.

It was too great a shock to be borne with calmness, and she immediately left the room. Elinor was disappointed too; but at the same time her regard for Colonel Brandon ensured his welcome with her, and she felt particularly hurt that a man so partial to her sister should perceive that she experienced nothing but grief and disappointment in seeing him. She instantly saw that it was not unnoticed by him, that he even observed Marianne as she quitted

16. Once a letter was written the paper, or papers, would be folded up and then sealed on the outside—there were no envelopes. The sealing would be done either by placing a sticky wafer between the folds of the paper or by melting wax onto the paper, and then stamping it with a seal. Then it could be directed, or addressed. The contents of this note are revealed on p. 344.

17. She would have pulled a cord to trigger a bell in the servants' quarters.

18. *footman:* low-ranking servant responsible for delivering messages, carrying things, and, in many households, answering the door and waiting on table.

19. The two-penny post conveyed letters within London. The system had started in 1680 and made it possible to send letters anywhere in the city for a penny. In 1801 the government's need for money to fight the wars with France caused it to increase the rate to two pennies, and a charge of three pennies for letters to and from suburban areas was instituted a few years later. London was the only city in England to have such a system, which was run separately from the rest of the postal service. Marianne's sending the letter by this means is a sign of her belief or knowledge that Willoughby is in London. A large number of receiving houses existed throughout the city to collect letters for the two-penny post. For a picture of someone posting a letter, see the next page.

20. Tea would be served in the early evening, so her expectation of visitors is not unreasonable.

21. The front doors of houses almost all had large knockers on them to allow people to signal their arrival. Doorbells had not been introduced: a passage in *Persuasion,* written six years after this novel was finished, contains one of the first known mentions of doorbells.

22. They are not too hasty in their expectation. Letters for the two-penny post were collected frequently, and delivered quickly and at various times during the day, so Marianne's letter to Willoughby would have reached his address well before this time.

23. London houses tended to be narrow and tall, with many stories and often only two or three rooms on each story. Thus people living in them would need to go up or down stairs frequently.

the room, with such astonishment and concern, as hardly left him
the recollection of what civility demanded towards herself.

"Is your sister ill?" said he.

Elinor answered in some distress that she was, and then talked
of head-aches, low spirits, and over fatigues; and of every thing to
which she could decently attribute her sister's behaviour.

He heard her with the most earnest attention, but seeming to recollect himself, said no more on the subject, and began directly to
speak of his pleasure at seeing them in London, making the usual
inquiries about their journey and the friends they had left behind.

In this calm kind of way, with very little interest on either side,
they continued to talk, both of them out of spirits, and the
thoughts of both engaged elsewhere. Elinor wished very much to
ask whether Willoughby were then in town, but she was afraid of
giving him pain by any inquiry after his rival; and at length by way
of saying something, she asked if he had been in London ever
since she had seen him last. "Yes," he replied, with some embarrassment, "almost ever since; I have been once or twice at
Delaford for a few days, but it has never been in my power to
return to Barton."

This, and the manner in which it was said, immediately brought
back to her remembrance, all the circumstances of his quitting
that place, with the uneasiness and suspicions they had caused to
Mrs. Jennings, and she was fearful that her question had implied
much more curiosity on the subject than she had ever felt.

Mrs. Jennings soon came in. "Oh! Colonel," said she, with her
usual noisy cheerfulness, "I am monstrous glad to see you—sorry
I could not come before—beg your pardon, but I have been
forced to look about me a little, and settle my matters;[24] for it is a
long while since I have been at home, and you know one has
always a world of little odd things to do after one has been away for
any time; and then I have had Cartwright to settle with[25]—Lord, I
have been as busy as a bee ever since dinner! But pray, Colonel,
how came you to conjure out[26] that I should be in town to-day?"

"I had the pleasure of hearing it at Mr. Palmer's, where I have
been dining."[27]

24. *matters:* household or financial affairs.

25. Her using Cartwright's last name rather than his first name indicates he is an upper servant; he is probably not somebody from outside the household, such as a merchant, for then she would say "Mr." He may be her butler, the highest-ranking male servant and someone who might manage the household. This would naturally make him a person she would need to spend time with after a lengthy absence.

26. *conjure out:* divine.

27. Mrs. Jennings does not seem to have contacted the Palmers since her arrival, so they presumably knew of her plans from letters.

Rowlandson Delin 1819
" Letters for post ? '

Posting a letter.

[From Andrew Tuer, *Old London Street Cries*, p. 57]

"Oh! you did; well, and how do they all do at their house? How does Charlotte do? I warrant you she is a fine size by this time."[28]

"Mrs. Palmer appeared quite well, and I am commissioned to tell you, that you will certainly see her to-morrow."

"Aye, to be sure, I thought as much. Well, Colonel, I have brought two young ladies with me, you see—that is, you see but one of them now, but there is another somewhere. Your friend Miss Marianne, too—which you will not be sorry to hear. I do not know what you and Mr. Willoughby will do between you about her. Aye, it is a fine thing to be young and handsome. Well! I was young once, but I never was very handsome—worse luck for me. However I got a very good husband, and I don't know what the greatest beauty can do more. Ah! poor man! he has been dead these eight years and better. But Colonel, where have you been to since we parted? And how does your business go on? Come, come, let's have no secrets among friends."

He replied with his accustomary mildness to all her inquiries, but without satisfying her in any. Elinor now began to make the tea, and Marianne was obliged to appear again.[29]

After her entrance, Colonel Brandon became more thoughtful and silent than he had been before, and Mrs. Jennings could not prevail on him to stay long. No other visitor appeared that evening, and the ladies were unanimous in agreeing to go early to bed.

Marianne rose the next morning with recovered spirits and happy looks. The disappointment of the evening before seemed forgotten in the expectation of what was to happen that day. They had not long finished their breakfast before Mrs. Palmer's barouche[30] stopt at the door, and in a few minutes she came laughing into the room; so delighted to see them all, that it was hard to say whether she received most pleasure from meeting her mother or the Miss Dashwoods again. So surprised at their coming to town, though it was what she had rather expected all along; so angry at their accepting her mother's invitation after having declined her own, though at the same time she would never have forgiven them if they had not come!

28. Charlotte was earlier described as expecting her baby in February. Since it is now early January she would be well advanced in her pregnancy.

29. Making tea was something the ladies of the house did—the servants simply brought in the hot water and materials. The interval between the arrival of the tea things and the making of tea was caused by the unexpected visit of Colonel Brandon. Marianne now feels obliged to reappear, since tea is a common meal and she, as an inhabitant of the house, should participate.

30. *barouche*: a popular carriage among the wealthy (see p. 29, note 18).

A woman in morning dress at a table.

[From *The Repository of arts, literature, fashions, manufactures, &c*, Vol. X (1813), p. 116]

"Mr. Palmer will be so happy to see you," said she; "what do you think he said when he heard of your coming with mama? I forget what it was now, but it was something so droll!"

After an hour or two spent in what her mother called comfortable chat, or in other words, in every variety of inquiry concerning all their acquaintance on Mrs. Jennings's side, and in laughter without cause on Mrs. Palmer's, it was proposed by the latter that they should all accompany her to some shops where she had business that morning, to which Mrs. Jennings and Elinor readily consented, as having likewise some purchases to make themselves;[31] and Marianne, though declining it at first, was induced to go likewise.

Wherever they went, she was evidently always on the watch. In Bond-street[32] especially, where much of their business lay, her eyes were in constant inquiry; and in whatever shop the party were engaged, her mind was equally abstracted from every thing actually before them, from all that interested and occupied the others. Restless and dissatisfied every where, her sister could never obtain her opinion of any article of purchase, however it might equally concern them both; she received no pleasure from any thing; was only impatient to be at home again, and could with difficulty govern her vexation at the tediousness of Mrs. Palmer, whose eye was caught by every thing pretty, expensive, or new; who was wild to buy all, could determine on none, and dawdled away her time in rapture and indecision.

It was late in the morning before they returned home; and no sooner had they entered the house than Marianne flew eagerly up stairs, and when Elinor followed, she found her turning from the table with a sorrowful countenance, which declared that no Willoughby had been there.[33]

"Has no letter been left here for me since we went out?" said she to the footman who then entered with the parcels.[34] She was answered in the negative. "Are you quite sure of it?" she replied. "Are you certain that no servant, no porter has left any letter or note?"[35]

The man replied that none had.

31. The wealth and variety of stores in London made shopping a prime activity for those visiting the city. In her letters chronicling visits to London Jane Austen often mentions shopping, including the fulfillment of commissions for other people. Elinor may be making some purchases for her mother or Margaret, or for their home in Barton. For a contemporary picture of the Wedgwood shop, one of the leading sellers of ceramics, see below.

32. *Bond-street:* a prominent street in London containing many shops. Willoughby later identifies it as the location of his lodgings (p. 610), and Marianne, having written to him, presumably knows this is his address. She could not simply call on him there because that would be improper.

33. She could be looking for a letter from Willoughby or a visiting card (see p. 311, note 7, and p. 313, note 17): either would be left on the table by the servants. A visiting card would be left personally, and so could arrive at any time, while the London two-penny post delivered throughout the day.

34. The footman would be fetching the parcels they had purchased from their carriage. Footmen would often accompany their employers on shopping excursions to carry things, but Marianne's question suggests this man has been at home. One important reason to bring a footman on errands was to impress others—footmen tended to have very gaudy uniforms—and announce one's status, but Mrs. Jennings is not one to care greatly about that.

35. A porter was in charge of the gate or door to a house. He, or a regular servant, most likely a footman, could be sent to deliver a letter by foot, for the affluent section of London was not extensive.

The Wedgwood shop in London.

[From *The Repository of arts, literature, fashions, manufactures, &c*, Vol. I (1809), p. 102]

"How very odd!" said she in a low and disappointed voice, as she turned away to the window.

"How odd indeed!" repeated Elinor within herself, regarding her sister with uneasiness. "If she had not known him to be in town she would not have written to him, as she did; she would have written to Combe Magna; and if he is in town, how odd that he should neither come nor write! Oh! my dear mother, you must be wrong in permitting an engagement between a daughter so young, a man so little known, to be carried on in so doubtful, so mysterious a manner! *I* long to inquire; but how will *my* interference be borne!"

She determined after some consideration, that if appearances continued many days longer, as unpleasant as they now were, she would represent in the strongest manner to her mother the necessity of some serious inquiry into the affair.

Mrs. Palmer and two elderly ladies of Mrs. Jennings's intimate acquaintance, whom she had met and invited in the morning, dined with them.[36] The former left them soon after tea to fulfil her evening engagements; and Elinor was obliged to assist in making a whist-table for the others. Marianne was of no use on these occasions, as she would never learn the game,[37] but though her time was therefore at her own disposal, the evening was by no means more productive of pleasure to her than to Elinor, for it was spent in all the anxiety of expectation and the pain of disappointment. She sometimes endeavoured for a few minutes to read; but the book was soon thrown aside, and she returned to the more interesting employment of walking backwards and forwards across the room, pausing for a moment whenever she came to the window, in hopes of distinguishing the long-expected rap.

36. Because Mrs. Jennings and the others returned "late in the morning," it would be natural for them to stay to dine; dinner, occurring around four or five, marked the end of the morning.

37. Marianne's refusal to learn would be unusual, for whist, which had arisen only in the eighteenth century, had by this time become the most popular card game in England. It is essentially bridge without bidding or a point system: the entire deck is distributed to four players; the last card, going to the dealer, is turned over to determine which suit is trumps; the highest card of each suit, or the highest trump, wins each trick; and victory is determined by how many tricks each pair of partners wins. It requires four people, which is why Elinor has to join Mrs. Jennings and her two friends to make up a table.

A London door of the period.

[From Reveirs-Hopkins, A. E., *The Sheraton Period* (New York, 1922), Figure 40]

Chapter Five

"*I*f this open weather¹ holds much longer," said Mrs. Jennings, when they met at breakfast the following morning, "Sir John will not like leaving Barton next week; 'tis a sad thing for sportsmen to lose a day's pleasure. Poor souls! I always pity them when they do; they seem to take it so much to heart."²

"That is true," cried Marianne in a cheerful voice, and walking to the window as she spoke, to examine the day. "I had not thought of *that*. This weather will keep many sportsmen in the country."

It was a lucky recollection, all her good spirits were restored by it. "It is charming weather for *them* indeed," she continued, as she sat down to the breakfast table with a happy countenance. "How much they must enjoy it! But" (with a little return of anxiety) "it cannot be expected to last long. At this time of year, and after such a series of rain, we shall certainly have very little more of it. Frosts will soon set in, and in all probability with severity. In another day or two perhaps; this extreme mildness can hardly last longer—nay, perhaps it may freeze to-night!"

"At any rate," said Elinor, wishing to prevent Mrs. Jennings from seeing her sister's thoughts as clearly as she did, "I dare say we shall have Sir John and Lady Middleton in town by the end of next week."³

"Aye, my dear, I'll warrant you we do. Mary always has her own way."⁴

"And now," silently conjectured Elinor, "she will write to Combe by this day's post."⁵

But if she *did*, the letter was written and sent away with a privacy which eluded all her watchfulness to ascertain the fact. Whatever the truth of it might be, and far as Elinor was from feeling thorough contentment about it, yet while she saw Marianne in spirits,⁶ she could not be very uncomfortable herself. And Mar-

1. *open weather*: absence of frost.

2. Early winter—it is now in January—was a prime period for hunting and shooting. But these activities would be curtailed by the onset of frost, something that in southern England might not happen substantially until January.

3. The original schedule was for the Middletons to leave approximately a week after Mrs. Jennings (p. 292).

4. The conflict between a husband who, dedicated to sport, prefers the country and a wife who wishes to go to London for its entertainments, shopping, and social life is a frequent theme in eighteenth-century literature, one that undoubtedly reflects a common social phenomenon.

5. Unlike the London two-penny post, the national postal service went out only once a day, and that is what Marianne would use to write to Willoughby's home of Combe Magna, in Somersetshire.

6. *in spirits*: cheerful, elated.

Grosvenor Square in London, in the heart of the Mayfair district where most of the characters reside.

[From *The Repository of arts, literature, fashions, manufactures, &c*, Vol. X (1813), p. 275]

ianne was in spirits; happy in the mildness of the weather, and still happier in her expectation of a frost.

The morning was chiefly spent in leaving cards at the houses of Mrs. Jennings's acquaintance to inform them of her being in town;[7] and Marianne was all the time busy in observing the direction of the wind, watching the variations of the sky and imagining an alteration in the air.[8]

"Don't you find it colder than it was in the morning, Elinor? There seems to me a very decided difference. I can hardly keep my hands warm even in my muff.[9] It was not so yesterday, I think. The clouds seem parting too, the sun will be out in a moment; and we shall have a clear afternoon."[10]

Elinor was alternately diverted and pained; but Marianne persevered, and saw every night in the brightness of the fire, and every morning in the appearance of the atmosphere, the certain symptoms of approaching frost.

The Miss Dashwoods had no greater reason to be dissatisfied with Mrs. Jennings's style of living, and set of acquaintance, than with her behaviour to themselves, which was invariably kind. Every thing in her household arrangements was conducted on the most liberal plan,[11] and excepting a few old city friends, whom, to Lady Middleton's regret, she had never dropped,[12] she visited no one, to whom an introduction could at all discompose the feelings of her young companions.[13] Pleased to find herself more comfortably situated in that particular[14] than she had expected, Elinor was very willing to compound for[15] the want of much real enjoyment from any of their evening parties, which, whether at home or abroad, formed only for cards, could have little to amuse her.

Colonel Brandon, who had a general invitation to the house, was with them almost every day; he came to look at Marianne and talk to Elinor, who often derived more satisfaction from conversing with him than from any other daily occurrence, but who saw at the same time with much concern his continued regard for her sister. She feared it was a strengthening regard. It grieved her to see the earnestness with which he often watched Marianne, and his spirits were certainly worse than when at Barton.[16]

7. This was part of the normal etiquette when a family arrived in a place. Soon after arrival the lady of the house would visit all the people they knew and leave a calling card with her name on it. The recipient was expected to reciprocate by leaving her own card or by actually visiting.

8. Though this period saw a gradual increase in the scientific study of weather and climate, there were no regular forecasts appearing in newspapers or elsewhere, so anyone wishing to predict the weather would have to rely on personal observations.

9. Large fur muffs were a popular fashion for women at this time. For a picture, see cover and p. 317.

10. The need to rely on personal observations to predict weather meant wide knowledge of such clues as clear skies in winter signaling a greater possibility of nighttime frost, even by someone as little concerned with practical matters as Marianne.

11. *on the most liberal plan:* in the most generous or bountiful manner.

12. The city, often capitalized, was the oldest section of London and its commercial center. Successful merchants often lived there to be close to their businesses, but wealthy and fashionable people disdained it, due to the low social status of trade as well as the noise and smells created by its traffic and factories. Mrs. Jennings, whose husband "traded with success in a less elegant part of the town" (p. 282), would have lived in or near the city while married to him and formed friendships among other merchant families there. Their lower status makes Lady Middleton, married to a country gentleman and highly conscious of elegance and gentility, wish her mother would drop the friendships. In *Pride and Prejudice* a similar attitude leads to sneers toward the Bennet girls for having an uncle with a business and residence in this part of London.

13. Even Elinor and Marianne have enough consciousness of social rank to be disconcerted by an introduction to those of lower status.

14. *particular:* regard.

15. *compound for:* accept (in return).

16. Colonel Brandon's character of a silent, despondent lover, pining for someone unattainable, makes him a figure often evoked sympathetically in Romantic literature.

About a week after their arrival it became certain that Willoughby was also arrived. His card was on the table,[17] when they came in from the morning's drive.[18]

"Good God!" cried Marianne, "he has been here while we were out." Elinor, rejoiced to be assured of his being in London, now ventured to say, "depend upon it he will call again to-morrow." But Marianne seemed hardly to hear her, and on Mrs. Jennings's entrance, escaped with the precious card.[19]

This event, while it raised the spirits of Elinor, restored to those of her sister, all, and more than all, their former agitation. From this moment her mind was never quiet; the expectation of seeing him every hour of the day, made her unfit for anything. She insisted on being left behind, the next morning, when the others went out.

Elinor's thoughts were full of what might be passing in Berkeley-street[20] during their absence; but a moment's glance at her sister when they returned was enough to inform her, that Willoughby had paid no second visit there. A note was just then brought in, and laid on the table.

"For me!" cried Marianne, stepping hastily forward.

"No, ma'am, for my mistress."

But Marianne, not convinced, took it instantly up.

"It is indeed for Mrs. Jennings; how provoking!"

"You are expecting a letter then?" said Elinor, unable to be longer silent.

"Yes, a little—not much."

After a short pause, "you have no confidence in me, Marianne."

"Nay, Elinor, this reproach from *you*—you who have confidence in no one!"

"Me!" returned Elinor in some confusion; "indeed, Marianne, I have nothing to tell."

"Nor I," answered Marianne with energy, "our situations then are alike. We have neither of us any thing to tell; you, because you communicate, and I, because I conceal nothing."[21]

Elinor, distressed by this charge of reserve[22] in herself, which

17. Mrs. Jennings may have left her card with him without necessarily knowing if he was in London. Willoughby could be responding to her or leaving his card on his own initiative; in either case, as a man living without a woman, he would have to perform the act himself.

18. They would have been driving out in Mrs. Jennings's carriage. Many people did this daily, even if they did not have any particular business, just for the sake of getting out and enjoying the fresh air.

19. This is extremely inconsiderate of Marianne. The card was left for Mrs. Jennings, yet Marianne has not only taken it away, but done so before its intended recipient even had a chance to see it. Her action also harms the giver of the card, who meant to notify Mrs. Jennings of his arrival and his consideration for her.

20. *Berkeley-street*: a short street extending west from Portman Square; this is the location of Mrs. Jennings's residence, which was earlier identified as being near Portman Square. This street was, and is, often called Upper Berkeley Street to distinguish it from a nearby, larger Berkeley Street that extends from Berkeley Square.

21. Marianne is probably thinking of her sister's silence concerning Edward, as well as her professed lack of interest in him in the conversation with Marianne and her mother regarding the trip to London, a profession that astonished Marianne and that she most likely considered insincere (p. 290). As for herself, Marianne has certainly failed to divulge the facts of her relationship to Willoughby, whatever they are. But she may believe that their earlier open expressions of affection and her own continued strong attachment to him constitute communication enough. From her perspective the union of hearts is all that really matters; prosaic details regarding actual engagement or marriage plans are a minor matter.

22. *reserve*: reticence, nondisclosure.

---

she was not at liberty to do away, knew not how, under such circumstances, to press for greater openness in Marianne.

Mrs. Jennings soon appeared, and the note being given her, she read it aloud. It was from Lady Middleton, announcing their arrival in Conduit-street[23] the night before, and requesting the company of her mother and cousins the following evening. Business on Sir John's part, and a violent cold on her own, prevented their calling in Berkeley-street. The invitation was accepted: but when the hour of appointment drew near, necessary as it was in common civility to Mrs. Jennings, that they should both attend her on such a visit, Elinor had some difficulty in persuading her sister to go, for still she had seen nothing of Willoughby; and therefore was not more indisposed for amusement abroad,[24] than unwilling to run the risk of his calling again in her absence.

Elinor found, when the evening was over, that disposition is not materially altered by a change of abode, for although scarcely settled in town, Sir John had contrived to collect around him, nearly twenty young people, and to amuse them with a ball. This was an affair, however, of which Lady Middleton did not approve. In the country, an unpremeditated dance was very allowable;[25] but in London, where the reputation of elegance was more important and less easily obtained,[26] it was risking too much for the gratification of a few girls,[27] to have it known that Lady Middleton had given a small dance of eight or nine couple, with two violins,[28] and a mere side-board collation.[29]

Mr. and Mrs. Palmer were of the party; from the former, whom they had not seen before since their arrival in town, as he was careful to avoid the appearance of any attention to his mother-in-law, and therefore never came near her, they received no mark of recognition on their entrance. He looked at them slightly, without seeming to know who they were, and merely nodded to Mrs. Jennings from the other side of the room. Marianne gave one glance round the apartment as she entered; it was enough, *he* was not there—and she sat down, equally ill-disposed to receive or communicate pleasure. After they had been assembled about an hour, Mr. Palmer sauntered towards the Miss Dashwoods to express his

23. *Conduit-street*: a street south of Hanover Square. All the London homes of the characters, with one notable exception, are in or near the Mayfair section of London. This area, which takes its name from a fair and market held there every May for a number of decades, was mostly developed in the early eighteenth century and quickly became the principal area of residence for the wealthy. Conduit Street, Bond Street, Hanover Square (the Palmers' residence), Park Street (Mrs. Ferrars's residence), and Sackville Street (site of a jewelers' shop where several characters meet) are all part of Mayfair. Mrs. Jennings's residence on Berkeley Street and John and Fanny Dashwood's home on Harley Street are in Marylebone, or St. Marylebone, an area to the immediate north of Mayfair that developed heavily in the later eighteenth century, after Mayfair could no longer accommodate all those seeking elegant housing in the most desirable part of London. For all these locations, see maps on pp. 740 and 742. For a picture of Grosvenor Square, in the heart of Mayfair, that shows the grandeur of the houses in this part of London, see p. 309.

24. *abroad*: away from home.

25. More casual manners prevailed in the country than in London, at least among the wealthy. Moreover, since it was harder in the country to gather people together for a dance, one would tend there to be less strict about numbers and more inclined to take advantage of any opportunity that arose, even if proper invitations had not been sent out beforehand.

26. Not only was there a stronger emphasis on elegance among people in London, but being surrounded by far greater numbers of wealthy and fashionable people, one would suffer by comparison for any defect in that regard. In the country, however, even a family of limited elegance might still outshine all its neighbors.

27. It would be for the gratification of the girls because dance, from everything shown in Jane Austen, seems to appeal particularly to women.

28. Two violins would be smaller than the orchestras at a regular ball.

29. A collation is a light meal, usually of snack-type foods and often gathered with little preparation. A sign of its size would be its being laid out on a sideboard rather than a full table, as would be done for a grander dance—it was normal to offer some refreshment at dances. A sideboard had drawers and cabinets underneath and was not just a side table. It had become a standard article of furniture in the fifty years preceding this novel. For a picture of one from this period, see p. 319.

surprise on seeing them in town, though Colonel Brandon had been first informed of their arrival at his house, and he had himself said something very droll on hearing that they were to come.

"I thought you were both in Devonshire," said he.

"Did you?" replied Elinor.[30]

"When do you go back again?"

"I do not know." And thus ended their discourse.

Never had Marianne been so unwilling to dance in her life, as she was that evening; and never so much fatigued by the exercise.[31] She complained of it as they returned to Berkeley-street.

"Aye, aye," said Mrs. Jennings, "we know the reason of all that very well; if a certain person who shall be nameless, had been there, you would not have been a bit tired: and to say the truth it was not very pretty[32] of him not to give you the meeting when he was invited."

"Invited!" cried Marianne.

"So my daughter Middleton told me, for it seems Sir John met him somewhere in the street this morning." Marianne said no more, but looked exceedingly hurt. Impatient in this situation to be doing something that might lead to her sister's relief, Elinor resolved to write the next morning to her mother, and hoped by awakening her fears for the health of Marianne, to procure those inquiries which had been so long delayed; and she was still more eagerly bent on this measure by perceiving after breakfast on the morrow, that Marianne was again writing to Willoughby, for she could not suppose it to be to any other person.[33]

About the middle of the day, Mrs. Jennings went out by herself on business, and Elinor began her letter directly, while Marianne, too restless for employment, too anxious for conversation, walked from one window to the other, or sat down by the fire in melancholy meditation. Elinor was very earnest in her application to her mother, relating all that had passed, her suspicions of Willoughby's inconstancy, urging her by every plea of duty and affection to demand from Marianne, an account of her real situation with respect to him.

Her letter was scarcely finished, when a rap foretold a visitor,

30. Colonel Brandon's account of hearing of their arrival and Mrs. Palmer's account of her husband's droll words were both spoken before Elinor (pp. 300–302 and 304), so she is understandably surprised at his apparent ignorance. He may have been too wrapped up in his newspaper, with his wife only imagining his reply, or his general inattention, especially to his wife, may have caused him to forget any conversation he had with her.

31. That she still dances some, despite her lack of interest, suggests the social pressure to dance, which in this case was probably strengthened by Sir John's insistence on everyone joining in whatever fun was on offer.

32. *pretty*: nice.

33. The contents of this note are revealed on pp. 344–346.

A woman with one of the popular large muffs of the time.

[From *The Repository of arts, literature, fashions, manufactures, &c*, Vol. XI (1814), p. 56]

and Colonel Brandon was announced. Marianne, who had seen him from the window, and who hated company of any kind, left the room before he entered it. He looked more than usually grave, and though expressing satisfaction at finding Miss Dashwood alone, as if he had somewhat[34] in particular to tell her, sat for some time without saying a word. Elinor, persuaded that he had some communication to make in which her sister was concerned, impatiently expected its opening. It was not the first time of her feeling the same kind of conviction; for more than once before, beginning with the observation of "your sister looks unwell to-day," or "your sister seems out of spirits," he had appeared on the point, either of disclosing, or of inquiring, something particular about her.[35] After a pause of several minutes, their silence was broken, by his asking her in a voice of some agitation, when he was to congratulate her on the acquisition of a brother?[36] Elinor was not prepared for such a question, and having no answer ready, was obliged to adopt the simple and common expedient, of asking what he meant? He tried to smile as he replied, "your sister's engagement to Mr. Willoughby is very generally known."

"It cannot be generally known," returned Elinor, "for her own family do not know it."

He looked surprised and said, "I beg your pardon, I am afraid my inquiry has been impertinent;[37] but I had not supposed any secrecy intended, as they openly correspond, and their marriage is universally talked of."

"How can that be? By whom can you have heard it mentioned?"

"By many—by some of whom you know nothing, by others with whom you are most intimate, Mrs. Jennings, Mrs. Palmer, and the Middletons.[38] But still I might not have believed it, for where the mind is perhaps rather unwilling to be convinced, it will always find something to support its doubts, if I had not, when the servant let me in to-day, accidentally seen a letter in his hand, directed to Mr. Willoughby in your sister's writing.[39] I came to inquire, but I was convinced before I could ask the question. Is

34. *somewhat*: something, especially a statement or piece of information.

35. Elinor will prove correct in her perception of his wavering inclination to communicate something when he explains what he was tempted to reveal (see pp. 378–388).

36. *brother*: brother-in-law. This is a common usage in Jane Austen. It reflects, at least in part, the general impossibility of divorce in this society, which meant that a relation by marriage was virtually as permanent as one by blood.

37. *impertinent*: inappropriate, presumptuous.

38. Mr. Palmer is not one of the sources. He is presumably too uninterested to discuss the matter.

39. The servant would have been preparing to mail Marianne's latest note to Willoughby. Their correspondence would constitute clear proof, according to prevailing standards, of their actual engagement.

A contemporary sideboard.

[From K. Warren Clouston, *The Chippendale Period in English Furniture* (New York, 1897), p. 200]

every thing finally settled? Is it impossible to—? But I have no right, and I could have no chance of succeeding. Excuse me, Miss Dashwood. I believe I have been wrong in saying so much, but I hardly know what to do, and on your prudence I have the strongest dependence. Tell me that it is all absolutely resolved on, that any attempt, that in short concealment, if concealment be possible, is all that remains."[40]

These words, which conveyed to Elinor a direct avowal of his love for her sister, affected her very much. She was not immediately able to say anything, and even when her spirits were recovered, she debated for a short time, on the answer it would be most proper to give. The real state of things between Willoughby and her sister was so little known to herself, that in endeavouring to explain it, she might be as liable to say too much as too little. Yet as she was convinced that Marianne's affection for Willoughby, could leave no hope of Colonel Brandon's success, whatever the event[41] of that affection might be, and at the same time wished to shield her conduct from censure,[42] she thought it most prudent and kind, after some consideration, to say more than she really knew or believed. She acknowledged, therefore, that though she had never been informed by themselves of the terms on which they stood with each other, of their mutual affection she had no doubt, and of their correspondence she was not astonished to hear.[43]

He listened to her with silent attention, and on her ceasing to speak, rose directly from his seat, and after saying in a voice of emotion,[44] "to your sister I wish all imaginable happiness; to Willoughby that he may endeavour to deserve her,"[45]—took leave, and went away.

Elinor derived no comfortable feelings from this conversation, to lessen the uneasiness of her mind on other points; she was left, on the contrary, with a melancholy impression of Colonel Brandon's unhappiness, and was prevented even from wishing it removed, by her anxiety for the very event that must confirm it.

40. He means concealment of his affection for Marianne, the only honorable and sensible course for him if she marries another.

41. *event:* result, outcome.

42. The censure would arise from Marianne's correspondence with, and passionate pursuit of, a man to whom she is not engaged or who has ceased to be interested in her. The first would be a clear violation of social rules, and the second would be considered improper in a woman, who was supposed to let a man take the initiative in essential romantic matters.

43. She avoids actually saying Marianne is engaged to Willoughby, while phrasing her words to give a clear impression to that effect. This allows her both to avoid a lie, since she has come to entertain serious doubts about Marianne's engagement and the possibility of a marriage, and to preserve her sister from censure, at least for now, and prevent Colonel Brandon from harboring unfounded hopes.

44. *emotion:* agitation.

45. The reasons for these last ominous words will soon appear.

Chapter Six

Nothing occurred during the next three or four days, to make Elinor regret what she had done, in applying to her mother; for Willoughby neither came nor wrote. They were engaged about the end of that time to attend Lady Middleton to a party, from which Mrs. Jennings was kept away by the indisposition of her youngest daughter;[1] and for this party, Marianne, wholly dispirited, careless of her appearance, and seeming equally indifferent whether she went or staid, prepared, without one look of hope, or one expression of pleasure. She sat by the drawing room fire after tea,[2] till the moment of Lady Middleton's arrival, without once stirring from her seat, or altering her attitude,[3] lost in her own thoughts and insensible of her sister's presence; and when at last they were told that Lady Middleton waited for them at the door, she started as if she had forgotten that any one was expected.[4]

They arrived in due time at the place of destination, and as soon as the string of carriages before them would allow,[5] alighted, ascended the stairs, heard their names announced from one landing-place to another in an audible voice,[6] and entered a room splendidly lit up, quite full of company, and insufferably hot.[7] When they had paid their tribute of politeness by curtseying to the lady of the house,[8] they were permitted to mingle in the croud, and take their share of the heat and inconvenience, to which their arrival must necessarily add. After some time spent in saying little and doing less, Lady Middleton sat down to Casino,[9] and as Marianne was not in spirits for moving about, she and Elinor luckily succeeding to[10] chairs, placed themselves at no great distance from the table.

They had not remained in this manner long, before Elinor perceived Willoughby, standing within a few yards of them, in

1. Mrs. Jennings would be attending Charlotte, who is toward the end of her pregnancy.

2. They have already dined and had tea, which usually came an hour or two after dinner. Fashionable parties, especially in London, often started late and continued well into the night.

3. *attitude*: position, posture.

4. Lady Middleton has come to fetch them in her carriage; because they are her mother's guests she would be the natural person to take them when Mrs. Jennings is unavailable.

5. The carriages would line up and the passengers in each would disembark with the aid of servants. This could take some time, for carriages were high off the ground and required some care to descend, especially at night and for ladies in elaborate ball dresses, which frequently had long trains. There would be numerous carriages because even guests who lived close enough to walk would use a carriage; not doing so, especially at a formal party, would be a humiliating mark of low status.

6. Servants standing on the landing-places, i.e., stair landings, would announce the names of the guests as they arrived.

7. Fashionable London parties were noted for often being extremely crowded and hot. The heat was caused not just by the large numbers of people, but also by the numerous candles used to light the rooms. Elaborate parties or balls were the only time when heavy indoor illumination would be used, for it was very expensive.

8. A curtsy to the hostess, or bow to her by a man, would be a standard greeting by guests.

9. Lady Middleton earlier had everyone play casino at her house (p. 266); it is evidently her favorite game. One reason she may prefer it to the more popular whist is that it is less challenging.

10. *succeeding to*: enjoying or possessing after someone else.

earnest conversation with a very fashionable looking young woman. She soon caught his eye, and he immediately bowed, but without attempting to speak to her, or to approach Marianne, though he could not but see her; and then continued his discourse with the same lady. Elinor turned involuntarily to Marianne, to see whether it could be unobserved by her. At that moment she first perceived him, and her whole countenance glowing with sudden delight, she would have moved towards him instantly, had not her sister caught hold of her.

"Good heavens!" she exclaimed, "he is there—he is there—Oh! why does he not look at me? why cannot I speak to him?"

"Pray, pray be composed," cried Elinor, "and do not betray what you feel to every body present. Perhaps he has not observed you yet."

This however was more than she could believe herself; and to be composed at such a moment was not only beyond the reach of Marianne, it was beyond her wish. She sat in an agony of impatience, which affected every feature.

At last he turned round again, and regarded them both; she started up, and pronouncing his name in a tone of affection, held out her hand to him. He approached, and addressing himself rather to Elinor than Marianne, as if wishing to avoid her eye,[11] and determined not to observe her attitude, inquired in a hurried manner after Mrs. Dashwood, and asked how long they had been in town. Elinor was robbed of all presence of mind by such an address, and was unable to say a word.[12] But the feelings of her sister were instantly expressed. Her face was crimsoned over, and she exclaimed in a voice of the greatest emotion, "Good God! Willoughby, what is the meaning of this? Have you not received my letters? Will you not shake hands with me?"[13]

He could not then avoid it, but her touch seemed painful to him, and he held her hand only for a moment. During all this time he was evidently struggling for composure. Elinor watched his countenance and saw its expression becoming more tranquil. After a moment's pause, he spoke with calmness.

"I did myself the honour of calling in Berkeley-street last Tues-

11. He will later explain his discomfort and avoidance of Marianne (p. 610).

12. That even Elinor is left speechless and discomposed indicates how startling his cold conduct toward Marianne is after all that passed earlier.

13. She has already held out her hand, and he has not taken it. Shaking

Women in evening dress.

[From *The Repository of arts, literature, fashions, manufactures, &c*, Vol. V (1811), p. 48]

day, and very much regretted that I was not fortunate enough to find yourselves and Mrs. Jennings at home. My card was not lost, I hope."[14]

"But have you not received my notes?" cried Marianne in the wildest anxiety. "Here is some mistake I am sure—some dreadful mistake. What can be the meaning of it? Tell me, Willoughby; for heaven's sake tell me, what is the matter?"

He made no reply; his complexion changed and all his embarrassment returned; but as if, on catching the eye of the young lady with whom he had been previously talking, he felt the necessity of instant exertion, he recovered himself again, and after saying, "Yes, I had the pleasure of receiving the information of your arrival in town, which you were so good as to send me," turned hastily away with a slight bow and joined his friend.

Marianne, now looking dreadfully white, and unable to stand, sunk into her chair, and Elinor, expecting every moment to see her faint, tried to screen her from the observation of others,[15] while reviving her with lavender water.[16]

"Go to him, Elinor," she cried, as soon as she could speak, "and force him to come to me. Tell him I must see him again—must speak to him instantly.—I cannot rest—I shall not have a moment's peace till this is explained—some dreadful misapprehension or other.—Oh go to him this moment."

"How can that be done? No, my dearest Marianne, you must wait. This is not a place for explanations. Wait only till tomorrow."

With difficulty however could she prevent her from following him herself; and to persuade her to check her agitation, to wait, at least, with the appearance of composure, till she might speak to him with more privacy and more effect, was impossible; for Marianne continued incessantly to give way in a low voice to the misery of her feelings, by exclamations of wretchedness. In a short time Elinor saw Willoughby quit the room by the door towards the staircase, and telling Marianne that he was gone, urged the impossibility of speaking to him again that evening, as a fresh argument for her to be calm. She instantly begged her sister

hands was a standard greeting between a man and a woman who were closely connected, but it was generally considered improper for those not so close. Thus this clearly indicates Marianne's belief in their engagement, and his rejection of such a state.

14. Willoughby shields himself behind a standard polite formulation, such as one would use toward the most casual acquaintance.

15. Elinor's actions indicate the high value placed on social appearances by almost every character.

16. She could be rubbing lavender water on her face or having her drink some (see p. 229, note 24). The popularity of the liquid is shown by her having some with her.

would entreat Lady Middleton to take them home, as she was too miserable to stay a minute longer.[17]

Lady Middleton, though in the middle of a rubber,[18] on being informed that Marianne was unwell, was too polite to object for a moment to her wish of going away, and making over her cards to a friend, they departed as soon as the carriage could be found. Scarcely a word was spoken during their return to Berkeley-street. Marianne was in a silent agony, too much oppressed even for tears; but as Mrs. Jennings was luckily not come home, they could go directly to their own room, where hartshorn[19] restored her a little to herself. She was soon undressed and in bed, and as she seemed desirous of being alone, her sister then left her, and while she waited the return of Mrs. Jennings, had leisure enough for thinking over the past.

That some kind of engagement had subsisted between Willoughby and Marianne she could not doubt; and that Willoughby was weary of it, seemed equally clear; for however Marianne might still feed her own wishes, *she* could not attribute such behaviour to mistake or misapprehension of any kind. Nothing but a thorough change of sentiment could account for it. Her indignation would have been still stronger than it was, had she not witnessed that embarrassment which seemed to speak[20] a consciousness of his own misconduct,[21] and prevented her from believing him so unprincipled as to have been sporting with the affections of her sister from the first, without any design that would bear investigation.[22] Absence might have weakened his regard, and convenience might have determined him to overcome it, but that such a regard had formerly existed she could not bring herself to doubt.

As for Marianne, on the pangs which so unhappy a meeting must already have given her, and on those still more severe which might await her in its probable consequence, she could not reflect without the deepest concern. Her own situation gained in the comparison; for while she could *esteem* Edward as much as ever, however they might be divided in future, her mind might be always supported. But every circumstance that could embitter

17. Again Marianne thinks only of her own feelings. In contrast, the heroine of *Pride and Prejudice*, when distressed, albeit not as much as Marianne, by an unexpected encounter with the hero while visiting his estate, never thinks of asking her aunt and uncle to cut their visit short because of her own wish to leave.

18. Casino is played in rubbers, or sets of three or five games, with score tabulated over the whole rubber, so one would always prefer to leave after a rubber is finished.

19. *hartshorn:* the scrapings of the horn of a hart, or male red deer. This was traditionally the main source of ammonia. A distilled form was used as a smelling salt to help revive people.

20. *speak:* indicate, signify.

21. Elinor's surmise as to his embarrassment and possible sense of guilt will eventually prove correct.

22. A design that would *not* bear investigation would be flirting with a woman for one's own amusement, something that could injure both her heart and her reputation by making her look foolish and overly eager. Another such design would be seeking to seduce her, though it is not clear if Elinor has this in mind, given the tremendous abhorrence with which even the thought of such a thing was regarded in this society.

such an evil seemed uniting to heighten the misery of Marianne in a final separation from Willoughby—in an immediate and irreconcileable rupture with him.

A postal delivery.

[From William Alexander, *Picturesque Representations of the dress & manners of the English* (1813), Plate 24]

A woman holding a letter.

[From *The Repository of arts, literature, fashions, manufactures, &c*, Vol. XI (1814), p. 56]

Chapter Seven

*B*efore the house-maid[1] had lit their fire the next day,[2] or the sun gained any power over a cold, gloomy morning in January, Marianne, only half dressed, was kneeling against one of the window-seats for the sake of all the little light she could command from it,[3] and writing as fast as a continual flow of tears would permit her. In this situation, Elinor, roused from sleep by her agitation and sobs, first perceived her; and after observing her for a few moments with silent anxiety, said, in a tone of the most considerate gentleness,

"Marianne, may I ask?" —

"No, Elinor," she replied, "ask nothing; you will soon know all."

The sort of desperate calmness with which this was said, lasted no longer than while she spoke, and was immediately followed by a return of the same excessive affliction. It was some minutes before she could go on with her letter, and the frequent bursts of grief which still obliged her, at intervals, to withhold her pen, were proofs enough of her feeling how more than probable it was that she was writing for the last time to Willoughby.

Elinor paid her every quiet and unobtrusive attention in her power; and she would have tried to sooth and tranquillize her still more, had not Marianne entreated her, with all the eagerness of the most nervous irritability, not to speak to her for the world. In such circumstances, it was better for both that they should not be long together; and the restless state of Marianne's mind not only prevented her from remaining in the room a moment after she was dressed, but requiring at once solitude and continual change of place, made her wander about the house till breakfast time, avoiding the sight of every body.[4]

At breakfast she neither ate, not attempted to eat any thing; and

1. *house-maid:* the maid responsible for cleaning the rooms and performing other general chores. Housemaids were the most common of all servants; wealthier households would usually have more than one.

2. Getting up early to light the fires was one of the housemaid's basic tasks, and an essential one, especially in winter, since the fires were the only source of heat. Marianne's rising before this indicates she is up very early.

3. Many windows in houses then were set in a deep recess or bay, which was often filled by a flat horizontal surface below the window that could serve as a seat. Such a seat would give Marianne a little illumination from the barely rising sun, while also providing a writing surface.

4. Given her early rising, and the lateness of breakfast then, this wandering could last a couple of hours.

A woman writing.

[From *The Masterpieces of Lawrence* (London, 1913), p. 42]

Elinor's attention was then all employed, not in urging her, not in pitying her, nor in appearing to regard her, but in endeavouring to engage Mrs. Jennings's notice entirely to herself.

As this was a favourite meal with Mrs. Jennings, it lasted a considerable time, and they were just setting themselves, after it, round the common working table,[5] when a letter was delivered to Marianne,[6] which she eagerly caught from the servant, and, turning of a death-like paleness, instantly ran out of the room. Elinor, who saw as plainly by this, as if she had seen the direction,[7] that it must come from Willoughby, felt immediately such a sickness at heart as made her hardly able to hold up her head, and sat in such a general tremour as made her fear it impossible to escape Mrs. Jennings's notice. That good lady, however, saw only that Marianne had received a letter from Willoughby, which appeared to her a very good joke, and which she treated accordingly, by hoping, with a laugh, that she would find it to her liking. Of Elinor's distress, she was too busily employed in measuring lengths of worsted for her rug,[8] to see any thing at all; and calmly continuing her talk, as soon as Marianne disappeared, she said,

"Upon my word I never saw a young woman so desperately in love in my life! My girls were nothing to her, and yet they used to be foolish enough; but as for Miss Marianne, she is quite an altered creature. I hope, from the bottom of my heart, he wo'nt keep her waiting much longer, for it is quite grievous to see her look so ill and forlorn. Pray, when are they to be married?"

Elinor, though never less disposed to speak than at that moment, obliged herself to answer such an attack as this, and, therefore, trying to smile, replied, "And have you really, Ma'am, talked yourself into a persuasion of my sister's being engaged to Mr. Willoughby? I thought it had been only a joke, but so serious a question seems to imply more; and I must beg, therefore, that you will not deceive yourself any longer. I do assure you that nothing would surprise me more than to hear of their being going[9] to be married."

"For shame, for shame, Miss Dashwood! how can you talk so! Don't we all know that it must be a match, that they were over

5. This would be a table where everyone could gather for various forms of work, especially needlework, which was often called just work. Various scenes in Jane Austen show women gathered together in this fashion.

6. This indicates the speed of the London two-penny post. Marianne's letter probably went out with the first delivery, which was at eight o'clock. If it reached Willoughby reasonably soon, he would have had time to write a letter that could be picked up during the next round at ten o'clock and then delivered to Marianne after a lengthy breakfast, probably eleven o'clock or a little earlier. For a contemporary picture of a postman delivering mail, see p. 330.

7. *direction*: address. Meaning if she had seen the handwriting.

8. Worsted wool was used for a variety of fabrics at this time, due to its strength and smoothness. Carpet work, which included making rugs by knitting pieces of wool together, was a common pastime of ladies, and it is later described as a regular activity of Mrs. Jennings.

9. *being going*: being in preparation. This construction is occasionally found in other passages in Jane Austen.

head and ears in love with each other from the first moment they met? Did not I see them together in Devonshire every day, and all day long; and did not I know that your sister came to town with me on purpose to buy wedding clothes?[10] Come, come, this wo'nt do. Because you are so sly[11] about it yourself, you think nobody else has any senses; but it is no such thing, I can tell you, for it has been known all over town this ever so long. I tell every body of it and so does Charlotte."

"Indeed, Ma'am," said Elinor, very seriously, "you are mistaken. Indeed, you are doing a very unkind thing in spreading the report, and you will find that you have, though you will not believe me now."

Mrs. Jennings laughed again, but Elinor had not spirits to say more, and eager at all events to know what Willoughby had written, hurried away to their room, where, on opening the door, she saw Marianne stretched on the bed, almost choked by grief, one letter in her hand, and two or three others lying by her. Elinor drew near, but without saying a word; and seating herself on the bed, took her hand, kissed her affectionately several times, and then gave way to a burst of tears, which at first was scarcely less violent than Marianne's.[12] The latter, though unable to speak, seemed to feel all the tenderness of this behaviour, and after some time thus spent in joint affliction, she put all the letters into Elinor's hands; and then covering her face with her handkerchief, almost screamed with agony. Elinor, who knew that such grief, shocking as it was to witness it, must have its course, watched by her till this excess of suffering had somewhat spent itself, and then turning eagerly to Willoughby's letter, read as follows:

Bond Street, January.

My Dear Madam,

I have just had the honour of receiving your letter, for which I beg to return my sincere acknowledgments.[13] I am much concerned to find there was any thing in my behaviour last night that did not meet your approbation; and though I am quite at a loss to discover in what point I could be so unfortunate as to offend you, I entreat

10. Buying wedding clothes was a standard part of marriage preparations. It meant not only clothes for the wedding, which at this time tended to be a restrained affair, but also items she could wear afterward that would help her start her new life. London would be the ideal place to buy wedding clothes because of its plethora of shops. In *Pride and Prejudice* the heroine's mother, on the occasion of one daughter's impending marriage, frets that she will not know which are the best stores in London to purchase her clothes.

11. *sly*: secretive.

12. This is a sign of both Elinor's acute sympathy with her sister and her own ability to experience strong emotions, however much she normally keeps her feelings under control.

13. In this opening sentence and hereafter the letter employs extremely studied and formal language, which forms a sharp contrast to what Marianne used in her letters (see below), as well as being unlike the language one would normally use in a highly personal and important letter to a friend.

your forgiveness of what I can assure you to have been perfectly
unintentional. I shall never reflect on my former acquaintance with
your family in Devonshire without the most grateful pleasure,[14] *and*
flatter myself it will not be broken by any mistake or misapprehen-
sion of my actions. My esteem for your whole family is very sin-
cere;[15] *but if I have been so unfortunate as to give rise to a belief of*
more than I felt, or meant to express, I shall reproach myself for not
having been more guarded in my professions of that esteem. That I
should ever have meant more you will allow to be impossible, when
you understand that my affections have been long engaged else-
where, and it will not be many weeks, I believe, before this engage-
ment is fulfilled.[16] *It is with great regret that I obey your commands*
of returning the letters, with which I have been honoured from you,
and the lock of hair, which you so obligingly bestowed on me.

> *I am, dear Madam,*
> *Your most obedient*
> *humble Servant,*
> *John Willoughby.*

With what indignation such a letter as this must be read by Miss
Dashwood, may be imagined. Though aware, before she began it,
that it must bring a confession of his inconstancy, and confirm
their separation for ever, she was not aware that such language
could be suffered to announce it! nor could she have supposed
Willoughby capable of departing so far from the appearance of
every honourable and delicate[17] feeling—so far from the common decorum of a gentleman,[18] as to send a letter so impudently[19] cruel: a letter which, instead of bringing with his desire of
a release any professions of regret,[20] acknowledged no breach of
faith, denied all peculiar[21] affection whatever—a letter of which
every line was an insult, and which proclaimed its writer to be
deep in hardened villany.

She paused over it for some time with indignant astonishment;
then read it again and again; but every perusal only served to
increase her abhorrence of the man, and so bitter were her feelings against him, that she dared not trust herself to speak, lest she

14. It is notable that he calls it a former acquaintance.

15. He speaks only of esteem, and that for the "whole family," not Marianne herself.

16. He will be married to another woman.

17. *delicate:* sensitive to others; attuned to what is proper.

18. An important part of the decorum of a gentleman was to express praise and admiration for the person one was addressing, especially if that person was a lady. Another was to be willing to accept blame for any disagreements or mishaps. Instead Willoughby says nothing to indicate any regard for Marianne, despite their past involvement, and nothing to indicate an awareness of any fault he may have committed. Instead, in mentioning a possible breach with the Dashwood family, he suggests it could occur only through some "mistake or misapprehension of my actions" — in other words, through some fault of Marianne's.

19. *impudently:* shamelessly.

20. His complete lack of regret or apology in this letter contrasts with the embarrassment Elinor perceived in his behavior at the party. The reason for the contrast will eventually be explained (pp. 610–614).

21. *peculiar:* particular.

might wound Marianne still deeper by treating their disengagement, not as a loss to her of any possible good but as an escape from the worst and most irremediable of all evils, a connection, for life, with an unprincipled man, as a deliverance the most real, a blessing the most important.[22]

In her earnest meditations on the contents of the letter, on the depravity of that mind which could dictate it, and, probably, on the very different mind[23] of a very different person, who had no other connection whatever with the affair than what her heart gave him with every thing that passed,[24] Elinor forgot the immediate distress of her sister, forgot that she had three letters on her lap yet unread, and so entirely forgot how long she had been in the room, that when on hearing a carriage drive up to the door, she went to the window to see who could be coming so unreasonably early,[25] she was all astonishment to perceive Mrs. Jennings's chariot,[26] which she knew had not been ordered till one.[27] Determined not to quit Marianne, though hopeless of contributing, at present, to her ease, she hurried away to excuse herself from attending Mrs. Jennings, on account of her sister being indisposed. Mrs. Jennings, with a thoroughly good-humoured concern for its cause, admitted the excuse most readily, and Elinor, after seeing her safe off,[28] returned to Marianne, whom she found attempting to rise from the bed, and whom she reached just in time to prevent her from falling on the floor, faint and giddy from a long want of proper rest and food; for it was many days since she had any appetite, and many nights since she had really slept; and now, when her mind was no longer supported by the fever of suspense, the consequence of all this was felt in an aching head, a weakened stomach, and a general nervous faintness. A glass of wine, which Elinor procured for her directly, made her more comfortable,[29] and she was at last able to express some sense of her kindness, by saying,

"Poor Elinor! how unhappy I make you!"

"I only wish," replied her sister, "there were any thing I *could* do, which might be of comfort to you."

This, as every thing else would have been, was too much for

22. The general impossibility of divorce, along with a woman's significantly inferior financial and legal position at the time, would make such a match especially terrible for Marianne.

23. *mind*: inner character.

24. Elinor's thoughts revert to Edward.

25. Etiquette dictated visits only later in the day, so that people had time at home to take care of important tasks.

26. A chariot was a small enclosed carriage that sat three people across. It was almost exactly like a chaise (see p. 283, note 4), except that a chaise was normally driven by someone, called a postilion, riding on one of the horses, and a chariot had a seat on top of the carriage for a driver. This made it more appropriate for transportation around town. A small and therefore less expensive carriage would be suitable for Mrs. Jennings, living on her own, while she would not want an open carriage, which could be even smaller, because it usually required one to drive oneself, which women generally did not do, and because she would wish for more protection from the elements while in London during the winter, the time when she is probably using her carriage the most. For a picture of a chariot, see the following page.

27. Carriages were often kept in alleys behind houses, and Mrs. Jennings would have told the servant what time to bring it to the door. Elinor, knowing the intended hour, is surprised because she has lost track of time: as mentioned above, the letter probably arrived at eleven or a little earlier, and she and Marianne have been together since then, absorbed in their thoughts and distress.

28. Elinor, despite her focus on Marianne, still takes the trouble to attend to her hostess.

29. Wine was often used for medicinal purposes then.

Marianne, who could only exclaim, in the anguish of her heart, "Oh! Elinor, I am miserable indeed," before her voice was entirely lost in sobs.

Elinor could no longer witness this torrent of unresisted grief in silence.

"Exert yourself, dear Marianne," she cried, "if you would not kill yourself and all who love you. Think of your mother; think of her misery while *you* suffer; for her sake you must exert yourself."

"I cannot, I cannot," cried Marianne; "leave me, leave me, if I distress you; leave me, hate me, forget me! but do not torture me so. Oh! how easy for those who have no sorrow of their own to talk of exertion! Happy, happy Elinor, *you* cannot have an idea of what I suffer."

"Do you call *me* happy, Marianne? Ah! if you knew!—And can you believe me to be so, while I see you so wretched!"

"Forgive me, forgive me," throwing her arms round her sister's neck; "I know you feel for me; I know what a heart you have; but yet you are—you must be happy; Edward loves you—what, oh! what can do away such happiness as that?"

"Many, many circumstances," said Elinor, solemnly.

"No, no, no," cried Marianne wildly,[30] "he loves you, and only you. You *can* have no grief."

"I can have no pleasure while I see you in this state."

"And you will never see me otherwise. Mine is a misery which nothing can do away."

"You must not talk so, Marianne. Have you no comforts? no friends?[31] Is your loss such as leaves no opening for consolation? Much as you suffer now, think of what you would have suffered if the discovery of his character had been delayed to a later period— if your engagement had been carried on for months and months, as it might have been, before he chose to put an end to it. Every additional day of unhappy confidence, on your side, would have made the blow more dreadful."

"Engagement!" cried Marianne, "there has been no engage-ment."

"No engagement!"

30. *wildly:* passionately, excitedly.

31. Elinor alludes to other aspects of life besides love, a principle she, in contrast to Marianne, has exemplified in her response to romantic disappointment.

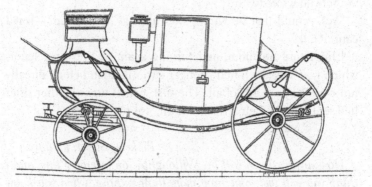

A chariot, such as Mrs. Jennings owns.

[From T. Fuller, *An Essay on Wheel Carriages* (London, 1828), Plate no. 1]

"No, he is not so unworthy as you believe him. He has broken no faith with me."

"But he told you that he loved you?"—[32]

"Yes—no—never absolutely. It was every day implied, but never professedly declared. Sometimes I thought it had been— but it never was."[33]

"Yet you wrote to him?"—

"Yes—could that be wrong after all that had passed?—But I cannot talk."

Elinor said no more, and turning again to the three letters which now raised a much stronger curiosity than before, directly ran over the contents of all. The first, which was what her sister had sent him on their arrival in town, was to this effect.

Berkeley Street, January.

How surprised you will be, Willoughby, on receiving this; and I think you will feel something more than surprise, when you know that I am in town. An opportunity of coming hither, though with Mrs. Jennings, was a temptation we could not resist.[34] I wish you may receive this in time to come here to-night, but I will not depend on it. At any rate I shall expect you to-morrow. For the present, adieu.

M. D.

Her second note, which had been written on the morning after the dance at the Middletons', was in these words:—

"I cannot express my disappointment in having missed you the day before yesterday, nor my astonishment at not having received any answer to a note which I sent you above a week ago. I have been expecting to hear from you, and still more to see you, every hour of the day. Pray call again as soon as possible, and explain the reason of my having expected this in vain. You had better come earlier another time, because we are generally out by one. We were last night at Lady Middleton's, where there was a dance. I have been told that you were asked to be of the party. But could it be so? You

32. A declaration of love was tantamount to a proposal, for a man normally never said that to a woman until he was asking her to marry him.

33. Willoughby's ability to keep implying this during his intense involvement with Marianne, without ever going beyond that, signals he knew exactly what he was doing, and perhaps that he had done this before. The strict rules governing sexual behavior meant that a man who wished to flirt with women without becoming trapped into a marriage commitment would need to be continually careful of what he said and did.

34. Marianne gratuitously insults Mrs. Jennings in her note. She is perhaps echoing Willoughby's sentiments: he, amid his frequent censure of others, had expressed his contempt for Mrs. Jennings and Lady Middleton (p. 96). Elinor had lamented this aspect of his behavior, one that Marianne had at times seconded, and here Marianne is being especially inconsiderate in denigrating someone who has kindly, and at her own expense, conveyed her to the place she dearly wanted to go.

*must be very much altered indeed since we parted, if that could be
the case, and you not there. But I will not suppose this possible, and
I hope very soon to receive your personal assurance of its being otherwise."*[35]

M. D.

The contents of her last note to him were these:—

*"What am I to imagine, Willoughby, by your behaviour last
night? Again I demand an explanation of it. I was prepared to meet
you with the pleasure which our separation naturally produced,
with the familiarity which our intimacy at Barton appeared to me
to justify. I was repulsed indeed! I have passed a wretched night in
endeavouring to excuse a conduct which can scarcely be called less
than insulting; but though I have not yet been able to form any reasonable apology for your behaviour, I am perfectly ready to hear
your justification of it. You have perhaps been misinformed, or purposely deceived, in something concerning me, which may have lowered me in your opinion. Tell me what it is, explain the grounds on
which you acted, and I shall be satisfied, in being able to satisfy
you.*[36] *It would grieve me indeed to be obliged to think ill of you; but
if I am to do it, if I am to learn that you are not what we have hitherto believed you, that your regard for us all was insincere, that your
behaviour to me was intended only to deceive, let it be told as soon
as possible. My feelings are at present in a state of dreadful indecision; I wish to acquit you, but certainty on either side will be ease to
what I now suffer.*[37] *If your sentiments are no longer what they were,
you will return my notes, and the lock of my hair which is in your
possession."*

M. D.

That such letters, so full of affection and confidence, could
have been so answered, Elinor, for Willoughby's sake, would have
been unwilling to believe. But her condemnation of him did not
blind her to the impropriety of their having been written at all;
and she was silently grieving over the imprudence which had haz-

35. By this point Marianne has spent more than a week pining for Willoughby and feeling surprised and distressed by his failure to appear or respond. She was "exceedingly hurt" after learning he had been invited to the party at the Middletons' that he did not attend. Yet in this note, written soon after, she avoids any expression of anguish or anger, confining herself to a simple request for an explanation and a brief expression of fear of his being altered, which she quickly dismisses. Her extreme confidence in him has still barely wavered.

36. Here Marianne, suffering acutely from Willoughby's behavior toward her at the party, begins to express some genuine despair, though even now it alternates with expectations of his vindication. The heartfelt appeal throughout the letter contrasts sharply with the completely cold and impersonal tone of Willoughby's reply.

37. This turns out to be wrong, for she is currently suffering far more than she ever did from the previous uncertainty. Of course, she probably did not imagine that Willoughby's rejection, even if it came, would be so callously and cruelly expressed.

arded such unsolicited proofs of tenderness, not warranted by anything preceding, and most severely condemned by the event,
when Marianne, perceiving that she had finished the letters,
observed to her that they contained nothing but what any one
would have written in the same situation.

"I felt myself," she added, "to be as solemnly engaged to him, as
if the strictest legal covenant had bound us to each other."

"I can believe it," said Elinor; "but unfortunately he did not feel
the same."[38]

"He *did* feel the same, Elinor—for weeks and weeks he felt it. I
know he did. Whatever may have changed him now, (and nothing but the blackest art employed against me can have done it,) I
was once as dear to him as my own soul could wish. This lock of
hair, which now he can so readily give up,[39] was begged of me
with the most earnest supplication.[40] Had you seen his look, his
manner, had you heard his voice at that moment! Have you forgot
the last evening of our being together at Barton? The morning
that we parted too! When he told me that it might be many weeks
before we meet again—his distress—can I ever forget his distress!"

For a moment or two she could say no more; but when this
emotion had passed away, she added, in a firmer tone,

"Elinor, I have been cruelly used; but not by Willoughby."

"Dearest Marianne, who but himself? By whom can he have
been instigated?"

"By all the world, rather than by his own heart. I could rather
believe every creature of my acquaintance leagued together to
ruin me in his opinion, than believe his nature capable of such
cruelty. This woman of whom he writes—whoever she be—or
any one, in short, but your own dear self, mama, and Edward,
may have been so barbarous to bely[41] me. Beyond you three, is
there a creature in the world whom I would not rather suspect of
evil than Willoughby, whose heart I know so well?"[42]

Elinor would not contend, and only replied, "Whoever may
have been so detestably your enemy, let them be cheated of their
malignant triumph, my dear sister, by seeing how nobly the consciousness of your own innocence and good intentions supports

38. Events have shown the hazards of dispensing with legal and social forms, for such forms create an external pressure to fulfill an agreement. Marianne, in contrast, relied only on another's feelings, and they proved either to have been always different from what she had supposed, or highly changeable.

39. Her lament over how easily he gave up the lock suggests that her request that he return it was really meant to stir him to a realization of what bound them together, not to inspire actual compliance.

40. Her account of how he obtained the lock, so sharply at odds with what he claims in his letter (as she complains below), conforms to Margaret's earlier description of the incident (p. 114).

41. *bely*: belie, i.e., slander, misrepresent.

42. Even now she insists on her profound knowledge of Willoughby's heart, privileging her feelings about him over the evidence before her eyes.

your spirits. It is a reasonable and laudable pride which resists such malevolence."[43]

"No, no," cried Marianne, "misery such as mine has no pride. I care not who knows that I am wretched. The triumph of seeing me so may be open to all the world. Elinor, Elinor, they who suffer little may be proud and independent as they like—may resist insult, or return mortification—but I cannot. I must feel—I must be wretched—and they are welcome to enjoy the consciousness of it that can."

"But for my mother's sake and mine"—

"I would do more than for my own. But to appear happy when I am so miserable—Oh! who can require it?"[44]

Again they were both silent. Elinor was employed in walking thoughtfully from the fire to the window, from the window to the fire, without knowing that she received warmth from one, or discerning objects through the other; and Marianne, seated at the foot of the bed, with her head leaning against one of its posts,[45] again took up Willoughby's letter, and after shuddering over every sentence, exclaimed—

"It is too much! Oh! Willoughby, Willoughby, could this be yours! Cruel, cruel—nothing can acquit you. Elinor, nothing can. Whatever he might have heard against me—ought he not to have suspended his belief? ought he not to have told me of it, to have given me the power of clearing myself? 'The lock of hair, (repeating it from the letter,) which you so obligingly bestowed on me'—That is unpardonable. Willoughby, where was your heart, when you wrote those words? Oh! barbarously insolent!—Elinor, can he be justified?"

"No, Marianne, in no possible way."

"And yet this woman—who knows what her art may have been—how long it may have been premeditated, and how deeply contrived by her![46]—Who is she?—Who can she be?—Whom did I ever hear him talk of as young and attractive among his female acquaintance?—Oh! no one, no one—he talked to me only of myself."

Another pause ensued; Marianne was greatly agitated, and it ended thus.

43. The idea of a form of pride that can be laudable in certain circumstances appears elsewhere in Jane Austen. It mostly means a pride in one's own merit that makes one act well to fulfill that ideal. Here it has a particular connotation, rather less noble, of not wishing to be humiliated in the eyes of others, especially an enemy. Elinor herself has displayed this pride in dealing with Lucy. She makes a case for it here because she perceives that Marianne is not yet ready to see that only Willoughby is to blame.

44. This is consistent with Marianne's general scorn for any form of disguise, even for the benefit of those she loves.

45. Beds then almost all had high posts around them. From the posts would hang a canopy, which would provide both additional decoration to the room and warmth during the wintertime.

46. *art:* wiles, cunning, artifices. The idea of a woman's artfulness in seducing a man is found elsewhere in Jane Austen.

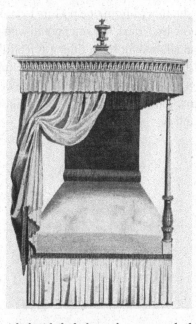

A bed, with the bedposts that were standard at the time.

[From A. E. Reveirs-Hopkins, *The Sheraton Period* (New York, 1922), Figure 13]

"Elinor, I must go home. I must go and comfort mama. Cannot we be gone to-morrow?"

"To-morrow, Marianne!"

"Yes; why should I stay here? I came only for Willoughby's sake—and now who cares for me? Who regards me?"

"It would be impossible to go to-morrow. We owe Mrs. Jennings much more than civility; and civility of the commonest kind must prevent such a hasty removal as that."[47]

"Well, then, another day or two, perhaps; but I cannot stay here long, I cannot stay to endure the questions and remarks of all these people.[48] The Middletons and Palmers—how am I to bear their pity? The pity of such a woman as Lady Middleton! Oh! what would *he* say to that!"[49]

Elinor advised her to lie down again, and for a moment she did so; but no attitude[50] could give her ease; and in restless pain of mind and body she moved from one posture to another, till growing more and more hysterical, her sister could with difficulty keep her on the bed at all, and for some time was fearful of being constrained to call for assistance. Some lavender drops,[51] however, which she was at length persuaded to take, were of use; and from that time till Mrs. Jennings returned, she continued on the bed quiet and motionless.

47. Marianne is not only neglecting her obligations to Mrs. Jennings, as Elinor immediately objects, but also any consideration for Elinor. Her mother had earlier indicated her hope that Elinor might see Edward in London, and since Marianne, like her mother, does not know of Edward's engagement to Lucy, she has every reason to think such an encounter would be of great benefit to her sister.

48. This contradicts her earlier statement that she has no pride and that all the world is welcome to witness her wretchedness. Her fears also demonstrate another drawback of her principle of openness and unreserve, for others would be far less aware of her misery and humiliation had she not behaved as if she were engaged to Willoughby at Barton, pined so openly for him in London, and written to him (thereby confirming the engagement in everyone's eyes). In contrast, Elinor, by keeping her affection for Edward as discreet as she can, runs far less danger of being the object of others' pity or attention.

49. Her statement shows the influence that Willoughby, whose contempt for Lady Middleton was just mentioned, continues to exercise on her. Marianne's ardent belief in a complete union of tastes and opinions with her beloved (p. 30) has been achieved to some extent—though not to her benefit.

50. *attitude:* position.

51. These would be drops of lavender water, the same substance that was applied the previous evening to help relieve her suffering.

Chapter Eight

*M*rs. Jennings came immediately to their room on her return, and without waiting to have her request of admittance answered, opened the door and walked in with a look of real concern.

"How do you do my dear?"—said she in a voice of great compassion to Marianne, who turned away her face without attempting to answer.

"How is she, Miss Dashwood?—Poor thing! she looks very bad.—No wonder. Aye, it is but too true. He is to be married very soon—a good-for-nothing fellow! I have no patience with him. Mrs. Taylor told me of it half an hour ago, and she was told it by a particular friend of Miss Grey herself, else I am sure I should not have believed it; and I was almost ready to sink[1] as it was. Well, said I, all I can say is, that if it is true, he has used a young lady of my acquaintance abominably ill, and I wish with all my soul his wife may plague his heart out. And so I shall always say, my dear, you may depend on it. I have no notion of men's going on in this way: and if ever I meet him again, I will give him such a dressing[2] as he has not had this many a day. But there is one comfort, my dear Miss Marianne; he is not the only young man in the world worth having; and with your pretty face you will never want admirers. Well, poor thing! I won't disturb her any longer, for she had better have her cry out at once and have done with it. The Parrys and Sandersons luckily are coming to-night you know, and that will amuse her."

She then went away, walking on tiptoe out of the room, as if she supposed her young friend's affliction could be increased by noise.

Marianne, to the surprise of her sister, determined on dining with them. Elinor even advised her against it. But "no, she would

1. *sink*: faint.

2. *dressing*: chastisement, castigation. This meaning survives in the expression "dressing down."

A butcher on his rounds.

[From William Pyne, *Costume of Great Britain* (London, 1804; 1989 reprint), Plate LVIII]

go down; she could bear it very well, and the bustle about her would be less." Elinor, pleased to have her governed for a moment by such a motive, though believing it hardly possible that she could sit out the dinner, said no more; and adjusting her dress³ for her as well as she could, while Marianne still remained on the bed, was ready to assist her into the dining room as soon as they were summoned to it.

When there, though looking most wretchedly, she ate more and was calmer than her sister had expected. Had she tried to speak, or had she been conscious of half Mrs. Jennings's well-meant but ill-judged attentions to her, this calmness could not have been maintained; but not a syllable escaped her lips, and the abstraction of her thoughts preserved her in ignorance of every thing that was passing before her.

Elinor, who did justice to Mrs. Jennings's kindness, though its effusions were often distressing, and sometimes almost ridiculous, made her those acknowledgments, and returned her those civilities, which her sister could not make or return for herself. Their good friend saw that Marianne was unhappy, and felt that every thing was due to her which might make her at all less so. She treated her therefore, with all the indulgent fondness of a parent towards a favourite child on the last day of its holidays.⁴ Marianne was to have the best place by the fire, was to be tempted to eat by every delicacy in the house, and to be amused by the relation of all the news⁵ of the day. Had not Elinor, in the sad countenance of her sister, seen a check to all mirth, she could have been entertained by Mrs. Jennings's endeavours to cure a disappointment in love, by a variety of sweetmeats⁶ and olives,⁷ and a good fire. As soon, however, as the consciousness of all this was forced by continual repetition on Marianne, she could stay no longer. With an hasty exclamation of Misery, and a sign to her sister not to follow her, she directly got up and hurried out of the room.

"Poor soul!" cried Mrs. Jennings, as soon as she was gone, "how it grieves me to see her! And I declare if she is not gone away without finishing her wine! And the dried cherries too!⁸ Lord! nothing seems to do her any good. I am sure if I knew of any thing she

3. *dress:* attire. The word then referred to everything one was wearing; the usual term for what we now call a dress was "gown."

4. Many children went to boarding schools, and had fairly long holidays when they were at home. Fond parents would, as the holidays neared their end, begin to regret the children's imminent departure and spoil them. This could be especially true of mothers with boys. Boys, more than girls, usually went to boarding schools, which could be harsh environments, due both to the discipline of the schoolmasters and the roughness of other boys. Mothers, who often lamented this but could not override their husbands' insistence — backed up by general social practice and opinion — that such an experience was necessary to make a boy a man, would fear what would happen to their sons back at school and wish to make them happy before this ordeal resumed. For a contemporary picture of a boy in a boarding school threatened with caning, see p. 361.

5. *news:* personal news or gossip.

6. *sweetmeats:* various sweet foods, including cakes.

7. Olives were a luxury item, since they were not cultivated in England and needed to be imported. Delicacies like this were more available in London than in the country, which is one reason for Mrs. Jennings to think they would please Marianne particularly.

8. Because of the lack of refrigeration, fruits were often dried or made into preserves. These would generally be the only fruits available during winter (it is currently January).

A London cherry seller.

[From Andrew Tuer, *Old London Street Cries*, p. 21]

would like, I would send all over the town for it. Well, it is the oddest thing to me, that a man should use such a pretty girl so ill! But when there is plenty of money on one side, and next to none on the other, Lord bless you! they care no more about such things!—"

"The lady then—Miss Grey I think you called her—is very rich?"

"Fifty thousand pounds, my dear. Did you ever see her? a smart, stilish girl they say, but not handsome. I remember her aunt very well, Biddy Henshawe; she married a very wealthy man. But the family are all rich together. Fifty thousand pounds![9] and by all accounts it wo'nt come before it's wanted; for they say he is all to pieces.[10] No wonder! dashing about with his curricle and hunters![11] Well, it don't signify talking, but when a young man, be he who he will, comes and makes love to[12] a pretty girl, and promises marriage, he has no business to fly off from his word only because he grows poor, and a richer girl is ready to have him. Why don't he, in such a case, sell his horses, let his house,[13] turn off[14] his servants, and make a thorough reform at once?[15] I warrant you, Miss Marianne would have been ready to wait till matters came round. But that won't do, now-a-days; nothing in the way of pleasure can ever be given up by the young men of this age."[16]

"Do you know what kind of a girl Miss Grey is? Is she said to be amiable?"[17]

"I never heard any harm of her; indeed I hardly ever heard her mentioned; except that Mrs. Taylor did say this morning, that one day Miss Walker hinted to her, that she believed Mr. and Mrs. Ellison would not be sorry to have Miss Grey married, for she and Mrs. Ellison could never agree."—

"And who are the Ellisons?"

"Her guardians, my dear. But now she is of age and may choose for herself;[18] and a pretty choice she has made!—What now," after pausing a moment—"your poor sister is gone to her own room I suppose to moan by herself. Is there nothing one can get to comfort her? Poor dear, it seems quite cruel to let her be alone. Well,

9. Fifty thousand pounds was a considerable sum then, much larger than any other female fortune mentioned in Austen novels. Landowning families normally left the bulk of their fortune to the eldest son, or to another male relation if no son existed, to preserve the family estate intact and in the male line. This suggests that Miss Grey comes from a wealthy commercial family, where such practices were less common. Many such families would provide their daughters with enormous dowries to enable them to marry men of higher social status, and thereby raise the entire family socially: someone like Willoughby with a landed estate but serious current debts would be an ideal candidate for such an exchange of money for status. In contrast, an aristocratic woman with this fortune would be able to attract a man of even higher rank than Willoughby. The likelihood of Miss Grey's lower background is strengthened by Mrs. Jennings's remembering her aunt, which suggests she knew the aunt when she was living in the commercial section of London with her husband.

10. *all to pieces*: in a state of disarray or dissolution.

11. A curricle was an expensive open carriage that required two horses, a further expense; hunters were special horses for hunting, which cost more than regular horses (see p. 173, note 17).

12. *makes love to*: courts, professes love to. The term had no further meaning then.

13. Many landowners rented their houses, whether due to debts or a wish to live elsewhere. They would rarely sell because of the strong emphasis on preserving the family estate for future generations.

14. *turn off*: dismiss.

15. Many wealthy people fell into debt—the need to keep up with others of one's own class who enjoyed even greater incomes was one reason—and this often led to programs of financial retrenchment.

16. Such laments can be found elsewhere in writings of the time, though there is no particular evidence for worse behavior among young men then than during other periods.

17. *amiable*: kind, good-natured.

18. People came of age when they reached twenty-one. Until that point Miss Grey would have been legally under the control of her guardians—presumably her parents are dead—and could have married only with their approval.

by-and-by we shall have a few friends, and that will amuse her a little. What shall we play at? She hates whist I know; but is there no round game she cares for?"[19]

"Dear Ma'am, this kindness is quite unnecessary. Marianne I dare say will not leave her room again this evening. I shall persuade her if I can to go early to bed, for I am sure she wants[20] rest."

"Aye, I believe that will be best for her. Let her name her own supper, and go to bed.[21] Lord! no wonder she has been looking so bad and so cast down this last week or two, for this matter I suppose has been hanging over her head as long as that. And so the letter that came to-day finished it! Poor soul! I am sure if I had had a notion of it, I would not have joked her about it for all my money. But then you know, how should I guess such a thing? I made sure of its being nothing but a common love letter, and you know young people like to be laughed at about them. Lord! how concerned Sir John and my daughters will be when they hear it! If I had had my senses about me I might have called in Conduit-street[22] in my way home, and told them of it. But I shall see them to-morrow."

"It would be unnecessary I am sure, for you to caution Mrs. Palmer and Sir John against ever naming Mr. Willoughby, or making the slightest allusion to what has passed, before my sister.[23] Their own good-nature must point out to them the real cruelty of appearing to know any thing about it when she is present; and the less that may ever be said to myself on the subject, the more my feelings will be spared, as you my dear madam will easily believe."

"Oh! Lord! yes, that I do indeed. It must be terrible for you to hear it talked of; and as for your sister, I am sure I would not mention a word about it to her for the world. You saw I did not all dinner time.[24] No more would Sir John nor my daughters, for they are all very thoughtful and considerate; especially if I give them a hint, as I certainly will. For my part, I think the less that is said about such things, the better, the sooner 'tis blown over and forgot. And what good does talking ever do you know?"[25]

"In this affair it can only do harm; more so perhaps than in

19. Marianne refused to join in a round game at Lady Middleton's on the grounds that she hated cards (p. 266). Mrs. Jennings was there, but has either forgotten or finds herself desperate to offer some other consolation to Marianne now that she has rejected the foods Mrs. Jennings offered.

20. *wants:* needs.

21. Again she thinks of what comfort Marianne might derive from food, a focus Mrs. Jennings will show on other occasions. Supper, a light meal, was eaten relatively late in the evening.

22. Conduit Street is where the Middletons live (see p. 314). Mrs. Jennings, even amid her genuine sympathy, reveals her love of gossip.

23. She does not mention Lady Middleton or Mr. Palmer, since she assumes they will be discreet, whether from good manners in her case or indifference in his (perhaps supplemented by a respect for certain forms of correct etiquette that he has shown).

24. To refrain from mentioning something important all through dinner constitutes significant self-restraint in Mrs. Jennings's eyes.

25. A truly extraordinary statement for Mrs. Jennings.

A student in a boarding school threatened with caning (see p. 357, note 4).

[From William Combe, *The Dance of Life* (London, 1817; 1903 reprint), p. 83]

many cases of a similar kind, for it has been attended by circumstances which, for the sake of every one concerned in it, make it
unfit to become the public conversation. I must do *this* justice to
Mr. Willoughby—he has broken no positive engagement with my
sister."

"Law, my dear! Don't pretend to defend him.[26] No positive
engagement indeed! after taking her all over Allenham House,
and fixing on the very rooms they were to live in hereafter!"[27]

Elinor, for her sister's sake, could not press the subject farther,
and she hoped it was not required of her for Willoughby's; since,
though Marianne might lose much, he could gain very little by the
inforcement[28] of the real truth.[29] After a short silence on both sides,
Mrs. Jennings, with all her natural hilarity,[30] burst forth again.

"Well, my dear, 'tis a true saying about an ill wind, for it will be
all the better for Colonel Brandon.[31] He will have her at last; aye,
that he will. Mind me, now, if they an't married by Midsummer.[32]
Lord! how he'll chuckle over this news! I hope he will come to-
night. It will be all to one a better match for your sister. Two thousand a year without debt or drawback[33]—except the little
love-child,[34] indeed; aye, I had forgot her; but she may be 'prenticed out at small cost,[35] and then what does it signify? Delaford is

A landscaped grounds with water, such as Delaford is described as having.

[From Humphrey Repton, *The Art of Landscape Gardening* (Boston, 1907; reprint ed.), p. 100]

26. Mrs. Jennings assumes Elinor just pretends to defend him for polite appearances' sake. She cannot imagine that Elinor might have a genuine spirit of justice toward a man who has wronged her sister. Of course, Elinor is not exculpating him, only saying his behavior is not as wrong as Mrs. Jennings assumes.

27. Their lengthy visit to Willoughby's probable future home at Allenham would be generally regarded as a sure sign of engagement (see p. 133, note 46).

28. *inforcement*: enforcement, i.e., urging, pressing.

29. The lack of an engagement would only partially excuse Willoughby, for most would consider him still bound in honor to marry Marianne after raising such expectations. The hero of *Persuasion* feels himself to be so bound after a far less assiduous courtship than Willoughby's. At the same time, the absence of an engagement would, if known, cause serious censure of Marianne's behavior, especially her correspondence with Willoughby.

30. *hilarity*: cheerfulness.

31. "It is an ill wind that blows nobody good" is a traditional saying that means most events, however bad, benefit at least somebody (hence the event, or wind, not doing that is truly an ill one). In this case Mrs. Jennings suggests that Willoughby's treachery will benefit Colonel Brandon.

32. *Midsummer*: June 24. Along with Michaelmas (September 29), Christmas, and Lady Day (March 25), it was one of the four rent days dividing the year.

33. *drawback*: diminution, deduction.

34. *love-child*: child born out of wedlock. Mrs. Jennings has already discussed Colonel Brandon's supposed natural daughter (p. 126).

35. Apprenticed out—"'prenticed" was a traditional form that had ceased to be standard English—meant binding someone as an apprentice, for a small fee, to learn a trade. Those who could afford it might instead send a natural child to a boarding school, as is done with such a character in *Emma*, Harriet Smith. In either case the idea would be to give the child a chance in life, while avoiding the shame, and the offense to one's neighbors and to the sanctity of marriage, of living with one's illegitimate child. Mrs. Jennings's suggestion would cost less than a boarding school and also consign the child to a lower position in life: her concluding words, "then what does it signify?," suggest a rather hard-hearted attitude.

a nice place, I can tell you; exactly what I call a nice old fashioned place, full of comforts and conveniences; quite shut in with great garden walls that are covered with the best fruit-trees in the country:[36] and such a mulberry tree in one corner![37] Lord! how Charlotte and I did stuff[38] the only time we were there! Then, there is a dove-cote, some delightful stewponds, and a very pretty canal;[39] and every thing, in short, that one could wish for: and, moreover, it is close to the church, and only a quarter of a mile from the turnpike-road, so 'tis never dull, for if you only go and sit up in an old yew arbour behind the house, you may see all the carriages that pass along.[40] Oh! 'tis a nice place! A butcher hard by[41] in the village, and the parsonage-house within a stone's throw.[42] To my fancy, a thousand times prettier than Barton Park, where they are forced to send three miles for their meat,[43] and have not a neighbour nearer than your mother.[44] Well, I shall spirit up[45] the Colonel as soon as I can. One shoulder of mutton, you know,

North Court, Isle of Wight: an older country house with walls around, partly fitting the description of Delaford.

[From John Preston Neale, *Views of the Seats of Noblemen and Gentlemen,* Vol. V (1822)]

36. Fruit trees were often surrounded by garden walls, which protected the trees from the cold and thereby lengthened their growing season. Sometimes the walls were heated to extend the growing season further, or to allow the cultivation of fruits that fared best in a warmer climate than England's.

37. Mulberry trees, which had first been imported into England because their leaves are the food of silkworms, grow best when protected by walls. They were not that common in England, though their fruit was considered by some a great delicacy; this is probably why Mrs. Jennings mentions it.

38. *stuff:* gorge ourselves. The term was not really proper English.

39. Dovecotes are houses for doves and pigeons, and there were many in England then to provide pigeons for eating. Stew ponds are fishponds, another feature of many estates for the purpose of providing food. Canals and other waterways were standard parts of the elaborate landscape gardens of the time; for an example, see picture on the preceding page. Mrs. Jennings's reference to the canal constitutes her one praise of something for its aesthetic value; otherwise she speaks only of the gastronomic or social benefits of Delaford.

40. Turnpikes were the main long-distance roads in Britain; they were constructed by private turnpike trusts, authorized by the government, that collected tolls. They would provide a regular stream of carriage traffic for the ever curious Mrs. Jennings. Yew trees, sometimes called English cedars, are a common conifer in England.

41. *hard by:* close by.

42. The parsonage house, where the minister of the parish lived, would usually be next to the church, which she just said was close to Colonel Brandon's house. Mrs. Jennings, as her next sentence indicates, values this especially for the social benefits, for clergy and their wives, being genteel, would be appropriate companions for those living at Delaford. The proximity of the local village helps mark Delaford as old-fashioned: a recent trend was to seclude country houses behind extensive landscaped parks.

43. Though most landowners would raise livestock, they would also purchase meat from a local butcher. Butchers in rural areas would often deliver meat to their customers; for a contemporary picture of a butcher on his way to a delivery, see p. 355.

44. The Dashwoods' residence at Barton is only half a mile from the Middletons' house, but even the difference between that and a closer proximity seems of great significance to the gregarious Mrs. Jennings.

45. *spirit up:* encourage.

drives another down.[46] If we *can* but put Willoughby out of her head!"

"Aye, if we can but do *that*, Ma'am," said Elinor, "we shall do very well with or without Colonel Brandon." And then rising, she went away to join Marianne, whom she found, as she expected, in her own room, leaning, in silent misery, over the small remains of a fire, which, till Elinor's entrance, had been her only light.[47]

"You had better leave me," was all the notice[48] that her sister received from her.

"I will leave you," said Elinor, "if you will go to bed." But this, from the momentary perverseness of impatient suffering, she at first refused to do. Her sister's earnest, though gentle persuasion, however, soon softened her to compliance, and Elinor saw her lay her aching head on the pillow, and saw her, as she hoped, in a way to get some quiet rest before she left her.

In the drawing-room, whither she then repaired,[49] she was soon joined by Mrs. Jennings, with a wine-glass, full of something, in her hand.

"My dear," said she, entering, "I have just recollected that I have some of the finest old Constantia wine[50] in the house, that ever was tasted, so I have brought a glass of it for your sister. My poor husband! how fond he was of it! Whenever he had a touch of his old cholicky gout,[51] he said it did him more good than any thing else in the world. Do take it to your sister."

"Dear Ma'am," replied Elinor, smiling at the difference of the complaints for which it was recommended, "how good you are! But I have just left Marianne in bed, and, I hope, almost asleep; and as I think nothing will be of so much service to her as rest, if you will give me leave, I will drink the wine myself."

Mrs. Jennings, though regretting that she had not been five minutes earlier, was satisfied with the compromise; and Elinor, as she swallowed the chief of it, reflected that, though its good effects on a cholicky gout were, at present, of little importance to her, its healing powers on a disappointed heart might be as reasonably tried on herself as on her sister.

Colonel Brandon came in while the party were at tea, and by

46. This is a proverbial expression, used sometimes to mean that eating makes one hungrier. Here it would mean that Marianne, having had her appetite whetted by Willoughby, will be all the more eager for another man to replace him.

47. Elinor would be carrying a candle or a lamp to light her way. Marianne's not procuring any light indicates her complete disdain of practicalities.

48. *notice:* acknowledgment.

49. *repaired:* returned, went.

50. *Constantia wine:* wine from the large Constantia farm near Cape Town in South Africa. This wine was developed by Dutch settlers in the late seventeenth century and soon became widely renowned for its high quality.

51. Gout involves inflammation and severe pain in the joints, especially those of the big toe. It was a common ailment of the time, especially among the wealthy, for it is caused by excessive consumption of alcohol and foods rich in purine, the most prominent of which are certain meats and fish. It also usually afflicted people as they grew older, and men were far more susceptible to it than women. "Cholicky" means his gout was accompanied by cholic, or colic, a term used then for severe stomach pains. This is a separate ailment, and was understood as such at the time, but it could easily exist with gout, since an overly rich diet also helped bring it on.

his manner of looking round the room for Marianne, Elinor immediately fancied that he neither expected, nor wished to see her there, and, in short, that he was already aware of what occasioned her absence. Mrs. Jennings was not struck by the same thought; for, soon after his entrance, she walked across the room to the tea-table where Elinor presided, and whispered—"The Colonel looks as grave as ever you see. He knows nothing of it; do tell him, my dear."

He shortly afterwards drew a chair close to her's, and, with a look which perfectly assured her of his good information, inquired after her sister.

"Marianne is not well," said she. "She has been indisposed all day, and we have persuaded her to go to bed."

"Perhaps, then," he hesitatingly replied, "what I heard this morning may be—there may be more truth in it than I could believe possible at first."

"What did you hear?"

"That a gentleman, whom I had reason to think—in short, that a man, whom I *knew* to be engaged—but how shall I tell you? If you know it already, as surely you must, I may be spared."[52]

"You mean," answered Elinor, with forced calmness, "Mr. Willoughby's marriage with Miss Grey. Yes, we *do* know it all. This seems to have been a day of general elucidation, for this very morning first unfolded it to us. Mr. Willoughby is unfathomable! Where did you hear it?"

"In a stationer's shop[53] in Pall Mall,[54] where I had business. Two ladies were waiting for their carriage, and one of them was giving the other an account of the intended match, in a voice so little attempting concealment, that it was impossible for me not to hear all.[55] The name of Willoughby, John Willoughby, frequently repeated, first caught my attention, and what followed was a positive assertion that every thing was now finally settled respecting his marriage with Miss Grey—it was no longer to be a secret[56]—it would take place even within a few weeks, with many particulars of preparations and other matters. One thing, especially, I remember, because it served to identify the man still more:—as soon as

52. His hesitation, which continues throughout this conversation, indicates how painful a subject he finds Willoughby's breach of faith with Marianne. He will shortly reveal further reasons why he finds any matter connected with Willoughby to be painful.

53. *stationer's shop:* shop selling writing materials. Writing then required a number of materials, including ink, quill pens, penknives (for sharpening pens), and sanders (for helping ink dry).

54. *Pall Mall:* a well-known street in London with many expensive shops and comparable houses. It is in the St. James neighborhood, a small area immediately south of Mayfair that had long been an aristocratic location, thanks to the royal residence at St. James Palace. Edward Ferrars will later be found living on this street, while Colonel Brandon lives on the nearby St. James Street. For a picture of Pall Mall, see next page.

55. His hearing news in this way indicates the relatively small upper-class society of the time. Even in London the number of people in this class would not be enormous, and they were concentrated in one section of the city. Hence it is not unlikely that those in that area would know of an important item of news such as an engagement, and that Colonel Brandon would overhear their gossip. Mrs. Jennings's hearing of the news earlier is another example of this.

56. It was probably a secret for a while because of negotiations over the marriage settlement. Elaborate legal and financial settlements were a standard aspect of marriage among the wealthy, and they could involve protracted bargains. In this case, an indebted groom would be acquiring a very large sum of money from the bride, so the negotiations could have been especially complicated. Once married the husband assumed general authority over the wife and her fortune, and Miss Grey's representative probably wished to provide her with good safeguards in return for her sizable contribution.

the ceremony was over, they were to go to Combe Magna, his seat in Somersetshire.[57] My astonishment!—but it would be impossible to describe what I felt. The communicative lady I learnt, on inquiry, for I staid in the shop till they were gone, was a Mrs. Ellison, and that, as I have been since informed, is the name of Miss Grey's guardian."[58]

"It is. But have you likewise heard that Miss Grey has fifty thousand pounds? In that, if in any thing, we may find an explanation."

"It may be so; but Willoughby is capable—at least I think"—he stopped a moment; then added in a voice which seemed to distrust itself, "And your sister—how did she—"

"Her sufferings have been very severe. I have only to hope that they may be proportionably short. It has been, it is a most cruel affliction. Till yesterday, I believe, she never doubted his regard; and even now, perhaps—but I am almost convinced that he never was really attached to her. He has been very deceitful! and, in some points, there seems a hardness of heart about him."

"Ah!" said Colonel Brandon, "there is, indeed! But your sister does not—I think you said so—she does not consider it quite as you do?"

"You know her disposition, and may believe how eagerly she would still justify him if she could."

He made no answer; and soon afterwards, by the removal of the tea-things, and the arrangement of the card parties,[59] the subject was necessarily dropped. Mrs. Jennings, who had watched them with pleasure while they were talking, and who expected to see the effect of Miss Dashwood's communication, in such an instantaneous gaiety on Colonel Brandon's side, as might have become a man in the bloom of youth, of hope and happiness, saw him, with amazement, remain the whole evening more serious and thoughtful than usual.[60]

57. Honeymoons were not typical then, though a newly married couple might travel somewhere for enjoyment.

58. Colonel Brandon, after first accidentally hearing the news, made an effort to gain further information. Generally only more vulgar characters would do this, but in this case his concern for Marianne prompted him to be more inquisitive.

59. Meaning groups for playing cards. Once tea was over this would be the normal way for many people to spend the evening.

60. This is a sign of Mrs. Jennings's limitations. Just as she cannot imagine that good food, and the prospect of Colonel Brandon's estate, would not quickly soothe Marianne's grief, so she cannot imagine that Colonel Brandon's affection for Marianne would make him think more of her current unhappiness than of his own enhanced marital prospects.

Pall Mall in London.
[From E. Beresford Chancellor, *The XVIIIth Century in London* (New York, 1921), p. 65]

Chapter Nine

*F*rom a night of more sleep than she had expected, Marianne awoke the next morning to the same consciousness of misery in which she had closed her eyes.

Elinor encouraged her as much as possible to talk of what she felt; and before breakfast was ready, they had gone through the subject again and again; with the same steady conviction and affectionate counsel on Elinor's side, the same impetuous feelings and varying opinions on Marianne's, as before. Sometimes she could believe Willoughby to be as unfortunate and as innocent as herself, and at others, lost every consolation in the impossibility of acquitting him. At one moment she was absolutely indifferent to the observation of all the world, at another she would seclude herself from it for ever, and at a third could resist it with energy. In one thing, however, she was uniform, when it came to the point, in avoiding, where it was possible, the presence of Mrs. Jennings, and in a determined silence when obliged to endure it. Her heart was hardened against the belief of Mrs. Jennings's entering into her sorrows with any compassion.

"No, no, no, it cannot be," she cried; "she cannot feel. Her kindness is not sympathy; her good nature is not tenderness. All that she wants is gossip, and she only likes me now because I supply it."[1]

Elinor had not needed this to be assured of the injustice to which her sister was often led in her opinion of others, by the irritable[2] refinement of her own mind, and the too great importance placed by her on the delicacies of a strong sensibility, and the graces of a polished manner. Like half the rest of the world, if more than half there be that are clever and good, Marianne, with excellent abilities[3] and an excellent disposition, was neither reasonable nor candid.[4] She expected from other people the same opinions

1.   The behavior of Mrs. Jennings earlier in the novel gave grounds for this dismissal of her motives, but her recent actions have revealed another, more favorable dimension of her character. Elinor has perceived this, thanks both to her careful observation and her steady fulfillment of the demands of social life, which causes her to interact with others continually. Marianne's quick, impulsive judgments and complete self-absorption deprive her of both these avenues of elucidation. Marianne also fails to distinguish between those like Mrs. Jennings and Sir John, whose vulgarities coexist with genuine benevolence of heart, and those like John and Fanny Dashwood who have few counterbalancing good qualities.

2.   *irritable:* excessively sensitive.

3.   *abilities:* mental powers or endowments.

4.   *candid:* fair, generous, benevolent. The meaning of the sentence is that even if more than half the world is clever and good, most of that group, including Marianne, are not reasonable and candid in judging others. Those who are clever and good as well as reasonable and candid must then be a tiny minority, one that presumably includes Elinor.

and feelings as her own, and she judged of their motives by the immediate effect of their actions on herself. Thus a circumstance occurred, while the sisters were together in their own room after breakfast, which sunk the heart of Mrs. Jennings still lower in her estimation; because, through her own weakness, it chanced to prove a source of fresh pain to herself, though Mrs. Jennings was governed in it by an impulse of the utmost good-will.

With a letter in her out-stretched hand, and countenance gaily smiling, from the persuasion of bringing comfort, she entered their room, saying,

"Now, my dear, I bring you something that I am sure will do you good."

Marianne heard enough. In one moment her imagination placed before her a letter from Willoughby, full of tenderness and contrition, explanatory of all that had passed, satisfactory, convincing; and instantly followed by Willoughby himself, rushing eagerly into the room to inforce,[5] at her feet, by the eloquence of his eyes, the assurances of his letter. The work of one moment was destroyed by the next. The hand writing of her mother, never till then unwelcome, was before her; and, in the acuteness of the disappointment which followed such an extasy of more than hope,[6] she felt as if, till that instant, she had never suffered.

The cruelty of Mrs. Jennings no language, within her reach in her moments of happiest eloquence, could have expressed;[7] and now she could reproach her only by the tears which streamed from her eyes with passionate violence—a reproach, however, so entirely lost on its object, that after many expressions of pity, she withdrew, still referring her to the letter for comfort. But the letter, when she was calm enough to read it, brought little comfort. Willoughby filled every page. Her mother, still confident of their engagement, and relying as warmly as ever on his constancy, had only been roused by Elinor's application,[8] to intreat from Marianne greater openness towards them both; and this, with such tenderness towards her, such affection for Willoughby, and such a conviction of their future happiness in each other, that she wept with agony through the whole of it.

5. *inforce*: enforce, i.e., strengthen or reinforce.

6. "More than hope" probably means her imagined scenario went so far beyond what she might reasonably hope that it was partly delusion or mental frenzy.

7. The inability to find words to express overpowering emotions is a theme found in various Romantic writings.

8. *application*: appeal (in Elinor's letter to her mother).

All her impatience to be at home again now returned; her mother was dearer to her than ever; dearer through the very excess of her mistaken confidence in Willoughby, and she was wildly[9] urgent to be gone. Elinor, unable herself to determine whether it were better for Marianne to be in London or at Barton, offered no counsel of her own except of patience till their mother's wishes could be known; and at length she obtained her sister's consent to wait for that knowledge.[10]

Mrs. Jennings left them earlier than usual; for she could not be easy till the Middletons and Palmers were able to grieve as much as herself; and positively refusing Elinor's offered attendance, went out alone for the rest of the morning. Elinor, with a very heavy heart, aware of the pain she was going to communicate, and perceiving by Marianne's letter how ill she had succeeded in laying any foundation for it, then sat down to write her mother an account of what had passed, and intreat her directions for the future; while Marianne, who came into the drawing-room on Mrs. Jennings's going away, remained fixed at the table where Elinor wrote, watching the advancement of her pen, grieving over her for the hardship of such a task, and grieving still more fondly over its effect on her mother.

In this manner they had continued about a quarter of an hour, when Marianne, whose nerves could not then bear any sudden noise, was startled by a rap at the door.

"Who can this be?" cried Elinor. "So early too! I thought we *had* been safe."[11]

Marianne moved to the window—

"It is Colonel Brandon!" said she, with vexation. "We are never safe from *him*."

"He will not come in, as Mrs. Jennings is from home."

"I will not trust to *that*," retreating to her own room. "A man who has nothing to do with his own time has no conscience in his intrusion on that of others."[12]

The event proved her conjecture right, though it was founded on injustice and error; for Colonel Brandon *did* come in; and Elinor, who was convinced that solicitude for Marianne brought

9. *wildly*: passionately, vehemently.

10. They will have to wait a little bit for this. Letters, which went by the very fast mail coach, would take almost two days to go between London and their home in Devonshire, so even if Elinor wrote immediately and Mrs. Dashwood responded likewise, it would be four or five days until they received her reply. The letter Marianne just received from her mother was in response to Elinor's letter sent around six days ago (see chronology, p. 714).

11. As seen at other points, etiquette generally forbade early calls so that people would have time to attend to their own affairs at home without disturbance.

12. This is a good example of Marianne's injustice in judging others' "motives by the immediate effect of their actions on herself." In addition, Marianne's exclusive focus on Willoughby has meant that she, unlike Elinor, never got to know Colonel Brandon; she also could still be influenced by Willoughby's dislike of Colonel Brandon (pp. 96–98).

378 SENSE AND SENSIBILITY

him thither, and who saw *that* solicitude in his disturbed and melancholy look, and in his anxious though brief inquiry after her, could not forgive her sister for esteeming him so lightly.

"I met Mrs. Jennings in Bond-street,"[13] said he, after the first salutation, "and she encouraged me to come on; and I was the more easily encouraged, because I thought it probable that I might find you alone, which I was very desirous of doing.[14] My object—my wish—my sole wish in desiring it—I hope, I believe it is—is to be a means of giving comfort;[15]—no, I must not say comfort—not present comfort—but conviction, lasting conviction to your sister's mind. My regard for her, for yourself, for your mother—will you allow me to prove it, by relating some circumstances, which nothing but a *very* sincere regard—nothing but an earnest desire of being useful—I think I am justified—though where so many hours have been spent in convincing myself that I am right, is there not some reason to fear I may be wrong?"[16] He stopped.

"I understand you," said Elinor. "You have something to tell me of Mr. Willoughby, that will open[17] his character farther. Your telling it will be the greatest act of friendship that can be shewn Marianne. *My* gratitude will be insured immediately by any information tending to that end, and *her's* must be gained by it in time. Pray, pray let me hear it."

"You shall; and, to be brief, when I quitted Barton last October,—but this will give you no idea—I must go farther back. You will find me a very awkward narrator, Miss Dashwood; I hardly know where to begin. A short account of myself, I believe, will be necessary, and it *shall* be a short one. On such a subject," sighing heavily, "I can have little temptation to be diffuse."[18]

He stopt a moment for recollection,[19] and then, with another sigh, went on.

"You have probably entirely forgotten a conversation—(it is not to be supposed that it could make any impression on you)—a conversation between us one evening at Barton Park—it was the evening of a dance—in which I alluded to a lady I had once known, as resembling, in some measure, your sister Marianne."[20]

13. A natural place to meet because it is a main shopping street.

14. Colonel Brandon's justification of himself shows that, contrary to Marianne's accusation, he is aware of the rules against calling early, especially when the mistress of the house is not at home.

15. In other words, he hopes that his motives are purely to give comfort, but he is conscious of other possible, less benevolent motives. His halting speech signals this consciousness, as well as perhaps other reasons for discomfort.

16. As will become apparent, he hesitates because he is about to reveal matters normally never mentioned in conversation, especially with a lady.

17. *open:* expose, reveal.

18. *diffuse:* wordy.

19. *for recollection:* to compose himself.

20. This happened on p. 106.

"Indeed," answered Elinor, "I have *not* forgotten it." He looked pleased by this remembrance, and added,

"If I am not deceived by the uncertainty, the partiality of tender recollection, there is a very strong resemblance between them, as well in mind as person. The same warmth of heart, the same eagerness of fancy and spirits. This lady was one of my nearest relations, an orphan from her infancy, and under the guardianship of my father.[21] Our ages were nearly the same, and from our earliest years we were playfellows and friends. I cannot remember the time when I did not love Eliza; and my affection for her, as we grew up, was such, as perhaps, judging from my present forlorn and cheerless gravity, you might think me incapable of having ever felt.[22] Her's, for me, was, I believe, fervent as the attachment of your sister to Mr. Willoughby, and it was, though from a different cause, no less unfortunate. At seventeen, she was lost to me for ever. She was married—married against her inclination to my brother. Her fortune was large, and our family estate much encumbered.[23] And this, I fear, is all that can be said for the conduct of one, who was at once her uncle and guardian. My brother did not deserve her; he did not even love her. I had hoped that her regard for me would support her under any difficulty, and for some time it did; but at last the misery of her situation, for she experienced great unkindness, overcame all her resolution, and though she had promised me that nothing—but how blindly I relate! I have never told you how this was brought on. We were within a few hours of eloping together for Scotland.[24] The treachery, or the folly, of my cousin's maid betrayed us.[25] I was banished to the house of a relation far distant, and she was allowed no liberty, no society,[26] no amusement, till my father's point was gained. I had depended on her fortitude too far, and the blow was a severe one[27]—but had her marriage been happy, so young as I then was, a few months must have reconciled me to it, or at least I should not have now to lament it. This however was not the case. My brother had no regard for her; his pleasures were not what they ought to have been,[28] and from the first he treated her unkindly. The consequence of this, upon a mind so young, so lively,[29] so

21. Because of the high mortality rate in this society many children were orphaned and raised by other relations, who served as their legal guardians.

22. Marriage between cousins, even first cousins, often occurred and was completely acceptable among the landed elite (it was less accepted lower in the social scale). One reason was the relative scarcity of socially suitable mates among this level of society.

23. *encumbered*: burdened with debt, especially a mortgage (which was the principal way landowners borrowed money). Many landowners fell into debt, and marriage to an heiress was a common solution. In this case, Eliza would be inheriting money from her parents: as long as she was a child others would manage the fortune for her, but they could not seize any of it; her uncle, as her guardian, was probably given the annual income from the money, such as the 5% it would earn if invested in government bonds, to help defray the costs of supporting her. His receipt of that money over the years could have inspired a wish to gain the principal as well for the sake of his family. He would wish her to marry his eldest son, rather than Colonel Brandon, because the former will inherit the family estate.

24. Scotland's laws allowed a couple younger than twenty-one to marry without the consent of parents or guardians; the marriage, once performed there, would be valid in England.

25. She probably had a lady's maid who attended her and helped her dress. Such a maid would tend to know her mistress's secrets, especially plans to go away, since the maid was in charge of her clothes and would pack them. The maid divulged the information either from folly or to curry favor and perhaps receive monetary compensation from the head of the family, Colonel Brandon's father.

26. *society*: company of other people.

27. He had harbored unrealistic expectations of her ability to resist the pressure to marry his brother.

28. This probably means he had affairs, among other things. It would be considered proper to employ a euphemism when speaking of sexual activity, especially if illicit.

29. *lively*: vivacious, lighthearted, merry.

inexperienced as Mrs. Brandon's, was but too natural. She resigned herself at first to all the misery of her situation; and happy had it been if she had not lived to overcome those regrets which the remembrance of me occasioned.[30] But can we wonder that with such a husband to provoke inconstancy, and without a friend to advise or restrain her, (for my father lived only a few months after their marriage, and I was with my regiment in the East Indies)[31] she should fall?[32] Had I remained in England, per-haps—but I meant to promote the happiness of both by removing from her for years, and for that purpose had procured my exchange.[33] The shock which her marriage had given me," he continued, in a voice of great agitation, "was of trifling weight—was nothing—to what I felt when I heard, about two years after-wards, of her divorce.[34] It was *that* which threw this gloom,—even now the recollection of what I suffered—"

He could say no more, and rising hastily walked for a few min-utes about the room. Elinor, affected by his relation, and still more by his distress, could not speak. He saw her concern, and coming to her, took her hand, pressed it, and kissed it with grate-ful respect.[35] A few minutes more of silent exertion enabled him to proceed with composure.

"It was nearly three years after this unhappy period before I returned to England.[36] My first care, when I *did* arrive, was of course to seek for her; but the search was as fruitless as it was melancholy. I could not trace her beyond her first seducer, and there was every reason to fear that she had removed from him only to sink deeper in a life of sin. Her legal allowance was not adequate to her fortune,[37] nor sufficient for her comfortable maintenance, and I learnt from my brother, that the power of receiving it had been made over some months before to another person. He imagined, and calmly could he imagine it, that her extravagance and consequent distress had obliged her to dispose of it for some immediate relief.[38] At last, however, and after I had been six months in England, I *did* find her. Regard for a former servant of my own, who had since fallen into misfortune, carried me to visit him in a spunging-house, where he was confined for

30. In other words, it would have been better if she had died than commit the terrible crime of adultery and experience the shame and guilt that followed. This was a standard sentiment at the time, a reflection of the firm insistence on female chastity.

31. It was revealed earlier that he had been in India, where many British troops were stationed to guard Britain's colonial interests. A regiment was the basic unit of the British army.

32. *fall:* lose her virtue, commit adultery.

33. He was already serving in a regiment stationed in England and exchanged his position there for one in India. Army officers usually purchased a commission for a particular regiment, so Colonel Brandon probably sold his existing commission and used the money to buy a new one. He went into the army in the first place because, as a younger son, he needed a profession, and the army was one of the leading choices of gentlemen. For more on this, see p. 194, and p. 195, note 12.

34. Divorce was almost nonexistent in this society, and considered a terrible calamity. It required a special act of Parliament, something available only to those wealthy enough to lobby for it, and was granted only under very serious circumstances, a wife's infidelity being a principal one.

35. This is a very intimate gesture, which Colonel Brandon, proper as he is, has performed only under the emotion of such a personal disclosure.

36. He could leave the army by selling his commission. He may have waited three years from a commitment to his regiment in India, or because of operations they were engaged in or shortages of other officers to replace him. As a colonel he would be the highest or almost highest-ranking officer in his regiment, and therefore of great importance.

37. She would have been given a legal allowance as part of the divorce—her husband would have gained her fortune by the marriage. The description suggests that her allowance was unfairly low relative to that fortune.

38. She probably went to moneylenders and agreed to hand over her allowance for a lump payment. Resorting to moneylenders was a common practice.

debt;[39] and there, in the same house, under a similar confinement, was my unfortunate sister. So altered—so faded—worn
down by acute suffering of every kind! hardly could I believe the
melancholy and sickly figure before me, to be the remains of the
lovely, blooming, healthful girl, on whom I had once doated.
What I endured in so beholding her—but I have no right to
wound your feelings by attempting to describe it—I have pained
you too much already.[40] That she was, to all appearance, in the
last stage of a consumption,[41] was—yes, in such a situation it was
my greatest comfort. Life could do nothing for her, beyond giving
time for a better preparation for death;[42] and that was given. I saw
her placed in comfortable lodgings, and under proper attendants;
I visited her every day during the rest of her short life; I was with
her in her last moments."

Again he stopped to recover himself; and Elinor spoke her feelings in an exclamation of tender concern, at the fate of his unfortunate friend.

"Your sister, I hope, cannot be offended," said he, "by the
resemblance I have fancied between her and my poor disgraced
relation. Their fates, their fortunes cannot be the same; and had
the natural sweet disposition of the one been guarded by a firmer
mind, or an happier marriage, she might have been all that you
will live to see the other be. But to what does all this lead? I seem
to have been distressing you for nothing. Ah! Miss Dashwood—a
subject such as this—untouched for fourteen years—it is dangerous to handle it at all! I *will* be more collected—more concise.
She left to my care her only child, a little girl, the offspring of her
first guilty connection,[43] who was then about three years old. She
loved the child, and had always kept it with her. It was a valued, a
precious trust to me; and gladly would I have discharged it in the
strictest sense, by watching over her education myself,[44] had the
nature of our situations allowed it; but I had no family, no home;
and my little Eliza was therefore placed at school. I saw her there
whenever I could, and after the death of my brother, (which happened about five years ago, and which left to me the possession of

39. Imprisonment for debt was a long-standing practice in England, and one that figures in many eighteenth- and nineteenth-century novels; it was also one reason moneylenders were willing to lend to so many people. Anybody whose debts exceeded a modest amount (except merchants, who were treated in a separate fashion) could be taken to court by their creditors and thrown in jail until they were able to repay the debt. Some people would end up spending years there. Those who had just been arrested and who expected to pay off their debts would reside in spunging houses, or lockup houses, while they tried to settle with their creditors. If they failed they would generally be transferred to the harsher conditions of a regular debtors' prison. Spunging houses mostly contained more affluent prisoners, who had the best expectations of resolving their debts and could afford the exorbitant fees charged by the houses—their name derived from their reputation for mercilessly sponging off their inmates with their charges. All this makes it unlikely that Colonel Brandon's former servant or sister-in-law, the latter now an outcast from all respectable society, would be in a spunging house instead of a regular debtors' prison. Thus this could be one of the very rare cases of a mistake by Jane Austen, probably a result of her dealing with a seamy side of life outside her own experience. She may have thought of a spunging house as the equivalent of a debtors' prison because the former was what any talk in her social circle about confinement for debt would refer to, or she may have been inspired by *Clarissa*, by one of her favorite novelists, Samuel Richardson, whose heroine's adventures involve a stay in a spunging house. For a picture of someone being arrested for debt, see p. 392.

40. Adultery, like any other sexual misbehavior, would normally be completely inappropriate to discuss before ladies, which is one reason he has hesitated to raise this matter earlier with Elinor, and is now apologetic about it.

41. *consumption:* tuberculosis. This was a frequent killer in those days, and people who were poor were even more susceptible to it, especially those living in cities and subject to poor sanitation and crowded conditions.

42. Again he speaks of death as a mercy for a fallen woman. By "better preparation for death" he means reconciling with God and receiving forgiveness and peace.

43. *connection:* affair.

44. Many children, especially girls, were educated at home. This was often done by the mother of the family, but a man could also undertake the charge. In this case, given the extreme youth of the child, he probably sent her first to a woman teaching and taking care of a few girls in her home; Jane Austen was sent briefly to such an establishment when she was seven. When older she could have been transferred to a boarding school for girls.

the family property,)[45] she frequently visited me at Delaford. I called her a distant relation; but I am well aware that I have in general been suspected of a much nearer connection with her.[46] It is now three years ago, (she had just reached her fourteenth year,) that I removed her from school, to place her under the care of a very respectable woman, residing in Dorsetshire,[47] who had the charge of four or five other girls of about the same time of life,[48] and for two years I had every reason to be pleased with her situation. But last February, almost a twelvemonth back, she suddenly disappeared. I had allowed her, (imprudently, as it has since turned out,) at her earnest desire, to go to Bath with one of her young friends, who was attending her father there for his health.[49] I knew him to be a very good sort of man, and I thought well of his daughter—better than she deserved, for, with a most obstinate and ill-judged secrecy, she would tell nothing, would give no clue, though she certainly knew all.[50] He, her father, a well-meaning, but not a quick-sighted man, could really, I believe, give no information; for he had been generally confined to the house, while the girls were ranging over the town and making what acquaintance they chose;[51] and he tried to convince me, as thoroughly as he was convinced himself, of his daughter's being entirely unconcerned in the business. In short, I could learn nothing but that she was gone; all the rest, for eight long months, was left to conjecture. What I thought, what I feared, may be imagined; and what I suffered too."

"Good heavens!" cried Elinor, "could it be—could Willoughby!"—[52]

"The first news that reached me of her," he continued, "came in a letter from herself, last October. It was forwarded to me from Delaford, and I received it on the very morning of our intended party to Whitwell;[53] and this was the reason of my leaving Barton so suddenly, which I am sure must at the time have appeared strange to every body, and which I believe gave offence to some. Little did Mr. Willoughby imagine, I suppose, when his looks censured me for incivility in breaking up the party, that I was

It is not clear how Colonel Brandon was supporting himself at this point. As a younger son his inheritance is unlikely to have been large enough to enable him to maintain a home for others besides himself. He could have procured a commission in a regiment stationed in England, but that would have made it difficult to establish a suitable home for a young girl.

45. His brother would have died without heirs, not surprising given his divorce and dissolute way of life, which would make him unlikely to marry again. The property would therefore descend to the next-oldest brother. Once Colonel Brandon inherited it he would have had a good home for the girl, as well as the means to hire a governess, but he may have decided it was better for her to continue in the school she was already attending.

46. He refers to the suspicions of Mrs. Jennings, and perhaps others, that the girl is his natural daughter.

47. *Dorsetshire*: a county in southwestern England (see map, p. 739).

48. Such informal arrangements for girls were not uncommon. It is not clear if this woman was continuing the girls' education or just supervising them.

49. Bath was the most popular resort town in England. Its warm springwaters were considered healthful both to bathe in and to drink. During the eighteenth century, with many people also coming for the various entertainments and active social life it offered, it boomed significantly. Thus it would have attracted the father of Eliza's friend for health reasons and lured the girls with its opportunities for enjoyment.

50. This would be after Eliza had disappeared from Bath, and Colonel Brandon came to locate her. The friend knew with whom Eliza had run away, but did not wish to betray the secret.

51. Bath was a prime destination for meeting people, especially those who were wealthy and leisured. The girls could have gone out frequently and encountered young men who were interested in them; with the father at home due to his health, they would have lacked normal adult supervision.

52. She guesses this partly because of what she has learned about Willoughby's character and partly because, without some connection to him, there would not be a clear reason for Colonel Brandon to tell his story. It would certainly be plausible that a pleasure-loving person like Willoughby would visit Bath.

53. When he received the letter he changed color upon looking at the address, which would have been in her handwriting (p. 120). The letter was probably forwarded by a servant at Delaford.

called away to the relief of one, whom he had made poor and miserable; but *had* he known it, what would it have availed? Would he have been less gay or less happy in the smiles of your sister? No, he had already done that, which no man who *can* feel for another, would do. He had left the girl whose youth and innocence he had seduced, in a situation of the utmost distress, with no creditable home,[54] no help, no friends, ignorant of his address! He had left her promising to return; he neither returned, nor wrote, nor relieved her."[55]

"This is beyond every thing!" exclaimed Elinor.

"His character is now before you; expensive,[56] dissipated,[57] and worse than both. Knowing all this, as I have now known it many weeks, guess what I must have felt on seeing your sister as fond of him as ever, and on being assured that she was to marry him; guess what I must have felt for all your sakes. When I came to you last week and found you alone, I came determined to know the truth; though irresolute what to do when it *was* known. My behaviour must have seemed strange to you then; but now you will comprehend it. To suffer you all to be so deceived; to see your sister—but what could I do? I had no hope of interfering with success; and sometimes I thought your sister's influence might yet reclaim him.[58] But now, after such dishonourable usage, who can tell what were his designs on her?[59] Whatever they may have been, however, she may now, and hereafter doubtless *will*, turn with gratitude towards her own condition, when she compares it with that of my poor Eliza, when she considers the wretched and hopeless situation of this poor girl, and pictures her to herself, with an affection for him as strong, still as strong as her own, and with a mind tormented by self-reproach, which must attend her through life.[60] Surely this comparison must have its use with her. She will feel her own sufferings to be nothing. They proceed from no misconduct, and can bring no disgrace. On the contrary, every friend must be made still more her friend by them. Concern for her unhappiness, and respect for her fortitude under it, must strengthen every attachment. Use your own

54. Meaning a decent or respectable home. The stigma attached to unchaste women would keep any normal lodging house from admitting her. It is not clear where she did find a home. Colonel Brandon never says where he went to find her. Earlier when Elinor asked Colonel Brandon if he had been continually in London, "he replied with some embarrassment" that he had been in Delaford (p. 300); his embarrassment may have come from his also having left London to see Eliza.

55. A woman in her situation would have been completely vulnerable, dependent on the man who seduced her for financial support as well as for whatever social respectability she might command, if he were willing to live with her and offer her his protection.

56. *expensive*: extravagant.

57. *dissipated*: intemperate, dissolute, without moral restraint. The term was a frequent one of censure then.

58. He had been tempted to tell Elinor at one point, when he also openly avowed his love for Marianne (see pp. 318–320). But if she were already engaged his news would be too late and his motives might have been questioned, especially since others like Mrs. Jennings had noticed his interest in Marianne.

59. Colonel Brandon thinks Willoughby might have intended to seduce Marianne as well. But Willoughby's later confession indicates that, bad as his behavior and motives were, he probably never had this intention (see p. 603, note 43).

60. Sexual misbehavior in a woman was a lifelong stain that would make her a permanent outcast from regular society. This could naturally lead to severe self-reproach, perhaps reinforced by feelings of moral or religious guilt.

discretion, however, in communicating to her what I have told you. You must know best what will be its effect; but had I not seriously, and from my heart believed it might be of service, might lessen her regrets, I would not have suffered myself to trouble you with this account of my family afflictions, with a recital which may seem to have been intended to raise myself at the expense of others."

Elinor's thanks followed this speech with grateful earnestness; attended too with the assurance of her expecting material advantage to Marianne, from the communication of what had passed.

"I have been more pained," said she, "by her endeavours to acquit him than by all the rest; for it irritates her mind more than the most perfect conviction of his unworthiness can do. Now, though at first she will suffer much, I am sure she will soon become easier. Have you," she continued, after a short silence, "ever seen Mr. Willoughby since you left him at Barton?"

"Yes," he replied gravely, "once I have. One meeting was unavoidable."

Elinor, startled by his manner, looked at him anxiously, saying, "What? have you met him to—"

"I could meet him in no other way. Eliza had confessed to me, though most reluctantly, the name of her lover; and when he returned to town, which was within a fortnight after myself,[61] we met by appointment, he to defend, I to punish his conduct.[62] We returned unwounded, and the meeting, therefore, never got abroad."[63]

Elinor sighed over the fancied necessity of this; but to a man and a soldier, she presumed not to censure it.[64]

"Such," said Colonel Brandon, after a pause, "has been the unhappy resemblance between the fate of mother and daughter! and so imperfectly have I discharged my trust!"[65]

"Is she still in town?"

"No; as soon as she recovered from her lying-in,[66] for I found her near delivery, I removed her and her child into the country, and there she remains."[67]

Recollecting, soon afterwards, that he was probably dividing

61. When Willoughby suddenly left the Dashwoods he was going to London. Since it was eight months at this point since she had disappeared her pregnancy would have been visible, and Colonel Brandon could have insisted on knowing the father.

62. He means they fought a duel. Dueling, though against the law, was a fairly common practice, especially among the upper classes and among soldiers; Colonel Brandon's service as an officer may have made him more likely to challenge someone. Men mostly fought duels to avenge insults to their own honor, but they would also fight for the sake of a woman's honor, as Colonel Brandon does here. One reason and justification for duels was that they provided a means to punish conduct such as sexual seduction or betrayal that was not punishable by law. The fear of having to fight a duel could serve as a deterrent: in *Pride and Prejudice* there is talk of a possible duel with a young man who has run off with an unmarried girl, and the girl's mother expresses a hope that this will make him marry her. The duelists would meet by appointment, usually in a relatively remote place to avoid attracting attention, especially by legal authorities. There were several open spaces on the outskirts of London that often served as dueling grounds.

63. *got abroad:* became generally known.

64. Women were less likely than men to approve of duels, though Elinor's thoughts show her awareness of how deeply entrenched, and accepted, the custom was among men. In one of Jane Austen's favorite novels, Richardson's *Sir Charles Grandison*, the hero, in a stance clearly approved by the author, refuses to fight duels out of principle, but his stance arouses mostly scorn and disagreement. Austen indicates her own attitude in a letter in which she describes an acquaintance in the army who accidentally shot himself. She writes, referring to his family, "*One* most material comfort however they have; the assurance of it's being really an accidental wound, which is not only positively declared by Earle himself, but is likewise testified by the particular direction of the bullet. Such a wound could not have been received in a duel" (Nov. 8, 1800; emphasis in original).

65. Meaning the trust of looking after the daughter. His acute regrets about his failure to protect her may be an additional reason for his hesitation to tell the story.

66. *lying-in:* confinement, i.e., period after a woman gives birth when she stays indoors and avoids activity (see p. 205, note 48).

67. He would be supporting them, probably in a remote location where they can avoid notice. That is also the fate of a woman in *Mansfield Park* who abandons her husband for another man.

Elinor from her sister, he put an end to his visit, receiving from her again the same grateful acknowledgments, and leaving her full of compassion and esteem for him.[68]

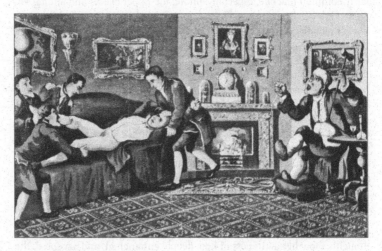

A man being arrested for debt.

[From William Combe, *The History of Johnny Quae Genus* (London, 1822; 1903 reprint), p. 222]

68. The story told by Colonel Brandon is by far the most melodramatic feature of the novel. Its main elements—childhood romance, attempted elopement, forced marriage, adultery and divorce, debtors' prison, death from consumption, illegitimate offspring, seduction and disappearance, and a duel—are those found in numerous novels of the time, the same sort that Jane Austen herself often satirizes for their overblown emotions and improbable plot devices. Thus the story fits uneasily into a novel criticizing the cult of sensibility and focusing on the realistic portrayal of ordinary life. Its main justification would be the further revelation it provides of Willoughby's character, along with the background it provides for Colonel Brandon, one showing that his current silence and gloominess are the result more of unfortunate circumstances than of inherent nature. It also gives him a particular affinity with Marianne by revealing both his passionate feelings and the resemblance between his history and that of many heroes of romantic fiction.

Chapter Ten

When the particulars of this conversation were repeated by Miss Dashwood to her sister, as they very soon were, the effect on her was not entirely such as the former had hoped to see. Not that Marianne appeared to distrust the truth of any part of it, for she listened to it all with the most steady and submissive attention, made neither objection nor remark, attempted no vindication of Willoughby, and seemed to shew by her tears that she felt it to be impossible. But though this behaviour assured Elinor that the conviction of his guilt *was* carried home to her mind, though she saw with satisfaction the effect of it, in her no longer avoiding Colonel Brandon when he called, in her speaking to him, even voluntarily speaking, with a kind of compassionate respect, and though she saw her spirits less violently irritated[1] than before, she did not see her less wretched. Her mind did become settled, but it was settled in a gloomy dejection. She felt the loss of Willoughby's character yet more heavily than she had felt the loss of his heart,[2] his seduction and desertion of Miss Williams, the misery of that poor girl, and the doubt of what his designs might *once* have been on herself, preyed altogether so much on her spirits, that she could not bring herself to speak of what she felt even to Elinor,[3] and brooding over her sorrows in silence, gave more pain to her sister than could have been communicated by the most open and most frequent confession of them.

To give the feelings or the language of Mrs. Dashwood on receiving and answering Elinor's letter, would be only to give a repetition of what her daughters had already felt and said; of a disappointment hardly less painful than Marianne's, and an indignation even greater than Elinor's. Long letters from her, quickly succeeding each other, arrived to tell all that she suffered and thought; to express her anxious solicitude for Marianne, and

1. *irritated*: excited, agitated.

2. Her situation thus contrasts with Elinor's, who while blaming Edward for some of his behavior at Norland, has no grounds for a severe reproach and therefore can continue to esteem him.

3. The idea of being the object of seduction would be a source of great shock and pain, both from moral revulsion at what was considered a terrible crime in itself and from knowledge of the ruin it would have caused if she had succumbed (as well as the damage to others, since a family would be severely tainted by a member's fall from respectability).

entreat she would bear up with fortitude under this misfortune. Bad indeed must the nature of Marianne's affliction be, when her mother could talk of fortitude! mortifying and humiliating must be the origin of those regrets, which *she* could wish her not to indulge!

Against the interest of her own individual comfort, Mrs. Dashwood had determined that it would be better for Marianne to be anywhere, at that time, than at Barton, where every thing within her view would be bringing back the past in the strongest and most afflicting manner, by constantly placing Willoughby before her, such as she had always seen him there. She recommended it to her daughters, therefore, by all means not to shorten their visit to Mrs. Jennings; the length of which, though never exactly fixed, had been expected by all to comprise at least five or six weeks.[4] A variety of occupations, of objects,[5] and of company, which could not be procured at Barton, would be inevitable there, and might yet, she hoped, cheat[6] Marianne, at times, into some interest beyond herself, and even into some amusement, much as the idea of both might now be spurned by her.

From all danger of seeing Willoughby again, her mother considered her to be at least equally safe in town as in the country, since his acquaintance must now be dropped by all who called themselves her friends. Design could never bring them in each other's way: negligence could never leave them exposed to a surprise; and chance had less in its favour in the croud of London than even in the retirement[7] of Barton, where it might force him before her while paying that visit at Allenham on his marriage,[8] which Mrs. Dashwood, from foreseeing at first as a probable event, had brought herself to expect as a certain one.

She had yet another reason for wishing her children to remain where they were; a letter from her son-in-law[9] had told her that he and his wife were to be in town before the middle of February,[10] and she judged it right that they should sometimes see their brother.

Marianne had promised to be guided by her mother's opinion, and she submitted to it therefore without opposition, though it

4. By now they have been in London more than three weeks (see chronology, p. 714). Long visits were common among genteel people at this time; Jane Austen shows them in her novels, and went on such visits to family members in her own life. One reason was the ample leisure of members of this class, especially the women. Another was the time, difficulty, and expense involved in travel, which made people wish to make the most of any trip they did take.

5. *objects*: objects of interest or enjoyment.

6. *cheat*: beguile.

7. *retirement*: seclusion.

8. Visiting a relative with one's new bride would be a standard courtesy, one Willoughby would have a particular reason to extend in this case because of his hope to inherit Allenham—though his wish not to encounter the Dashwoods or anybody else in that neighborhood could also be a powerful deterrent.

9. *son-in-law*: stepson.

10. They left for London during the first week in January and arrived three days later (pp. 292–294). Thus a stay of five to six weeks or longer would keep them there until the arrival of John Dashwood and his wife.

proved perfectly different from what she wished and expected, though she felt it to be entirely wrong, formed on mistaken grounds, and that by requiring her longer continuance in London it deprived her of the only possible alleviation of her wretchedness, the personal sympathy of her mother, and doomed her to such society and such scenes[11] as must prevent her ever knowing a moment's rest.

But it was a matter of great consolation to her, that what brought evil[12] to herself would bring good to her sister; and Elinor, on the other hand, suspecting that it would not be in her power to avoid Edward entirely, comforted herself by thinking, that though their longer stay would therefore militate against her own happiness, it would be better for Marianne than an immediate return into Devonshire.

Her carefulness in guarding her sister from ever hearing Willoughby's name mentioned, was not thrown away. Marianne, though without knowing it herself, reaped all its advantage; for neither Mrs. Jennings, nor Sir John, nor even Mrs. Palmer herself, ever spoke of him before her. Elinor wished that the same forbearance could have extended towards herself, but that was impossible, and she was obliged to listen day after day to the indignation of them all.

Sir John could not have thought it possible. "A man of whom he had always had such reason to think well! Such a good-natured fellow! He did not believe there was a bolder rider in England![13] It was an unaccountable business. He wished him at the devil with all his heart. He would not speak another word to him, meet him where he might, for all the world! No, not if it were to be by the side of Barton covert, and they were kept waiting for two hours together.[14] Such a scoundrel of a fellow! such a deceitful dog! It was only the last time they met that he had offered him one of Folly's puppies![15] and this was the end of it!"

Mrs. Palmer, in her way, was equally angry. "She was determined to drop his acquaintance immediately, and she was very thankful that she had never been acquainted with him at all. She wished with all her heart Combe Magna was not so near Cleve-

11. Meaning the company of Mrs. Jennings and other acquaintances in London, as well as probably the general crowds and busyness of the city. Marianne has long demonstrated a love of solitude, and she sought it especially when she experienced the heartbreak of Willoughby's departure from Barton; she would naturally yearn for it even more now.

12. *evil:* trouble. The term had a weaker connotation then.

13. Sir John had earlier praised Willoughby for his bold riding, an important virtue among hunters (see p. 83, note 21).

14. A covert is a thicket or other place where animals hide. They would be standing outside Barton covert—which is presumably a fairly large one, having gained this name—to wait for the prey to emerge, either on their own initiative or after being chased out by dogs.

15. Sir John presumably had more puppies than he wished to raise, and Willoughby was interested in one, perhaps from admiring the qualities of the puppy's parent. Dogs were a major preoccupation of sportsmen, since they were central to most types of hunting and shooting.

land; but it did not signify, for it was a great deal too far off to visit; she hated him so much that she was resolved never to mention his name again, and she should tell everybody she saw, how good-for-nothing he was."

The rest of Mrs. Palmer's sympathy was shewn in procuring all the particulars in her power of the approaching marriage, and communicating them to Elinor. She could soon tell at what coachmaker's the new carriage was building,[16] by what painter Mr. Willoughby's portrait was drawn,[17] and at what warehouse Miss Grey's clothes might be seen.[18]

The calm and polite unconcern of Lady Middleton on the occasion was an happy relief to Elinor's spirits, oppressed as they often were by the clamorous kindness of the others. It was a great comfort to her, to be sure of exciting no interest in *one* person at least among their circle of friends; a great comfort to know that there was *one* who would meet her without feeling any curiosity after particulars, or any anxiety for her sister's health.

Every qualification is raised at times, by the circumstances of the moment, to more than its real value; and she was sometimes worried down by officious condolence to rate good-breeding as more indispensable to comfort than good-nature.[19]

Lady Middleton expressed her sense of the affair about once every day, or twice, if the subject occurred very often, by saying, "It is very shocking indeed!" and by the means of this continual though gentle vent, was able not only to see the Miss Dashwoods from the first without the smallest emotion, but very soon to see them without recollecting a word of the matter;[20] and having thus supported the dignity of her own sex,[21] and spoken her decided censure of what was wrong in the other, she thought herself at liberty to attend to the interest of her own assemblies,[22] and therefore determined (though rather against the opinion of Sir John) that as Mrs. Willoughby would at once be a woman of elegance and fortune, to leave her card with her as soon as she married.[23]

Colonel Brandon's delicate unobtrusive inquiries were never unwelcome to Miss Dashwood. He had abundantly earned the privilege of intimate discussion of her sister's disappointment, by

16. *building*: being built. This construction is found occasionally in Jane Austen. A coachmaker would make any type of carriage, not just a coach. Acquiring a new carriage upon marriage was common, especially since the carriage would take the couple away after the ceremony and could display their wealth and good taste to everyone. In Jane Austen's satirical story "Three Sisters," a dispute between a prospective bride and groom about what new carriage they will purchase threatens to derail the match, while in *Mansfield Park* the only criticism made of an elegant wedding is that the vehicle conveying the couple from the scene was not a new one.

17. Having one's portrait painted was a basic ritual for those in the landowning class; the portraits of each generation were usually displayed prominently in the family home.

18. "Warehouse" was a more dignified term for a store. Some stores would display the wedding clothes of very wealthy brides in their windows as a way to advertise.

19. This gives a sense of Jane Austen's own scale of values. She consistently presents good breeding, or manners, as a worthy quality, but just as consistently prizes goodness of heart even more.

20. This indication of Lady Middleton's indifference, and the behavior that follows, give the immediate lie to any idea of actually rating good breeding over good nature.

21. An ideal of female solidarity appears at points in Austen's novels. In *Emma* the heroine wonders if, by discussing with a man the possibility of another woman's illicit love, "she had not transgressed the duty of woman by woman." In a letter Jane Austen comments on the running public feud between the princess of Wales and her husband, the reigning prince regent, who was notorious for sexual misconduct and for mistreating his wife, and declares that, while disappointed in the princess's latest behavior, "I shall support her as long as I can, because she *is* a Woman, & because I hate her Husband" (Feb. 16, 1813). At the same time, Jane Austen shows many women disregarding such female solidarity, as Lady Middleton does here.

22. *assemblies*: social gatherings, parties.

23. She would leave her visiting card, a sign of her wish to become acquainted.

the friendly zeal with which he had endeavoured to soften it, and they always conversed with confidence. His chief reward for the painful exertion of disclosing past sorrows and present humiliations, was given in the pitying eye with which Marianne sometimes observed him, and the gentleness of her voice whenever (though it did not often happen) she was obliged, or could oblige herself to speak to him.[24] *These* assured him that his exertion had produced an increase of good-will towards himself, and *these* gave Elinor hopes of its being farther augmented hereafter; but Mrs. Jennings, who knew nothing of all this, who knew only that the Colonel continued as grave as ever, and that she could neither prevail on him to make the offer himself, nor commission her to make it for him, began, at the end of two days, to think that, instead of Midsummer, they would not be married till Michaelmas,[25] and by the end of a week that it would not be a match at all. The good understanding between the Colonel and Miss Dashwood seemed rather to declare that the honours of the mulberry-tree, the canal, and the yew arbour,[26] would all be made over[27] to *her*; and Mrs. Jennings had for some time ceased to think at all of Mr. Ferrars.[28]

Early in February, within a fortnight from the receipt of Willoughby's letter, Elinor had the painful office of informing her sister that he was married. She had taken care to have the intelligence conveyed to herself, as soon as it was known that the ceremony was over, as she was desirous that Marianne should not receive the first notice of it from the public papers, which she saw her eagerly examining every morning.[29]

She received the news with resolute composure; made no observation on it, and at first shed no tears; but after a short time they would burst out, and for the rest of the day, she was in a state hardly less pitiable than when she first learnt to expect the event.

The Willoughbys left town as soon as they were married; and Elinor now hoped, as there could be no danger of her seeing either of them, to prevail on her sister, who had never yet left the house since the blow first fell, to go out again by degrees as she had done before.[30]

24. This signals that Marianne appreciates the Romantic quality of his story.

25. Midsummer is June 24, Michaelmas September 29. For more, see p. 19, note 16.

26. These are some of the features of Colonel Brandon's Delaford estate that were extolled by Mrs. Jennings (see pp. 362–364).

27. *made over*: transferred, handed over.

28. Here Mrs. Jennings's relative intellectual shallowness, and tendency to focus only on what is immediately before her proves beneficial to Elinor.

29. Newspapers would announce recent weddings. In *Pride and Prejudice* the heroine's mother is disappointed that the recent marriage of one of her daughters, which occurred under a cloud of prior scandalous conduct, received only a brief mention in the papers, with no information given on the family or residence of the bride.

30. Willoughby's wedding marks the end of this phase of Marianne's story. The transition to Elinor and her travails is marked in the next line by the arrival of the Miss Steeles in London.

A public coach.

[From John Ashton, *The Dawn of the XIXth Century in England* (London, 1906), p. 183]

About this time, the two Miss Steeles, lately arrived at their cousin's house in Bartlett's Buildings, Holborn,[31] presented themselves again before their more grand relations in Conduit and Berkeley-street;[32] and were welcomed by them all with great cordiality.

Elinor only was sorry to see them. Their presence always gave her pain, and she hardly knew how to make a very gracious return to the overpowering delight of Lucy in finding her *still* in town.

"I should[33] have been quite disappointed if I had not found you here *still*," said she repeatedly, with a strong emphasis on the word. "But I always thought I *should*. I was almost sure you would not leave London yet awhile; though you *told* me, you know, at Barton, that you should not stay above a *month*.[34] But I thought, at the time, that you would most likely change your mind when it came to the point. It would have been such a great pity to have went away before your brother and sister came. And now to be sure you will be in no *hurry* to be gone. I am amazingly[35] glad you did not keep to *your word*."[36]

Elinor perfectly understood her, and was forced to use all her self-command to make it appear that she did *not*.[37]

"Well, my dear," said Mrs. Jennings, "and how did you travel?"

"Not in the stage, I assure you," replied Miss Steele, with quick exultation; "we came post all the way,[38] and had a very smart beau to attend us. Dr. Davies was coming to town, and so we thought we'd join him in a post-chaise,[39] and he behaved very genteelly, and paid ten or twelve shillings more than we did."[40]

"Oh, oh!" cried Mrs. Jennings; "very pretty, indeed! and the Doctor is a single man, I warrant you."

"There now," said Miss Steele, affectedly simpering, "everybody laughs at me so about the Doctor, and I cannot think why. My cousins say they are sure I have made a conquest; but for my part I declare I never think about him from one hour's end to another. 'Lord! here comes your beau, Nancy,' my cousin said t'other day, when she saw him crossing the street to the house. My beau, indeed! said I—I cannot think who you mean. The Doctor is no beau of mine."

31. Bartlett's Buildings was a very small cul-de-sac extending south off High Holborn (it was near the current Holborn Circus); see map, p. 740. Holborn is a long-inhabited area on the western edge of the city of London; it is thus near the commercial part of London, and removed from the more fashionable vicinity of Mayfair that all the other characters in the novel inhabit. This marks the lower social status of the relations with which the Miss Steeles are staying, and is why the sentence goes on to mention "their more grand relations" elsewhere. At the time Holborn was occupied principally by lawyers, who would be near the law courts, and merchants, so the Steeles' relations are certainly not poor. Lucy mentioned them to Elinor in a conversation about her trip to London (p. 278). For a picture of Bartlett's Buildings, see p. 408.

32. This would be Mrs. Jennings and the Middletons. They do not present themselves to the Palmers, who are as much their relations and are probably richer, because they have not met them yet.

33. *should:* would.

34. By this time they have barely exceeded a month in London (see chronology, p. 714), but Lucy is quick to detect any transgression of Elinor's stated intentions. For Elinor's earlier hopes, see p. 288.

35. *amazingly:* exceedingly.

36. Lucy's tremendous delight is mostly her usual insincerity. But she may feel some genuine satisfaction in Elinor's supposed failure to keep her word.

37. Elinor may understand particularly the meaning of "no *hurry* to be gone," which insinuates that Elinor wants to remain in London until Edward arrives because of her affection for him and her hope to win him in the end.

38. "The stage" means the stage, or public, coach, which offered regular service throughout Britain. Coming post meant renting a private carriage (both means involved hiring horses); for more, see p. 125, note 18. Characters in Jane Austen novels almost always travel post, for while more expensive and not faster than the public coach, it offered privacy and social exclusiveness. Someone using the stagecoach could be accompanied by poorer people, such as Mrs. Jennings's servant Betty, whom she sent by this means when coming to London. This is why Miss Steele exultingly points out that they traveled post. It is likely she and her sister have been forced before to use the public coach. For a picture of a public coach, see the previous page.

39. A post chaise is a carriage rented to travel post. It seats three people, so Dr. Davies would have been able to take two companions.

40. Shillings were one of the three basic monetary units in Britain then: they

"Aye, aye, that is very pretty talking—but it won't do—the Doctor is the man, I see."[41]

"No, indeed!" replied her cousin, with affected earnestness, "and I beg you will contradict it, if you ever hear it talked of."

Mrs. Jennings directly gave her the gratifying assurance that she certainly would *not*, and Miss Steele was made completely happy.

"I suppose you will go and stay with your brother and sister, Miss Dashwood, when they come to town," said Lucy, returning, after a cessation of hostile hints, to the charge.[42]

"No, I do not think we shall."

"Oh, yes, I dare say you will."

Elinor would not humour her by farther opposition.

"What a charming thing it is that Mrs. Dashwood can spare you both for so long a time together!"

"Long a time, indeed!" interposed Mrs. Jennings. "Why, their visit is but just begun!"

Lucy was silenced.[43]

"I am sorry we cannot see your sister, Miss Dashwood," said Miss Steele. "I am sorry she is not well;" for Marianne had left the room on their arrival.

"You are very good. My sister will be equally sorry to miss the pleasure of seeing you;[44] but she has been very much plagued lately with nervous head-aches,[45] which make her unfit for company or conversation."

"Oh, dear, that is a great pity! but such old friends as Lucy and me!—I think she might see *us*; and I am sure we would not speak a word."

Elinor, with great civility, declined the proposal. Her sister was perhaps laid down upon the bed, or in her dressing gown,[46] and therefore not able to come to them.

"Oh, if that's all," cried Miss Steele, "we can just as well go and see *her*."

Elinor began to find this impertinence[47] too much for her temper; but she was saved the trouble of checking it, by Lucy's sharp reprimand, which now, as on many occasions, though it did not

were worth twelve pence, and twenty of them made a pound. Dr. Davies's paying more suggests it was only his presence that allowed the Miss Steeles to come by this means. He may have been traveling post anyway, which would be standard for someone of his social rank (see next note), and have invited Anne and Lucy to join him.

41. Dr. Davies would not be a medical man, who were usually called physicians or surgeons or apothecaries, depending on their status and skills, but a doctor of divinity, i.e., a clergyman—Miss Steele later speaks of his new clerical living, or position, and his ability to hire a curate (p. 510). Clergy who had earned an advanced degree received this title. Most lacked it, for it was not needed for ordination; of the various clergy in Jane Austen the only other doctor is Dr. Grant of *Mansfield Park*. This gave the title prestige, and would have added to Miss Steele's elation at the idea of a romance between herself and Dr. Davies, who as a clergyman would be a gentleman even if not a doctor.

42. Lucy suggests they will do that because Elinor wishes to put herself in closer proximity to Edward.

43. This indicates that Lucy, in contradiction to her first words to Elinor, is not at all pleased with their presence. Her comment about Mrs. Dashwood sparing them was probably made in the hope that Elinor or Mrs. Jennings would speak of their imminent departure.

44. This line is a good example of the polite lies that Elinor, unlike Marianne, is willing to speak. Marianne hardly has pleasure in seeing anybody, and would have none at all in seeing the Miss Steeles.

45. Many ailments were described as nervous because human physiology was frequently understood then in terms of nerves (for more, see p. 425, note 60). Earlier Marianne was described as suffering from "nervous faintness" (p. 340).

46. A dressing gown was a robe worn while grooming and preparing to dress, hence the name, or when relaxing privately.

47. *impertinence*: offensive inquisitiveness or familiarity.

give much sweetness to the manners of one sister, was of advantage in governing those of the other.

Bartlett's Buildings in London, where the Miss Steeles stay with their cousins. Its houses were less grand than those in Mayfair locations such as Hanover Square and Grosvenor Square (see pictures on pp. 209 and 309). The clothing in this picture is from a few decades later.

[From E. Beresford Chancellor, *The XVIIIth Century in London* (New York, 1921), p. 258]

A fashionable young man, such as Elinor is about to observe.

[From *The Repository of arts, literature, fashions, manufactures, &c*, Vol. III (1810), p. 262]

Chapter Eleven

After some opposition, Marianne yielded to her sister's entreaties, and consented to go out with her and Mrs. Jennings one morning for half an hour. She expressly conditioned, however, for paying no visits, and would do no more than accompany them to Gray's in Sackville-street,[1] where Elinor was carrying on a negociation for the exchange of a few old-fashioned jewels of her mother.[2]

When they stopped at the door, Mrs. Jennings recollected that there was a lady at the other end of the street, on whom she ought to call; and as she had no business at Gray's, it was resolved, that while her young friends transacted their's, she should pay her visit and return for them.

On ascending the stairs, the Miss Dashwoods found so many people before them in the room, that there was not a person at liberty to attend to their orders; and they were obliged to wait.[3] All that could be done was, to sit down at that end of the counter which seemed to promise the quickest succession;[4] one gentleman only was standing there, and it is probable that Elinor was not without hope of exciting his politeness to a quicker dispatch. But the correctness[5] of his eye, and the delicacy of his taste, proved to be beyond[6] his politeness. He was giving orders for a toothpick-case[7] for himself, and till its size, shape, and ornaments were determined, all of which, after examining and debating for a quarter of an hour over every toothpick-case in the shop, were finally arranged by his own inventive fancy,[8] he had no leisure to bestow any other attention on the two ladies, than what was comprised in three or four very broad stares; a kind of notice which served to imprint on Elinor the remembrance of a person and face, of strong, natural, sterling insignificance, though adorned in the first style of fashion.[9]

1.   Gray's was an actual jewelry store of the time. Sackville Street is in May-fair (close to Piccadilly Circus); see map, p. 742. Though in the same general part of London, it was far enough from Mrs. Jennings's residence that they would certainly have taken her carriage, which is why below she speaks of returning for Elinor and Marianne.

2.   Jewelry styles, after remaining fairly stable during the eighteenth cen-tury, began to change significantly around 1800. The changes introduced included a variety of new patterns and arrangements, a greater use of classi-cal motifs, and a wider range of stones and colors. This would naturally make people like Elinor or Mrs. Dashwood wish to trade in older pieces for newer ones. This process would not necessarily be a financial hardship, an impor-tant consideration for the Dashwoods, since the newer styles tended to employ less expensive materials; thus Mrs. Dashwood's older pieces probably contained more expensive stones, and that could make the jeweler willing to pay well in order to reset them in a newer style and sell them to customers who still sought finer stones.

3.   London shops were often crowded. At the same time, shops catering to the affluent were spacious and offered chairs to make their customers com-fortable (for pictures of such shops, see pp. 179 and 305).

4.   *quickest succession*: shortest wait.

5.   *correctness*: exactness.

6.   *beyond*: superior to, greater than.

7.   Toothpicks had long been in existence, and for at least a couple of cen-turies prior to this toothpick cases had been an accoutrement for the wealthy. In this period cases were made of an endless array of decorative materials and often lined with velvet; their luxurious quality is indicated by their being sold in a jewelry store. The toothpicks themselves could even be made of gold, though many were wooden. Some cases were built in the form of a tube that allowed one to slide the toothpick out when needed. The cases would be attached to one's clothing by a chain or placed in a pocket.

8.   He did not simply choose one of the existing cases, but designed his own. The need for a special order to make such a case is why the text speaks below of when he will return to pick up his completed case.

9.   "Adorned" refers to his overall attire. It does not necessarily mean he is wearing adornments such as jewelry.

Marianne was spared from the troublesome feelings of contempt and resentment, on this impertinent examination of their features, and on the puppyism[10] of his manner in deciding on all the different horrors of the different toothpick-cases presented to his inspection, by remaining unconscious of it all; for she was as well able to collect her thoughts within herself, and be as ignorant of what was passing around her, in Mr. Gray's shop, as in her own bed-room.[11]

At last the affair was decided. The ivory, the gold, and the pearls, all received their appointment,[12] and the gentleman having named the last day on which his existence could be continued without the possession of the toothpick-case, drew on his gloves with leisurely care,[13] and bestowing another glance on the Miss Dashwoods, but such a one as seemed rather to demand than express admiration, walked off with an happy air of real conceit and affected indifference.[14]

Elinor lost no time in bringing her business forward, and was on the point of concluding it, when another gentleman presented himself at her side. She turned her eyes towards his face, and found him with some surprise to be her brother.

Their affection and pleasure in meeting, was just enough to make a very creditable appearance in Mr. Gray's shop. John Dashwood was really far from being sorry to see his sisters again; it rather gave them satisfaction; and his inquiries after their mother were respectful and attentive.

Elinor found that he and Fanny had been in town two days.

"I wished very much to call upon you yesterday," said he, "but it was impossible, for we were obliged to take Harry to see the wild beasts at Exeter Exchange:[15] and we spent the rest of the day with Mrs. Ferrars.[16] Harry was vastly pleased. *This* morning I had fully intended to call on you, if I could possibly find a spare half hour, but one has always so much to do on first coming to town. I am come here to bespeak[17] Fanny a seal.[18] But to-morrow I think I shall certainly be able to call in Berkeley-street, and be introduced to your friend Mrs. Jennings. I understand she is a woman of very good fortune.[19] And the Middletons too, you must intro-

10. *puppyism*: conceit, affectation. "Puppy" was a popular term for a foppish man.

11. This shows an advantage of Marianne's extreme inwardness.

12. *appointment*: assignment. His choice of all three materials shows how fancy a toothpick case he desired.

13. Both men and women would frequently wear gloves when going outside in any season.

14. This currently unnamed character will appear again and play an important role in the plot. This episode provides a useful introduction, for he will continue to exhibit the same characteristics he does here.

15. Exeter Exchange was the leading zoo in London at this time. From the time of the Renaissance many wealthy and titled individuals in Europe had collected animals from around the world; in England, starting in the late Middle Ages, the monarchy had established a collection at the Tower of London, the Tower Menagerie, which had long been open to the public. Its collection was limited, however, and had declined during this period. Exeter Exchange, or Change, was a large building containing a variety of shops and entertainments (at the current location of the Strand Palace Hotel); toward the end of the eighteenth century a small menagerie was installed, and in the years after 1800 it grew to become one of the best zoos in Europe and a leading attraction in London. It contained all the big cats (which had long been the focus of zoos), along with an enormous array of other mammals, birds, and reptiles from all parts of the world. It also had an excellent guidebook to the animals, an innovation at the time. Its main drawback was a very high admission price, but this did not stop many from coming, and money was certainly not an object to someone as wealthy as John Dashwood—at least when he is spending on his child, as opposed to helping his sisters. For a picture of Exeter Exchange, see next page.

16. John and Fanny Dashwood's priorities are shown by their visiting the zoo, rather than his sisters, on their first day in London. Exeter Exchange was open every day from 9 to 9 and, being completely indoors, was unaffected by weather, so they easily could have postponed their visit.

17. *bespeak*: order.

18. A seal was used to seal letters closed by stamping on wax. Seals, made of very hard material, would often be fancy and decorated.

19. This suggests even his belated call on his sisters is motivated partly by a wish to meet Mrs. Jennings, whose wealth makes her worthy of his respect.

duce me to *them*. As my mother-in-law's[20] relations, I shall be happy to shew them every respect. They are excellent neighbours to you in the country, I understand."

"Excellent indeed. Their attention to our comfort, their friendliness in every particular, is more than I can express."

"I am extremely glad to hear it, upon my word; extremely glad indeed. But so it ought to be; they are people of large fortune, they are related to you, and every civility, and accommodation that can serve to make your situation pleasant, might be reasonably expected.[21] And so you are most comfortably settled in your little cottage and want for nothing! Edward brought us a most charming account of the place; the most complete thing of its kind, he said, that ever was, and you all seemed to enjoy it beyond any thing. It was a great satisfaction to us to hear it, I assure you."

Elinor did feel a little ashamed of her brother;[22] and was not sorry to be spared the necessity of answering him, by the arrival of Mrs. Jennings's servant, who came to tell her that his mistress waited for them at the door.

Mr. Dashwood attended them down stairs, was introduced to Mrs. Jennings at the door of her carriage, and repeating his hope of being able to call on them the next day, took leave.

His visit was duly paid. He came with a pretence at an apology from their sister-in-law, for not coming too; "but she was so much engaged with her mother, that really she had no leisure for going any where."[23] Mrs. Jennings, however, assured him directly, that she should not stand upon ceremony, for they were all cousins, or something like it, and she should certainly wait on[24] Mrs. John Dashwood very soon, and bring her sisters to see her. His manners to *them*, though calm, were perfectly kind;[25] to Mrs. Jennings most attentively civil; and on Colonel Brandon's coming in soon after himself, he eyed him with a curiosity which seemed to say, that he only wanted to know him to be rich, to be equally civil to *him*.

After staying with them half an hour, he asked Elinor to walk with him to Conduit-street, and introduce him to Sir John and

20. *mother-in-law's:* stepmother's.

21. An ironic statement considering that he, though much more closely related to Elinor's family and probably wealthier than Sir John, has not been the picture of generosity toward them.

22. Elinor is a little ashamed because she knows her brother's enthusiastic delight with their current situation, which is hardly as wonderful as he suggests, stems from his feeling that it helps absolve him of having reneged on his promise to assist them. It is notable that Elinor feels shame rather than resentment: despite her brother's stinginess, and the harm it has caused her, she would still prefer to think well of him.

23. Presumably his wife does not wish to see Elinor, because of her strong aversion to any possibility of marriage between Elinor and her brother Edward.

24. *wait on:* call upon, visit.

25. His conduct to his sisters was less warm and affectionate than one might expect, especially after his not having seen them in many months, but still courteous.

Polito's Menagerie, Exeter Exchange.

[From *The Repository of arts, literature, fashions, manufactures, &c*, Vol. VIII (1812), p. 27]

Lady Middleton. The weather was remarkably fine, and she readily consented. As soon as they were out of the house, his enquiries began.

"Who is Colonel Brandon? Is he a man of fortune?"

"Yes; he has very good property in Dorsetshire."

"I am glad of it. He seems a most gentlemanlike man; and I think, Elinor, I may congratulate you on the prospect of a very respectable establishment[26] in life."

"Me, brother! what do you mean?"

"He likes you. I observed him narrowly,[27] and am convinced of it.[28] What is the amount of his fortune?"

"I believe about two thousand a-year."

"Two thousand a-year;" and then working himself up to a pitch of enthusiastic generosity, he added, "Elinor, I wish, with all my heart, it were *twice* as much, for your sake."

"Indeed I believe you," replied Elinor; "but I am very sure that Colonel Brandon has not the smallest wish of marrying *me*."

"You are mistaken, Elinor; you are very much mistaken. A very little trouble on your side secures[29] him. Perhaps just at present he may be undecided; the smallness of your fortune may make him hang back; his friends may all advise him against it.[30] But some of those little attentions and encouragements which ladies can so easily give, will fix him,[31] in spite of himself. And there can be no reason why you should not try for him. It is not to be supposed that any prior attachment on your side—in short, you know as to an attachment of that kind, it is quite out of the question, the objections are insurmountable—you have too much sense not to see all that. Colonel Brandon must be the man; and no civility shall be wanting on my part, to make him pleased with you and your family. It is a match that must give universal satisfaction. In short, it is a kind of thing that"—lowering his voice to an important whisper—"will be exceedingly welcome to *all parties*."[32] Recollecting himself, however, he added, "That is, I mean to say—your friends[33] are all truly anxious to see you well settled;

26. *establishment*: settlement in life, particularly through marriage.

27. *narrowly*: closely, carefully.

28. He observed him closely because he hoped to discover an affection for Elinor on Colonel Brandon's part. His doing so indicates how much John Dashwood is focused on specific practical goals during social occasions.

29. *secures*: will secure. There are other examples in Jane Austen of this use of the present tense for the future.

30. His friends would advise him to prefer someone with a greater fortune — at least this is what John Dashwood assumes friends would advise.

31. *fix him*: fix his love.

32. By "*all parties*" he means his wife and her mother, who wish Elinor to be eliminated as a potential wife for Edward. This is one reason for his eagerness to see her married to Colonel Brandon. His statement shows his obtuseness and insensitivity: not only does he fail to grasp that Elinor is unlikely to base her marital decisions on what would best please his wife and mother, who have never shown any consideration for her, but it also does not occur to him that an allusion to their wishes is an insult to the person he is speaking to, for they welcome Elinor's marriage with someone else because they do not consider her good enough for Edward.

33. *friends*: relatives.

Fanny particularly, for she has your interest very much at heart, I assure you. And her mother too, Mrs. Ferrars, a very good-natured woman, I am sure it would give her great pleasure; she said as much the other day."

Elinor would not vouchsafe any answer.

"It would be something remarkable now," he continued, "something droll, if Fanny should have a brother and I a sister settling[34] at the same time. And yet it is not very unlikely."

"Is Mr. Edward Ferrars," said Elinor, with resolution, "going to be married?"

"It is not actually settled, but there is such a thing in agitation.[35] He has a most excellent mother. Mrs. Ferrars, with the utmost liberality, will come forward, and settle on him a thousand a-year, if the match takes place.[36] The lady is the Hon. Miss Morton,[37] only daughter of the late Lord Morton, with thirty thousand pounds.[38] A very desirable connection on both sides, and I have not a doubt of its taking place in time. A thousand a-year is a great deal for a mother to give away, to make over for ever; but Mrs. Ferrars has a noble spirit. To give you another instance of her liberality:—The other day, as soon as we came to town, aware that money could not be very plenty[39] with us just now, she put bank-notes into Fanny's hands to the amount of two hundred pounds.[40] And extremely acceptable it is, for we must live at a great expense while we are here."

He paused for her assent and compassion; and she forced herself to say,

"Your expenses both in town and country must certainly be considerable, but your income is a large one."

"Not so large, I dare say, as many people suppose. I do not mean to complain, however; it is undoubtedly a comfortable one, and I hope will in time be better. The inclosure of Norland Common, now carrying on, is a most serious drain.[41] And then I have made a little purchase within this half year; East Kingham Farm, you must remember the place, where old Gibson used to live. The land was so very desirable for me in every respect, so imme-

34. *settling*: getting married.

35. *in agitation*: under consideration or discussion. He hopes, by suggesting the probability of Edward's marriage, to discourage any hopes of Elinor.

36. This means she will transfer to him, in a legally binding manner, a sum of money or an estate producing an income of a thousand a year.

37. *Hon. Miss Morton*: Honourable Miss Morton. This was a courtesy title granted to the children of viscounts and barons, the two lowest ranks of the nobility, or peerage. Daughters of higher-ranking nobles were called "Lady" plus their full name. Being a child of a noble conferred no legal privilege, but it was a great source of prestige, and someone like John Dashwood or Mrs. Ferrars would be eager to be connected with such a person by marriage.

38. This is a considerable fortune, one that would yield 1,500 pounds a year in income. Her being an only daughter is one reason for the sum: prevailing inheritance practices usually put a ceiling on the amount that could go to daughters and younger sons, in order to ensure that most of the family fortune went to the eldest son. Her fortune, along with her rank, makes her a very desirable marital choice. In fact, from a social and economic perspective she is far superior to Edward, since he has no title and his fortune, even with Mrs. Ferrars's promised gift, is smaller than hers, when men's fortunes were usually considerably larger than women's. It is possible it is mostly Edward's family who are considering or discussing the match, not Miss Morton's family.

39. *plenty*: plentiful, abundant.

40. Banknotes were notes pledging payment of a certain amount; hence they were the equivalent of money. Many banks in England at this time had the right to issue their own notes, which other banks would honor. Two hundred pounds is 40% of the annual income of Mrs. Dashwood and her daughters.

41. Enclosure of land by large landowners was a prominent practice in the late eighteenth and early nineteenth centuries. It often meant, as it does here, transferring commons, frequently uncultivated areas available for use by the community, to individual owners. This usually happened as the result of an act of Parliament. The costs of enclosure for those sponsoring it could be high, including the legal and political costs of getting the bill passed and the property surveyed as well as the physical costs of transforming the land by building fences, bridges, or roads, draining and clearing wild areas, and planting new crops. This is what makes it a serious drain on John Dashwood's resources. Of course, he, like others, could reasonably expect an increase of income in the long run. Enclosure reached its peak during the war with France, when the cutting off of food imports from overseas increased markets and prices for agricultural producers in England.

diately adjoining my own property, that I felt it my duty to buy it.[42] I could not have answered it to my conscience to let it fall into any other hands. A man must pay for his convenience; and it *has* cost me a vast deal of money."

"More than you think it really and intrinsically worth."

"Why, I hope not that. I might have sold it again the next day, for more than I gave:[43] but with regard to the purchase-money, I might have been very unfortunate indeed; for the stocks were at that time so low, that if I had not happened to have the necessary sum in my banker's hands, I must have sold out to very great loss."[44]

Elinor could only smile.

"Other great and inevitable expenses too we have had on first coming to Norland. Our respected father, as you well know, bequeathed all the Stanhill effects[45] that remained at Norland (and very valuable they were) to your mother. Far be it from me to repine at his doing so; he had an undoubted right to dispose of his own property as he chose. But, in consequence of it, we have been obliged to make large purchases of linen, china, &c. to supply the place of what was taken away. You may guess, after all these expenses, how very far we must be from being rich, and how acceptable Mrs. Ferrars's kindness is."

"Certainly," said Elinor; "and assisted by her liberality, I hope you may yet live to be in easy circumstances."

"Another year or two may do much towards it," he gravely replied;[46] "but however there is still a great deal to be done. There is not a stone laid of Fanny's greenhouse,[47] and nothing but the plan of the flower-garden marked out."[48]

"Where is the green-house to be?"

"Upon the knoll behind the house. The old walnut trees are all come down to make room for it.[49] It will be a very fine object from many parts of the park, and the flower-garden will slope down just before it, and be exceedingly pretty.[50] We have cleared away all the old thorns that grew in patches over the brow."

Elinor kept her concern and her censure to herself; and was

42. The further growth of large estates through the purchase of smaller parcels of land—"farm" generally designated a modest parcel—was another trend of the time. John Dashwood speaks of it as a duty because enhancing the family estate, which would be passed on to future generations, was an important imperative among the landowning classes.

43. This exchange offers a good insight into the psychology of a greedy man. On the one hand, he naturally complains of the costs he has incurred and the impoverishment he has suffered; on the other hand, when asked if he has actually lost money on a deal, he immediately retorts no, both because his concern for money makes him unlikely to have struck a bad bargain and because his pride in his financial acumen makes him reluctant to admit to having made such a bargain, even if that were the case.

44. It is soon revealed that he was "within some thousand pounds" of being forced to sell at a loss, an enormous sum at the time (p. 436).

45. *effects:* movable property.

46. His obliviousness appears again, this time with regard to Elinor's obvious sarcasm.

47. Greenhouses were popular at the time. Some landowners would have enormous complexes of them. They were often the only means of procuring fresh produce or flowers during the winter, due to the prohibitive cost of transporting such products from overseas. The products of greenhouses, especially flowers, were often seen as a female province, which is probably why he speaks of it as Fanny's.

48. Flower gardens had also become increasingly popular in this period, and could be very elaborate. For a picture, see p. 426.

49. He may be cutting down the walnut trees for the profit to be made from the wood as well as from landscaping considerations. Walnut wood was valuable because of its frequent use in furniture, and, being also used to make gun stocks, its price had soared during the Napoleonic Wars, which were raging at the time of this novel.

50. Elaborate landscaping for the purpose of creating attractive views, from various positions, was a major preoccupation of estate owners at this time. The park refers to the lawns and groves of trees surrounding the house. Sloping terrain was highly valued, so much that major work was often done to create or enhance slopes and hills.

very thankful that Marianne was not present, to share the provocation.[51]

Having now said enough to make his poverty clear, and to do away the necessity of buying a pair of ear-rings for each of his sisters, in his next visit at Gray's, his thoughts took a cheerfuller turn, and he began to congratulate Elinor on having such a friend as Mrs. Jennings.[52]

"She seems a most valuable woman indeed.—Her house, her style of living, all bespeak an exceeding good income; and it is an acquaintance that has not only been of great use[53] to you hitherto, but in the end may prove materially advantageous.—Her inviting you to town is certainly a vast thing in your favour; and indeed, it speaks[54] altogether so great a regard for you, that in all probability when she dies you will not be forgotten.—She must have a great deal to leave."

"Nothing at all, I should rather suppose; for she has only her jointure,[55] which will descend to her children."

"But it is not to be imagined that she lives up to her income.[56] Few people of common prudence will do *that*; and whatever she saves, she will be able to dispose of."

"And do you not think it more likely that she should leave it to her daughters, than to us?"

"Her daughters are both exceedingly well married, and therefore I cannot perceive the necessity of her remembering them farther. Whereas, in my opinion, by her taking so much notice of you, and treating you in this kind of way, she has given you a sort of claim on her future consideration, which a conscientious woman would not disregard.[57] Nothing can be kinder than her behaviour; and she can hardly do all this, without being aware of the expectation she raises."

"But she raises none in those most concerned. Indeed, brother, your anxiety for our welfare and prosperity carries you too far."

"Why to be sure," said he, seeming to recollect himself, "people have little, have very little in their power.[58] But, my dear Elinor, what is the matter with Marianne?—she looks very unwell, has lost her colour, and is grown quite thin. Is she ill?"[59]

51. Marianne was earlier shown apostrophizing the trees at Norland when they left (p. 50), so cutting them down would arouse her indignation. Both picturesque and Romantic taste celebrated trees and deplored their disappearance; in *Mansfield Park* the heroine quotes lines from the poet William Cowper, one of Marianne's favorites, that lament the cutting down of avenues of trees. Even the clearing away of the old thorns might upset Marianne, since such rough natural features, especially if scattered irregularly in patches, were considered of particular picturesque value. At the same time, some landscaping ideas encouraged cutting down trees in certain places to create better vistas. For a picture of what the leading landscape designer of the time, Humphrey Repton, considers to represent the improvement that can result from clearing a clump of trees, see p. 427.

52. John Dashwood continues to raise topics with a specific end in mind, in this case the financial generosity his sisters might expect from Mrs. Jennings.

53. *use:* benefit.

54. *speaks:* signifies, indicates.

55. A jointure is a fixed sum paid annually to a widow. It, or more specifically the capital generating it, would normally go to her children, or to other heirs of her husband if they lack children, after she dies.

56. His statement undoubtedly expresses his own financial practice, which, with his lack of imagination, he automatically extrapolates to everyone else. It also reveals the falsity of his earlier lament of poverty.

57. Of course, the claim Elinor and her sister have on Mrs. Jennings as her temporary guests is nothing compared to the claim they have on him, their half brother and someone who had promised his father to aid them.

58. He may be thinking of his own inability, in his eyes, to give something to his sisters, due to the other demands on his income.

59. Thinness at this time could be considered not simply a sign of bad health, but also unattractive. A figure of moderate proportions, rather than an extremely slender one, was the ideal of beauty.

"She is not well, she has had a nervous complaint on her for several weeks."[60]

"I am sorry for that. At her time of life, any thing of an illness destroys the bloom for ever![61] Her's has been a very short one! She was as handsome a girl last September, as any I ever saw; and as likely to attract the men. There was something in her style of beauty, to please them particularly. I remember Fanny used to say that she would marry sooner and better than you did; not but what she is exceedingly fond of *you*, but so it happened to strike her.[62] She will be mistaken, however. I question whether Marianne *now*, will marry a man worth more than five or six hundred a-year, at the utmost, and I am very much deceived if *you* do not do better.[63] Dorsetshire! I know very little of Dorsetshire; but, my dear Elinor, I shall be exceedingly glad to know more of it; and I think I can answer for your having Fanny and myself among the earliest and best pleased of your visitors."[64]

Elinor tried very seriously to convince him that there was no likelihood of her marrying Colonel Brandon; but it was an expectation of too much pleasure to himself to be relinquished, and he was really resolved on seeking an intimacy with that gentleman, and promoting the marriage by every possible attention. He had just compunction enough for having done nothing for his sisters himself, to be exceedingly anxious that everybody else should do a great deal; and an offer from Colonel Brandon, or a legacy from Mrs. Jennings, was the easiest means of atoning for his own neglect.

They were lucky enough to find Lady Middleton at home, and Sir John came in before their visit ended. Abundance of civilities passed on all sides. Sir John was ready to like anybody, and though Mr. Dashwood did not seem to know much about horses,[65] he soon set him down as[66] a very good-natured fellow: while Lady Middleton saw enough of fashion[67] in his appearance, to think his acquaintance worth having; and Mr. Dashwood went away delighted with both.

"I shall have a charming account to carry to Fanny," said he, as he walked back with his sister. "Lady Middleton is really a most

60. The eighteenth century witnessed an increasing tendency to explain human physiology and ailments in terms of nerves; this replaced older theories that explained the body and its workings in terms of different humors. A medical book of 1807 proclaimed that "nervous diseases make up two-thirds of the whole with which civilized society is infested" (Thomas Trotter, *A View of the Nervous Temperament*, p. iv). Similarly, "the enormously influential Edinburgh medical professor, William Cullen, argued . . . that all disease was strictly speaking 'nervous,' i.e., typified by pain mediated through nervous stimuli" (from Roy and Dorothy Porter, *In Sickness and in Health: The British Experience 1650–1850*, p. 69). One source for this focus on nerves was the increasing interest in various sensations, which had affinities and connections to the cult of sensibility. Marianne's extreme sensitivity and irritability would make her an ideal candidate for being regarded as suffering from nervous difficulties.

61. A woman's beauty is often discussed in Jane Austen in terms of her bloom, which refers particularly to her prime of loveliness and freshness. A contemporary book on beauty (*The Mirror of the Graces*, 1811), in a chapter on how best to preserve "the bloom of beauty," compares the progression of a woman's appearance to the progression of the seasons from spring to winter and the progression of a flower from blossom to decay and death. Thus John Dashwood speaks of the bloom being destroyed forever, and of the tragic shortness of Marianne's bloom (since it cannot be repeated).

62. Fanny may have genuinely considered Marianne more attractive than Elinor; the narrator describes the former as "handsomer" (p. 88). But Fanny's hostility toward Elinor would give her extra reason to denigrate her.

63. The idea of a woman's looks having a specific monetary value can be found elsewhere in this society, though usually not in so crass a form. Beauty was certainly a crucial asset, perhaps the most important one for gaining a husband and through that financial security and a comfortable home.

64. Visiting a new couple within one's family circle or neighborhood was a standard courtesy.

65. Sir John's love of sport gives him a natural interest in horses, and since they tended to be a popular topic for gentlemen in general, he is probably surprised as well as disappointed by John Dashwood's lack of knowledge.

66. *set him down as:* reckoned or determined him to be.

67. *fashion:* elegance, high social rank.

elegant woman! Such a woman as I am sure Fanny will be glad to know.[68] And Mrs. Jennings too, an exceeding well-behaved woman, though not so elegant as her daughter. Your sister[69] need not have any scruple even of[70] visiting *her*, which, to say the truth, has been a little the case, and very naturally; for we only knew that Mrs. Jennings was the widow of a man who had got all his money in a low way;[71] and Fanny and Mrs. Ferrars were both strongly prepossessed[72] that neither she nor her daughters were such kind of women as Fanny would like to associate with. But now I can carry her a most satisfactory account of both."

An elaborate flower garden of the time.

[From Humphrey Repton, *The Art of Landscape Gardening* (Boston, 1907; reprint ed.), p. 144]

68. As on so many occasions, he is thinking of his wife. Thus he describes Lady Middleton and Mrs. Jennings, and not Sir John, for his wife would be dealing mainly with other women if she visited the family.

69. *sister*: sister-in-law, i.e., Fanny.

70. *scruple . . . of*: hesitation . . . in.

71. Money from trade, which is how Mrs. Jennings's husband acquired his fortune, would be considered low, i.e., socially inferior.

72. *prepossessed*: predisposed to believe.

A landscape that has had trees removed to improve the view.

[From Humphrey Repton, *The Art of Landscape Gardening* (Boston, 1907; reprint ed.), p. 26]

Chapter Twelve

*M*rs. John Dashwood had so much confidence in her husband's judgment that she waited the very next day both on Mrs. Jennings and her daughter;[1] and her confidence was rewarded by finding even the former, even the woman with whom her sisters were staying, by no means unworthy her notice; and as for Lady Middleton, she found her one of the most charming women in the world!

Lady Middleton was equally pleased with Mrs. Dashwood. There was a kind of cold hearted selfishness on both sides, which mutually attracted them; and they sympathised with each other in an insipid propriety of demeanour, and a general want of understanding.[2]

The same manners however, which recommended Mrs. John Dashwood to the good opinion of Lady Middleton, did not suit the fancy of Mrs. Jennings, and to *her* she appeared nothing more than a little proud-looking woman of uncordial address,[3] who met her husband's sisters without any affection, and almost without having any thing to say to them; for of the quarter of an hour bestowed on Berkeley-street, she sat at least seven minutes and a half in silence.[4]

Elinor wanted very much to know, though she did not chuse to ask, whether Edward was then in town; but nothing would have induced Fanny voluntarily to mention his name before her, till able to tell her that his marriage with Miss Morton was resolved on, or till her husband's expectations on Colonel Brandon were answered; because she believed them still so very much attached to each other, that they could not be too sedulously divided in word and deed on every occasion. The intelligence however, which *she* would not give, soon flowed from another quarter. Lucy came very shortly to claim Elinor's compassion on being

1. Her confidence contrasts with the attitude of Lady Middleton, who considered her husband's earlier assurances of the Miss Steeles' gentility to be worthless (p. 222).

2. *understanding:* intelligence.

3. *address:* outward demeanor or manner, especially in conversation.

4. Etiquette dictated an introductory visit be fifteen minutes. The precision of "seven minutes and a half" gives a sense of how closely Lady Middleton and Mrs. John Dashwood, sticklers for strict etiquette, adhered to the time limit.

unable to see Edward, though he had arrived in town with Mr. and Mrs. Dashwood.[5] He dared not come to Bartlett's Buildings for fear of detection, and though their mutual impatience to meet, was not to be told, they could do nothing at present but write.[6]

Edward assured them himself of his being in town, within a very short time, by twice calling in Berkeley-street. Twice was his card found on the table,[7] when they returned from their morning's engagements. Elinor was pleased that he had called; and still more pleased that she had missed him.

The Dashwoods were so prodigiously delighted with the Middletons, that though not much in the habit of giving any thing, they determined to give them—a dinner; and soon after their acquaintance began, invited them to dine in Harley-street,[8] where they had taken a very good house for three months. Their sisters and Mrs. Jennings were invited likewise,[9] and John Dashwood was careful to secure Colonel Brandon, who, always glad to be where the Miss Dashwoods were, received his eager civilities with some surprise,[10] but much more pleasure. They were to meet Mrs. Ferrars; but Elinor could not learn whether her sons were to be of the party. The expectation of seeing *her*, however, was enough to make her interested in the engagement; for though she could now meet Edward's mother without that strong anxiety which had once promised to attend such an introduction, though she could now see her with perfect indifference as to her opinion of herself, her desire of being in company with Mrs. Ferrars, her curiosity to know what she was like, was as lively as ever.[11]

The interest with which she thus anticipated the party, was soon afterwards increased, more powerfully than pleasantly, by her hearing that the Miss Steeles were also to be at it.

So well had they recommended themselves to Lady Middleton, so agreeable had their assiduities made them to her, that though Lucy was certainly not elegant, and her sister not even genteel,[12] she was as ready as Sir John to ask them to spend a week or two in Conduit-street: and it happened to be particularly convenient to the Miss Steeles, as soon as the Dashwoods' invitation

5.   Lucy probably wishes to tell Elinor of his arrival because it reveals her intimate knowledge of him. She may also fear that Elinor, due to her family connection with John Dashwood and his wife, will see Edward before she does.

6.   Since Lucy's location at Bartlett's Buildings is far from the residences of others they know, including Edward's mother and sister (see p. 405, note 31, and map on p. 740), there would probably be little danger of detection if he visited Lucy. He may simply prefer not to see her and be using this as a convenient excuse.

7.   His calling twice suggests a stronger wish to see Elinor than Lucy. In the next chapter he will call for a third time. The card is his visiting card.

8.   Harley Street is just north of Mayfair in Marylebone. It would be a distinguished address, and not far from those of other characters.

9.   Elinor and Marianne, as close friends of the Middletons and as John Dashwood's sisters, have to be invited. It is notable that he and his wife give a dinner for new acquaintances but seem never to have considered giving one for his sisters' sake.

10.   Colonel Brandon's surprise results from his complete lack of connection to or acquaintance with John Dashwood.

11.   Her curiosity may stem from continued concern for Edward, as well as a natural interest in seeing someone of whom she has heard so much. It may also indicate a lingering hope, perhaps not even acknowledged, for a marriage to Edward.

12.   Lucy is genteel because she, unlike her sister, has decent outward manners, however nasty she is in reality. An example would be Lucy's checking her sister when she rudely insisted on visiting Marianne in her bedroom. Lady Middleton was earlier shown worrying whether the two sisters would be elegant, or even genteel; that she has ceased to do so, despite the importance of these qualities to her, testifies to how susceptible she is to flattery.

was known, that their visit should begin a few days before the party took place.[13]

Their claims to the notice of Mrs. John Dashwood, as the nieces of the gentleman who for many years had had the care of her brother, might not have done much, however, towards procuring them seats at her table; but as Lady Middleton's guests they must be welcome; and Lucy, who had long wanted to be personally known to the family, to have a nearer view of their characters and her own difficulties, and to have an opportunity of endeavouring to please them, had seldom been happier in her life than she was on receiving Mrs. John Dashwood's card.

On Elinor its effect was very different. She began immediately to determine that Edward who lived with his mother, must be asked as his mother was, to a party given by his sister; and to see him for the first time after all that passed, in the company of Lucy!—she hardly knew how she could bear it!

These apprehensions perhaps were not founded entirely on reason, and certainly not at all on truth.[14] They were relieved however, not by her own recollection,[15] but by the good will of Lucy, who believed herself to be inflicting a severe disappointment when she told her that Edward certainly would not be in Harley-street on Tuesday, and even hoped to be carrying the pain still farther by persuading her, that he was kept away by that extreme affection for herself, which he could not conceal when they were together.

The important Tuesday came that was to introduce the two young ladies to this formidable mother-in-law.

"Pity me, dear Miss Dashwood!" said Lucy, as they walked up the stairs together—for the Middletons arrived so directly[16] after Mrs. Jennings, that they all followed the servant at the same time[17]—"There is nobody here but you, that can feel for me.—I declare I can hardly stand. Good gracious!—In a moment I shall see the person that all my happiness depends on—that is to be my mother!"[18]—

Elinor could have given her immediate relief by suggesting the possibility of its being Miss Morton's mother, rather than her own,

13. They know that their presence at the Middletons' will ensure them an invitation. In deciding to move the Miss Steeles show themselves as ready to drop their London relatives as they were to abandon those in Exeter with whom they had been staying before they met Sir John.

14. The flaw in Elinor's reasoning, a rare one for her, comes from not guessing that Edward would stay away, given both the embarrassing nature of the situation for him and his general shyness and discomfort in company.

15. *recollection*: recovery of composure.

16. *directly*: immediately.

17. The servant would open the door and lead them to the place, probably the drawing room, where the hosts and any other guests were gathered.

18. She will become Lucy's mother, i.e., mother-in-law, if she marries Edward. The phrase "all my happiness" is frequently used in reference to marriage. It is notable that Lucy sees all her happiness depending on Mrs. Ferrars rather than Edward himself, for it is his mother's attitude that will determine whether the marriage is financially opportune for Lucy.

whom they were about to behold; but instead of doing that, she assured her, and with great sincerity, that she did pity her,—to the utter amazement of Lucy, who, though really uncomfortable herself, hoped at least to be an object of irrepressible envy to Elinor.

Mrs. Ferrars was a little, thin woman, upright, even to formality, in her figure, and serious, even to sourness, in her aspect.[19] Her complexion was sallow; and her features small, without beauty, and naturally without expression; but a lucky contraction of the brow had rescued her countenance from the disgrace of insipidity, by giving it the strong characters of pride and ill nature. She was not a woman of many words: for, unlike people in general, she proportioned them to the number of her ideas;[20] and of the few syllables that did escape her, not one fell to the share of Miss Dashwood, whom she eyed with the spirited determination of disliking her at all events.

Elinor could not *now* be made unhappy by this behaviour.—A few months ago it would have hurt her exceedingly; but it was not in Mrs. Ferrars's power to distress her by it now;—and the difference of her manners to the Miss Steeles, a difference which seemed purposely made to humble her more, only amused her. She could not but smile to see the graciousness of both mother and daughter towards the very person—for Lucy was particularly distinguished—whom of all others, had they known as much as she did, they would have been most anxious to mortify; while she herself, who had comparatively no power to wound them, sat pointedly slighted by both. But while she smiled at a graciousness so misapplied, she could not reflect on the mean-spirited folly from which it sprung, nor observe the studied attentions with which the Miss Steeles courted its continuance, without thoroughly despising them all four.[21]

Lucy was all exultation on being so honourably distinguished; and Miss Steele wanted only to be teazed about Dr. Davies to be perfectly happy.

The dinner was a grand one, the servants were numerous, and every thing bespoke the Mistress's inclination for shew, and the

19. *aspect:* look, facial expression.

20. In other words, Mrs. Ferrars says little because she has few ideas, or thoughts, to express; people in general do not thus restrict themselves—the clear implication is that most also have few thoughts to express but are happy to chatter anyway. Hence in a very brief space the author manages to skewer both this character and most people.

21. The four are the Miss Steeles, Mrs. Ferrars, and her daughter Fanny. Elinor's conclusion is an example of how critical and independent she can be in her private judgment, even as she always maintains outward politeness and respect.

A coffeepot of the time.

[From MacIver Percival, *Old English Furniture and its Surroundings* (New York, 1920), Plate XII]

Master's ability to support it.[22] In spite of the improvements and additions which were making to the Norland estate, and in spite of its owner having once been within some thousand pounds of being obliged to sell out at a loss,[23] nothing gave any symptom of that indigence which he had tried to infer from it;—no poverty of any kind, except of conversation, appeared—but there, the deficiency was considerable. John Dashwood had not much to say for himself that was worth hearing, and his wife had still less. But there was no peculiar[24] disgrace in this, for it was very much the case with the chief[25] of their visitors, who almost all laboured under one or other of these disqualifications for being agreeable—Want[26] of sense, either natural or improved[27]—want of elegance—want of spirits[28]—or want of temper.[29]

When the ladies withdrew to the drawing-room after dinner, this poverty was particularly evident, for the gentlemen *had* supplied the discourse with some variety—the variety of politics, inclosing land, and breaking horses[30]—but then it was all over; and one subject only engaged the ladies till coffee came in,[31] which was the comparative heights of Harry Dashwood, and Lady Middleton's second son William, who were nearly of the same age.

Had both the children been there, the affair might have been determined too easily by measuring them at once; but as Harry only was present, it was all conjectural assertion on both sides, and every body had a right to be equally positive in their opinion, and to repeat it over and over again as often as they liked.

The parties stood thus:[32]

The two mothers, though each really convinced that her own son was the tallest, politely decided in favour of the other.

The two grandmothers, with not less partiality, but more sincerity, were equally earnest in support of their own descendant.

Lucy, who was hardly less anxious to please one parent than the other, thought the boys were both remarkably tall for their age, and could not conceive that there could be the smallest difference in the world between them; and Miss Steele, with yet greater address[33] gave it, as fast as she could, in favour of each.[34]

22. In organizing and hosting an affair like this, the mistress of the house would display the family wealth. A large number of servants would be needed to serve all the courses in a dinner party and attend to the guests' needs; their presence would be a further testament to the family's fortune.

23. This is in reference to a farm he recently bought (pp. 418–420).

24. *peculiar:* particular.

25. *chief:* greater part.

26. *want:* lack.

27. *improved:* cultivated (especially by education).

28. *spirits:* animation, cheer.

29. *temper:* composure, equanimity.

30. Politics were a favorite subject of gentlemen, while enclosing land and horses have already been revealed as fascinating to John Dashwood and Sir John Middleton, respectively. Breaking horses means taming them and making them obedient.

31. Coffee was frequently served after dinner. Evening tea could include coffee, though tea was more popular in England. For a picture of a contemporary coffeepot, see previous page.

32. The following conversation is an excellent example of Jane Austen's ability, within a short space and using an ordinary incident, to display the distinctive characteristics of a variety of people.

33. *address:* dexterity.

34. Miss Steele's tactic is a little less refined than her sister's, since it involves saying opposite things in succession, and thereby obviously lying about one. It is not clear which sister's method works better in its object of flattering both sides.

Elinor, having once delivered her opinion on William's side, by which she offended Mrs. Ferrars and Fanny still more, did not see the necessity of enforcing[35] it by any farther assertion; and Marianne, when called on for her's, offended them all, by declaring that she had no opinion to give, as she had never thought about it.[36]

Before her removing from Norland, Elinor had painted a very pretty pair of screens for her sister-in-law,[37] which being now just mounted and brought home,[38] ornamented her present drawing room; and these screens, catching the eye of John Dashwood on his following the other gentlemen into the room, were officiously handed by him to Colonel Brandon for his admiration.

"These are done by my eldest sister," said he; "and you, as a man of taste, will, I dare say, be pleased with them.[39] I do not know whether you ever happened to see any of her performances before, but she is in general reckoned to draw extremely well."[40]

The Colonel, though disclaiming all pretensions to connoisseurship, warmly admired the screens, as he would have done any thing painted by Miss Dashwood; and the curiosity of the others being of course excited, they were handed round for general inspection. Mrs. Ferrars, not aware of their being Elinor's work, particularly requested to look at them; and after they had received the gratifying testimony of Lady Middleton's approbation, Fanny presented them to her mother, considerately informing her at the same time, that they were done by Miss Dashwood.

"Hum"—said Mrs. Ferrars—"very pretty,"—and without regarding them at all, returned them to her daughter.

Perhaps Fanny thought for a moment that her mother had been quite rude enough,—for, colouring[41] a little, she immediately said,

"They are very pretty, ma'am—an't[42] they?" But then again, the dread of having been too civil, too encouraging herself, probably came over her, for she presently added,

"Do you not think they are something in Miss Morton's style of painting, ma'am?—*She does* paint most delightfully!—How beautifully her last landscape is done![43]

35. *enforcing:* urging, reaffirming.

36. Their order of speaking follows a clear hierarchy, as it often did in this society. The two mothers, having the strongest claim on the matter, speak first. The two grandmothers follow. Finally, both the Miss Dashwoods and Miss Steeles have an equal claim to speak next, but the latter's eagerness to curry favor makes them interject first.

37. A screen was used to shield people from the heat of the fire: because fires were the only source of heat in a room, they would need to burn strongly, especially in a large room, and people near the fire could be too hot. Larger screens would be placed on a stand and moved between a person and the fire; smaller screens would be attached to a handle and held. The screens mentioned here are the latter type, since they are passed around for inspection. Screens could be decorated with embroidery or painted; both were common pastimes of ladies, and Elinor's artistic skill would make painting a screen a natural gift for her sister-in-law.

38. They may have been recently mounted, or placed in an appropriate frame, because the Dashwoods wished to have it done by a skilled craftsman in London. Thus this does not necessarily indicate a disdain for Elinor's gift on their part.

Homes were often decorated with pictures or other objects created by female family members, due to the popularity of decorative projects among ladies. Other examples already seen are the drawings by Elinor placed on the walls of the Dashwoods' cottage (p. 54), and the embroidered landscape by Mrs. Palmer that is hung in the room in Mrs. Jennings's house currently inhabited by Elinor and Marianne (p. 296).

39. Female accomplishments such as painting or drawing were often seen as ways to attract men.

40. He can rely only on others' opinions in evaluating her talent, not offer his own.

41. *colouring:* blushing.

42. "An't" or "ain't" was incorrect grammar.

43. Since a landscape painting is usually larger than a handheld screen, their praise of Miss Morton is probably intended to make Elinor's work look less impressive.

"Beautifully indeed! But *she* does every thing well."

Marianne could not bear this.—She was already greatly displeased with Mrs. Ferrars; and such ill-timed praise of another, at Elinor's expense, though she had not any notion of what was principally meant by it, provoked her immediately to say with warmth,

"This is admiration of a very particular[44] kind!—what is Miss Morton to us?—who knows, or who cares, for her?—it is Elinor of whom *we* think and speak."

And so saying, she took the screens out of her sister-in-law's hands, to admire them herself as they ought to be admired.

Mrs. Ferrars looked exceedingly angry, and drawing herself up more stiffly than ever, pronounced in retort this bitter phillippic; "Miss Morton is Lord Morton's daughter."[45]

Fanny looked very angry too, and her husband was all in a fright at his sister's audacity. Elinor was much more hurt by Marianne's warmth, than she had been by what produced it;[46] but Colonel Brandon's eyes, as they were fixed on Marianne, declared that he noticed only what was amiable[47] in it, the affectionate heart which could not bear to see a sister slighted in the smallest point.

Marianne's feelings did not stop here. The cold insolence of Mrs. Ferrars's general behaviour to her sister, seemed, to her, to foretel such difficulties and distresses to Elinor, as her own wounded heart taught her to think of with horror; and urged by a strong impulse of affectionate sensibility, she moved, after a moment, to her sister's chair, and putting one arm round her neck, and one cheek close to her's, said in a low, but eager, voice,

"Dear, dear Elinor, don't mind them. Don't let them make *you* unhappy."

She could say no more; her spirits were quite overcome, and hiding her face on Elinor's shoulder, she burst into tears.[48]— Every body's attention was called, and almost every body was concerned.—Colonel Brandon rose up and went to them without knowing what he did.—Mrs. Jennings, with a very intelligent[49] "Ah! poor dear," immediately gave her, her salts;[50] and Sir John felt so desperately enraged against the author of this nervous dis-

44. *particular:* peculiar.

45. She considers it a philippic, or denunciation, because identifying some-one as a lord's daughter indicates her importance and shows the folly of any-one who dares to speak slightingly of her. The use of such a strong, rarely used term as "philippic" may be intended as an ironic commentary on Mrs. Ferrars's own sense of self-importance, especially as the term, which derives from the great Greek orator Demosthenes, was usually applied to a long for-mal speech rather than to one simple, banal sentence, as here.

46. Marianne's interventions on Elinor's behalf often have this effect.

47. *amiable:* kind, benevolent.

48. Though acting from genuine sympathy for her sister, Marianne ends up turning everyone's attention toward herself.

49. *intelligent:* knowing.

50. These are smelling salts. Usually consisting of ammonium carbonate, they were frequently used to rouse people who fainted or were otherwise incapacitated. Women often carried them.

tress,[51] that he instantly changed his seat to one close by Lucy Steele, and gave her, in a whisper, a brief account of the whole shocking affair.

In a few minutes, however, Marianne was recovered enough to put an end to the bustle, and sit down among the rest; though her spirits retained the impression of what had passed, the whole evening.[52]

"Poor Marianne!" said her brother to Colonel Brandon in a low voice, as soon as he could secure his attention,—"She has not such good health as her sister,—she is very nervous,[53]—she has not Elinor's constitution;—and one must allow that there is something very trying to a young woman who *has been* a beauty, in the loss of her personal attractions. You would not think it perhaps, but Marianne *was* remarkably handsome a few months ago; quite as handsome as Elinor.—Now you see it is all gone."

51. As already discussed (p. 425, note 60), many ailments were described then as nervous.

52. That such a brief episode could affect her the entire evening indicates her extreme sensitivity.

53. *nervous:* inclined to nervous disorders or weakness.

Lady Mary Grenville; an example of the prestige of drawing for upper-class ladies.
[From *The Masterpieces of Hoppner* (London, 1912, p. 15)]

Chapter Thirteen

*E*linor's curiosity to see Mrs. Ferrars was satisfied.—She had found in her every thing that could tend to make a farther connection between the families, undesirable.—She had seen enough of her pride, her meanness,[1] and her determined prejudice against herself, to comprehend all the difficulties that must have perplexed[2] the engagement, and retarded the marriage, of Edward and herself, had he been otherwise free;—and she had seen almost enough to be thankful for her *own* sake, that one greater obstacle preserved her from suffering under any other of Mrs. Ferrars's creation, preserved her from all dependence upon her caprice, or any solicitude for her good opinion. Or at least, if she did not bring herself quite to rejoice in Edward's being fettered to Lucy, she determined, that had Lucy been more amiable, she *ought* to have rejoiced.

She wondered that Lucy's spirits could be so very much elevated by the civility of Mrs. Ferrars;—that her interest and her vanity should so very much blind her, as to make the attention which seemed only paid her because she was *not Elinor*, appear a compliment to herself—or to allow her to derive encouragement from a preference only given her, because her real situation was unknown. But that it was so, had not only been declared by Lucy's eyes at the time, but was declared over again the next morning more openly, for at her particular desire, Lady Middleton set her down in Berkeley-street on the chance of seeing Elinor alone, to tell her how happy she was.

The chance proved a lucky one, for a message from Mrs. Palmer soon after she arrived, carried Mrs. Jennings away.[3]

"My dear friend," cried Lucy as soon as they were by themselves, "I come to talk to you of my happiness. Could any thing be so flattering as Mrs. Ferrars's way of treating me yesterday? So

1. *meanness*: pettiness, baseness.

2. *perplexed*: complicated.

3. It is now February (see chronology, pp. 714–715), which is the month when Mrs. Palmer's baby is expected, so her message may be a request for her mother's assistance with something relating to that.

exceeding affable as she was!—You know how I dreaded the thoughts of seeing her;—but the very moment I was introduced, there was such an affability in her behaviour as really should seem to say, she had quite took a fancy to me. Now was not it so?—You saw it all; and was not you quite struck with it?"

"She was certainly very civil to you."

"Civil!—Did you see nothing but only civility?—I saw a vast deal more. Such kindness as fell to the share of nobody but me!—No pride, no hauteur, and your sister just the same—all sweetness and affability!"

Elinor wished to talk of something else, but Lucy still pressed her to own[4] that she had reason for her happiness; and Elinor was obliged to go on.—

"Undoubtedly, if they had known your engagement," said she, "nothing could be more flattering than their treatment of you;—but as that was not the case"—

"I guessed you would say so"—replied Lucy quickly—"but there was no reason in the world why Mrs. Ferrars should seem to like me, if she did not, and her liking me is every thing. You shan't talk me out of my satisfaction. I am sure it will all end well, and there will be no difficulties at all, to what I used to think. Mrs. Ferrars is a charming woman, and so is your sister. They are both delightful women indeed!—I wonder I should never hear you say how agreeable Mrs. Dashwood was!"

To this, Elinor had no answer to make, and did not attempt any.

"Are you ill, Miss Dashwood?—you seem low—you don't speak;—sure you an't well."

"I never was in better health."

"I am glad of it with all my heart, but really you did not look it. I should be so sorry to have *you* ill; you, that have been the greatest comfort to me in the world!—Heaven knows what I should have done without your friendship."—

Elinor tried to make a civil answer, though doubting her own success. But it seemed to satisfy Lucy, for she directly replied,

"Indeed I am perfectly convinced of your regard for me, and next to Edward's love, it is the greatest comfort I have.—Poor

4. *own*: acknowledge, allow.

Edward!—But now, there is one good thing, we shall be able to meet, and meet pretty often, for Lady Middleton's delighted with Mrs. Dashwood, so we shall be a good deal in Harley-street, I dare say, and Edward spends half his time with his sister—besides, Lady Middleton and Mrs. Ferrars will visit now;—and Mrs. Ferrars and your sister were both so good to say more than once, they should always be glad to see me.—They are such charming women!—I am sure if ever you tell your sister what I think of her, you cannot speak too high."[5]

But Elinor would not give her any encouragement to hope that she *should* tell her sister. Lucy continued.

"I am sure I should have seen it in a moment, if Mrs. Ferrars had took a dislike to me. If she had only made me a formal curtsey, for instance, without saying a word, and never after had took any notice of me, and never looked at me in a pleasant way—you know what I mean,—if I had been treated in that forbidding sort of way,[6] I should have gave it all up in despair. I could not have stood it. For where she *does* dislike, I know it is most violent."

Elinor was prevented from making any reply to this civil triumph,[7] by the door's being thrown open, the servant's announcing Mr. Ferrars, and Edward's immediately walking in.

It was a very awkward moment; and the countenance of each shewed that it was so. They all looked exceedingly foolish; and Edward seemed to have as great an inclination to walk out of the room again, as to advance farther into it. The very circumstance, in its unpleasantest form, which they would each have been most anxious to avoid, had fallen on them—They were not only all three together, but were together without the relief of any other person. The ladies recovered themselves first. It was not Lucy's business to put herself forward, and the appearance of secrecy must still be kept up. She could therefore only *look* her tenderness, and after slightly addressing him, said no more.

But Elinor had more to do;[8] and so anxious was she, for his sake and her own, to do it well, that she forced herself, after a moment's recollection, to welcome him, with a look and manner that were almost easy,[9] and almost open; and another struggle,

5. *high:* highly. Lucy's grammar is often incorrect. Lucy will later write a letter to Elinor that is full of Mrs. Jennings's praises, in the apparent hope that Elinor will show Mrs. Jennings the letter. This use of a third party to convey flattery may be a favorite technique of hers.

6. She clearly refers to Mrs. Ferrars's forbidding look and general hostility toward Elinor, which both gratify Lucy and prove to her that she has better chances.

7. *triumph:* expression of triumph.

8. Since Elinor is staying in this house she, unlike Lucy, must function as hostess. She also may have "more to do" because she must hide her knowledge of the engagement from Edward.

9. *easy:* unembarrassed; free from awkwardness or stiffness.

another effort still improved them.[10] She would not allow the presence of Lucy, nor the consciousness of some injustice towards herself, to deter her from saying that she was happy to see him, and that she had very much regretted being from home, when he called before in Berkeley-street. She would not be frightened from paying him those attentions which, as a friend and almost a relation, were his due, by the observant eyes of Lucy, though she soon perceived them to be narrowly watching her.

Her manners gave some re-assurance to Edward, and he had courage enough to sit down; but his embarrassment still exceeded that of the ladies in a proportion, which the case rendered reasonable, though his sex might make it rare;[11] for his heart had not the indifference of Lucy's, nor could his conscience have quite the ease of Elinor's.

Lucy, with a demure and settled air, seemed determined to make no contribution to the comfort of the others, and would not say a word; and almost every thing that *was* said, proceeded from Elinor, who was obliged to volunteer all the information about her mother's health, their coming to town, &c. which Edward ought to have inquired about, but never did.[12]

Her exertions did not stop here; for she soon afterwards felt herself so heroically disposed as to determine, under pretence of fetching Marianne, to leave the others by themselves: and she really did it, and *that* in the handsomest manner, for she loitered away several minutes on the landing-place,[13] with the most high-minded fortitude,[14] before she went to her sister. When that was once done, however, it was time for the raptures of Edward to cease;[15] for Marianne's joy hurried her into the drawing-room immediately. Her pleasure in seeing him was like every other of her feelings, strong in itself, and strongly spoken. She met him with a hand that would be taken, and a voice that expressed the affection of a sister.

"Dear Edward!" she cried, "this is a moment of great happiness!—This would almost make amends for every thing!"

Edward tried to return her kindness as it deserved, but before such witnesses he dared not say half what he really felt. Again they

10. The achievement of composure is not a simple or quick task. But her persistence does allow her eventually to manage it.

11. As a man he is naturally less subject to embarrassment, but the specifics of this case cause him to suffer more from it right now.

12. These were the normal polite inquiries one would make to an acquaintance not seen for a while.

13. The numerous floors of houses in London meant there would be many landing places, or stair landings.

14. This suggests a consciousness of her own fortitude, and may be a mild irony directed at Elinor by the author. Her prolonged absence may be to help her steady her nerves.

15. According to convention a man should be in raptures when he is with his lady love, especially if he has not seen her for a long time. But everything known about Edward so far suggests that he will neither feel nor express many raptures upon seeing Lucy.

all sat down, and for a moment or two all were silent; while Marianne was looking with the most speaking[16] tenderness, sometimes at Edward and sometimes at Elinor, regretting only that their delight in each other should be checked by Lucy's unwelcome presence. Edward was the first to speak, and it was to notice Marianne's altered looks, and express his fear of her not finding London agree with her.

"Oh! don't think of me!" she replied, with spirited earnestness, though her eyes were filled with tears as she spoke, "don't think of *my* health. Elinor is well, you see. That must be enough for us both."[17]

This remark was not calculated to make Edward or Elinor more easy, nor to conciliate the good will of Lucy, who looked up at Marianne with no very benignant expression.

"Do you like London?" said Edward, willing to say any thing that might introduce another subject.

"Not at all. I expected much pleasure in it, but I have found none. The sight of you, Edward, is the only comfort it has afforded; and thank Heaven! you are what you always were!"[18]

She paused—no one spoke.

"I think, Elinor," she presently added, "we must employ Edward to take care of us in our return to Barton. In a week or two, I suppose, we shall be going; and, I trust, Edward will not be very unwilling to accept the charge."[19]

Poor Edward muttered something, but what it was, nobody knew, not even himself. But Marianne, who saw his agitation, and could easily trace it to whatever cause best pleased herself,[20] was perfectly satisfied, and soon talked of something else.

"We spent such a day, Edward, in Harley-street yesterday! So dull, so wretchedly dull!—But I have much to say to you on that head, which cannot be said now."

And with this admirable discretion did she defer the assurance of her finding their mutual relatives more disagreeable than ever, and of her being particularly disgusted with his mother,[21] till they were more in private.

16. *speaking*: expressive, eloquent.

17. Marianne once more shows her genuine benevolence, even as again her actions have a less than beneficent effect. In this case, she is also being rude to Lucy, who as a visitor to the house deserves, whatever her personal faults, to be greeted by Marianne and included in the conversation.

18. Marianne is obviously failing to notice Edward's discomfort, which, given its acuteness, must be at least somewhat apparent.

19. Unmarried young women were not supposed to travel on their own. Edward could serve as chaperone on their journey—as an indirect relation of theirs this would not be improper. Jane Austen's own travel plans were frequently arranged to allow her to be accompanied by one of her brothers.

20. Marianne's tendency to evaluate the world according to her own wishes and feelings causes her to overlook others' real situation and needs.

21. Edward, whatever his feelings about his mother, might not necessarily be pleased to hear Marianne express her pointed dislike of her.

"But why were you not there, Edward?—Why did you not come?"

"I was engaged elsewhere."

"Engaged! But what was that, when such friends were to be met?"

"Perhaps, Miss Marianne," cried Lucy, eager to take some revenge on her, "you think young men never stand upon engagements, if they have no mind to keep them, little as well as great."[22]

Elinor was very angry, but Marianne seemed entirely insensible of the sting; for she calmly replied,

"Not so, indeed; for, seriously speaking, I am very sure that conscience only kept Edward from Harley-street.[23] And I really believe he *has* the most delicate conscience in the world; the most scrupulous in performing every engagement however minute, and however it may make against[24] his interest or pleasure.[25] He is the most fearful of giving pain, of wounding expectation, and the most incapable of being selfish, of any body I ever saw. Edward, it is so and I will say it. What! are you never to hear yourself praised![26]—Then, you must be no friend of mine; for those who will accept of my love and esteem, must submit to my open commendation."

The nature of her commendation, in the present case, however, happened to be particularly ill-suited to the feelings of two thirds of her auditors, and was so very unexhilarating to Edward,[27] that he very soon got up to go away.

"Going so soon!" said Marianne; "my dear Edward, this must not be."

And drawing him a little aside, she whispered her persuasion that Lucy could not stay much longer. But even this encouragement failed, for he would go; and Lucy, who would have outstaid him had his visit lasted two hours, soon afterwards went away.

"What can bring her here so often!" said Marianne, on her leaving them. "Could she not see that we wanted her gone!—how teazing[28] to Edward!"

"Why so?—we were all his friends, and Lucy has been the

22. The allusion is to Willoughby's abandonment of Marianne: it would be the great, or important, engagement, while Edward's attendance at another social event would be the little one.

23. Marianne probably means that Edward, knowing his mother's disapproval of his love for Elinor, decided the most conscientious course would be to stay away and avoid creating discomfort or ill will among the others.

24. *make against:* go against, be unfavorable to.

25. This has a pointed meaning that Marianne cannot conceive but that probably strikes everybody else: namely that Edward's willingness to stand by his engagement to Lucy for four years is a superb example of his keeping a commitment however much it goes against his pleasure.

26. By this point even Marianne notices Edward's discomfort, but this does not induce restraint in her.

27. Her praise of Edward for fulfilling unpleasant engagements reminds Elinor of the unpleasant fact of the engagement and Lucy of his lack of affection for her.

28. *teazing:* annoying.

longest known to him of any. It is but natural that he should like to see her as well as ourselves."

Marianne looked at her steadily, and said, "You know, Elinor, that this is a kind of talking which I cannot bear. If you only hope to have your assertion contradicted, as I must suppose to be the case, you ought to recollect that I am the last person in the world to do it. I cannot descend to be tricked out of assurances, that are not really wanted."[29]

She then left the room; and Elinor dared not follow her to say more, for bound as she was by her promise of secrecy to Lucy, she could give no information that would convince Marianne;[30] and painful as the consequences of her still continuing in an error might be, she was obliged to submit to it. All that she could hope, was that Edward would not often expose her or himself, to the distress of hearing Marianne's mistaken warmth, nor to the repetition of any other part of the pain that had attended their recent meeting—and this she had every reason to expect.

29. *wanted:* needed.

30. Marianne's ignorance, and indiscretion based on that ignorance, have added to the many difficulties of Elinor's situation.

Chapter Fourteen

Within a few days after this meeting, the newspapers announced to the world, that the Lady of Thomas Palmer, Esq.[1] was safely delivered of a son and heir; a very interesting and satisfactory paragraph, at least to all those intimate connections who knew it before.[2]

This event, highly important to Mrs. Jennings's happiness, produced a temporary alteration in the disposal of her time, and influenced, in a like degree, the engagements of her young friends; for as she wished to be as much as possible with Charlotte, she went thither every morning as soon as she was dressed and did not return till late in the evening; and the Miss Dashwoods, at the particular request of the Middletons, spent the whole of every day in Conduit-street. For their own comfort, they would much rather have remained, at least all the morning,[3] in Mrs. Jennings's house; but it was not a thing to be urged against the wishes of everybody.[4] Their hours were therefore made over to Lady Middleton and the two Miss Steeles, by whom their company was in fact as little valued, as it was professedly sought.

They had too much sense to be desirable companions to the former; and by the latter they were considered with a jealous eye, as intruding on *their* ground, and sharing the kindness which they wanted to monopolize. Though nothing could be more polite than Lady Middleton's behaviour to Elinor and Marianne, she did not really like them at all. Because they neither flattered herself nor her children, she could not believe them good-natured; and because they were fond of reading, she fancied them satirical: perhaps without exactly knowing what it was to be satirical;[5] but *that* did not signify. It was censure in common use, and easily given.

Their presence was a restraint both on her and on Lucy. It

1. Esq. stands for "esquire," an informal title generally placed after the names of untitled gentlemen. It derives from the medieval squire, who served and ranked below a knight, the lowest of titled positions. It would be especially likely to be employed in a formal announcement like this one. In some of her letters Jane Austen affixes Esq. to the names of some male relatives; in one to a nephew who has just finished school and can now be considered an adult gentleman, she declares, "One reason for my writing to you now, is that I may have the pleasure of directing to you Esqre" (Dec. 16, 1816).

2. The suggestion is that few not intimately connected with the family would bother paying much attention to the newspaper announcement; its main function was to make the family feel good about seeing their important news receiving such official proclamation.

3. At this time this would mean most of the day.

4. This is a good example of the ultimate primacy of social obligations in this world. Such obligations weighed particularly on women, who were in a more dependent situation than men.

5. "Satirical" could have a sharper meaning then, one that included a strong tendency toward sarcasm or the condemnation of others. The term would have additional resonance because satire was a popular literary genre in the eighteenth century.

checked the idleness of one, and the business of the other. Lady Middleton was ashamed of doing nothing before them, and the flattery which Lucy was proud to think of and administer at other times, she feared they would despise her for offering. Miss Steele was the least discomposed of the three, by their presence; and it was in their power to reconcile her to it entirely. Would either of them, only have given her a full and minute account of the whole affair between Marianne and Mr. Willoughby, she would have thought herself amply rewarded for the sacrifice of the best place by the fire after dinner, which their arrival occasioned.[6] But this conciliation was not granted; for though she often threw out expressions of pity for her sister to Elinor, and more than once dropt a reflection on the inconstancy of beaux before Marianne, no effect was produced, but a look of indifference from the former, or of disgust in the latter. An effort even yet lighter might have made her their friend. Would they only have laughed at her about the Doctor! But so little were they, any more than the others, inclined to oblige her, that if Sir John dined from home, she might spend a whole day without hearing any other raillery on the subject, than what she was kind enough to bestow on herself.

All these jealousies and discontents, however, were so totally unsuspected by Mrs. Jennings, that she thought it a delightful thing for the girls to be together; and generally congratulated her young friends every night, on having escaped the company of a stupid[7] old woman so long. She joined them sometimes at Sir John's, and sometimes at her own house; but wherever it was, she always came in excellent spirits, full of delight and importance, attributing Charlotte's well doing to her own care, and ready to give so exact, so minute a detail of her situation, as only Miss Steele had curiosity enough to desire. One thing *did* disturb her; and of that she made her daily complaint. Mr. Palmer maintained the common, but unfatherly opinion among his sex, of all infants being alike; and though she could plainly perceive at different times, the most striking resemblance between this baby and every one of his relations on both sides, there was no convincing his father of it; no persuading him to believe that it was not exactly

6. As the guests, since the Miss Steeles are staying with the Middletons, Elinor and Marianne would be given priority next to the fire. Anne Steele's focus on a matter like that is a good sign of her general concern with the material and the trivial.

7. *stupid*: dull, tiresome.

A woman in evening dress.

[From *The Repository of arts, literature, fashions, manufactures, &c,* Vol. IV (1810), p. 27]

like every other baby of the same age; nor could he even be brought to acknowledge the simple proposition of its being the finest child in the world.

I come now to the relation of a misfortune, which about this time befell Mrs. John Dashwood. It so happened that while her two sisters with Mrs. Jennings were first calling on her in Harley-street, another of her acquaintance had dropt in—a circumstance in itself not apparently likely to produce evil to her. But while the imaginations of other people will carry them away to form wrong judgments of our conduct, and to decide on it by slight appearances, one's happiness must in some measure be always at the mercy of chance. In the present instance, this last-arrived lady allowed her fancy so far to outrun truth and probability, that on merely hearing the name of the Miss Dashwoods, and understanding them to be Mr. Dashwood's sisters, she immediately concluded them to be staying in Harley-street; and this misconstruction produced within a day or two afterwards, cards of invitation for them as well as for their brother and sister, to a small musical party at her house.[8] The consequence of which was, that Mrs. John Dashwood was obliged to submit not only to the exceedingly great inconvenience of sending her carriage for the Miss Dashwoods;[9] but, what was still worse, must be subject to all the unpleasantness of appearing to treat them with attention: and who could tell that they might not expect to go out with her a second time? The power of disappointing them, it was true, must always be her's. But that was not enough; for when people are determined on a mode of conduct which they know to be wrong, they feel injured by the expectation of any thing better from them.

Marianne had now been brought by degrees, so much into the habit of going out every day, that it was become a matter of indifference to her, whether she went or not: and she prepared quietly and mechanically for every evening's engagement, though without expecting the smallest amusement from any, and very often without knowing till the last moment, where it was to take her.

To her dress and appearance she was grown so perfectly indif-

8. *musical party*: gathering to listen to music. Private concerts in people's homes were one of the principal ways to experience music at this time. The large number of people, particularly ladies, who played musical instruments provided a basis for such concerts. In London they had become especially popular among the wealthy toward the end of the eighteenth century, a time when public concerts were increasing significantly in number and size and were therefore becoming less socially exclusive. Some of these private concerts were fairly grand and formal. Others, like this one, were smaller, in part because this would guarantee greater exclusivity—it is likely this consideration would appeal to John and Fanny Dashwood. Professional musicians, including famous ones, might perform at private concerts, though they were mainly only amateurs (as is the case here—see p. 464).

9. Since they received the cards for Elinor and Marianne, they would be expected to bring them to the party.

ferent, as not to bestow half the consideration on it, during the whole of her toilette, which it received from Miss Steele in the first five minutes of their being together, when it was finished. Nothing escaped *her* minute observation and general curiosity; she saw every thing, and asked every thing; was never easy till she knew the price of every part of Marianne's dress;[10] could have guessed the number of her gowns altogether with better judgment than Marianne herself, and was not without hopes of finding out before they parted, how much her washing cost per week,[11] and how much she had every year to spend upon herself.[12] The impertinence of these kind of scrutinies, moreover, was generally concluded with a compliment, which though meant as its douceur,[13] was considered by Marianne as the greatest impertinence of all; for after undergoing an examination into the value and make of her gown, the colour of her shoes, and the arrangement of her hair,[14] she was almost sure of being told that upon "her word she looked vastly smart, and she dared to say would make a great many conquests."[15]

With such encouragement as this, was she dismissed on the present occasion to her brother's carriage; which they were ready to enter five minutes after it stopped at the door, a punctuality not very agreeable to their sister-in-law, who had preceded them to the house of her acquaintance, and was there hoping for some delay on their part that might inconvenience either herself or her coachman.[16]

The events of the evening were not very remarkable. The party, like other musical parties, comprehended a great many people who had real taste for the performance, and a great many more who had none at all; and the performers themselves were, as usual, in their own estimation, and that of their immediate friends, the first private performers[17] in England.

As Elinor was neither musical, nor affecting to be so,[18] she made no scruple of turning away her eyes from the grand pianoforté,[19] whenever it suited her, and unrestrained even by the presence of a harp, and a violoncello,[20] would fix them at pleasure on any other object in the room. In one of these excursive glances

10. *dress:* attire.

11. Washing, or laundry, was an elaborate task in those days and could represent a significant cost. Country houses often had a laundry maid and more than one laundry room for various stages of the process. Those lacking such means could either hire a woman to come to their home and wash or send their clothes out to be laundered.

12. In many families girls would be given a fixed allowance for personal spending. Questions about one's personal finances would be considered inappropriate, especially when directed to someone who was not a close friend or relative.

13. *douceur:* conciliatory gift or gesture.

14. Women were likely to have some knowledge of the make, or construction, of their gowns because they were not purchased already made. The woman would select the material and color she wanted and then order it to be made in the style she preferred. As for hair, its arrangement was often undertaken by a maid, though women like Miss Steele or Marianne who lacked a personal maid would have to do it themselves.

15. Marianne had earlier expressed strong revulsion at the idea of a woman's making a conquest of a man (pp. 84–86).

16. A servant who drives one's carriage; most carriages required such a driver. He also helped take care of the carriage (and sometimes the horses).

17. *private performers:* amateur musicians.

18. The preceding paragraph spoke of the great many who had no taste for the musical performance (more than those who did). Yet many would affect a love of music, for it was considered a mark of gentility and refinement. Lady Middleton did this earlier (p. 66). Elinor's willingness to avoid such affectation is a sign of her independent spirit.

19. Grand pianofortes, or pianos, were a recent innovation, having appeared around 1790, a little more than fifty years after the appearance of pianofortes, when an English manufacturer, John Broadwood, created a large, wing-shaped version. Its richer sound would be especially appropriate for a musical party. Thanks to Broadwood's manufacturing improvements, the cost of a grand pianoforte was only around fifty pounds, not an exorbitant sum.

20. Harps were, after pianos, the most popular instruments for women, the principal amateur musicians to play. "Violoncello" is an older term for a cello. The sentence suggests that most would regard these additional instruments as a great treat.

she perceived among a group of young men, the very he, who had given them a lecture on toothpick-cases at Gray's.[21] She perceived him soon afterwards looking at herself, and speaking familiarly to her brother; and had just determined to find out his name from the latter, when they both came towards her, and Mr. Dashwood introduced him to her as Mr. Robert Ferrars.[22]

He addressed her with easy civility, and twisted his head into a bow which assured her as plainly as words could have done,[23] that he was exactly the coxcomb[24] she had heard him described to be by Lucy. Happy had it been for her, if her regard for Edward had depended less on his own merit, than on the merit of his nearest relations! For then his brother's bow must have given the finishing stroke to what the ill-humour of his mother and sister would have begun. But while she wondered at the difference of the two young men, she did not find that the emptiness and conceit of the one, put her at all out of charity with the modesty and worth of the other. Why they *were* different, Robert explained to her himself in the course of a quarter of an hour's conversation; for, talking of his brother, and lamenting the extreme *gaucherie*[25] which he really believed kept him from mixing in proper society, he candidly[26] and generously attributed it much less to any natural deficiency, than to the misfortune of a private education; while he himself, though probably without any particular, any material superiority by nature, merely from the advantage of a public school,[27] was as well fitted to mix in the world[28] as any other man.

"Upon my soul," he added, "I believe it is nothing more; and so I often tell my mother, when she is grieving about it. 'My dear Madam,' I always say to her, 'you must make yourself easy. The evil is now irremediable, and it has been entirely your own doing. Why would you be persuaded by my uncle, Sir Robert, against your own judgment, to place Edward under private tuition, at the most critical time of his life? If you had only sent him to Westminster[29] as well as myself, instead of sending him to Mr. Pratt's, all this would have been prevented.' This is the way in which I always consider the matter, and my mother is perfectly convinced of her error."[30]

21. For the incident, see pp. 410–412.

22. He is called "Mr. Robert Ferrars" because he is a younger son. Edward, the older son, is plain "Mr. Ferrars."

23. Bowing was a formal gesture that most men would not bother with when simply meeting someone. His bow, and especially the elaborate twist of the head accompanying it, suggest a tendency to parade his fine manners.

24. *coxcomb*: conceited, foolish man, excessively concerned with his appearance and inclined to show off; fop.

25. *gaucherie*: awkwardness, lack of grace.

26. *candidly*: courteously, fair-mindedly.

27. A public school was a boys' school open to the public, but under private ownership (there were no state schools then). The name distinguishes it from a private education for one or a few persons in someone's home.

28. *the world*: elite society.

29. *Westminster*: one of the most distinguished public schools in England.

30. It is curious that Mrs. Ferrars did not send Edward to public school. Most boys from elite families went to public schools, which gave them the opportunity to form friendships and connections with others of similar background. An ambitious mother like Mrs. Ferrars would thus have strong reason to send her eldest son to such a school. The explanation given here is the influence of Edward and Robert's uncle, Sir Robert (Robert was probably named after him, while Edward, like many eldest sons, was probably named after his father). Sir Robert may have disliked public schools, and he may have known and liked Mr. Pratt, Edward's tutor. His title and his sex may have caused Mrs. Ferrars to defer to him on the issue of boys' schooling.

The difference between Robert and Sir Robert over public schools mirrors a debate in this period over their value, especially regarding their moral effects. Most men of the upper classes supported them. They argued in particular that the principal feature of the schools, the autonomy of the boys outside the classroom, inculcated toughness, the ability to socialize with others, and qualities of leadership and self-government. At the same time, an increasing number of people criticized this same atmosphere for fostering tyranny and brutality on the part of the older and stronger boys and for encouraging immoral behavior and the neglect of religious duties.

Elinor would not oppose his opinion, because, whatever might be her general estimation of the advantage of a public school,[31] she could not think of Edward's abode in Mr. Pratt's family, with any satisfaction.

"You reside in Devonshire, I think"—was his next observation, "in a cottage near Dawlish."[32]

Elinor set him right as to its situation,[33] and it seemed rather surprising to him that anybody could live in Devonshire, without living near Dawlish. He bestowed his hearty approbation however on their species of house.

"For my own part," said he, "I am excessively fond of a cottage; there is always so much comfort, so much elegance about them. And I protest, if I had any money to spare, I should buy a little land and build one myself, within a short distance of London, where I might drive myself down at any time, and collect a few friends about me, and be happy.[34] I advise every body who is going to build, to build a cottage.[35] My friend Lord Courtland came to me the other day on purpose to ask my advice, and laid before me three different plans of Bonomi's.[36] I was to decide on the best of them. 'My dear Courtland,' said I, immediately throw-

An elegant cottage of the time (for this cottage's plan, see next page).

[From *The Repository of arts, literature, fashions, manufactures, &c,* Series Two, Vol. I (1816), p. 1]

31. Jane Austen's own attitude on public versus private schools is not clear. Her father took in private students; at the same time, in a letter, speaking of a boy she and her sister knew, she writes that his going soon to a public school "will do him good I dare say" (Jan. 30, 1809).

32. Dawlish was a popular seaside resort in Devonshire, which is probably why Robert, who seems very much a man of leisure, would have heard of it. It is in a somewhat different part of Devonshire from the Dashwoods' home north of Exeter (see map, p. 739). Jane Austen visited Dawlish once; all we know of her attitude toward it is that many years later she commented that its library was "pitiful and wretched" (Aug. 10, 1814).

33. *situation:* location.

34. Many wealthy people at this time constructed houses in the vicinity of London that could serve as rural retreats.

35. This period witnessed a brief vogue for cottages among the wealthy. Cottages were traditionally small, humble dwellings, most often inhabited by the poor. But their simplicity and rustic associations gave them a particular appeal in the prevailing Romantic mood of the day. This inspired a new form of cottage, the cottage ornée (from the French for "adorned" or "decorated") — in Austen's unfinished novel, *Sanditon*, one character is constructing such a dwelling, while in *Persuasion* one couple inhabits a cottage recently built in this style. These cottages, while smaller than grand country houses, were larger than traditional cottages and contained more amenities — the wish of the wealthy for a more rustic existence did not extend to denying themselves physical comforts. But they did incorporate rustic elements such as uncut stone for walls and thatch for roofs, numerous gables and other items jutting out from walls, irregularities of proportion and design, earth tones, and vegetation all around the house. Thus when the Dashwoods moved into their cottage the author commented that "as a cottage it was defective, for the building was regular, the roof was tiled, the window shutters were not painted green, nor were the walls covered with honeysuckles" (p. 52). These cottages also appealed greatly to current taste for the picturesque. For a contemporary picture of a cottage, see facing page. Many publications of the time offered pictures and architectural plans of cottages.

36. Joseph Bonomi (1739–1808), who was originally from Italy, was one of the leading architects in England during this period. He worked on grand private homes as well as churches and public buildings. His work represents the complete antithesis of the ideals behind the vogue for cottages, which is probably why he is chosen as the figure whose designs are rejected in favor of a cottage. Bonomi was a firm advocate and practitioner of classical architecture, which had dominated England during the eighteenth century but was

ing them all into the fire, 'do not adopt either[37] of them, but by all means build a cottage.' And that, I fancy, will be the end of it.[38]

"Some people imagine that there can be no accommodations, no space in a cottage; but this is all a mistake. I was last month at my friend Elliott's near Dartford.[39] Lady Elliott wished to give a dance.[40] 'But how can it be done?' said she; 'my dear Ferrars, do tell me how it is to be managed. There is not a room in this cottage that will hold ten couple, and where can the supper be?'[41] I immediately saw that there could be no difficulty in it, so I said, 'My dear Lady Elliott, do not be uneasy. The dining parlour will admit eighteen couple with ease;[42] card-tables may be placed in the drawing-room;[43] the library may be open for tea and other refreshments;[44] and let the supper be set out in the saloon.'[45] Lady Elliott was delighted with the thought. We measured the dining-room, and found it would hold exactly eighteen couple, and the affair was arranged precisely after my plan. So that, in fact, you see, if people do but know how to set about it, every comfort may be as well enjoyed in a cottage as in the most spacious dwelling."

Elinor agreed to it all, for she did not think he deserved the compliment of rational opposition.[46]

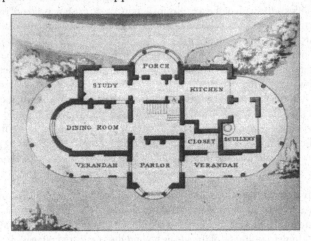

A plan for a cottage (see preceding page for the cottage).

[From *The Repository of arts, literature, fashions, manufactures, &c,* Series Two, Vol. I (1816), p. 1]

beginning to be displaced by new, more Romantic tastes (he himself expressed contempt for Gothic architecture, whose revival in this period was inspired by the same principles that spurred the construction of cottages). He favored buildings on a grand scale, with strict harmony in all proportions, voluminous space, imposing walls and columns, restraint in surface decoration, and a general austerity—all these being the opposite of what fashionable cottages attempted to achieve.

37. *either:* any. The term could be used for more than two items then.

38. Robert's tremendous confidence in his own judgment will continue to be one of his most prominent characteristics.

39. Dartford is a town about ten to fifteen miles east of London. It would thus be a good location for a close rural retreat. See map on p. 738.

40. The two friends he has mentioned, Lord Courtland and Lady Elliott, both have titles. This reflects his participation in elite London society, which included many aristocrats, as well as his propensity to boast of his intimacy with such figures.

41. Having a substantial supper was standard at balls, which involved hours of dancing and could go well past midnight. In *Emma*, when someone proposes that sandwiches rather than a regular supper be served at a ball, this is immediately rejected: "A private dance, without sitting down to supper, was pronounced an infamous fraud upon the rights of men and women."

42. Dining rooms in wealthy houses were often very large, for dinner parties could require numerous people to sit around the dining table, with plenty of space for servants to bring the food and attend to the guests.

43. Most dances had places for playing cards, for many guests, especially men and older people, would not wish to dance at all, or at least not for the whole time.

44. Libraries had become standard features of wealthy homes during the eighteenth century. By the end of the century they also frequently served as the most popular general living rooms, used for a variety of informal occupations. Hence the idea to serve refreshments there would not be so unusual, though most people would probably be more wary than Robert and Lady Elliott of the potential danger to the books of serving drinks there to a large party of people.

45. A saloon was a large room that could serve various functions.

46. Elinor's own experience of living in a cottage, after inhabiting a grand country house, would give her a clear sense of the complete folly of someone who claimed that there is no difference in comfort between the two.

As John Dashwood had no more pleasure in music than his eldest sister, his mind was equally at liberty to fix on any thing else; and a thought struck him during the evening, which he communicated to his wife, for her approbation, when they got home. The consideration of Mrs. Dennison's mistake, in supposing his sisters their guests, had suggested the propriety of their being really invited to become such, while Mrs. Jennings's engagements kept her from home. The expense would be nothing, the inconvenience not more; and it was altogether an attention, which the delicacy of his conscience pointed out to be requisite to its complete enfranchisement from his promise to his father. Fanny was startled at the proposal.

"I do not see how it can be done," said she, "without affronting Lady Middleton, for they spend every day with her; otherwise I should be exceedingly glad to do it. You know I am always ready to pay them any attention in my power, as my taking them out this evening shews.[47] But they are Lady Middleton's visitors. How can I ask them away from her?"

Her husband, but with great humility, did not see the force of her objection. "They had already spent a week in this manner in Conduit-street, and Lady Middleton could not be displeased at their giving the same number of days to such near relations."

Fanny paused a moment, and then, with fresh vigour, said,

"My love, I would ask them with all my heart, if it was in my power. But I had just settled within myself to ask the Miss Steeles to spend a few days with us. They are very well behaved, good kind of girls; and I think the attention is due to them, as their uncle did so very well by Edward. We can ask your sisters some other year, you know; but the Miss Steeles may not be in town any more. I am sure you will like them; indeed, you *do* like them, you know, very much already, and so does my mother; and they are such favourites with Harry!"[48]

Mr. Dashwood was convinced. He saw the necessity of inviting the Miss Steeles immediately, and his conscience was pacified by the resolution of inviting his sisters another year; at the same time,

47. Of course, the real reason she took them in her carriage was because of someone else's mistake, and she very much resented it.

48. The Miss Steeles were probably as flattering in their attention to John and Fanny's son as they were to Lady Middleton's children.

"*A Fashionable Mama*": *a satirical print on the growing popularity of breast-feeding among the wealthy.*

[From *Works of James Gillray* (London, 1849)]

however, slyly[49]suspecting that another year would make the invitation needless, by bringing Elinor to town as Colonel Brandon's wife, and Marianne as *their* visitor.

Fanny, rejoicing in her escape, and proud of the ready wit that had procured it, wrote the next morning to Lucy, to request her company and her sister's, for some days, in Harley-street, as soon as Lady Middleton could spare them. This was enough to make Lucy really and reasonably happy. Mrs. Dashwood seemed actually working for her, herself; cherishing all her hopes, and promoting all her views![50] Such an opportunity of being with Edward and his family was, above all things, the most material to her interest, and such an invitation the most gratifying to her feelings! It was an advantage that could not be too gratefully acknowledged, nor too speedily made use of; and the visit to Lady Middleton, which had not before had any precise limits, was instantly discovered to have been always meant to end in two days time.

When the note was shewn to Elinor, as it was within ten minutes after its arrival, it gave her, for the first time, some share in the expectations of Lucy; for such a mark of uncommon kindness, vouchsafed[51] on so short an acquaintance, seemed to declare that the good will towards her arose from something more than merely malice against herself; and might be brought, by time and address,[52] to do every thing that Lucy wished. Her flattery had already subdued the pride of Lady Middleton, and made an entry into the close heart of Mrs. John Dashwood; and these were effects that laid open the probability of greater.

The Miss Steeles removed to Harley-street, and all that reached Elinor of their influence there, strengthened her expectation of the event. Sir John, who called on them more than once, brought home such accounts of the favour they were in, as must be universally striking. Mrs. Dashwood had never been so much pleased with any young women in her life, as she was with them; had given each of them a needle book,[53] made by some emigrant;[54] called Lucy by her christian name;[55] and did not know whether she should ever be able to part with them.

49. *slyly*: secretly.

50. *views*: expectations, aims.

51. *vouchsafed*: bestowed.

52. *address*: skill, dexterity.

53. *needle book*: case shaped like a book that holds needles and other materials for sewing and embroidery. It was a common accessory for ladies, who frequently engaged in needlework. Jane Austen's House Museum in Chawton, England, has a needle case on display that she made as a gift for her niece.

54. This refers to the large numbers of people, mostly of aristocratic background, who fled France during the French Revolution to escape execution or imprisonment. Many took refuge in England, especially in London, and remained there until 1814–1815, when Napoleon was overthrown and the monarchy was restored. Jane Austen had some personal contact with the world of emigrants through Eliza de Feuillide, her cousin who had married an upper-class Frenchman and lived in France for many years before her husband was guillotined during the revolution and she had to flee to England. She lived in London and maintained ties to the community of French exiles, and she eventually married Jane Austen's brother; Jane would stay with them when visiting London. Many of these emigrants were poor, having lost most or all of their property during the revolution, and there were various charitable endeavors to assist them. Buying a needle book would be one logical though modest way to help them: making items like this was a common activity of upper-class women, so the background of many emigrants would make this one means for them to earn a little money.

55. Calling Lucy by her Christian, or first, name would be a sign of intimacy and friendliness.

VOLUME THREE

Chapter One

Mrs. Palmer was so well at the end of a fortnight, that her mother felt it no longer necessary to give up the whole of her time to her; and contenting herself with visiting her once or twice a day, returned from that period to her own home, and her own habits, in which she found the Miss Dashwoods very ready to reassume their former share.

About the third or fourth morning after their being thus re-settled in Berkeley-street, Mrs. Jennings, on returning from her ordinary visit to Mrs. Palmer, entered the drawing-room, where Elinor was sitting by herself, with an air of such hurrying importance as prepared her to hear something wonderful;[1] and giving her time only to form that idea, began directly to justify it by saying,

"Lord! my dear Miss Dashwood! have you heard the news!"

"No, ma'am. What is it?"

"Something so strange! But you shall hear it all.[2]—When I got to Mr. Palmer's, I found Charlotte quite in a fuss about the child. She was sure it was very ill—it cried, and fretted, and was all over pimples. So I looked at it directly, and, 'Lord! my dear,' says I, 'it is nothing in the world but the red-gum;'[3] and nurse said just the same.[4] But Charlotte, she would not be satisfied, so Mr. Donavan was sent for;[5] and luckily he happened to be just come in from Harley-street,[6] so he stepped over directly, and as soon as ever he saw the child, he said just as we did, that it was nothing in the world but the red-gum, and then Charlotte was easy. And so, just as he was going away again, it came into my head, I am sure I do not know how I happened to think of it,[7] but it came into my head

476

1. *wonderful:* astonishing.

2. Mrs. Jennings's love of gossip makes her want to relate every detail and not just go directly to the main points. This also allows the reader to learn the whole story.

3. *red-gum:* a rash of red pimples and irregular patches on the skin, found especially in infants who are teething (which would account for the child's crying and fretting). A medical writer of the period, Alexander Hamilton, states that "it frequently disappears suddenly, without any inconvenience to the child," and that it poses little risk or need for action (quoted in David Selwyn, *Jane Austen and Children*, p. 25). Hence Mrs. Jennings sees no cause for alarm.

4. Among the wealthy, it was standard to hire a nurse for a new mother; she would normally start her employment just before the delivery and continue through the end of the mother's confinement, which would be four or five weeks after the birth. The nurse is probably not a wet nurse, someone who supplied the infant with milk. The use of wet nurses was a long-standing practice among the wealthy that had declined, though not disappeared, during the late eighteenth century due to an increasing emphasis, connected to Romanticism, on following the more natural course of breast-feeding. For a contemporary picture of a wealthy and fashionable woman breast-feeding her baby, see p. 473.

5. Mr. Donavan would be a medical doctor. Sending for a doctor, after first making a home diagnosis, was a common practice then. The high death rate and the limits of professional medicine caused people to develop their own knowledge of ailments and treatments; one study of upper-class women found accounts of illness and recommendations for treating them to be the single largest subject in the women's letters to one another. But even after arriving at conclusions on their own, people would still frequently send for a professional to hear his opinion.

6. *Harley-street:* the street on which John and Fanny Dashwood live.

7. That Mrs. Jennings cannot know how she happened to think of inquiring after the latest news indicates her complete lack of self-awareness. It is probable that she has inquired of many doctors before, for since doctors almost always visited patients at home, they would be excellent sources for gossip.

to ask him if there was any news. So upon that, he smirked, and simpered, and looked grave, and seemed to know something or other, and at last he said in a whisper, 'For fear any unpleasant report should reach the young ladies under your care as to their sister's indisposition, I think it advisable to say, that I believe there is no great reason for alarm; I hope Mrs. Dashwood will do very well.' "

"What! is Fanny ill?"[8]

"That is exactly what I said, my dear. 'Lord!' says I, 'is Mrs. Dashwood ill?' So then it all came out; and the long and the short of the matter, by all I can learn, seems to be this. Mr. Edward Ferrars, the very young man I used to joke with you about (but however, as it turns out, I am monstrous glad there never was any thing in it), Mr. Edward Ferrars, it seems, has been engaged above this twelvemonth to my cousin Lucy!—There's for you, my dear!—And not a creature knowing a syllable of the matter except Nancy![9]—Could you have believed such a thing possible?— There is no great wonder in their liking one another; but that matters should be brought so forward[10] between them, and nobody suspect it! *That* is strange!—I never happened to see them together, or I am sure I should have found it out directly. Well, and so this was kept a great secret, for fear of Mrs. Ferrars, and neither she nor your brother or sister suspected a word of the matter;—till this very morning, poor Nancy, who, you know, is a well-meaning creature, but no conjurer,[11] popt it all out. 'Lord!' thinks she to herself, 'they are all so fond of Lucy, to be sure they will make no difficulty about it;'[12] and so, away she went to your sister, who was sitting all alone at her carpet-work,[13] little suspecting what was to come—for she had just been saying to your brother, only five minutes before, that she thought to make a match between Edward and some Lord's daughter or other, I forget who.[14] So you may think what a blow it was to all her vanity and pride. She fell into violent hysterics immediately, with such screams as reached your brother's ears, as he was sitting in his own dressing-room down stairs,[15] thinking about writing a letter to his steward in the country.[16] So up he flew directly, and a terrible

8. Elinor can call her "Fanny" because she is her sister-in-law. The doctor and Mrs. Jennings call her "Mrs. Dashwood."

9. *Nancy*: Anne Steele.

10. *so forward*: to such an advanced stage.

11. *no conjurer*: far from clever.

12. Sir John just reported on Mrs. Dashwood's apparent great favor toward the Miss Steeles.

13. Carpet work involved stitching colored wool onto a canvas to make rugs, hangings, coverings (such as bed valances), or cushions. Like other decorative activities, it was a frequent pursuit of wealthy ladies, including a number of characters in Jane Austen. It seems to be especially popular among older or married women in her novels: the heroine of *Emma* muses that it may become an occupation of hers in later years. Mrs. Jennings, who was earlier described as making a rug, is the other figure engaged in carpet work in this novel.

14. She and her husband and Mrs. Ferrars have already indicated their high hopes for the daughter of Lord Morton as a mate for Edward.

15. As mentioned earlier, houses in London contained numerous floors, so a dressing room, which would normally not be on the ground floor, is on a lower level than the room Fanny is in. Dressing rooms were places where people would undertake various activities, including writing letters.

16. The steward is someone who manages a wealthy man's estate. This could include directing any work done on the land, supervising the servants and other laborers, and taking care of basic financial transactions. He would be a natural person for John Dashwood to write to while in London, especially since he is currently enclosing common land and making major alterations in the gardens and landscaping around the house (pp. 418–420).

scene took place, for Lucy was come[17] to them by that time, little dreaming what was going on. Poor soul! I pity *her*. And I must say, I think she was used very hardly; for your sister scolded like any fury, and soon drove her into a fainting fit. Nancy, she fell upon her knees, and cried bitterly; and your brother, he walked about the room, and said he did not know what to do. Mrs. Dashwood declared they should not stay a minute longer in the house; and your brother was forced to go down upon *his* knees too, to persuade her to let them stay till they had packed up their clothes.[18] *Then* she fell into hysterics again, and he was so frightened that he would send for Mr. Donavan, and Mr. Donavan found the house in all this uproar. The carriage was at the door ready to take my poor cousins away, and they were just stepping in as he came off; poor Lucy in such a condition, he says, she could hardly walk; and Nancy, she was almost as bad. I declare, I have no patience with your sister; and I hope, with all my heart, it will be a match in spite of her. Lord! what a taking[19] poor Mr. Edward will be in when he hears of it! To have his love used so scornfully! for they say he is monstrous fond of her, as well he may. I should not wonder, if he was to be in the greatest of a passion!—and Mr. Donavan thinks just the same. He and I had a great deal of talk about it; and the best of all is, that he is gone back again to Harley-street, that he may be within call when Mrs. Ferrars is told of it,[20] for she was sent for as soon as ever my cousins left the house, for your sister was sure *she* would be in hysterics too; and so she may, for what I care. I have no pity for either of them. I have no notion of people's making such a to-do about money and greatness.[21] There is no reason on earth why Mr. Edward and Lucy should not marry; for I am sure Mrs. Ferrars may afford to do very well by her son, and though Lucy has next to nothing herself, she knows better than any body how to make the most of every thing; and I dare say, if Mrs. Ferrars would only allow him five hundred a-year, she would make as good an appearance with it as any body else would with eight. Lord! how snug they might live in such another cottage as yours—or a little bigger—with two maids and two men;[22]

17. *was come:* had come. The past tense was occasionally formed then with "to be" instead of "to have." Thus this is not a case of bad grammar.

18. As the mistress of the house Mrs. Dashwood would be the person who usually invited, or disinvited, guests. Mr. Dashwood's need, and willingness, to go down on his knees to persuade her not to commit a flagrant act of rudeness indicates the nature of their marital relationship. In the previous chapter he is described as expressing a simple disagreement "with great humility" (p. 472).

19. *taking:* passion, agitation of mind.

20. Their long talk, and Mrs. Jennings's glee that Mr. Donovan will return and learn more, indicate that he is also a great lover of gossip. It also makes plausible Mrs. Jennings's long account of the incident, something important for the plot but also something that Elinor would not be able to witness herself.

21. *greatness:* high rank or social position.

22. Elinor's mother is able to afford one male and two female servants on five hundred a year. Mrs. Jennings's expectation for Edward and Lucy to have one more servant, and perhaps a slightly larger cottage, may be based on the two thousand pounds that Edward already has (p. 270), which would give him an additional hundred pounds a year.

and I believe I could help them to a housemaid, for my Betty has a sister out of place,[23] that would fit them exactly."[24]

Here Mrs. Jennings ceased, and as Elinor had had time enough to collect her thoughts, she was able to give such an answer, and make such observations, as the subject might naturally be supposed to produce. Happy to find that she was not suspected of any extraordinary interest in it; that Mrs. Jennings (as she had of late often hoped might be the case) had ceased to imagine her at all attached to Edward; and happy above all the rest, in the absence of Marianne, she felt very well able to speak of the affair without embarrassment, and to give her judgment, as she believed, with impartiality on the conduct of every one concerned in it.

She could hardly determine what her own expectation of its event[25] really was; though she earnestly tried to drive away the notion of its being possible to end otherwise at last, than in the marriage of Edward and Lucy. What Mrs. Ferrars would say and do, though there could not be a doubt of its nature, she was anxious to hear; and still more anxious to know how Edward would conduct himself. For *him* she felt much compassion;—for Lucy very little—and it cost her some pains to procure that little;—for the rest of the party none at all.[26]

As Mrs. Jennings could talk on no other subject, Elinor soon saw the necessity of preparing Marianne for its discussion. No time was to be lost in undeceiving her, in making her acquainted with the real truth, and in endeavouring to bring her to hear it talked of by others, without betraying that she felt any uneasiness for her sister, or any resentment against Edward.[27]

Elinor's office[28] was a painful one.—She was going to remove what she really believed to be her sister's chief consolation,[29]—to give such particulars of Edward, as she feared would ruin him for ever in her good opinion,—and to make Marianne, by a resemblance in their situations, which to *her* fancy would seem strong, feel all her own disappointment over again. But unwelcome as such a task must be, it was necessary to be done, and Elinor therefore hastened to perform it.

She was very far from wishing to dwell on her own feelings, or

23. *place*: employment.

24. Finding a job for servants one has some connection with was a frequent activity of those employing them. Other characters in Jane Austen do it, and she refers to several cases of this in her letters. It reflected a strong upper-class ethos of paternalism: such beneficence was considered the rightful return for the deference servants were supposed to give their employers. Mrs. Jennings, being both generous and a busybody, would be especially inclined to undertake such a task, and Betty, the servant she took to London, is probably a particular favorite of hers.

25. *event*: outcome.

26. She presumably feels a little compassion for Lucy, and not for the others, because Lucy, however bad her general behavior, has been subject to unjustifiably harsh treatment, and is suffering for being engaged, something that is not intrinsically bad, whereas the others are suffering because of their unworthy obsession with making Edward marry someone of wealth and position. Of course, Elinor's dislike of Lucy makes her strongly disinclined to feel any sympathy, but her sense of duty makes her struggle, with some success, to extend the modicum of sympathy she considers justified.

27. Elinor is glad that Mrs. Jennings has ceased to suspect her of any particular affection for Edward, as has everyone else to all appearances, and she fears that any display of resentment by Marianne would reawaken those suspicions.

28. *office*: duty or service to be performed.

29. Marianne has consistently shown great pleasure in the prospect of Elinor's happiness. The joy she displayed when she saw Edward, when he visited Elinor while Lucy Steele was also there, was the only time since Willoughby's abandonment of her that she exhibited any emotion like that.

to represent herself as suffering much, any otherwise than as the self-command she had practised since her first knowledge of Edward's engagement, might suggest a hint of what was practicable to Marianne. Her narration was clear and simple; and though it could not be given without emotion, it was not accompanied by violent agitation, nor impetuous[30] grief. — *That* belonged rather to the hearer, for Marianne listened with horror, and cried excessively. Elinor was to be the comforter of others in her own distresses, no less than in theirs; and all the comfort that could be given by assurances of her own composure of mind, and a very earnest vindication of Edward from every charge but of imprudence,[31] was readily offered.

But Marianne for some time would give credit to neither. Edward seemed a second Willoughby; and acknowledging as Elinor did, that she *had* loved him most sincerely, could she feel less than herself! As for Lucy Steele, she considered her so totally unamiable, so absolutely incapable of attaching a sensible man, that she could not be persuaded at first to believe, and afterwards to pardon, any former affection of Edward for her. She would not even admit it to have been natural; and Elinor left her to be convinced that it was so, by that which only could convince her, a better knowledge of mankind.[32]

Her first communication had reached no farther than to state the fact of the engagement, and the length of time it had existed. — Marianne's feelings had then broken in, and put an end to all regularity[33] of detail; and for some time all that could be done was to sooth her distress, lessen her alarms, and combat her resentment. The first question on her side, which led to farther particulars, was,

"How long has this been known to you, Elinor? has he written to you?"

"I have known it these four months. When Lucy first came to Barton-park last November, she told me in confidence of her engagement."[34]

At these words, Marianne's eyes expressed the astonishment,

30. *impetuous:* vehement, violent.

31. This goes further in vindication of Edward than Elinor went earlier, for upon first learning of his prior engagement she considered him definitely blamable for spending time at Norland after feeling an attraction for her, and thus raising her hopes. Since then Elinor's affection for him, and compassion for his entrapment in an unhappy engagement, may have softened her verdict, or she may simply be softening her indictment here to calm Marianne.

32. With a better knowledge of mankind Marianne would recognize that even virtuous and wise people are capable of doing foolish things under certain influences, such as personal beauty and outer good nature, the main reasons Elinor gave earlier for Edward's initial infatuation with Lucy (p. 256).

33. *regularity:* orderliness.

34. It is now early March, which means Elinor and Marianne have been in London for two months. Elinor learned of the engagement in early November (see chronology, pp. 714 and 715).

which her lips could not utter. After a pause of wonder, she exclaimed,

"Four months!—Have you known of this four months?"—

Elinor confirmed it.

"What!—while attending me in all my misery, has this been on your heart?—and I have reproached you for being happy!"—

"It was not fit that you should then know how much I was the reverse!"—

"Four months!"—cried Marianne again.—"So calm!—so cheerful!—how have you been supported?"—

"By feeling that I was doing my duty.—My promise to Lucy, obliged me to be secret. I owed it to her, therefore, to avoid giving any hint of the truth; and I owed it to my family and friends, not to create in them a solicitude about me, which it could not be in my power to satisfy."[35]

Marianne seemed much struck.—

"I have very often wished to undeceive yourself and my mother," added Elinor; "and once or twice I have attempted it;[36]—but without betraying my trust, I never could have convinced you."

"Four months!—and yet you loved him!"—

"Yes. But I did not love only him;[37]—and while the comfort of others was dear to me, I was glad to spare them from knowing how much I felt. Now, I can think and speak of it with little emotion.[38] I would not have you suffer on my account; for I assure you I no longer suffer materially myself. I have many things to support me. I am not conscious of having provoked the disappointment by any imprudence of my own,[39] and I have borne it as much as possible without spreading it farther. I acquit Edward of all essential misconduct. I wish him very happy; and I am so sure of his always doing his duty, that though now he may harbour some regret, in the end he must become so.[40] Lucy does not want sense, and that is the foundation on which every thing good may be built.—And after all, Marianne, after all that is bewitching in the idea of a single and constant attachment, and all that can be said of one's happiness depending entirely on any particular person, it is not

35. She needed to disguise her feelings, because if her friends had noticed her unhappiness, she would not have been in a position to explain it.

36. The incidents she has in mind are probably the two occasions when she expressed relative indifference toward Edward, first when discussing their trip to London with their mother (p. 290) and then after she and Marianne saw Edward in London (pp. 454–456).

37. This ideal of still caring for a larger circle of people even while strongly in love with a particular person is an important one in Jane Austen (see also p. 103, note 8).

38. *emotion*: agitation.

39. In this she contrasts notably with Marianne.

40. His knowledge of having done his duty will eventually make him happy, despite any current regret. This idea of finding happiness in doing one's duty, or suffering unhappiness from reneging on it, often appears in Austen's novels, and it is a concept Elinor would naturally be inclined to uphold.

meant—it is not fit—it is not possible that it should be so.[41]— Edward will marry Lucy; he will marry a woman superior in person[42] and understanding to half her sex; and time and habit will teach him to forget that he ever thought another superior to her." —

"If such is your way of thinking," said Marianne, "if the loss of what is most valued is so easily to be made up by something else, your resolution, your self-command, are, perhaps, a little less to be wondered at. — They are brought more within my comprehension."[43]

"I understand you. — You do not suppose that I have ever felt much. — For four months, Marianne, I have had all this hanging on my mind, without being at liberty to speak of it to a single creature; knowing that it would make you and my mother most unhappy whenever it were explained to you, yet unable to prepare you for it in the least. — It was told me, — it was in a manner forced on me by the very person herself, whose prior engagement ruined all my prospects; and told me, as I thought, with triumph. — This person's suspicions, therefore, I have had to oppose, by endeavouring to appear indifferent where I have been most deeply interested; — and it has not been only once; — I have had her hopes and exultation to listen to again and again. — I have known myself to be divided from Edward for ever, without hearing one circumstance that could make me less desire the connection. — Nothing has proved him unworthy; nor has any thing declared him indifferent to me.[44] — I have had to contend against the unkindness of his sister, and the insolence of his mother; and have suffered the punishment of an attachment, without enjoying its advantages. — And all this has been going on at a time, when, as you too well know, it has not been my only unhappiness. — If you can think me capable of ever feeling — surely you may suppose that I have suffered *now*. The composure of mind with which I have brought myself at present to consider the matter, the consolation that I have been willing to admit,[45] have been the effect of constant and painful exertion;[46] — they did not spring up of themselves; — they did not occur to relieve my spirits at first — No, Marianne. — *Then*,

41. As indicated in other places, Jane Austen rejects the idea of only one person being right for another person, and irrevocable disappointment if one loses that person. In *Persuasion,* after describing the deep love the heroine felt for the hero before being persuaded to reject him, the author suggests that she could have recovered from her dejection through a "second attachment, the only thoroughly natural, happy, and sufficient cure," while in a letter to her niece on whether to reject a man in love with her, she writes, "it is no creed of mine, as you must be well aware, that such sort of Disappointments kill anybody" (Nov. 18, 1814). At the same time, Elinor's halting speech at the end of the sentence gives a sense of her struggle to accept this idea herself.

42. *person:* physical appearance.

43. Marianne also concluded that Elinor must not have strong feelings for Edward when she witnessed Elinor's composed behavior after his visit at Barton ended (p. 198).

44. Elinor may consider Edward's three visits to her (she was not home for the first two), compared with the apparent absence of visits to Lucy, for Lucy certainly would have mentioned such visits if they had occurred, to constitute further proof of his greater interest in herself.

45. *admit:* allow, permit myself.

46. Her consolation is probably what she said above about Edward's being neither unworthy nor indifferent. But this is a struggle because her wounded feelings regarding his engagement to Lucy would incline her to think badly of him and doubt whether he loved her.

if I had not been bound to silence, perhaps nothing could have kept me entirely—not even what I owed to my dearest friends—from openly shewing that I was *very* unhappy."—[47]

Marianne was quite subdued.—

"Oh! Elinor," she cried, "you have made me hate myself for ever.—How barbarous have I been to you!—you, who have been my only comfort, who have borne with me in all my misery, who have seemed to be only suffering for me!—Is this my gratitude!—Is this the only return I can make you?[48]—Because your merit cries out upon myself, I have been trying to do it away."

The tenderest caresses followed this confession. In such a frame of mind as she was now in, Elinor had no difficulty in obtaining from her whatever promise she required; and at her request, Marianne engaged never to speak of the affair to any one with the least appearance of bitterness;—to meet Lucy without betraying the smallest increase of dislike to her;—and even to see Edward himself, if chance should bring them together, without any diminution of her usual cordiality.—These were great concessions;—but where Marianne felt that she had injured, no reparation could be too much for her to make.[49]

She performed her promise of being discreet, to admiration.[50]—She attended to all that Mrs. Jennings had to say upon the subject, with an unchanging complexion, dissented from her in nothing, and was heard three times to say, "Yes, ma'am."—She listened to her praise of Lucy with only moving from one chair to another, and when Mrs. Jennings talked of Edward's affection, it cost her only a spasm in her throat.—Such advances towards heroism in her sister, made Elinor feel equal to any thing herself.

The next morning brought a farther trial of it,[51] in a visit from their brother, who came with a most serious aspect[52] to talk over the dreadful affair, and bring them news of his wife.

"You have heard, I suppose," said he with great solemnity, as soon as he was seated, "of the very shocking discovery that took place under our roof yesterday."

47. Elinor's distress is shown by the frequent dashes and emphases in the last part of this paragraph, a very rare instance of unpolished speech on her part.

48. This acknowledgment of one's own wrong or mistaken conduct is an important moment for many Jane Austen heroines, for it is only through a recognition of their own fallibility that people can undertake the difficult task of amending themselves. Marianne's statement parallels those of other heroines, though she makes hers aloud, since she is not the person through whom the story is being told. Her initial declaration that she will hate herself forever also goes further in self-reproach, a product of the same emotional ardor that led to her mistakes.

49. As with other heroines, Marianne's acknowledgment of her faults leads quickly to a resolution of atonement and better behavior, though she, unlike the others, requires the prompting and instructions of someone else to set her on this course.

50. *admiration*: astonishment, or admiration. Both meanings were possible then, and both are probably intended here.

51. Just as Elinor has faced a series of trials of her fortitude and composure over the course of the novel, so Marianne, now that she has resolved to attain those same qualities, faces her own series of tests.

52. *aspect*: look, facial expression.

They all looked their assent; it seemed too awful a moment for speech.

"Your sister," he continued, "has suffered dreadfully. Mrs. Ferrars too—in short it has been a scene of such complicated[53] distress—but I will hope that the storm may be weathered without our being any of us quite overcome. Poor Fanny! she was in hysterics all yesterday. But I would not alarm you too much. Donavan[54] says there is nothing materially to be apprehended; her constitution is a good one, and her resolution equal to any thing. She has borne it all, with the fortitude of an angel! She says she never shall think well of anybody again; and one cannot wonder at it, after being so deceived!—meeting with such ingratitude, where so much kindness had been shewn, so much confidence had been placed! It was quite out of the benevolence of her heart, that she had asked these young women to her house; merely because she thought they deserved some attention, were harmless, well-behaved girls, and would be pleasant companions;[55] for otherwise we both wished very much to have invited you and Marianne to be with us, while your kind friend there, was attending her daughter. And now to be so rewarded! 'I wish with all my heart,' says poor Fanny in her affectionate way, 'that we had asked your sisters instead of them.'"

Here he stopped to be thanked; which being done, he went on.

"What poor Mrs. Ferrars suffered, when first Fanny broke it to her, is not to be described. While she with the truest affection had been planning a most eligible connection[56] for him, was it to be supposed that he could be all the time secretly engaged to another person!—such a suspicion could never have entered her head! If she suspected *any* prepossession[57] elsewhere, it could not be in *that* quarter.[58] 'There, to be sure,' said she, 'I might have thought myself safe.' She was quite in an agony. We consulted together, however, as to what should be done, and at last she determined to send for Edward. He came. But I am sorry to relate what ensued. All that Mrs. Ferrars could say to make him put an end to the engagement, assisted too as you may well suppose by my arguments, and Fanny's entreaties, was of no avail. Duty,[59] affection,

53. *complicated:* involved, confused.

54. He calls him "Donavan" rather than "Mr. Donavan" as Mrs. Jennings does. This greater familiarity may be because he is the Dashwoods' family doctor, whereas Mrs. Jennings seems to know him only through his attendance on her daughter, or it may reflect John Dashwood's greater status consciousness. People generally used "Mr." or "Miss/Mrs." when speaking of or to social equals, but only last names for social inferiors. The great majority of medical practitioners were not considered gentlemen; physicians, the only ones to receive a formal education, were an exception, but they were few in number and consulted only for special cases, so an ordinary practitioner like Mr. Donavan would not be one. At the same time, since they were not drastically inferior, characters in Jane Austen sometimes use "Mr." when referring to medical men.

55. In fact, the real reason she invited the Miss Steeles was to give herself a good excuse not to invite the Miss Dashwoods (see pp. 472–474).

56. *eligible connection:* desirable or suitable match.

57. *prepossession:* predisposition.

58. Meaning she thought it would be in Elinor's quarter.

59. Duty to parents was an important principle in this society.

every thing was disregarded. I never thought Edward so stubborn, so unfeeling before. His mother explained to him her liberal[60] designs, in case of his marrying Miss Morton; told him she would settle on him the Norfolk estate,[61] which, clear of land-tax, brings in a good thousand a-year;[62] offered even, when matters grew desperate, to make it twelve hundred;[63] and in opposition to this, if he still persisted in this low[64] connection, represented to him the certain penury that must attend the match. His own two thousand pounds she protested should be his all; she would never see him again; and so far would she be from affording[65] him the smallest assistance, that if he were to enter into any profession with a view of better support, she would do all in her power to prevent his advancing in it."[66]

Here Marianne, in an ecstacy of indignation, clapped her hands together, and cried, "Gracious God! can this be possible!"

"Well may you wonder, Marianne," replied her brother, "at the obstinacy which could resist such arguments as these. Your exclamation is very natural."

Marianne was going to retort, but she remembered her promises, and forbore.[67]

"All this, however," he continued, "was urged in vain. Edward said very little; but what he did say, was in the most determined manner. Nothing should prevail on him to give up his engagement. He would stand to it, cost him what it might."[68]

"Then," cried Mrs. Jennings with blunt sincerity, no longer able to be silent, "he has acted like an honest man! I beg your pardon, Mr. Dashwood, but if he had done otherwise, I should have thought him a rascal. I have some little concern in the business, as well as yourself, for Lucy Steele is my cousin, and I believe there is not a better kind of girl in the world, nor one who more deserves a good husband."[69]

John Dashwood was greatly astonished; but his nature was calm, not open to provocation, and he never wished to offend anybody, especially anybody of good fortune. He therefore replied without any resentment,

"I would by no means speak disrespectfully of any relation of

60. *liberal:* generous (in a financial sense).

61. She would transfer legal ownership of the estate to him. Norfolk is a county in eastern England (see map p. 738).

62. The land tax had been a basic feature of English taxation since the late seventeenth century. In 1798 the government's urgent need for money to finance the war with France led it to allow owners to free land permanently from the tax through the payment of a large lump sum. The size of the sum kept most owners from seizing the opportunity. But where they had, as here, and the land was consequently clear and free of the tax, its value would be considerably greater, for the annual rate of the tax was 20% of the assessed value of the land (though in practice it was often less, since the assessments were antiquated and tended to understate the value). The issue of taxation would tend to be on people's minds when making financial calculations, especially if they were as concerned with money as John Dashwood, for taxes of various kinds had risen to unprecedented rates at this time due to the government's need to finance the long and difficult war against Napoleonic France.

63. Their inclination is to assume that the amount of money is all that matters. The additional two hundred would presumably come from a transfer of other assets, such as government bonds, to Edward.

64. *low:* socially inferior.

65. *affording:* providing.

66. Since professional advancement was frequently determined by patronage and personal connections, such a threat could be significant, depending on Mrs. Ferrars's connections in a particular profession.

67. Another sign of Marianne's incipient reformation.

68. Edward displays great strength of character here, though he does it in his usual quiet way. This episode is one of the only places in the novel where he is able to demonstrate the qualities that make him worthy of Elinor's love.

69. In praising Lucy Mrs. Jennings reveals her intellectual limitations, even as her defense of Edward shows her moral integrity and decency.

yours, madam. Miss Lucy Steele is, I dare say, a very deserving young woman, but in the present case you know, the connection must be impossible. And to have entered into a secret engagement with a young man under her uncle's care, the son of a woman especially of such very large fortune as Mrs. Ferrars, is perhaps altogether a little extraordinary.[70] In short, I do not mean to reflect upon the behaviour of any person whom you have a regard for, Mrs. Jennings. We all wish her extremely happy, and Mrs. Ferrars's conduct throughout the whole, has been such as every conscientious, good mother, in like circumstances, would adopt. It has been dignified and liberal. Edward has drawn his own lot, and I fear it will be a bad one."

Marianne sighed out her similar apprehension; and Elinor's heart wrung for the feelings of Edward, while braving his mother's threats, for a woman who could not reward him.

"Well, sir," said Mrs. Jennings, "and how did it end?"[71]

"I am sorry to say, ma'am, in a most unhappy rupture:— Edward is dismissed for ever from his mother's notice.[72] He left her house yesterday, but where he is gone or whether he is still in town, I do not know; for *we* of course can make no inquiry."

"Poor young man!—and what is to become of him?"

"What, indeed, ma'am! It is a melancholy consideration. Born to the prospect of such affluence! I cannot conceive a situation more deplorable. The interest of two thousand pounds—how can a man live on it![73]—and when to that is added the recollection, that he might, but for his own folly, within three months have been in the receipt of two thousand, five hundred a-year, (for Miss Morton has thirty thousand pounds,)[74] I cannot picture to myself a more wretched condition. We must all feel for him; and the more so, because it is totally out of our power to assist him."

"Poor young man!" cried Mrs. Jennings, "I am sure he should be very welcome to bed and board at my house; and so I would tell him if I could see him. It is not fit that he should be living about at his own charge now, at lodgings and taverns."[75]

Elinor's heart thanked her for such kindness towards Edward, though she could not forbear smiling at the form of it.

70. His idea is that respect for high social rank and wealth should have added to her scruples about undertaking a secret engagement. This idea of respect for rank was a basic part of this society, though most people would not go as far as John Dashwood in arguing that this meant owing such a signifi-cant extra obligation to someone simply because he or she was of high rank.

71. Mrs. Jennings's curiosity has now returned, superseding her moral indig-nation.

72. *notice*: favor; acknowledgment as her son.

73. The interest would be one hundred pounds a year, and from the per-spective of those in the genteel class this would be a paltry sum. Among other things, it would virtually preclude having a servant, which was regarded as a basic necessity. In a letter Jane Austen comments on a recently married cou-ple who lived "without keeping a servant of any kind.—What a prodigious innate love of virtue she must have, to marry under such circumstances!" (Oct. 27, 1798).

74. Her thirty thousand pounds would produce fifteen hundred a year in income, to be added to the thousand a year promised by Mrs. Ferrars. John Dashwood may have temporarily forgotten about Mrs. Ferrars's offer to raise the sum to twelve hundred, or he may simply find two thousand, five hun-dred an easier figure than two thousand, seven hundred. In either case, the difference between that and a hundred pounds is substantial.

75. Mrs. Jennings is naturally inclined to think of such prosaic matters, at a time when Edward is probably too absorbed in larger issues to worry about that.

"If he would only have done as well by himself," said John Dashwood, "as all his friends were disposed to do by him, he might now have been in his proper situation, and would have wanted for nothing. But as it is, it must be out of anybody's power to assist him. And there is one thing more preparing against him, which must be worse than all—his mother has determined, with a very natural kind of spirit, to settle *that* estate upon Robert immediately, which might have been Edward's, on proper conditions. I left her this morning with her lawyer, talking over the business."

"Well!" said Mrs. Jennings, "that is *her* revenge. Everybody has a way of their own. But I don't think mine would be, to make one son independent, because another had plagued me."[76]

Marianne got up, and walked about the room.

"Can any thing be more galling to the spirit of a man," continued John, "than to see his younger brother in possession of an estate which might have been his own? Poor Edward! I feel for him sincerely."[77]

A few minutes more spent in the same kind of effusion, concluded his visit; and with repeated assurances to his sisters that he really believed there was no material danger in Fanny's indisposition, and that they need not therefore be very uneasy about it, he went away; leaving the three ladies unanimous in their sentiments on the present occasion, as far at least as it regarded Mrs. Ferrars's conduct, the Dashwoods' and Edward's.

Marianne's indignation burst forth as soon as he quitted the room; and as her vehemence made reserve impossible in Elinor, and unnecessary in Mrs. Jennings,[78] they all joined in a very spirited critique upon the party.

76. This shrewd statement indicates the practical blindness induced by Mrs. Ferrars's anger and foreshadows a crucial plot development.

77. As an only son who inherited almost all his family's property, John Dashwood is inclined to see this as particularly tragic.

78. Elinor is naturally inclined to remain composed and reserved, but with her strong affection for Edward she cannot remain silent when her sister is voicing her own feelings of indignation on his behalf. Politeness would require Mrs. Jennings not to criticize the relatives of Elinor and Marianne in their presence, but when one of them begins the denunciation Mrs. Jennings is no longer bound by such a rule.

Contemporary hats and headdresses.

[From *The Repository of arts, literature, fashions, manufactures, &c*, Vol. V (1811), p. 361]

Chapter Two

Mrs. Jennings was very warm in her praise of Edward's conduct, but only Elinor and Marianne understood its true merit. They only knew how little he had had to tempt him to be disobedient, and how small was the consolation, beyond the consciousness of doing right, that could remain to him in the loss of friends and fortune. Elinor gloried in his integrity; and Marianne forgave all his offences in compassion for his punishment. But though confidence[1] between them was, by this public discovery,[2] restored to its proper state, it was not a subject on which either of them were fond of dwelling when alone. Elinor avoided it upon principle, as tending to fix still more upon her thoughts, by the too warm, too positive assurances of Marianne, that belief of Edward's continued affection for herself which she rather wished to do away;[3] and Marianne's courage soon failed her, in trying to converse upon a topic which always left her more dissatisfied with herself than ever, by the comparison it necessarily produced between Elinor's conduct and her own.

She felt all the force of that comparison; but not as her sister had hoped, to urge her to exertion now; she felt it with all the pain of continual self-reproach, regretted most bitterly that she had never exerted herself before; but it brought only the torture of penitence, without the hope of amendment. Her mind was so much weakened that she still fancied present exertion impossible, and therefore it only dispirited her more.[4]

Nothing new was heard by them, for a day or two afterwards, of affairs in Harley-street, or Bartlett's Buildings.[5] But though so much of the matter was known to them already, that Mrs. Jennings might have had enough to do in spreading that knowledge farther, without seeking after more, she had resolved from the first to pay a visit of comfort and inquiry to her cousins as soon as she

1. *confidence:* intimacy—based upon fully confiding in each other.

2. *discovery:* disclosure.

3. Elinor probably doesn't want to think about Edward's continued affection for her because it will make her regret her loss of him. This is a change from earlier, when she drew consolation from his continued regard. It may be that Edward and Lucy's apparent determination to stick to their engagement, despite all opposition, has convinced Elinor of its inevitability, whereas before she harbored a hope that something would occur to terminate it. Thus she now finds it best to cease considering the matter. She may also feel, with Edward firmly committed to Lucy, that any affection on his part for another woman is wrong.

4. This represents a relapse from the previous chapter, when Marianne resolved to act better and showed some progress in conversations with Mrs. Jennings and John Dashwood. It now appears her improvement was mostly due to Elinor's urging, at a point when Marianne was especially susceptible. A more persistent and lasting reformation must wait for further stimulus.

5. Harley Street is where the Dashwoods live, and Bartlett's Buildings is the residence of the Steeles' cousins. They have evidently returned there after being ejected from the Dashwoods'.

could;[6] and nothing but the hindrance of more visitors than usual, had prevented her going to them within that time.[7]

The third day succeeding their knowledge of the particulars, was so fine, so beautiful a Sunday as to draw many to Kensington Gardens,[8] though it was only the second week in March. Mrs. Jennings and Elinor were of the number; but Marianne, who knew that the Willoughbys were again in town, and had a constant dread of meeting them, chose rather to stay at home, than venture into so public a place.

An intimate acquaintance of Mrs. Jennings joined them soon after they entered the Gardens, and Elinor was not sorry that by her continuing with them, and engaging all Mrs. Jennings's conversation, she was herself left to quiet reflection. She saw nothing of the Willoughbys, nothing of Edward, and for some time nothing of anybody who could by any chance whether grave or gay, be interesting to her. But at last she found herself with some surprise, accosted by Miss Steele, who, though looking rather shy, expressed great satisfaction in meeting them, and on receiving encouragement from the particular kindness of Mrs. Jennings, left her own party for a short time, to join their's. Mrs. Jennings immediately whispered to Elinor,

"Get it all out of her, my dear. She will tell you any thing if you ask. You see I cannot leave Mrs. Clarke."

It was lucky, however, for Mrs. Jennings's curiosity and Elinor's too, that she would tell any thing *without* being asked, for nothing would otherwise have been learnt.[9]

"I am so glad to meet you"; said Miss Steele, taking her familiarly by the arm—"for I wanted to see you of all things in the world." And then lowering her voice, "I suppose Mrs. Jennings has heard all about it. Is she angry?"

"Not at all, I believe, with you."

"That is a good thing. And Lady Middleton, is *she* angry?"

"I cannot suppose it possible that she should."

"I am monstrous glad of it.[10] Good gracious! I have had such a time of it! I never saw Lucy in such a rage in my life. She vowed at

6.   Meaning she is determined to acquire still more knowledge of the affair.

7.   It seems a little unlikely that Mrs. Jennings, given her craving for more news of Lucy, would not have managed to visit them at least briefly during a two-day period. But it does make Elinor the one who hears Anne Steele's story, thus allowing it to be told at second- rather than thirdhand.

8.   Kensington Gardens are extensive grounds, basically forming one large park, next to Kensington Palace in what was then the western edge of London (see map, p. 740). They had been developed during the eighteenth century to adjoin Kensington Palace, which was the principal royal residence from 1690 to 1760. Kensington Gardens contained numerous walks and were popular, both for exercise and fresh air and for seeing and meeting others. They were far enough from the main residential areas of the time that most people would use a carriage to get there.

9.   Elinor would not have asked, despite her genuine curiosity, because it would have been impolite to inquire about personal affairs.

10. She is worried about their anger; that is why she looked uncharacteristically shy when she first saw Elinor. The dependence of her and her sister on others' hospitality, and their assiduous efforts to court Mrs. Jennings and the Middletons, make her fearful of upsetting them. She may assume that because John and Fanny Dashwood are furious, other wealthy people will also be offended by Lucy's attempt to marry someone above her rank.

People of the time promenading in Hyde Park, which adjoins Kensington Gardens.

[From Max von Boehn, *Modes & Manners of the Nineteenth Century*, Vol. I (London, 1909), p. 81]

first she would never trim me up a new bonnet,[11] nor do any thing else for me again, so long as she lived; but now she is quite come to, and we are as good friends as ever. Look, she made me this bow to my hat, and put in the feather last night.[12] There now, *you* are going to laugh at me too. But why should not I wear pink ribbons?[13] I do not care if it *is* the Doctor's favourite colour. I am sure, for my part, I should never have known he *did* like it better than any other colour, if he had not happened to say so. My cousins have been so plaguing me!—I declare sometimes I do not know which way to look before them."

She had wandered away to a subject on which Elinor had nothing to say, and therefore soon judged it expedient to find her way back again to the first.

"Well, but Miss Dashwood," speaking triumphantly, "people may say what they chuse about Mr. Ferrars's declaring he would not have Lucy, for it's no such a thing I can tell you; and it's quite a shame for such ill-natured reports to be spread abroad.[14] Whatever Lucy might think about it herself,[15] you know, it was no business of other people to set it down for[16] certain."

"I never heard anything of the kind hinted at before, I assure you," said Elinor.

"Oh! did not you? But it *was* said, I know, very well, and by more than one; for Miss Godby told Miss Sparks, that nobody in their senses could expect Mr. Ferrars to give up a woman like Miss Morton, with thirty thousand pounds to her forture, for Lucy Steele that had nothing at all; and I had it from Miss Sparks myself. And besides that, my cousin Richard said himself, that when it came to the point, he was afraid Mr. Ferrars would be off;[17] and when Edward did not come near us for three days,[18] I could not tell what to think myself; and I believe in my heart Lucy gave it up all for lost; for we came away from your brother's Wednesday, and we saw nothing of him not all Thursday, Friday, and Saturday, and did not know what was become with him. Once Lucy thought to write to him, but then her spirit rose against that.[19] However this morning he came just as we came home from church;[20] and then it all came out, how he had been

11. To trim a bonnet or hat was to decorate it. This was a common practice, especially among women who were less wealthy, since it was cheaper to embellish a plain bonnet or hat than to buy one that already had elaborate decorations. Jane Austen refers to trimming hats in her letters. In one she mentions a place where one can buy hats cheaply, while also discussing the popularity of flowers and fruit as decorations and the various types of fruit being used. For a contemporary picture of various hats and headdresses, see p. 499.

12. Bows, or ribbons, and feathers were two of the most popular trimmings to add to hats. Lucy's renewed affection for her sister probably resulted from her learning of Edward's fidelity to their engagement, which means that Anne's mistake in revealing it has not turned out to be so harmful to Lucy.

13. If she is wearing a feather bow, a common style at the time, the ribbons would be part of it.

14. *abroad*: at large, among people in general.

15. This suggests Lucy thought Edward would abandon their engagement, a point made more explicitly by her sister in her next speech. Lucy's own greedy nature and lack of scruples probably made it hard for her to imagine someone else making such a great monetary sacrifice out of honor, especially as she already was aware of Edward's lack of real affection for her.

16. *set it down for*: reckon or determine it as.

17. This shows how widespread the assumption was that a man would never sacrifice so much financially when he had a choice—and thus it reveals how courageous and honorable Edward's behavior is.

18. Her use of Edward's first name is fairly familiar for someone who is not a relative. She may feel justified by the public confirmation of Edward's engagement to her sister, for once they were married and he became Anne's brother-in-law she would use his first name. Most people, however, would wait until that happened.

19. Her spirit, or pride, rose against the idea of entreating him, especially as she seemed to assume at this point that he had decided to reject her.

20. All the characters in Austen's novels would attend church on a regular basis. She herself frequently went twice on Sundays. Edward may have appeared at this time because he knew they would be returning from church and he would be sure to find them. For a picture of a church service in London, see p. 521.

sent for Wednesday to Harley-street, and been talked to by his mother and all of them, and how he had declared before them all that he loved nobody but Lucy, and nobody but Lucy would he have. And how he had been so worried by what passed, that as soon as he had went away from his mother's house, he had got upon his horse, and rid into the country some where or other; and how he had staid about at an inn all Thursday and Friday, on pur- pose to get the better of it. And after thinking it all over and over again, he said, it seemed to him as if, now he had no fortune, and no nothing at all, it would be quite unkind to keep her on to the engagement, because it must be for her loss, for he had nothing but two thousand pounds, and no hope of any thing else; and if he was to go into orders,[21] as he had some thoughts, he could get nothing but a curacy,[22] and how was they to live upon that? — He could not bear to think of her doing no better, and so he begged, if she had the least mind for it, to put an end to the matter directly, and leave him to shift for himself.[23] I heard him say all this as plain as could possibly be. And it was entirely for *her* sake, and upon *her* account, that he said a word about being off, and not upon his own. I will take my oath he never dropt a syllable of being tired of her, or of wishing to marry Miss Morton, or any- thing like it. But, to be sure, Lucy would not give ear to such kind of talking; so she told him directly (with a great deal about sweet and love, you know, and all that—Oh, la! one can't repeat such kind of things you know)—she told him directly, she had not the least mind in the world to be off, for she could live with him upon a trifle, and how little so ever he might have, she should be very glad to have it all, you know, or something of the kind.[24] So then he was monstrous happy, and talked on some time about what they should do, and they agreed he should take orders directly, and they must wait to be married till he got a living.[25] And just then I could not hear any more, for my cousin called from below to tell me Mrs. Richardson was come in her coach, and would take one of us to Kensington Gardens;[26] so I was forced to go into the room and interrupt them, to ask Lucy if she would like to go,[27] but she did not care to leave Edward; so I just run up stairs and

21. *go into orders*: become ordained as a clergyman. He said earlier he favored this profession, and his education at Oxford would help qualify him, for it and Cambridge, the other English university then, were principally devoted to training people for the church.

22. *curacy*: position as a curate, someone who performed the clerical duties for the clergyman actually holding the living (see p. 117, note 25). Curates received low salaries.

23. His account of his probable poverty and his indication that he would understand if she renounced him would be what a man should say to a woman under such circumstances, for an honorable man would not wish her to feel bound to a marriage that could cause her hardship. But the very stark picture he paints of their probable situation, along with his statement that she should end the matter "if she had the least mind for it," go beyond what honor would require, and probably stem from his hope that she will break the engagement. In fact, most people at the time, even those who expected Edward to remain true to his vow, would expect her to release him from his obligation, for holding him to it means forcing the person she ostensibly loves to make a terrible sacrifice—of his fortune, his social position, and his ties to his family.

24. Such a firm avowal of love would be important in convincing Edward to remain faithful, since Lucy knows that he could break their engagement if he wishes, even if it transgressed general ideas of proper behavior.

25. A living is a position as a clergyman for a parish, which he would be qualified to fill once he took orders, or became ordained.

26. Mrs. Richardson presumably had room for one more person and decided to offer one of them a place. The great distance from their lodgings to Kensington Gardens would necessitate going in a carriage (see map, p. 740). Riding in a carriage would also be socially prestigious, which is probably why Miss Steele is pleased to come, just as she would enjoy walking through Kensington Gardens, whose location at the western edge of London meant that it was popular among the wealthy, for they lived closer to the park than most in London and had carriages to drive them there.

27. She may ask Lucy rather than simply going herself from her contrition at having foolishly spilled Lucy's secret.

put on a pair of silk stockings,[28] and came off with the Richard-sons."

"I do not understand what you mean by interrupting them," said Elinor; "you were all in the same room together, were not you?"

"No, indeed, not us. La! Miss Dashwood, do you think people make love[29] when any body else is by? Oh for shame!—To be sure you must know better than that. (Laughing affectedly.)—No, no; they were shut up in the drawing-room together, and all I heard was only by listening at the door."

"How!" cried Elinor; "have you been repeating to me what you only learnt yourself by listening at the door? I am sorry I did not know it before; for I certainly would not have suffered you to give me particulars of a conversation which you ought not to have known yourself. How could you behave so unfairly by your sister?"[30]

"Oh, la! there is nothing in *that*. I only stood at the door, and heard what I could. And I am sure Lucy would have done just the same by me; for a year or two back, when Martha Sharpe and I had so many secrets together, she never made any bones of hiding in a closet, or behind a chimney-board,[31] on purpose to hear what we said."[32]

Elinor tried to talk of something else; but Miss Steele could not be kept beyond a couple of minutes, from what was uppermost in her mind.

"Edward talks of going to Oxford soon," said she, "but now he is lodging at No. ——, Pall Mall.[33] What an ill-natured woman his mother is, an't she? And your brother and sister were not very kind! However, I shan't say anything against them to *you*; and to be sure they did send us home in their own chariot,[34] which was more than I looked for. And for my part, I was all in a fright for fear your sister should ask us for the huswifes[35] she had gave us a day or two before; but however, nothing was said about them, and I took care to keep mine out of sight. Edward have got some busi-ness at Oxford, he says; so he must go there for a time; and after *that*, as soon as he can light upon[36] a Bishop, he will be

28. Stockings, which went to just above the knee and were fixed in place with a garter, were a basic part of a woman's wardrobe. Jane Austen refers to buying ones at various points in her letters. They could be cotton or wool as well as silk; the latter were more expensive, and Anne Steele's boasting of silk ones is probably because she and Lucy may not always have been able to afford silk. Silk was especially scarce, and therefore expensive, at this time due to the Napoleonic Wars.

29. *make love:* court, profess love.

30. The impropriety of eavesdropping is consistently upheld by the better characters in Jane Austen, along with a general respect for others' privacy and personal secrets. Elinor's willingness to remain silent about Lucy's engagement, despite the pain it causes, is one example of this sort of integrity. In *Pride and Prejudice* the heroine leaves the room rather than talking more to her sister, when she learns that this sister is ready to tell her information she was not meant to divulge, even though the information is of great importance to the heroine.

31. A closet usually meant a small room then. A chimney board was a large wooden panel placed in front of the hearth during the summer, when the fireplace was not being used.

32. This gives a sense of Lucy's moral character.

33. *Pall Mall:* a well-known and expensive street in London (see p. 369, note 54). Edward's lodging there does not suggest much effort at economizing, though, as his talk of going to Oxford indicates, he is staying in London only briefly. He may even have a friend who lives there and is willing to accommodate him for a few days.

34. *chariot:* small, enclosed carriage (see p. 341, note 26).

35. A huswife, or housewife, was a small case for needlework and sewing supplies. The ones here are the same as the needle books that were earlier mentioned as gifts from Fanny Dashwood (p. 474).

36. *light upon:* find, come across.

ordained.[37] I wonder what curacy he will get!—Good gracious! (giggling as she spoke) I'd lay my life I know what my cousins will say, when they hear of it. They will tell me I should write to the Doctor, to get Edward the curacy of his new living.[38] I know they will; but I am sure I would not do such a thing for all the world.—'La!' I shall say directly, 'I wonder how you could think of such a thing. *I* write to the Doctor, indeed!' "

"Well," said Elinor, "it is a comfort to be prepared against[39] the worst. You have got your answer ready."[40]

Miss Steele was going to reply on the same subject, but the approach of her own party made another more necessary.

"Oh, la! here come the Richardsons. I had a vast deal more to say to you, but I must not stay away from them not any longer. I assure you they are very genteel people.[41] He makes a monstrous deal of money, and they keep their own coach.[42] I have not time to speak to Mrs. Jennings about it myself, but pray tell her I am quite happy to hear she is not in anger against[43] us, and Lady Middleton the same; and if any thing should happen to take you and your sister away, and Mrs. Jennings should want company, I am sure we should be very glad to come and stay with her for as long a time as she likes. I suppose Lady Middleton won't ask us any more this bout.[44] Good bye; I am sorry Miss Marianne was not here. Remember me kindly to her. La! if you have not got your spotted muslin on!—I wonder you was not afraid of its being torn."[45]

Such was her parting concern; for after this, she had time only to pay her farewell compliments to Mrs. Jennings, before her company was claimed by Mrs. Richardson; and Elinor was left in possession of knowledge which might feed her powers of reflection some time, though she had learnt very little more than what had been already foreseen and foreplanned in her own mind. Edward's marriage with Lucy was as firmly determined on, and the time of its taking place remained as absolutely uncertain, as she had concluded it would be;—every thing depended, exactly after[46] her expectation, on his getting that preferment, of which, at present, there seemed not the smallest chance.[47]

37. A bishop was in charge of a diocese, a large region consisting of numerous parishes. The approval of a bishop was required to become ordained as a clergyman.

38. The doctor's new living would be his new position as clergyman for a parish; he, like many holders of a living, could hire a curate to perform the duties.

39. *against*: for.

40. Elinor means that it is good she is prepared for the terrible eventuality of being asked to write to the doctor and has her answer of "not for all the world" ready. Elinor is being ironic at Miss Steele's expense, since she knows that the latter eagerly hopes people will think her attachment to the doctor strong enough to justify asking her to write to him, and she would certainly love to send such a letter. The statement, like some others in the novel, indicates that Elinor, as generally serious and high-minded as she is, does have a sense of humor and can be witty.

41. It is possible that the Richardsons are not genteel, for their stopping at the Miss Steeles' current residence in Bartlett's Buildings to offer one of them a ride suggests they live in the vicinity, and that area was not inhabited mostly by those who were genteel. Nevertheless, they probably are wealthy, as many doing business in London became during this period.

42. Keeping a carriage indicated wealth, and a coach was the largest and most expensive of all carriages.

43. *in anger against*: angry with.

44. *bout*: time, i.e., this stay in London.

45. Muslin was a lightweight cotton fabric originally from India that had become extremely popular in Britain in the late eighteenth century and was the most widely used material for women's gowns during this period—a muslin meant a dress of this fabric. Muslin came in a variety of patterns and decorations; *Northanger Abbey*, on the subject of muslins, mentions "the spotted, the sprigged, the mull, or the jackonet." Muslin's delicate nature meant it was in danger of being torn.

46. *after*: according to.

47. The preferment would be his appointment to a clerical position. His chances seem remote because personal connections were vital for obtaining a living, and Edward, with his family turned against him, probably does not have any connections to assist him.

As soon as they returned to the carriage, Mrs. Jennings was eager for information; but as Elinor wished to spread as little as possible intelligence[48] that had in the first place been so unfairly obtained, she confined herself to the brief repetition of such simple particulars, as she felt assured that Lucy, for the sake of her own consequence, would chuse to have known. The continuance of their engagement, and the means that were to be taken for promoting its end, was all her communication; and this produced from Mrs. Jennings the following natural remark.

"Wait for his having a living!—aye, we all know how *that* will end;—they will wait a twelvemonth, and finding no good comes of it, will set down[49] upon a curacy of fifty pounds a-year, with the interest of his two thousand pounds, and what little matter[50] Mr. Steele and Mr. Pratt can give her.—Then they will have a child every year! and Lord help 'em! how poor they will be!—I must see what I can give them towards furnishing their house. Two maids and two men indeed!—as I talked of t'other day.—No, no, they must get a stout[51] girl of all works.[52]—Betty's sister would never do for them *now*."

The next morning brought Elinor a letter by the two-penny post[53] from Lucy herself. It was as follows:

Bartlett's Buildings, March.

I hope my dear Miss Dashwood will excuse the liberty I take of writing to her;[54] but I know your friendship for me will make you pleased to hear such a good account of myself and my dear Edward,[55] after all the troubles we have went through lately, therefore will make no more apologies, but proceed to say that, thank God! though we have suffered dreadfully, we are both quite well now, and as happy as we must always be in one another's love. We have had great trials, and great persecutions,[56] but however, at the same time, gratefully acknowledge many friends, yourself not the least among them, whose great kindness I shall always thankfully remember, as will Edward too, who I have told of it.[57] I am sure you will be glad to hear, as likewise dear Mrs. Jennings, I spent two

48. *intelligence*: news, information.

49. *set down*: settle down.

50. *matter*: amount.

51. *stout*: strong, robust.

52. A girl of all works would be the sole servant in a household and have to perform a variety of chores. Such servants would always be female, since women comprised the great majority of servants and were significantly cheaper than male servants—someone who could afford a male servant could probably afford two female ones, which would make far more sense on a budget. Among the tasks of such a servant would be cooking, cleaning, washing clothes, and waiting at table. The labor involved would require substantial strength, though even with that the mistress of the house would certainly have to help the servant with many of her tasks.

53. *two-penny post*: local London postal service (see p. 299, note 22).

54. She calls it a liberty because people usually wrote only to relatives and close friends, and Elinor has certainly not indicated any wish to correspond with Lucy. But correspondence between two women would not be considered improper, since there would be no danger of sexual misbehavior.

55. This suggests one motive of Lucy's letter: a wish of exulting in her triumph over Elinor with regard to Edward. Another motive appears toward the end.

56. Much of her language, such as "great trials, and great persecutions," is hackneyed, echoing both the Bible and romantic fiction.

57. Her sister, in reporting their conversation to Elinor, never described any mention of Elinor, which she presumably would have if it had occurred. Lucy, knowing Edward's affection for Elinor, would have had little reason to say anything good of her.

*happy hours with him yesterday afternoon, he would not hear of
our parting, though earnestly did I, as I thought my duty required,
urge him to it for prudence sake, and would have parted for ever on
the spot, would he consent to it;*[58] *but he said it should never be, he
did not regard*[59] *his mother's anger, while he could have my affections; our prospects are not very bright, to be sure, but we must wait,
and hope for the best; he will be ordained shortly, and should it ever
be in your power to recommend him to any body that has a living to
bestow, am very sure you will not forget us, and dear Mrs. Jennings
too, trust she will speak a good word for us to Sir John, or Mr.
Palmer, or any friend that may be able to assist us.*[60] *—Poor Anne
was much to blame for what she did, but she did it for the best, so I
say nothing; hope Mrs. Jennings won't think it too much trouble to
give us a call, should she come this way any morning, 'twould be a
great kindness, and my cousins would be proud to know her.*[61] *—My
paper reminds me to conclude,*[62] *and begging to be most gratefully
and respectfully remembered to her, and to Sir John, and Lady
Middleton, and the dear children, when you chance to see them,
and love to Miss Marianne,*

I am, &c. &c.

As soon as Elinor had finished it, she performed what she concluded to be its writer's real design, by placing it in the hands of
Mrs. Jennings, who read it aloud with many comments of satisfaction and praise.

"Very well indeed!—how prettily she writes!—aye, that was
quite proper to let him be off if he would. That was just like
Lucy.—Poor soul! I wish I could get him a living with all my
heart.—She calls me dear Mrs. Jennings, you see. She is a good-
hearted girl as ever lived.—Very well upon my word. That sentence is very prettily turned. Yes, yes, I will go and see her, sure
enough. How attentive she is, to think of every body![63] —Thank
you, my dear, for shewing it me. It is as pretty a letter as ever I saw,
and does Lucy's head and heart great credit."

58. This is the direct opposite of what Anne Steele reported, which was that Edward encouraged Lucy to drop the engagement for her sake if she wished, and that Lucy insisted on maintaining it.

59. *regard:* heed or fear.

60. As already mentioned, personal recommendations played a central role in procuring livings.

61. Her humble phrasing suggests the lower status of her cousins, who probably would be happy to know, or become friendly with, someone of higher status like Mrs. Jennings. It also suggests Lucy's wish to appeal to Mrs. Jennings, whom she has just called "dear." Lucy, knowing where Elinor is staying, would assume that Mrs. Jennings would also see the letter, for letters were often shared among members of the same household. Writing to Elinor allows her to flatter Mrs. Jennings in a way that is less awkward than if she were writing to the latter directly.

62. This means she is running out of space on her sheet of paper. Paper was expensive then, and postage was determined by the number of sheets sent in each letter. Therefore people tried to minimize the sheets used: in her own letters Jane Austen at various times wrote between existing lines, wrote new lines perpendicular to existing ones, and wrote in blank spaces near the address, all to fit more writing on a given number of sheets.

63. Mrs. Jennings's response shows her susceptibility to flattery, and thus the shrewdness of Lucy in appealing to her in this way.

Chapter Three

*T*he Miss Dashwoods had now been rather more than two months in town, and Marianne's impatience to be gone increased every day. She sighed for the air,[1] the liberty, the quiet of the country; and fancied that if any place could give her ease, Barton must do it. Elinor was hardly less anxious than herself for their removal, and only so much less bent on its being effected immediately, as that she was conscious of the difficulties of so long a journey, which Marianne could not be brought to acknowledge.[2] She began, however, seriously to turn her thoughts towards its accomplishment, and had already mentioned their wishes to their kind hostess, who resisted them with all the eloquence of her good-will,[3] when a plan was suggested, which, though detaining them from home yet a few weeks longer, appeared to Elinor altogether[4] much more eligible[5] than any other. The Palmers were to remove to Cleveland about the end of March, for the Easter holidays;[6] and Mrs. Jennings, with both her friends, received a very warm invitation from Charlotte to go with them. This would not, in itself, have been sufficient for the delicacy[7] of Miss Dashwood;—but it was inforced[8] with so much real politeness by Mr. Palmer himself, as, joined to the very great amendment of his manners towards them since her sister had been known to be unhappy, induced her to accept it with pleasure.[9]

When she told Marianne what she had done, however, her first reply was not very auspicious.

"Cleveland!"—she cried, with great agitation. "No, I cannot go to Cleveland."—

"You forget," said Elinor, gently, "that its situation is not . . . that it is not in the neighbourhood of. . . ."[10]

"But it is in Somersetshire.—I cannot go into Somersetshire.—

1.   London was known for the poor quality of its air, which was considered unhealthful as well as unpleasant, for medical opinion attributed many ailments to bad air.

2.   It took them two and a half days to reach London from Barton, and their return will be more difficult, since Mrs. Jennings has not indicated an intention of going to Barton (as mentioned later, the Middletons are remaining in London, so she would have no good reason to go there now). This means they will have to pay for transportation and find a chaperone (see note 14 below).

3.   The phrasing suggests Mrs. Jennings lacks other forms of eloquence.

4.   *altogether*: on the whole.

5.   *eligible*: suitable, proper.

6.   Elinor saw Anne Steele in Kensington Gardens during the second week of March, so this would be in a few weeks (see chronology, p. 715).

7.   *delicacy*: refined sense of what is proper and becoming.

8.   *inforced*: enforced, i.e., seconded, reaffirmed.

9.   Elinor may have hesitated to accept Mrs. Palmer's invitation from a sense that she was asking them only as part of her invitation to Mrs. Jennings, or from a fear that Mrs. Palmer's word was unreliable due to her flightiness and her deference to her far less accommodating husband. In either case, Mr. Palmer's invitation, which was presumably made in a more rational and clearer fashion, would remove her hesitation.

10.   Elinor avoids saying Willoughby's name or the name of his estate, Combe Magna. She clearly knows that even their mention upsets her sister. In this Marianne contrasts with Elinor, who has always been able to speak and hear of Edward and Lucy with calmness.

There, where I looked forward to going . . . No, Elinor, you cannot expect me to go there."[11]

Elinor would not argue upon the propriety of overcoming such feelings;—she only endeavoured to counteract them by working on others;—and represented it, therefore, as a measure which would fix the time of her returning to that dear mother, whom she so much wished to see, in a more eligible, more comfortable[12] manner, than any other plan could do, and perhaps without any greater delay. From Cleveland, which was within a few miles of Bristol, the distance to Barton was not beyond one day, though a long day's journey;[13] and their mother's servant might easily come there to attend them down;[14] and as there could be no occasion for their staying above a week at Cleveland, they might now be at home in little more than three weeks time. As Marianne's affection for her mother was sincere, it must triumph, with little difficulty, over the imaginary evils she had started.[15]

Mrs. Jennings was so far from being weary of her guests, that she pressed them very earnestly to return with her again from Cleveland. Elinor was grateful for the attention, but it could not alter their design; and their mother's concurrence being readily gained, every thing relative to their return was arranged as far as it could be;—and Marianne found some relief in drawing up a statement of the hours, that were yet to divide her from Barton.

"Ah! Colonel, I do not know what you and I shall do without the Miss Dashwoods";—was Mrs. Jennings's address to him when he first called on her, after their leaving her was settled—"for they are quite resolved upon going home from the Palmers;—and how forlorn we shall be, when I come back!—Lord! we shall sit and gape at one another as dull[16] as two cats."

Perhaps Mrs. Jennings was in hopes, by this vigorous sketch of their future ennui, to provoke him to make that offer, which might give himself an escape from it;—and if so, she had soon afterwards good reason to think her object gained; for, on Elinor's moving to the window to take more expeditiously the dimensions of a print, which she was going to copy for her friend,[17] he followed her to it with a look of particular meaning, and conversed

11. Though both Cleveland and Combe Magna are in Somersetshire, they were earlier stated to be almost thirty miles apart (p. 210), a point Elinor was just trying to make.

12. *comfortable:* pleasant.

13. The distance is later described as eighty miles (p. 564). The standard travel speed on main roads was seven to eight miles an hour, so it would take a little more than ten hours. For the location of Bristol, a main port city at the time, see maps on pp. 738 and 739.

14. Since it was considered improper for unmarried young women to travel on their own, the male servant who worked for Mrs. Dashwood could accompany them. When two young women in *Pride and Prejudice* travel they use the same arrangement. The servant would take the public coach to reach Elinor and Marianne.

15. *started:* introduced.

16. *dull:* listless.

17. Copying prints was a common activity of those who drew; in fact, the long-standing method for teaching drawing was to have the student engage in continual copying from books. Mrs. Jennings may have expressed admiration for this print, one Elinor presumably purchased for herself. The copy Elinor is making would cost far less than another new print. She would move to the window because artificial light at this time was far too weak to be effective for drawing.

with her there for several minutes. The effect of his discourse on the lady too, could not escape her observation, for though she was too honourable to listen, and had even changed her seat, on purpose that she might not hear, to one close by the piano forté on which Marianne was playing,[18] she could not keep herself from seeing that Elinor changed colour, attended with agitation, and was too intent on what he said, to pursue her employment.[19]— Still farther in confirmation of her hopes, in the interval of Marianne's turning from one lesson[20] to another, some words of the Colonel's inevitably reached her ear, in which he seemed to be apologizing for the badness of his house. This set the matter beyond a doubt. She wondered indeed at his thinking it necessary to do so;—but supposed it to be the proper etiquette. What Elinor said in reply she could not distinguish, but judged from the motion of her lips that she did not think that any material objection;—and Mrs. Jennings commended her in her heart for being so honest. They then talked on for a few minutes longer without her catching a syllable, when another lucky stop in Marianne's performance brought her these words in the Colonel's calm voice,

"I am afraid it cannot take place very soon."

Astonished and shocked at so unlover-like a speech, she was almost ready to cry out, "Lord! what should hinder it?"—but checking her desire, confined herself to this silent ejaculation.

"This is very strange!—sure he need not wait to be older."—

This delay on the Colonel's side, however, did not seem to offend or mortify his fair companion in the least, for on their breaking up the conference soon afterwards, and moving different ways, Mrs. Jennings very plainly heard Elinor say, and with a voice which shewed her to feel what she said,

"I shall always think myself very much obliged to you."

Mrs. Jennings was delighted with her gratitude, and only wondered, that after hearing such a sentence, the Colonel should be able to take leave of them, as he immediately did, with the utmost sang-froid, and go away without making her any reply!—She had not thought her old friend could have made so indifferent a suitor.

18. Mrs. Jennings's refusal to listen, despite her insatiable curiosity, indicates she has some sense of honor and courtesy, despite her frequent disregard for the finer points of etiquette. It distinguishes her from the two Miss Steeles.

19. Meaning her copying of the print. Women often talked while pursuing various domestic employments, particularly embroidery.

20. *lesson:* exercise, piece (on the pianoforte).

A contemporary church service at St. Stephen, Walbrook, one of the many churches in the city of London designed by Sir Christopher Wren.

[From Fiona St. Aubyn, *Ackermann's Illustrated London*—illustrations by Augustus Pugin and Thomas Rowlandson (Ware, 1985), p. 29]

What had really passed between them was to this effect.

"I have heard," said he, with great compassion, "of the injustice your friend Mr. Ferrars has suffered from his family; for if I understand the matter right, he has been entirely cast off by them for persevering in his engagement with a very deserving young woman—Have I been rightly informed?—Is it so?"—

Elinor told him that it was.

"The cruelty, the impolitic cruelty,"—he replied, with great feeling—"of dividing, or attempting to divide, two young people long attached to each other, is terrible—Mrs. Ferrars does not know what she may be doing—what she may drive her son to. I have seen Mr. Ferrars two or three times in Harley-street, and am much pleased with him. He is not a young man with whom one can be intimately acquainted in a short time, but I have seen enough of him to wish him well for his own sake, and as a friend of yours, I wish it still more. I understand that he intends to take orders. Will you be so good as to tell him that the living of Delaford, now just vacant, as I am informed by this day's post,[21] is his, if he think it worth his acceptance[22]—But *that*, perhaps, so unfortunately circumstanced as he is now, it may be nonsense to appear to doubt,[23] I only wish it were more valuable.—It is a rectory, but a small one;[24] the late incumbent, I believe, did not make more than 200*l*. per annum, and though it is certainly capable of improvement, I fear, not to such an amount as to afford him a very comfortable income.[25] Such as it is, however, my pleasure in presenting him to it, will be very great. Pray assure him of it."[26]

Elinor's astonishment at this commission could hardly have been greater, had the Colonel been really making her an offer of his hand. The preferment, which only two days before she had considered as hopeless for Edward, was already provided to enable him to marry;—and *she*, of all people in the world, was fixed on to bestow it!—Her emotion was such as Mrs. Jennings had attributed to a very different cause;—but whatever minor feelings less pure, less pleasing, might have a share in that emotion, her esteem for the general benevolence, and her gratitude for the particular friendship, which together prompted Colonel Brandon

21. *post*: mail.

22. The living, or position as clergyman at Delaford, is controlled by Colonel Brandon. Wealthy landowners often controlled the livings of the parish where they resided, which meant they could appoint a new person whenever it became vacant, something that usually happened with the death of the existing holder. All that was required was for the appointee to be ordained and for the appointment to receive the consent of the bishop for the diocese, which was usually not a great barrier. Thus someone like Colonel Brandon was free to use this power to confer benefits on someone he liked, though most people controlling livings were conscientious enough to select someone they also thought would perform the duties adequately.

23. The normal etiquette would be for someone offering an appointment to express doubt about its acceptance, as a gesture of respect for the recipient, but he knows that in the present case such a gesture would be particularly artificial.

24. A rectory gave the holder the right to receive all the tithes in his parish. A vicarage, the other principal type of clerical position, gave the holder the right to receive only some of them. Thus rectories were generally better, but in some cases their income could be smaller than that of certain vicarages, since parishes varied greatly in the amount of tithes they could produce.

25. Most livings would provide more than two hundred pounds a year. To improve a living was to raise the tithes, often through reassessing property values to reflect recent improvements and thereby the amount of tithes owed. In a letter Jane Austen refers to her father's attempts to raise his tithes (Jan. 3, 1801).

26. Colonel Brandon's benevolence to someone he does not even know provides proof of his good character. This is valuable, since he, while playing an important role in the story, is absent or withdrawn for a good part of it.

to this act, were strongly felt, and warmly expressed. She thanked him for it with all her heart, spoke of Edward's principles and disposition[27] with that praise which she knew them to deserve; and promised to undertake the commission with pleasure, if it were really his wish to put off so agreeable an office[28] to another. But at the same time, she could not help thinking that no one could so well perform it as himself. It was an office in short, from which, unwilling to give Edward the pain of receiving an obligation from *her*, she would have been very glad to be spared herself;—but Colonel Brandon, on motives of equal delicacy, declining it likewise, still seemed so desirous of its being given through her means, that she would not on any account make farther opposition. Edward, she believed, was still in town, and fortunately she had heard his address from Miss Steele. She could undertake therefore to inform him of it, in the course of the day. After this had been settled, Colonel Brandon began to talk of his own advantage in securing so respectable and agreeable a neighbour, and *then* it was that he mentioned with regret, that the house was small and indifferent;[29]—an evil[30] which Elinor, as Mrs. Jennings had supposed her to do, made very light of, at least as far as regarded its size.

"The smallness of the house," said she, "I cannot imagine any inconvenience to them, for it will be in proportion to their family and income."

By which the Colonel was surprised to find that *she* was considering Mr. Ferrars's marriage as the certain consequence of the presentation;[31] for he did not suppose it possible that Delaford living could supply such an income, as any body in his style of life would venture to settle[32] on—and he said so.

"This little rectory *can* do no more than make Mr. Ferrars comfortable as a bachelor; it cannot enable him to marry. I am sorry to say that my patronage ends with this; and my interest[33] is hardly more extensive. If, however, by any unforeseen chance it should be in my power to serve him farther, I must think very differently of him from what I now do, if I am not as ready to be useful to him then, as I sincerely wish I could be at present. What I am now

27. *disposition:* mental tendencies or bent.

28. *put off so agreeable an office:* transfer so pleasant a task.

29. *indifferent:* of middling quality. A house, or parsonage, for the clergyman to reside in was a standard part of a living.

30. *evil:* difficulty.

31. *presentation:* conferral, bestowal (of the clerical position).

32. *settle:* marry, establish a married home.

33. *interest:* influence, especially through personal connections. He refers to his influence in the church.

doing indeed, seems nothing at all, since it can advance him so little towards what must be his principal, his only object of happiness. His marriage must still be a distant good;—at least, I am afraid it cannot take place very soon.—"

Such was the sentence which, when misunderstood, so justly offended the delicate feelings of Mrs. Jennings;[34] but after this narration of what really passed between Colonel Brandon and Elinor, while they stood at the window, the gratitude expressed by the latter on their parting, may perhaps appear in general, not less reasonably excited, nor less properly worded than if it had arisen from an offer of marriage.[35]

34. This is when Mrs. Jennings "was almost ready to cry out, 'Lord! what should hinder it?' " (p. 520).

35. Her final words were, "I shall always think myself very much obliged to you" (p. 520).

Chapter Four

"Well, Miss Dashwood," said Mrs. Jennings, sagaciously smiling, as soon as the gentleman had withdrawn, "I do not ask you what the Colonel has been saying to you; for though, upon my honour, I *tried* to keep out of hearing, I could not help catching enough to understand his business. And I assure you I never was better pleased in my life, and I wish you joy of it with all my heart."

"Thank you, ma'am," said Elinor. "It *is* a matter of great joy to me; and I feel the goodness of Colonel Brandon most sensibly.[1] There are not many men who would act as he has done. Few people who have so compassionate an heart! I never was more astonished in my life."

"Lord! my dear, you are very modest! I an't the least astonished at it in the world, for I have often thought of late, there was nothing more likely to happen."

"You judged from your knowledge of the Colonel's general benevolence; but at least you could not foresee that the opportunity would so very soon occur."[2]

"Opportunity!" repeated Mrs. Jennings—"Oh! as to that, when a man has once made up his mind to such a thing, somehow or other he will soon find an opportunity. Well, my dear, I wish you joy of it again and again; and if ever there was a happy couple in the world, I think I shall soon know where to look for them."[3]

"You mean to go to Delaford after them I suppose," said Elinor, with a faint smile.

"Aye, my dear, that I do, indeed. And as to the house being a bad one, I do not know what the Colonel would be at, for it is as good a one as ever I saw."[4]

"He spoke of its being out of repair."

1. *sensibly*: acutely.

2. No one could know when Colonel Brandon would be able to bestow the clerical living, because it would become available only upon the death or resignation, most likely the former, of the previous holder.

3. Mrs. Jennings's complete misunderstanding of what is really happening is something that often occurred in the fiction of the time. It was a favorite device of writers to create suspense or drama; sometimes it was even a principal engine of the plot. Jane Austen ridicules it in *Northanger Abbey* for its implausibility, so her use of it here conflicts with her normal procedure, especially since the sustained miscommunication between Elinor and Mrs. Jennings, in which each makes numerous statements without ever realizing that the other person is speaking of a completely different subject, strains credibility somewhat. The main difference in Jane Austen's use of this device is that she employs it purely to generate a brief comic episode, and it has no effect on the plot.

4. Elinor is talking about the parsonage house, and Mrs. Jennings of Colonel Brandon's own house.

"Well, and whose fault is that? why don't he repair it?—who should do it but himself?"

They were interrupted by the servant's coming in to announce the carriage being at the door; and Mrs. Jennings immediately preparing to go, said—

"Well, my dear, I must be gone before I have had half my talk out. But, however, we may have it all over in the evening, for we shall be quite alone. I do not ask you to go with me, for I dare say your mind is too full of the matter to care for company; and besides, you must long to tell your sister all about it."

Marianne had left the room before the conversation began.

"Certainly, ma'am, I shall tell Marianne of it; but I shall not mention it at present to any body else."

"Oh! very well," said Mrs. Jennings rather disappointed. "Then you would not have me tell it Lucy, for I think of going as far as Holborn to-day."

"No, ma'am, not even Lucy if you please. One day's delay will not be very material; and till I have written to Mr. Ferrars, I think it ought not to be mentioned to any body else. I shall do *that* directly. It is of importance that no time should be lost with him, for he will of course have much to do relative to his ordination."

This speech at first puzzled Mrs. Jennings exceedingly. Why Mr. Ferrars was to be written to about it in such a hurry, she could not immediately comprehend. A few moments' reflection, however, produced a very happy idea, and she exclaimed;—

"Oh ho!—I understand you. Mr. Ferrars is to be the man. Well, so much the better for him. Aye, to be sure, he must be ordained in readiness;[5] and I am very glad to find things are so forward[6] between you. But, my dear, is not this rather out of character? Should not the Colonel write himself?—sure, he is the proper person."

Elinor did not quite understand the beginning of Mrs. Jennings's speech; neither did she think it worth inquiring into; and therefore only replied to its conclusion.

"Colonel Brandon is so delicate a man, that he rather wished any one to announce his intentions to Mr. Ferrars than himself."

5. She thinks Edward will be the clergyman to perform the marriage ceremony, and for that he needs to be ordained. This is why she considers Elinor's talk of the matter a sign that the wedding is imminent, and why she
finds it odd that Colonel Brandon does not write to Edward.

6. *so forward*: at such an advanced stage.

*A bishop; he would be necessary for the ordination of Edward that Mrs. Jennings is
speaking of.*

[From William Pyne, *Costume of Great Britain* (London, 1804; 1989 reprint), Plate XXII]

"And so *you* are forced to do it. Well, *that* is an odd kind of delicacy! However, I will not disturb you (seeing her preparing to write.) You know your own concerns best. So good bye, my dear. I have not heard of any thing to please me so well since Charlotte was brought to bed."[7]

And away she went; but returning again in a moment,

"I have just been thinking of Betty's sister, my dear. I should be very glad to get her so good a mistress.[8] But whether she would do for a lady's maid, I am sure I can't tell.[9] She is an excellent housemaid, and works very well at her needle.[10] However, you will think of all that at your leisure."

"Certainly, ma'am," replied Elinor, not hearing much of what she said, and more anxious to be alone, than to be mistress of the subject.

How she should begin—how she should express herself in her note to Edward, was now all her concern. The particular circumstances between them made a difficulty of that which to any other person would have been the easiest thing in the world; but she equally feared to say too much or too little, and sat deliberating over her paper, with the pen in her hand,[11] till broken in on by the entrance of Edward himself.

He had met Mrs. Jennings at the door in her way to the carriage, as he came to leave his farewell card;[12] and she, after apologising for not returning herself, had obliged him to enter, by saying that Miss Dashwood was above, and wanted to speak with him on very particular business.

Elinor had just been congratulating herself, in the midst of her perplexity, that however difficult it might be to express herself properly by letter, it was at least preferable to giving the information by word of mouth, when her visitor entered, to force her upon this greatest exertion of all.[13] Her astonishment and confusion were very great on his so sudden appearance. She had not seen him before since his engagement became public, and therefore not since his knowing her to be acquainted with it; which, with the consciousness of what she had been thinking of, and what she had to tell him, made her feel particularly uncomfort-

7. *was brought to bed:* had her child.

8. Earlier Mrs. Jennings thought of Betty's sister when she was speculating about a servant for Edward and Lucy (see pp. 480–482, and p. 483, note 24). Thus she shows a particular zeal for the paternalist assistance toward servants common in this society.

9. A lady's maid would dress and groom her mistress and take care of her clothes. It was a high-ranking position, for it required knowledge of clothes and fashion, skill at hairdressing, and, since she would be closer to her mistress than a typical servant, some education and relatively polished speech and manners. This is why Mrs. Jennings wonders if Betty's sister would be suited for the job. At present Elinor lacks a lady's maid, since her mother's household has only three servants and they would be needed for more essential chores. But if married to Colonel Brandon she would be in a position to hire one.

10. A housemaid's principal job was cleaning the house, but she was also frequently expected to do sewing or needlework.

11. Elinor's writing to Edward raises no problem of impropriety, in contrast to Marianne's writing to Willoughby, because of her family connection with Edward.

12. Leaving his farewell card would, like leaving his visiting card when arriving in a place, be a sign of respect and friendship. His interest in speaking to Elinor before his departure from London is a mark of his regard for her. His departure from London, already mentioned, would be a logical move in his new circumstances, for living there was more expensive. He will struggle to live on his remaining income, especially after being used to luxuries like frequent travel, his own horse, and a servant, also with his own horse, to attend him wherever he goes. It was undoubtedly an allowance from his mother, common for sons in wealthy families, that enabled him to afford all that.

13. Elinor is forced to undergo one more difficult test to her fortitude and self-command. This one is particularly difficult because she must give Edward news that makes his marriage to Lucy much more likely.

able for some minutes. He too was much distressed, and they sat down together in a most promising state of embarrassment.— Whether he had asked her pardon for his intrusion on first coming into the room, he could not recollect; but determining to be on the safe side, he made his apology in form as soon as he could say any thing, after taking a chair.

"Mrs. Jennings told me," said he, "that you wished to speak with me, at least I understood her so—or I certainly should not have intruded on you in such a manner; though at the same time, I should have been extremely sorry to leave London without seeing you and your sister; especially as it will most likely be some time—it is not probable that I should soon have the pleasure of meeting you again. I go to Oxford tomorrow."

"You would not have gone, however," said Elinor, recovering herself, and determined to get over what she so much dreaded as soon as possible, "without receiving our good wishes, even if we had not been able to give them in person. Mrs. Jennings was quite right in what she said. I have something of consequence to inform you of, which I was on the point of communicating by paper. I am charged with a most agreeable office, (breathing rather faster than usual as she spoke.) Colonel Brandon, who was here only ten minutes ago, has desired me to say that, understanding you mean to take orders, he has great pleasure in offering you the living of Delaford, now just vacant, and only wishes it were more valuable. Allow me to congratulate you on having so respectable and well-judging a friend, and to join in his wish that the living—it is about two hundred a-year—were much more considerable,[14] and such as might better enable you to—as might be more than a temporary accommodation to yourself[15]—such in short, as might establish all your views[16] of happiness."[17]

What Edward felt, as he could not say it himself, it cannot be expected that any one else should say for him. He *looked* all the astonishment which such unexpected, such unthought-of information could not fail of exciting; but he said only these two words,

"Colonel Brandon!"[18]

"Yes," continued Elinor, gathering more resolution, as some of

14. Her statement of congratulation is very formal, echoing the language found in official communications. She may be falling back on standard wording to restrain her emotions.

15. The halting nature of her speech indicates how difficult and painful this is for her.

16. *views:* expectations, plans.

17. "Establishing all one's views of happiness" was a standard formulation for speaking about the prospect of marriage.

18. The reason for his emphatic utterance of this name, and nothing else, upon hearing the news will become clearer.

the worst was over; "Colonel Brandon means it as a testimony of his concern for what has lately passed—for the cruel situation in which the unjustifiable conduct of your family has placed you—a concern which I am sure Marianne, myself, and all your friends must share; and likewise as a proof of his high esteem for your general character, and his particular approbation of your behaviour on the present occasion."

"Colonel Brandon give *me* a living!—Can it be possible?"

"The unkindness of your own relations has made you astonished to find friendship any where."

"No," replied he, with sudden consciousness, "not to find it in *you*; for I cannot be ignorant that to you, to your goodness I owe it all.—I feel it—I would express it if I could[19]—but, as you well know, I am no orator."

"You are very much mistaken. I do assure you that you owe it entirely, at least almost entirely, to your own merit, and Colonel Brandon's discernment of it. I have had no hand in it. I did not even know, till I understood his design, that the living was vacant; nor had it ever occurred to me that he might have had such a living in his gift. As a friend of mine, of my family, he may perhaps—indeed I know he *has*, still greater pleasure in bestowing it; but, upon my word, you owe nothing to my solicitation."

Truth obliged her to acknowledge some small share in the action, but she was at the same time so unwilling to appear as the benefactress of Edward, that she acknowledged it with hesitation; which probably contributed to fix that suspicion in his mind which had recently entered it.[20] For a short time he sat deep in thought, after Elinor had ceased to speak;—at last, and as if it were rather an effort, he said,

"Colonel Brandon seems a man of great worth and respectability. I have always heard him spoken of as such, and your brother I know esteems him highly. He is undoubtedly a sensible man, and in his manners perfectly the gentleman."[21]

"Indeed," replied Elinor, "I believe that you will find him, on farther acquaintance, all that you have heard him to be; and as you will be such very near neighbours, (for I understand the par-

19. It is notable that he begins to stumble over his words just after expressing his conviction that Elinor is the source of this unexpected benefit.

20. His statements have already hinted at what this suspicion might be, and further clues will shortly appear.

21. His thanks are very formal, and while complimenting Colonel Brandon's general character, he never expresses any actual satisfaction or pleasure regarding what the colonel has done for him.

sonage is almost close to the mansion-house,)[22] it is particularly important that he *should* be all this."

Edward made no answer; but when she had turned away her head, gave her a look so serious, so earnest, so uncheerful, as seemed to say, that he might hereafter wish the distance between the parsonage and the mansion-house much greater.[23]

"Colonel Brandon, I think, lodges in St. James's-street," said he, soon afterwards, rising from his chair.[24]

Elinor told him the number of the house.

"I must hurry away then, to give him those thanks which you will not allow me to give *you*; to assure him that he has made me a very—an exceedingly happy man."

Elinor did not offer to detain him; and they parted, with a very earnest assurance on *her* side of her unceasing good wishes for his happiness in every change of situation that might befal him; on *his*, with rather an attempt to return the same good will, than the power of expressing it.

"When I see him again," said Elinor to herself, as the door shut him out, "I shall see him the husband of Lucy."[25]

And with this pleasing anticipation, she sat down to re-consider the past, recal the words and endeavour to comprehend all the feelings of Edward; and, of course, to reflect on her own with discontent.

When Mrs. Jennings came home, though she returned from seeing people whom she had never seen before, and of whom therefore she must have a great deal to say, her mind was so much more occupied by the important secret in her possession, than by anything else, that she reverted to it again as soon as Elinor appeared.

"Well, my dear," she cried, "I sent you up the young man. Did not I do right?—And I suppose you had no great difficulty—You did not find him very unwilling to accept your proposal?"

"No, ma'am; *that* was not very likely."

"Well, and how soon will he be ready?—For it seems all to depend upon that."

"Really," said Elinor, "I know so little of these kind of forms,

22. Mrs. Jennings earlier said the two were close in her description of Delaford (pp. 362–364). Such proximity was common, for the wealthiest landowner and the clergyman were normally the two leading figures in a rural parish, and there was usually a strong wish on both sides for a good working relationship.

23. His reason for wishing the two farther apart has already been suggested and will later be confirmed (p. 682): he believes Elinor will marry Colonel Brandon, and is jealous and naturally disinclined to be near the new couple. Elinor's close friendship with the colonel and frequent meetings with him would certainly make that plausible. Edward may have even heard a rumor to that effect, for Mrs. Jennings has been speculating about it already and would naturally spread the idea, and, if Lucy heard it, she would want to tell Edward, in order to drive the thought of Elinor from his head. Thus Edward attributes Colonel Brandon's gift to Elinor's influence and finds the idea of thanking him an awkward one. He also has a new reason for gloom.

24. Edward is conscientious enough that, after a pause, he rises still to go and perform the duty of thanking Colonel Brandon.

25. Elinor senses that the Delaford living will permit the marriage of Edward and Lucy, and she faces the unpleasant fact squarely and unhesitatingly.

that I can hardly even conjecture as to the time, or the preparation necessary; but I suppose two or three months will complete
his ordination."[26]

"Two or three months!" cried Mrs. Jennings; "Lord! my dear,
how calmly you talk of it; and can the Colonel wait two or three
months! Lord bless me! — I am sure it would put *me* quite out of
patience! — And though one would be very glad to do a kindness
by poor Mr. Ferrars, I do think it is not worth while to wait two or
three months for him. Sure, somebody else might be found that
would do as well; somebody that is in orders already."

"My dear ma'am," said Elinor, "what can you be thinking of? —
Why, Colonel Brandon's only object is to be of use[27] to Mr. Ferrars."

"Lord bless you, my dear! — Sure you do not mean to persuade
me that the Colonel only marries you for the sake of giving ten
guineas to Mr. Ferrars!"[28]

The deception could not continue after this; and an explanation immediately took place, by which both gained considerable
amusement for the moment, without any material loss of happiness to either, for Mrs. Jennings only exchanged one form of
delight for another, and still without forfeiting her expectation of
the first.[29]

"Aye, aye, the parsonage is but a small one," said she, after the
first ebullition of surprise and satisfaction was over, "and very
likely *may* be out of repair; but to hear a man apologising, as I
thought, for a house that to my knowledge has five sitting rooms
on the ground-floor,[30] and I think the housekeeper told me, could
make up fifteen beds![31] — and to you too, that had been used to
live in Barton cottage! — It seemed quite ridiculous. But, my dear,
we must touch up[32] the Colonel to do something to the parsonage, and make it comfortable for them,[33] before Lucy goes to it."

"But Colonel Brandon does not seem to have any idea of the
living's being enough to allow them to marry."

"The Colonel is a ninny, my dear; because he has two thousand
a-year himself, he thinks that nobody else can marry on less. Take

26. The principal step for becoming ordained was to pass an examination administered by a bishop. A candidate would need to locate a bishop and make arrangements for the examination, something that might take a little time but rarely many months.

27. *use:* benefit.

28. Ten guineas was the wedding officiant's fee. A guinea was a coin worth a pound and a shilling.

29. This means she still hopes for Elinor's marriage to Colonel Brandon.

30. "Sitting room" was a general term for a room in which people could socialize, play games, or engage in other indoor activities. Mrs. Dashwood's house has only two sitting rooms, and they are relatively small, so Colonel Brandon's house is on a much larger scale.

31. The large number of beds was not unusual for country houses. In addition to the sizable families that their inhabitants often had, the owners of the houses liked to be able to host friends and relatives for extended visits. This has already been seen with the lengthy stays of Mrs. Jennings and Colonel Brandon at the Middletons', or the earlier one of Mrs. Dashwood and her three daughters with John and Fanny Dashwood. The housekeeper, the leading female servant in a household, would be in charge of maintaining the beds, and thus the best person for someone as curious as Mrs. Jennings to ask in order to gather information about the house.

32. *touch up:* remind.

33. The patron of a clerical living was responsible for the construction and maintenance of the parsonage. Many parsonages were in poor shape, in part because the person responsible for their maintenance was not the person living in them. The resident of the house could spend money on it, but he would do so knowing that he could neither recoup his investment from selling the house nor pass it on to his descendants. Since Colonel Brandon's father and brother, the previous owners of Delaford and also the previous patrons of the living, were described as irresponsible and dissolute, it is likely that the house suffered neglect for a while.

my word for it, that, if I am alive, I shall be paying a visit at Delaford Parsonage before Michaelmas;[34] and I am sure I sha'nt go if Lucy an't there."

Elinor was quite of her opinion, as to the probability of their not waiting for any thing more.

34. *Michaelmas:* September 29. Mrs. Jennings's opinion of the possibility of marriage on such an income, however challenging it may be, has a basis in Jane Austen's own life, for when her parents married, her father's clerical position paid him less than two hundred.

Chapter Five

*E*dward, having carried his thanks to Colonel Brandon, proceeded with his happiness to Lucy; and such was the excess of it by the time he reached Bartlett's Buildings, that she was able to assure Mrs. Jennings, who called on her again the next day with her congratulations, that she had never seen him in such spirits[1] before in her life.

Her own happiness, and her own spirits, were at least very certain;[2] and she joined Mrs. Jennings most heartily in her expectation of their being all comfortably together in Delaford Parsonage before Michaelmas. So far was she, at the same time, from any backwardness[3] to give Elinor that credit which Edward *would* give her, that she spoke of her friendship for them both with the most grateful warmth, was ready to own[4] all their obligation to her, and openly declared that no exertion for their good on Miss Dashwood's part, either present or future, would ever surprise her, for she believed her capable of doing anything in the world for those she really valued. As for Colonel Brandon, she was not only ready to worship him as a saint, but was moreover truly anxious that he should be treated as one in all worldly concerns;[5] anxious that his tythes should be raised to the utmost;[6] and secretly resolved to avail herself, at Delaford, as far as she possibly could, of his servants, his carriage, his cows, and his poultry.[7]

It was now above a week since John Dashwood had called in Berkeley-street, and as since that time no notice had been taken by them of his wife's indisposition, beyond one verbal inquiry, Elinor began to feel it necessary to pay her a visit.—This was an obligation, however, which not only opposed her own inclination, but which had not the assistance of any encouragement from her companions. Marianne, not contented with absolutely

1. *in such spirits*: so elated.

2. The sentence implies that Edward's happiness was far from certain — for Lucy's report of his supposed elation can hardly be relied on.

3. *backwardness*: reluctance, disinclination.

4. *own*: acknowledge.

5. Meaning someone who in worldly, or monetary, matters was happy to renounce his own interest completely.

6. Since tithes were owed on the produce of property, a large landowner would naturally be a major source of them.

7. The proximity of the parsonage to Colonel Brandon's house would make such appropriation easier. In thinking of Colonel Brandon's livestock she probably hopes to get some of the eggs and milk; it would be unrealistic to expect even a generous man to give another family livestock he is raising for meat.

refusing to go herself, was very urgent to prevent her sister's going at all; and Mrs. Jennings, though her carriage was always at Elinor's service, so very much disliked Mrs. John Dashwood, that not even her curiosity to see how she looked after the late discovery,[8] nor her strong desire to affront her by taking Edward's part, could overcome her unwillingness to be in her company again. The consequence was, that Elinor set out by herself to pay a visit, for which no one could really have less inclination, and to run the risk of a tête-à-tête with a woman, whom neither of the others had so much reason to dislike.[9]

Mrs. Dashwood was denied; but before the carriage could turn from the house, her husband accidentally came out.[10] He expressed great pleasure in meeting Elinor, told her that he had been just going to call in Berkeley-street, and assuring her that Fanny would be very glad to see her, invited her to come in.

They walked up stairs into the drawing-room.—Nobody was there.

"Fanny is in her own room, I suppose," said he;—"I will go to her presently, for I am sure she will not have the least objection in the world to seeing *you*.—Very far from it indeed. *Now* especially there cannot be[11]—but however, you and Marianne were always great favourites.—Why would not Marianne come?"—

Elinor made what excuse she could for her.

"I am not sorry to see you alone," he replied, "for I have a good deal to say to you. This living of Colonel Brandon's—can it be true?—has he really given it to Edward?—I heard it yesterday by chance, and was coming to you on purpose to inquire farther about it."[12]

"It is perfectly true.—Colonel Brandon has given the living of Delaford to Edward."

"Really!—Well, this is very astonishing!—no relationship!—no connection between them!—and now that livings fetch such a price![13]—what was the value of this?"

"About two hundred a-year."

"Very well—and for the next presentation[14] to a living of that

8. *discovery:* disclosure (of Edward's engagement).

9. Elinor has particular reason for disliking her because of her previous rudeness to Elinor and her current harsh attitude toward Edward.

10. The servant at the door claimed that his mistress was not at home, a standard message from those not wishing to see someone. Elinor had come in Mrs. Jennings's carriage, and carriages could take a little time to turn around because of the need to maneuver the horses.

11. Since there is now no danger of a marriage between Elinor and Edward, Fanny no longer has a special reason to dislike Elinor—though John Dashwood refrains from saying that explicitly.

12. He has a reason for inquiring because he, his wife, and Mrs. Ferrars wish to see Edward renounce Lucy, and this gift to Edward makes that less likely.

13. Most livings were either granted to those with whom the presenter had a personal connection or family tie, or they were sold.

14. *presentation:* appointment.

value—supposing the late incumbent to have been old and sickly, and likely to vacate it soon—he might have got I dare say—fourteen hundred pounds.[15] And how came he not to have settled that matter before this person's death?[16]—Now indeed it would be too late to sell it, but a man of Colonel Brandon's sense!—I wonder he should be so improvident in a point of such common, such natural, concern!—Well, I am convinced that there is a vast deal of inconsistency in almost every human character. I suppose, however—on recollection—that the case may probably be *this*. Edward is only to hold the living till the person to whom the Colonel has really sold the presentation, is old enough to take it.[17]—Aye, aye, that is the fact, depend upon it."

Elinor contradicted it, however, very positively; and by relating that she had herself been employed in conveying the offer from Colonel Brandon to Edward, and therefore must understand the terms on which it was given, obliged him to submit to her authority.

"It is truly astonishing!"—he cried, after hearing what she said—"what could be the Colonel's motive?"

"A very simple one—to be of use to Mr. Ferrars."

"Well, well; whatever Colonel Brandon may be, Edward is a very lucky man!—You will not mention the matter to Fanny, however, for though I have broke it to her, and she bears it vastly well,—she will not like to hear it much talked of."

Elinor had some difficulty here to refrain from observing, that she thought Fanny might have borne with composure, an acquisition of wealth to her brother, by which neither she nor her child could be possibly impoverished.[18]

"Mrs. Ferrars," added he, lowering his voice to the tone becoming so important a subject, "knows nothing about it at present, and I believe it will be best to keep it entirely concealed from her as long as may be.—When the marriage takes place, I fear she must hear of it all."

"But why should such precaution be used?—Though it is not to be supposed that Mrs. Ferrars can have the smallest satisfaction in knowing that her son has money enough to live upon,—for

15. The right to appoint someone to a clerical living was a form of property. It could be passed to one's heir or sold, and there was an active market in livings. The normal price was five to seven times the annual income it generated. In this case, the incumbent was likely to die soon, which would make it more valuable because the new appointment could be made sooner, so John Dashwood's estimate is very accurate. He may have engaged in such transactions himself, or, being very concerned with money, may have taken the trouble to learn the value of various forms of property.

16. Once a living became vacant the right to appoint a new person could no longer be sold.

17. Often a wealthy person would purchase the right of presentation to a living in order to provide for a son or other young relative. If the living became available before the intended beneficiary was old enough to be ordained, then someone else would be hired for the intervening years; he would sign a contract allowing him to collect the income but requiring him to resign eventually.

18. Though Elinor's indignation is understandable, she is a little unfair in ascribing a purely malicious motive to Fanny. Edward's marriage to a woman without money or prestige would taint their entire family's social position. Thus Fanny and Mrs. Ferrars would dislike any development that would make Edward's marriage to Lucy more likely.

that must be quite out of the question; yet why, after her late behaviour, is she supposed to feel at all?—she has done with her son, she has cast him off for ever, and has made all those over whom she had any influence, cast him off likewise. Surely, after doing so, she cannot be imagined liable to any impression of sorrow or of joy on his account—she cannot be interested in any thing that befalls him.—She would not be so weak as to throw away the comfort of a child, and yet retain the anxiety of a parent!"

"Ah! Elinor," said John, "your reasoning is very good, but it is founded on ignorance of human nature.[19] When Edward's unhappy match takes place, depend upon it his mother will feel as much as if she had never discarded him; and therefore every circumstance that may accelerate that dreadful event, must be concealed from her as much as possible. Mrs. Ferrars can never forget that Edward is her son."

"You surprise me; I should think it must nearly have escaped her memory by *this* time."

"You wrong her exceedingly. Mrs. Ferrars is one of the most affectionate mothers in the world."

Elinor was silent.

"We think *now*"—said Mr. Dashwood, after a short pause, "of *Robert's* marrying Miss Morton."

Elinor, smiling at the grave and decisive importance of her brother's tone, calmly replied,

"The lady, I suppose, has no choice in the affair."

"Choice!—how do you mean?"—[20]

"I only mean, that I suppose from your manner of speaking, it must be the same to Miss Morton whether she marry[21] Edward or Robert."

"Certainly, there can be no difference; for Robert will now to all intents and purposes be considered as the eldest son;—and as to any thing else, they are both very agreeable young men, I do not know that one is superior to the other."

Elinor said no more, and John was also for a short time silent.—His reflections ended thus.

19. Elinor's speech is ironic, direct criticism being too impolite and too likely to strain her relationship with her brother. But irony is lost on him, and he treats her arguments as if she meant them seriously.

20. Here, in response to Elinor's irony, John Dashwood is so befuddled that he cannot even respond.

21. *whether she marry*: an example of the use of the subjunctive mood, which is more frequent in Jane Austen than in current English.

"Of *one* thing, my dear sister," kindly taking her hand, and speaking in an awful[22] whisper—"I may assure you;—and I *will* do it, because I know it must gratify you. I have good reason to think—indeed I have it from the best authority, or I should not repeat it, for otherwise it would be very wrong to say any thing about it—but I have it from the very best authority—not that I ever precisely heard Mrs. Ferrars say it herself—but her daughter *did*, and I have it from her[23]—That in short, whatever objections there might be against a certain—a certain connection[24]—you understand me—it would have been far preferable to her, it would not have given her half the vexation that *this* does. I was exceedingly pleased to hear that Mrs. Ferrars considered it in that light—a very gratifying circumstance you know to us all. 'It would have been beyond comparison,' she said, 'the least evil of the two, and she would be glad to compound[25] *now* for nothing worse.' But however, all that is quite out of the question—not to be thought of or mentioned—as to any attachment you know—it never could be—all that is gone by. But I thought I would just tell you of this, because I knew how much it must please you.[26] Not that you have any reason to regret, my dear Elinor. There is no doubt of your doing exceedingly well—quite as well, or better, perhaps, all things considered. Has Colonel Brandon been with you lately?"

Elinor had heard enough, if not to gratify her vanity, and raise her self-importance, to agitate her nerves and fill her mind;—and she was therefore glad to be spared from the necessity of saying much in reply herself, and from the danger of hearing any thing more from her brother, by the entrance of Mr. Robert Ferrars.[27] After a few moments' chat, John Dashwood, recollecting that Fanny was yet uninformed of his sister's being there, quitted the room in quest of her; and Elinor was left to improve her acquaintance with Robert, who, by the gay unconcern, the happy self-complacency of his manner while enjoying so unfair a division of his mother's love and liberality, to the prejudice of his banished brother, earned only by his own dissipated course of life,[28] and

22. *awful:* solemn, respectful.

23. The hesitating nature of his words indicates the respect, if not fear, with which he regards Mrs. Ferrars. He has already shown himself to be very deferential toward his wife, and his mother-in-law, with at least as forceful and acerbic a personality, greater age, and far more financial power, could inspire even greater obsequiousness.

24. The "certain connection" is Elinor's marriage to Edward.

25. *compound:* settle (especially as part of an agreement or exchange).

26. His naivety and obtuseness are shown by his belief that Elinor would take it as a compliment to be told that her marriage to Edward would be a lesser evil than Lucy's.

27. Robert's entrance has been announced by the servant, who uses the formal designation of Mr. Robert Ferrars.

28. Robert has already been shown associating with aristocratic and fashionable people in London, and many such people, especially young men, were known for their dissipated, i.e., dissolute and profligate, lifestyles.

that brother's integrity, was confirming her most unfavourable opinion of his head and heart.

They had scarcely been two minutes by themselves, before he began to speak of Edward; for he too had heard of the living, and was very inquisitive on the subject. Elinor repeated the particulars of it, as she had given them to John; and their effect on Robert, though very different, was not less striking than it had been on *him*. He laughed most immoderately. The idea of Edward's being a clergyman, and living in a small parsonage-house, diverted him beyond measure;—and when to that was added the fanciful imagery of Edward reading prayers in a white surplice,[29] and publishing[30] the banns of marriage between John Smith and Mary Brown,[31] he could conceive nothing more ridiculous.

Elinor, while she waited in silence, and immovable gravity, the conclusion of such folly, could not restrain her eyes from being fixed on him with a look that spoke all the contempt it excited. It was a look, however, very well bestowed, for it relieved her own feelings, and gave no intelligence[32] to him. He was recalled from wit to wisdom, not by any reproof of her's, but by his own sensibility.[33]

"We may treat it as a joke," said he at last, recovering from the affected laugh which had considerably lengthened out the genuine gaiety of the moment—"but upon my soul, it is a most serious business. Poor Edward! he is ruined for ever. I am extremely sorry for it—for I know him to be a very good-hearted creature; as well-meaning a fellow perhaps, as any in the world. You must not judge of him, Miss Dashwood, from *your* slight acquaintance.— Poor Edward!—His manners[34] are certainly not the happiest in nature.—But we are not all born, you know, with the same powers—the same address.[35]—Poor fellow!—to see him in a circle of strangers!—to be sure it was pitiable enough!—but, upon my soul, I believe he has as good a heart as any in the kingdom; and I declare and protest to you I never was so shocked in my life, as when it all burst forth. I could not believe it.—My mother was the first person who told me of it, and I, feeling myself called on to act

29. A white surplice, a long loose robe worn over other clothing, was used by Anglican clergy when conducting services.

30. *publishing*: announcing.

31. The reading of banns was one of two ways to get married. On three successive Sundays the impending marriage of two people would be announced in church; the idea was that if there were any impediment, such as an existing marriage of one of the betrothed or parental opposition to someone who was not twenty-one, anyone knowing of this impediment would learn of the marriage and have time to step forward to prevent it. The other way was to procure a license from a clergyman, who would check the couple's qualifications. This method was generally preferred because it offered greater privacy, but it also cost money. Hence poor people used banns. This is why Robert imagines the banns of two people with very ordinary names, and he undoubtedly finds the prospect of Edward's performing clerical duties for such humble folk to add to the absurdity of his proposed profession.

32. *gave no intelligence*: communicated no meaning.

33. *sensibility*: consciousness.

34. *manners*: general conduct and demeanor.

35. *address*: outward manner, especially in conversation.

with resolution, immediately said to her, 'My dear madam, I do not know what you may intend to do on the occasion, but as for myself, I must say, that if Edward does marry this young woman, *I* never will see him again.' That was what I said immediately,—I was most uncommonly shocked indeed!—Poor Edward!—he has done for himself completely—shut himself out for ever from all decent society!—but, as I directly said to my mother, I am not in the least surprised at it; from his style of education it was always to be expected.[36] My poor mother was half frantic."

"Have you ever seen the lady?"

"Yes; once, while she was staying in this house, I happened to drop in for ten minutes; and I saw quite enough of her. The merest awkward country girl,[37] without style, or elegance, and almost without beauty.—I remember her perfectly. Just the kind of girl I should suppose likely to captivate poor Edward. I offered immediately, as soon as my mother related the affair to me, to talk to him myself, and dissuade him from the match; but it was too late *then*, I found, to do any thing, for unluckily, I was not in the way[38] at first, and knew nothing of it till after the breach had taken place, when it was not for me, you know, to interfere. But had I been informed of it a few hours earlier—I think it is most probable—that something might have been hit on. I certainly should have represented it to Edward in a very strong light. 'My dear fellow,' I should have said, 'consider what you are doing. You are making a most disgraceful connection,[39] and such a one as your family are unanimous in disapproving.' I cannot help thinking, in short, that means might have been found.[40] But now it is all too late. He must be starved, you know;—that is certain; absolutely starved."

He had just settled this point with great composure, when the entrance of Mrs. John Dashwood put an end to the subject. But though *she* never spoke of it out of her own family, Elinor could see its influence on her mind,[41] in the something like confusion of countenance with which she entered, and an attempt at cordiality in her behaviour to herself. She even proceeded so far as to be concerned to find that Elinor and her sister were so soon to

36. Robert earlier gave his opinion on the folly of Edward's private education (p. 466).

37. The awkwardness of the manners, speech, dress, and culture of country people was a commonly accepted stereotype among members of elite London society like Robert.

38. *in the way:* at hand; in a position to be found or to know what is happening.

39. *connection:* match, marriage.

40. Robert's conviction that he could have resolved the problem easily, a conviction perfectly suiting his consistent arrogance, will have important effects on the plot later.

41. Edward's engagement to Lucy has removed Fanny's reason for disliking Elinor—though having long harbored and nurtured this dislike, she adopts a new course only with some difficulty and awkwardness.

leave town, as she had hoped to see more of them;—an exertion in which her husband, who attended her into the room, and hung enamoured over her accents,[42] seemed to distinguish every thing that was most affectionate and graceful.

A *dairymaid.*

[From William Pyne, *Costume of Great Britain* (London, 1804; 1989 reprint), Plate XIII]

42. *accents:* utterances—with reference both to the words and the tone of voice.

A genteel lady feeding her poultry (her clothing is from a slightly earlier period).
[From George Williamson, *George Morland: his life and works* (London, 1907), p. 112]

Chapter Six

O ne other short call in Harley-street, in which Elinor received her brother's congratulations on their travelling so far towards Barton without any expense,[1] and on Colonel Brandon's being to follow them to Cleveland in a day or two, completed the intercourse of the brother and sisters in town;—and a faint invitation from Fanny, to come to Norland whenever it should happen to be in their way, which of all things was the most unlikely to occur, with a more warm, though less public, assurance, from John to Elinor, of the promptitude with which he should come to see her at Delaford,[2] was all that foretold any meeting in the country.

It amused her to observe that all her friends seemed determined to send her to Delaford;—a place, in which, of all others, she would now least chuse to visit, or wish to reside; for not only was it considered as her future home by her brother and Mrs. Jennings, but even Lucy, when they parted, gave her a pressing invitation to visit her there.

Very early in April, and tolerably early in the day, the two parties from Hanover-square and Berkeley-street set out from their respective homes, to meet, by appointment, on the road.[3] For the convenience of Charlotte and her child, they were to be more than two days on their journey, and Mr. Palmer, travelling more expeditiously with Colonel Brandon, was to join them at Cleveland soon after their arrival.[4]

Marianne, few as had been her hours of comfort in London, and eager as she had long been to quit it, could not, when it came to the point, bid adieu to the house in which she had for the last time enjoyed those hopes, and that confidence, in Willoughby, which were now extinguished for ever, without great pain. Nor

1. Because they will accompany Mrs. Jennings to Cleveland they will not have to pay for that, and Cleveland, near Bristol, represents more than half the total journey (see map, p. 738).

2. He looks forward to seeing her at Delaford because he hopes she will soon be the wife of Colonel Brandon, but, knowing Fanny's long-standing dislike of Elinor, he promises the visit only when speaking to Elinor privately.

3. The two parties are Mrs. Palmer, her baby, and probably a nurse or servant to help with the baby, all coming from Hanover Square, and Mrs. Jennings, Elinor, and Marianne. They would go in two separate carriages, because the main carriage for long-distance travel, a chaise, sat only three people. But the carriages, once they meet up outside London, will stay together and make the same stops for food and lodging.

4. The distance by existing roads from London to Cleveland was approximately 120 miles. At standard speeds of seven to eight miles an hour, this would take fifteen to seventeen hours, but they will lengthen the trip with frequent stops to allow Mrs. Palmer and the baby to rest: carriage rides were bumpy, and people often felt sick and tired after them.

could she leave the place in which Willoughby remained, busy in new engagements, and new schemes,[5] in which *she* could have no share, without shedding many tears.

Elinor's satisfaction at the moment of removal, was more positive. She had no such object for her lingering thoughts to fix on, she left no creature behind, from whom it would give her a moment's regret to be divided for ever, she was pleased to be free herself from the persecution of Lucy's friendship, she was grateful for bringing her sister away unseen by Willoughby since his marriage, and she looked forward with hope to what a few months of tranquillity at Barton might do towards restoring Marianne's peace of mind, and confirming her own.

Their journey was safely performed. The second day brought them into the cherished, or the prohibited, county of Somerset, for as such was it dwelt on by turns in Marianne's imagination; and in the forenoon[6] of the third they drove up to Cleveland.

Cleveland was a spacious, modern-built house, situated on a sloping lawn.[7] It had no park, but the pleasure-grounds were tolerably extensive;[8] and like every other place of the same degree of importance,[9] it had its open shrubbery, and closer wood walk,[10] a

A view such as landowners aspired to have on their property.

[From Humphrey Repton, *The Art of Landscape Gardening* (Boston, 1907; reprint ed.), p. 118]

5. *schemes:* plans, designs, projects.

6. *forenoon:* morning. Since "morning" then meant most of the day, this term, the counterpart of "afternoon," was used for the early part of the day.

7. Houses that were modern in 1811, the publication date of the novel, were located on high ground to give them good views. Older houses had been built in lower positions for the sake of shelter; *Emma*, in describing such a house's position, refers to "the old neglect of prospect [view]." For an example of a then-modern house, see below; for an example of what the leading landscape gardener of the time Humphrey Repton (discussed in *Mansfield Park*) considers a desirable view, see facing page.

8. The park and pleasure grounds were the two principal areas of landscaping surrounding a house. The pleasure grounds consisted of areas, including walkways, shrubberies, and gardens that had obviously been designed by human hands; the park, which was usually farther afield and often very extensive, consisted of lawns and woodlands that, while often carefully landscaped, looked as if they could be natural.

9. *importance:* dignity.

10. Shrubberies were popular in landscaped gardens and usually contained winding paths, often with scattered places to sit. This one is open because, like most shrubberies, its spacious paths allow those walking in it to see all around them—as Marianne does below. In this it would contrast with "the closer [i.e., more enclosed] wood walk."

Earl Stoke Park: an example of a modern country house (from the perspective of 1811), with some features similar to the Palmers'.

[From John Preston Neale, *Views of the Seats of Noblemen and Gentlemen*, Vol. V (1822)]

road of smooth gravel winding round a plantation,[11] led to the front, the lawn was dotted over with timber, the house itself was under the guardianship of the fir, the mountain-ash, and the acacia, and a thick screen of them altogether, interspersed with tall Lombardy poplars,[12] shut out the offices.[13]

Marianne entered the house with an heart swelling with emotion from the consciousness of being only eighty miles from Barton,[14] and not thirty from Combe Magna; and before she had been five minutes within its walls, while the others were busily helping Charlotte shew her child to the housekeeper,[15] she quitted it again, stealing away through the winding shrubberies, now just beginning to be in beauty, to gain a distant eminence;[16] where, from its Grecian temple,[17] her eye, wandering over a wide tract of country to the south-east, could fondly rest on the farthest ridge of hills in the horizon, and fancy that from their summits Combe Magna might be seen.

In such moments of precious, of invaluable misery, she rejoiced in tears of agony to be at Cleveland;[18] and as she returned by a different circuit to the house,[19] feeling all the happy privilege

A classical structure on landscaped grounds.

[From Humphrey Repton, *The Art of Landscape Gardening* (Boston, 1907; reprint ed.), p. 180]

11. *plantation*: wood of planted trees.

12. Lombardy poplars had recently been introduced into England. While their timber was of no worth, they were valued for their great height, which would make them stand out when interspersed with other trees. Trees were often planted near houses for aesthetic reasons.

13. *offices*: buildings near a house where necessary work was performed (the term was also used for similar rooms within, such as the kitchen, pantry, or cellar, but it probably does not mean that in this context). Here it would mean the stables and barns. Blocking such practical elements from view was an important part of landscaping, intended to allow people to engage in appreciation and contemplation of natural beauty without being reminded of more sordid realities.

14. This indicates Jane Austen's precision with regard to distances, for the journey from Bristol to Exeter was a little more than seventy-five miles by the main routes of the day, and Cleveland and Barton were described, respectively, as "within a few miles of Bristol" (p. 518) and "within four miles northward of Exeter" (p. 46). Thus eighty miles could be exactly right.

15. The housekeeper was the highest-ranking female servant, who would run much of the household and supervise other servants. She would remain at the house when the family was gone, which is why she has not seen the child. Because her job required her to have frequent consultations with the mistress of the house, and because she usually was more educated than other servants, the mistress would know her better and might naturally make a point of showing her new baby to her.

16. *eminence*: elevation, high ground. Having raised places to allow people to enjoy views of the surrounding countryside was standard.

17. Landscaped grounds would often have various buildings scattered around to blend with the natural scenery; classical structures were especially popular. The Grecian temple has been placed in a high position, both to allow it to be seen easily from elsewhere and to offer expansive views. For an example of a classical structure designed to enhance the beauty of grounds, see facing page.

18. Marianne's conscious indulgence in misery, a prominent feature of Romanticism, appeared earlier in response to her father's death and to Willoughby's departure from Barton.

19. Meaning a route along the paths surrounding the house. Landscaping of the time emphasized the creation of multiple circuits that would offer a variety of picturesque views as people walked around them.

of country liberty, of wandering from place to place in free and luxurious solitude, she resolved to spend almost every hour of every day while she remained with the Palmers, in the indulgence of such solitary rambles.[20]

She returned just in time to join the others as they quitted the house, on an excursion through its more immediate premises; and the rest of the morning was easily whiled away,[21] in lounging round the kitchen garden, examining the bloom upon its walls,[22] and listening to the gardener's lamentations upon blights, — in dawdling through the green-house,[23] where the loss of her favourite plants, unwarily exposed, and nipped by the lingering frost, raised the laughter of Charlotte, — and in visiting her poultry-yard, where, in the disappointed hopes of her dairy-maid, by hens forsaking their nests, or being stolen by a fox, or in the rapid decease of a promising young brood, she found fresh sources of merriment.[24]

The morning was fine and dry, and Marianne, in her plan of employment abroad,[25] had not calculated for any change of weather during their stay at Cleveland.[26] With great surprise therefore, did she find herself prevented by a settled rain from going out again after dinner. She had depended on a twilight walk to the Grecian temple, and perhaps all over the grounds, and an evening merely cold or damp would not have deterred her from it; but an heavy and settled rain even *she* could not fancy dry or pleasant weather for walking.

Their party was small, and the hours passed quietly away. Mrs. Palmer had her child, and Mrs. Jennings her carpet-work;[27] they talked of the friends they had left behind, arranged Lady Middleton's engagements, and wondered whether Mr. Palmer and Colonel Brandon would get farther than Reading that night.[28] Elinor, however little concerned in it, joined in their discourse, and Marianne, who had the knack of finding her way in every house to the library, however it might be avoided by the family in general, soon procured herself a book.[29]

Nothing was wanting on Mrs. Palmer's side that constant and friendly good-humour could do, to make them feel themselves welcome. The openness and heartiness of her manner, more than

20. She has long enjoyed solitary rambles, especially when wrapped up in her unhappiness, but was unable to pursue them while in London. Thus it is not surprising that she seizes her first opportunity in months. At the same time, her plan to spend all her time alone while visiting the Palmers represents a distinct lack of consideration for her hosts.

21. Since they arrived before noon they still had many hours of morning left, by the meaning of the term then.

22. Kitchen gardens, which grew fruits and vegetables, were frequently enclosed by walls, for the shelter from the cold and wind would extend the growing season of the crops. Sometimes walls were heated with fires to lengthen the season even further.

23. Many estates contained greenhouses.

24. Poultry yards were a basic feature of farms and estates, and poultry was something that was often a particular concern of the lady of the house. The dairymaid was in charge of hens or milk cows. For contemporary pictures of a dairymaid and a lady feeding her poultry, see pp. 558 and 559.

25. *abroad*: out of doors.

26. Marianne's refusal to accept the weather is emblematic of her character. It will soon have significant consequences.

27. She may be still working on the rug she had been taking measurements for earlier (see p. 334). For more on carpet work, see p. 479, note 13.

28. Reading was approximately forty miles west of London by the roads of the time; see map, p. 738. If they reach it only by the evening, they did not leave London until the middle of the day, as Mrs. Jennings and Mrs. Palmer presumably know they planned to do. Because the total distance from London to the Palmers' home would require fifteen to seventeen hours of travel time (see page 561, note 4), they would not have been able to make the journey in a day and decided to divide it in this fashion.

29. Almost all grand houses had libraries. They frequently contained books accumulated over many generations, which could be a point of family pride. Yet there was no guarantee that the current generation inhabiting the house would have any taste for reading.

atoned for that want of recollection[30] and elegance, which made her often deficient in the forms of politeness; her kindness, recommended by so pretty a face, was engaging; her folly, though evident, was not disgusting, because it was not conceited; and Elinor could have forgiven every thing but her laugh.

The two gentlemen arrived the next day to a very late dinner,[31] affording a pleasant enlargement of the party, and a very welcome variety to their conversation, which a long morning of the same continued rain had reduced very low.

Elinor had seen so little of Mr. Palmer, and in that little had seen so much variety in his address to her sister and herself, that she knew not what to expect to find him in his own family. She found him, however, perfectly the gentleman in his behaviour to all his visitors, and only occasionally rude to his wife and her mother; she found him very capable of being a pleasant companion, and only prevented from being so always, by too great an aptitude to fancy himself as much superior to people in general, as he must feel himself to be to Mrs. Jennings and Charlotte. For the rest of his character and habits, they were marked, as far as Elinor could perceive, with no traits at all unusual in his sex and time of life. He was nice[32] in his eating, uncertain in his hours; fond of his child, though affecting to slight it; and idled away the mornings at billiards,[33] which ought to have been devoted to business.[34] She liked him, however, upon the whole much better than she had expected, and in her heart was not sorry that she could like him no more;—not sorry to be driven by the observation of his Epicurism,[35] his selfishness, and his conceit, to rest with complacency[36] on the remembrance of Edward's generous temper,[37] simple taste, and diffident feelings.[38]

Of Edward, or at least of some of his concerns, she now received intelligence from Colonel Brandon, who had been into Dorsetshire lately; and who, treating her at once as the disinterested friend of Mr. Ferrars, and the kind confidante of himself, talked to her a great deal of the Parsonage at Delaford, described its deficiencies, and told her what he meant to do himself towards removing them.[39]—His behaviour to her in this, as well as in

30. *recollection:* composure, self-possession.

31. Dinner was usually at four or five o'clock. If they did reach Reading the previous night, and thus still had eighty of the 120 miles to go, they would have been ten or eleven hours on the road and could not have arrived until the evening.

32. *nice:* fastidious, delicate.

33. Mr. Palmer complained of the lack of a billiard table at Sir John's house.

34. The main business of a landowner would be managing his estate, which would include supervising agricultural or other activities on his own land and dealing with farmers who rented large tracts of land from him.

35. *Epicurism:* devotion to fine eating; cultivated taste in food. Other male characters in Jane Austen have this characteristic.

36. *complacency:* pleasure.

37. *temper:* disposition, emotional constitution.

38. Diffident feelings are praised elsewhere in Austen's novels, because they mean modesty and lack of pride.

39. Improving the parsonage was the responsibility of the person controlling the appointment to the clerical position (see p. 541, note 33).

Playing billiards.

[From William Combe, *The Dance of Life* (London, 1817; 1903 reprint), p. 197]

every other particular, his open pleasure in meeting her after an absence of only ten days, his readiness to converse with her, and his deference for her opinion, might very well justify Mrs. Jennings's persuasion of his attachment, and would have been enough, perhaps, had not Elinor still, as from the first, believed Marianne his real favourite, to make her suspect it herself. But as it was, such a notion had scarcely ever entered her head, except by Mrs. Jennings's suggestion; and she could not help believing herself the nicest observer of the two;—she watched his eyes, while Mrs. Jennings thought only of his behaviour;—and while his looks of anxious solicitude on Marianne's feeling, in her head and throat, the beginning of an heavy cold, because unexpressed by words, entirely escaped the latter lady's observation;—*she* could discover in them the quick feelings, and needless alarm of a lover.

Two delightful twilight walks on the third and fourth evenings of her being there, not merely on the dry gravel of the shrubbery,[40] but all over the grounds, and especially in the most distant parts of them, where there was something more of wildness than in the rest, where the trees were the oldest, and the grass was the longest and wettest,[41] had—assisted by the still greater imprudence of sitting in her wet shoes and stockings[42]—given Marianne a cold so violent, as, though for a day or two trifled with or denied, would force itself by increasing ailments, on the concern of every body, and the notice of herself. Prescriptions poured in from all quarters, and as usual, were all declined.[43] Though heavy and feverish, with a pain in her limbs, a cough, and a sore throat, a good night's rest was to[44] cure her entirely; and it was with difficulty that Elinor prevailed on her, when she went to bed, to try one or two of the simplest of the remedies.

40. Gravel walks were standard in shrubberies, which were designed for frequent use and not intended to look natural.

41. The wilder parts of the grounds presumably include the wood walk. An interest in less manicured areas would fit naturally with Marianne's tastes.

42. She is probably sitting on a seat on the grounds. Garden seats were popular, to allow for rest amid walks and for the enjoyment of the views.

43. Because illness was mostly treated at home, and domestic remedies were often as effective as ones prescribed by doctors, almost everyone would have their own remedies for ailments and be eager to share them.

44. *was to*: was likely to (in the opinion of Marianne).

Two women outdoors.

[From *The Repository of arts, literature, fashions, manufactures, &c*, Vol. IV (1810), p. 178]

Chapter Seven

Marianne got up the next morning at her usual time; to every inquiry replied that she was better, and tried to prove herself so, by engaging in her accustomary employments. But a day spent in sitting shivering over the fire with a book in her hand, which she was unable to read, or in lying, weary and languid, on a sofa,[1] did not speak much in favour of her amendment; and when, at last, she went early to bed, more and more indisposed, Colonel Brandon was only astonished at her sister's composure, who, though attending and nursing her the whole day, against Marianne's inclination, and forcing proper medicines on her at night, trusted, like Marianne, to the certainty and efficacy of sleep, and felt no real alarm.[2]

A very restless and feverish night, however, disappointed the expectation of both; and when Marianne, after persisting in rising, confessed herself unable to sit up, and returned voluntarily to her bed, Elinor was very ready to adopt Mrs. Jennings's advice, of sending for the Palmers' apothecary.[3]

He came, examined his patient, and though encouraging Miss Dashwood to expect that a very few days would restore her sister to health, yet, by pronouncing her disorder to have a putrid tendency,[4] and allowing the word "infection" to pass his lips, gave instant alarm to Mrs. Palmer on her baby's account. Mrs. Jennings, who had been inclined from the first to think Marianne's complaint more serious than Elinor, now looked very grave on Mr. Harris's report, and confirming Charlotte's fears and caution, urged the necessity of her immediate removal with her infant; and Mr. Palmer, though treating their apprehensions as idle, found the anxiety and importunity of his wife too great to be withstood. Her departure therefore was fixed on; and, within an hour after

1.   Sofas had developed as a piece of furniture only in the decade or two preceding this novel. Lying on one, or on other pieces of furniture, was generally frowned upon, with the exception of those whose health justified it. For
a picture of a contemporary sofa, see below.

2.   Colonel Brandon's alarm indicates the depth of his feelings for Marianne. Since he is consistently shown to be intelligent as well as calm and
careful in responding to difficulties, it also suggests the seriousness of her ailment.

3.   The apothecary was the most basic medical practitioner, who would
respond to normal illnesses, give advice, and prescribe medicines.

4.   Putrid fever was the name given to typhus then, though terminology was
not always precise (a putrid sore throat could mean other afflictions of the
throat, including diphtheria). It was known to be a serious condition: in a letter Jane Austen refers to a family who lost their eldest son to a putrid fever
(Jan. 7, 1807).

A sofa.

[From A. E. Reveirs-Hopkins, *The Sheraton Period* (New York, 1922), Figure 7]

Mr. Harris's arrival, she set off, with her little boy and his nurse,[5] for the house of a near relation of Mr. Palmer's, who lived a few miles on the other side of Bath;[6] whither her husband promised, at her earnest entreaty, to join her in a day or two; and whither she was almost equally urgent with her mother to accompany her. Mrs. Jennings, however, with a kindness of heart which made Elinor really love her, declared her resolution of not stirring from Cleveland as long as Marianne remained ill, and of endeavouring, by her own attentive care, to supply to her the place of the mother she had taken her from; and Elinor found her on every occasion a most willing and active helpmate, desirous to share in all her fatigues, and often by her better experience in nursing, of material use.[7]

Poor Marianne, languid and low from the nature of her malady, and feeling herself universally ill, could no longer hope that to-morrow would find her recovered; and the idea of what to-morrow would have produced, but for this unlucky illness, made every ailment more severe; for on that day they were to have begun their journey home; and, attended the whole way by a servant of Mrs. Jennings, were to have taken their mother by surprise on the following forenoon.[8] The little that she said, was all in lamentation of this inevitable delay; though Elinor tried to raise her spirits, and make her believe, as she *then* really believed herself, that it would be a very short one.

The next day produced little or no alteration in the state of the patient; she certainly was not better, and except that there was no amendment, did not appear worse. Their party was now farther reduced; for Mr. Palmer, though very unwilling to go, as well from real humanity and good-nature, as from a dislike of appearing to be frightened away by his wife, was persuaded at last by Colonel Brandon to perform his promise of following her; and while he was preparing to go, Colonel Brandon himself, with a much greater exertion, began to talk of going likewise.[9]—Here, however, the kindness of Mrs. Jennings interposed most acceptably; for to send the Colonel away while his love was in so much uneasiness on her sister's account, would be to deprive them both,

5. "Nurse" was also used then for someone who took care of small children (the term "nanny" did not develop until later). Thus this woman would be different from the nurse who attended Mrs. Palmer during her recovery after giving birth.

6. Since they are a few miles from Bristol, Bath would not be far away (see map, p. 738).

7. Because most nursing was done at home by women, someone older like Mrs. Jennings, and who had two children of her own, would have acquired considerable experience.

8. They had earlier spoken of having Mrs. Dashwood's manservant accompany them home, due to the impropriety of young unmarried ladies traveling alone (p. 518). They had also discussed the trip as being feasible in a day, but a long day. They have evidently decided now not to attempt this but to arrive in the forenoon, i.e., before noon, of the second day.

9. Colonel Brandon probably feels he should offer to leave, since the Palmers, his hosts, are now gone, and unlike Mrs. Jennings and Elinor, he has neither a family connection with the Palmers nor a job of nursing a sick person to justify his presence. But his wish to remain there and watch Marianne's progress makes this offer an exertion.

she thought, of every comfort; and therefore telling him at once that his stay at Cleveland was necessary to herself, that she should want him to play at piquet of an evening,[10] while Miss Dashwood was above with her sister, &c. she urged him so strongly to remain, that he, who was gratifying the first wish of his own heart by a compliance, could not long even affect to demur; especially as Mrs. Jennings's entreaty was warmly seconded by Mr. Palmer, who seemed to feel a relief to himself, in leaving behind him a person so well able to assist or advise Miss Dashwood in any emergence.[11]

Marianne was of course kept in ignorance of all these arrangements. She knew not that she had been the means of sending the owners of Cleveland away, in about seven days from the time of their arrival. It gave her no surprise that she saw nothing of Mrs. Palmer; and as it gave her likewise no concern, she never mentioned her name.

Two days passed away from the time of Mr. Palmer's departure, and her situation continued, with little variation, the same. Mr. Harris, who attended her every day, still talked boldly of a speedy recovery, and Miss Dashwood was equally sanguine; but the expectation of the others was by no means so cheerful. Mrs. Jennings had determined very early in the seisure that Marianne would never get over it,[12] and Colonel Brandon, who was chiefly of use in listening to Mrs. Jennings's forebodings, was not in a state of mind to resist their influence. He tried to reason himself out of fears, which the different judgment of the apothecary seemed to render absurd; but the many hours of each day in which he was left entirely alone, were but too favourable for the admission of every melancholy idea, and he could not expel from his mind the persuasion that he should see Marianne no more.[13]

On the morning of the third day however, the gloomy anticipations of both were almost done away; for when Mr. Harris arrived, he declared his patient materially better. Her pulse was much stronger, and every symptom more favourable than on the preceding visit. Elinor, confirmed in every pleasant hope, was all cheerfulness; rejoicing that in her letters to her mother, she had

10. Piquet is a two-person card game, so Mrs. Jennings can claim she needs his presence to entertain her, even though she is actually saying this to give him a good excuse to stay.

11. *emergence*: emergency.

12. "Seisure," or seizure, often meant a stroke at this time, but it could also be applied to a variety of serious ailments that incapacitated the sufferer.

13. Colonel Brandon's pessimism is probably caused in part by the tragic death years earlier of the young woman he loved.

pursued her own judgment rather than her friend's, in making very light of the indisposition which delayed them at Cleveland; and almost fixing on the time when Marianne would be able to travel.

But the day did not close so auspiciously as it began.—Towards the evening, Marianne became ill again, growing more heavy, restless, and uncomfortable than before.[14] Her sister, however, still sanguine, was willing to attribute the change to nothing more than the fatigue of having sat up to have her bed made;[15] and carefully administering the cordials prescribed,[16] saw her with satisfaction sink at last into a slumber, from which she expected the most beneficial effects. Her sleep, though not so quiet as Elinor wished to see it, lasted a considerable time; and anxious to observe the result of it herself, she resolved to sit with her during the whole of it. Mrs. Jennings, knowing nothing of any change in the patient, went unusually early to bed; her maid, who was one of the principal nurses,[17] was recreating herself[18] in the housekeeper's room, and Elinor remained alone with Marianne.

The repose of the latter became more and more disturbed; and her sister, who watched with unremitting attention her continual change of posture, and heard the frequent but inarticulate sounds of complaint which passed her lips, was almost wishing to rouse her from so painful a slumber, when Marianne, suddenly awakened by some accidental noise in the house, started hastily up, and with feverish wildness, cried out—

"Is mama coming?—"

"Not yet," replied the other, concealing her terror, and assisting Marianne to lie down again, "but she will be here, I hope, before it is long. It is a great way, you know, from hence to Barton."[19]

"But she must not go round by London," cried Marianne, in the same hurried manner, "I shall never see her, if she goes by London."[20]

Elinor perceived with alarm that she was not quite herself, and while attempting to sooth her, eagerly felt her pulse. It was lower and quicker than ever! and Marianne, still talking wildly of mama, her alarm increased so rapidly, as to determine her on

14. She confounds the doctor's prognostications. His predictions and diagnoses will prove wrong again, as will those of others attending Marianne. One reason was the extreme limitations of medical knowledge at this time. People then understood human anatomy well and developed a general understanding of various diseases and their probable causes. But with no knowledge of microorganisms, no ability to see inside living persons, and no large-scale epidemiological studies, medical thinkers and practitioners were severely handicapped in both comprehending and treating serious ailments.

15. The lack of effective medicines meant that people often relied on simpler remedies like changing sheets.

16. Cordials could refer to a variety of substances meant to revive people or improve their condition; many contained alcohol. These have been prescribed by the apothecary.

17. Nursing was also a frequent activity of female servants, who could develop as great an expertise as their mistresses.

18. *recreating herself*: refreshing herself through a pleasant activity. She is probably talking with the housekeeper.

19. As already mentioned, it is a day or a little longer to Barton from where they are now.

20. London would be completely out of the way when going between their home near Exeter and the Palmers' near Bristol (see map, p. 738). Thus Marianne's speculation indicates something seriously wrong with her.

sending instantly for Mr. Harris, and dispatching a messenger to Barton for her mother. To consult with Colonel Brandon on the best means of effecting the latter, was a thought which immediately followed the resolution of its performance; and as soon as she had rung up the maid to take her place by her sister,[21] she hastened down to the drawing-room, where she knew he was generally to be found at a much later hour than the present.

It was no time for hesitation. Her fears and her difficulties were immediately before him. Her fears, he had no courage, no confidence to attempt the removal of;—he listened to them in silent despondence;—but her difficulties were instantly obviated, for with a readiness that seemed to speak[22] the occasion, and the service pre-arranged in his mind, he offered himself as the messenger who should fetch Mrs. Dashwood.[23] Elinor made no resistance that was not easily overcome.[24] She thanked him with brief, though fervent gratitude, and while he went to hurry off his servant with a message to Mr. Harris, and an order for post-horses directly,[25] she wrote a few lines to her mother.

The comfort of such a friend at that moment as Colonel Brandon—of such a companion for her mother,—how gratefully was it felt!—a companion whose judgment would guide, whose attendance must relieve, and whose friendship might sooth her!—as far as the shock of such a summons *could* be lessened to her, his presence, his manners, his assistance, would lessen it.

He, meanwhile, whatever he might feel, acted with all the firmness of a collected mind,[26] made every necessary arrangement with the utmost dispatch, and calculated with exactness the time in which she might look for his return.[27] Not a moment was lost in delay of any kind. The horses arrived, even before they were expected, and Colonel Brandon only pressing her hand with a look of solemnity, and a few words spoken too low to reach her ear, hurried into the carriage. It was then about twelve o'clock, and she returned to her sister's apartment to wait for the arrival of the apothecary, and to watch by her the rest of the night. It was a night of almost equal suffering to both. Hour after hour passed away in sleepless pain and delirium on Marianne's side, and in

21. Since the maid is in the housekeeper's room, she would quickly hear the bell calling for her, for the bells, activated by ropes and pulleys extending throughout the house, sounded in the servants' quarters.

22. *speak*: express, signify.

23. This episode gives Colonel Brandon the opportunity to play an active, heroic role, particularly in relation to Marianne.

24. She would feel that politeness required a few words of dissuasion, since Colonel Brandon is volunteering to undertake a very long journey on her sister's behalf.

25. *directly*: immediately. Post horses were hired to pull carriages on main roads; for more on the elaborate system of transportation by post, see p. 125, note 18. Colonel Brandon already has a chaise of his own, so he needs only to hire horses.

26. He suffers from strong feelings, probably of fear and distress, but does not allow them to interfere with his actions.

27. Because of the general uniformity of long-distance roads at this time, it was possible to estimate travel times fairly exactly.

the most cruel anxiety on Elinor's, before Mr. Harris appeared. Her apprehensions once raised, paid by their excess for all her former security;[28] and the servant who sat up with her, for she would not allow Mrs. Jennings to be called, only tortured her more, by hints of what her mistress had always thought.

Marianne's ideas[29] were still, at intervals, fixed incoherently on her mother, and whenever she mentioned her name, it gave a pang to the heart of poor Elinor, who, reproaching herself for having trifled with so many days of illness, and wretched for some immediate relief, fancied that all relief might soon be in vain, that every thing had been delayed too long, and pictured to herself her suffering mother arriving too late to see this darling child, or to see her rational.[30]

She was on the point of sending again for Mr. Harris, or if *he* could not come, for some other advice, when the former—but not till after five o'clock—arrived. His opinion, however, made some little amends for his delay, for though acknowledging a very unexpected and unpleasant alteration in his patient, he would not allow the danger to be material, and talked of the relief which a fresh mode of treatment must procure, with a confidence which, in a lesser degree, was communicated to Elinor. He promised to call again in the course of three or four hours, and left both the patient and her anxious attendant more composed than he had found them.

With strong concern, and with many reproaches for not being called to their aid, did Mrs. Jennings hear in the morning of what had passed. Her former apprehensions, now with greater reason restored, left her no doubt of the event;[31] and though trying to speak comfort to Elinor, her conviction of her sister's danger would not allow her to offer the comfort of hope. Her heart was really grieved. The rapid decay, the early death of a girl so young, so lovely as Marianne, must have struck a less interested person with concern. On Mrs. Jennings's compassion she had other claims. She had been for three months her companion, was still under her care, and she was known to have been greatly injured, and long unhappy. The distress of her sister too, particularly a

28. Meaning her former confidence in Marianne's quick recovery.

29. *ideas*: thoughts.

30. Elinor's mistaken diagnosis, which now causes her to feel so penitent, could be seen as an unusual instance of her fallibility. At the same time, Mrs. Jennings and the apothecary also prove to be wrong, at least in part.

31. *event*: outcome.

favourite, was before her;—and as for their mother, when Mrs. Jennings considered that Marianne might probably be to *her* what Charlotte was to herself, her sympathy in *her* sufferings was very sincere.

Mr. Harris was punctual in his second visit;—but he came to be disappointed in his hopes of what the last would produce. His medicines had failed;—the fever was unabated; and Marianne only more quiet—not more herself—remained in an heavy stupor. Elinor, catching all, and more than all, his fears in a moment, proposed to call in farther advice.[32] But he judged it unnecessary; he had still something more to try, some fresh application, of whose success he was almost as confident as the last, and his visit concluded with encouraging assurances which reached the ear, but could not enter the heart, of Miss Dashwood. She was calm, except when she thought of her mother, but she was almost hopeless; and in this state she continued till noon, scarcely stirring from her sister's bed, her thoughts wandering from one image of grief, one suffering friend[33] to another, and her spirits oppressed to the utmost by the conversation of Mrs. Jennings, who scrupled not[34] to attribute the severity and danger of this attack, to the many weeks of previous indisposition which Marianne's disappointment had brought on. Elinor felt all the reasonableness of the idea, and it gave fresh misery to her reflections.[35]

About noon, however, she began—but with a caution—a dread of disappointment, which for some time kept her silent, even to her friend—to fancy, to hope she could perceive a slight amendment in her sister's pulse;—she waited, watched, and examined it again and again;—and at last, with an agitation more difficult to bury under exterior calmness, than all her foregoing distress, ventured to communicate her hopes. Mrs. Jennings, though forced, on examination, to acknowledge a temporary revival, tried to keep her young friend from indulging a thought of its continuance;—and Elinor, conning over every injunction of distrust,[36] told herself likewise not to hope. But it was too late. Hope had already entered; and feeling all its anxious flutter, she bent over her sister

32. She could mean consulting another apothecary, or she could mean calling in a physician. Physicians were the only medical men who had undergone formal study. They were much fewer in number, cost more, and would generally be called only when a case was serious.

33. *friend:* friend or relative.

34. *scrupled not:* did not hesitate. Putting "not" after the verb, rather than "do/did not" before, was a frequent formulation in the language of the time.

35. It may increase Elinor's misery because it reflects badly on her sister, by showing how much Marianne caused her current suffering and danger. Elinor may also feel some responsibility herself, because she did not acquiesce to Marianne's wish to return home from London earlier.

36. *conning over every injunction of distrust:* reviewing every reason or observation suggesting that Marianne would not recover.

to watch—she hardly knew for what. Half an hour passed away, and the favourable symptom yet blessed her. Others even arose to confirm it. Her breath, her skin, her lips, all flattered Elinor with signs of amendment, and Marianne fixed her eyes on her with a rational, though languid, gaze. Anxiety and hope now oppressed her in equal degrees, and left her no moment of tranquillity till the arrival of Mr. Harris at four o'clock;—when his assurances, his felicitations on a recovery in her sister even surpassing his expectation, gave her confidence, comfort, and tears of joy.

Marianne was in every respect materially better, and he declared her entirely out of danger. Mrs. Jennings, perhaps satisfied with the partial justification of her forebodings which had been found in their late alarm, allowed herself to trust in his judgment, and admitted with unfeigned joy, and soon with unequivocal cheerfulness, the probability of an entire recovery.

Elinor could not be cheerful. Her joy was of a different kind, and led to anything rather than to gaiety. Marianne restored to life, health, friends, and to her doating mother, was an idea to fill her heart with sensations of exquisite comfort, and expand it in fervent gratitude;—but it led to no outward demonstrations of joy, no words, no smiles. All within Elinor's breast was satisfaction, silent and strong.

She continued by the side of her sister with little intermission the whole afternoon, calming every fear, satisfying every inquiry of her enfeebled spirits, supplying every succour, and watching almost every look and every breath. The possibility of a relapse would of course, in some moments, occur to remind her of what anxiety was—but when she saw, on her frequent and minute examination, that every symptom of recovery continued, and saw Marianne at six o'clock sink into a quiet, steady, and to all appearance comfortable, sleep, she silenced every doubt.

The time was now drawing on, when Colonel Brandon might be expected back. At ten o'clock, she trusted, or at least not much later,[37] her mother would be relieved from the dreadful suspense in which she must now be travelling towards them. The Colonel

37. Colonel Brandon left around midnight of the previous night, so ten o'clock would be twenty-two hours later. The distance is eighty miles in each direction. At seven to eight miles an hour this would take twenty to twenty-three hours; Elinor's estimate may be on the slow side from knowing that it would take her mother a little time, once she received Colonel Brandon's unexpected visit, to get ready to depart, especially since she would have to make arrangements for Margaret.

too!—perhaps scarcely less an object of pity!—Oh!—how slow was the progress of time which yet kept them in ignorance!

At seven o'clock, leaving Marianne still sweetly asleep, she joined Mrs. Jennings in the drawing-room to tea. Of breakfast she had been kept by her fears, and of dinner by their sudden reverse, from eating much;—and the present refreshment, therefore, with such feelings of content as she brought to it, was particularly welcome.[38] Mrs. Jennings would have persuaded her at its conclusion to take some rest before her mother's arrival, and allow *her* to take her place by Marianne; but Elinor had no sense of fatigue, no capability of sleep at that moment about her, and she was not to be kept away from her sister an unnecessary instant. Mrs. Jennings therefore attending her up stairs into the sick chamber, to satisfy herself that all continued right, left her there again to her charge and her thoughts, and retired to her own room to write letters and sleep.

The night was cold and stormy. The wind roared round the house, and the rain beat against the windows;[39] but Elinor, all happiness within, regarded it not. Marianne slept through every blast, and the travellers—they had a rich reward in store, for every present inconvenience.

The clock struck eight. Had it been ten, Elinor would have been convinced that at that moment she heard a carriage driving up to the house; and so strong was the persuasion that she *did*, in spite of the *almost* impossibility of their being already come, that she moved into the adjoining dressing-closet[40] and opened a window-shutter,[41] to be satisfied of the truth. She instantly saw that her ears had not deceived her. The flaring lamps of a carriage were immediately in view.[42] By their uncertain light she thought she could discern it to be drawn by four horses; and this, while it told the excess of her poor mother's alarm, gave some explanation to such unexpected rapidity.[43]

Never in her life had Elinor found it so difficult to be calm, as at that moment. The knowledge of what her mother must be feeling as the carriage stopt at the door,—of her doubt—her dread—perhaps her despair!—and of what *she* had to tell!—with such

38. Since breakfast and dinner were the only meals during the day, she would be very hungry. Snacks were usually served with evening tea.

39. The stormy setting of this scene is appropriate for the dramatic event that will conclude it.

40. *dressing-closet*: small dressing room.

41. Most windows had solid shutters attached to them to protect against wind and keep the room warmer during the night.

42. Carriages had lamps to enable them to travel at night. The flame of the lamps causes them to be flaring, i.e., burning with varying intensity.

43. A chaise, the standard long-distance carriage, was normally driven by two horses. Four horses would be more expensive but faster.

knowledge it was impossible to be calm. All that remained to be done, was to be speedy; and therefore staying only till she could leave Mrs. Jennings's maid with her sister, she hurried down stairs.

The bustle in the vestibule,[44] as she passed along an inner lobby,[45] assured her that they were already in the house. She rushed forwards towards the drawing-room,—she entered it,[46]— and saw only Willoughby.

44. Vestibules were common in large houses then. The bustle would be the servant letting somebody in, and probably speaking to him and taking his things.

45. Lobby usually referred specifically to a hall or corridor.

46. She would wait in the drawing room and the servant would conduct those arriving to her.

An inner doorway from a house of the period.

[From A. E. Reveirs-Hopkins, *The Sheraton Period* (New York, 1922), Figure 39]

Chapter Eight

*E*linor, starting back with a look of horror at the sight of him,[1] obeyed the first impulse of her heart in turning instantly to quit the room, and her hand was already on the lock,[2] when its action was suspended by his hastily advancing, and saying, in a voice rather of command than supplication,

"Miss Dashwood, for half an hour—for ten minutes—I entreat you to stay."

"No, sir," she replied with firmness, "I shall *not* stay. Your business cannot be with *me*. The servants, I suppose, forgot to tell you that Mr. Palmer was not in the house."

"Had they told me," he cried with vehemence, "that Mr. Palmer and all his relations were at the devil,[3] it would not have turned me from the door. My business is with you, and only you."

"With me!"—in the utmost amazement—"well, sir—be quick—and if you can—less violent."[4]

"Sit down, and I will be both."

She hesitated; she knew not what to do. The possibility of Colonel Brandon's arriving and finding him there, came across her. But she had promised to hear him, and her curiosity no less than her honour was engaged. After a moment's recollection, therefore, concluding that prudence required dispatch, and that her acquiescence would best promote it, she walked silently towards the table, and sat down. He took the opposite chair, and for half a minute not a word was said by either.

"Pray be quick, sir"—said Elinor impatiently—"I have no time to spare."

He was sitting in an attitude[5] of deep meditation, and seemed not to hear her.

"Your sister," said he, with abruptness, a moment afterwards—

1. Willoughby's sudden appearance is one of the least expected and most dramatic events in the novel. It performs the crucial function of finally revealing the full story behind his earlier, often mysterious actions.

2. Inner doors in houses normally had locks, and turning them was often necessary to open and close the door.

3. *at the devil*: in perdition.

4. *violent*: excessively vehement (in speech). She is not expressing a fear of physical violence from him.

5. *attitude*: posture.

"is out of danger. I heard it from the servant. God be praised!⁶ —
But is it true? — is it really true?"

Elinor would not speak. He repeated the inquiry with yet
greater eagerness.

"For God's sake tell me, is she out of danger, or is she not?"

"We hope she is."

He rose up, and walked across the room.

"Had I known as much half an hour ago — But since I *am*
here" — speaking with a forced vivacity as he returned to his seat —
"what does it signify? — For once, Miss Dashwood — it will be the
last time, perhaps — let us be cheerful together. — I am in a fine
mood for gaiety. — Tell me honestly" — a deeper glow overspread-
ing his cheeks — "do you think me most a knave or a fool?"⁷

Elinor looked at him with greater astonishment than ever. She
began to think that he must be in liquor; — the strangeness of such
a visit, and of such manners, seemed no otherwise intelligible;
and with this impression she immediately rose, saying,

"Mr. Willoughby, I advise you at present to return to Combe. —
I am not at leisure to remain with you longer. — Whatever your
business may be with me, it will be better recollected and
explained to-morrow."

"I understand you," he replied, with an expressive smile, and a
voice perfectly calm, "yes, I am very drunk.⁸ A pint of porter⁹ with
my cold beef at Marlborough was enough to over-set¹⁰ me."

"At Marlborough!"¹¹ — cried Elinor, more and more at a loss to
understand what he would be at.

"Yes — I left London this morning at eight o'clock,¹² and the
only ten minutes I have spent out of my chaise¹³ since that time,
procured me a nuncheon¹⁴ at Marlborough."

The steadiness of his manner, and the intelligence of his eye as
he spoke, convincing Elinor, that whatever other unpardonable
folly might bring him to Cleveland, he was not brought there by
intoxication, she said, after a moment's recollection,

"Mr. Willoughby, you *ought* to feel, and I certainly *do* — that
after what has passed — your coming here in this manner, and

6. This expression, from a man who has never seemed religious, signals the ubiquity of Christian language in this society, especially when speaking of matters of life and death.

7. After beginning with a question and a heartfelt exclamation about Marianne, Willoughby soon reverts to speaking of himself.

8. Willoughby's immediate grasp of her thoughts signals his intelligence, which makes the unworthiness in his behavior especially unfortunate.

9. *porter:* a dark, bitter beer, usually drunk by porters and manual laborers because it was considered strengthening. That may be why Willoughby selected it, along with cold beef, during a long journey; it also may have been readily available and quick to swallow at his stopping place. He says below that he stopped for only ten minutes.

10. *over-set:* discompose, mentally and physically overcome.

11. Marlborough is almost fifty miles east of their current location near Bristol. Thus one would not expect someone who arrived at eight in the evening to have eaten a midday meal there.

12. The distance from London is 120 miles. Carriages with four horses averaged ten miles an hour, as opposed to the seven to eight of ones with two horses: thus, it has taken him twelve hours. Willoughby's willingness to pay extra for four horses shows both his eagerness to arrive and the wealth he now enjoys thanks to his marriage.

13. He probably means the chaise he rented. He earlier was shown owning a curricle, an open carriage and more fashionable vehicle, and he probably had something else expensive and stylish for London.

14. *nuncheon:* a light meal or snack during the day.

forcing yourself upon my notice, requires a very particular excuse.—What is it, that you mean by it?"—

"I mean"—said he, with serious energy—"if I can, to make you hate me one degree less than you do *now*.[15] I mean to offer some kind of explanation, some kind of apology, for the past; to open my whole heart to you, and by convincing you, that though I have been always a blockhead, I have not been always a rascal, to obtain something like forgiveness from Ma—from your sister."[16]

"Is this the real reason of your coming?"

"Upon my soul it is,"—was his answer, with a warmth which brought all the former Willoughby to her remembrance, and in spite of herself made her think him sincere.

"If that is all, you may be satisfied already,—for Marianne *does*—she has *long* forgiven you."

"Has she!"—he cried, in the same eager tone.—"Then she has forgiven me before she ought to have done it. But she shall forgive me again, and on more reasonable grounds.—*Now* will you listen to me?"

Elinor bowed her assent.

"I do not know," said he, after a pause of expectation on her side, and thoughtfulness on his own,—"how *you* may have accounted for my behaviour to your sister, or what diabolical motive you may have imputed to me.—Perhaps you will hardly think the better of me,—it is worth the trial however, and you shall hear every thing. When I first became intimate in your family, I had no other intention, no other view in the acquaintance than to pass my time pleasantly while I was obliged to remain in Devonshire,[17] more pleasantly than I had ever done before. Your sister's lovely person and interesting[18] manners[19] could not but please me; and her behaviour to me almost from the first, was of a kind[20]—It is astonishing, when I reflect on what it was, and what *she* was, that my heart should have been so insensible!—But at first I must confess, my vanity only was elevated by it. Careless of her happiness, thinking only of my own amusement, giving way to feelings which I had always been too much in the habit of indulging, I endeavoured, by every means in my power, to make

15. Willoughby's declared motive shows him not to be a simple villain, since he does care what others think of him, though it also shows his limits, since he is principally concerned with repairing his reputation. Better characters in Jane Austen generally prefer to let their actions speak for themselves.

16. He stops before saying "Marianne" in full. As someone who now has no connection to her, it would not be proper to use only her first name. Later in the conversation, when he has become more comfortable, and perhaps less fearful of Elinor's refusing to listen, he does call her "Marianne."

17. His obligation in Devonshire is to visit his cousin Mrs. Smith, whose estate he hopes to inherit.

18. *interesting*: engaging, inclined to arouse curiosity or emotion.

19. *manners*: outward conduct and demeanor.

20. Willoughby's statement confirms what the description of their initial conversation suggested (pp. 88–90), that he was mostly responding to her enthusiasm and affection.

A contemporary picture of extravagant living.

[From William Combe, *The History of Johnny Quae Genus* (London, 1822; 1903 reprint), p. 150]

myself pleasing to her,[21] without any design of returning her affection."[22]

Miss Dashwood at this point, turning her eyes on him with the most angry contempt, stopped him, by saying,

"It is hardly worth while, Mr. Willoughby, for you to relate, or for me to listen any longer. Such a beginning as this cannot be followed by any thing.—Do not let me be pained by hearing any thing more on the subject."

"I insist on your hearing the whole of it," he replied. "My fortune was never large, and I had always been expensive, always in the habit of associating with people of better income than myself.[23] Every year since my coming of age,[24] or even before, I believe, had added to my debts;[25] and though the death of my old cousin, Mrs. Smith, was to set me free; yet that event being uncertain, and possibly far distant, it had been for some time my intention to re-establish my circumstances by marrying a woman of fortune.[26] To attach myself to your sister, therefore, was not a thing to be thought of;—and with a meanness,[27] selfishness, cruelty—which no indignant, no contemptuous look, even of yours, Miss Dashwood, can ever reprobate too much—I was acting in this manner, trying to engage her regard, without a thought of returning it.—But one thing may be said for me, even in that horrid state of selfish vanity, I did not know the extent of the injury I meditated, because I did not *then* know what it was to love. But have I ever known it?[28]—Well may it be doubted; for, had I really loved, could I have sacrificed my feelings to vanity, to avarice?—or, what is more, could I have sacrificed her's?—But I have done it. To avoid a comparative poverty, which her affection and her society would have deprived of all its horrors,[29] I have, by raising myself to affluence, lost every thing that could make it a blessing."

"You did then," said Elinor, a little softened, "believe yourself at one time attached to her."

"To have resisted such attractions, to have withstood such tenderness!—Is there a man on earth who could have done it!—Yes, I found myself, by insensible degrees, sincerely fond of her;[30] and

21. His conscious efforts to please her show why they were able to achieve the seemingly perfect union of tastes that Marianne believed in so ardently.

22. Willoughby would have been especially wrong in the context of a society in which marriage was so essential for a woman and she had only a limited number of years before losing her eligibility. His behavior would not only cause a woman to suffer heartbreak, but might also undermine her chances of ever marrying, due to the time she spent focused on him, as well as the time she might need to recover before being able to accept and encourage the attentions of other men.

23. His estate at Combe Magna, which seemed to be his only source of income, gave him six to seven hundred pounds a year (p. 136). This was not a lot compared to what many upper-class men enjoyed, especially those in London or resort towns like Bath, the places where Willoughby seemed to spend much of his time.

24. One came of age at twenty-one and would be freed from the legal guardianship of a parent or other relative. This enabled Willoughby to contract debts easily.

25. The young man who, tempted by pleasure and bad company, fell into a dissolute life and became heavily indebted was a favorite figure in literary works of the time. A famous series of paintings and engravings by the eighteenth-century artist William Hogarth, *A Rake's Progress*, presented a widely circulated vision of such a man. For a picture from a contemporary book whose main character fell into such trouble, see preceding page.

26. Marrying a woman of fortune was a typical remedy for men in Willoughby's position. His own good looks and charm may have made him especially inclined to consider it.

27. *meanness*: baseness.

28. He explains immediately below when he did know love, or at least some semblance of it.

29. Meaning he would not have suffered any of the pains from poverty with Marianne as his wife. Such a declaration of complete indifference to money echoes Marianne's expression of disdain for any relationship of wealth and happiness (p. 174). Both cases suggest a lack of realism.

30. Elinor's question focused on the crucial issue of whether he really loved her. Willoughby's answer here indicates that he did, even if it took him a while. This means Marianne was right to perceive his affection for her. Her principal mistake was to behave as if they were engaged, when Willoughby was not willing to make an open commitment and declaration of love.

the happiest hours of my life were what I spent with her, when I felt my intentions were strictly honourable, and my feelings blameless. Even *then*, however, when fully determined on paying my addresses to[31] her, I allowed myself most improperly to put off, from day to day, the moment of doing it, from an unwillingness to enter into an engagement while my circumstances were so greatly embarrassed.[32] I will not reason here—nor will I stop for *you* to expatiate on the absurdity, and the worse than absurdity, of scrupling to engage my faith where my honour was already bound.[33] The event has proved, that I was a cunning fool,[34] providing with great circumspection for a possible opportunity of making myself contemptible and wretched for ever. At last, however, my resolution was taken, and I had determined, as soon as I could engage her alone, to justify the attentions I had so invariably paid her, and openly assure her of an affection which I had already taken such pains to display.[35] But in the interim—in the interim of the very few hours that were to pass, before I could have an opportunity of speaking with her in private—a circumstance occurred—an unlucky circumstance, to ruin all my resolution, and with it all my comfort. A discovery took place,"—here he hesitated and looked down.—"Mrs. Smith had somehow or other been informed,[36] I imagine by some distant relation, whose interest it was to deprive me of her favour,[37] of an affair, a connection—but I need not explain myself farther," he added, looking at her with an heightened colour and an inquiring eye,—"your particular intimacy—you have probably heard the whole story long ago."[38]

"I have," returned Elinor, colouring likewise and hardening her heart anew against any compassion for him, "I have heard it all. And how you will explain away any part of your guilt in that dreadful business, I confess is beyond my comprehension."

"Remember," cried Willoughby, "from whom you received the account. Could it be an impartial one? I acknowledge that her situation and her character ought to have been respected by me. I do not mean to justify myself, but at the same time cannot leave

31. *paying my addresses to*: courting and, in this case, proposing.

32. He did not want to propose while he was in such a troubled financial situation.

33. His affectionate behavior toward Marianne, and the intimacy they had established, bound him in honor to marry her, even if he had not actually pledged his faith by asking her. Willoughby's statement indicates his awareness of the moral principle he violated.

34. This refers to his consistently avoiding any actual words or deeds that would truly bind him to Marianne. Men who liked to flirt with women, without any intention of marriage, would need a certain amount of cunning to do this safely. Among the friends who helped lead Willoughby into debt, he may have met some who were practiced at this and showed him how to play the game successfully.

35. An open declaration of love would be tantamount to a proposal. Willoughby's careful avoidance of this shows how well he knew what he was doing.

36. Willoughby's hesitation could result from his embarrassment at discussing a subject that places him in such a terrible light, and from his awareness that this subject is improper to speak about before ladies.

37. The distant relation would have been hoping to displace Willoughby as Mrs. Smith's heir. Because inheritance was the principal way to acquire wealth among the genteel classes in this society, conflicts among relatives over the will of a wealthy person were frequent.

38. His discomfort returns. He figures that Elinor has already heard the story of Eliza Williams from Colonel Brandon.

you to suppose that I have nothing to urge—that because she was injured she was irreproachable, and because I was a libertine, *she* must be a saint.[39] If the violence of her passions, the weakness of her understanding—I do not mean, however, to defend myself.[40] Her affection for me deserved better treatment, and I often, with great self-reproach, recal the tenderness which, for a very short time, had the power of creating any return.[41] I wish—I heartily wish it had never been. But I have injured more than herself; and I have injured one, whose affection for me—(may I say it?) was scarcely less warm than her's; and whose mind[42]—Oh! how infinitely superior!"—[43]

"Your indifference, however, towards that unfortunate girl—I must say it, unpleasant to me as the discussion of such a subject may well be—your indifference is no apology for your cruel neglect of her. Do not think yourself excused by any weakness, any natural defect of understanding on her side, in the wanton cruelty so evident on yours. You must have known that while you were enjoying yourself in Devonshire, pursuing fresh schemes, always gay, always happy, she was reduced to the extremest indigence."

"But, upon my soul, I did *not* know it," he warmly replied; "I did not recollect that I had omitted to give her my direction;[44] and common sense might have told her how to find it out."[45]

"Well, sir, and what said Mrs. Smith?"

"She taxed[46] me with the offence at once, and my confusion may be guessed. The purity of her life, the formality of her notions, her ignorance of the world[47]—every thing was against me. The matter itself I could not deny, and vain was every endeavour to soften it. She was previously disposed, I believe, to doubt the morality of my conduct in general, and was moreover discontented with the very little attention, the very little portion of my time that I had bestowed on her, in my present visit.[48] In short, it ended in a total breach. By one measure I might have saved myself. In the height of her morality, good woman! she offered to forgive the past, if I would marry Eliza. That could not

39. Willoughby may have a point here. In Colonel Brandon's account of the affair, Eliza's close friend refused to divulge any details, even though it was leading Eliza to social ruin, and Eliza's having such a friend suggests that she was not extremely scrupulous, or at least not very wise.

40. The implication of his words is that she took much of the initiative. But after saying that he draws back, for he knows it is dishonorable to defend himself at her expense after what he has done. Here, as elsewhere, Willoughby shows a knowledge of good principles, even as he frequently transgresses them.

41. That is, her tenderness sparked him to feel a brief tenderness in return. In the case of Marianne he was also mostly responding to her passion.

42. *mind:* inner character, both emotional and intellectual.

43. His recognition of Marianne's superiority suggests that he may never have contemplated seducing her, as Marianne had shuddered to imagine. A further deterrent may have come from knowing that seducing a young woman of a respectable family, in a quiet rural neighborhood, would ruin his own standing there, including with the cousin whose property he hoped to inherit. In contrast, in Bath he was able to operate under the cover of relative anonymity, for it contained large numbers of visitors who knew little of one another; it was a place where he did not live, and the girl in question had no family there.

44. *direction:* address.

45. This still means Willoughby himself took no trouble to learn of her fate or location. Even now he asks nothing about Eliza's current state, though he knows that Elinor's acquaintance with Colonel Brandon means she might have some information, nor does he ask about his own child, though he must suspect the possibility of a child and may even have been told of it by Colonel Brandon when he challenged Willoughby to a duel.

46. *taxed:* accused, charged.

47. This means specifically her ignorance of other cases of such behavior, which might make Willoughby's deed seem less unusual or shocking. One meaning of "the world" was wealthy and fashionable society, and Willoughby, who has lived among rich friends, may be suggesting that someone conversant with this milieu would not be so censorious.

48. After Willoughby met Marianne he spent most of his time with her and her family (p. 136), at the expense of Mrs. Smith. His neglect of her indicates both his selfishness, since she was his relative and his hostess, and his imprudence, since he was expecting to inherit her money.

be[49]—and I was formally dismissed from her favour and her house.[50] The night following this affair—I was to go the next morning—was spent by me in deliberating on what my future conduct should be. The struggle was great—but it ended too soon. My affection for Marianne, my thorough conviction of her attachment to me—it was all insufficient to outweigh that dread of poverty,[51] or get the better of those false ideas of the necessity of riches, which I was naturally inclined to feel, and expensive society[52] had increased. I had reason to believe myself secure of my present wife, if I chose to address her, and I persuaded myself to think that nothing else in common prudence remained for me to do. An heavy scene however awaited me, before I could leave Devonshire;—I was engaged to dine with you on that very day; some apology was therefore necessary for my breaking the engagement. But whether I should write this apology, or deliver it in person, was a point of long debate. To see Marianne, I felt would be dreadful, and I even doubted whether I could see her again and keep to my resolution. In that point, however, I under-valued my own magnanimity,[53] as the event declared; for I went, I saw her, and saw her miserable, and left her miserable—and left her hoping never to see her again."

"Why did you call, Mr. Willoughby?" said Elinor, reproach-fully; "a note would have answered every purpose.—Why was it necessary to call?"

"It was necessary to my own pride. I could not bear to leave the country[54] in a manner that might lead you, or the rest of the neighbourhood, to suspect any part of what had really passed between Mrs. Smith and myself—and I resolved therefore on call-ing at the cottage, in my way to Honiton.[55] The sight of your dear sister, however, was really dreadful; and to heighten the matter, I found her alone. You were all gone I do not know where. I had left her only the evening before, so fully, so firmly resolved within myself on doing right! A few hours were to have engaged her to me for ever; and I remember how happy, how gay were my spirits, as I walked from the cottage to Allenham, satisfied with myself, delighted with every body! But in this, our last interview of friend-

49. His absolute dismissal of the possibility of marrying her could result from the importance of female chastity, which would make him reluctant to marry an unchaste woman even if he was the cause of her fall, from his wish to find a wife with a large fortune, from Eliza's social position, from lack of affection, or from some combination of these. Her illegitimate birth would taint her by itself, as would her lack of family and fortune, since Colonel Brandon was not in a position to give her a substantial amount; most people placed great importance on such considerations when choosing a mate, and Willoughby's association with the wealthy may have made him especially prone to such judgments.

50. By "dismissed from her favor" he means disinherited.

51. As with other characters in the novel he defines poverty according to the standards of his class. The six to seven hundred pounds a year from his estate at Combe Magna, which Mrs. Smith could not take away, would by itself give him a higher income than the great majority of the population at the time.

52. *expensive society*: the society or company of those who spent lavishly.

53. *magnanimity*: fortitude; in other words, his ability to endure her misery without weakening his resolution of leaving her.

54. *country*: county.

55. Honiton, a town in eastern Devonshire, was already mentioned as the first important stop when journeying east from Barton (p. 124); see also map, p. 739.

ship, I approached her with a sense of guilt that almost took from me the power of dissembling. Her sorrow, her disappointment, her deep regret, when I told her that I was obliged to leave Devonshire so immediately—I never shall forget it—united too with such reliance, such confidence in me!—Oh, God!—what an hard-hearted rascal I was!"

They were both silent for a few moments. Elinor first spoke.

"Did you tell her that you should soon return?"

"I do not know what I told her," he replied, impatiently; "less than was due to the past, beyond a doubt, and in all likelihood much more than was justified by the future. I cannot think of it.—It won't do.—Then came your dear mother to torture me farther, with all her kindness and confidence. Thank Heaven! it *did* torture me. I was miserable. Miss Dashwood, you cannot have an idea of the comfort it gives me to look back on my own misery. I owe such a grudge to myself for the stupid, rascally folly of my own heart, that all my past sufferings under it are only triumph and exultation to me now.[56] Well, I went, left all that I loved, and went to those to whom, at best, I was only indifferent. My journey to town—travelling with my own horses, and therefore so tediously[57]—no creature to speak to—my own reflections so cheerful—when I looked forward everything so inviting!—when I looked back at Barton, the picture so soothing!—oh! it was a blessed journey!"

He stopt.

"Well, sir," said Elinor, who, though pitying him, grew impatient for his departure, "and this is all?"

"All!—no,—have you forgot what passed in town?—That infamous letter—Did she shew it you?"

"Yes, I saw every note that passed."

"When the first of her's reached me, (as it immediately did, for I was in town the whole time,) what I felt is—in the common phrase, not to be expressed; in a more simple one—perhaps too simple to raise any emotion—my feelings were very, very painful.[58]—Every line, every word was—in the hackneyed metaphor which their dear writer, were she here, would forbid—

56. He speaks almost solely of what he suffered and makes no attempt to imagine what Marianne was certainly suffering during this same time.

57. *tediously:* slowly, in a wearisome fashion. Traveling with his own horses would be much less expensive, but it would also be much slower, since the horses would have to stop frequently to eat, drink, and rest; the reason for normally changing horses approximately every ten miles on long journeys was that each new set of horses would be well rested and fed and ready to gallop at maximum speed. Willoughby presumably chose this means of travel because his rupture with Mrs. Smith made him worry about his finances. He says he was confident of marrying a rich woman, but may have hesitated to rely on that until he saw her in London.

58. "Not to be expressed" was a common way of describing feelings that were overwhelming.

a dagger to my heart. To know that Marianne was in town was—in the same language—a thunderbolt.—Thunderbolts and daggers!—what a reproof would she have given me![59]—her taste, her opinions—I believe they are better known to me than my own,—and I am sure they are dearer."[60]

Elinor's heart, which had undergone many changes in the course of this extraordinary conversation, was now softened again;—yet she felt it her duty to check such ideas in her companion as the last.

"This is not right, Mr. Willoughby.—Remember that you are married. Relate only what in your conscience you think necessary for me to hear."[61]

"Marianne's note, by assuring me that I was still as dear to her as in former days, that in spite of the many, many weeks we had been separated, she was as constant in her own feelings, and as full of faith in the constancy of mine as ever, awakened all my remorse. I say awakened, because time and London, business and dissipation, had in some measure quieted it, and I had been growing a fine hardened villain, fancying myself indifferent to her, and chusing to fancy that she too must have become indifferent to me; talking to myself of our past attachment as a mere idle, trifling, business, shrugging up my shoulders in proof of its being so, and silencing every reproach, overcoming every scruple, by secretly saying now and then, 'I shall be heartily glad to hear she is well married.'—But this note made me know myself better. I felt that she was infinitely dearer to me than any other woman in the world, and that I was using her infamously. But everything was then just settled between Miss Grey and me. To retreat was impossible. All that I had to do, was to avoid you both. I sent no answer to Marianne, intending by that means to preserve myself from her farther notice; and for some time I was even determined not to call in Berkeley-street;—but at last, judging it wiser to affect the air of a cool, common acquaintance than anything else, I watched you all safely out of the house one morning, and left my name."[62]

"Watched us out of the house!"

59. Thunderbolts and daggers were clichéd metaphors used frequently in conventional fiction of the time. Marianne scorned all jargon or hackneyed language (pp. 84–86 and 182–186), a sentiment in keeping with the Romantic emphasis on originality. It also corresponds to some of Jane Austen's attitudes: in a letter to a niece on her draft of a novel, she wishes her niece would not have a character "plunge into a vortex of Dissipation. I do not object to the Thing, but I cannot bear the expression;—it is such thorough novel slang—and so old, that I dare say Adam met with it in the first novel he opened" (Sept. 28, 1814).

60. Marianne had ardently expressed her strong opinions to Willoughby, and obviously succeeded in imparting them to him, someone who had probably not thought much about many of these matters before.

61. Avowing such passionate and high regard for another woman is disrespectful to his current wife.

62. Meaning he left his visiting card with his name on it; this occurred on p. 312.

"Even so. You would be surprised to hear how often I watched
you, how often I was on the point of falling in with you.[63] I have
entered many a shop to avoid your sight, as the carriage drove
by.[64] Lodging as I did in Bond-street,[65] there was hardly a day in
which I did not catch a glimpse of one or other of you; and nothing but the most constant watchfulness on my side, a most invariably prevailing desire to keep out of your sight, could have
separated us so long. I avoided the Middletons as much as possible, as well as everybody else who was likely to prove an acquaintance in common. Not aware of their being in town, however, I
blundered on Sir John, I believe, the first day of his coming, and
the day after I had called at Mrs. Jennings's. He asked me to a
party, a dance at his house in the evening.—Had he *not* told me as
an inducement that you and your sister were to be there, I should
have felt it too certain a thing, to trust myself near him. The next
morning brought another short note from Marianne—still affectionate, open, artless,[66] confiding—everything that could make
my conduct most hateful. I could not answer it. I tried—but could
not frame a sentence. But I thought of her, I believe, every
moment of the day. If you *can* pity me, Miss Dashwood, pity my
situation as it was *then*. With my head and heart full of your sister,
I was forced to play the happy lover to another woman!—Those
three or four weeks were worse than all. Well, at last, as I need not
tell you, you were forced on me; and what a sweet figure I cut!—
what an evening of agony it was![67]—Marianne, beautiful as an
angel on one side, calling me Willoughby in such a tone!—Oh!
God!—holding out her hand to me, asking me for an explanation
with those bewitching eyes fixed in such speaking[68] solicitude on
my face!—and Sophia, jealous as the devil on the other hand,
looking all that was[69]—Well, it does not signify; it is over now.—
Such an evening!—I ran away from you all as soon as I could; but
not before I had seen Marianne's sweet face as white as death.—
That was the last, last look I ever had of her;—the last manner in
which she appeared to me. It was a horrid sight!—Yet when I
thought of her to-day as really dying, it was a kind of comfort to
me to imagine that I knew exactly how she would appear to those,

63. *falling in with you*: coming upon you by chance, meeting you.

64. Elinor and Marianne were repeatedly described riding in Mrs. Jennings's carriage in London. They could have easily caught a glimpse of Willoughby through the carriage windows.

65. Bond Street was a main shopping street where Elinor and Marianne, as well as other characters, went on various errands. Marianne in fact watched out particularly for Willoughby when on the street (p. 304).

66. *artless*: guileless, sincere.

67. Willoughby was shown experiencing acute discomfort in this scene (pp. 324–326), which made Elinor reflect immediately afterward that he seemed conscious of his bad behavior—as he now confirms.

68. *speaking*: expressive, eloquent.

69. In the same sentence he compares Marianne to an angel and his wife to a devil. In describing the latter he cannot even finish the thought, since it would mean using language one should not employ when speaking of one's wife. The hyperbole of his language, even when recounting an incident of several months earlier, shows his strong feelings, though it also calls his character into question, for in Austen's novels the use of exaggerated expression generally indicates some flaw, whether insincerity or a weak intellect or excessive indulgence of emotion.

who saw her last in this world. She was before me, constantly before me, as I travelled, in the same look and hue."

A short pause of mutual thoughtfulness succeeded. Willoughby first rousing himself, broke it thus:

"Well, let me make haste and be gone. Your sister is certainly better, certainly out of danger?"

"We are assured of it."

"Your poor mother too!—doting on Marianne."

"But the letter, Mr. Willoughby, your own letter; have you anything to say about that?"

"Yes, yes, *that* in particular. Your sister wrote to me again, you know, the very next morning. You saw what she said. I was breakfasting at the Ellisons,[70]—and her letter, with some others, was brought to me there from my lodgings.[71] It happened to catch Sophia's eye before it caught mine—and its size, the elegance of the paper, the hand-writing altogether,[72] immediately gave her a suspicion. Some vague report had reached her before of my attachment to some young lady in Devonshire, and what had passed within her observation the preceding evening had marked who the young lady was, and made her more jealous than ever. Affecting that air of playfulness, therefore, which is delightful in a woman one loves, she opened the letter directly, and read its contents. She was well paid for her impudence.[73] She read what made her wretched. Her wretchedness I could have borne,[74] but her passion—her malice—At all events it must be appeased. And in short—what do you think of my wife's style of letter-writing?— delicate—tender—truly feminine—was it not?"[75]

"Your wife!—The letter was in your own hand-writing."

"Yes, but I had only the credit of servilely copying such sentences as I was ashamed to put my name to.[76] The original was all her own—her own happy thoughts and gentle diction. But what could I do?—we were engaged, every thing in preparation, the day almost fixed—But I am talking like a fool. Preparation!— day!—In honest words, her money was necessary to me, and in a situation like mine, any thing was to be done to prevent a rupture. And after all, what did it signify to my character[77] in the opinion of

70. The Ellisons were Miss Grey's guardians, with whom she would have been staying until her marriage, since social conventions would forbid a single young woman to lodge on her own.

71. Marianne sent her letter very early in the morning, and the fast and frequent deliveries of the London two-penny post meant it could have arrived at Willoughby's lodgings before breakfast, which was often at nine or ten o'clock for the wealthy, and then been carried to the Ellisons' by a servant.

72. Other ladies in Jane Austen use elegant paper. As for the handwriting, men's and women's handwriting were generally spoken of as different, partly because women were taught a special ladies' hand that was particularly graceful and ornamental.

73. *impudence*: shamelessness.

74. The words indicate his callousness toward the woman who would become his wife.

75. Prevailing ideas of femininity emphasized tenderness and delicacy, in particular a sensitivity to others and propriety, as being natural to women and important virtues for them to cultivate and possess.

76. Willoughby's servile copying is in keeping with much of his behavior, in which bad actions frequently result more from weakness and an inclination to follow the path of least resistance than from active villainy or malice. This is true of other characters in Jane Austen, including several who are of a similar type as Willoughby, that is, a charming and agreeable young man who attracts a heroine before proving untrustworthy to some degree. Other examples are Wickham of *Pride and Prejudice*, Henry Crawford of *Mansfield Park*, and Frank Churchill of *Emma*.

77. *character*: reputation, standing.

Marianne and her friends, in what language my answer was couched?—It must have been only to one end. My business was to declare myself a scoundrel, and whether I did it with a bow or a bluster was of little importance.—'I am ruined for ever in their opinion—said I to myself—I am shut out for ever from their society, they already think me an unprincipled fellow, this letter will only make them think me a blackguard one.' Such were my reasonings, as, in a sort of desperate carelessness, I copied my wife's words, and parted with the last relics of Marianne. Her three notes—unluckily they were all in my pocket-book,[78] or I should have denied their existence, and hoarded them for ever—I was forced to put them up, and could not even kiss them. And the lock of hair—that too I had always carried about me in the same pocket-book, which was now searched by Madam with the most ingratiating virulence,[79]—the dear lock—all, every memento was torn from me."

"You are very wrong, Mr. Willoughby, very blameable," said Elinor, while her voice, in spite of herself, betrayed her compassionate emotion; "you ought not to speak in this way, either of Mrs. Willoughby or my sister. You have made your own choice. It was not forced on you. Your wife has a claim to your politeness, to your respect, at least. She must be attached to you, or she would not have married you. To treat her with unkindness, to speak of her slightingly is no atonement to Marianne—nor can I suppose it a relief to your own conscience."

"Do not talk to me of my wife," said he with an heavy sigh.—"She does not deserve your compassion.—She knew I had no regard for her when we married.[80]—Well, married we were, and came down to Combe Magna to be happy, and afterwards returned to town to be gay.—And now do you pity me, Miss Dashwood?—or have I said all this to no purpose?—Am I—be it only one degree—am I less guilty in your opinion than I was before?—My intentions were not always wrong. Have I explained away any part of my guilt?"

"Yes, you have certainly removed something—a little.—You have proved yourself, on the whole, less faulty than I had believed

78. *pocket-book*: small book kept in a pocket where items could be stored (see p. 115, note 23).

79. His calling his wife "Madam," almost as if he would rather not speak her name, and his description of her "ingratiating virulence" constitute his strongest expression yet of hostility toward her. The more he speaks of her, and remembers the contrasting character of Marianne, the more disgusted he becomes with his current choice—though, as Elinor immediately points out, his disgust, however justified, is no excuse for exhibiting and articulating it before a stranger.

80. Her motive was presumably to gain the prestige of being married to someone who had a landed estate (see p. 359, note 9) and whose charm, wit, and good looks made him cut a fine figure in fashionable society. She also may have been motivated to marry by the animosity earlier described between herself and Mrs. Ellison, one of her guardians with whom she would have been living since young women could not live on their own (p. 358).

you. You have proved your heart less wicked, much less wicked. But I hardly know—the misery that you have inflicted—I hardly know what could have made it worse."

"Will you repeat to your sister when she is recovered, what I have been telling you?—Let me be a little lightened too in her opinion as well as in yours. You tell me that she has forgiven me already. Let me be able to fancy that a better knowledge of my heart, and of my present feelings, will draw from her a more spontaneous, more natural, more gentle, less dignified, forgiveness. Tell her of my misery and my penitence—tell her that my heart was never inconstant to her, and if you will, that at this moment she is dearer to me than ever."

"I will tell her all that is necessary to what may comparatively be called, your justification. But you have not explained to me the particular reason of your coming now, nor how you heard of her illness."

"Last night, in Drury-lane lobby,[81] I ran against[82] Sir John Middleton, and when he saw who I was—for the first time these two months—he spoke to me.—That he had cut me ever since my marriage, I had seen without surprise or resentment.[83] Now, however, his good-natured, honest, stupid[84] soul, full of indignation against me, and concern for your sister, could not resist the temptation of telling me what he knew ought to—though probably he did not think it *would*—vex me horridly.—As bluntly as he could speak it, therefore, he told me that Marianne Dashwood was dying of a putrid fever[85] at Cleveland—a letter that morning received from Mrs. Jennings declared her danger most imminent[86]—the Palmers all gone off in a fright, &c.—I was too much shocked to be able to pass myself off as insensible[87] even to the undiscerning Sir John. His heart was softened in seeing mine suffer; and so much of his ill-will was done away, that when we parted, he almost shook me by the hand while he reminded me of an old promise about a pointer puppy.[88] What I felt on hearing that your sister was dying—and dying too, believing me the greatest villain upon earth, scorning, hating me in her latest moments—for how could I tell what horrid projects might not

81. Drury Lane was, with Covent Garden, one of the two London theaters licensed to perform spoken drama during most of the year. Ironically it was not actually open at the time this novel was written and published: it had burned down in 1809, and a new building was completed only in 1812. Sir John's attendance at a play shows that he enjoys other forms of amusement besides sport. For a picture of the newly built theater, see below.

82. *ran against:* encountered, ran into.

83. To cut someone meant to refuse to acknowledge or speak to that person. It was a standard means of indicating strong disapproval.

84. *stupid:* simple, undiscerning.

85. *putrid fever:* typhus (see p. 573, note 4).

86. Marianne first caught cold seven days before this, and her illness was pronounced to have a "putrid tendency" three days later (see chronology, p. 716). Mrs. Jennings would have sent the letter mentioned by Sir John a day or two after that, meaning two or three days before the current conversation, and it arrived in London a day or two later (mail service was fairly rapid then). Mrs. Jennings's pessimism about Marianne's sickness would have made her write of her death as probable.

87. *insensible:* indifferent. He would prefer to look indifferent in order not to acknowledge publicly his consciousness of his wrong behavior.

88. Sir John, in execrating Willoughby after his abandonment of Marianne, had mentioned offering him one of his dog's puppies (p. 398)

Drury Lane Theatre.

[From *The Repository of arts, literature, fashions, manufactures, &c,* Vol. VIII (1812), p. 287]

have been imputed?[89] *One* person I was sure would represent me as capable of anything[90] — What I felt was dreadful! — My resolution was soon made, and at eight o'clock this morning I was in my carriage. Now you know all."

Elinor made no answer. Her thoughts were silently fixed on the irreparable injury which too early an independence[91] and its consequent habits of idleness, dissipation, and luxury, had made in the mind, the character, the happiness, of a man who, to every advantage of person and talents, united a disposition naturally open and honest, and a feeling, affectionate temper.[92] The world had made him extravagant and vain — Extravagance and vanity had made him cold-hearted and selfish. Vanity, while seeking its own guilty triumph at the expense of another, had involved him in a real attachment, which extravagance, or at least its offspring, necessity, had required to be sacrificed.[93] Each faulty propensity in leading him to evil, had led him likewise to punishment. The attachment, from which against honour, against feeling, against every better interest he had outwardly torn himself, now, when no longer allowable, governed every thought; and the connection, for the sake of which he had, with little scruple, left her sister to misery, was likely to prove a source of unhappiness to himself of a far more incurable nature.[94] From a reverie of this kind she was recalled at the end of some minutes by Willoughby, who, rousing himself from a reverie at least equally painful, started up in preparation for going, and said,

"There is no use in staying here; I must be off."

"Are you going back to town?"

"No — to Combe Magna. I have business there; from thence to town in a day or two. Good bye."

He held out his hand. She could not refuse to give him her's; — he pressed it with affection.[95]

"And you *do* think something better of me than you did?" — said he, letting it fall, and leaning against the mantle-piece as if forgetting he was to go.

Elinor assured him that she did; — that she forgave, pitied, wished him well — was even interested in his happiness — and

89. The horrid project he is probably thinking of particularly is that of seducing her. It is notable that, in describing his sudden wish to see Marianne, he speaks more of saving his own reputation in her eyes than in learning of her condition and chances for recovery.

90. The one person is Colonel Brandon, who would naturally have reason to speak ill of Willoughby, and in particular to impute a design of seduction to him.

91. *independence:* financial independence.

92. His good temper and other positive qualities make his case particularly unfortunate, as well as a powerful lesson in the dangers of privilege and idleness. In *Emma* the rich and spoiled title character, who suffers from the "power of having rather too much her own way," acts heedlessly and willfully and ends up causing great harm to herself and others—though in her case she manages to reform in time.

93. Elinor's reflections summarize the moral lesson, though her language, which echoes that found in moral essays, seems a little formal for a personal reflection made in the midst of a highly charged dialogue. The treatment of abstractions—vanity, extravagance, necessity—almost as living entities that act and engender others is common in eighteenth-century writing.

94. Thus there is a poetic justice in his fate, compared to Marianne's.

95. His eagerness to shake her hand, at the end of what will almost certainly be his last conversation with any of the Dashwoods, contrasts with his extreme reluctance to shake hands with Marianne in his previous, and final, encounter with her.

added some gentle counsel as to the behaviour most likely to promote it. His answer was not very encouraging.

"As to that," said he, "I must rub through[96] the world as well as I can. Domestic happiness is out of the question. If, however, I am allowed to think that you and yours feel an interest in my fate and actions, it may be the means—it may put me on my guard—at least, it will be something to live for. Marianne to be sure is lost to me for ever. Were I even by any blessed chance at liberty again"—[97]

Elinor stopped him with a reproof.

"Well"—he replied—"once more good bye. I shall now go away and live in dread of one event."

"What do you mean?"

"Your sister's marriage."

"You are very wrong. She can never be more lost to you than she is now."

"But she will be gained by some one else. And if that some one should be the very he whom, of all others, I could least bear[98]— But I will not stay to rob myself of all your compassionate good-will, by shewing that where I have most injured I can least forgive.[99] Good bye,—God bless you!"

And with these words, he almost ran out of the room.

96. *rub through*: contrive to keep going through, with more or less difficulty.

97. By "at liberty" he means not married, which would almost certainly require his wife's death. That is why Elinor immediately interrupts and reproves him.

98. He means Colonel Brandon.

99. This inability to forgive shows the limits of his character, though his awareness and admission of that flaw, and of his injury to Colonel Brandon, reveal once more the capacities that could have led him to become a better person.

Chapter Nine

E linor, for some time after he left her, for some time even after
the sound of his carriage had died away, remained too much
oppressed by a croud of ideas, widely differing in themselves, but
of which sadness was the general result, to think even of her sister.

Willoughby, he, whom only half an hour ago she had abhorred
as the most worthless of men, Willoughby, in spite of all his faults,
excited a degree of commiseration for the sufferings produced by
them, which made her think of him as now separated for ever
from her family with a tenderness, a regret, rather in proportion,
as she soon acknowledged within herself—to his wishes than to
his merits.[1] She felt that his influence over her mind was heightened by circumstances which ought not in reason to have weight;
by that person[2] of uncommon attraction, that open, affectionate,
and lively[3] manner which it was no merit to possess; and by that
still ardent love for Marianne, which it was not even innocent to
indulge. But she felt that it was so, long, long before she could feel
his influence less.[4]

When at last she returned to the unconscious Marianne, she
found her just awaking, refreshed by so long and sweet a sleep to
the extent of her hopes. Elinor's heart was full. The past, the present, the future, Willoughby's visit, Marianne's safety, and her
mother's expected arrival, threw her altogether into an agitation
of spirits which kept off every indication of fatigue, and made her
only fearful of betraying herself to her sister. Short was the time,
however, in which that fear could affect her, for within half an
hour after Willoughby's leaving the house, she was again called
down stairs by the sound of another carriage.[5]—Eager to save her
mother from every unnecessary moment's horrible suspense, she
ran immediately into the hall, and reached the outward door just
in time to receive and support her as she entered it.[6]

1. Her feelings correspond to his strong wish to be forgiven rather than to how much he actually deserves this forgiveness.

2. *person*: physical person.

3. *lively*: vivacious, lighthearted, merry.

4. Her admission indicates the power of Willoughby's attractions, and makes his enticement of Marianne more understandable. At the same time, it shows the dangers of such external charms.

5. They just missed Willoughby, which, given the hostility between him and Colonel Brandon, was fortunate for everyone; it also shows how close Willoughby came to being unable to meet Elinor and deliver his confession. Colonel Brandon and Mrs. Dashwood have arrived around an hour earlier than Elinor anticipated: she expected them at ten, Willoughby arrived at eight, his visit lasted around half an hour (see above), and it is now half an hour later. One reason for their early arrival may be that Mrs. Dashwood was already preparing to leave and had arranged for Margaret to be picked up by friends, which would have allowed them to depart soon after Colonel Brandon reached Barton (p. 626).

6. Presumably her mother needs support because of her extreme anguish. The outward door would open to the exterior, in contrast to the inner door between the vestibule and the rest of the house.

Mrs. Dashwood, whose terror as they drew near the house had produced almost the conviction of Marianne's being no more, had no voice to inquire after her, no voice even for Elinor; but *she*, waiting neither for salutation nor inquiry, instantly gave the joyful relief;—and her mother, catching it with all her usual warmth, was in a moment as much overcome by her happiness, as she had been before by her fears. She was supported into the drawing-room between her daughter and her friend;—and there, shedding tears of joy, though still unable to speak, embraced Elinor again and again, turning from her at intervals to press Colonel Brandon's hand, with a look which spoke at once her gratitude, and her conviction of his sharing with herself in the bliss of the moment. He shared it, however, in a silence even greater than her own.[7]

As soon as Mrs. Dashwood had recovered herself, to see Marianne was her first desire; and in two minutes she was with her beloved child, rendered dearer to her than ever by absence, unhappiness, and danger. Elinor's delight, as she saw what each felt in the meeting, was only checked by an apprehension of its robbing Marianne of farther sleep;—but Mrs. Dashwood could be calm, could be even prudent, when the life of a child was at stake, and Marianne, satisfied in knowing her mother was near her, and conscious of being too weak for conversation, submitted readily to the silence and quiet prescribed by every nurse around her.[8] Mrs. Dashwood *would* sit up with her all night, and Elinor, in compliance with her mother's entreaty, went to bed. But the rest, which one night entirely sleepless, and many hours of the most wearing anxiety seemed to make requisite, was kept off by irritation[9] of spirits. Willoughby, "poor Willoughby," as she now allowed herself to call him, was constantly in her thoughts; she would not but have heard his vindication for the world, and now blamed, now acquitted herself for having judged him so harshly before. But her promise of relating it to her sister was invariably painful.[10] She dreaded the performance of it, dreaded what its effect on Marianne might be; doubted whether after such an explanation she could ever be happy with another; and for a

7. She, though not speaking, is still expressing her feelings through strong gestures and looks; he is not even doing that.

8. The nurses probably include Mrs. Jennings, her maid (described earlier as one of the principal nurses), Elinor, and Mrs. Dashwood, who as the mother of three would have had ample nursing experience.

9. *irritation:* excitement, agitation.

10. Elinor is strongly swayed back and forth by her emotions, a state that brings her closer to Marianne. But unlike her sister, she attempts to combat the influence of nonrational factors in her thinking.

moment wished Willoughby a widower.[11] Then, remembering
Colonel Brandon, reproved herself, felt that to *his* sufferings and
his constancy far more than to his rival's, the reward of her sister
was due, and wished any thing rather than Mrs. Willoughby's
death.

The shock of Colonel Brandon's errand at Barton had been
much softened to Mrs. Dashwood by her own previous alarm;[12]
for so great was her uneasiness about Marianne, that she had
already determined to set out for Cleveland on that very day, without waiting for any farther intelligence, and had so far settled her
journey before his arrival, that the Careys were then expected
every moment to fetch Margaret away, as her mother was unwilling to take her where there might be infection.

Marianne continued to mend every day, and the brilliant
cheerfulness of Mrs. Dashwood's looks and spirits proved her to
be, as she repeatedly declared herself, one of the happiest women
in the world. Elinor could not hear the declaration, nor witness its
proofs without sometimes wondering whether her mother ever
recollected Edward.[13] But Mrs. Dashwood, trusting to the tem-
perate account of her own disappointment which Elinor had sent
her, was led away by the exuberance of her joy to think only of
what would increase it. Marianne was restored to her from a danger in which, as she now began to feel, her own mistaken judgment in encouraging the unfortunate attachment to Willoughby,
had contributed to place her; — and in her recovery she had yet
another source of joy unthought of by Elinor. It was thus imparted
to her, as soon as any opportunity of private conference between
them occurred.

"At last we are alone. My Elinor, you do not yet know all my
happiness. Colonel Brandon loves Marianne. He has told me so
himself."

Her daughter, feeling by turns both pleased and pained,[14] surprised and not surprised, was all silent attention.

"You are never like me, dear Elinor, or I should wonder at your
composure now. Had I sat down to wish for any possible good to
my family, I should have fixed on Colonel Brandon's marrying

11. This wish for Willoughby to be free again, after all he has done, is a sign of his dangerous influence on her.

12. Mrs. Dashwood was already alarmed, presumably by the delay in her daughters' return home and by letters from Elinor telling of Marianne's illness.

13. Elinor cannot help thinking of her own situation, and perhaps feeling a little resentment at her mother's neglect of her own sufferings in favor of Marianne's more visible ones.

14. Elinor is probably pained because of her fear that Marianne may not be able to return Colonel Brandon's love, and he will be doomed to disappointment.

one of you as the object most desirable. And I believe Marianne will be the most happy with him of the two."

Elinor was half inclined to ask her reason for thinking so, because satisfied that none founded on an impartial consideration of their age, characters, or feelings, could be given;[15]—but her mother must always be carried away by her imagination on any interesting subject, and therefore instead of an inquiry, she passed it off with a smile.

"He opened his whole heart to me yesterday as we travelled. It came out quite unawares, quite undesignedly. I, you may well believe, could talk of nothing but my child;—he could not conceal his distress; I saw that it equalled my own, and he perhaps, thinking that mere friendship, as the world now goes, would not justify so warm a sympathy—or rather not thinking at all, I suppose—giving way to irresistible feelings, made me acquainted with his earnest, tender, constant, affection for Marianne. He has loved her, my Elinor, ever since the first moment of seeing her."

Here, however, Elinor perceived,—not the language, not the professions of Colonel Brandon, but the natural embellishments of her mother's active fancy, which fashioned every thing delightful to her, as it chose.

"His regard for her, infinitely surpassing anything that Willoughby ever felt or feigned, as much more warm, as more sincere or constant—which ever we are to call it—has subsisted through all the knowledge of dear Marianne's unhappy prepossession[16] for that worthless young man!—and without selfishness— without encouraging a hope!—could he have seen her happy with another[17]—Such a noble mind!—such openness, such sincerity!—no one can be deceived in *him*."[18]

"Colonel Brandon's character," said Elinor, "as an excellent man, is well established."[19]

"I know it is"—replied her mother seriously, "or after such a warning, *I* should be the last to encourage such affection, or even to be pleased by it. But his coming for me as he did, with such active, such ready friendship, is enough to prove him one of the worthiest of men."

15. Elinor perceives, from long acquaintance with Colonel Brandon, the strong differences between his character and Marianne's. Also, her recent encounter with Willoughby has reminded her of his attractions and of the eagerness and vivacity that he shares with Marianne.

16. *prepossession:* liking, partiality.

17. In other words, Colonel Brandon feared for Marianne's involvement with Willoughby from a genuine concern for her happiness, rather than because he harbored hopes at that time of gaining her for himself.

18. Mrs. Dashwood is thinking of her, and others', misplaced faith in Willoughby.

19. As usual Elinor refers not simply to her own feelings, or even her own observations based on particular incidents or conversations (as her mother is now doing), but to his public reputation, which, as she proceeds to explain, constitutes even more solid proof of his excellence.

"His character, however," answered Elinor, "does not rest on *one* act of kindness, to which his affection for Marianne, were humanity out of the case, would have prompted him. To Mrs. Jennings, to the Middletons, he has been long and intimately known; they equally love and respect him;[20] and even my own knowledge of him, though lately acquired, is very considerable; and so highly do *I* value and esteem him, that if Marianne can be happy with him, I shall be as ready as yourself to think our connection[21] the greatest blessing to us in the world. What answer did you give him?—Did you allow him to hope?"

"Oh! my love, I could not then talk of hope to him or to myself. Marianne might at that moment be dying. But he did not ask for hope or encouragement. His was an involuntary confidence,[22] an irrepressible effusion to a soothing friend—not an application to a parent. Yet after a time I *did* say, for at first I was quite overcome—that if she lived, as I trusted she might, my greatest happiness would lie in promoting their marriage; and since our arrival, since our delightful security[23] I have repeated it to him more fully, have given him every encouragement in my power. Time, a very little time, I tell him, will do everything;—Marianne's heart is not to be wasted for ever on such a man as Willoughby.—His own merits must soon secure it."

"To judge from the Colonel's spirits, however, you have not yet made him equally sanguine."

"No.—He thinks Marianne's affection too deeply rooted for any change in it under a great length of time, and even supposing her heart again free, is too diffident of himself to believe, that with such a difference of age and disposition, he could ever attach her.[24] There, however, he is quite mistaken. His age is only so much beyond her's, as to be an advantage, as to make his character and principles fixed;—and his disposition, I am well convinced, is exactly the very one to make your sister happy. And his person, his manners too, are all in his favour. My partiality does not blind me; he certainly is not so handsome as Willoughby—but at the same time, there is something much more pleasing in his countenance.—There was always a something,—if you

20. In this he contrasts with Willoughby, who was not known by anyone of their acquaintance, except for Sir John, who simply praised him as a good sportsman and pleasant companion.

21. *connection:* family connection through marriage.

22. *confidence:* confiding of private information.

23. They can feel secure of Marianne's recovery.

24. *attach her:* win her affection.

remember,—in Willoughby's eyes at times, which I did not like."

Elinor could *not* remember it;—but her mother, without wait-ing for her assent, continued,

"And his manners, the Colonel's manners are not only more pleasing to me than Willoughby's ever were, but they are of a kind I well know to be more solidly attaching to Marianne. Their gen-tleness, their genuine attention to other people, and their manly unstudied simplicity[25] is much more accordant with her real dis-position, than the liveliness—often artificial, and often ill-timed of the other. I am very sure myself, that had Willoughby turned out as really amiable, as he has proved himself the contrary, Mar-ianne would yet never have been so happy with *him*, as she will be with Colonel Brandon."

She paused.—Her daughter could not quite agree with her, but her dissent was not heard, and therefore gave no offence.

"At Delaford, she will be within an easy distance of me,"[26] added Mrs. Dashwood, "even if I remain at Barton; and in all probability,—for I hear it is a large village,—indeed there cer-tainly *must* be some small house or cottage close by, that would suit us quite as well as our present situation."

Poor Elinor!—here was a new scheme for getting her to Delaford!—but her spirit was stubborn.[27]

"His fortune too!—for at my time of life you know, everybody cares about *that*;—and though I neither know, nor desire to know, what it really is, I am sure it must be a good one."[28]

Here they were interrupted by the entrance of a third person, and Elinor withdrew to think it all over in private, to wish success to her friend, and yet in wishing it, to feel a pang for Willoughby.

25. *simplicity:* sincerity, straightforwardness, freedom from artifice. In *Emma* the heroine articulates a similar ideal of manly behavior when she says that a deceptive character is "So unlike what a man should be!—None of that upright integrity, that strict adherence to truth and principle, that disdain of trick and littleness, which a man should display in every transaction of his life."

26. Delaford is in Dorsetshire, which is immediately east of Devonshire (see map, p. 739). Their home in Barton is in the eastern part of the latter county, so if Colonel Brandon's home is in western Dorsetshire, it could be an easy distance. Of course, Mrs. Dashwood could be exaggerating, due to her general inclination to emphasize the positive in every circumstance.

27. Elinor would not wish to go to Delaford because it would mean seeing a married Edward and Lucy there.

28. Mrs. Dashwood's disdain for knowing the exact extent of others' fortunes contrasts with almost every other character in Jane Austen. While few worry about financial details as much as John Dashwood, most, including the good characters, consider it valuable to know the basic amount of a person's income, especially a potential son-in-law.

Chapter Ten

Marianne's illness, though weakening in its kind,[1] had not been long enough to make her recovery slow; and with youth, natural strength, and her mother's presence in aid, it proceeded so smoothly as to enable her to remove, within four days after the arrival of the latter, into Mrs. Palmer's dressing-room.[2] When there, at her own particular request, for she was impatient to pour forth her thanks to him for fetching her mother, Colonel Brandon was invited to visit her.

His emotion in entering the room, in seeing her altered looks, and in receiving the pale hand which she immediately held out to him, was such, as, in Elinor's conjecture, must arise from something more than his affection for Marianne, or the consciousness of its being known to others; and she soon discovered in his melancholy eye and varying complexion as he looked at her sister, the probable recurrence of many past scenes of misery to his mind, brought back by that resemblance between Marianne and Eliza already acknowledged, and now strengthened by the hollow eye, the sickly skin, the posture of reclining weakness, and the warm acknowledgment of peculiar[3] obligation.

Mrs. Dashwood, not less watchful of what passed than her daughter, but with a mind very differently influenced, and therefore watching to very different effect, saw nothing in the Colonel's behaviour but what arose from the most simple and self-evident sensations, while in the actions and words of Marianne she persuaded herself to think that something more than gratitude already dawned.[4]

At the end of another day or two, Marianne growing visibly stronger every twelve hours, Mrs. Dashwood, urged equally by her own and her daughter's wishes, began to talk of removing to Barton. On *her* measures depended those of her two friends; Mrs.

1. *weakening in its kind:* naturally inclined to weaken its sufferer.

2. The dressing room was usually a large room attached to the bedroom, where one could receive visitors and conduct other business.

3. *peculiar:* special, particular.

4. She has persuaded herself that Marianne is falling in love with him. The

A woman at the opera.

[From *The Repository of arts, literature, fashions, manufactures, &c,* Vol. XI (1814), p. 302]

Jennings could not quit Cleveland during the Dashwoods' stay,[5] and Colonel Brandon was soon brought, by their united request, to consider his own abode there as equally determinate,[6] if not equally indispensable. At his and Mrs. Jennings's united request in return, Mrs. Dashwood was prevailed on to accept the use of his carriage on her journey back, for the better accommodation of her sick child; and the Colonel, at the joint invitation of Mrs. Dashwood and Mrs. Jennings, whose active good-nature made her friendly and hospitable for other people as well as herself,[7] engaged with pleasure to redeem it by a visit at the cottage, in the course of a few weeks.[8]

The day of separation and departure arrived; and Marianne, after taking so particular and lengthened a leave of Mrs. Jennings, one so earnestly grateful, so full of respect and kind wishes as seemed due to her own heart from a secret acknowledgment of past inattention, and bidding Colonel Brandon farewel with the cordiality of a friend, was carefully assisted by him into the carriage, of which he seemed anxious that she should engross at least half.[9] Mrs. Dashwood and Elinor then followed, and the others were left by themselves, to talk of the travellers, and feel their own dulness, till Mrs. Jennings was summoned to her chaise to take comfort in the gossip of her maid for the loss of her two young companions;[10] and Colonel Brandon immediately afterwards took his solitary way to Delaford.[11]

The Dashwoods were two days on the road,[12] and Marianne bore her journey on both, without essential fatigue. Every thing that the most zealous affection, the most solicitous care could do to render her comfortable, was the office of each watchful companion, and each found their reward in her bodily ease, and her calmness of spirits. To Elinor, the observation of the latter was particularly grateful. She, who had seen her week after week so constantly suffering, oppressed by anguish of heart which she had neither courage to speak of, nor fortitude to conceal, now saw with a joy, which no other could equally share, an apparent composure of mind, which, in being the result as she trusted of serious reflection, must eventually lead her to contentment and cheerfulness.

reference below to Marianne's "bidding Colonel Brandon farewel with the cordiality of a friend" suggests this has not happened and Mrs. Dashwood is being overly optimistic in her perceptions.

5.   Mrs. Jennings needs to perform the role of hostess, for she is the one person with a close connection to the owners of the house.

6.   *determinate:* fixed.

7.   Mrs. Jennings is extending Mrs. Dashwood's hospitality.

8.   He would be redeeming his carriage.

9.   A chaise, Colonel Brandon's carriage, holds three people, and Marianne will travel with Elinor and her mother.

10. Mrs. Jennings is returning to London. Servants are shown in Austen's novels as a frequent source of information, and Mrs. Jennings is a great lover of gossip. She was earlier described having her servant inquire of another servant for information (p. 128).

11. Colonel Brandon, lacking his own carriage, may hire one, or he may go on horseback. Men often traveled that way for short distances, and Cleveland's location near Bristol would make it reasonably close to his home in Dorsetshire (see map, p. 739).

12. The distance has earlier been stated to be eighty miles. That would be ten to eleven hours at prevailing speeds, but they probably proceeded more slowly, with frequent rests, because of Marianne's condition. Below they are described as being home for dinner, which was usually at four or five o'clock, so they were not on the road the entire second day.

As they approached Barton, indeed, and entered on scenes, of which every field and every tree brought some peculiar, some painful recollection, she grew silent and thoughtful, and turning away her face from their notice, sat earnestly gazing through the window. But here, Elinor could neither wonder nor blame; and when she saw, as she assisted Marianne from the carriage, that she had been crying, she saw only an emotion too natural in itself to raise anything less tender than pity, and in its unobtrusiveness entitled to praise. In the whole of her subsequent manner, she traced the direction[13] of a mind awakened to reasonable exertion; for no sooner had they entered their common sitting-room, than Marianne turned her eyes around it with a look of resolute firmness, as if determined at once to accustom herself to the sight of every object with which the remembrance of Willoughby could be connected.[14]—She said little, but every sentence aimed at cheerfulness, and though a sigh sometimes escaped her, it never passed away without the atonement of a smile. After dinner she would try her piano-forté. She went to it; but the music on which her eye first rested was an opera,[15] procured for her by Willoughby, containing some of their favourite duets,[16] and bearing on its outward leaf her own name in his hand writing.[17]— That would not do.—She shook her head, put the music aside, and after running over the keys for a minute complained of feebleness in her fingers, and closed the instrument again; declaring however with firmness as she did so, that she should in future practise much.[18]

The next morning produced no abatement in these happy symptoms. On the contrary, with a mind and body alike strengthened by rest, she looked and spoke with more genuine spirit, anticipating the pleasure of Margaret's return, and talking of the dear family party which would then be restored, of their mutual pursuits and cheerful society as the only happiness worth a wish.

"When the weather is settled, and I have recovered my strength," said she, "we will take long walks together every day. We will walk to the farm at the edge of the down,[19] and see how

13. *direction:* disposition.

14. Marianne's new spirit of resolution and improvement will be confirmed by her subsequent words and behavior.

15. Opera music was very popular then. Even at public concerts a large proportion of the music would be songs from operas. For a picture of a woman at the opera, see p. 635.

16. Duets were a favorite type of song in opera, and an opportunity to sing together would have naturally appealed to Marianne and Willoughby.

17. This would be the outward page of the opera score. Many people bought or copied musical scores to play at home.

18. Marianne's misery in London, and the severe illness she suffered just after it, could call into question the decision to have her remain in London after her rejection by Willoughby. Her behavior here, however, suggests that her mother may have been right to keep her from scenes that had such distressing associations with Willoughby. Even now, after more time and with a spirit of fortitude opposite to her earlier state of mind, she is powerfully affected by every reminder of him.

19. A farm usually meant a relatively small plot of land cultivated by someone of modest income; it often was rented from a wealthy landowner. The initial description of Barton spoke of it as full of downs, or expanses of elevated, generally treeless land.

the children go on; we will walk to Sir John's new plantations at Barton-Cross,[20] and the Abbeyland; and we will often go to the old ruins of the Priory, and try to trace its foundations as far as we are told they once reached.[21] I know we shall be happy. I know the summer will pass happily away. I mean never to be later in rising than six; and from that time till dinner I shall divide every moment between music and reading.[22] I have formed my plan, and am determined to enter on a course of serious study. Our own library is too well known to me, to be resorted to for anything beyond mere amusement.[23] But there are many works well worth reading, at the Park; and there are others of more modern production which I know I can borrow of Colonel Brandon.[24] By reading only six hours a-day, I shall gain in the course of a twelvemonth a great deal of instruction which I now feel myself to want."

Elinor honoured her for a plan which originated so nobly as this; though smiling to see the same eager fancy which had been leading her to the extreme of languid indolence and selfish repining, now at work in introducing excess into a scheme of such rational employment and virtuous self-controul. Her smile however changed to a sigh when she remembered that her promise to Willoughby was yet unfulfilled, and feared she had that to communicate which might again unsettle the mind of Marianne, and ruin at least for a time this fair prospect of busy tranquillity. Willing therefore to delay the evil hour, she resolved to wait till her sister's health were more secure, before she appointed[25] it. But the resolution was made only to be broken.

Marianne had been two or three days at home, before the weather was fine enough for an invalid like herself to venture out. But at last a soft, genial morning appeared; such as might tempt the daughter's wishes and the mother's confidence; and Marianne, leaning on Elinor's arm, was authorised to walk as long as she could without fatigue, in the lane before the house.

The sisters set out at a pace, slow as the feebleness of Marianne in an exercise hitherto untried since her illness required;—and they had advanced only so far beyond the house as to admit a full

20. The plantations are probably woods of planted trees that Sir John has recently established, perhaps for timber.

21. A priory is a monastery or nunnery, especially one that is an offshoot of a larger abbey; this priory may have been connected to the institution on what she calls the Abbeyland. All such institutions were dissolved in England during the sixteenth century when Henry VIII created the Church of England and rejected Roman Catholicism; the buildings frequently fell into ruin. Interest in ruins of various kinds had grown in England during the preceding century, and both Romanticism, which was fascinated by the past and tragic fates, and the taste for the picturesque, which considered ruins an invaluable part of a picturesque landscape, encouraged this interest further (see picture on p. 181 for an example). The taste for them was so prevalent that many landowners installed manufactured ruins on their grounds. In her youthful satire "The History of England," Jane Austen, after denouncing the cruelties of Henry VIII, jokes that "nothing can be said in his vindication, but that his abolishing Religious Houses & leaving them to the ruinous depredations of time has been of infinite use to the landscape of England in general." For a contemporary picture of the ruins of an abbey, see p. 645.

22. It is currently late April (see chronology, pp. 716–717). Marianne can anticipate many months when the days will be long enough for her to rise early in the morning and enjoy sufficient daylight for reading.

23. *amusement:* enjoyment, diversion.

24. The Park is the Middletons' residence, which, like any grand country house, would contain a library. Marianne's mention of getting more modern books from Colonel Brandon suggests that Sir John and Lady Middleton are not readers and have not bothered to add to the collections developed by previous generations. It also suggests that she knows, either from her own discussions with Colonel Brandon or from Elinor, that he is a reader. This would be a further affinity between them.

25. *appointed:* determined the time for.

view of the hill, the important hill behind, when pausing with her eyes turned towards it, Marianne calmly said,

"There, exactly there"—pointing with one hand, "on that projecting mound,—there I fell; and there I first saw Willoughby."

Her voice sunk with the word, but presently reviving she added,

"I am thankful to find that I can look with so little pain on the spot!—shall we ever talk on that subject, Elinor?"—hesitatingly it was said.—"Or will it be wrong?—I *can* talk of it now, I hope, as I ought to do."—

Elinor tenderly invited her to be open.

"As for regret," said Marianne, "I have done with that, as far as *he* is concerned. I do not mean to talk to you of what my feelings have been for him, but what they are *now*.—At present, if I could be satisfied on one point, if I could be allowed to think that he was not *always* acting a part, not *always* deciving me;—but above all, if I could be assured that he never was so *very* wicked as my fears have sometimes fancied him, since the story of that unfortunate girl"—

She stopt.—Elinor joyfully treasured her words as she answered,

"If you could be assured of that, you think you should be easy."

"Yes. My peace of mind is doubly involved in it;—for not only is it horrible to suspect a person, who has been what *he* has been to *me*, of such designs,—but what must it make me appear to myself?—What in a situation like mine, but a most shamefully unguarded affection could expose me to"—[26]

"How then," asked her sister, "would you account for his behaviour?"

"I would suppose him,—Oh! how gladly would I suppose him, only fickle, very, very fickle."

Elinor said no more. She was debating within herself on the eligibility[27] of beginning her story directly, or postponing it till Marianne were in stronger health;—and they crept on for a few minutes in silence.

"I am not wishing him too much good," said Marianne at last

26. What troubles Marianne is that if Willoughby never loved her but was only out to seduce her, then her quickness to show her feelings for him and her disregard of decorum would appear especially immodest and imprudent—"shamefully unguarded," as she puts it. In effect, she would have exposed herself to a shocking attempt on her virtue through her own recklessness and impropriety. Her peace is "doubly involved" in this scenario, because it would force her to think much less both of Willoughby and herself. The seriousness of this matter is indicated by the incomplete termination of her final sentence, caused either by her inability to continue or by Elinor's interruption to keep her from dwelling on such gloomy thoughts.

27. *eligibility:* desirability, suitableness.

A woman looking at an engraving by Michelangelo; an example of the kind of worthy reading Marianne has resolved to do.

[From Sir Walter Armstrong, *Lawrence* (London, 1913), p. 90]

with a sigh, "when I wish his secret reflections may be no more unpleasant than my own. He will suffer enough in them."

"Do you compare your conduct with his?"

"No. I compare it with what it ought to have been; I compare it with yours."

"Our situations have borne little resemblance."

"They have borne more than our conduct.—Do not, my dearest Elinor,[28] let your kindness defend what I know your judgment must censure. My illness has made me think—It has given me leisure and calmness for serious recollection.[29] Long before I was enough recovered to talk, I was perfectly able to reflect. I considered the past; I saw in my own behaviour since the beginning of our acquaintance with him last autumn, nothing but a series of imprudence towards myself, and want of kindness to others. I saw that my own feelings had prepared my sufferings, and that my want of fortitude under them had almost led me to the grave. My illness, I well knew, had been entirely brought on by myself, by such negligence of my own health, as I had felt even at the time to be wrong. Had I died,—it would have been self-destruction. I did not know my danger till the danger was removed; but with such feelings as these reflections gave me, I wonder at my recovery,— wonder that the very eagerness of my desire to live, to have time for atonement to my God, and to you all, did not kill me at once.[30] Had I died,—in what peculiar misery should I have left you, my nurse, my friend, my sister!—You, who had seen all the fretful selfishness of my latter days; who had known all the murmurings of my heart!—How should I have lived in *your* remembrance!— My mother too! How could you have consoled her![31]—I cannot express my own abhorrence of myself. Whenever I looked towards the past, I saw some duty neglected, or some failing indulged. Every body seemed injured by me. The kindness, the unceasing kindness of Mrs. Jennings, I had repaid with ungrateful contempt. To the Middletons, the Palmers, the Steeles, to every common acquaintance even, I had been insolent and unjust; with an heart hardened against their merits, and a temper irritated by their very attention.—To John, to Fanny,—yes, even to them, little as they

28. "My dearest Elinor" is a particularly affectionate designation. "Dear" and "my dear" are used frequently, but this is rarer, a product of Marianne's heightened emotion.

29. "Serious" often meant religious and probably does here in part, for below Marianne will discuss the profound religious implications of her case. But her "serious recollection" was also probably more general, as her subsequent words indicate. This long speech, in which she recognizes her various mistakes, traces their causes, identifies the means of correction, and resolves to undertake them, is similar to speeches of other Austen heroines.

30. She believes that her death, had it occurred, would have been self-destruction. This means in her mind she came close to committing suicide, a mortal sin that would require atonement to God, even if uncompleted. Jane Austen was sincerely, if not fervently, religious, though her novels for the most part do not touch overtly on religious issues. A case of near suicide necessitates an exception.

31. Her language becomes more halting and emotional as she proceeds.

Old Abbey, Evesham. One of many pictures of the ruins of an abbey by a leading painter of the time, J. M. W. Turner.

[From Geoffrey Holme, ed., *Early English Water-colour Drawings* (London, 1919), Plate I]

deserve, I had given less than their due.[32] But you,—you above all, above my mother, had been wronged by me. I, and only I, knew your heart and its sorrows; yet, to what did it influence me?—not to any compassion that could benefit you or myself.— Your example was before me: but to what avail?—Was I more considerate of you and your comfort? Did I imitate your forbearance, or lessen your restraints, by taking any part in those offices[33] of general complaisance[34] or particular gratitude which you had hitherto been left to discharge alone?[35]—No;—not less when I knew you to be unhappy, than when I had believed you at ease, did I turn away from every exertion of duty or friendship; scarcely allowing sorrow to exist but with me, regretting only *that* heart which had deserted and wronged me, and leaving you, for whom I professed an unbounded affection, to be miserable for my sake."

Here ceased the rapid flow of her self-reproving spirit; and Elinor, impatient to sooth, though too honest to flatter, gave her instantly that praise and support which her frankness and her contrition so well deserved. Marianne pressed her hand and replied,

"You are very good.—The future must be my proof. I have laid down my plan, and if I am capable of adhering to it—my feelings shall be governed and my temper improved.[36] They shall no longer worry others, nor torture myself. I shall now live solely for my family. You, my mother, and Margaret, must henceforth be all the world to me; you will share my affections entirely between you. From you, from my home, I shall never again have the smallest incitement[37] to move;[38] and if I do mix in other society it will be only to shew that my spirit is humbled, my heart amended, and that I can practise the civilities, the lesser duties of life,[39] with gentleness, and forbearance. As for Willoughby—to say that I shall soon or that I shall ever forget him, would be idle. His remembrance can be overcome by no change of circumstances or opinions. But it shall be regulated, it shall be checked by religion, by reason, by constant employment."[40]

She paused—and added in a lower voice, "If I could but know *his* heart, everything would become easy."

Elinor, who had now been for some time reflecting on the pro-

32. John and Fanny deserve some consideration as her brother and his wife. This is why Elinor paid them visits in London and spoke cordially to John, even though she was as contemptuous as Marianne of their principles and conduct and had more personal reason for resentment because they opposed a marriage between herself and Edward. Marianne's words show her accepting the need to fulfill social obligations, regardless of the unpleasantness of the people involved.

33. *offices*: duties, tasks.

34. *complaisance*: civility, agreeableness, willingness to please others.

35. Elinor had performed the duty of being civil to people in general and showing gratitude to those, such as Mrs. Jennings, who were particularly kind.

36. Marianne's vow of reformation climaxes her story. It has been well prepared by all that has happened. Unfortunately, in contrast to some other Austen heroines, she will not have a chance to demonstrate her new virtue and self-control in the remainder of the story.

37. *incitement*: incentive, motive.

38. Marianne's vow never to leave home shows that she is not thinking of the marriage to Colonel Brandon that her mother contemplates. It also shows her again going to extremes — even in her worthy resolutions.

39. The "lesser duties of life" would be the social obligations she has just discussed.

40. The idea of religion and reason as the forces that could subdue bad passions and make people act correctly was a long-standing one, articulated in various writings of the time. Employment would add to their effect in this case by taking Marianne's mind off Willoughby.

priety[41] or impropriety of speedily hazarding her narration, without feeling at all nearer decision than at first, heard this; and perceiving that as reflection did nothing, resolution must do all, soon found herself leading to the fact.[42]

She managed the recital, as she hoped, with address;[43] prepared her anxious listener with caution; related simply and honestly the chief points on which Willoughby grounded his apology; did justice to his repentance, and softened only his protestations of present regard.[44] Marianne said not a word.—She trembled, her eyes were fixed on the ground, and her lips became whiter than even sickness had left them. A thousand inquiries sprung up from her heart, but she dared not urge one. She caught every syllable with panting eagerness; her hand, unknowingly to herself, closely pressed her sister's, and tears covered her cheeks.

Elinor, dreading her being tired, led her towards home; and till they reached the door of the cottage, easily conjecturing what her curiosity must be though no question was suffered to speak it,[45] talked of nothing but Willoughby, and their conversation together; and was carefully minute[46] in every particular of speech and look, where minuteness could be safely indulged.[47] As soon as they entered the house, Marianne with a kiss of gratitude and these two words just articulate through her tears, "Tell mama," withdrew from her sister and walked slowly up stairs. Elinor would not attempt to disturb a solitude so reasonable as what she now sought; and with a mind anxiously pre-arranging its result, and a resolution of reviving the subject again, should Marianne fail to do it, she turned into the parlour to fulfil her parting injunction.

41. *propriety*: wisdom and appropriateness. She would not be thinking of etiquette here.

42. Not able to figure out when to speak, she realizes she must simply resolve and act.

43. *address*: skill, dexterity.

44. She would not want Marianne to know the strength of his current regard for her, and preference for her over his wife, because that might make it harder for Marianne to get over him. Willoughby's sentiments were also improper in themselves and not appropriate to repeat.

45. Marianne could not bring herself to ask any questions to betray her curiosity.

46. *minute*: precise, attentive to detail.

47. She could not be specific on dangerous subjects, such as Willoughby's continuing affection for Marianne.

Chapter Eleven

Mrs. Dashwood did not hear unmoved the vindication of her former favourite. She rejoiced in his being cleared from some part of his imputed guilt;—she was sorry for him;—she wished him happy.[1] But the feelings of the past could not be recalled.—Nothing could restore him with a faith unbroken—a character unblemished, to Marianne. Nothing could do away the knowledge of what the latter had suffered through his means, nor remove the guilt of his conduct towards Eliza.[2] Nothing could replace him, therefore, in her former esteem, nor injure the interests of Colonel Brandon.

Had Mrs. Dashwood, like her daughter, heard Willoughby's story from himself—had she witnessed his distress, and been under the influence of his countenance and his manner, it is probable that her compassion would have been greater. But it was neither in Elinor's power, nor in her wish, to rouse such feelings in another, by her retailed explanation,[3] as had at first been called forth in herself. Reflection had given calmness to her judgment, and sobered her own opinion of Willoughby's deserts;—she wished, therefore, to declare only the simple truth, and lay open such facts as were really due to his character, without any embellishment of tenderness to lead the fancy astray.

In the evening, when they were all three together, Marianne began voluntarily to speak of him again;—but that it was not without an effort, the restless, unquiet thoughtfulness in which she had been for some time previously sitting—her rising colour, as she spoke—and her unsteady voice, plainly shewed.

"I wish to assure you both," said she, "that I see every thing—as you can desire me to do."

Mrs. Dashwood would have interrupted her instantly with soothing tenderness, had not Elinor, who really wished to hear

1. This indicates the benevolence of Mrs. Dashwood, who has consistently shown a strong wish to think well of everybody.

2. Willoughby in fact had little to say in his defense when it came to this matter.

3. *her retailed explanation:* her retold explanation, or detailed explanation. Either meaning is possible, and both may be intended.

her sister's unbiassed opinion, by an eager sign, engaged her silence. Marianne slowly continued—

"It is a great relief to me—what Elinor told me this morning— I have now heard exactly what I wished to hear."—For some moments her voice was lost; but recovering herself, she added, and with greater calmness than before[4]—"I am now perfectly satisfied, I wish for no change. I never could have been happy with him, after knowing, as sooner or later I must have known, all this.—I should have had no confidence, no esteem. Nothing could have done it away to my feelings."

"I know it—I know it," cried her mother. "Happy with a man of libertine practices!—With one who had so injured the peace of the dearest of our friends, and the best of men![5]—No—my Marianne has not a heart to be made happy with such a man!—Her conscience, her sensitive conscience, would have felt all that the conscience of her husband ought to have felt."

Marianne sighed, and repeated—"I wish for no change."

"You consider the matter," said Elinor, "exactly as a good mind and a sound understanding must consider it; and I dare say, you perceive, as well as myself, not only in this, but in many other circumstances, reason enough to be convinced that your marriage must have involved you in many certain troubles and disappointments, in which you would have been poorly supported by an affection, on his side, much less certain. Had you married, you must have been always poor. His expensiveness[6] is acknowledged even by himself, and his whole conduct declared that self-denial is a word hardly understood by him. His demands and your inexperience together on a small, very small income,[7] must have brought on distresses which would not be the *less* grievous to you, from having been entirely unknown and unthought of before. *Your* sense of honour and honesty would have led you, I know, when aware of your situation, to attempt all the economy that would appear to you possible; and perhaps, as long as your frugality retrenched only on your own comfort, you might have been suffered to practise it, but beyond that—and how little could the utmost of your single management do to stop the ruin which had

4. Marianne's emotions keep her from speaking steadily, but like Elinor under similar circumstances, she struggles to control her feelings.

5. "The best of men" is Colonel Brandon, whose peace was severely injured by Willoughby's seduction of Eliza Williams.

6. *expensiveness*: extravagance.

7. Marianne has no experience as a housekeeper, someone who would order meals, purchase items for the house, hire and supervise servants, and perform other basic tasks of the mistress of the house. In *Northanger Abbey* the mother of the heroine, who is also seventeen and shows some of the same romantic tendencies as Marianne, worries that when she marries she "would make a sad, heedless young housekeeper." She consoles herself that her daughter will eventually learn to do the job well, but in Marianne's case any initial mistakes would have been harder to amend because of Willoughby's debts and irresponsible habits. Elinor describes it as a "very small income" even though, at "six or seven hundred a year" (p. 136), it is greater than their family's current income and not much below the thousand a year she had earlier defined as wealth (p. 172). She is probably thinking of how small it would be for someone with Willoughby's extravagant tastes.

begun before your marriage?[8]—Beyond *that*, had you endeavoured, however reasonably, to abridge *his* enjoyments, is it not to be feared, that instead of prevailing on feelings so selfish to consent to it, you would have lessened your own influence on his heart, and made him regret the connection[9] which had involved him in such difficulties?"

Marianne's lips quivered, and she repeated the word "Selfish?" in a tone that implied—"do you really think him selfish?"

"The whole of his behaviour," replied Elinor, "from the beginning to the end of the affair, has been grounded on selfishness. It was selfishness which first made him sport with your affections; which afterwards, when his own were engaged, made him delay the confession of it, and which finally carried him from Barton. His own enjoyment, or his own ease, was, in every particular, his ruling principle."

"It is very true. *My* happiness never was his object."

"At present," continued Elinor, "he regrets what he has done. And why does he regret it?—Because he finds it has not answered towards himself.[10] It has not made him happy. His circumstances are now unembarrassed[11]—he suffers from no evil of that kind; and he thinks only that he has married a woman of a less amiable temper than yourself. But does it thence follow that had he married you, he would have been happy?—The inconveniences would have been different. He would then have suffered under the pecuniary distresses which, because they are removed, he now reckons as nothing. He would have had a wife of whose temper he could make no complaint, but he would have been always necessitous—always poor; and probably would soon have learnt to rank the innumerable comforts of a clear estate[12] and good income as of far more importance, even to domestic happiness, than the mere temper of a wife."[13]

"I have not a doubt of it," said Marianne; "and I have nothing to regret—nothing but my own folly."

"Rather say your mother's imprudence, my child," said Mrs. Dashwood; "*she* must be answerable."

Marianne would not let her proceed;—and Elinor, satisfied

8. If he was already heading toward financial ruin while single, his situation would have become more acute once he also needed to support a wife, and probably children.

9. *connection*: marriage.

10. *answered towards himself*: satisfied him, fulfilled his wishes.

11. *His circumstances are now unembarrassed*: He is now free from financial troubles.

12. *clear estate*: estate clear of debts.

13. In delivering such a comprehensive verdict, in which almost every aspect of the situation has been carefully considered, Elinor is serving as a useful mouthpiece for the author, though perhaps also showing greater and more systematic wisdom than is completely realistic.

that each felt their own error, wished to avoid any survey of the past that might weaken her sister's spirits; she therefore, pursuing the first subject, immediately continued,

"*One* observation may, I think, be fairly drawn from the whole of the story—that all Willoughby's difficulties have arisen from the first offence against virtue, in his behaviour to Eliza Williams. That crime has been the origin of every lesser one, and of all his present discontents."

Marianne assented most feelingly to the remark; and her mother was led by it to an enumeration of Colonel Brandon's injuries and merits, warm as friendship and design could unitedly dictate.[14] Her daughter did not look, however, as if much of it were heard by her.

Elinor, according to her expectation, saw on the two or three following days, that Marianne did not continue to gain strength as she had done; but while her resolution was unsubdued, and she still tried to appear cheerful and easy, her sister could safely trust to the effect of time upon her health.

Margaret returned,[15] and the family were again all restored to each other, again quietly settled at the cottage, and if not pursuing their usual studies with quite so much vigour as when they first came to Barton,[16] at least planning a vigorous prosecution of them in future.

Elinor grew impatient for some tidings of Edward.[17] She had heard nothing of him since her leaving London, nothing new of his plans, nothing certain even of his present abode. Some letters had passed between her and her brother, in consequence of Marianne's illness; and in the first of John's, there had been this sentence:—"We know nothing of our unfortunate Edward, and can make no inquiries on so prohibited a subject, but conclude him to be still at Oxford";[18] which was all the intelligence[19] of Edward afforded her by the correspondence, for his name was not even mentioned in any of the succeeding letters. She was not doomed, however, to be long in ignorance of his measures.[20]

Their man-servant had been sent one morning to Exeter on business;[21] and when, as he waited at table,[22] he had satisfied the

14. She is motivated both by her genuine friendship with Colonel Brandon and her design to promote a match between him and Marianne.

15. Margaret had gone to stay with friends just before Mrs. Dashwood departed for the Palmers'. Her return may have been delayed from a fear of a lingering infection in Marianne, or from a belief that her presence would tax Marianne while she was still recovering.

16. The distraction and heartbreak of previous events may have sapped some of their vigor. This also indicates that Marianne has not yet embarked on the program of voluminous reading she outlined when they first returned.

17. The latest phase of Marianne's story is now complete, so the situation of Elinor and Edward can return to the fore.

18. John Dashwood's letter does indicate some concern, despite his disapproval of Edward's conduct, as well as some concern on Fanny's part, if the letter is accurate in reporting her sentiments (John has exaggerated her compassion on other occasions). It also shows Mrs. Ferrars's continued obstinacy, which is why the subject of Edward is still prohibited.

19. *intelligence:* news.

20. *measures:* plans, course of action.

21. He would probably go to Exeter regularly, for he would be the servant to run most errands.

22. Waiting at table would be another of his duties. It was something male or female servants could do, but men were preferred, and their two female servants would have their hands full with the essential tasks of cooking, cleaning, and washing clothes, all of which were normally female chores.

inquiries of his mistress as to the event[23] of his errand, this was his voluntary communication—

"I suppose you know, ma'am, that Mr. Ferrars is married."

Marianne gave a violent start, fixed her eyes upon Elinor, saw her turning pale, and fell back in her chair in hysterics. Mrs. Dashwood, whose eyes, as she answered the servant's inquiry, had intuitively taken the same direction, was shocked to perceive by Elinor's countenance how much she really suffered, and in a moment afterwards, alike distressed by Marianne's situation, knew not on which child to bestow her principal attention.

The servant, who saw only that Miss Marianne was taken ill, had sense enough to call one of the maids, who, with Mrs. Dashwood's assistance, supported her into the other room. By that time, Marianne was rather better, and her mother leaving her to the care of Margaret and the maid, returned to Elinor, who, though still much disordered, had so far recovered the use of her reason and voice as to be just beginning an inquiry of Thomas, as to the source of his intelligence. Mrs. Dashwood immediately took all that trouble on herself; and Elinor had the benefit of the information without the exertion of seeking it.

"Who told you that Mr. Ferrars was married, Thomas?"

"I see Mr. Ferrars myself, ma'am, this morning in Exeter, and his lady too, Miss Steele as was. They was stopping in a chaise at the door of the New London Inn,[24] as I went there with a message from Sally at the Park to her brother, who is one of the post-boys.[25] I happened to look up as I went by the chaise, and so I see directly it was the youngest Miss Steele; so I took off my hat, and she knew me and called to me, and inquired after you, ma'am, and the young ladies, especially Miss Marianne, and bid me I should give her compliments and Mr. Ferrars's, their best compliments and service,[26] and how sorry they was they had not time to come on and see you,[27] but they was in a great hurry to go forwards, for they was going further down[28] for a little while, but howsever, when they come back, they'd make sure to come and see you."[29]

"But did she tell you she was married, Thomas?"

"Yes, ma'am. She smiled, and said how she had changed her

23. *event*: result.

24. The chaise would be stopping there because an inn was usually where those traveling could hire fresh horses.

25. A postboy rides the post horses serving travelers. Thomas's message gives a glimpse of servant society, in which those working in different households could be tied by family relationship or friendship. Thomas and Sally may have been more than friends; servants often married other servants. He probably went first to the Park, the Middletons' residence, on some business of the Dashwoods and then received the commission from Sally. His casual mention of this indicates he has no fear that his employers will object to his conducting business of his own while on an errand for them.

26. *service*: respects.

27. Lucy (i.e., the youngest Miss Steele) recognized Thomas from her stay at Barton and took advantage of the opportunity to send a message by him. Her full reasons for doing this will appear later.

28. *further down*: farther away from London. It later turns out they were going to Dawlish, which is farther south in Devonshire (see map, p. 739).

29. This speech constitutes the most sustained example of servant speech in any Austen novel. As with other servants, his language is less polished and grammatical than that of the genteel characters; while servants frequently could read, they would have received little or no formal education. At the same time, Austen does not caricature Thomas's speech, as some writers of the time did when presenting servants: he gets his points across clearly and arranges his thoughts with reasonable coherence.

name since she was in these parts. She was always a very affable and free-spoken[30] young lady, and very civil behaved. So, I made free to wish her joy."

"Was Mr. Ferrars in the carriage with her?"

"Yes, ma'am, I just see him leaning back in it, but he did not look up;—he never was a gentleman much for talking."[31]

Elinor's heart could easily account for his not putting himself forward; and Mrs. Dashwood probably found the same explanation.

"Was there no one else in the carriage?"

"No, ma'am, only they two."

"Do you know where they came from?"

"They come straight from town,[32] as Miss Lucy—Mrs. Ferrars told me."

"And are going farther westward?"

"Yes, ma'am—but not to bide[33] long. They will soon be back again, and then they'd be sure and call here."

Mrs. Dashwood now looked at her daughter; but Elinor knew better than to expect them. She recognised the whole of Lucy in the message, and was very confident that Edward would never come near them. She observed, in a low voice, to her mother, that they were probably going down to Mr. Pratt's, near Plymouth.[34]

Thomas's intelligence seemed over. Elinor looked as if she wished to hear more.

"Did you see them off, before you came away?"

"No, ma'am—the horses was just coming out,[35] but I could not bide any longer; I was afraid of being late."

"Did Mrs. Ferrars look well?"

"Yes, ma'am, she said how she was very well; and to my mind she was always a very handsome young lady—and she seemed vastly contented."

Mrs. Dashwood could think of no other question, and Thomas and the table-cloth, now alike needless, were soon afterwards dismissed.[36] Marianne had already sent to say that she should eat nothing more. Mrs. Dashwood's and Elinor's appetites were equally lost, and Margaret might think herself very well off, that

30. *free-spoken:* unreserved.

31. Thomas would know about Edward from his extended stay with the Dashwoods at Norland (their current servants were all taken from Norland), and from the week Edward spent visiting the Dashwoods in Barton.

32. *town:* London.

33. *bide:* stay, remain. This meaning of the word was somewhat archaic by then; it is used by nobody else in Austen's novels. Older words and grammar were more likely to persist among the less educated.

34. This is a logical surmise, since Mr. Pratt is Lucy's uncle with whom Edward studied, and Plymouth is west of Exeter and therefore "further down."

35. The fresh horses they were hiring for the next stage of their journey were about to be harnessed to their carriage.

36. The removal of the tablecloth, like the dismissal of Thomas, signifies the end of the meal.

with so much uneasiness as both her sisters had lately experienced, so much reason as they had often had to be careless of their
meals, she had never been obliged to go without her dinner
before.

When the dessert and the wine were arranged,[37] and Mrs.
Dashwood and Elinor were left by themselves, they remained
long together in a similarity of thoughtfulness and silence. Mrs.
Dashwood feared to hazard any remark, and ventured not to offer
consolation. She now found that she had erred in relying on Elinor's representation of herself; and justly concluded that every
thing had been expressly softened at the time, to spare her from
an increase of unhappiness, suffering as she then had suffered for
Marianne. She found that she had been misled by the careful, the
considerate attention of her daughter, to think the attachment,
which once she had so well understood, much slighter in reality,
than she had been wont to believe, or than it was now proved to
be. She feared that under this persuasion she had been unjust,
inattentive, nay, almost unkind, to her Elinor;—that Marianne's
affliction, because more acknowledged, more immediately before
her, had too much engrossed her tenderness, and led her away to
forget that in Elinor she might have a daughter suffering almost as
much, certainly with less self-provocation, and greater fortitude.[38]

37. Dessert and wine normally appeared after the tablecloth was gone. The term "dessert" derives from the French *desservir*, meaning "to clear the table," because dessert was traditionally served after the tablecloth and regular dishes had been removed.

38. This disclosure functions, among other things, to show Mrs. Dashwood her injustice to Elinor, as well as her daughter's merit in hiding her own suffering for the sake of the others.

Chapter Twelve

*E*linor now found the difference between the expectation of an unpleasant event, however certain the mind may be told to consider it, and certainty itself. She now found, that in spite of herself, she had always admitted a hope, while Edward remained single, that something would occur to prevent his marrying Lucy; that some resolution of his own, some mediation of friends, or some more eligible opportunity of establishment[1] for the lady, would arise to assist the happiness of all. But he was now married, and she condemned her heart for the lurking flattery, which so much heightened the pain of the intelligence.

That he should be married so soon, before (as she imagined) he could be in orders, and consequently before he could be in possession of the living,[2] surprised her a little at first. But she soon saw how likely it was that Lucy, in her self-provident care,[3] in her haste to secure him, should overlook every thing but the risk of delay. They were married, married in town, and now hastening down to her uncle's. What had Edward felt on being within four miles of Barton, on seeing her mother's servant, on hearing Lucy's message!

They would soon, she supposed, be settled at Delaford. — Delaford, — that place in which so much conspired to give her an interest; which she wished to be acquainted with, and yet desired to avoid. She saw them in an instant in their parsonage-house; saw in Lucy, the active, contriving[4] manager, uniting at once a desire of smart appearance, with the utmost frugality, and ashamed to be suspected of half her economical practices; — pursuing her own interest in every thought, courting the favour of Colonel Brandon, of Mrs. Jennings, and of every wealthy friend. In Edward — she knew not what she saw, nor what she wished to see; — happy or

1. *establishment:* settlement in life, specifically through marriage.

2. She had speculated it might take him a few months to be ordained, though she admitted her lack of knowledge of the matter (pp. 538–540). Only an ordained clergyman could perform the functions of the living.

3. *self-provident care:* careful foresight regarding herself.

4. *contriving:* skillful, inventive.

unhappy,—nothing pleased her; she turned away her head from every sketch of him.[5]

Elinor flattered herself that some one of their connections[6] in London would write to them to announce the event, and give farther particulars,[7]—but day after day passed off, and brought no letter, no tidings. Though uncertain that any one were to blame, she found fault with every absent friend. They were all thoughtless or indolent.

"When do you write to Colonel Brandon, ma'am?" was an inquiry which sprung from the impatience of her mind to have something going on.

"I wrote to him, my love, last week, and rather expect to see, than to hear from him again. I earnestly pressed his coming to us, and should not be surprised to see him walk in to-day or to-morrow, or any day."[8]

This was gaining something, something to look forward to. Colonel Brandon *must* have some information to give.

Scarcely had she so determined it, when the figure of a man on horseback drew her eyes to the window. He stopt at their gate. It was a gentleman,[9] it was Colonel Brandon himself. Now she should hear more; and she trembled in expectation of it. But—it was *not* Colonel Brandon—neither his air[10]—nor his height. Were it possible, she should say it must be Edward. She looked again. He had just dismounted;—she could not be mistaken;—it *was* Edward. She moved away and sat down. "He comes from Mr. Pratt's purposely to see us. I *will* be calm; I *will* be mistress of myself."

In a moment she perceived that the others were likewise aware of the mistake. She saw her mother and Marianne change colour; saw them look at herself, and whisper a few sentences to each other. She would have given the world to be able to speak—and to make them understand that she hoped no coolness, no slight, would appear in their behaviour to him;—but she had no utterance,[11] and was obliged to leave all to their own discretion.

Not a syllable passed aloud. They all waited in silence for the appearance of their visitor. His footsteps were heard along the

5. Meaning a mental picture of him in his new situation.

6. *connections*: relatives.

7. The self-flattery would be that her relatives would consider her important enough to inform of such news.

8. Mrs. Dashwood continues to harbor boundless optimism about Colonel Brandon's soon marrying Marianne.

9. A gentleman's dress differed from that of men of lower station (see p. 165, note 20).

10. *air*: outward character, demeanor.

11. *utterance*: power of speech.

gravel path;[12] in a moment he was in the passage; and in another, he was before them.

His countenance, as he entered the room, was not too happy, even for Elinor. His complexion was white with agitation, and he looked as if fearful of his reception, and conscious that he merited no kind one. Mrs. Dashwood, however, conforming, as she trusted, to the wishes of that daughter, by whom she then meant in the warmth of her heart to be guided in everything, met him with a look of forced complacency,[13] gave him her hand, and wished him joy.[14]

He coloured,[15] and stammered out an unintelligible reply. Elinor's lips had moved with her mother's, and when the moment of action was over, she wished that she had shaken hands with him too. But it was then too late, and with a countenance meaning to be open, she sat down again and talked of the weather.

Marianne had retreated as much as possible out of sight, to conceal her distress; and Margaret, understanding some part, but not the whole, of the case, thought it incumbent on her to be dignified, and therefore took a seat as far from him as she could, and maintained a strict silence.

When Elinor had ceased to rejoice in the dryness of the season, a very awful pause took place. It was put an end to by Mrs. Dashwood, who felt obliged to hope that he had left Mrs. Ferrars very well. In an hurried manner, he replied in the affirmative.

Another pause.

Elinor, resolving to exert herself, though fearing the sound of her own voice, now said,

"Is Mrs. Ferrars at Longstaple?"[16]

"At Longstaple!" he replied, with an air of surprise — "No, my mother is in town."

"I meant," said Elinor, taking up some work[17] from the table, "to inquire after Mrs. *Edward* Ferrars."

She dared not look up;—but her mother and Marianne both turned their eyes on him. He coloured, seemed perplexed, looked doubtingly, and after some hesitation, said,

12. Gravel was often used to form paths.

13. *complacency*: pleasure, delight.

14. Wishing someone joy was a standard formulation for congratulating someone on a recent marriage.

15. *coloured*: blushed.

16. Longstaple is the place near Plymouth where Mr. Pratt lives.

17. *work*: needlework.

"Perhaps you mean—my brother—you mean Mrs.—Mrs. *Robert* Ferrars."

"Mrs. Robert Ferrars!"—was repeated by Marianne and her mother, in an accent[18] of the utmost amazement;—and though Elinor could not speak, even *her* eyes were fixed on him with the same impatient wonder. He rose from his seat and walked to the window, apparently from not knowing what to do; took up a pair of scissars that lay there, and while spoiling both them and their sheath by cutting the latter to pieces as he spoke,[19] said, in an hurried voice,

"Perhaps you do not know—you may not have heard that my brother is lately married to—to the youngest—to Miss Lucy Steele."[20]

His words were echoed with unspeakable astonishment by all but Elinor, who sat with her head leaning over her work, in a state of such agitation as made her hardly know where she was.

"Yes," said he, "they were married last week, and are now at Dawlish."[21]

Elinor could sit it[22] no longer. She almost ran out of the room,[23] and as soon as the door was closed,[24] burst into tears of joy, which at first she thought would never cease. Edward, who had till then looked any where, rather than at her, saw her hurry away, and perhaps saw—or even heard, her emotion;[25] for immediately afterwards he fell into a reverie, which no remarks, no inquiries, no affectionate address of Mrs. Dashwood could penetrate, and at last, without saying a word, quitted the room, and walked out towards the village—leaving the others in the greatest astonishment and perplexity on a change in his situation, so wonderful and so sudden;—a perplexity which they had no means of lessening but by their own conjectures.

18. *accent*: tone

19. Scissors would often be found lying around in a house inhabited by ladies because they were used for needlework, a basic female activity in this society.

20. Now it is Edward who is nervous and hesitant in speaking.

21. For more on Dawlish, see p. 469, note 32.

22. *sit it*: endure it.

23. Ladies were not supposed to run, and nobody was supposed to run inside a house. Her excitement stirs her to a speedy exit, but her self-control keeps her from actually running.

24. Elinor's self-control is also indicated by her still taking the trouble to close the door after herself, the correct behavior whenever leaving a room.

25. *emotion*: agitation.

Chapter Thirteen

*U*naccountable, however, as the circumstances of his release might appear to the whole family, it was certain that Edward was free: and to what purpose that freedom would be employed was easily pre-determined by all;—for after experiencing the blessings of *one* imprudent engagement, contracted without his mother's consent, as he had already done for more than four years, nothing less could be expected of him in the failure of *that*, than the immediate contraction of another.[1]

His errand at Barton, in fact, was a simple one. It was only to ask Elinor to marry him;—and considering that he was not altogether inexperienced in such a question, it might be strange that he should feel so uncomfortable in the present case as he really did, so much in need of encouragement and fresh air.

How soon he had walked himself into the proper resolution, however, how soon an opportunity of exercising it occurred, in what manner he expressed himself, and how he was received, need not be particularly told.[2] This only need be said;—that when they all sat down to table at four o'clock,[3] about three hours after his arrival, he had secured his lady, engaged her mother's consent, and was not only in the rapturous profession of the lover, but in the reality of reason and truth, one of the happiest of men.[4] His situation indeed was more than commonly joyful. He had more than the ordinary triumph[5] of accepted love to swell his heart, and raise his spirits. He was released without any reproach to himself, from an entanglement which had long formed his misery, from a woman whom he had long ceased to love;—and elevated at once to that security with another, which he must have thought of almost with despair, as soon as he had learnt to consider it with desire.[6] He was brought, not from doubt or suspense, but from misery to happiness;[7]—and the change was openly spo-

1. Jane Austen is being humorous here, because of course Edward no longer has to worry about parental consent, since he has been effectively renounced by his one remaining parent.

2. This silence on the actual words exchanged during a proposal is standard in Jane Austen. She may have found the heightened emotion of such a scene unsuitable to her general manner of presentation.

3. Their having dinner at four o'clock shows that they do not worry too much about status, for a later dinner hour was a sign of greater wealth and rank. Edward's joining them and fitting into their normal family life corresponds to the usual practice in Jane Austen, in which romantic love does not exclude other ties or override general social obligations.

4. "Please make me the happiest of men" was a standard formulation for proposing, but here it is more than just a phrase.

5. *triumph*: exultation.

6. His security with Elinor, i.e., secure possession of her hand in marriage, was something that, from the time he began to desire it, he had despaired of ever obtaining.

7. The typical lover would go only from some degree of uncertainty about his acceptance, or perhaps only a need to wait to ask, to the happiness of being accepted; Edward has reached the latter state after having suffered miserably from a positive conviction that happiness was forever denied him.

ken[8] in such a genuine, flowing, grateful cheerfulness, as his
friends had never witnessed in him before.

His heart was now open to Elinor, all its weaknesses, all its
errors confessed, and his first boyish attachment to Lucy treated
with all the philosophic dignity of twenty-four.

"It was a foolish, idle inclination on my side," said he, "the consequence of ignorance of the world—and want of employment.
Had my mother given me some active profession when I was
removed at eighteen from the care of Mr. Pratt, I think—nay, I am
sure, it would never have happened; for though I left Longstaple
with what I thought, at the time, a most unconquerable preference for his niece, yet had I then had any pursuit, any object to
engage my time and keep me at a distance from her for a few
months, I should very soon have outgrown the fancied attachment, especially by mixing more with the world, as in such a case
I must have done. But instead of having anything to do, instead of
having any profession chosen for me, or being allowed to chuse
any myself, I returned home to be completely idle; and for the
first twelvemonth afterwards, I had not even the nominal employment, which belonging to the university would have given me, for
I was not entered at Oxford till I was nineteen.[9] I had therefore
nothing in the world to do, but to fancy myself in love; and as my
mother did not make my home in every respect comfortable, as I
had no friend, no companion in my brother, and disliked new
acquaintance, it was not unnatural for me to be very often at
Longstaple, where I always felt myself at home, and was always
sure of a welcome; and accordingly I spent the greatest part of my
time there from eighteen to nineteen: Lucy appeared everything
that was amiable and obliging.[10] She was pretty too—at least I
thought so *then*, and I had seen so little of other women, that I
could make no comparisons, and see no defects. Considering
everything, therefore, I hope, foolish as our engagement was, foolish as it has since in every way been proved, it was not at the time
an unnatural, or an inexcusable piece of folly."

The change which a few hours had wrought in the minds and
the happiness of the Dashwoods, was such—so great—as

8. *spoken:* revealed, indicated.

9. As a student at Oxford, Edward would have been in the group known as "gentleman commoners," to distinguish them from the small number of noblemen above them and the larger number below of simple commoners who were not from wealthy backgrounds. Gentleman commoners often enjoyed ample sums to spend and were notorious for devoting most of their time and attention to various leisure pursuits. They could pursue serious studies if they wished, but the university imposed few requirements on them, and most knew that their academic attainments would have little affect on their future. The many who stood to inherit property often left before even finishing a normal degree. Those planning on a career in the church, the principal profession a university education led to, did need to finish and did study more, but if from a wealthy background their personal and family connections would probably be decisive in securing them a position. Moreover, the social segregation of gentleman commoners from other students meant that someone like Edward, even with his professed discomfort among those of gentility, would spend his time with other wealthy, and therefore idle, students.·

10. Edward earlier spoke of his general shyness and discomfort with genteel company (p. 178). Lucy, who was from a humbler background, was probably less intimidating, especially after he had spent time in the same house with her. Her interest in securing someone of his wealth and status would have made her, calculating as she is, do everything in her power to encourage and make him comfortable, which could have had a powerful effect on him.

Oxford.

[From A. D. Godley, *Oxford in the Eighteenth Century* (New York, 1908), frontispiece]

promised them all, the satisfaction of a sleepless night. Mrs. Dash-wood, too happy to be comfortable, knew not how to love Edward, nor praise Elinor enough, how to be enough thankful for his release without wounding his delicacy,[11] nor how at once to give them leisure for unrestrained conversation together, and yet enjoy, as she wished, the sight and society of both.

Marianne could speak *her* happiness only by tears. Compar-isons would occur—regrets would arise;[12]—and her joy, though sincere as her love for her sister, was of a kind to give her neither spirits[13] nor language.

But Elinor—How are *her* feelings to be described?—From the moment of learning that Lucy was married to another, that Edward was free, to the moment of his justifying the hopes which had so instantly followed, she was everything by turns but tran-quil. But when the second moment had passed, when she found every doubt, every solicitude removed, compared her situation with what so lately it had been,—saw him honourably released from his former engagement, saw him instantly profiting by the release, to address herself and declare an affection as tender, as constant as she had ever supposed it to be,—she was oppressed,[14] she was overcome by her own felicity;—and happily disposed as is the human mind to be easily familiarized with any change for the better, it required several hours to give sedateness to her spirits, or any degree of tranquillity to her heart.[15]

Edward was now fixed[16] at the cottage at least for a week;—for whatever other claims might be made on him, it was impossible that less than a week should be given up to the enjoyment of Eli-nor's company, or suffice to say half that was to be said of the past, the present, and the future;—for though a very few hours spent in the hard labour of incessant talking will dispatch more subjects than can really be in common between any two rational crea-tures, yet with lovers it is different. Between *them* no subject is fin-ished, no communication is even made, till it has been made at least twenty times over.

Lucy's marriage, the unceasing and reasonable wonder among

11. To express fulsome thanks for his release from Lucy would implicitly belittle her, and this could offend Edward's delicacy, since Lucy is the woman to whom he was engaged for a long time and the current wife of his brother.

12. Marianne compares her own situation with Elinor's, just as Elinor earlier compared her situation to Marianne's. Each is genuinely devoted to the other and joyful to see her sister happy, but both are human enough to think of themselves, even when something significant happens to the other.

13. *spirits*: vigor, animation (such as might spur her to speak).

14. *oppressed*: overwhelmed.

15. Elinor is striving for calmness as always, though here the struggle takes a particularly long time.

16. *fixed*: settled.

them all, formed of course one of the earliest discussions of the lovers;—and Elinor's particular knowledge of each party made it appear to her in every view, as one of the most extraordinary and unaccountable circumstances she had ever heard. How they could be thrown together, and by what attraction Robert could be drawn on to marry a girl, of whose beauty she had herself heard him speak without any admiration,—a girl too already engaged to his brother, and on whose account that brother had been thrown off by his family—it was beyond her comprehension to make out. To her own heart it was a delightful affair, to her imagination it was even a ridiculous one, but to her reason, her judgment, it was completely a puzzle.

Edward could only attempt an explanation by supposing, that perhaps at first accidentally meeting, the vanity of the one had been so worked on by the flattery of the other, as to lead by degrees to all the rest.[17] Elinor remembered what Robert had told her in Harley-street, of his opinion of what his own mediation in his brother's affairs might have done, if applied to in time. She repeated it to Edward.

"*That* was exactly like Robert,"—was his immediate observation.—"And *that*," he presently added, "might perhaps be in *his* head when the acquaintance between them first began. And Lucy perhaps at first might think only of procuring his good offices in my favour. Other designs might afterwards arise."

How long it had been carrying on between them, however, he was equally at a loss with herself to make out; for at Oxford, where he had remained by choice ever since his quitting London, he had had no means of hearing of her but from herself, and her letters to the very last were neither less frequent, nor less affectionate than usual.[18] Not the smallest suspicion, therefore, had ever occurred to prepare him for what followed;—and when at last it burst on him in a letter from Lucy herself, he had been for some time, he believed, half stupified between the wonder, the horror, and the joy of such a deliverance. He put the letter into Elinor's hands.

17. Robert has consistently demonstrated an overweening vanity, while Lucy has just as consistently demonstrated an assiduous willingness to flatter anyone in a position to confer benefits on her.

18. This indicates Lucy's care and calculation. She would not do anything to mar her relationship with Edward until she was completely sure of someone else.

"DEAR SIR,

BEING very sure I have long lost your affections, I have thought myself at liberty to bestow my own on another, and have no doubt of being as happy with him as I once used to think I might be with you; but I scorn to accept a hand while the heart was another's.[19] Sincerely wish you happy in your choice, and it shall not be my fault if we are not always good friends, as our near relationship now makes proper. I can safely say I owe you no ill-will, and am sure you will be too generous to do us any ill offices.[20] Your brother has gained my affections entirely, and as we could not live without one another, we are just returned from the altar, and are now on our way to Dawlish for a few weeks, which place your dear brother has great curiosity to see,[21] but thought I would first trouble you with these few lines, and shall always remain,

Your sincere well-wisher, friend, and sister,
LUCY FERRARS.

I have burnt all your letters, and will return your picture the first opportunity. Please to destroy my scrawls — but the ring with my hair you are very welcome to keep."

Elinor read and returned it without any comment.[22]

"I will not ask your opinion of it as a composition," said Edward. — "For worlds would not I have had a letter of her's seen by *you* in former days. — In a sister it is bad enough, but in a wife! — how I have blushed over the pages of her writing! — and I believe I may say that since the first half year of our foolish — business[23] — this is the only letter I ever received from her, of which the substance made me any amends for the defect of the style."

"However it may have come about," said Elinor, after a pause — "they are certainly married. And your mother has brought on herself a most appropriate punishment. The independence[24] she settled on Robert, through resentment against you, has put it in his power to make his own choice; and she has actually been bribing one son with a thousand a-year, to do the very deed which she disinherited the other for intending to do. She

19. For the first time, she openly acknowledges Edward's affection for Elinor, even though her awareness of this affection has long been obvious to Elinor and has spurred much of Lucy's conduct throughout the novel.

20. She expects a match between Edward and Elinor. Her conclusion that he will not do her any ill offices, or harm, is ironic in light of her deliberately malicious deception of the Dashwoods about her supposed marriage to Edward (for more on this, see note 27 below).

21. When Elinor mentioned her residence in Devonshire on first meeting Robert, he spoke of Dawlish and seemed to consider it the only place of significance in the county. Since it was a popular seaside resort, his wealthy friends may have been there and spoken of it. Lucy would be happy to oblige his interest in going, because a visit to the area where she used to live would serve purposes of her own (see p. 703, note 25).

22. Elinor, who probably can say nothing sincere about the letter that is not critical, prefers to remain silent, perhaps because she will soon be sister-in-law to Lucy's husband.

23. He struggles with the appropriate word to describe his entanglement with Lucy.

24. *independence*: financial independence.

will hardly be less hurt, I suppose, by Robert's marrying Lucy, than she would have been by your marrying her."

"She will be more hurt by it, for Robert always was her favourite. — She will be more hurt by it, and on the same principle will forgive him much sooner."

In what state the affair stood at present between them, Edward knew not, for no communication with any of his family had yet been attempted by him. He had quitted Oxford within four and twenty hours after Lucy's letter arrived, and with only one object before him, the nearest road to Barton, had had no leisure to form any scheme of conduct, with which that road did not hold the most intimate connection. He could do nothing till he were assured of his fate with Miss Dashwood; and by his rapidity in seeking *that* fate, it is to be supposed, in spite of the jealousy with which he had once thought of Colonel Brandon,[25] in spite of the modesty with which he rated his own deserts, and the politeness with which he talked of his doubts, he did not, upon the whole, expect a very cruel reception. It was his business, however, to say that he *did*, and he said it very prettily.[26] What he might say on the subject a twelvemonth after, must be referred to the imagination of husbands and wives.

That Lucy had certainly meant to deceive, to go off with a flourish of malice against him in her message by Thomas, was perfectly clear to Elinor;[27] and Edward himself, now thoroughly enlightened on her character, had no scruple[28] in believing her capable of the utmost meanness of wanton ill-nature. Though his eyes had been long opened, even before his acquaintance with Elinor began, to her ignorance and a want of liberality in some of her opinions—they had been equally imputed, by him, to her want of education; and till her last letter reached him, he had always believed her to be a well-disposed, good-hearted girl, and thoroughly attached to himself. Nothing but such a persuasion could have prevented his putting an end to an engagement, which, long before the discovery[29] of it laid him open to his mother's anger, had been a continual source of disquiet and regret to him.[30]

25. His jealousy of Colonel Brandon appeared in the scene when Elinor conveyed Colonel Brandon's gift of the Delaford living (see pp. 534–538), though it was not identified explicitly then.

26. According to the conventions of proposing, a man should express great doubt about the woman's answer, regardless of what he really felt about his probable reception. This would be a sign of respect, since it suggested that her charms were such that she could expect many worthy offers of marriage. In *Pride and Prejudice* the heroine becomes incensed by the hero's first proposal because of his smug assurance, which he cannot help displaying, that she will accept him.

27. Lucy's malice was principally directed against Edward rather than Elinor. The reason would be her anger that he came to prefer another. She may have thought that making Elinor unhappy would be a way of inflicting harm on Edward, or that Elinor's false belief about his marriage would lead her to actions or words that would injure Edward or create difficulties for him. The deception also shows the malice of Robert, who had no cause to hurt Edward or Elinor, for it required him to remain quiet and hidden away in the carriage, a reversal of his normal behavior, and allow Thomas to believe that he was Edward.

28. *scruple:* hesitation.

29. *discovery:* disclosure.

30. Edward could have ended the engagement, but considered himself bound in honor to uphold it because of his belief in her fundamental decency and her affection for himself: to break an engagement to such a woman would be cruel.

"I thought it my duty," said he, "independent of my feelings, to give her the option of continuing the engagement or not, when I was renounced by my mother, and stood to all appearance without a friend in the world to assist me.[31] In such a situation as that, where there seemed nothing to tempt the avarice or the vanity of any living creature, how could I suppose, when she so earnestly, so warmly insisted on sharing my fate, whatever it might be, that any thing but the most disinterested affection was her inducement? And even now, I cannot comprehend on what motive she acted, or what fancied advantage it could be to her, to be fettered to a man for whom she had not the smallest regard, and who had only two thousand pounds in the world. She could not foresee that Colonel Brandon would give me a living."

"No, but she might suppose that something would occur in your favour; that your own family might in time relent. And at any rate, she lost nothing by continuing the engagement, for she has proved that it fettered neither her inclination nor her actions. The connection was certainly a respectable one, and probably gained her consideration among her friends;[32] and, if nothing more advantageous occurred, it would be better for her to marry *you* than be single."[33]

Edward was of course immediately convinced that nothing could have been more natural than Lucy's conduct, nor more self-evident than the motive of it.

Elinor scolded him, harshly as ladies always scold the imprudence which compliments themselves, for having spent so much time with them at Norland, when he must have felt his own inconstancy.[34]

"Your behaviour was certainly very wrong," said she, "because—to say nothing of my own conviction, our relations were all led away by it to fancy and expect *what*, as you were *then* situated, could never be."

He could only plead an ignorance of his own heart, and a mistaken confidence in the force of his engagement.

"I was simple enough to think, that because my *faith* was plighted to another, there could be no danger in my being with

31. His feelings made him wish to give her the option of dissolving the engagement, after his mother renounced him, because he had long hoped to end it. But he also believed it was his duty, since the engagement now threatened to bind her to a life of poverty.

32. Since married women had far higher status than single women, being engaged would add a little to Lucy's stature in the eyes of other women. Also, an engagement to a man of much higher rank was probably more than any of her friends could boast.

33. As Jane Austen wrote in a letter, "Single Women have a dreadful propensity for being poor" (March 13, 1817). Marriage offered the great majority of women greater income and financial security. It also gave a woman social position and the opportunity to be the mistress of a household, instead of having to spend her life as a dependent and powerless guest in others' homes. The foolish desperation of Lucy's elder sister regarding the doctor and other supposed "beaux" is a fate that Lucy would be eager to avoid.

34. She means his inconstancy to Lucy.

you; and that the consciousness of my engagement was to[35] keep my heart as safe and sacred as my honour. I felt that I admired you, but I told myself it was only friendship; and till I began to make comparisons between yourself and Lucy, I did not know how far I was got.[36] After that, I suppose, I *was* wrong in remaining so much in Sussex, and the arguments with which I reconciled myself to the expediency of it, were no better than these:—The danger is my own; I am doing no injury to anybody but myself."

Elinor smiled, and shook her head.[37]

Edward heard with pleasure of Colonel Brandon's being expected at the Cottage, as he really wished not only to be better acquainted with him, but to have an opportunity of convincing him that he no longer resented his giving him the living of Delaford—"Which, at present," said he, "after thanks so ungraciously delivered as mine were on the occasion, he must think I have never forgiven him for offering."[38]

Now he felt astonished himself that he had never yet been to the place. But so little interest had he taken in the matter that he owed all his knowledge of the house, garden, and glebe,[39] extent of the parish, condition of the land, and rate of the tythes,[40] to Elinor herself, who had heard so much of it from Colonel Brandon, and heard it with so much attention, as to be entirely mistress of the subject.[41]

One question after this only remained undecided, between them, one difficulty only was to be overcome. They were brought together by mutual affection, with the warmest approbation of their real friends, their intimate knowledge of each other seemed to make their happiness certain—and they only wanted something to live upon. Edward had two thousand pounds, and Elinor one, which, with Delaford living, was all that they could call their own; for it was impossible that Mrs. Dashwood should advance anything, and they were neither of them quite enough in love to think that three hundred and fifty pounds a-year would supply them with the comforts of life.[42]

Edward was not entirely without hopes of some favourable change in his mother towards him; and on *that* he rested for the

35. *was to:* was likely or bound to.

36. *was got:* had gotten.

37. Elinor shakes her head in outward disapproval of his behavior, which was wrong, as he admitted. But she smiles because the entire reason his behavior was wrong was that he failed to recognize how much his attraction to her would override his prior commitment to Lucy and was too enamored to tear himself away from her even after he did sense his peril.

38. Edward's ungracious reception of Colonel Brandon's gift would have been spurred by his jealousy of the latter's supposed amorous relationship with Elinor, perhaps supplemented by mixed feelings about a gift that would advance his marriage to Lucy.

39. The glebe was the land given to the holder of a living to raise his own crops and livestock. The garden, right next to the house, could also provide food for him and his family. When Jane Austen's father held his living, he and his wife grew vegetables, fruit, and herbs in their garden, maintained a dairy farm, engaged in beekeeping, and raised pigs, sheep, and various types of fowl (this did not mean they did all the work themselves, for hired farm labor was inexpensive).

40. The size of the parish and condition of the land would, like the rate of tithes, affect their income, in addition to affecting his pastoral duties.

41. Elinor's being chosen as Colonel Brandon's agent in this transaction ends up proving very useful.

42. The living is worth two hundred pounds a year. Edward's two thousand pounds and Elinor's one thousand would produce, at the prevailing 5% rate of return on investments, one hundred fifty pounds a year.

residue of their income. But Elinor had no such dependence;[43] for since Edward would still be unable to marry Miss Morton, and his chusing herself had been spoken of in Mrs. Ferrars's flattering language as only a lesser evil than his chusing Lucy Steele, she feared that Robert's offence would serve no other purpose than to enrich Fanny.

About four days after Edward's arrival Colonel Brandon appeared, to complete Mrs. Dashwood's satisfaction, and to give her the dignity of having, for the first time since her living at Barton, more company with her than her house would hold. Edward was allowed to retain the privilege of first comer, and Colonel Brandon therefore walked every night to his old quarters at the Park; from whence he usually returned in the morning, early enough to interrupt the lovers' first tête-à-tête before breakfast.

A three weeks' residence at Delaford, where, in his evening hours at least, he had little to do but to calculate the disproportion between thirty-six and seventeen,[44] brought him to Barton in a temper of mind which needed all the improvement in Marianne's looks, all the kindness of her welcome, and all the encouragement of her mother's language, to make it cheerful. Among such friends, however, and such flattery, he did revive. No rumour of Lucy's marriage had yet reached him;—he knew nothing of what had passed; and the first hours of his visit were consequently spent in hearing and in wondering. Every thing was explained to him by Mrs. Dashwood, and he found fresh reason to rejoice in what he had done for Mr. Ferrars, since eventually it promoted the interest of Elinor.

It would be needless to say, that the gentlemen advanced in the good opinion of each other, as they advanced in each other's acquaintance, for it could not be otherwise. Their resemblance in good principles and good sense, in disposition and manner of thinking, would probably have been sufficient to unite them in friendship, without any other attraction; but their being in love with two sisters, and two sisters fond of each other, made that mutual regard inevitable and immediate, which might otherwise have waited the effect of time and judgment.

43. *dependence*: confidence, expectation.

44. This is the difference between his age and Marianne's.

The letters from town, which a few days before would have made every nerve in Elinor's body thrill with transport,[45] now arrived to be read with less emotion than mirth. Mrs. Jennings wrote to tell the wonderful[46] tale, to vent her honest indignation against the jilting girl, and pour forth her compassion towards poor Mr. Edward, who, she was sure, had quite doted upon the worthless hussey, and was now, by all accounts, almost broken-hearted, at Oxford. — "I do think," she continued, "nothing was ever carried on so sly; for it was but two days before Lucy called and sat a couple of hours with me. Not a soul suspected anything of the matter, not even Nancy who, poor soul! came crying to me the day after, in a great fright for fear of Mrs. Ferrars,[47] as well as not knowing how to get to Plymouth; for Lucy it seems borrowed all her money before she went off to be married, on purpose we suppose to make a shew with, and poor Nancy had not seven shillings in the world;[48] — so I was very glad to give her five guineas[49] to take her down to Exeter, where she thinks of staying three or four weeks with Mrs. Burgess,[50] in hopes, as I tell her, to fall in with the Doctor again. And I must say that Lucy's crossness not to take her along with them in the chaise is worse than all.[51] Poor Mr. Edward! I cannot get him out of my head, but you must send for him to Barton, and Miss Marianne must try to comfort him."[52]

Mr. Dashwood's strains were more solemn. Mrs. Ferrars was the most unfortunate of women — poor Fanny had suffered agonies of sensibility[53] — and he considered the existence of each, under such a blow, with grateful wonder. Robert's offence was unpardonable, but Lucy's was infinitely worse.[54] Neither of them was ever again to be mentioned to Mrs. Ferrars; and even, if she might hereafter be induced to forgive her son, his wife should never be acknowledged as her daughter, nor be permitted to appear in her presence. The secrecy with which every thing had been carried on between them, was rationally treated as enormously heightening the crime, because, had any suspicion of it occurred to the others, proper measures would have been taken to prevent the marriage; and he called on Elinor to join with him in

45. *transport:* overwhelming emotion.

46. *wonderful:* astonishing.

47. Miss Steele's fearfulness of offending those who were wealthy and powerful appeared earlier, when she worried that Mrs. Jennings and Lady Middleton might be angry after learning of Lucy's engagement to Edward (pp. 502–504).

48. There was a seven-shilling coin at the time, since seven shillings was a third of a guinea (a coin worth a pound and a shilling).

49. *five guineas:* this would be a little more than five pounds (see above note).

50. Mrs. Burgess is probably the friend or relative with whom both Miss Steeles were staying when Sir John and Mrs. Jennings ran into them in Exeter and invited them to stay at Barton Park.

51. A woman who married would often be accompanied after the wedding by her sister; a character in *Mansfield Park* does that. As for Anne Steele's pursuit of Dr. Davies, Jane Austen's nephew J. E. Austen-Leigh, who wrote a memoir of Jane Austen based on the memories of himself and other family members, said that his aunt would often speak of her characters' later fates, and "Miss Steele never succeeded in catching the Doctor."

52. Mrs. Jennings's zeal for matchmaking, along with her continued belief in an impending marriage between Elinor and Colonel Brandon, leads her to think immediately of coupling Edward and Marianne.

53. *sensibility:* acute feeling.

54. This is a sign of their unreasonableness, for Lucy, unlike Robert, owed no duty to them, especially after Fanny had cruelly ejected her from her house and they had denounced her as completely unworthy of Edward.

regretting that Lucy's engagement with Edward had not rather been fulfilled, than that she should thus be the means of spreading misery farther in the family. — He thus continued:

"Mrs. Ferrars has never yet mentioned Edward's name, which does not surprise us; but to our great astonishment, not a line has been received from him on the occasion. Perhaps, however, he is kept silent by his fear of offending, and I shall, therefore, give him a hint, by a line to Oxford, that his sister and I both think a letter of proper submission from him, addressed perhaps to Fanny, and by her shewn to her mother, might not be taken amiss;[55] for we all know the tenderness of Mrs. Ferrars's heart, and that she wishes for nothing so much as to be on good terms with her children."

This paragraph was of some importance to the prospects and conduct of Edward. It determined him to attempt a reconciliation, though not exactly in the manner pointed out by their brother and sister.

"A letter of proper submission!" repeated he; "would they have me beg my mother's pardon for Robert's ingratitude to *her*, and breach of honour to *me*?[56] — I can make no submission — I am grown neither humble nor penitent by what has passed. — I am grown very happy, but that would not interest. — I know of no submission that *is* proper for me to make."

"You may certainly ask to be forgiven," said Elinor, "because you have offended;[57] — and I should think you might *now* venture so far as to profess some concern for having ever formed the engagement which drew on you your mother's anger."

He agreed that he might.

"And when she has forgiven you, perhaps a little humility may be convenient while acknowledging a second engagement, almost as imprudent in *her* eyes, as the first."

He had nothing to urge against it, but still resisted the idea of a letter of proper submission; and therefore, to make it easier to him, as he declared a much greater willingness to make mean[58] concessions by word of mouth than on paper, it was resolved that, instead of writing to Fanny, he should go to London, and personally intreat her good offices in his favour. — "And if they really *do*

55. John Dashwood's advice is actually an example of real benevolence on his part. A narrower self-interest could make him glad that both Edward and Robert are out of Mrs. Ferrars's favor, for then she might leave all her money to Fanny. But that has apparently been overridden by a genuine wish to maintain harmonious family relations, something he has generally exhibited, as well as perhaps a belief in the rightness of an eldest son receiving his inheritance and being treated justly (he had spoken with sincere pity of Edward's seeing his younger brother supplant him on p. 498).

56. Robert's breach of honor was stealing his own brother's fiancée.

57. He has offended by entering and maintaining an engagement without his mother's consent. Prevailing norms would consider this wrong.

58. *mean:* undignified, low.

interest themselves," said Marianne, in her new character of candour,[59] "in bringing about a reconciliation, I shall think that even John and Fanny are not entirely without merit."

After a visit on Colonel Brandon's side of only three or four days, the two gentlemen quitted Barton together.—They were to go immediately to Delaford, that Edward might have some personal knowledge of his future home, and assist his patron and friend in deciding on what improvements were needed to it; and from thence, after staying there a couple of nights, he was to proceed on his journey to town.

59. *candour:* inclination to think favorably of others.

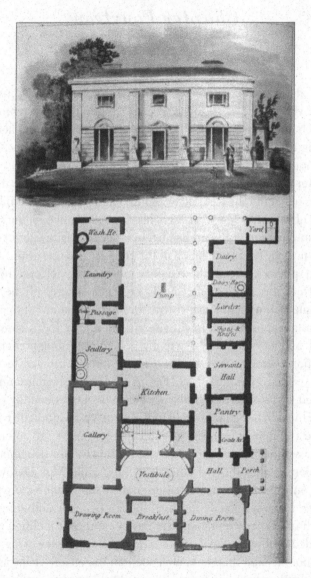

A magnificent cottage, such as Robert Ferrars would draw plans for—see following chapter.

[From *The Repository of arts, literature, fashions, manufactures, &c,* Vol. IX (1813), p. 53]

Chapter Fourteen

*A*fter a proper resistance on the part of Mrs. Ferrars, just so violent and so steady as to preserve her from that reproach which she always seemed fearful of incurring, the reproach of being too amiable,[1] Edward was admitted to her presence, and pronounced to be again her son.

Her family had of late been exceedingly fluctuating. For many years of her life she had had two sons; but the crime and annihilation of Edward a few weeks ago, had robbed her of one; the similar annihilation of Robert had left her for a fortnight without any; and now, by the resuscitation of Edward, she had one again.

In spite of his being allowed once more to live, however, he did not feel the continuance of his existence secure, till he had revealed his present engagement; for the publication[2] of that circumstance, he feared, might give a sudden turn[3] to his constitution, and carry him off[4] as rapidly as before. With apprehensive caution therefore it was revealed, and he was listened to with unexpected calmness. Mrs. Ferrars at first reasonably endeavoured to dissuade him from marrying Miss Dashwood, by every argument in her power; — told him, that in Miss Morton he would have a woman of higher rank and larger fortune; — and enforced[5] the assertion, by observing that Miss Morton was the daughter of a nobleman with thirty thousand pounds, while Miss Dashwood was only the daughter of a private gentleman,[6] with no more than *three*; but when she found that, though perfectly admitting the truth of her representation,[7] he was by no means inclined to be guided by it, she judged it wisest, from the experience of the past, to submit — and therefore, after such an ungracious delay as she owed to her own dignity, and as served to prevent every suspicion of good-will, she issued her decree of consent to the marriage of Edward and Elinor.

1. *amiable:* kind, friendly, good-natured.

2. *publication:* promulgation, announcement.

3. *turn:* change, including an attack of illness.

4. *carry him off:* kill him (that is, as a son in Mrs. Ferrars's eyes).

5. *enforced:* bolstered, urged further.

6. A private gentleman was one who did not occupy a leading social position, as someone with a title would, and therefore did not play a prominent public role.

7. *representation:* argument, remonstrance.

Contemporary wallpapers and borders.

[From MacIver Percival, *Old English Furniture and Its Surroundings* (New York, 1920), Plate XI]

What she would engage to do towards augmenting their income, was next to be considered; and here it plainly appeared, that though Edward was now her only son, he was by no means her eldest; for while Robert was inevitably endowed with a thousand pounds a-year, not the smallest objection was made against Edward's taking orders for the sake of two hundred and fifty at the utmost;[8] nor was any thing promised either for the present or in future, beyond the ten thousand pounds, which had been given with Fanny.

It was as much, however, as was desired, and more than was expected by Edward and Elinor; and Mrs. Ferrars herself, by her shuffling excuses, seemed the only person surprised at her not giving more.[9]

With an income quite sufficient to their wants thus secured to them,[10] they had nothing to wait for after Edward was in possession of the living, but the readiness of the house, to which Colonel Brandon, with an eager desire for the accommodation of Elinor, was making considerable improvements;[11] and after waiting some time for their completion, after experiencing, as usual, a thousand disappointments and delays, from the unaccountable dilatoriness of the workmen, Elinor, as usual, broke through the first positive resolution of not marrying till every thing was ready,[12] and the ceremony took place in Barton church early in the autumn.[13]

The first month after their marriage was spent with their friend at the Mansion-house, from whence they could superintend the progress of the Parsonage, and direct every thing as they liked on the spot;—could chuse papers, project shrubberies, and invent a sweep.[14] Mrs. Jennings's prophecies, though rather jumbled together, were chiefly fulfilled; for she was able to visit Edward and his wife in their Parsonage by Michaelmas,[15] and she found in Elinor and her husband, as she really believed, one of the happiest couple in the world. They had in fact nothing to wish for, but the marriage of Colonel Brandon and Marianne, and rather better pasturage for their cows.[16]

They were visited on their first settling by almost all their rela-

8. Normally the elder son received the principal family inheritance, and the younger son entered a profession. The two hundred and fifty mentioned here is higher than the two hundred a year previously specified as the income of the living. But the living was also stated to be "capable of improvement" (p. 522), which would mean raising the tithes and hence the income. The words "at the utmost" suggest the lack of precision about how much the tithes could be raised.

9. She knows how much more the elder son normally received than younger sons or daughters. Also, the ten thousand is far less necessary to Fanny and her husband, because of John Dashwood's ample fortune, than it is to Edward and Elinor.

10. The ten thousand pounds would produce five hundred a year in income. Combined with the two hundred and fifty just mentioned for the living, and the one hundred and fifty from the three thousand Edward and Elinor already have, their income would be nine hundred a year. In her earlier discussion of money with Marianne, at which Edward was present, Elinor stated one thousand a year to be the wealth she considered essential to happiness (p. 172). Thus she has come very close to her imagined sum.

11. Colonel Brandon is especially eager to accommodate Elinor since, once she is at the parsonage, Marianne will be able to visit her.

12. The words "as usual" are probably meant to suggest that brides are usually more eager for a marriage.

13. Edward proposed to Elinor in May (see chronology, p. 717), so they have not waited very long. Since the main action of the novel began in the summer of the preceding year, when the attraction between Edward and Elinor was noticed at Norland and Mrs. Dashwood decided to leave, approximately a year has passed. Jane Austen's longer novels transpire over a similar period of time (her shortest novels, Northanger Abbey and Persuasion, take place over approximately half a year).

14. Papers means wallpapers, a popular feature of interior decoration at this time; for a picture of designs from the time for wallpapers and borders, see the preceding page. Shrubberies were standard features of gardens. A sweep was a curved carriage drive leading to a house.

15. She had prophesied that Colonel Brandon and Elinor would be married by Michaelmas, September 29 (p. 402).

16. They would raise cows on their glebe land, and this would be a basic part of their income. The passage suggests how quickly they have become absorbed in the humdrum practicalities of married life.

tions and friends. Mrs. Ferrars came to inspect the happiness which she was almost ashamed of having authorised; and even the Dashwoods were at the expense of a journey from Sussex to do them honour.[17]

"I will not say that I am disappointed, my dear sister," said John, as they were walking together one morning before the gates of Delaford House, "*that* would be saying too much, for certainly you have been one of the most fortunate young women in the world, as it is. But, I confess, it would give me great pleasure to call Colonel Brandon brother.[18] His property here, his place, his house, every thing in such respectable and excellent condition!— and his woods!—I have not seen such timber any where in Dorsetshire, as there is now standing in Delaford Hanger![19]—And though, perhaps, Marianne may not seem exactly the person to attract him—yet I think it would altogether[20] be adviseable for you to have them now frequently staying with you, for as Colonel Brandon seems a great deal at home, nobody can tell what may happen—for, when people are much thrown together, and see little of anybody else—and it will always be in your power to set her off to advantage, and so forth;—in short, you may as well give her a chance—You understand me."—

But though Mrs. Ferrars *did* come to see them, and always treated them with the make-believe of decent affection, they were never insulted by her real favour and preference. *That* was due to the folly of Robert, and the cunning of his wife; and it was earned by them before many months had passed away. The selfish sagacity of the latter, which had at first drawn Robert into the scrape, was the principal instrument of his deliverance from it; for her respectful humility, assiduous attentions, and endless flatteries, as soon as the smallest opening was given for their exercise, reconciled Mrs. Ferrars to his choice, and re-established him completely in her favour.

The whole of Lucy's behaviour in the affair, and the prosperity which crowned it, therefore, may be held forth as a most encouraging instance of what an earnest, an unceasing attention to self-interest, however its progress may be apparently obstructed, will

17. Visiting a new couple was a standard courtesy. John Dashwood had earlier congratulated Elinor on avoiding much of the expense of the trip home because she was traveling partway with Mrs. Jennings, and is presumably mindful of such costs for himself, even though they would represent a small portion of his income.

18. He is disappointed that she has not married the wealthier Colonel Brandon.

19. A hanging wood was one on a steep hillside, so Delaford Hanger is presumably such a wood on Colonel Brandon's property. Since Norland was mentioned as possessing valuable woods (p. 4), John Dashwood may have a particular interest in timber. This is further suggested by his comparison with the timber of other places in Dorsetshire. He had earlier spoken of not knowing Dorsetshire, and his only exposure has been in his voyage here. He presumably observed the features of the land as they passed and carefully assessed the value of any woods he saw.

20. *altogether:* on the whole.

Cows grazing.

[From Humphrey Repton, *The Art of Landscape Gardening* (Boston, 1907; reprint edition), p. 42]

do in securing every advantage of fortune, with no other sacrifice than that of time and conscience. When Robert first sought her acquaintance, and privately visited her in Bartlett's Buildings, it was only with the view imputed to him by his brother. He merely meant to persuade her to give up the engagement; and as there could be nothing to overcome but the affection of both, he naturally expected that one or two interviews would settle the matter.[21] In that point, however, and that only, he erred;[22]—for though Lucy soon gave him hopes that his eloquence would convince her in *time*, another visit, another conversation, was always wanted to produce this conviction. Some doubts always lingered in her mind when they parted, which could only be removed by another half hour's discourse with himself. His attendance was by this means secured, and the rest followed in course. Instead of talking of Edward, they came gradually to talk only of Robert,—a subject on which he had always more to say than on any other, and in which she soon betrayed an interest even equal to his own; and in short, it became speedily evident to both, that he had entirely supplanted his brother.[23] He was proud of his conquest, proud of tricking Edward, and very proud of marrying privately without his mother's consent.[24] What immediately followed is known. They passed some months in great happiness at Dawlish; for she had many relations and old acquaintance to cut[25]—and he drew several plans for magnificent cottages;[26]—and from thence returning to town, procured the forgiveness of Mrs. Ferrars, by the simple expedient of asking it, which, at Lucy's instigation, was adopted. The forgiveness at first, indeed, as was reasonable,[27] comprehended only Robert; and Lucy, who had owed his mother no duty, and therefore could have transgressed none, still remained some weeks longer unpardoned. But perseverance in humility of conduct and messages, in self-condemnation for Robert's offence, and gratitude for the unkindness she was treated with, procured her in time the haughty notice which overcame her by its graciousness,[28] and led soon afterwards, by rapid degrees, to the highest state of affection and influence. Lucy became as necessary to Mrs. Ferrars, as either Robert or Fanny;

21. Robert's assumption reflects both his contempt for affection as an important factor in determining people's actions and his confidence in his own powers of persuasion, a confidence he earlier proclaimed (p. 556).

22. In other words, he was right to consider affection no significant barrier, at least in this case, and right to believe he could persuade Lucy to renounce Edward. He erred only in thinking he could accomplish this quickly.

23. It became evident to her as soon as she saw she had a chance to catch him, a man whose new fortune made him a far more desirable target than his brother, and it became evident to him as soon as she displayed this interest in him (his vanity and her adroitness probably kept him from perceiving its mercenary nature).

24. If Robert is under twenty-one (his age is not specified) his mother would be in a position to prevent a marriage by withholding her consent when the clergyman providing the license asked her for it. The ways to circumvent this were to go to Scotland, where it was possible to get married immediately without a parent's consent and still have a marriage that was valid, or to find a parish in London where the growth in population meant the clergy were unable to check the qualifications of all the people seeking permission to marry. Even if he were twenty-one, he would still be circumventing the social custom dictating parental consent.

25. By cutting them, or refusing to acknowledge their acquaintance, Lucy would be establishing her superiority over those she knew earlier, as well as getting revenge for any perceived slights they had inflicted on her. This would give her a reason for happily consenting to Robert's plan of going to Dawlish, since it would put her in proximity to those she knew when living in Devonshire.

26. Robert had expressed his taste for fancy cottages to Elinor (pp. 468–470); the incongruous phrase "magnificent cottages" suggests the absurdities of the current fashion. Drawing up plans would be a natural pastime for Robert— many wealthy people at the time functioned as their own amateur architects. For an example of a contemporary picture and plan of a cottage, showing the grand heights such cottages could reach, see p. 695.

27. Mrs. Ferrars, and her daughter and son-in-law, exhibited a similar "reasonableness" earlier when they considered Lucy especially culpable for having entered a secret engagement with someone from a wealthy family (p. 496).

28. Lucy, in her attempt to flatter Mrs. Ferrars and break down her hostility, claimed the latter was showing graciousness when she conferred her haughty notice, or acknowledgment.

and while Edward was never cordially forgiven for having once intended to marry her, and Elinor, though superior to her in fortune and birth, was spoken of as an intruder, *she* was in every thing considered, and always openly acknowledged, to be a favourite child. They settled in town, received very liberal assistance from Mrs. Ferrars, were on the best terms imaginable with the Dashwoods; and setting aside the jealousies and ill-will continually subsisting between Fanny and Lucy, in which their husbands of course took a part, as well as the frequent domestic disagreements between Robert and Lucy themselves, nothing could exceed the harmony in which they all lived together.

What Edward had done to forfeit the right of eldest son, might have puzzled many people to find out; and what Robert had done to succeed to[29] it, might have puzzled them still more. It was an arrangement, however, justified in its effects, if not in its cause; for nothing ever appeared in Robert's style of living or of talking, to give a suspicion of his regretting the extent of his income, as either leaving his brother too little, or bringing himself too much; — and if Edward might be judged from the ready discharge of his duties in every particular,[30] from an increasing attachment to his wife and his home, and from the regular cheerfulness of his spirits, he might be supposed no less contented with his lot, no less free from every wish of an exchange.

Elinor's marriage divided her as little from her family as could well be contrived, without rendering the cottage at Barton entirely useless, for her mother and sisters spent much more than half their time with her.[31] Mrs. Dashwood was acting on motives of policy as well as pleasure in the frequency of her visits at Delaford; for her wish of bringing Marianne and Colonel Brandon together was hardly less earnest, though rather more liberal than what John had expressed.[32] It was now her darling object. Precious as was the company of her daughter to her, she desired nothing so much as to give up its constant enjoyment to her valued friend; and to see Marianne settled at the mansion-house was equally the wish of Edward and Elinor. They each felt his sorrows,

29. *succeed to*: enjoy or possess in the wake of someone else.

30. Clerical duties would include conducting regular services, presiding at marriages and funerals, and visiting parishioners. Edward, though obviously a conscientious man who would perform his duties faithfully, never exhibits any particular religious zeal. This was not unusual at the time, for while religious faith was almost universal in this society, it frequently involved no great fervor, and the clergy was regarded as a profession that could be pursued, like any other, with a view in part to the advantages and opportunities it offered.

31. Mrs. Dashwood spoke earlier of the closeness of Barton and Delaford.

32. She wants to bring them together from a belief that Colonel Brandon is a worthy man and they would form a happy couple, not from a wish to procure his wealth for her daughter.

A marriage ceremony.

[From William Combe, *The Dance of Life* (London, 1817; 1903 reprint), p. 234]

and their own obligations,[33] and Marianne, by general consent, was to be the reward of all.

With such a confederacy against her—with a knowledge so intimate of his goodness—with a conviction of his fond attachment to herself, which at last, though long after it was observable to everybody else—burst on her[34]—what could she do?[35]

Marianne Dashwood was born to an extraordinary fate. She was born to discover the falsehood of her own opinions, and to counteract, by her conduct, her most favourite maxims. She was born to overcome an affection formed so late in life as at seventeen, and with no sentiment superior to strong esteem and lively friendship, voluntarily to give her hand to another![36]—and *that* other, a man who had suffered no less than herself under the event of a former attachment, whom, two years before, she had considered too old to be married,[37]—and who still sought the constitutional safeguard of a flannel waistcoat!

But so it was. Instead of falling a sacrifice to an irresistible passion, as once she had fondly flattered herself with expecting,— instead of remaining even for ever with her mother, and finding her only pleasures in retirement[38] and study, as afterwards in her more calm and sober judgment she had determined on,—she found herself at nineteen, submitting to new attachments, entering on new duties, placed in a new home, a wife, the mistress of a family,[39] and the patroness of a village.[40]

Colonel Brandon was now as happy, as all those who best loved him, believed he deserved to be;—in Marianne he was consoled for every past affliction;—her regard and her society restored his mind to animation, and his spirits to cheerfulness;[41] and that Marianne found her own happiness in forming his, was equally the persuasion and delight of each observing friend. Marianne could never love by halves; and her whole heart became, in time, as much devoted to her husband, as it had once been to Willoughby.[42]

Willoughby could not hear of her marriage without a pang; and his punishment was soon afterwards complete in the voluntary forgiveness of Mrs. Smith, who, by stating his marriage with a

33. They are obliged to Colonel Brandon for the clerical living they now enjoy, as well as the considerable effort he took to improve their home and make it ready for them quickly.

34. Marianne is the last to perceive it; her absorption in her own thoughts has often made her obtuse about what is happening around her.

35. This succumbing to external pressure represents a highly unromantic path to marriage, the least romantic of any Austen heroine. It thus forms a sharp irony in light of Marianne's earlier opinions about love and marriage. In addition, Colonel Brandon, like Edward, contrasts with the dashing hero presented in much Romantic literature and initially desired by Marianne. At the same time, her choice of a man whose steady good sense makes him similar to Elinor, and whose close residence to her sister forms one of his attractions, is appropriate for a novel in which the ties between the two sisters have been central to the story—in many respects more important than either of their romantic relationships.

36. She had early on castigated Elinor for speaking of only her esteem and liking of Edward (p. 38). Now she is willingly entering a marriage in which she feels nothing more for her husband.

37. Since Elinor's marriage took place approximately one year after they first came to Barton, Marianne's is happening a year later.

38. *retirement:* seclusion.

39. Her duties would involve managing the household, as well as supervising the raising of their children—and the phrase "mistress of a family" suggests they eventually have children.

40. The leading landowner in a village played an important role; he would provide employment, charity, and hospitality and frequently would act as a local legal authority. His wife would host events for people in the neighborhood and visit local poor families and assist them.

41. It is notable that, amid this account of his cheerfulness, the fate of Eliza Williams and her child is never mentioned. He presumably continues to provide for them, but may not maintain any other ties. Those who had transgressed fundamental social laws were generally cast out from society, and kept from tainting or influencing others. Jane Austen may have refrained from further mentioning them because of her own discomfort with the subject, which she introduced mostly as a background story for Willoughby and Colonel Brandon.

42. Thus Marianne eventually does fall in love; despite the humorous comments of the narrator above, her final fate is not completely unromantic.

woman of character, as the source of her clemency, gave him reason for believing that had he behaved with honour towards Marianne, he might at once have been happy and rich. That his repentance of misconduct, which thus brought its own punishment, was sincere, need not be doubted;—nor that he long thought of Colonel Brandon with envy, and of Marianne with regret. But that he was for ever inconsolable, that he fled from society, or contracted an habitual gloom of temper, or died of a broken heart, must not be depended on[43]—for he did neither.[44] He lived to exert, and frequently to enjoy himself. His wife was not always out of humour, nor his home always uncomfortable;[45] and in his breed of horses and dogs, and in sporting of every kind, he found no inconsiderable degree of domestic felicity.[46]

For Marianne, however—in spite of his incivility in surviving her loss—he always retained that decided regard which interested him in everything that befell her, and made her his secret standard of perfection in woman;—and many a rising beauty would be slighted by him in after-days as bearing no comparison with Mrs. Brandon.

Mrs. Dashwood was prudent enough to remain at the cottage, without attempting a removal to Delaford; and fortunately for Sir John and Mrs. Jennings, when Marianne was taken from them, Margaret had reached an age highly suitable for dancing, and not very ineligible for being supposed to have a lover.[47]

Between Barton and Delaford, there was that constant communication which strong family affection would naturally dictate;— and among the merits and the happiness of Elinor and Marianne, let it not be ranked as the least considerable, that though sisters, and living almost within sight of each other, they could live without disagreement between themselves, or producing coolness between their husbands.[48]

FINIS

43. These were the conventions of many novels, which showed people who behaved badly always suffering fully for their misdeeds.

44. *neither*: none of these things. "Neither" was sometimes used then for more than two items.

45. *uncomfortable*: unpleasant.

46. Fervent devotion to sport was characteristic of many country gentlemen, even those who loved their wives and had no reason to wish to escape their company.

47. Margaret was thirteen at the beginning of the novel, and thus would be fifteen now. This would be around the age that girls started dancing at social events and were considered at least potentially romantic figures.

48. The suggestion is that this is unusual. Their sisterly harmony is similar to that seen in *Pride and Prejudice*, in which the heroine and her sister maintain a close relationship throughout the novel and end up settling down with husbands who are close friends and live in proximity to each other, though not as great a proximity as Elinor and Marianne. Their situation also contrasts with the frequent discord between the other linked couples, John and Fanny Dashwood and Robert and Lucy Ferrars.

Chronology

Jane Austen did not provide any exact dates in *Sense and Sensibility*, in contrast to most of her novels, but she provides enough indications of times of year and intervals between events to allow for a fairly precise chronology of the action.

VOLUME II PAGE

VOLUME III   PAGE

Middle of March	Elinor and Marianne plan trip home	516
	Colonel Brandon calls, tells Elinor of gift to Edward	518–22
	Elinor tells Edward of gift *This was the same day as above.*	532–34
Next Day	Mrs. Jennings calls on Lucy Steele	544
Mid- to Late March	Elinor calls on John Dashwood *"It was now above a week since" his telling her and Mrs. Jennings of Edward's engagement.*	544
First Half of April	Elinor, Marianne, Mrs. Jennings, and Mrs. Palmer leave London together *It was "very early in April."*	560
Day 3	Arrival at the Palmers' house	562
Day 4	Mr. Palmer and Colonel Brandon arrive	568
Days 5 & 6	Marianne takes two twilight walks	570
Day 7	Marianne develops a violent cold *This is the most likely day. The cold, acquired during the walks, was "for a day or two trifled with or denied."*	570
Day 8	Marianne's condition worsens	572
Day 9	Apothecary examines Marianne, speaks of infection; Mrs. Palmer and baby evacuate the house	572–74
Day 10	Mr. Palmer joins his wife	574
Days 11 & 12	Marianne's condition remains the same	576
Day 13	Marianne seems to improve, then worsens	576–78
	Colonel Brandon leaves to get Mrs. Dashwood	580
	Sir John receives a letter from Mrs. Jennings about Marianne, later tells Willoughby of it	616
Day 14	Marianne begins to improve	584
	Willoughby arrives and is met with Elinor	590–92
	Colonel Brandon and Mrs. Dashwood arrive	622–24
Mid- to Late April	Marianne moved to dressing room *This was "within four days after" above event.*	634
Late April	The Dashwoods leave for home *The day is not specified; it seems to be several days to a week after the above.*	636

The Dashwoods arrive home   638
It was late during the next day.

Marianne goes for a walk; Elinor tells of   640–44
Willoughby
She had been "two or three days at home."

Early May   Elinor hears of Lucy's marriage   656–58
*Elinor was not "long in ignorance" of news
of the matter. Counting backward from Colonel
Brandon's arrival in Barton (see below), this would
be almost two weeks after they left the Palmers'.*

Edward leaves Oxford   682
*This would be soon after above event. Lucy had
written him a letter while traveling to Dawlish
(p. 680), and thus just before she sent message of
her marriage to Elinor, and he left Oxford "within
four and twenty hours after receiving the letter."*

Early to Mid-   Edward arrives in Barton, proposes to Elinor   666, 672
May   *This would be two days after his departure from
Oxford, according to prevailing travel speeds.*

Middle of May   Colonel Brandon's arrival in Barton   688
*This was "about four days after Edward's arrival."
He had been at home for three weeks after
everyone's departure from the Palmers'.*

Latter Part of   Edward and Colonel Brandon leave for Delaford   694
May   *This was "three or four days" after Brandon arrived.*

Edward leaves for London   694
He stayed at Delaford "a couple of nights" first.

Edward secures his mother's consent to his marriage 696
*He would have been two days, or a little more, on the
road; she agreed after a little delay. At this point it
was two weeks after Lucy and Robert's marriage.*

Mid- to Late   Elinor and Edward marry   698
August   *This was one month before the following event. It is
described as "early in the autumn," but in Britain
this included August.*

Late September   Elinor and Edward move into their parsonage   698

They are visited by their relations and friends   698–700
*This happened soon after their move, and Mrs.
Jennings came "by Michaelmas," i.e., September 29.*

Later in Year   Mrs. Ferrars forgives Robert and Lucy   700
                     This occurred "before many months had passed
                     away."

Latter Part of   Marianne and Colonel Brandon marry   706
Next Year   *They married two years after she had judged him*
                     "too old to be married," which was in September
                     of the first year of the novel.

Bibliography

EDITIONS OF *SENSE AND SENSIBILITY*

Chapman, R. W., ed., *The Novels of Jane Austen, Vol. I: Sense and Sensibility* (Oxford, 1933)

Copeland, Edward, ed., *The Cambridge Edition of the Works of Jane Austen: Sense and Sensibility* (Cambridge, 2006)

Johnson, Claudia, ed., *Sense and Sensibility: A Norton Critical Edition* (New York, 2001)

Lamont, Claire, ed., *Sense and Sensibility* (London, 1970)

WORKS BY JANE AUSTEN

The Cambridge Edition of the Works of Jane Austen (Cambridge, 2005–2009)

Jane Austen's Letters, ed. by Deirdre Le Faye (Oxford, 1995)

Jane Austen's "Sir Charles Grandison," ed. by Brian Southam (Oxford, 1980)

The Oxford Illustrated Jane Austen, 6 Vols., ed. by R. W. Chapman (Oxford, 1933)

WORKS RELATING TO JANE AUSTEN

Biographical

Austen, Caroline, *Reminiscences of Caroline Austen* (Guildford, 1986)

Austen-Leigh, J. E., *A Memoir of Jane Austen and Other Family Recollections* (Oxford, 2002; originally published 1871)

Austen-Leigh, William, and Richard Arthur Austen-Leigh, *Jane Austen: A Family Record*, revised and enlarged by Deirdre Le Faye (Boston, 1989)

Harman, Claire, *Jane's Fame: How Austen Conquered the World* (Edinburgh, 2009)

Honan, Park, *Jane Austen: Her Life* (New York, 1989)

Le Faye, Deirdre, *Jane Austen: The World of Her Novels* (New York, 2002)

Mitton, G. E., *Jane Austen and Her Times* (Philadelphia, 2003; originally 1905)
Myer, Valerie Grosvenor, *Jane Austen: Obstinate Heart* (New York, 1997)
Ross, Josephine, *Jane Austen: A Companion* (New Brunswick, NJ, 2003)
Tucker, George Holbert, *Jane Austen the Woman* (New York, 1994)

Critical

Auerbach, Emily, *Searching for Jane Austen* (Madison, 2004)
Babb, Howard S., *Jane Austen's Novels: The Fabric of Dialogue* (Columbus, OH, 1962)
Bush, Douglas, *Jane Austen* (New York, 1975)
Butler, Marilyn, *Jane Austen and the War of Ideas* (Oxford, 1975)
Cecil, Lord David, *A Portrait of Jane Austen* (New York, 1979)
Craik, W. A., *Jane Austen: The Six Novels* (London, 1965)
Dwyer, June, *Jane Austen* (New York, 1989)
Emsley, Sarah, *Jane Austen's Philosophy of the Virtues* (New York, 2005)
Fergus, Jan, *Jane Austen and the Didactic Novel: "Northanger Abbey," "Sense and Sensibility" and "Pride and Prejudice"* (Totowa, NJ, 1983)
Gard, Roger, *Jane Austen's Novels: The Art of Clarity* (New Haven, 1992)
Gooneratne, Yasmine, *Jane Austen* (Cambridge, 1970)
Grey, J. David, ed., *The Jane Austen Companion* (New York, 1986)
Halperin, John, ed., *Jane Austen: Bicentenary Essays* (Cambridge, 1975)
Hardy, Barbara, *A Reading of Jane Austen* (New York, 1979)
Hardy, John, *Jane Austen's Heroines: Intimacy in Human Relationships* (London, 1984)
Horwitz, Barbara, *Jane Austen and the Question of Women's Education* (New York, 1991)
Hudson, Glenda, *Sibling Love and Incest in Jane Austen's Fiction* (New York, 1999)
Jenkyns, Richard, *A Fine Brush on Ivory: An Appreciation of Jane Austen* (New York, 2004)
Jones, Vivien, *How to Study a Jane Austen Novel* (Basingstoke, Hampshire, 1987)
Lascelles, Mary, *Jane Austen and Her Art* (Oxford, 1939)
Liddell, Robert, *The Novels of Jane Austen* (London, 1963)
Litz, J. Walton, *Jane Austen* (New York, 1965)
MacDonagh, Oliver, *Jane Austen: Real and Imagined Worlds* (New Haven, 1991)
Mansell, Darrel, *The Novels of Jane Austen: An Interpretation* (London, 1973)
McMaster, Juliet, *Jane Austen the Novelist* (Basingstoke, 1996)
Mews, Hazel, *Frail Vessels: Women's Roles in Women's Novels from Fanny Burney to George Eliot* (London, 1969)

Moler, Kenneth L., *Jane Austen's Art of Illusion* (Lincoln, NE, 1968)

Mooneyham, Laura, *Romance, Language and Education in Jane Austen's Novels* (New York, 1988)

Morini, Massimiliano, *Jane Austen's Narrative Techniques* (Farnham, 2009)

Morris, Ivor, *Jane Austen and the Interplay of Character* (London, 1999)

Nardin, Jane, *Those Elegant Decorums: The Concept of Propriety in Jane Austen's Novels* (Albany, NY, 1973)

Paris, J. Bernard, *Character and Conflict in Jane Austen's Novels* (Detroit, 1978)

Ruderman, Anne C., *The Pleasures of Virtue: Political Thought in the Novels of Jane Austen* (Lanham, MD, 1995)

Scott, P. J. M., *Jane Austen* (London, 1982)

Southam, B. C., ed., *Jane Austen: The Critical Heritage*, 2 Vols. (London, 1968–1987)

Stovel, Bruce, and Lynn Weinlos Gregg, eds., *The Talk in Jane Austen* (Alberta, 2002)

Tave, Stuart, *Some Words of Jane Austen* (Chicago, 1973)

Ten Harmsel, Henrietta, *Jane Austen: A Study in Fictional Conventions* (The Hague, 1964)

Thomson, Clara Linklater, *Jane Austen: A Survey* (London, 1929)

Watt, Ian, ed., *Jane Austen: A Collection of Critical Essays* (Englewood Cliffs, NJ, 1963)

WORKS OF HISTORICAL BACKGROUND

General Histories and Reference

Burton, Elizabeth, *The Pageant of Georgian England* (New York, 1967)

Craik, W. A., *Jane Austen in Her Time* (London, 1969)

Halevy, Elie, *A History of the English People in the Nineteenth Century, Vol. I: England in 1815*, translated by E. I. Watkin and D. A. Barker, 2nd ed. (London, 1949)

Harvey, A. D., *Britain in the Early Nineteenth Century* (New York, 1978)

McKendrick, Neil, John Brewer, and J. H. Plumb, *The Birth of a Consumer Society: The Commercialization of Eighteenth-Century England* (Bloomington, IN, 1982)

Olsen, Kirstin, *All Things Austen: An Encyclopedia of Austen's World*, 2 Vols. (Westport, CT, 2005)

Parreaux, Andre, *Daily Life in England in the Reign of George III* (London, 1969)

Porter, Roy, *English Society in the Eighteenth Century*, rev. ed. (London, 1990)

Rule, John, *Albion's People: English Society, 1714–1815* (London, 1992)
Todd, Janet, ed. *Jane Austen in Context* (New York, 2005)
White, R. J., *Life in Regency England* (London, 1963)

Language of the Period

The Compact Edition of the Oxford English Dictionary (Oxford, 1971)
Johnson, Samuel, *Dictionary of the English Language*, ed. by Alexander
     Chalmers (London, 1994; reprint of 1843 ed.)
Page, Norman, *The Language of Jane Austen* (Oxford, 1972)
Phillipps, K. C., *Jane Austen's English* (London, 1970)
Pinion, F. B., *A Jane Austen Companion* (London, 1973)
Room, Adrian, *Dictionary of Changes in Meaning* (New York, 1986)
Schapera, I., *Kinship Terminology in Jane Austen's Novels* (London, 1977)
Stokes, Myra, *The Language of Jane Austen: A Study of Some Aspects of Her
     Vocabulary* (New York, 1991)
Tucker, Susie, *Protean Shape: A Study in Eighteenth-Century Vocabulary
     and Usage* (London, 1967)

Cultural and Literary Background

Baker, Ernest, *The Novel of Sentiment and the Gothic Romance*, in *The His-
     tory of the English Novel*, Vol. V (London, 1929)
Bate, Walter Jackson, *From Classic to Romantic: Premises of Taste in Eigh-
     teenth Century England* (New York, 1946)
Black, Jeremy, *Culture in Eighteenth-Century England: A Subject for Taste*
     (London, 2005)
Bradbrook, Frank W., *Jane Austen and Her Predecessors* (Cambridge, 1966)
Bredvold, Louis I., *The Natural History of Sensibility* (Detroit, 1962)
Brewer, John, *The Pleasures of the Imagination: English Culture in the Eigh-
     teenth Century* (New York, 1997)
Feingold, Richard, *Nature and Society: Later Eighteenth-Century Uses of the
     Pastoral and Georgic* (New Brunswick, 1978)
Foster, James, *The History of the Pre-Romantic Novel in England* (New York,
     1949)
Gaull, Marilyn, *English Romanticism: The Human Context* (New York,
     1988)
Kelly, Gary, *English Fiction of the Romantic Period, 1789–1830* (London,
     1989)
Lane, Maggie, *Jane Austen and Names* (Bristol, 2002)
McCalman, Iain, ed., *An Oxford Companion to the Romantic Age: British
     Culture, 1776–1832* (Oxford, 1999)
Railo, Eino, *Haunted Castle: A Study of the Elements of English Romanti-
     cism* (New York, 1964)

Sweet, Rosemary, *Antiquaries: The Discovery of the Past in Eighteenth-Century Britain* (London, 2004)

Tompkins, Joyce, *The Popular Novel in England, 1770–1800* (Lincoln, 1961)

Marriage and the Family

Jones, Hazel, *Jane Austen and Marriage* (London, 2009)

Outhwaite, R. B., *Clandestine Marriage in England 1500–1850* (London, 1995)

Stone, Lawrence, *The Family, Sex and Marriage in England 1500–1800* (London, 1977)

———, *Road to Divorce: England 1530–1987* (Oxford, 1990)

Tadmor, Naomi, *Family and Friends in Eighteenth-Century England: Household, Kinship, and Patronage* (Cambridge, 2001)

Trumbach, Randolph, *The Rise of the Egalitarian Family: Aristocratic Kinship and Domestic Relations in Eighteenth-Century England* (New York, 1978)

Wolfram, Sybil, *In-Laws and Outlaws: Kinship and Marriage in England* (Beckenham, Kent, 1987)

The Position of Women

Barker, Hannah, and Elaine Chalus, eds., *Women's History: Britain, 1700–1850: An Introduction* (London, 2005)

Brophy, Elizabeth Bergen, *Women's Lives and the 18th-Century English Novel* (Tampa, 1991)

Horn, Pamela, *Victorian Countrywomen* (Oxford, 1991)

Perkin, Joan, *Women and Marriage in Nineteenth-Century England* (London, 1989)

Shoemaker, Robert B., *Gender in English Society, 1650–1850: The Emergence of Separate Spheres?* (London, 1998)

Tague, Ingrid H., *Women of Quality: Accepting and Contesting Ideals of Femininity in England, 1690–1760* (Woodbridge, UK, 2002)

Vickery, Amanda, *The Gentleman's Daughter: Women's Lives in Georgian England* (London, 1998)

Children and Childbearing

Bayne-Powell, Rosamond, *The English Child in the Eighteenth Century* (New York, 1939)

Fletcher, Anthony, *Growing Up in England: The Experience of Childhood 1600–1914* (New Haven, 2008)

Lewis, Judith Schneid, *In the Family Way: Childbearing in the British Aristocracy, 1760–1860* (New Brunswick, NJ, 1986)

Selwyn, David, *Jane Austen and Children* (New York, 2010)

Steward, James Christen, *The New Child: British Art and the Origins of Modern Childhood* (Berkeley, 1995)

Housekeeping and Servants

Adams, Samuel and Sarah, *The Complete Servant* (Lewes, 1989; originally published 1825)

Bayne-Powell, Rosamond, *Housekeeping in the Eighteenth Century* (London, 1956)

Davidson, Caroline, *A Woman's Work Is Never Done: A History of Housework in the British Isles, 1650–1950* (London, 1982)

Dillon, Maureen, *Artificial Sunshine: A Social History of Domestic Lighting* (London, 2002)

Gerard, Jessica, *Country House Life: Family and Servants, 1815–1914* (Oxford, 1994)

Hardyment, Christina, *Home Comfort: A History of Domestic Arrangements* (Chicago, 1992)

Hecht, J. Jean, *The Domestic Servant Class in Eighteenth-Century England* (London, 1956)

Hill, Bridget, *Servants: English Domestics in the Eighteenth Century* (Oxford, 1996)

Horn, Pamela, *Flunkeys and Scullions: Life Below Stairs in Georgian England* (Stroud, 2004)

———, *The Rise and Fall of the Victorian Servant* (Stroud, 2004)

Laing, Alastair, *Lighting* (London, 1982)

Sambrook, Pamela, *The Country House Servant* (Stroud, 1999)

Stuart, Dorothy Margaret, *The English Abigail* (London, 1946)

Turner, E. S., *What the Butler Saw: 250 Years of the Servant Problem* (New York, 1962)

Entails and Settlements

English, Barbara, and John Saville, *Strict Settlement: A Guide for Historians* (Hull, 1983)

Erickson, Amy Louise, *Women and Property in Early Modern England* (London, 1993)

Habakkuk, John, *Marriage, Debt, and the Estates System: English Landownership, 1650–1950* (Oxford, 1994)

Holcombe, Lee, *Wives and Property: Reform of the Married Women's Property Law in Nineteenth-Century England* (Oxford, 1983)

Spring, Eileen, *Law, Land, and Family: Aristocratic Inheritance in England, 1300 to 1800* (Chapel Hill, 1993)

Money and Finance

Burnett, John, *A History of the Cost of Living* (Harmondsworth, Middlesex, 1969)

Daunton, M. J., *Progress and Poverty: An Economic and Social History of Britain, 1700–1850* (New York, 1995)

Dowell, Stephen, *A History of Taxes and Taxation in England* (London, 1884)

Friedberg, Robert, *Coins of the British World: Complete from 500 A.C. to the Present* (New York, 1962)

Landed Society

Baugh, Daniel A., ed., *Aristocratic Government and Society in Eighteenth-Century England: The Foundations of Stability* (New York, 1975)

Beckett, J. V. *The Aristocracy in England, 1660–1914* (Oxford, 1986)

Bence-Jones, Mark, and Hugh Montgomery-Massingberd, *The British Aristocracy* (London, 1979)

Book of the Ranks and Dignities of British Society, attributed to Charles Lamb (London, 1805; reprinted 1924)

Cannon, John, *Aristocratic Century: The Peerage of Eighteenth-Century England* (Cambridge, 1984)

Greene, D. J., "Jane Austen and the Peerage," *PMLA* 68 (1953): 1017–1031.

Langford, Paul, *Public Life and the Propertied Englishman, 1689–1798* (Oxford, 1991)

Mingay, G. E., *English Landed Society in the Eighteenth Century* (London, 1963)

———, *The Gentry: The Rise and Fall of a Ruling Class* (New York, 1976)

Stone, Lawrence, and Jeanne C. Fawtier Stone, *An Open Elite? England 1540–1880* (Oxford, 1984)

Thompson, F. M. L., *English Landed Society in the Nineteenth Century* (London, 1963)

The Rural World

Bovill, E. W., *English Country Life, 1780–1830* (London, 1962)

Harte, Negley, and Roland Quinault, eds., *Land and Society in Britain, 1700–1914* (Manchester, 1996)

Horn, Pamela, *The Rural World, 1780–1850: Social Change in the English Countryside* (New York, 1980)

Keith-Lucas, Brian, *The Unreformed Local Government System* (London, 1980)

Rackham, Oliver, *The History of the Countryside* (London, 1986)

Wade Martins, Susanna, *Farmers, Landlords and Landscapes: Rural Britain, 1720 to 1870* (Macclesfield, Cheshire, 2004)

Wild, Trevor, *Village England: A Social History of the Countryside* (London, 2004)

Williamson, Tom, *The Transformation of Rural England: Farming and the Landscape, 1700–1870* (Exeter, UK, 2002)

Williamson, Tom, and Liz Bellamy, *Property and Landscape* (London, 1987)

Urban Life

Berg, Maxine, *Luxury and Pleasure in Eighteenth-Century Britain* (New York, 2005)

Cox, Nancy, *The Complete Tradesman: A Study of Retailing, 1550–1820* (Aldershot, 2000)

Cruickshank, Daniel, and Neil Burton, *Life in the Georgian City* (London, 1990)

Ellis, Joyce M., *The Georgian Town 1680–1840* (Basingstoke, 2001)

Girouard, Mark, *The English Town: A History of Urban Life* (New Haven, 1990)

Mui, Hoh-Cheung, and Lorna H. Mui, *Shops and Shopkeeping in Eighteenth-Century England* (Kingston, Ontario, 1989)

London

A to Z of Regency London (London, 1985)

Adburgham, Alison, *Shopping in Style: London from the Restoration to Edwardian Elegance* (London, 1979)

Altick, Richard, *The Shows of London* (Cambridge, MA, 1978)

Bayne-Powell, Rosamund, *Eighteenth-Century London Life* (New York, 1938)

Borer, Mary, *Illustrated Guide to London, 1800* (New York, 1988)

Fox, Celina, ed., *London—World City, 1800–1840* (New Haven, 1992)

Kisling, Jr., Vernon N., ed., *Zoo and Aquarium History: Ancient Animal Collections to Zoological Gardens* (Boca Raton, 2001)

Margetson, Stella, *Regency London* (London, 1971)

Mingay, G. E., *Georgian London* (London, 1975)

Picard, Liza, *Dr. Johnson's London* (New York, 2000)

Porter, Roy, *London: A Social History* (Cambridge, MA, 1994)

Schwartz, Richard B., *Daily Life in Johnson's London* (Madison, WI, 1983)

Sheppard, Francis, *London: A History* (New York, 1998)

Stewart, Rachel, *The Town House in Georgian London* (New Haven, 1992)

Thorold, Peter, *The London Rich: The Creation of a Great City, from 1666 to the Present* (New York, 1999)

Weinreb, Ben, and Christopher Hibbert, *The London Encyclopedia* (Bethesda, 1986)

The Professions

Corfield, Penelope J., *Power and the Professions in Britain, 1700–1850* (New York, 1995)

Reader, W. J., *Professional Men: The Rise of the Professional Classes in Nineteenth-Century England* (London, 1966)

The Church and the Clergy

Collins, Irene, *Jane Austen and the Clergy* (London, 1994)

Francis Brown, C. K., *A History of the English Clergy, 1800–1900* (London, 1953)

Hart, A. Tindal, *The Country Priest in English History* (London, 1959)

Jacob, W. M., *The Clerical Profession in the Long Eighteenth Century, 1680–1840* (Oxford, 2007)

Legg, J. Wickham, *English Church Life from the Restoration to the Tractarian Movement* (London, 1914)

Sykes, Norman, *Church and State in England in the XVIIIth Century* (Hamden, CT, 1962)

Virgin, Peter, *The Church in an Age of Negligence* (Cambridge, 1989)

Yates, Nigel, *Eighteenth-Century Britain: Religion and Politics, 1714–1815* (Harlow, 2008)

The Navy and Army

Haythornthwaite, Philip J., *The Armies of Wellington* (New York, 1994)

Holmes, Richard, *Redcoat: The British Soldier in the Age of Horse and Musket* (London, 2001)

Lavery, Brian, *Nelson's Navy: The Ships, Men and Organisation 1793–1815* (London, 1989)

Lewis, Michael, *A Social History of the Navy 1793–1815* (London, 1960)

Medicine

Buchan, William, *Domestic Medicine* (New York, 1815; based on London ed.)

Digby, Anne, *Making a Medical Living: Doctors and Patients in the English Market for Medicine, 1720–1911* (Cambridge, UK, 1994)

English, Peter, *Rheumatic Fever in America and Britain* (New Brunswick, NJ, 1999)

French, Roger, and Andrew Wear, eds., *British Medicine in an Age of Reform* (London, 1991)

Heberden, William, *Commentaries on the History and Cure of Diseases* (London, 1802)

King, Lester, *The Medical World of the Eighteenth Century* (Chicago, 1958)

Lane, Joan, *A Social History of Medicine: Health, Healing and Disease in England, 1750–1950* (London, 2001)

Loudon, Irvine, *Medical Care and the General Practitioner, 1750–1850* (Oxford, 1986)

Porter, Roy, and Dorothy Porter, *In Sickness and in Health: The British Experience, 1650–1850* (New York, 1989)

——, *Patient's Progress: Doctors and Doctoring in Eighteenth-Century England* (Stanford, 1989)

Trotter, Thomas, *A View of the Nervous Temperament* (Troy, NY, 1808; originally published, London, 1807)

Law and Lawyers

Duman, Daniel, *The Judicial Bench in England, 1727–1875: The Reshaping of a Professional Elite* (London, 1982)

Lemmings, David, *Professors of the Law: Barristers and English Legal Culture in the Eighteenth Century* (Oxford, 2000)

Education

Brock, M. G., and M. C. Curthoys, eds., *The History of the University of Oxford* Vol. VI: *Nineteenth-Century Oxford, Part 1* (Oxford, 1997)

Chandos, John, *Boys Together: English Public Schools, 1800–1864* (New Haven, 1984)

Gardiner, Dorothy, *English Girlhood at School: A Study of Women's Education Through Twelve Centuries* (London, 1929)

Hans, Nicholas, *New Trends in Education in the Eighteenth Century* (London, 1951)

Kamm, Josephine, *Hope Deferred: Girls' Education in English History* (London, 1965)

Mack, Edward C., *Public Schools and British Opinion, 1780–1860* (New York, 1941)

Midgley, Graham, *University Life in Eighteenth-Century Oxford* (New Haven, 1996)

Roach, John, *A History of Secondary Education in England, 1800–1870* (London, 1986)

Sutherland, L. S., and L. G. Mitchell, eds., *The History of the University of Oxford* Vol. V: *The Eighteenth Century* (Oxford, 1986)

Books and Newspapers

Altick, Robert, *The English Common Reader: A Social History of the Mass Reading Public, 1800–1900* (Chicago, 1957)

Black, Jeremy, *The English Press, 1621–1861* (Stroud, 2001)

Bronson, Bertrand H., *Printing as an Index of Taste in Eighteenth-Century England* (New York, 1958)

Clarke, Bob, *From Grub Street to Fleet Street: An Illustrated History of English Newspapers to 1899* (Aldershot, 2004)

St. Clair, William, *The Reading Nation in the Romantic Period* (Cambridge, UK, 2004)

Writing

Finlay, Michael, *Western Writing Implements in the Age of the Quill Pen* (Carlisle, Cumbria, 1990)

Whalley, Joyce Irene, *English Handwriting, 1540–1853* (London, 1969)

———, *Writing Implements and Accessories: From the Roman Stylus to the Typewriter* (Newton Abbot, Devon, 1975)

The Postal Service

Hemmeon, J. C., *The History of the British Post Office* (Cambridge, MA, 1912)

Joyce, Herbert, *The History of the Post Office* (London, 1893)

Robinson, Howard, *The British Post Office: A History* (Princeton, 1948)

Transportation

Copeland, John, *Roads and Their Traffic* (Newton Abbot, Devon, 1968)

Dyos, H. J., and D. H. Aldcroft, *British Transport: An Economic Survey from the Seventeenth Century to the Twentieth* (Leicester, 1969)

Felton, William, *A Treatise on Carriages* (London, 1796)

Jackman, W. T., *The Development of Transportation in Modern England* (London, 1962)

Luton Museum and Art Gallery, *The Turnpike Age* (Luton, 1970—reprint of contemporary work by G. Gray)

MacKinnon, Honourable Mr. Justice (F. D.), "Topography and Travel in Jane Austen's Novels," *The Cornhill Magazine*, series 3, vol. 59 (1925): 184–199.

McCausland, Hugh, *The English Carriage* (London, 1948)

Pawson, Eric, *Transport and Economy: The Turnpike Roads of Eighteenth-Century Britain* (New York, 1977)

Reid, James, *Evolution of Horse Drawn Vehicles* (London, 1933)

Sparkes, Ivan, *Stagecoaches and Carriages* (Bourne End, 1975)

Stratton, Ezra, *World on Wheels* (New York, 1878)

Whatney, Marylilan, *The Elegant Carriage* (London, 1961)

Wilkinson, T. W., *From Track to By-Pass: A History of the English Road* (London, 1934)

Leisure and Amusement

Battiscombe, Georgina, *English Picnics* (London, 1949)
Gurney, Jackie, *The National Trust Book of Picnics* (Newton Abbot, 1982)
Parlett, David, *A Dictionary of Card Games* (New York, 1992)
———, *A History of Card Games* (New York, 1991)
Pimlott, J. A. R., *The Englishman's Christmas: A Social History* (Atlantic Highlands, NJ, 1998)

Music

Hart, Miriam, *Hardly an Innocent Diversion: Music in the Life and Writings of Jane Austen* (Ohio U., 1999)
Loesser, Arthur, *Men, Women and Pianos: A Social History* (New York, 1954)
Piggott, Patrick, *The Innocent Diversion: A Study of Music in the Life and Writings of Jane Austen* (London, 1979)
Weber, William, *The Great Transformation of Musical Taste: Concert Programming from Haydn to Brahms* (Cambridge, UK, 2008)
Wollenberg, Susan, and Simon McVeigh, eds., *Concert Life in Eighteenth-Century Britain* (Aldershot, 2004)

Outdoor Sports

Arkwright, William, *The Pointer and His Predecessors* (London, 1906)
Billett, Michael, *A History of English Country Sports* (London, 1994)
Carr, Raymond, *English Fox Hunting: A History* (London, 1986)
Griffin, Emma, *Blood Sport: Hunting in Britain Since 1066* (New Haven, 2007)
Itzkowitz, David C., *Peculiar Privilege: A Social History of English Foxhunting, 1753–1885* (Hassocks, 1977)
Landry, Donna, *The Invention of the Countryside: Hunting, Walking and Ecology in English Literature, 1671–1831* (New York, 2001)
Lascelles, Robert, *Letters on Sporting* (London, 1815)
Longrigg, Roger, *The English Squire and His Sport* (New York, 1977)
[Magne de Marolles], adapted and translated by John Acton, *An Essay on Shooting* (London, 1791)
Munsche, P. B., *Gentlemen and Poachers: The English Game Laws, 1671–1831* (Cambridge, UK, 1981)
Needham, T. H. [pseud.], *The Complete Sportsman* (London, 1817)
Selwyn, David, *Jane Austen and Leisure* (London, 1999)
The Sportsman's Dictionary (London, 1807)

Weather and the Seaside

Feltham, John, *A Guide to All the Watering and Sea-Bathing Places* (London, 1804)

Walton, John K., *The English Seaside Resort: A Social History, 1750–1914* (New York, 1983)
Wheeler, Dennis, and Julian Mayes, eds., *Regional Climates of the British Isles* (New York, 1997)

The Idea of the Picturesque

Andrews, Malcolm, *The Search for the Picturesque: Landscape, Aesthetics and Tourism in Britain, 1760–1800* (Stanford, 1989)
Everett, Nigel, *The Tory View of Landscape* (New Haven, 1994)
Gilpin, William, *Observations, on Several Parts of England, particularly the Mountains and Lakes of Cumberland and Westmoreland, relative chiefly to Picturesque Beauty, made in the year 1772*, 3rd ed. (London, 1802)
———, *Observations on the River Wye* (London, 1800)
———, *Remarks on Forest Scenery and other Woodland Views* (London, 1791)
———, *Three Essays: on Picturesque Beauty, on Picturesque Travel, and on Sketching Landscape* (London, 1808)
Hunt, John Dixon, *Gardens and the Picturesque: Studies in the History of Landscape Architecture* (Cambridge, MA, 1992)
Hussey, Christopher, *The Picturesque: Studies in a Point of View* (London, 1927; reprint 1967)
Watkin, David, *The English Vision: The Picturesque in Architecture, Landscape and Garden Design* (London, 1982)

Gardens and Landscaping

Batey, Mavis, *Jane Austen and the English Landscape* (Chicago, 1996)
Campbell, Susan, *A History of Kitchen Gardening* (London, 2005)
Coffin, David, *The English Garden: Meditation and Memorial* (Princeton, 1994)
Jackson-Stops, Gervase, *The Country House Garden: A Grand Tour* (Boston, 1987)
Jacques, David, *Georgian Gardens: The Reign of Nature* (Portland, OR, 1984)
Laird, Mark, *The Flowering of the Landscape Garden: English Pleasure Grounds, 1720–1800* (Philadelphia, 1999)
Quest-Ritson, Charles, *The English Garden: A Social History* (London, 2001)
Stuart, David, *Georgian Gardens* (London, 1979)
———, *The Kitchen Garden: A Historical Guide to Traditional Crops* (London, 1984)
Williamson, Tom, *Polite Landscapes: Gardens and Society in Eighteenth-Century England* (Baltimore, 1995)
Wilson, C. Anne, ed., *The Country House Kitchen Garden, 1600–1950* (Thrupp, Stroud, 1998)

Cottages

Crowley, John, *The Invention of Comfort: Sensibilities & Design in Early Modern Britain & Early America* (Baltimore, 2001)

Evans, Tony, and Candida Lycett Green, *English Cottages* (New York, 1983)

Gandy, Joseph, *Designs for Cottages, Cottage Farms & Other Rural Buildings* (London, 1805)

Gyfford, E., *Designs for Elegant Cottages and Small Villas* (London, 1806)

———, *Designs for Small Picturesque Cottages and Hunting Boxes* (London, 1807)

Tinniswood, Adrian, *Life in the English Country Cottage* (London, 1995)

Houses

Arnold, Dana, *The Georgian Country House: Architecture, Landscape and Society* (Stroud, Gloucestershire, 1998)

Aslet, Clive, *The National Trust Book of the English House* (Harmondsworth, Middlesex, 1985)

Christie, Christopher, *The British Country House in the Eighteenth Century* (New York, 2000)

Clemenson, Heather, *English Country Houses and Landed Estates* (New York, 1982)

Cook, Olive, *The English House through Seven Centuries* (New York, 1983)

Girouard, Mark, *Life in the English Country House: A Social and Architectural History* (New Haven, 1978)

———, *Town and Country* (New Haven, 1992)

Jackson-Stops, Gervase, ed., *The Fashioning and Functioning of the British Country House* (Hanover, 1989)

Meadows, Peter, *Joseph Bonomi, Architect* (London, 1988)

Reid, Richard, *The Georgian House and Its Details* (Bath, 1989)

Woodforde, John, *Georgian Houses for All* (London, 1978)

Interior Decoration

Edwards, Ralph, and L. G. G. Ramsey, *The Connoisseur's Period Guides to the Houses, Decoration, Furnishing and Chattels of the Classic Periods*, Vol. 4: *The Late Georgian Period, 1760–1810*, Vol. 5: *The Regency Period, 1810–1830* (London, 1958)

Gloag, John, *Georgian Grace: A Social History of Design from 1660 to 1830* (London, 1956)

Harrison, Molly, *People and Furniture: A Social Background to the English Home* (London, 1971)

Jourdain, Margaret, *Regency Furniture, 1795–1830* (London, 1965)

Morley, John, *Regency Design, 1790–1840* (London, 1993)

Musgrave, Clifford, *Regency Furniture, 1800–1830* (London, 1970)

Parissien, Steven, *The Georgian House in America and Britain* (New York, 1995)

———, *Regency Style* (Washington, D.C., 1992)

Pilcher, Donald, *The Regency Style, 1800 to 1830* (New York, 1948)

Ponsonby, Margaret, *Stories from Home: English Domestic Interiors, 1750–1850* (Aldershot, 2007)

Rogers, John, *English Furniture* (Feltham, 1967)

Vickery, Amanda, *Behind Closed Doors: At Home in Georgian England* (New Haven, 2009)

Watkins, Susan, *Jane Austen in Style* (New York, 1996)

Female Decorative Activities

Allen, B. Sprague, *Tides in English Taste (1690–1800): A Background for the Study of Literature*, Vol. I (New York, 1958)

Beck, Thomasina, *The Embroiderer's Story: Needlework from the Renaissance to the Present Day* (Devon, 1995)

Bermingham, Ann, *Learning to Draw: Studies in the Cultural History of a Polite and Useful Art* (New Haven, 2000)

Bicknell, Peter, and Jane Munro, eds., *Gilpin to Ruskin: Drawing Masters and their Manuals, 1800–1860* (London, 1987)

Forest, Jennifer, *Jane Austen's Sewing Box* (Millers Point, New South Wales, 2009)

Gandee, B. F., *The Artist, or Young Ladies Instructor in Ornamental Painting, Drawing, &c.* (London, 1835)

Hughes, Therle, *English Domestic Needlework, 1660–1860* (London, 1961)

Robertson, Hannah, *The Young Ladies School of Arts* (York, 1777)

Synge, Lanto, *Antique Needlework* (Poole, 1982)

Taunton, Nerylla, *Antique Needlework Tools and Embroideries* (Woodbridge, 1997)

Fashion and Adornment

Ashelford, Jane, *The Art of Dress: Clothes and Society, 1500–1914* (New York, 1996)

Bennion, Elisabeth, *Antique Dental Instruments* (New York, 1986)

Buck, Anne, *Dress in Eighteenth-Century England* (London, 1979)

Byrde, Penelope, *A Frivolous Distinction: Fashion and Needlework in the Works of Jane Austen* (Bristol, 1979)

Cunnington, C. Willett, *English Women's Clothing in the Nineteenth Century* (Mineola, NY, 1990; originally published 1937)

———, and Phyllis Cunnington, *A Handbook of English Costume in the Eighteenth Century* (Boston, 1972)

Downing, Sarah Jane, *Fashion in the Time of Jane Austen* (Oxford, 2010)

Ewing, Elizabeth, *Everyday Dress, 1650–1900* (London, 1984)

Farrell, Jeremy, *Socks & Stockings* (London, 1992)

Lady of Distinction, *The Mirror of the Graces; or, The English Lady's Costume* (London, 1811)

McKendrick, Neil, and John Brewer, and J. H. Plumb, *The Birth of a Consumer Society* (London, 1982)

Petroski, Henry, *The Toothpick: Technology and Culture* (New York, 2007)

Pratt, Lucy, and Linda Woolley, *Shoes* (London, 1999)

Food and Dining

Black, Maggie, and Deirdre Le Faye, *The Jane Austen Cookbook* (Chicago, 1995)

Grigson, Jane, *English Food* (London, 1992)

Hartley, Dorothy, *Food in England* (London, 1954)

Hickman, Peggy, *A Jane Austen Household Book, with Martha Lloyd's Recipes* (North Pomfret, VT, 1977)

Johnson, Hugh, *Vintage: The Story of Wine* (New York, 1989)

Lane, Maggie, *Jane Austen and Food* (London, 1995)

Lehmann, Gilly, *The British Housewife: Cookery Books, Cooking and Society in Eighteenth-Century Britain* (Totnes, 2003)

Palmer, Arnold, *Movable Feasts* (New York, 1952)

Paston-Williams, Sara, *The Art of Dining: A History of Cooking and Eating* (London, 1993)

Roberts, Jonathan, *The Origins of Fruit and Vegetables* (New York, 2001)

Trusler, John, *The Honours of the Table, or Rules for Behaviour during Meals* (London, 1791)

Wilson, C. Anne, *Food and Drink in Britain: From the Stone Age to Recent Times* (London, 1973)

Etiquette

Banfield, Edwin, *Visiting Cards and Cases* (Trowbridge, 1989)

Curtin, Michael, "A Question of Manners," *Journal of Modern History* 57:3 (Sept. 1985), pp. 396–423

Fritzer, Penelope Joan, *Jane Austen and Eighteenth-Century Courtesy Books* (Westport, CT, 1997)

Morgan, Marjorie, *Manners, Morals and Class in England, 1774–1858* (New York, 1994)

Ross, Josephine, *Jane Austen's Guide to Good Manners* (New York, 2006)

Wildeblood, Joan, *The Polite World: A Guide to the Deportment of the English in Former Times* (London, 1973)

Female Conduct Books

Advice of a Mother to Her Daughter, by the Marchioness of Lambert; *A Father's Legacy to His Daughters*, by Dr. Gregory; *The Lady's New Year's Gift, or, Advice to a Daughter*, by Lord Halifax, in *Angelica's Ladies Library* (London, 1794)

Burton, John, *Lectures on Female Education and Manners* (London, 1793; reprint ed., New York, 1970)

Chapone, Hester, *Letters on the Improvement of the Mind* (Walpole, NH, 1802; first published London, 1773)

Gisborne, Thomas, *An Enquiry into the Duties of the Female Sex* (London, 1796)

Murry, Ann, *Mentoria, or, the Young Ladies' Instructor* (London, 1785)

Pennington, Sarah, *An Unfortunate Mother's Advice to Her Absent Daughters* (London, 1770)

Trusler, John, *Principles of Politeness, and of Knowing the World, in Two Parts* (London, 1800)

Ideas of the Gentleman

Carter, Philip, *Men and the Emergence of Polite Society, Britain 1660–1800* (Harlow, Essex, 2001)

Castronovo, David, *The English Gentleman: Images and Ideals in Literature and Society* (New York, 1987)

Dueling and Clubs

Baldick, Robert, *The Duel: A History of Duelling* (London, 1965)

Clark, Peter, *British Clubs and Societies, 1580–1800: The Origins of an Associational World* (Oxford, 2000)

Fullerton, Susannah, *Jane Austen and Crime* (Madison, 2006)

Kiernan, V. G., *The Duel in European History: Honour and the Reign of Aristocracy* (Oxford, 1988)

Maps

ENGLAND

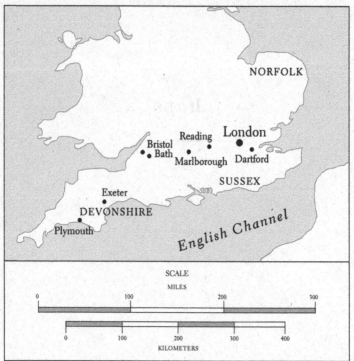

Plymouth: Town near which Lucy Steele's uncle Mr. Pratt lives.

Devonshire: County containing Plymouth, Exeter, and Barton, where Mrs. Dashwood's family and the Middletons reside.

Exeter: Town four miles south of Barton.

Bristol: City, just north of the Palmers' residence.

Bath: Leading resort town; where Willoughby seduces Eliza Williams.

Marlborough: Town where Willoughby stops on his trip from London.

Reading: Town on the route from London to the Palmers'.

Sussex: County containing Norland, the Dashwood estate.

Dartford: Town near which Robert Ferrars visits his friends the Elliotts.

Norfolk: County containing the estate Mrs. Ferrars bequeaths to Robert.

SOUTHWEST ENGLAND

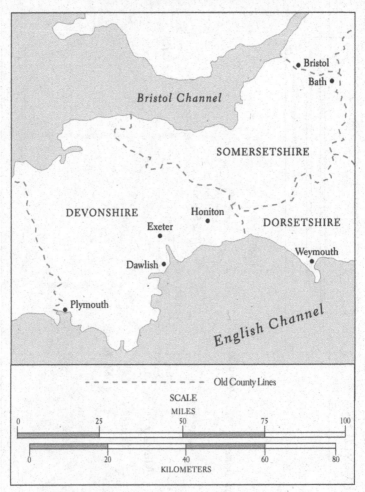

Plymouth, Devonshire, Exeter, Bath: See previous page.

Dawlish: Seaside resort that Robert Ferrars wishes to visit.

Honiton: First important stop traveling east from Barton.

Somersetshire: County in which Willoughby and the Palmers live
(the latter are at the northern edge, just below Bristol).

Dorsetshire: County containing Colonel Brandon's residence.

Weymouth: Seaside resort that Mrs. Palmer visits.

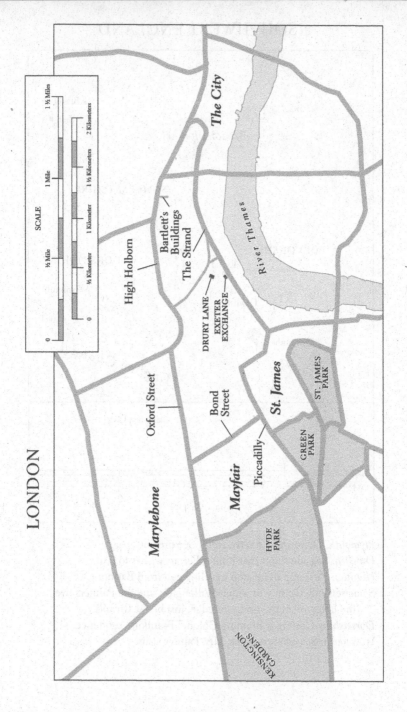

LONDON

Marylebone

Mayfair

St. James

The City

High Holborn

Bartlett's
Buildings
The Strand

DRURY LANE
EXETER
EXCHANGE

Oxford Street

Bond
Street

Piccadilly

GREEN
PARK

ST. JAMES
PARK

HYDE
PARK

KENSINGTON
GARDENS

River Thames

SCALE

0   ½ Mile   1 Mile   1½ Miles

0   ½ Kilometer   1 Kilometer   1½ Kilometers   2 Kilometers

Kensington Gardens: Where Elinor drives with Mrs. Jennings, and sees Lucy Steele.

Mayfair: Wealthy and fashionable area where most of the novel's characters reside while in London.

Marylebone: Fashionable area that developed after Mayfair did; Mrs. Jennings and John and Fanny Dashwood live there.

Bond Street: See next page.

St. James: Old aristocratic area where Colonel Brandon resides, and Edward stays briefly.

Exeter Exchange: Popular zoo where John and Fanny Dashwood take their son, Harry, on their first full day in London.

Drury Lane: One of the two principal London theaters; where John Dashwood tells Willoughby of Marianne's illness.

Bartlett's Buildings: Small street where the Miss Steeles spend most of their time in London, staying with their cousins.

The City: Principal commercial section of London.

LONDON — MAYFAIR AND VICINITY

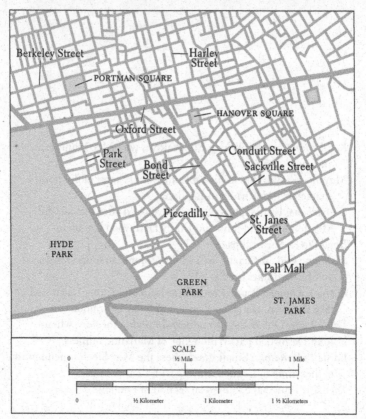

Berkeley Street: Where Mrs. Jennings lives, and where Elinor and Marianne stay when in London.

Harley Street: Where John and Fanny Dashwood reside in London.

Park Street: Where Mrs. Ferrars lives.

Hanover Square: Where the Palmers reside in London.

Bond Street: Main shopping street, and where Willoughby lives.

Conduit Street: Where the Middletons reside in London.

Sackville Street: Location of Gray's jewelry shop, where Elinor meets John Dashwood.

St. James Street: Where Colonel Brandon is staying.

Pall Mall: Where Edward Ferrars resides briefly.